THE PENGUIN BOOK OF FRENCH SHORT STORIES

'Patrick McGuinness's two-volume *The Penguin Book of French Short Stories* is outstanding' Philip Hensher, *Spectator*, Books of the Year

'A French version of *The Thousand and One Nights* . . . Both volumes tell us something new about writing in French . . . Such a creative arrangement forces us to rethink what we expect a short story to be or do . . . Perhaps all short fiction reminds us that the end is nigh, in which case not the least of Patrick McGuinness's achievements is that of showing us how to read and live accordingly' Annabel Kim, *The Times Literary Supplement*

'It's hard to imagine a better introduction to French literature than this glorious two-volume bran tub of short fiction . . . outstanding masterpieces all . . . There's a welcome playfulness throughout' John Self, *Guardian*

'Beautiful and deep, *The Penguin Book of French Short Stories* is a sumptuous treat for any book lover' Martin Chilton, *Independent*

'Tales with a certain ooh la la . . . an eclectic, often steamy collection charting the history of the French short story [with] some gems by less famous figures . . . high marks for quality and variety' Matthew Reisz, *Observer*

'Patrick McGuinness's magisterial anthology teems with universes . . . There is so much to discover in these stories – both history and food for short story lovers everywhere' *Irish Times*

'Impeccably edited by Patrick McGuinness. The first volume stretches from the 16th century to the early 20th century . . . Volume two takes us from there to the early 21st century, featuring more women and non-white authors than the first volume. Treat yourself: buy both' Tomiwa Owolade, *Sunday Times*

'What a collection it is . . . Both volumes fizz with the enthusiasm with which McGuinnes[s] range across centuries and contine[nts] out to be the definitive antholog[y] fiction' Charlie Connelly, [...]

T0322044

ABOUT THE AUTHOR

Patrick McGuinness is Professor of French and Comparative Literature at the University of Oxford, and a Fellow of St Anne's College. Born in Tunisia and raised in Belgium, he is a poet, novelist and translator. His novel *The Last Hundred Days* was longlisted for the 2011 Man Booker Prize and shortlisted for the 2011 Costa First Novel Award, and his second novel, *Throw me to the Wolves*, won the 2020 Encore Award. His other books include two collections of poems, *The Canals of Mars* (2004), *Jilted City* (2010), *Blood Feather* (2023), and a memoir, *Other People's Countries* (2015), which won the Duff Cooper Prize. He was made a Chevalier des Arts et des Lettres in 2011, and is a Fellow of the Royal Society of Literature.

The Penguin Book of French Short Stories

Volume 1

Edited by
PATRICK McGUINNESS

PENGUIN BOOKS

PENGUIN CLASSICS

UK | USA | Canada | Ireland | Australia
India | New Zealand | South Africa

Penguin Books is part of the Penguin Random House group of companies
whose addresses can be found at global.penguinrandomhouse.com

First published in Allen Lane 2022
First published in Penguin Classics 2024
003

Printed and bound in Great Britain by Clays Ltd, Elcograf S.p.A.

The authorized representative in the EEA is Penguin Random House Ireland,
Morrison Chambers, 32 Nassau Street, Dublin D02 YH68

A CIP catalogue record for this book is available from the British Library

ISBN: 978–0–241–46200–3

www.greenpenguin.co.uk

MIX
Paper | Supporting
responsible forestry
FSC® C018179
www.fsc.org

Penguin Random House is committed to a
sustainable future for our business, our readers
and our planet. This book is made from Forest
Stewardship Council® certified paper.

Contents

Contents

Contents

Contents

Introduction

The reader opening this anthology will quickly realise that short stories come in different shapes and sizes. I mention this at the outset because short stories have been the subject of many theories and definitions over the centuries, often considerably longer than the stories themselves. These theories and definitions prescribe on matters of length, of subject, of voice and point of view, or on how the short story should handle time, place and action. We are told that the short story explores a single mood or situation; that it aims for a single effect; that it must finish with a click, like a box snapping shut; or we are told the opposite – that it must end on ambiguity or tension. The short story should resolve. It should refuse resolution. It must tie up its loose ends, it must close on suspenseful ellipses . . .

Luckily, it is easier – as well as more enjoyable – to read short stories than to define them. This is just as well, because the French short story tradition is rich and innovative and contains as many classic examples of the genre as it does oddballs, eccentrics and radical misfits. While there are plenty of both in these pages, it is nonetheless useful to establish some parameters – if only to see how far writers can stretch, blur or subvert them.

Though the words 'short' and 'story' impose basic requirements and raise basic expectations, these are, fortunately, permissive. They are also dependent on period and culture: a thirty-page short story in the nineteenth century reads very differently from a thirty-page short story in the twenty-first. There are also practical questions: at what point does a short story edge over into a novella? Or, at the other end of the scale, how to differentiate between a very short short story and a prose poem, or what we call today 'microfiction' or 'flash fiction', forms which existed long before the names arrived to bed them down among our literary categories? And who decides on these labels? Is it the author? The publisher? The marketing department?

Rather than focusing on 'page count' and 'word limit' as undifferentiated slabs of matter from which the short story hews its duration, it would better serve to think of it as a genre that puts the reader in a unique relationship with time. Stories are woven into our lives, but not all stories weave in the same way. Whether it's a medieval audience listening to a tale that has been transmitted orally over generations, or a commuter reading a piece of fiction among the advertisements and lifestyle features in their magazine, the short story fits in and around a day made up of different kinds of time, attention and activity.

In 1966, the Hungarian writer István Örkény published a volume of what he called 'one-minute stories'. In his preface – which he described, with demystifying practicality, as 'handling instructions' – he writes:

> While the soft-boiled egg is boiling or the number you are dialing answers (provided it is not engaged, of course) you have ample time to read one of these short stories which, because of their brevity, I have come to think of as one-minute stories.

Though each age imagines itself busier than the last, the short story is the genre that has most ingeniously adapted to the competing claims on our time and attention. It can insert itself into the cracks in our timetables and infiltrate our slack hours. The most productive thinking about short stories starts out from the question of time rather than the fact of length or size. Thirty pages will always be thirty pages, but one minute is never just one minute.

More than half a century before Örkény, Félix Fénéon had gone even further: his 'three-line novellas', several of which are included in this anthology, are masterpieces of suggestive compression. They can be read in a matter of seconds, though their effect is much harder to measure. Decanted from the 'fait divers' or the 'news in brief' section of regional newspapers, and then rewritten with wit and waspish aplomb, these brisk, lapidary tales expand in inverse proportion to the number of words they contain.

Fénéon's skill lies in showing us how much irony, social observation, pathos and drama a writer can fit into a few words. One of his most barbed 'novellas' goes as follows: 'Verniot, septuagenarian beggar from Clichy, has died of hunger. 2000 francs were hidden in his mattress. But let's not generalize.' At twenty words long, we have a novel's worth of plotlines and psychological questions, and a narrative voice whose ironic final observation leaves us at once amused and uncomfortably implicated. Fénéon is an extreme example, but he shows us that the best short stories use their length as a resource, rather than just inhabiting it as a limit: they combine the immediacy of theatre, the compression of a poem and the latitude of a novel.

A further advantage of the short story is uninterruptedness, the way it can be read (or heard) in one sitting. Although some people can sit for longer than others, we all know what we mean by 'a sitting': an arrangement between the mind and the body, between the limits of our attention span and the moment pins and needles set in. The playwright August Strindberg claimed that the one-act play was the most effective kind of drama because it lacked intervals, and because, as he put it, the audience was 'prisoner' for the duration. Something similar can be said of the short story: that it shares with the one-act play the pressure of an imminent ending as it bears down upon the *nowness* of reading or listening.

Fénéon's three-line novellas appeared in the daily newspaper *Le Matin* between May and November 1906 and remind us that everyday life is a mine of scenarios as full of drama, mystery, absurdity and plot twists as the most *outré* fiction. They also remind us that the literary short story – a piece of artistically-designed and mostly (but not exclusively) fictional prose – is just one strand of narrative in a world saturated with stories. It is no coincidence that the high point of the modern short story – the nineteenth and early twentieth century – is also a high point in print media, in news and reportage, and in an experience of speed and connectivity that, despite changes in technology, remains remarkably consistent with today's. Newspapers and magazines were hospitable to the short story and the first readers of many of the stories in this anthology encountered them in a patchwork of different kinds of narrative: news stories, court reports, 'true crime', gossip columns, journalistic scoops, political commentary and philosophical tales. They will also have picked them out from the mixed page: advertisements, recipes (which are also stories), polemics, letters, puzzles, notices and personal ads. The short story is a pragmatic, nimble genre, responsive and topical, reaching the parts of a culture other genres cannot, and reaching them fast. Where the novel stretches across our days and accompanies us through them, the short story thrives in the busy ecosystem of everyday narratives and everyday reading habits. Several of the stories in this anthology reflect that: there are stories in the form of news items, political or philosophical parables, topical polemics, dialogues and monologues, letters, psychological case studies, dream-notation and even a multiple-choice questionnaire. There are fine-tuned classics of the 'well-made' tale and works that seem to conform to no genre, or sit proudly and unfazed between genres.

Volume One begins with a bawdy, innuendo-laden tale from Philippe de Laon's *One Hundred New Tales*, written between 1464 and 1467. The final story in Volume Two dates from the early 2000s, written by Virginie Despentes, one of the most thrilling and taboo-breaking contemporary French writers.

Laon's *One Hundred New Tales* have been described both as 'the first French literary work in prose' and as 'a museum of obscenities'. Although only the first of these judgments was a compelling argument for their inclusion, the second reminds us that the short story is not some remote high-cultural object to be entombed in a university syllabus, but a diversion and an entertainment. Both *One Hundred New Tales* and Marguerite de Navarre's *The Heptameron*, from which the volume's second story 'The Substitute' is taken, are inspired (like Chaucer's *The Canterbury Tales*) by Boccaccio's *The Decameron*. They follow their model in setting stories told by diverse voices into an overarching frame narrative. In *The Decameron*, travellers who have been thrown together by circumstances tell stories as they escape the Black Death. In *The Canterbury Tales*, they are travelling on a pilgrimage. In *The Heptameron*, they are in an abbey, waiting for the bridge that will bear them to safety to be completed. What these early examples of storytelling have in common is sophistication and playfulness, tricky narrators and slippery perspectives. From the very start, the short story is testing its limits, pushing the boundaries, defying expectations.

These classic tales also show us that once we are together, around a table or in a room, and once we have assured ourselves of food and shelter, we want stories. The earliest storytellers show us that stories are our first non-physical need, and what medieval and Renaissance audiences have in common with today's readers and listeners is the understanding that we are narrative creatures: that whatever our ends and goals, however full our agendas and busy our days, there will always be time for stories.

The advantage of beginning the anthology with *The Heptameron* is that it opens up the field to include more than just the classics from the Golden Age of the short story. To have started with Voltaire or Diderot, and moved smoothly to Colette and Marcel Aymé via Maupassant and Balzac, would have been to impose an artificial beginning on a thrillingly messy and hybrid tradition. Diverging from the familiar path, this anthology contains hitherto untranslated sixteenth-century stories by Jean-Pierre Camus and François de Rosset. These garish, sensational narratives, nicknamed 'histoires sanglantes' or 'bloody tales', are the ancestors of today's 'true crime' genre.

As we move through the centuries, we encounter works, many of them little known in English, that might be considered to stretch the definition of a story. But the short story has never been a pure, clear-cut genre, and I have been fascinated by the way in which classic stories share so much of their narrative DNA with other forms of writing: the prose poem, for instance, with Baudelaire, Mallarmé and Charles Cros, who are included here; or with strange dream-narratives such as Xavier Forneret's 'A Dream'. In Forneret's short tale, the nineteenth century's fascination with the unconscious, and with the sleeping mind's bizarre connectivity, is distilled into a single, surreal text. As Forneret claimed: 'Since I write while I'm dreaming, you can read me while you're sleeping.' No wonder the surrealists claimed him as a trailblazing predecessor. Closer to the twenty-first century, Simone de Beauvoir's 'Monologue' or Béatrix Beck's 'The Adam Affair', a dialogue between God and a particularly obtuse Adam, give the short story the dynamism of drama.

The question is not 'what is a short story?' but 'what can a short story *be*?'. French thought has a reputation for classifying and defining, and French literary history is the home of ' – isms': Naturalism, Symbolism, Surrealism, Existentialism, to name just a few movements that enjoyed worldwide influence. This fondness for categorizing has the unexpected and paradoxical effect of giving writers more categories to blur. When Diderot titled his story 'This Is Not a Story' and included 'a character whose role is more or less that of the reader', he was breaking down the fourth wall. When, 200 years later, Raymond Queneau wrote 'A Tale for Your Shaping' as a questionnaire in which the reader chooses outcomes, he was playing with the complex interrelationship between formal structure and readerly expectation in a similar spirit. That playfulness can be seen in the work of OuLiPo, or 'Ouvroir de littérature potentielle' ('Workshop of Potential Literature'), a group of writers that included Queneau, Italo Calvino and Georges Perec, who exploited the inventive licence granted by writing to particular rules and constraints. It can also be seen in the more ludic strains of French literary theory, in the work of Roland Barthes, and in that other dominant ' – ism', Structuralism: an understanding that the rules themselves are the best route to subverting the rules. It would not be too much to say that the fondness for categorizing is exactly what makes the French literary tradition so varied and experimental.

With Voltaire, Diderot and Sade, the short story is both a self-aware genre, sophisticated and amusing, and a place to think – an opportunity for reflection, to test political and social ideas. In Voltaire's 'Micromégas', an early science-fiction story that is also a philosophical parable, an extraterrestrial character is used to make us see ourselves from the outside. Funny, absurd, by turns intellectually playful and serious, Voltaire gives humanity – or at any rate French humanity – the sort of cultural out-of-body experience that enables it to scrutinize itself. Seriousness and play are not incompatible, and the French short story from the eighteenth to the twenty-first centuries has often directly or obliquely engaged in philosophical and social concerns.

Of the many continuities in this anthology, the reader will notice how the French short story is imbricated in its culture, in the febrile politics of its time. It has addressed injustice and discrimination, and often intervened publicly in the big debates. From Voltaire testing the tolerance of the French state and official religion to Victor Hugo's 'Claude Gueux', about the barbarism of the death penalty, writers have used the short story not just for its brevity but for the ways in which it circulates. More widely and quickly disseminated than novels and more easily digested than political tracts, it blends the efficacy of polemic with the attractions of entertainment.

Another continuity the reader will notice is the relationship between the ordinary and extraordinary, and the French short story's attraction to the 'fantastic'. Traditionally understood as a nineteenth-century speciality, its roots lie earlier and its offshoots extend into the twentieth and twenty-first centuries. This anthology contains classics such as Gautier's 'The Mummy's Foot' and Mérimée's 'The Venus of Ille', along with lesser-known masterpieces such as Villiers de l'Isle-Adam's moving story 'Véra', in which, through a sustained refusal to believe in his wife's death, a widower succeeds in returning her to life (or does he . . .?). The *'fantastique'* is one of the dominant genres and thrives on bringing the everyday and the extraordinary into explosive contact. In Marcel Aymé's 'The Man who Walked Through Walls' and Jacques Sternberg's 'The Execution', fantastical events are told in such matter-of-fact, deadpan prose that the flatness of the narration accentuates rather than dulls the narrative. Meanwhile, writers such as Renée Vivien and Claude Cahun are the heirs of Perrault and his fairy tales, and Jules Verne's science fiction is in the lineage of Voltaire's space travel. While all this speaks to a desire for escapism and supernatural thrill, it reflects something more serious in all of us: the feeling that there is more to life than just the here and now. We may think of the 'fantastic' and related genres – science fiction, horror, gothic – as expressions of our need for an *'au-delà'*, a 'beyond', in a utilitarian and post-religious age.

The short story is also a place where authors experiment with themes and styles that are at an angle to the work for which they are best known. Thus Apollinaire, the great modern poet of *Calligrammes* and *Alcools*, appears here with a short story about a man with the gift of blending in with his surroundings. Émile Zola, the Naturalist author of the twenty-novel Rougon Macquart cycle, features with a sharp and prescient story about advertising and the media. His fellow one-time Naturalist, Joris-Karl Huysmans, the decadent-turned-catholic author of *Against Nature*, is represented by the bleakly comic tale of Mr Bougran, a sacked bureaucrat who cannot bear to retire. A taste of the *fin de siècle* and decadent period is offered in a range of stories, from the erotic and depraved tales of Rachilde and Jean Lorrain to Marcel Schwob's harrowing war story, 'The *Sans Gueules*'.

Some of the major twentieth century writers I would have wished to include – notably Jean-Paul Sartre, Albert Camus, Georges Simenon and Jean Giono – were unavailable for reasons of copyright, but I have also sought to expand the range of authors traditionally available to the

English-speaking audience. As well as the canonical and the classic (Colette, Marguerite Duras, Marguerite Yourcenar, Georges Perec, Françoise Sagan), I have included authors who are less familiar to readers in the anglosphere. These include Emmanuel Bove, Béatrix Beck, Charles-Albert Cingria, Jacqueline Harpman, Madeleine Bourdouxhe and Thomas Owen, as well as contemporary writers such as Gilles Ortlieb, Ananda Devi and Christian Garcin. In the works of Birago Diop, Boualem Sansal, Leïla Sebbar and Assia Djebar, among others, the short story brings its unique focus to bear on the legacies of colonialism and the cultural, linguistic and religious fault lines of contemporary France and its former colonies. Many authors are translated here for the first time; their work enriches not just the French literary tradition, but the range of French writing available in English.

I think of every story not just as a standalone fiction, but as part of a whole, a busy, imbricated set of contexts. In theatrical terms, I like to imagine the 'noises off' behind and to the side of them. They may be free-standing works of art but they are not sealed off from the worlds that produced them. They are also little keys to their cultures, their times and places: from Renaissance France to the multicultural global *francophonie* of the twentieth and twenty-first centuries.

My aim in this selection has been to entertain, to provide variety and to reveal the unexpected continuities between different periods and different literary traditions. I have aimed for variety among the stories and diversity among the authors. The pluralism of my definition of the short story is matched by the pluralism of my definition of French, and I include many writers from the francophone world. I have chosen writers substantially published in France, or resident there, or writers who are part of the literary culture in terms of their publishing houses, their eligibility for prizes, or their media presence. Here, too, I have been permissive: though they have all written French short stories, none of the authors in these pages has been required to show their passport or provide proof of residence.

Acknowledgements

Preparing an anthology like this, an editor runs up a marathon of debts. My first *tranche* of thanks goes to Simon Winder, who commissioned it and tracked its progress attentively and with encouragement. I am also grateful to Eva Hodgkin for her advice and for her careful and nuanced reading of both French originals and English translations. Claire Péligry was a tremendous copy editor and Anna Wilson at Penguin turned complicated manuscripts into clear and elegant pages.

I have benefited from the advice of several friends and colleagues at Oxford and elsewhere: Clément Dessy, Catherine Emerson, Andrew Kahn, Will McMorran, Stephen Romer, Catriona Seth, Helen Swift, Kate Tunstall, Caroline Warman and Jenny Yee. At St Anne's College, I am grateful to my fellow modern languages tutors, Geraldine Hazbun and Simon Park, and to my students, whose curiosity has kept me abreast of French literature over almost three decades of teaching. My greatest thanks go to the translators who have contributed to these volumes: translation is how cultures speak to each other, and we continue to be indebted to those who practice it.

PHILIPPE DE LAON

The Husband as Doctor

It is well known that in the province of Champagne you are sure to meet heavy and dull-witted persons, which has seemed strange to many persons, seeing that the district is so near to the country of Mischief. Many stories could be told of the stupidity of the Champenois, but this present story will suffice.

In this province, there lived a young man, an orphan, who at the death of his father and mother had become rich and powerful. He was stupid, ignorant and disagreeable, but hard-working and knew well how to take care of himself and his affairs, and for this reason, many persons, – even people of condition, – were willing to give him their daughter in marriage.

One of these damsels, above all others, pleased the friends and relations of our Champenois, for her beauty, goodness, riches, and so forth. They told him that it was time he married.

'You are now,' they said, 'twenty-three years old, and there could not be a better time. And if you will listen to us, we have searched out for you a fair and good damsel who seems to us just suited to you. It is such a one – you know her well;' and they told him her name.

The young man, who cared little whether he was married or not, as long as he lost no money by it, replied that he would do whatever they wished. 'Since you think it will be to my advantage, manage the business the best way you can, and I will follow your advice and instructions.'

'You say well,' replied these good people. 'We will select your wife as carefully as though it were for ourselves, or one of our children.'

To cut matters short, a little time afterwards our Champenois was married; but on the first night, when he was sleeping with his wife, he, never having mounted on any Christian woman, soon turned his back to her, and a few poor kisses was all she had of him, but nothing on her back. You may guess his wife was not well pleased at this; nevertheless, she concealed her discontent.

This unsatisfactory state of things lasted ten days, and would have continued longer if the girl's mother had not put a stop to it.

It should be known to you that the young man was unskilled in the mysteries of wedlock, for during the lifetime of his parents he had been kept with a tight hand, and, above all things, had been forbidden to play at the beast with two backs, lest he should take too much delight therein, and waste all his patrimony. This was wise of his parents, for he was not a young man likely to be loved for his good looks.

As he would do nothing to anger his father or mother, and was, moreover, not of an amorous disposition, he had always preserved his chastity, though his wife would willingly have deprived him of it, if she had known how to do so honestly.

One day the mother of the bride came to her daughter, and asked her all about her husband's state and condition, and the thousand other things which women like to know. To all of these questions the bride replied that her husband was a good man, and she hoped and believed that she would be happy with him.

But the old woman knew by her own experience that there are more things in married life than eating and drinking, so she said to her daughter:

'Come here, and tell me, on your word of honour, how does he acquit himself at night?'

When the girl heard this question, she was so vexed and ashamed that she could not reply, and her eyes filled with tears. Her mother understood what these tears meant, and said:

'Do not weep, my child! Speak out boldly! I am your mother, and you ought not to conceal anything from me, or be afraid of telling me. Has he done nothing to you yet?'

The poor girl, having partly recovered, and being reassured by her mother's words, ceased her tears, but yet could make no reply. Thereupon, her mother asked again:

'Lay aside your grief and answer me honestly: has he done nothing to you yet?'

In a low voice, mingled with tears, the girl replied, 'On my word, mother, he has never yet touched me, but, except for that, there is no more kind or affectionate man.'

'Tell me,' said the mother; 'do you know if he is properly furnished with all his members? Speak out boldly, if you know.'

'By St John! he is all right in that respect,' replied the bride. 'I have often, by chance, felt his luggage as I turned to and fro in our bed when I could not sleep.'

'That is enough,' said the mother; 'leave the rest to me. This is what you must do. In the morning you must pretend to be very ill – even as though your soul were departing from your body. Your husband will, I fully expect, seek me out and bid me come to you, and I will play my part so well that your business will be soon settled, for I shall take your water to a certain doctor, who will give such advice as I order.'

All was done as arranged, for on the morrow, as soon as it was dawn, the girl, who was sleeping with her husband, began to complain and to sham sickness as though a strong fever racked her body.

Her booby husband was much vexed and astonished, and knew not what to say or do. He sent forthwith for his mother-in-law, who was not long in coming. As soon as he saw her, 'Alas! mother!' said he, 'your daughter is dying.'

'My daughter?' said she. 'What does she want?' And whilst she was speaking she walked to the patient's chamber.

As soon as the mother saw her daughter, she asked what was the matter; and the girl, being well instructed what she was to do, answered not at first, but, after a little time, said, 'Mother, I am dying.'

'You shall not die, please God! Take courage! But how comes it that you are taken ill so suddenly?'

'I do not know! I do not know!' replied the girl. 'It drives me wild to answer all these questions.'

The old woman took the girl's hand, and felt her pulse; then she said to her son-in-law:

'On my word she is very ill. She is full of fire, and we must find some remedy. Have you any of her water?'

'That which she made last night is there,' said one of the attendants.

'Give it me,' said the mother.

3

She took the urine, and put it in a proper vessel, and told her son-in-law that she was about to show it to such-and-such a doctor, that he might know what he could do to her daughter to cure her.

'For God's sake, spare nothing,' said she. 'I have yet some money left, but I love my daughter better than money.'

'Spare!' quoth he. 'If money can help, you shall not want.'

'No need to go so fast,' said she. 'Whilst she is resting, I will go home; but I will come back if I am wanted.'

Now you must know that the old woman had on the previous day, when she left her daughter, instructed the doctor, who was well aware of what he ought to say. So the young man carried his wife's water to the doctor, and when he had saluted him, related how sick and suffering his wife was.

'And I have brought you some of her water that you may judge how ill she is, and more easily cure her.'

The doctor took the vessel of urine, and turned it about and examined it, then said:

'Your wife is afflicted with a sore malady, and is in danger of dying unless help be forthcoming; her water shows it.'

'Ah, master, for God's sake tell me what to do, and I will pay you well if you can restore her to health, and prevent her from dying.'

'She need not die,' said the doctor; 'but unless you make haste, all the money in the world will not save her life.'

'Tell me, for God's sake,' said the other, 'what to do, and I will do it.'

'She must,' said the doctor, 'have connection with a man, or she will die.'

'Connection with a man?' said the other. 'What is that?'

'That is to say,' continued the doctor, 'that you must mount on the top of her, and speedily ram her three or four times, or more if you can; for, if not, the great heat which is consuming her will not be put out.'

'Ah! Will that be good for her?'

'There is no chance of her living,' said the doctor, 'if you do not do it, and quickly too.'

'By St John,' said the other, 'I will try what I can do.'

With that he went home and found his wife, who was groaning and lamenting loudly.

'How are you, my dear?' said he.

'I am dying, my dear,' she replied.

'You shall not die, please God,' said he. 'I have seen the doctor, who has told me what medicine will cure you,' and as he spoke, he undressed himself, and lay down by his wife, and began to execute the orders he had received from the doctor.

'What are you doing?' said she. 'Do you want to kill me?'

'No! I am going to cure you,' he replied. 'The doctor said so;' and Nature instructing him, and the patient helping, he performed on her two or three times.

When he was resting from his labours, much astonished at what had happened, he asked his wife how she was.

'I am a little better than I was before,' she replied.

'God be praised,' said he. 'I hope you will get well and that the doctor told me truly.' And with that he began again.

To cut matters short, he performed so well that his wife was cured in a few days, at which he was very joyful, and so was her mother when she knew it.

The young man after this became a better fellow than he was before, and his wife being now restored to health, he one day invited all his relations and friends to dinner, and also the father and mother of his wife, and he served grand cheer after his own fashion. They drank to him, and he drank to them, and he was marvellous good company.

But hear what happened to him: in the midst of the dinner he began to weep, which much astonished all his friends who were at table with him, and they demanded what was the matter, but he could not reply for weeping scalding tears. At last he spoke, and said:

'I have good cause to weep.'

'By my oath you have not,' replied his mother-in-law. 'What ails you? You are rich and powerful, and well housed, and have good friends; and you must not forget that you have a fair and good wife whom God brought back to health when she was on the edge of the grave. In my opinion you ought to be light-hearted and joyful.'

'Alas!' said he, 'woe is me! My father and mother, who both loved me, and who amassed and left me so much wealth, are both dead, and by my fault, for they died of a fever, and if I had well towzled them both when they were ill, as I did to my wife, they would still be on their feet.'

There was no one at table who, on hearing this, would not have liked to laugh, nevertheless they restrained themselves as best they could. The tables were removed, and each went his way, and the young man continued to live with his wife, and – in order that she might continue in good health – he failed not to tail her pretty often.

Translated by Robert B. Douglas

MARGUERITE DE NAVARRE

The Substitute

In the Duchy of Milan, at the time when the Grand Master of Chaumont was governor, there lived a nobleman called Bonnivet, who later, for his merits, was made an Admiral of France. Greatly loved by the aforementioned Grand Master and everyone else in Milan for the virtues he possessed, he was often to be seen at those assemblies where all the ladies gathered together, and was more popular with them than any Frenchman had ever been, as much for his beauty, grace and eloquence as for the reputation everyone accorded him of being one of the best and bravest swordsmen of his time. One day, at a masked ball during the Carnival, he danced with one of the most beautiful ladies in the city; and, whenever there was a pause in the music, he did not fail to address those amorous compliments to her which he knew how to devise better than any other. But she, who was not supposed to answer him, suddenly decided to discourage him and halt him by saying that she did not love and would never love anyone but her husband, and that he should not entertain any hopes whatever. Despite this reply, the nobleman did not consider himself beaten, and he pursued her vigorously until the middle of Lent. The only result was that he found her firm in her determination to love neither him nor anyone else, which he found hard to believe, in that her husband was ill-favoured and she was extremely beautiful. He decided, since she was practising deception, to use trickery himself; and promptly abandoning his pursuit of her, he made such thorough inquiries about her way of life that he found she was in love with an Italian nobleman who was both worthy and honourable.

The aforementioned Bonnivet gradually won the friendship of this nobleman, so gently and craftily that the Italian did not perceive his intentions, but liked him so well that he came second only to his lady in his affections. Bonnivet, in order to wrest his secret from him, pretended to tell him his own – namely that he was in love with a certain lady to whom he had really never given a thought – and begged him not to reveal it, so that they might have only one heart and mind between them. The poor nobleman, in order to show him equal friendship, told him at great length about the love he bore the lady on whom Bonnivet wished to be avenged; and once a day the two of them met at a certain place to tell each other what luck each had had during the day, one telling lies and the other the truth. The nobleman confessed to having been in love with his lady for three years, without having received anything from her but fair words and assurances of her love for him. The aforementioned Bonnivet explained to him all the means by which he might attain his end, and he found these so effective that within a few days she agreed to grant him all he asked; all that remained was to find an opportunity, and with Bonnivet's help this was soon found.

One day, before supper, the nobleman said to him:

'Sir, I am more deeply indebted to you than to anyone else in the world, for thanks to your advice I hope to have tonight what I have desired for so many years.'

'I beg you,' said Bonnivet, 'to tell me all about it, so that I may see whether there is any trickery or danger involved, and help you as a true friend.'

The nobleman told him that the lady had found a means of leaving the main door of the house open, on the pretext of some illness of a brother of hers, which made it necessary to send for medicines from the town at all hours; so that he could certainly enter the courtyard, but was to take care not to go up the main staircase, making his way instead up some steps on the right and entering the first gallery he came to, where he would find the doors leading into the rooms of her father-in-law and brothers-in-law. He was to pick out carefully the third door from the top of the stairs, and if, pushing it gently, he found it closed, he must go away, for that would mean that her husband had returned, although he was not due to come home for two days. But if he found it open, he was to enter softly and shut the door behind him, bolting it fast, knowing that she was alone in the room. Above all, he was not to forget to wear felt slippers, for fear of making a noise, and to be careful not to come until two o'clock in the morning, because her brothers-in-law, who were very fond of playing cards, never went to bed before one. Bonnivet replied:

'Go ahead, my dear fellow! May God be with you and keep you from any mishap, and if my presence can be of any help to you, I shall not spare anything in my power.'

The nobleman thanked him warmly, but said that in this matter he could not be too much alone, and went off to attend to it.

For his part, Bonnivet did not sleep; and, seeing that the time had come for him to take his revenge on his cruel lady, he retired early to his lodgings and had his beard cut to the same length and breadth as the nobleman's; he had his hair cut in the same way, so that it was impossible to tell the difference between them by touching him. Nor did he forget to put on felt slippers and to make sure that the rest of his clothing was similar to the nobleman's. Because he was on friendly terms with the lady's father-in-law, he was not afraid of going to the house early, thinking that if he were seen he would go straight to the room of the good man, with whom he had some business.

At midnight he entered the lady's house, where he found quite a few people coming and going; but he passed among them without being recognized and reached the gallery. Touching the first two doors, he found them closed, but not the third, which he gently pushed open. Once he was inside the lady's room, he bolted the door behind him. He saw the whole room hung with white, and the floor and ceiling white too; and in the room there was a bed of fine linen, with a curtain admirably worked in white. The lady was alone in the bed, with her nightcap and shift covered with pearls and precious stones; this he saw through one corner of the curtain without her seeing him, for there was a large candle of white wax in the room which made it as light as day. For fear of being recognized, he blew out the candle first of all, then took off his clothes and got into bed beside her. She, thinking it was the man who had loved her for so long, gave him as warm a welcome as she could; but he, knowing it was meant for another, took care not to say a single word to her and thought of nothing but carrying out his revenge, in other words of taking away her honour and chastity without owing her gratitude or favour. But willy-nilly, the lady was so pleased with this revenge that she thought he had been repaid in full for all his services by the time the clock struck one and the moment came to say farewell. Then, as quietly as he could, he asked her if she was as pleased with him as he with her. She, thinking he was her sweetheart, told him she was not only pleased but astonished at the fervour of his love, which had prevented him from speaking to her for a whole hour. He promptly burst into loud laughter, and said to her:

'Tell me, my lady, will you reject me again, as you have been accustomed to doing till now?'

Recognizing him by his voice and his laughter, she was so overwhelmed with grief and shame that she called him a villain, traitor and deceiver a thousand times, and tried to jump out of bed to look for a knife with which to kill herself, since she had been unfortunate enough to lose her honour for a man whom she did not love and who, to revenge himself upon her, might spread the story abroad. But he held her back with his arms, and speaking to her kindly and gently, assured her that he loved her more than the Italian nobleman and would conceal her dishonour so well that it would never be held against her. This poor foolish woman believed; and hearing from him the scheme he had devised and the pains he had taken to win her, she swore to him that she loved him more than the other man who had been unable to keep her secret, and that she was now convinced that what was commonly said about the French was untrue, for they were more clever, persevering and discreet than the Italians. Accordingly, from then on she would abandon the opinion of her fellow countrymen and of the French, and cleave to him. But she begged him not to come for some time to any gathering where she was, unless he was masked, for she knew she would feel so ashamed that her face would betray her to everyone. He gave his word, and then asked her, when her sweetheart came at two o'clock, to receive him well, after which she could then gradually part company with him. To this she objected so strongly that if it had not been for the love she bore him she would never have agreed to it. However, in taking leave of her, he gave her such satisfaction that she would have dearly wished him to stay longer.

After he had got up and put on his clothes he went out of the room, leaving the door ajar as he had found it. As it was nearly two o'clock, and he was afraid of meeting the Italian nobleman on the way, he withdrew to the top of the stairs, where soon afterwards he saw him pass by and go into his lady's room. He for his part went home to his lodgings to rest from his labours, so that at nine o'clock in the morning he was still in bed. While he was getting up, the Italian nobleman arrived and did not fail to tell him of his good fortune, though it had not been as good as he had hoped. He said that when he entered his lady's room, he found her out of bed, wearing her dressing gown and in a high fever; her pulse was beating fast, her face was flushed, and she was beginning to perspire heavily. She accordingly begged him to leave her at once, for she had not dared to call her women, for fear of causing a scandal; and she felt so ill that she had more cause to think of death than love, and to hear about God than Cupid. She told him she was sorry about the risks he had run for her, since she was unable to give him in this world the happiness she hoped to enjoy soon in the next. At this he was so astonished and distressed that his ardour and joy turned to ice and sadness, and he left her at once. At daybreak he had sent for news of her, and she was really very sick.

While he was recounting his misfortunes, he wept so copiously that it seemed as if his soul were going to leave his body with his tears. Bonnivet, who felt as much like laughing as the other felt tearful, comforted him as best he could, telling him that long-lasting love affairs always had a difficult beginning, and that Love was imposing this delay on him so that his enjoyment should be greater later on. With these words they parted. The lady kept to her bed for a few days, and when she recovered her health she dismissed her first sweetheart, explaining her conduct by her remorse and the fear she had had of dying. But she continued to favour Bonnivet, whose love, as is usual, lasted as long as the flowers of the field.

Translated by Paul Chilton

FRANÇOIS DE ROSSET

*The True Story of a Woman Who Killed Her Husband
and Subsequently Performed Unheard-of Acts
of Violence on His Body*

While previous centuries have given us several examples of the barbarism and cruelty of some women, we should not be surprised if our present times, being more wicked than earlier eras, produce monsters of nature who are indeed more brutal that the fiercest beasts. Witness the cruel acts of a violent Spanish woman – violent both in name and deed – in the unprecedented vengeance she wreaked on the man who boasted of having slept with her. There are countless stories, both ancient and modern, telling of the wrath of a woman driven to revenge, because, disregarding the attributes of her sex, traditionally gentle and amiable by nature, there is no cruel or evil act she will not commit when fury unleashes her passions. Seething with emotions, she becomes a Procne and a Medea, forgiving neither husbands nor children.

In Soirans, a village one league's distance from Auxerre, a woman called Marguerite, knowing that her husband was carousing at the tavern with some friends – and he had even sent someone to fetch two chickens from his home –, this wife waiting impatiently for her husband, on seeing him coming with one of his companions, started spewing a torrent of abuse against him, calling him a drunkard, a glutton, a lecher, an idler, a stinker, a seducer and other insults sparked by her anger. Once inside the house, she continued her tirade and, seeing that she could not be appeased, her husband fetched a double-edged sword, which he kept in his bedroom, intending to charge at her, but he missed his footing and fell to the floor. In a flash, the woman stopped him from getting up. She grabbed a three-legged stool and gave him such a hard blow to the head that he was knocked senseless and, redoubling her blows, she killed him stone dead. When she realized that he was not moving, she dragged him over to the fireside and gave him wine, but it was in vain, because he was well and truly dead. Grasping the seriousness of the situation, she tried to think of solutions to hide this murder and, unable to hide it from God, she resolved to conceal it from men. She removed the body and placed it under the straw mattress on her bed, and, after it had lain there some time, the devil tempted her into carrying out unheard-of acts of violence.

She dragged the body out from beneath the straw mattress, laid it out in the centre of the room and, without feeling the slightest compassion, began to vent her rage on her dead husband's private parts, which she cut off. Then, she picked up an axe and delivered a heavy blow, thinking to disguise his sex. She chopped off his head and cut it into four quarters, then severed his arms above the elbow and his legs above the knee.

O executioner, do you not regret butchering your poor husband? Can your barbaric hands be thus reddened with his blood without your being repulsed? The blood of the man who slept beside you for so many years and with whom you have had two beautiful children? Do you believe your crime will escape punishment, and that the all-seeing eye of Heaven will allow your viciousness to go unchastised? Do you not feel the Furies tormenting your soul, and a parasitic worm gnawing your conscience? What! Your fanatical rage driven by the devil is not yet assuaged? You want to perform the penultimate act of this bloody tragedy, whose horrendous outcome will be no less gruesome?

This shrew took the head, rolled it, spat out evil words in a croaking voice, then came to the eyes, which she stabbed with the point of a spindle. She took a pair of pincers with which she ripped off his nose and ears. And she was not done, there was still more violence to come: she plucked out his beard, leaving not a single hair.

What did she do next? She gathered up all the scattered pieces – in other words, the head, the eyes, the nose, the ears, the lower part of the arm with the hands, the legs and the innards – and buried all those butchered parts in a corner of the house. Then she picked up a bag and put one of the quarters in it and went to throw it into the River Arvesan. She then did the same with the remaining three quarters.

Finally, there she was, her hands still red with blood, trying to erase the bloodstains from her bedroom. The more water she threw on them, the redder the blood became; the colour was so deep that the water could not wash it away.

A few days went by, and people were surprised not to see her husband. Even the local lord asked her where he was. She replied that he had left the house late one night in his nightshirt and that she had not seen him since. The wheelwright's wife asked her the same thing and she told her that he had gone to war.

Finally, the lord of Soirans sent one of his servants to enquire further, and the servant asked where her husband was. She answered that he had gone to Chalon and that, if she had money, she would go looking for him.

These three different replies provided seemingly incontrovertible evidence pointing to this evil woman's crime. Nevertheless, God requires much clearer and stronger proof of her offence, and for suspicions and evidence to be confirmed by that same veracity.

So now it was Epiphany. While the procession was making its way around Soirans church, the local lord, on seeing the woman beside the river, went to her and asked her what she was doing there. She said that she was watching some crows and magpies on the bank of the river, whose water level had dropped drastically since she had thrown her husband's quarters into it, and she had already spotted one, after which she subsequently confessed.

It seems that God wished to make use of those macabre birds, as He did in the past with the cranes that acted as witnesses against the thieves that had killed Ibycus! On seeing her alone and pensive by the river, the lord of Soirans began to have suspicions, and the cawing crows appeared to be saying in their language that the carrion was close at hand, which prompted him to ask whether she might have killed her husband. She denied it loudly and emphatically, saying that the truth would out.

Then the lord of Soirans mulled over the different replies she had given when asked about her husband's absence. His misgivings grew and he resolved that after mass he would try to uncover the truth of which she had spoken.

Once mass was over, he took a good number of parishioners, his subjects, who began searching the riverbanks, where they found three of the deceased's quarters, and a dog found the fourth, which it dragged out of the water. Although he could not be identified from his quartered body, having been mutilated and decapitated, even so, the lord of Soirans had the woman arrested and imprisoned and, as he made her touch the body parts, the blood spurted out.

They then went to her house where they encountered the scene where she had committed this butchery, even though she had tried, as we have already described, to wash away the blood. And now there was new evidence calling for vengeance against this cruel woman. Even though she would not accuse herself from her own lips, it was sufficient to have her brought to trial and to subject her to the sentence warranted by her crime.

Finally, the judge having extracted the truth through her own confession, she was sentenced to make honourable amends, in her nightdress and brandishing a torch, to beg mercy from God, the king and from Justice.

After she had made honourable amends in front of Sourans church, she was transported by cart to the Bouteran woods, on the main road to Dijon, where the gallows had been erected.

Her confessor exhorted her to call on the Divine Majesty and beg for His mercy to receive forgiveness for her wrongs and recognize that Our Lord always has open arms to receive the sinner who bows down in shame and repents. Even the lord of Soirans said to her: 'Be brave, Marguerite, ask the Lord for mercy with a contrite and humble heart! Beg His forgiveness, meet death willingly and repent for having thus slaughtered your husband!' That wretched woman, as I am so bold as to call her, refused all these holy remonstrances, remained obdurate and obstinate in her sin and did not allow her heart of stone to soften or demonstrate the least contrition by shedding a few tears. But alas! It seemed she was possessed by the Devil, telling her to say that her deed was a good thing, and were it to be done again, she would do so.

Oh, wicked woman, what are you thinking of? Where will despair lead you? Can you not see the gates of Hell opening if you do not change your mind and the Devil holding you in his clutches ready to throw you in? Call on the mercy of your Saviour, who does not wish for the death of the sinner, but for him to convert! Give the heavenly angels cause to rejoice by your conversion! But alas, I cannot see you ready to relinquish your stubborn stance, because you persist in your obduracy. You are close to the port where you can find your salvation, but you prefer to sink.

After being hanged and strangled, her body was burned, and the ashes scattered to the winds. Ultimately, that evil woman, that terrible monster, died in her obstinacy, refusing through true contrition to patiently resign herself to temporal torment, insignificant compared to her crime, in order to avoid eternal damnation.

Translated by Ros Schwartz

JEAN-PIERRE CAMUS

The Phantom

These tidings are so fresh that it has only been a few days since their principal character yielded to the grave the tribute all flesh must pay. The object which strikes our senses without the distance it requires to serve its purpose deprives them of understanding; things which happen on our own doorstep are much less remarked upon than those which reach us from afar. Some occurrences are like flowers: the foreign ones are more valued, not for their price but for their rarity, than those which grow on our own soil.

In that capital of our Gauls, the grandeur of which is reflected in its very name, at the home of a wearer of those robes said to be long, meaning belonging to the Judicature, a dreadful phantom appeared several times in the night, on occasion to his clerks, and on others to his maidservants.

Now not all the phantoms which appear to such folk during the hours of darkness are pure spirits without flesh or bone, which renders these apparitions somewhat dubious in the eyes of masters and mistresses, and makes them keep their eyes on the behaviour of these young people to ensure that nothing dishonourable is happening in their households. Now it was mainly in the clerks' bedroom that this spectre would show itself quite frequently, and so terrify these poor boys that they would be quite dumbstruck and beside themselves. This led the master to judge that their fear was not feigned. He was a resolute and God-fearing man, and so he decided to find out what could be the cause.

He wanted to spend a night in this bedroom, where his wife did not care to keep him company, having done all she could to dissuade him. He has his bed made, readies candles and books there, and decides to spend the time occupied thus to prevent sleep from overcoming him. He also gave orders for watch to be kept in the bedroom beneath, which was his own, and, should he make the slightest noise moving a chair, they were to climb the stairs and come to him.

Notwithstanding all these watches and sentries, an hour after he had gone to bed, while he was reading a book, the phantom did not fail to appear. It was a large man, a wearer of the same robes, tall beyond measure, with a hideous face, a long, bristly and ragged beard, and horrible eyes that blazed like two torches. This sight alone so terrified him that he remained motionless and pulseless, as if he had been stunned or enchanted. The spectre walked two or three times around the room at a furious pace and then, taking the candlestick from a bedside stool, places it on the table, takes a large book which was lying on it and opens it, and, having sat down, starts to read it, or rather to say things as if he were reading them – appalling things which this man, lying in his bed, more dead than alive, distinctly heard, so overwhelmed with horror that he could no more move than a statue. This continued a while, for what seemed an age to this stupefied man, who then summoned the strength to reach out from under the sheets with his hand and shake the stool to ask for help. At that moment, this tall man rises, and, casting a look his way capable of turning a man into stone, so horrible it was, knocks over the table, book, chair and candlestick, putting out the candle, and leaves the room full of darkness and horror, disappearing with a sound that led the man in bed and even those below to believe the house was going to ruin.

They rushed up the stairs with light and found the master unconscious in bed, as stiff and as cold as if he were dead. Someone dashes off for water and restoratives; he does not stir for at least half an hour, his wife weeping and despairing. At last he comes round, but so dejected and agitated that it was as if he had risen from the grave like a second Lazarus. A high fever took hold which led him almost to death's door. Nonetheless, care and succour saved him from this mortal illness, though for the two years he lived thereafter he was left with such palpitations, along with such agitation and melancholy, that his health was far from perfect. A very virtuous man of the Church, his relative, who aided and consoled him from the time of this accident to his death, told of these matters which spread far and wide in every tongue, with each teller adding to it, either by his invention or by his lies.

To speak now of the apparition of spirits, about which many have written great volumes, would you not judge it pointless, and would it not be an unbearable abuse of Scripture, to offer in evidence that passage against the return of spirits, that they leave and do not return (the Prophet saying at that point that human will is by itself led into sin, but cannot by itself escape it without the assistance of celestial grace)? Scripture is so full of apparitions of angels and demons, and even the souls of the dead, and yet there are people of little faith who remain incredulous after such clear examples.

And when Our Lord appeared to His Apostles after His Resurrection, is it not written that they thought they had seen a spirit? And He said to them: 'Touch and see.' But if they thought they had seen a spirit, they must have believed in the return of spirits. The story I have just told, which took place in our time and on our doorstep, and one might say before our eyes, seems to me as remarkable as it is urgent.

Translated by Will McMorran

CHARLES PERRAULT

Bluebeard

Once upon a time there lived a man who possessed fine houses in town and in the country, dishes and plates of silver and gold, furniture all covered in embroidery, and carriages all gilded; but unfortunately the man's beard was blue, and this made him so ugly and fearsome that all the women and girls, without exception, would run away from him. Nearby there lived a noble lady, who had two daughters of the greatest beauty. The man asked her permission to marry one or other of them, leaving it to her to decide which daughter she would give to him. Neither of them wanted him, and each said that the other one could be his wife, for they could not bring themselves to marry a man with a blue beard. What put them off even more was that he had already been married several times, and nobody knew what had become of the wives.

Bluebeard, in order to get better acquainted, took them and their mother, with three or four of their best friends, and some young men who lived in the neighbourhood, to visit one of his country houses, where they stayed for a whole week. They had outings all the time, hunting parties, fishing trips and banquets; nor did they ever go to sleep, but spent all the night playing practical jokes on one another; and they enjoyed themselves so much that the younger of the two sisters began to think that their host's beard was not as blue as it had been, and that he was just what a gentleman should be. As soon as they were back in town, it was settled that they should marry.

After a month had passed, Bluebeard told his wife that he had to go away for at least six weeks to another part of the country, on an important business matter. He told her to make sure that she enjoyed herself properly while he was away, to invite her friends to stay and to take them out into the country if she wanted to, and not to stint herself wherever she was. 'Here are the keys of the two big storerooms,' he said, 'the keys for the cupboards with the gold and silver dinner service that is not for every day, and for my strongboxes with my gold and silver coins, and for my jewel-boxes, and here is the master key for all the rooms. As for this small key here, it will unlock the private room at the end of the long gallery in my apartment downstairs. You may open everything and go everywhere, except for this private room, where I forbid you to go; and I forbid it to you so absolutely that, if you did happen to go into it, there is no knowing what I might do, so angry would I be.' She promised to obey his commands exactly; and he kissed her, got into his carriage, and set off on his journey.

Her neighbours and friends came to visit the new bride without waiting to be invited, so impatient were they to see all the expensive things in the house; they had not dared to come while her husband was there, because of his blue beard, which scared them. And off they went to look at the bedrooms, the sitting rooms, and the dressing rooms, each one finer and more luxurious than the one before. Then they went up to the store-rooms, and words failed them when they saw how many beautiful things there were, tapestries, beds, sofas, armchairs, side-tables, dining-tables, and mirrors so tall that you could see yourself from head to foot, some with frames of glass, some of silver, and some of silver-gilt, which were the most beautiful and splendid that they had ever seen. They kept on saying how lucky their friend was and how much they envied her; she, however, took no pleasure in the sight of all this wealth, because of the impatience that she felt to go and open the door to the private room downstairs.

So keen was her curiosity that, without reflecting how rude it was to leave her guests, she went down by a little secret staircase at the back; and she was in such a hurry that two or three times she nearly broke her neck. When the door of the little room was in front of her she stood looking at it for a while, remembering how her husband had forbidden her to open it, and wondering whether something bad might happen to her if she disobeyed, but the temptation was strong and she could not resist it; so she took the little key and, trembling all over, opened the door. At first, she could see nothing, because the shutters were closed. After a few moments, she began to see that the floor was all covered in clotted blood, and that it reflected the bodies of several women, dead, and tied up along the wall (they were the wives whom Bluebeard had married, and whose throats he had cut one after the other). She nearly died of fright, and the key, which she had taken out of the lock, fell out of her hand.

When she had recovered herself a little, she picked up the key again, and locking the door behind her she went upstairs to her room to try to collect her thoughts, but she was unable to, because the shock had been too great. She noticed that the key was stained with blood, and although she cleaned it two or three times the blood would not go away. However much she washed it, and even scoured it with sand and pumice, the blood stayed on it; it was a magic key, and there was no way of cleaning it completely: when the blood was removed from one side, it came back on the other.

Bluebeard returned from his journey that very night, saying that while he was still on his way, he had received letters telling him that the business he had gone to arrange had already been settled to his advantage. His wife did all she could to make him believe that she was delighted at his returning so soon. The next day, he asked for his keys back, and she gave them to him, but her hand was trembling so much that he easily guessed what had happened.

'Why is it,' he asked, 'that the key to my private room is not here with the others?'

She replied: 'I must have left it upstairs on my table.'

'Then don't forget to give it to me later,' said Bluebeard.

She made excuses several times, but finally she had to bring him the key. Bluebeard examined it, and said to his wife: 'Why is there blood on this key?'

'I know nothing about it,' said the poor woman, as pale as death.

'You know nothing about it?' said Bluebeard; 'but I do: you have tried to get into my private room. Very well, madam, that is where you will go; and there you will take your place, beside the ladies you have seen.'

She threw herself at her husband's feet, weeping and pleading to be forgiven, and all her actions showed how truly she repented being so disobedient. So beautiful was she, and in such distress, that she would have moved the very rocks to pity; but Bluebeard's heart was harder than rock. 'You must die, madam,' he said, 'this very instant.'

'If I must die,' she said, looking at him with her eyes full of tears, 'give me some time to say my prayers to God.'

'I will give you ten minutes,' said Bluebeard, 'and not a moment longer.'

As soon as she was alone, she called to her sister and said: 'Sister Anne' (for that was her name), 'go up to the top of the tower, I beg you, to see if my brothers are coming, for they promised to come today; and if you can see them, make them a signal to hurry.'

Her sister Anne went to the top of the tower, and the poor woman below cried up to her at every moment: *'What can you see, sister Anne, sister Anne? Is anyone coming this way?'*

And her sister would reply: *'All I can see is the dust in the sun, and the green of the grass all round.'*

Meanwhile, Bluebeard, holding a great cutlass in his hand, shouted as loud as he could to his wife: 'Come down from there at once, or else I'll come and fetch you.'

'Please, just a minute longer,' his wife answered, and immediately called out, but quietly: *'What can you see, sister Anne, sister Anne? Is anyone coming this way?'*

And her sister Anne replied: *'All I can see is the dust in the sun, and the green of the grass all round.'*

'Down you come at once,' Bluebeard was shouting, 'or I will fetch you down.'

'I'm coming now,' his wife kept saying; and then she would call: *'What can you see, sister Anne, sister Anne? Is anyone coming this way?'*

And then her sister Anne replied: 'I can see a great cloud of dust, and it is coming towards us.'

'Is that our brothers on their way?'

'Alas! sister, no; it is only a flock of sheep.'

'Do you refuse to come down?' shouted Bluebeard.

'Just a moment more,' his wife answered, and called out: *'What can you see, sister Anne, sister Anne? Is anyone coming this way?'*

'I can see,' she replied, 'two horsemen riding towards us, but they are still a long way off . . . God be praised,' she cried a moment later, 'it's our brothers; I shall wave to them as hard as I can, so that they will hurry.'

Bluebeard began to shout so loudly that the whole house shook. His poor wife came down, and fell at his feet in tears, with her hair all dishevelled. 'That will not save you,' cried Bluebeard; 'you must die.' And taking her hair in one hand, and raising his cutlass in the air with the other, he was on the point of chopping off her head. The poor woman, turning towards him and looking at him with despair in her eyes, begged him to give her a minute or two to prepare herself for death.

'No, no,' he said, 'commend your soul to God,' and raising his arm . . .

At that moment, there was heard such a loud banging at the door that Bluebeard stopped short; the door opened, and at once the two horsemen came in; they drew their swords and ran straight at Bluebeard. He recognized them for his wife's brothers: one was a dragoon guard, the other a musketeer; immediately he ran to escape, but the two brothers went after him so fast that they caught him before he could get out of the front door. They cut him open with their swords, and left him dead. His poor wife was almost as dead as her husband, without even enough strength to get up and embrace her two brothers.

It turned out that Bluebeard had no heirs, so that his wife became the mistress of all his riches. She used some to marry her sister Anne to a young gentleman who had loved her for years; some she used to buy captains' commissions for her two brothers; and the remainder, to marry herself to a man of true worth, with whom she forgot all about the bad time she had had with Bluebeard.

THE MORAL OF THIS TALE

> Curiosity's all very well in its way,
> But satisfy it and you risk much remorse,
> Examples of which can be seen every day.
> The feminine sex will deny it, of course,
> But the pleasure you wanted, once taken, is lost,
> And the knowledge you looked for is not worth the cost.

ANOTHER MORAL

> People with sense who use their eyes,
> Study the world and know its ways,
> Will not take long to realize

Bluebeard

That this is a tale of bygone days,
And what it tells is now untrue:
Whether his beard be black or blue,
The modern husband does not ask
His wife to undertake a task
Impossible for her to do,
And even when dissatisfied,
With her he's quiet as a mouse.
It isn't easy to decide
Which is the master in the house.

Translated by Christopher Betts

MADAME DE LAFAYETTE

La Comtesse de Tende

In the first year of the regency of Queen Catherine de Médicis, Mademoiselle de Strozzi, the daughter of the Maréchal and a close relation of the Queen, married the Comte de Tende of the house of Savoy. He was rich and handsome; he lived with greater magnificence than any other nobleman at court, though more in a manner to attract esteem than to give pleasure. His wife nonetheless loved him passionately at first. She was very young; he regarded her as a mere child, and he soon fell in love with another woman. The Comtesse de Tende, who was spirited and of Italian descent, became jealous. She allowed herself no rest; she gave none to her husband; he avoided her presence and ceased to live with her as a man lives with his wife.

The beauty of the Comtesse de Tende increased; she showed that she was well endowed with wit; she was regarded in society with admiration; she busied herself with her own affairs and gradually recovered from her jealousy and passion.

She became the intimate friend of the Princesse de Neufchâtel, the young and beautiful widow of the prince of that house. On his death, he had bequeathed her a sovereign position that made her the most high-ranking and brilliant match at court.

The Chevalier de Navarre, a descendant of the former monarchs of that kingdom, was also at that time young, handsome, full of wit and nobility; but fortune had endowed him with no other goods than his illustrious birth. His glance fell on the Princesse de Neufchâtel – with whose character he was acquainted – as a woman capable of a passionate attachment and well suited to making the fortune of a man like himself. With this in mind, he paid court to her and attracted her interest: she did not discourage him, but he found that he was still very far from the success he desired. His intentions were known to nobody except one of his friends, to whom he had confided them; this friend was also an intimate of the Comte de Tende. He made the Chevalier de Navarre consent to entrust the Comte de Tende with his secret, in the hope that he might be persuaded to further his cause with the Princesse de Neufchâtel. The Comte de Tende already liked the Chevalier de Navarre; he spoke of the matter to his wife, for whom he was beginning to have greater consideration, and persuaded her, in fact, to do what was wanted.

The Princesse de Neufchâtel had already told her in confidence about her inclination for the Chevalier de Navarre, and she gave her friend her support and encouragement. The Chevalier came to see her; they established connections and made arrangements together; but, on seeing her, he also conceived a violent passion for her. At first, he refused to give himself up to it; he saw the obstacles that would be put in the way of his plans if he were subject to conflicting feelings of love and ambition; he tried to resist; but, in order to succeed, he would have had to avoid seeing the Comtesse de Tende frequently, whereas in fact he saw her every day when he visited the Princesse de Neufchâtel. In this way, he fell hopelessly in love with her. He was unable to hide his passion from her entirely; this flattered her self-regard and she began to feel a violent love for him.

As she was speaking to him one day of his good fortune in marrying the Princesse de Neufchâtel, he gave her a look in which his passion was fully declared and said:

'Do you then believe, Madame, that there is no good fortune I would prefer to that of marrying the princess?'

The Comtesse de Tende was struck by his expression and his words; she returned his look, and there was a moment of troubled silence between them more eloquent than words. From that time on, she was in a state of constant agitation and could find no rest; she felt remorse at depriving her friend of the heart of a man she intended to marry solely for the sake of his love, amid universal disapproval, and at the expense of her high rank.

The treachery horrified her. The shame and misery of a love affair presented themselves to her imagination; she saw the abyss into which she was about to cast herself, and resolved to avoid it.

Her resolutions were ill kept. The Princesse de Neufchâtel was almost persuaded that she should marry the Chevalier de Navarre; however, she was not satisfied that he loved her sufficiently and, despite her own passion and the care he took to deceive her, she discerned that his feelings were no more than lukewarm. She complained of it to the Comtesse de Tende, who reassured her; but Madame de Neufchâtel's complaints added the final touch to her disquiet, making apparent to her the extent of her treachery, which might perhaps cost her lover his fortune. She warned him of the Princesse de Neufchâtel's suspicions. He declared that he was indifferent to everything except her love for him; nonetheless, he mastered his feelings at her command and succeeded in reassuring the princess, who indicated to her friend that she was now entirely satisfied with the Chevalier de Navarre.

Then jealousy took possession of the Comtesse de Tende. She feared that her lover really did love the princess; she perceived all the reasons he had for loving her; their marriage, which she had earlier desired, horrified her; yet she did not wish him to break it off, and she found herself in a state of cruel uncertainty. She allowed the Chevalier de Navarre to see the remorse she felt towards the princess; but she resolved to hide her jealousy from him and believed she had in fact done so.

The Princesse de Neufchâtel's passion finally triumphed over her hesitations; she determined upon marriage, but resolved that it should be consecrated in secret and only made public afterwards.

The Comtesse de Tende felt she would die of grief. On the day the wedding was to take place, there was also a public ceremony; her husband attended. She sent all her women there; she let it be known that she was receiving no one and shut herself in her private room, where she lay on a couch and gave herself up to the most cruel torments of remorse, love and jealousy.

The room had a secret door. While she was in this state, she heard the door open and saw the Chevalier de Navarre, finely dressed and more elegant and charming than she had ever seen him.

'Chevalier! What are you doing here?' she cried. 'What do you want? Have you lost your reason? What has become of your marriage? Do you care nothing for my reputation?'

'Have no fear for your reputation, Madame,' he replied; 'no one can know I am here; there is no question of my marriage; I care no longer for my fortune, I care only for your heart, Madame; all the rest I willingly renounce. You have allowed me to see that you did not hate me; yet you have tried to conceal from me that I am fortunate enough to have caused you pain by marrying the Princesse de Neufchâtel. I have come to tell you, Madame, that I will not proceed with the marriage, that it would be a torment to me, and that I want to live only for you. They are waiting for me as I speak to you now, everything is ready, but I shall break it all off, if, in doing so, I do something that is pleasing to you and that convinces you of my passion.'

The Comtesse de Tende fell back on her couch, from which she had half risen, and looked at the Chevalier with eyes full of love and tears.

'Do you then wish me to die?' she said. 'What heart could contain everything you make me feel? That you should abandon for my sake the fortune that awaits you! I cannot even bear to think of such a thing. Go to the Princesse de Neufchâtel, go to the high position destined for you; you will have my heart as well. I shall deal with my remorse, my hesitations and my jealousy – since I am forced to admit it – in whatever way my feeble reason dictates; but I shall never see you again if you do not go immediately and consecrate your marriage. Go, don't hesitate an instant; but, for my sake and yours, give up this unreasoning passion you have revealed to me; it could lead us into terrible misfortunes.'

The Chevalier was at first enraptured to see how genuinely the Comtesse de Tende loved him; but the horror of giving himself to another woman presented itself anew to his gaze. He wept, he lamented, he promised her everything she wanted, provided that she would agree to see him again in this same place. She asked him, before he left, how he had found his way in. He told her that he had entrusted himself to an equerry in her service who had once been in his own; this man had brought him through the stable yard and up a little staircase that led to the private room as well as to the equerry's own room.

Meanwhile, the time for the wedding was drawing near and the Chevalier, urged on by the Comtesse de Tende, was at last obliged to go. He went to the greatest and most desirable gift of fortune to which a penniless younger son has ever been raised up; but he went as if to the scaffold. The Comtesse de Tende passed the night, as may well be imagined, in a state of agitation and disquiet. When morning came, she called her women;

not long after her room was open, she saw her equerry approach her bed and put a letter on it without anyone noticing. The sight of this letter disturbed her, both because she recognized it as coming from the Chevalier de Navarre and because it was so improbable that, during a night which was supposed to have been his wedding night, he had had the opportunity to write to her – so improbable was it, indeed, that she feared he or others might have put obstacles in the way of his marriage. She opened the letter with deep emotion and read these words, or something like them:

'I think only of you, Madame, I care for nothing else: in the first moments of legitimate possession of the highest-born match in France, when the day has hardly begun to break, I have left the chamber where I spent the night in order to tell you that I have already repented a thousand times of having obeyed your will and of failing to renounce everything to live for you alone.'

The Comtesse de Tende was much moved by this letter and by the circumstances in which it was written. She went to dine at the house of the Princesse de Neufchâtel, who had invited her. The princess's marriage had now been made public. The Comtesse de Tende found the room full of people; but as soon as the Princesse de Neufchâtel caught sight of her, she left the gathering and asked her to come with her to her private room. Hardly had they sat down before the princess's face was covered in tears. Her friend believed the cause to be the public declaration of her marriage: she must be finding this more difficult to bear than she had imagined. She soon saw, however, that she was wrong.

'Ah! Madame,' the Princesse de Neufchâtel said to her, 'what have I done? I have married a man for love; I have entered into an unequal match which is universally disapproved of and which drags me down; and the man I have placed above everything else loves another woman!'

The Comtesse de Tende thought she would faint when she heard these words; she did not believe that the princess could have fathomed her husband's passion without having also unravelled its cause. She was unable to reply. The Princesse de Navarre, as she was now called, noticed nothing and continued thus:

'The Prince de Navarre, Madame, far from showing the impatience one would have expected once the wedding was over, kept me waiting yesterday night. When he came, he was joyless, distracted and preoccupied. At dawn, he left my room on some pretext or other. But he had been writing: I saw it on his hands. To whom could he have been writing if not to a mistress? Why did he keep me waiting, and what was it that preoccupied him?'

At that moment the conversation was interrupted because the Princesse de Condé was arriving; the Princesse de Navarre went to receive her and the Comtesse de Tende remained, beside herself. That very evening, she wrote to the Prince de Navarre to warn him of the suspicions of his wife and to urge him to restrain his behaviour.

Their passion was in no way diminished by the perils and obstacles they faced. The Comtesse de Tende could not rest, and sleep no longer came to alleviate her distress. One morning, after she had called her women, her equerry approached and told her quietly that the Prince de Navarre was in her private room and that he begged her to let him tell her something it was absolutely necessary for her to know. It is easy to yield to what gives pleasure: the Comtesse de Tende knew that her husband had gone out; she said that she wished to sleep, and told her women to close her doors again and not to return unless she called them.

The Prince de Navarre came in from the private room and fell on his knees by her bed.

'What have you to tell me?' she said.

'That I love you, Madame, that I adore you, that I cannot live with Madame de Navarre. This morning, I was overcome by such a violent desire to see you that I was unable to resist it. I have come here at the risk of all the consequences that might follow and without even hoping to be able to speak to you.'

The Comtesse de Tende rebuked him at first for compromising her so heedlessly; then their passion drew them into such a long conversation that the Comte de Tende returned from town. He went to his wife's apartment; he was told that she was not yet awake. It was late; he insisted on entering her room and found the Prince de Navarre on his knees by her bed, as he had been from the start. Never was a man so astonished as the Comte de Tende; never was a woman so dismayed as his wife. The Prince de Navarre alone retained some presence of mind; without losing his poise or getting up, he said to the Comte de Tende:

'Come, I beg you, and help me to obtain a favour: I have gone down on my knees to ask for it, yet it has not been granted.'

The tone and manner of the Prince de Navarre allayed the astonishment of the Comte de Tende. 'I am not sure,' he replied in the same tone as the prince, 'that a favour that you ask of my wife on bended knees, when she is said to be asleep and I find you alone with her, and with no carriage at my door, is likely to be of the kind that I would wish to grant.'

The Prince de Navarre, who had overcome the embarrassment of the first moments and regained his assurance, rose from his knees and sat down with the greatest self-possession. The Comtesse de Tende, trembling and distraught, was able to hide her confusion because her bed was in shadow. The Prince de Navarre addressed her husband thus:

'I shall surprise you: you will no doubt blame my conduct, but you will nonetheless be obliged to help me. I love and am loved by the person at court most worthy of love. Yesterday evening, I slipped away from the company of the Princesse de Navarre and all my servants in order to go to an assignation with this lady. My wife, who has already fathomed that I have something other than herself on my mind and who is keeping my conduct under observation, found out from my servants that I was no longer with them; her jealousy and despair are beyond bounds. I told her that I had spent the time that gave her anxiety as a guest of the Maréchale de Saint-André, who is unwell and who is seeing hardly anyone; I told her that only Madame la Comtesse de Tende was there and that she could ask her if it were not true that she had seen me there the whole evening. I decided to come and place myself in your wife's hands. I went to the house of La Châtre, which is only a few steps away from here; I left the house without my servants seeing me and was told that Madame la Comtesse was awake. I found no one in her antechamber and made so bold as to enter. She is refusing to tell lies on my behalf; she protests that she is unwilling to betray her friend and is very properly rebuking me, as I have vainly rebuked myself. It is imperative to relieve Madame la Princesse de Navarre of her anxiety and jealousy so that I may be spared the mortal embarrassment of her reproaches.'

The Comtesse de Tende was hardly less surprised by the Prince de Navarre's presence of mind than by the arrival of her husband; she recovered her composure, and the Comte de Tende's doubts were entirely set at rest. He joined his wife in pointing out to the Prince de Navarre the depths of misfortune and misery into which he was about to cast himself, and what he owed to the princess; the Comtesse de Tende promised to tell her whatever her husband wanted.

As the Prince de Navarre was about to leave, the Comte de Tende stopped him. 'To reward us,' he said, 'for the service we are to perform for you at the expense of the truth, at least tell us who this charming mistress is. She cannot be a person worthy of any esteem, since she loves you and maintains a liaison with you when you are committed to a woman as beautiful as the Princesse de Navarre, married to her, and deeply in her debt. This person can have neither wit, nor courage, nor delicacy; the truth is that it is not worth spoiling for her sake such great good fortune as yours and making yourself guilty of such ingratitude.'

The Prince de Navarre could find nothing to say; he pretended to be in a hurry. The Comte de Tende showed him out personally so that he would not be seen.

The Comtesse de Tende remained deeply distressed by the risk she had run, by the thoughts her husband's words inspired, and by her perception of the misfortunes to which her passion left her exposed; but she lacked the strength to withdraw from it. She continued her relations with the Prince de Navarre; she saw him sometimes through the offices of her equerry La Lande. She considered herself, and was indeed, one of the most unhappy women in the world. Every day, the Princesse de Navarre confided to her a jealousy of which she was the cause and which filled her with remorse; when the Princesse de Navarre was satisfied with her husband's behaviour, she was herself consumed with jealousy in her turn.

A new torment was added to those she already suffered: the Comte de Tende became as much enamoured of her as if she had not been his wife; he no longer left her alone and tried to avail himself of all the rights he had previously despised.

She refused him forcefully, bitterly, even scornfully. Her feelings being already committed to the Prince de Navarre, she was wounded and offended by any passion but his. The Comte de Tende was sensitive to the full severity of her behaviour. Cut to the quick, he assured her that he would never trouble her again: he left her, in fact, in the abruptest manner possible.

The campaign was about to begin: the Prince de Navarre had to leave to join the army. The Comtesse de Tende began to feel the pain his absence would cause and to be fearful for the perils to which he would be exposed. She resolved to evade the necessity of hiding her affliction and made a plan to spend the summer on an estate she owned thirty miles from Paris.

She put this plan into effect. Their farewell was so painful that they could only consider it a bad omen for them both. The Comte de Tende remained with the King, to whom he was attached by virtue of his office.

The court was to move closer to the army; Madame de Tende's house was not far removed from it; her husband told her that he would visit the house for a single night to see to some building work that he had set in train. He did not wish her to have any reason to believe that the purpose of the visit was to see her; his resentment towards her was of the kind that only passion brings. Madame de Tende had found the Prince de Navarre so respectful at first, and she had felt herself capable of so much virtue, that she had mistrusted neither him nor herself. But time and opportunity had triumphed over her virtue and his respect, and, not long after she had arrived at her house, she realized that she was pregnant. One need only reflect on the reputation she had acquired and preserved, and on the state of her relations with her husband, in order to measure her despair. She came near several times to making an attempt on her life; yet she conceived some slight hope on the basis of her husband's impending visit, and resolved to await its outcome. While thus oppressed, she endured the further pain of knowing that La Lande, whom she had left in Paris to pass on her lover's letters and her own, had died after a short illness, and she found herself deprived of all help at a time when she needed it most.

Meanwhile the army had undertaken a siege. Because of her passion for the Prince de Navarre, she was subject to incessant fears, even amidst the mortal horrors that racked her.

Her fears proved to be only too well founded. She received letters from the army informing her that the siege was over; but they informed her at the same time that the Prince de Navarre had been killed on the last day. She lost her senses and her reason; both, at times, deserted her entirely. There were moments when this extreme misery seemed to her a kind of consolation. She no longer feared for her peace of mind, her reputation, or her life. Death alone seemed desirable to her. She hoped her grief would bring it about; if not, she was resolved to make an end of herself. A last trace of shame persuaded her to say that she was suffering severe pains as a pretext for her cries and tears. When her many afflictions forced her gaze to turn inward, she saw that she had deserved them, and her natural feelings as well as her Christian ones dissuaded her from becoming her own murderer and suspended the execution of her resolve.

She had not long been a prey to these violent torments when the Comte de Tende arrived. She believed she had experienced all the feelings her unhappy state could inspire in her; but the arrival of her husband brought with it a further agitation and confusion that she had not felt before. He learned on his arrival that she was ill and, as he had always maintained proper forms of behaviour in the eyes of the public and of his household servants, he came at once to her room. She seemed, when he saw her, like a woman beside herself, a woman distracted; she was unable to hold back her tears, attributing them as before to the pains that tormented her. The Comte de Tende, touched by the state he found her in, felt compassion for her and, believing that he might thereby divert her mind from her pain, spoke to her of the death of the Prince de Navarre and of his wife's grief.

Madame de Tende's own grief could not withstand these remarks; her tears became so copious that the Comte de Tende was taken aback and almost guessed the truth. He left the room in a state of great turmoil and agitation; it seemed to him that his wife's condition was not one caused by physical pain; the way she had wept still more bitterly when he had spoken to her of the death of the Prince de Navarre had struck him, and all at once the singular incident when he had found him kneeling by her bed presented itself to his imagination. He remembered how she had treated him when he had wanted to come back to her, and, in the end, thought he saw the truth; yet there still remained in his mind that trace of doubt which our self-regard always allows us in cases where belief exacts too high a price.

His despair was extreme, and all his thoughts were violent; but he was wise enough to master his first reactions and resolved to leave the next day at dawn without seeing his wife, trusting that time would bring him greater certainty and enable him to determine his course of action.

Deeply immersed in her misery as Madame de Tende was, she had not failed to notice her own lack of self-possession and the manner in which her husband had left her room; she guessed a part of the truth and, feeling only horror now for her mortal life, she resolved to end it in a way that might not cost her the hope of salvation.

She considered carefully what she should do; then, shaken to the depths of her soul and overwhelmed by a sense of her misfortunes, repenting of her very life, she finally brought herself to write these words to her husband:

'This letter will cost me my life; but I deserve death and desire it. I am pregnant. The man who caused my misfortune is no longer on this earth, nor is the only other person who knew of our liaison; the world at large has never suspected it. I had resolved to put an end to my life by my own hand, but I offer it instead to God and to you in expiation of my crime. I had no wish to dishonour myself in public, since my reputation concerns you also; preserve it for your own sake. I shall reveal the state I find myself in; you must conceal its shameful cause and bring about my death when you wish and by what means you wish.'

Day was beginning to break as she finished this letter, perhaps the most difficult to write that has ever been written. She sealed it, went to the window, and, seeing the Comte de Tende in the courtyard about to get into his carriage, sent one of her women to take it to him and tell him that there was no hurry and that he could read it at his leisure. The Comte de Tende was surprised to receive the letter; it gave him a kind of presentiment, not of everything he would in fact find in it, but of something connected with his reflections the day before. He got into his carriage alone, full of disquiet and not even daring to open the letter, impatient as he was to read it. Finally, he did read it and discovered his misfortune. It is difficult to imagine the thoughts that came into his mind at that moment. The violent state he was in would have led anyone who had been present to believe that he had lost his reason or was about to die. Jealousy and well-founded suspicions ordinarily prepare husbands for their misfortunes; it may even be that they always have their doubts; yet they are spared the certainty afforded by an open confession, which it is beyond our capacity to comprehend.

The Comte de Tende had always found his wife worthy of love, even though he had not loved her constantly himself; but, of all the women he had ever known, she had always appeared to him to be also the most worthy of esteem. Thus, he felt no less astonishment than rage, and through these emotions he still felt, despite himself, a pain in which tenderness had its part.

He stopped at a house that happened to be on his road and passed several days there in a state of agitation and affliction, as one can well imagine. His first reflections were those it was natural to have on such an occasion. He thought only of killing his wife, but the death of the Prince de Navarre and La Lande, whom he recognized without difficulty as the confidant, gave his fury some pause. He had no doubt that his wife had told him the truth in claiming that her liaison had never been suspected; he judged that the marriage of the Prince de Navarre could easily have deceived the world at large, since he had himself been deceived. Now that he had been made so palpably aware of the truth, the fact that everyone else was wholly ignorant of his misfortune was a consolation; but the circumstances, making evident to him how far and in what way he had been deceived, pierced his heart, and his only desire was for vengeance. Yet he reflected that, if he killed his wife and it was noticed that she was pregnant, people would easily guess the truth. As he was the proudest of men, he decided on the course of action which would best protect his reputation and resolved to let nothing emerge in public. With this in mind, he sent a gentleman to the Comtesse de Tende with this note:

'The desire to prevent my shame from becoming a public spectacle must have precedence for the time being over my vengeance; I shall consider later how to dispose of your worthless life. Conduct yourself as if you had continued to be what you ought to have been.'

Madame de Tende received this message with joy; she believed it to be her death sentence and, when she saw that she had her husband's consent to make her pregnancy known, she became keenly aware that shame is the most violent of the passions. She discovered a kind of peace in believing herself sure to die and to see her reputation safeguarded; her sole thought now was to prepare herself for death; and, as she was a woman whose every feeling was lively, she embraced virtue and penitence as ardently as she had followed the dictates of her passion. Besides, her soul was disabused and steeped in affliction; she could turn her gaze on nothing in life that was not more harsh than death itself, so that she saw no other remedy for her misfortunes than the ending of her unhappy life. She spent some time in this state, appearing more dead than alive. Finally, in about the sixth month of her pregnancy, her body succumbed, a continuous fever took hold of her and the very violence of her illness caused her to give birth. She had the consolation of seeing her child alive, of being certain that he could not live and that she would not give her husband an illegitimate heir. She herself died a few days later, receiving death with a joy no mortal has ever felt; she instructed her confessor to deliver to her husband the news of her death, to ask his pardon on her behalf, and to beg him to forget her memory, which could only be odious to him.

The Comte de Tende received the news without inhumanity, and even with some sentiments of pity, but nonetheless with joy. Although he was very young, he never had the desire to marry again, and he lived to a very advanced age.

Translated by Terence Cave

VOLTAIRE

Micromégas
A Philosophical Story

I

Voyage of an inhabitant of the star Sirius to the planet Saturn

On one of those planets which orbit the star named Sirius there lived a young man of great intelligence, whom I had the honour of meeting during the last visit he made to our little ant hill; he was called Micromégas, a most suitable name for any man of parts. He was eight leagues tall: by which I mean twenty-four thousand geometrical paces, each measuring five feet.

A number of the algebraists, people ever useful to the public, will now reach for their pens and discover that, since Monsieur Micromégas, inhabitant of the land of Sirius, measures twenty-four thousand paces from tip to toe (the equivalent of one hundred and twenty thousand royal feet), and since we on Earth measure scarcely five feet and our globe is nine thousand leagues in circumference, they will find, as I say, that the globe which fostered him must be exactly twenty-one million, six hundred thousand times greater in circumference than our little Earth. Nothing in nature could be simpler or more straightforward. To compare the territories of certain German or Italian sovereigns – which may be toured in half an hour – with the Turkish or Muscovite or Chinese empires, would be to give but a feeble idea of the prodigious differences which nature has contrived between all her creatures.

His Excellency's height being as I have stated, our sculptors and painters will all readily agree that his waist probably measures fifty thousand royal feet; which makes for very handsome proportions.

As to his mind, it was among the most cultivated in existence; he knew a great number of things, some of which he worked out for himself: while not yet two hundred and fifty years of age and still a pupil at the Jesuit college of his planet (as was the custom), he independently solved more than fifty of Euclid's Problems. Which is eighteen more than Blaise Pascal, who solved thirty-two of them for his own amusement (or so his sister says), only to develop into a fairly average geometer and a very poor metaphysician. By the age of four hundred and fifty, as childhood was drawing to a close, Micromégas was busy dissecting quantities of those tiny insects which are scarcely a hundred feet in diameter and invisible under ordinary Sirian microscopes. He wrote a most original work on the subject, which nonetheless landed him in trouble. The local Mufti, a celebrated pedant and ignoramus, found some of the arguments in this book to be suspect, offensive, reckless, and unorthodox to the point of heresy. He proceeded against it vigorously. The case turned on whether the substantial form of the fleas on Sirius was of the same nature as that of the snails. Micromégas mounted a spirited defence; he won over all the ladies; the trial lasted two hundred and twenty years. At last the Mufti had the book condemned by jurists who had not opened it, and the author was ordered not to show his face at court for the next eight hundred years.

He was only moderately grieved to be banished from a court so full of squabbling and petty intrigue. He wrote a very amusing song about the Mufti, who was not especially bothered; after which he set out on a voyage from planet to planet to complete his education 'in heart and mind', as the saying goes. Those who travel only by post-chaise or berlin coach will no doubt be amazed at the methods of transport in the world above: down here on our little mud-heap we have no conception of customs other than our own.

Our traveller was wonderfully acquainted with the laws of gravity and with all the forces of attraction and repulsion. These he put to such use that, sometimes with the aid of a sunbeam, at other times through the convenient offices of a comet, he and his retinue went from one globe to the next as a bird hops from branch to branch. He travelled the length of the Milky Way in no time at all, though I am bound to record that not once on his way past the stars with which it is strewn did he glimpse the lovely empyreal heaven which the celebrated Reverend Derham boasts of having seen at the end of his telescope. I do not suggest that the Reverend Derham has poor eyes, Heaven forbid! But Micromégas was there in person, is a good observer, and ... I have no wish to contradict anyone.

After a lengthy tour, Micromégas arrived on Saturn. Though accustomed to novelties, on seeing the smallness of this globe and its inhabitants he could not at first suppress that smile of superiority which even the wisest of us is occasionally guilty of. Saturn is after all barely nine hundred times the size of the Earth, and its citizens are dwarfs a mere thousand fathoms or so tall. At first he and his retinue amused themselves a little at the expense of their hosts, just as an Italian musician arriving in France invariably laughs at Lully's compositions. However, as the Sirian was not stupid he soon came to appreciate that a thinking being may be far from ridiculous even if he is only six thousand feet tall. He became well acquainted with the Saturnians, after their initial surprise had worn off. He formed a close friendship with the Secretary of the Academy of Saturn, a most intelligent fellow who had not, it is true, made any discoveries of his own, but who could give a very good account of the discoveries of others and was moderately adept at both light verse and heavy computations. I shall here record, for the satisfaction of readers, a singular conversation which Micromégas had one day with Monsieur Secretary.

II

Conversation between the inhabitants of Sirius and Saturn

After His Excellency had gone to bed, and the Secretary had drawn close to his face, the former began:

'One has to admit,' he said, 'that nature is full of variety.'

'Why yes,' said the Saturnian, 'nature is like a flower-bed whose blooms –'

'No,' said the other, 'let's not go into your flower beds.'

'Nature,' resumed the Secretary, 'is an assembly of blondes and brunettes, whose costumes –'

'What do I care for your brunettes?' said the other.

'Well, then, nature is like a portrait gallery whose individual features –'

'No!' said the visitor. 'Once and for all, nature is like nature. Why search for comparisons?'

'To please you,' answered the Secretary.

'I don't want to be pleased,' the visitor replied, 'I want to be instructed. You can begin by telling me how many senses the inhabitants of your globe possess.'

'We have seventy-two,' said the Academician; 'and every day we complain at having so few. Our imaginations surpass our needs; with our seventy-two senses, our ring of Saturn and our five moons, we feel too circumscribed; despite all our curiosity, and the profusion of passions arising from our seventy-two senses, we have all the time in the world to be bored.'

'I can well believe it,' said Micromégas. 'We on our globe possess nearly a thousand senses, yet there remains in us some vague unease, some nameless longing which ceaselessly reminds us that we are of little consequence, and that there are beings who enjoy a more perfect state. I have travelled a little. I have seen mortals who are far inferior to us; I have seen others far superior, but I have never seen any who did not have more desires than real needs, and more needs than means to satisfy them. Some day perhaps I shall find the land where nothing is lacking; but so far no one has given me positive news of such a place.'

The Saturnian and the Sirian went on to exhaust themselves in conjecture; but after much ingenious and unsettled argument they were forced to return to facts.

'How long do you live for?' asked the Sirian.

'Ah! All too short a time,' replied the little man from Saturn.

'Just as with us,' said the Sirian. 'We are always lamenting the brevity of life. It must be a universal law of nature.'

'Alas,' said the Saturnian, 'we live for only five hundred entire revolutions of the sun.' (The equivalent, by human reckoning, of fifteen thousand years or thereabouts.) 'Which, as you can see, is to die almost the moment one is born; our existence is a point in time, our span is but an instant, our globe a mere atom. No sooner do we begin to educate ourselves a little than death arrives before we have any experience of life. For myself I do not dare to make plans; I feel like a drop of water in an immense ocean. I am ashamed, particularly in front of you, of the ridiculous figure I cut in this world.'

'Were you not a philosopher,' Micromégas answered, 'I should be afraid of distressing you with the news that our life span is seven hundred times greater than yours; but as you know too well, when the moment comes to return our body to the elements and reanimate nature under another form – what is called dying – when that moment of metamorphosis arrives, to have lived for an eternity or for a single day amounts to precisely the same. I have been in places where they live a thousand times longer than we do, and found that still they grumbled. Yet everywhere there are to be found people of sense, who accept their lot and give thanks to the author of nature. He has distributed through this universe a wealth of varieties with a kind of admirable uniformity. All thinking beings differ, for example, but all are fundamentally alike in sharing the gift of thought and of possessing desires. Matter everywhere has extension, but on each globe it has different properties. On Saturn how many such properties do you recognize in matter?'

'If you mean,' replied the Saturnian, 'properties without which we believe this globe could not exist in its present form, then we count three hundred: extension, impenetrability, mobility, gravity, divisibility, and so forth.'

'No doubt so small a number suffices for the ends the Creator had in mind for your little dwelling,' replied the visitor. 'I marvel at His wisdom in all things; everywhere I see difference, but also everywhere proportion. Your globe is small, so too are its inhabitants; you have few sensations; your matter has few properties – all this is the work of Providence. Of what colour is your sun, examined closely?'

'White, tending strongly to yellow,' said the Saturnian. 'And when we separate out one of its rays, we find it to contain seven colours.'

'Ours tends towards red,' said the Sirian, 'and we have thirty-nine primary colours. Of all the suns I have approached not one resembles another, just as on your planet each and every face differs from all the others.'

After several questions of this nature, the Sirian asked how many essentially distinct substances were recognized on Saturn. He learned that only thirty or so had been identified, such as God, space, matter, beings with extension that are sentient, beings with extension that are sentient and cognizant, beings with cognition but without extension, those which interpenetrate, those which do not interpenetrate, and so forth. The philosopher

43

from Saturn was in turn prodigiously astonished to hear that the Sirian came from a world which recognized three hundred substances, and that he had discovered for himself a further three thousand in the course of his travels. Finally, after acquainting each other with a little of what they knew and a lot of what they did not, and having passed in discussion an entire revolution of the sun, they resolved to make a little philosophical voyage together.

III

The voyage of two inhabitants of Sirius and Saturn

Our two philosophers were ready to launch themselves into the atmosphere of Saturn, with a fine array of mathematical instruments, when the Saturnian's mistress heard the news and arrived in tears to make her reproaches. She was a pretty little brunette, barely six hundred and sixty fathoms tall, but whose many charms made up for her tiny stature.

'Ah, cruel man!' she cried out. 'After resisting you for fifteen hundred years, when at last I was beginning to yield, when I have spent barely two hundred years in your arms, now you leave me to go off on your travels with a giant from another world. Away with you! It was just idle curiosity, you never truly loved me; were you a true Saturnian you would stay by my side. Where are you going? What are you after? Our five moons are less fickle, our ring of Saturn less changeable than you are. Well, what's done is done, I shall never love another.'

The philosopher embraced her and wept in turn, for all that he was a philosopher; and the lady, having swooned, took her leave and found consolation in the arms of a local dandy.

Meanwhile our two seekers after knowledge departed. They began by leaping on to the ring of Saturn, which they found to be rather flat, as has been independently deduced by an illustrious inhabitant of our own little globe; from here they went without difficulty from moon to moon. A comet happened to be passing close by the last of these, so they leapt on board complete with servants and instruments. After being carried approximately a hundred and fifty million leagues they arrived at the satellites of Jupiter. They continued on to Jupiter itself, where they tarried for a year, during which time they discovered a number of wonderful secrets, which would now be at the printer's were it not that the gentlemen of the Inquisition found some of their propositions a little hard to swallow. I have nevertheless consulted the manuscript of these discoveries in the library of the illustrious Bishop of—, who, with a kindness and generosity I cannot sufficiently praise, has allowed me to consult his collection.

But let us return to our travellers. After leaving Jupiter they crossed a distance of approximately one hundred million leagues, passing close by the planet Mars, which, as we know, is five times smaller than our little globe; they observed two moons which serve that planet and which have escaped the attention of our astronomers. I am aware that Father Castel will now write (entertainingly, even) against the existence of these two moons; but I take my stand with those who reason by analogy. The good philosophers of that school know how difficult it would be for Mars, so far from the sun, to make do with any less than two moons. Whatever the facts of the case, our friends thought Mars so small that, fearing they would not find room to lay their heads, they continued on their way: like two travellers who scorn a miserable village inn and press on to the next town. But the Sirian and his companion were soon to regret their decision. They carried on for a long time and found nothing. At last they made out a small gleam of light: it was the Earth. A pitiable sight, for people coming from Jupiter. However, fearing they should have cause to repent a second time, they resolved to disembark. They moved along the tail of the comet and, finding an aurora borealis ready and waiting, boarded it and landed on Earth, on the northern shore of the Baltic Sea, on the fifth day of July in the year seventeen hundred and thirty-seven, new style.

IV

What happened to them on planet Earth

After resting for a while, they breakfasted off two mountains, which their servants had prepared for them moderately well. Now they were ready to explore the diminutive place in which they found themselves. First they went from north to south. The average step of the Sirian and his retinue covered about thirty thousand royal feet; the dwarf from Saturn lagged far behind, panting, for he had to take about twelve steps to each of the other's strides: picture to yourself (if the comparison be allowed) a tiny lapdog following a captain in the King of Prussia's guards.

Since these particular visitors move fairly quickly, they had circled the globe within thirty-six hours. It is of course true that the sun, or rather the Earth, makes the same journey in a single day; but you must remember that better progress is made turning on an axis than marching on foot. Here they were, then, back where they started, having seen that pond called the 'Mediterranean' (almost imperceptible to them) and that other pond by the name of the 'Great Ocean', which surrounds our molehill. At no point had the water reached above the dwarf's knee, and his companion scarcely got his heels wet. On their way there and on their way back they had tried their utmost to discover whether this globe was inhabited or not. They stooped, they lay down, they groped in every corner; but, their eyes and hands being out of all proportion to the little creatures crawling about here, they received not the slightest impression which might lead them to suspect that we and our fellow beings inhabiting this globe have the honour to exist.

The dwarf, who was sometimes a little rash in his judgements, concluded at first that there was no one on Earth. His primary reason was that he had seen no one. Micromégas politely pointed out that this was rather a poor way of reasoning.

'For,' said he, 'you with your little eyes cannot see certain stars of the fiftieth magnitude which I can make out quite clearly; do you conclude from this that such stars do not exist?'

'But,' said the dwarf, 'I have had a good feel around the whole place.'

'But,' replied the other, 'you may have a poor sense of touch.'

'But,' said the dwarf, 'look how badly constructed, irregular and ridiculously shaped this globe is! Everything seems to be in a state of chaos: look at these tiny streams, none of which flows in a straight line; these ponds which are neither round, square, oval, nor any other regular form; these little sharp things (he was referring to mountains) which stick up all over the place and have taken the skin off my feet! And look at the overall shape of the globe, how it flattens out at the poles, how it moves round the sun in that awkward way so that the climates at either pole are bound to be hostile to life! But what really makes me think there is no one here is that in my view no one with any sense would want to live here.'

'Very well,' said Micromégas, 'but perhaps the people who live here have no sense. And yet there are signs that all this was not created for nothing. Everything seems irregular, in your words, because everything on Saturn and Jupiter is laid out in straight lines. So, perhaps that is precisely why there is a measure of confusion here. Have I not told you that in my travels I have always met with variety?'

The Saturnian replied to these arguments point by point. The debate might have gone on for ever, had not Micromégas in the heat of argument fortunately chanced to break the string of his diamond necklace. The diamonds dropped; they were pretty little stones, of different sizes, the largest weighing four hundred pounds and the smallest fifty. The dwarf picked up one or two of them and noticed, as he held them to his eye, that from the way they had been cut these diamonds made excellent microscopes. So he took one little microscope, a hundred and sixty feet in diameter, and applied it to his pupil; Micromégas picked another measuring two thousand five hundred feet. Excellent though these were, however, nothing could be seen through them at first: adjustment was needed. At length the Saturnian saw something imperceptible moving about just beneath the surface of the Baltic Sea: it was a whale. He picked it up adroitly with his little finger and, placing it on his thumbnail, he showed it to the Sirian, who for the second time began laughing at the immoderately small size of the inhabitants of our globe. The Saturnian, satisfied by now that our world was inhabited, at once imagined that it must be exclusively so by whales; and, since he was much given to rational analysis, he wanted to work out where so tiny an atom derived its movement, and whether it had ideas, a will and freedom. Micromégas for his part was much perplexed: he examined the creature very patiently, and came to the conclusion that there could be no grounds for believing a soul to be lodged in such a body. The two travellers were thus inclining to the view that there was no intelligent life on Earth, when they saw through their microscopes something larger than a whale floating on the Baltic Sea. It will be recalled that at this moment in time a flock of philosophers was just returning from the Arctic Circle, where they had gone to carry out observations which no one had hitherto taken it into their heads to make. The gazettes merely record that the vessel ran aground on the shores of the Gulf of Bothnia, and that they had a good deal of trouble escaping with their lives; but in this world one never knows what takes place behind the scenes. I shall here relate simply what occurred, and without additions of my own, which is no small effort for a historian.

V

Observations and arguments of the two travellers

Micromégas extended his hand very gently towards the spot where the object had appeared, and stretched out two fingers which he instantly withdrew for fear of making a mistake; then, opening and closing them, he delicately lifted the vessel bearing these gentlemen and placed it on his nail, as before, without squeezing too tightly for fear of crushing it.

'This is a quite different animal from the earlier one,' pronounced the dwarf from Saturn. Micromégas placed the alleged animal in the palm of his hand. The passengers and crew, who thought they had been swept up by a hurricane and now believed they were on some sort of rock, all started to bustle about. The sailors picked up barrels of wine, throwing them on to Micromégas's hand and leaping down after them. The geometers took their quadrants, their sextants and a few Lapp girls, and climbed down on to the Sirian's fingers. There was so much action that finally he felt something moving and tickling his fingers: the iron tip of an alpenstock was being driven a foot deep into his index finger; from which prickling he concluded that something sharp had projected from the tiny animal he was holding. But at first he suspected nothing more. The microscope, which barely allowed them to see a whale or a ship, had no purchase on a creature as imperceptible as man. I have no wish to offend anyone's vanity, but I must ask those convinced of their own importance to make a preliminary observation with me: if we take the average height of mankind to be approximately five feet, then we cut no more imposing a figure on this Earth than a creature approximately one six-hundred-thousandth of an inch high standing on a ball with a circumference of ten feet.

Now imagine a form of matter capable of holding the Earth in its hand, whose organs are in proportion to our own (and there may well exist any number of such forms of matter): then consider, I beg you, what they would make of those battles of ours, where we gain a couple of villages in one skirmish, only to lose them in the next.

I have no doubt that if some captain in the great Grenadiers ever reads this work, he will raise by at least two good feet the height of his company's bearskin bonnets; but I can tell him now that try as he may, he and his men will never be more than infinitesimally small.

What marvellous skill was required, then, for our philosopher from Sirius to spy out the atoms I have just been describing! When Leeuwenhoek and Hartsoeker first saw, or thought they saw, the seed from which we all grow, they were making a far less astonishing discovery. What pleasure Micromégas felt in seeing these tiny machines moving about, in scrutinizing their comings and goings, in following them in all their operations! How he shouted out! With what joy he handed one of his microscopes to his travelling companion!

'I can see them!' they both cried out at once. 'Look at them ferrying their loads, bending down and straightening up again!'

As they spoke their hands trembled with the excitement of seeing such novel objects and with the fear of losing them. The Saturnian, passing from extreme scepticism to extreme credulity, thought he could see some of them engaged in propagating themselves. 'Aha!' he said, 'I have caught nature in the act.' But he was deceived by appearances, which happens all too often, whether one uses microscopes or not.

VI

How they fared in the company of humans

Micromégas, a far better observer of things than his dwarf, could clearly see that the atoms were talking to one other; he drew the attention of his companion who, ashamed at his mistake over procreation, was now somewhat reluctant to credit such species with the power to communicate ideas. He had the gift of languages as much as the Sirian; but since he could not hear these human atoms talking, he concluded that they could not talk. Besides, how should such imperceptible beings have speech organs, and what could they possibly have to say to each other? In order to speak one must be able to think, more or less. But if they could think, they must have the equivalent of a soul. Now to attribute the equivalent of a soul to this species seemed to him absurd.

'But,' said the Sirian, 'just now you thought they were making love. Do you think one can make love without having thoughts, without uttering the odd word here and there, without at least making oneself understood? Do you further suppose that it is a harder thing to produce an argument than an infant? To my mind how one does either is a great mystery.'

'I no longer dare to believe or disbelieve,' said the dwarf. 'I have no opinions left. We must endeavour to examine these insects, and reason afterwards.'

'Very well said,' Micromégas replied, and he immediately took out a pair of scissors. With these he cut his nails, and with a clipping from his thumbnail he fashioned on the spot a sort of large speaking-trumpet shaped like a vast funnel, the smaller end of which he placed to his ear. The rim of the funnel embraced the ship and its entire company. The faintest voice could be picked up by the circular fibres of the nail; such that, thanks to his industry, the philosopher up above now heard perfectly the buzzing of the human insects down below. Within a few hours he could distinguish words, and succeeded finally in understanding French. The dwarf did likewise, though with greater difficulty. The astonishment of the visitors redoubled by the minute. They were listening to tiny microbes making reasonable sense: this trick on the part of nature seemed wholly unaccountable. You may imagine the impatience with which the Sirian and his dwarf burned to engage these atoms in conversation; but the latter feared that his thunderous voice, not to mention that of Micromégas, would deafen the microbes without being understood by them. They must find a way of diminishing its force. Each therefore placed in his mouth a sort of miniature toothpick, whose finely sharpened end reached down close to the ship. The Sirian held the dwarf on his knee and the ship and company on one nail. He bent his head and began speaking in a low voice. With the aid of these precautions and many more, he addressed them at last:

'Invisible insects, whom the hand of the Creator has been pleased to bring to life in the abyss of the infinitely small, I give thanks to Him for deigning to reveal to me secrets which had seemed impenetrable. Perhaps nobody at my court would deign to look upon you; but I disdain no creature, and I hereby offer you my protection.'

If ever there was astonishment, it was to be found among the company who heard these words, and who could not imagine where they were coming from. The ship's chaplain fell to reciting the prayers for casting out devils; the sailors swore; the philosophers on board invented a system: but whatever the system, they could not explain who was talking to them. The dwarf from Saturn, whose voice was gentler than Micromégas's, informed them briefly as to what manner of beings they were dealing with. He recounted the voyage from Saturn, put them in the picture as to the identity of Monsieur Micromégas, and, after commiserating with them for being so small, enquired whether they had always been in this miserable condition bordering on nothingness and what were they doing on a planet which appeared to be run by whales, whether they were happy, whether they multiplied, whether they had a soul, and a hundred other such questions.

One quibbler on board, bolder than the rest and offended at having doubts cast upon his soul, scrutinized their interlocutor through sights mounted on his quadrant, took two bearings, and on the third said: 'You appear to think, sir, that because you measure a thousand fathoms from head to toe, you are therefore –'

'A thousand fathoms!' exclaimed the dwarf. 'Good heavens! How can he possibly know my height? A thousand fathoms! He is not an inch out in his calculation. What! This atom has actually measured me! He is a geometer, and he knows my size; whereas I, who can only see him through a microscope, have yet to discover his!'

'Yes, I have your measure,' said the physicist, 'and what's more I am now going to measure your big friend.'

This proposal was accepted, and His Excellency stretched out full length on the ground, since had he remained standing his head would have been too far above the clouds. Our philosophers planted a tall tree into him, at a spot which the good Doctor Swift would call by its name but which I shall certainly refrain from specifying, out of my great respect for the ladies. Next, by a series of triangulations, they deduced that they were in fact looking at a young man one hundred and twenty thousand royal feet long.

Micromégas now spoke again: 'I see more than ever that one must not judge anything by its apparent size. O God, who has endowed with intelligence forms of matter that seem so contemptible, the infinitely small evidently costs you as little effort as the infinitely great; moreover, if there can possibly exist creatures smaller than these, they may well be of greater intelligence than those superb animals I have seen in the heavens, whose foot alone would cover this globe on which I have landed.'

One of the philosophers replied that he could rest assured; there were indeed intelligent beings far smaller than man. He described for him, not Virgil's fabulations about the bees, but what Swammerdam has discovered and Réaumur dissected. Lastly he informed him that there are creatures which are to bees as bees are to humans, or as the Sirian himself was to those prodigious animals he had mentioned, and as those animals are to yet other forms, beside which they seem but atoms. By degrees the conversation began to flow, and Micromégas spoke as follows.

VII

Conversation with the humans

'O intelligent atoms, in whom the Supreme Being has been pleased to manifest His skill and His might, the joys you experience on your globe must doubtless be extremely pure; for, having so little matter and being apparently all mind, you must pass your lives in thinking and loving – in leading the true life of the spirit. Nowhere have I witnessed real happiness, but surely it is to be found here.'

At this all the philosophers shook their heads, and one of them, more forthright than the rest, owned frankly that, except for a small number of individuals held in low esteem, the rest were a confederacy of the mad, the bad and the miserable.

'We have more than enough matter to do plenty of evil, if evil comes from matter; and too much spirit, if evil comes from the spirit. For instance, do you realize that as I speak a hundred thousand lunatics of our species, wearing hats, are busy killing or being killed by a hundred thousand other animals in turbans, and that almost everywhere on Earth this is how we have carried on since time immemorial?'

The Sirian shuddered and asked what could be the subject of such terrible quarrels between such puny creatures.

'It is all for the sake of a few mud-heaps,' replied the philosopher, 'no bigger than your heel. Not that any of the millions who are cutting each other's throats lay claim to the least particle of these heaps. The issue is simply whether it shall belong to one man known as "Sultan" or to another known, for some reason, as "Tsar". Neither man has ever seen or ever will see the little piece of land in question, and almost none of the creatures slaughtering each other has ever seen the animal on whose behalf they are slaughtering.'

'Ah! The devils!' cried the Sirian indignantly. 'Is such fanatical fury conceivable? I am tempted to take three strides and with each stride to trample this whole ant-hill of ridiculous assassins.'

'Spare yourself the trouble,' came the reply. 'They are making a fair job of their own destruction. The truth is that, ten years on, there is never one in a hundred of the wretches left; even those who have not drawn a sword are carried off by hunger, exhaustion or debauchery. Besides, it is not they who should be punished, but the sedentary barbarians holed up in their offices, who command the massacre of a million men while digesting a good meal, and afterwards have a *Te Deum* offered up in thanks to God.'

The traveller felt moved to pity for this tiny species, in whom he was discovering such surprising contradictions.

'Since you are among the few who are enlightened,' he said to these gentlemen, 'and seem not to murder people for a living, tell me, how do you pass your time?'

'We dissect flies,' said the philosopher, 'we measure lines, we combine numbers, we agree upon the two or three things that we do understand, and argue over the two or three thousand that we do not.'

Immediately it occurred to both Sirian and Saturnian to elicit from these thinking atoms what it was that they did agree upon.

'What do you reckon to be the distance,' the former asked, 'from the Dog Star to the great star in Gemini?'

'Thirty-two and a half degrees,' they answered in unison.

'And from here to the moon?'

'Sixty times the radius of the Earth, in round numbers.'

'And how heavy is your air?'

He intended to catch them out, but they all replied that air weighs approximately nine hundred times less than the equivalent volume of the lightest water, and nineteen hundred times less than gold for ducats. The little dwarf from Saturn, amazed at their answers, was inclined to take for sorcerers the same people to whom a quarter of an hour earlier he had refused a soul.

Finally Micromégas said to them:

'Since you know so much about what is outside of you, no doubt you know even more about what is within. Tell me what your soul is, and how you form your ideas.'

The philosophers all replied in unison, as before; but now they all gave different answers. The oldest cited Aristotle, another uttered the name of Descartes, another Malebranche, another Leibniz, and yet another Locke.

An aged peripatetic confidently declared in loud tones: 'The soul is an "entelechy",[24] and is the reason by which it has the power to be what it is. So Aristotle specifically states, on page 633 of the Louvre edition: "Ἐντελεχεῖά ἐστι, etc."'

'My Greek is limited,' said the giant.

'Mine too,' said the philosophizing microbe.

'Why, then,' pursued the Sirian, 'do you cite this Aristotle fellow in Greek?'

'Because,' replied the scholar, 'one should always cite what one does not understand in the language one least understands.'

The Cartesian now spoke up: 'The soul is pure spirit; it imbibes all metaphysical ideas in the mother's womb, on leaving which it has to go to school, to relearn from scratch what it knew so well and will never know again.'

'So,' replied the animal eight leagues tall, 'there was little point in your soul being so learned inside your mother's womb, if it was to become so ignorant by the time you had some hairs on your chin. And what do you mean by spirit?'

'What a question!' said the theoretician. 'I have no idea. They say it is not the same thing as matter.'

'Do you at least know what matter is?'

'Certainly,' the man replied. 'This stone, for example, is grey and of a certain shape, has three dimensions and weight, and is divisible.'

'So!' said the Sirian. 'This thing which seems to you divisible, weighty and grey – would you mind telling me what it is? You observe some of its attributes, but do you know what it is in itself?'

'No,' said the other.

'Then you have no idea what matter is.'

Monsieur Micromégas now addressed another of the sages perched on his thumb, asking him what his soul was and what it did.

'Not a thing,' replied this disciple of Malebranche. 'It is God who does everything for me. I see everything in Him, I do everything through Him. It is He who arranges everything, without my involvement.'

'One might as well not exist,' countered the sage from Sirius. 'And you, my friend,' he said to a Leibnizian who was present, 'what is your soul?'

'It is the hand that tells the time, just as my body is the clock that chimes; or, if you prefer, it is what chimes while my body tells the time; in other words, my soul is the mirror of the universe and my body the frame on the mirror. That much is clear.'

A tiny partisan of Locke was standing by, who, when spoken to at last, replied: 'I do not know by what means I think, but I know that I have never thought except with the aid of my senses. That there are non-material intelligent substances I don't doubt; but that God should be incapable of bestowing mind on matter I doubt very much. I revere the eternal power, and it is not for me to set bounds to it; I affirm nothing, and am content to believe that more things are possible than we think.'

The animal from Sirius smiled. He found the last speaker by no means the most foolish; and the dwarf from Saturn would have embraced this follower of Locke but for their extreme disparity in size. Unfortunately for everyone, there was present a little animalcule in an academic square cap, who interrupted all the philosopher animalcules. He claimed he had all the answers, and that they were in the Summa of St Thomas Aquinas. He looked the two celestial visitors up and down, then informed them that everything – their persons, their worlds, their suns, their stars – had been created uniquely for Man.

On hearing this speech, our two travellers fell upon each other, choking with that inextinguishable laughter which, according to Homer, is the portion of the gods. Their shoulders and stomachs heaved and fell, and during these convulsions the vessel, which the Sirian had been balancing on his finger-nail, fell into the Saturnian's trouser pocket. These two good people spent a great deal of time searching for it; at last they found both ship and company, and set everything very neatly to rights again. The Sirian picked up the little microbes once more. He still spoke to them with great kindness, despite being privately a little vexed to find that the infinitely small should have a pride almost infinitely large. He promised to write a fine work of philosophy for them, in suitably tiny script, in which they would discover the nature of things. True to his word, he gave them the volume before leaving. It was taken to Paris, to the Academy of Sciences. But when the Secretary opened it, he found nothing but blank pages.

'*Aha*,' said he, '*I suspected as much.*'

Translated by Theo Cuffe

DENIS DIDEROT

This Is Not a Story

When somebody tells a story, however short it may be, and somebody is listening, it is unusual for the storyteller not to be interrupted occasionally by the listener. That is why I have introduced into the narrative you are about to read, and which is not a story – or, if you like, is a poor story – a character whose role is more or less that of the reader. Now I shall begin.

'So what do you conclude from that?'

'That such an interesting subject should set us agog with excitement, provide a topic of conversation for every club in town, be discussed there over and over again until it is exhausted, give rise to a thousand arguments, at least a score of pamphlets, and a few hundred pieces of verse one way or the other; and that in spite of all the author's subtlety, knowledge and wit, seeing that his work has created no great stir, it is mediocre, indeed very mediocre.'

'But it seems to me that he has given us quite a pleasant evening, and that this reading has produced . . .'

'What? A string of worn-out anecdotes we fired at one another, and which said only something known since time immemorial – that man and woman are two very evil animals.'

'All the same, you were infected by the epidemic and contributed your share like everybody else.'

'That's because, willy-nilly, we adapt ourselves to the company in which we find ourselves. When we enter a room full of people, we usually arrange even our expression to match those we see; we feign gaiety when we are sad, and sadness when we are tempted to be gay. We don't want to be left out of anything; the man of letters talks politics, the politician metaphysics, the metaphysician morals, the moralist finance, and the financier literature or geometry. Instead of listening or keeping quiet, everybody prefers to chatter about subjects he knows nothing about, and everybody is bored out of stupid vanity or politeness.'

'You're in a peevish mood.'

'As usual.'

'I think I would be well advised to keep my anecdote for a more favourable occasion.'

'In other words you'll wait until I'm not here.'

'No, it isn't that.'

'Or you're afraid I'd be less indulgent towards you, now we are alone together, than I would be with just anybody in a group of people.'

'No, it isn't that.'

'Then will you be kind enough to tell me what it is?'

'It's that my anecdote doesn't prove anything more than those which annoyed you so much.'

'Well, tell it to me anyway.'

'No, no; you've had enough.'

'Do you know that of all the ways people have of infuriating me, yours is the one I dislike most?'

'And what is mine?'

'That of getting people to beg you to do what you're simply dying to do anyway. Well, my dear fellow, I beg you, I implore you to be good enough to satisfy yourself.'

'Satisfy myself!'

'Begin, for heaven's sake, begin.'

'I'll try to be brief.'

'That won't do your story any harm.'

At this point, somewhat mischievously, I coughed, spat, slowly unfolded my handkerchief, blew my nose, opened my snuffbox, and took a pinch of snuff. I heard my friend muttering between his teeth: 'The story may be short, but the preliminaries aren't . . .' I felt tempted to call a servant, on the pretext of sending him on some errand; but I restrained myself, and said:

'It must be admitted that some men are very good and some women very bad.'

'Anybody can see that, sometimes without leaving his own house. What next?'

'What next? I once knew a beautiful Alsatian woman, beautiful enough to make old men come running and to halt young men dead in their tracks.'

'I knew her too; her name was Madame Reymer.'

'That's right. A fellow called Tanié, who had just arrived from Nancy, fell madly in love with her. He had no money; he was one of those poor wretches who are driven out of their homes by hard-hearted parents with too many children, and who throw themselves into the world with no idea of what will become of them, impelled by an instinct which tells them they cannot suffer any fate worse than the one they are fleeing. Tanié, in love with Madame Reymer and exalted by a passion which sustained his courage and ennobled in his eyes everything he did, submitted himself without repugnance to the most painful indignities in order to relieve his mistress's poverty. During the day he worked in the docks; at nightfall he went begging in the streets.'

'That was all very fine, but it couldn't last.'

'Consequently Tanié, tired of fighting poverty, or rather of keeping in a state of indigence a charming woman who was beset by rich men urging her to get rid of that vagabond Tanié . . .'

'Which she would have done two or three weeks later.'

'. . . and to accept their riches, decided to leave her and try to obtain a passage on one of the King's ships. The moment of his departure arrived. He went to take his leave of Madame Reymer. "My dear," he said, "I can no longer take advantage of your affection. I have made up my mind: I am leaving." "You are leaving?" "Yes." "And where are you going?" "To the West Indies. You deserve a better fate, and I cannot keep you from it any longer . . ."'

'Good for Tanié!'

'"'And what is to become of me?"'

'The deceitful woman!'

'"You are surrounded by men who want nothing better than to please you. I release you from your promises and vows. See which of your suitors you like best and accept him; it is I who beg you to do so . . ." "Oh, Tanié! You of all people are suggesting that I . . ."'

'You can spare me Madame Reymer's pantomime. I can see it all, I know it all ...'

'"As I take my leave, the only favour I demand of you is to enter into no engagement which would separate us for ever. Swear that to me, my love. Whatever part of the world I may inhabit I shall have to be in a sorry plight if I let a year go by without giving you positive proof of my tender affection. Don't cry ..."'

'They all cry when they want to.'

'"... and don't oppose a plan which the reproaches of my heart have finally inspired in me, and to which they would soon bring me back." And off went Tanié on his way to Santo Domingo.'

'Just at the right time for Madame Reymer and himself.'

'What do you know about it?'

'I know, just as surely as it is possible to know anything, that when Tanié advised her to make a choice, that choice was already made.'

'Right!'

'Go on with your story.'

'Tanié was an intelligent fellow and he had a considerable talent for business. It was not long before he made a reputation for himself. He was appointed to the Supreme Council of the tape, and in that position distinguished himself by his knowledge and impartiality. He did not aspire to great wealth; he simply wished to make his fortune honestly and speedily. Every year he sent a portion of it to Madame Reymer. He came back at the end of ... nine or ten years; no, I don't think he was away longer than that ... and presented his beloved with a little wallet containing the product of his talents and labours ... and fortunately for Tanié, this was at the time she had just parted company with the last of his successors.'

'The last?'

'Yes.'

'You mean there had been several?'

'Certainly.'

'Go on, go on!'

'But perhaps I have nothing to tell you that you don't know better than I do.'

'Never mind, go ahead anyway.'

'Madame Reymer and Tanié lived in quite a fine house in the Rue

Sainte-Marguerite, next door to me. I thought highly of Tanié and was a frequent visitor to his house, which, if not luxurious, was very well appointed.

'Although I never counted it with Madame Reymer, I can tell you for certain that she had an income of over fifteen thousand livres before Tanié returned.'

'And she concealed her wealth from him?'

'Yes.'

'Why?'

'Because she was miserly and grasping.'

'Grasping, I'll grant you; but miserly! A courtesan miserly! . . . Why, the two lovers lived for five or six years in the closest harmony.'

'Thanks to the extreme cunning of the one and the boundless trust of the other.'

'Oh, it's true that it was impossible for the shadow of a suspicion to enter a soul as pure as Tanié's. The only thing which I occasionally noticed was that Madame Reymer had soon forgotten her original poverty, that she was tormented by a love of wealth and ostentation, that she felt humiliated that a woman as lovely as herself should have to go about on foot . . .'

'Why didn't she ride in a carriage?'

'. . . and that the splendour of vice concealed its baseness from her eyes. You're laughing? . . . It was then that Monsieur de Maurepas decided to set up a trading company in North America. To be successful, this enterprise required an active, intelligent man. His choice fell on Tanié, whom he had entrusted with several important affairs during his sojourn at the Cape, and who had always acquitted himself to the Minister's satisfaction. Tanié was deeply distressed by this mark of distinction. He was so contented, so happy with his beautiful mistress! He loved her; and she loved him; or so he thought.'

'That was well said.'

'What could money add to his happiness? Nothing. However, the Minister insisted. He had to make up his mind and confide in Madame Reymer. I called at his house just at the end of this unhappy scene. Poor Tanié was dissolving in tears. "What's the matter, my dear fellow?" I asked him. He answered with a sob: "It's this woman!" Madame Reymer was peacefully working at a tapestry frame. Tanié got up abruptly and went out. I remained alone with his mistress, who promptly told me all about what she described as Tanié's folly. She gave me an exaggerated account of the slenderness of her means, pleading her cause with all the art by which a subtle mind can palliate the sophistries of ambition. "Why is he making such a fuss? He will be away two or three years at the most." "That's a long time for a man you love and who loves you as much as he does." "He loves me, you say? If he really loved me, would he hesitate to satisfy my wishes?" "But, Madame, why don't you go with him?" "Go with him? I would never go out there, and mad as he is, he has never taken it into his head to ask me. Does he distrust me?" "I don't think so for a moment." "Seeing that I waited for him for twelve years, he can surely rely on my good faith for two or three more. Monsieur, this is one of those rare opportunities which present themselves only once in a lifetime; and I don't want him one day to regret not having taken it, and perhaps blame me for having missed it." "Tanié will never regret anything, as long as he has the good fortune to please you." "That's all very well; but you may be sure he'll be very pleased to be rich when I'm an old woman. The great failing of women is that they never think of the future; that isn't a failing of mine . . ." The Minister was in Paris at the time. From the Rue Sainte-Marguerite to his house was only a step. Tanié had gone there and accepted the appointment. He came home dry-eyed but with a heavy heart. "Madame," he said, "I have been to see Monsieur de Maurepas; he has my word. I shall go, I shall go; and you will be satisfied." "Oh, my love!" Madame Reymer pushed aside her tapestry frame, rushed towards Tanié threw her arms around his neck, and overwhelmed him with caresses and sweet nothings. "Oh!" she said, "now I see that you love me." Tanié answered coldly: "You want to be rich . . ."

'She was, the minx, ten times richer than she deserved to be.'

'". . . and you shall be. Since it is gold that you love, I must go to look for gold for you." It was Tuesday: and the Minister had fixed his departure for Friday without fail. I called to say good-bye to him just as he was struggling with himself and trying to tear himself away from the arms of the beautiful, cruel, unworthy Madame Reymer. He was in the grip of a frenzy, a despair, an agony of which I have never seen the like. It was not a lament so much as a prolonged cry. Madame Reymer was still in bed.

He was holding one of her hands, and kept on saying over and over again: "Cruel woman, cruel woman! What more do you need than the comfort you now enjoy and a friend, a lover such as me? I have been to seek a fortune for her in the burning regions of America; now she wants me to seek another for her in the frozen north. My dear friend, I feel sure that this woman is mad and that I am a fool, but it would be less terrible for me to die than to grieve her. You want me to leave you; I shall leave you." He was on his knees beside her bed, his lips pressed to her hand and his face buried in the bedclothes, which, stifling his murmurs, made them all the more melancholy and frightening. The bedroom door opened; he raised his head abruptly and saw the postilion who had come to tell him that the horses had been harnessed to the chaise. He gave a cry and hid his face in the bedclothes again. After a moment of silence he stood up and said to his mistress: "Kiss me, Madame; kiss me once more, for you will never see me again." His presentiment was only too true. He set off, and three days after reaching Petersburg, caught a fever, from which he died on the fourth.'

'I knew all about that.'

'Were you by any chance one of Tanié's successors?'

'That's right; it was with that abominable beauty that all my fortunes went awry.'

'Poor Tanié!'

'There are those who would tell you he was a fool.'

'I won't defend him; but I hope with all my heart that ill fate will place those you mention in the clutches of a woman as beautiful and cunning as Madame Reymer.'

'You are cruel in your sense of vengeance.'

'Besides, if there are evil women and good men, there are also women who are very good and men who are very evil; and what I'm going to tell you now is no more a story than what you have just heard.'

'I believe you.'

'Monsieur d'Hérouville . . .'

'The one who's still alive? The Lieutenant General of the King's armies? The one who married that charming creature called Lolotte?'

'That's the one.'

'He's a man of honour and a friend of scholarship.'

'And of scholars. He has been working for a long time on a universal history of war in all ages and all nations.'

'That's a huge undertaking.'

'To carry it out, he gathered round him a few young men of considerable merit, such as Monsieur de Montucla, the author of the *History of Mathematics*.'

'Good heavens! Did he have many men of that calibre?'

'Well, there was a fellow called Gardeil, the hero of the story I'm going to tell you, who was almost his equal in his own field. A common passion for the study of Greek led to a relationship between Gardeil and me which time, reciprocal advice, a taste for seclusion, and above all the possibility of seeing each other at any time, developed into quite a close friendship.'

'At that time you were living in the Place de l'Estrapade.'

'While he lived in the Rue Sainte-Hyacinthe, and his mistress, Mademoiselle de La Chaux, in the Place Saint-Michel. I call her by her real name because the poor woman is no more, and because her life can only bring her honour in the eyes of right-minded people and win her the admiration, regrets and tears of those whom Nature has favoured or punished with some small portion of her sensitivity.'

'But your voice is trembling, and I think you're crying.'

'It seems to me that I can still see her big black eyes, soft and shining, and, hear the sound of her touching voice ringing in my ears and disturbing my heart. Unique and charming creature, you are dead! You have been dead for nearly twenty years; and the memory of you still saddens my heart.'

'Were you in love with her?'

'No. Oh, La Chaux! Oh, Gardeil! Both of you were marvels, one of woman's affection, the other of man's ingratitude. Mademoiselle de La Chaux came from a respectable family. She left her parents to throw herself into Gardeil's arms. Gardeil had nothing, while Mademoiselle de La Chaux had a modest fortune, and this fortune was entirely sacrificed to Gardeil's needs and fancies. She regretted neither the fortune she had dissipated nor the honour she had tarnished. Her lover took the place of everything in her eyes.'

'That fellow Gardeil must have been very charming and attractive, then?'

'Not a bit of it. He was a surly little man, caustic and taciturn, with a thin, swarthy face; altogether, he was a gaunt, puny figure of a man; ugly, if a man can be ugly with an intelligent face.'

'And that was what had turned the head of a charming girl?'

'Does that surprise you?'

'Always.'

'You?'

'Me.'

'So you no longer remember your affair with the Deschamps woman and the profound despair into which you sank when that creature closed her door against you?'

'Let's forget about that: go on.'

'I used to say to you: "I suppose she's very beautiful?" And you would answer sadly: "No." "Then is she intelligent?" "She's a fool." "So is it her talents that attract you?" "She has only one." "And what is that rare, sublime, marvellous talent?" "That of making me happier in her arms than I have ever been in the arms of any other woman." But Mademoiselle de La Chaux, the respectable, sensitive Mademoiselle de La Chaux, promised herself, secretly, instinctively and without knowing it, that happiness which you enjoyed, and which made you say of the Deschamps woman: "If that vile, wretched creature goes on driving me out of her house, I shall take a pistol and blow my brains out in her anteroom." Did you say that or didn't you?'

'I said it; and even now I don't know why I didn't do it.'

'You agree with me, then?'

'I'll agree with anything you like.'

'My dear fellow, the wisest man among us is fortunate indeed not to have met that woman, beautiful or ugly, witty or stupid, who could have driven him mad enough to be shut up in the Petites-Maisons. Let us be generous in our pity for men and sparing in our blame; let us look back on our past years as so many moments rescued from the evil which pursues us; and let us never think without trembling of the violence of certain natural attractions, particularly for passionate souls and ardent imaginations. A spark falling by accident on a keg of powder doesn't produce a more terrible effect. The finger destined to shake that fateful spark on to you or me may be already raised.

'Monsieur d'Hérouville, eager to speed up his work, tired out his colleagues. Gardeil's health was affected. In order to lighten his burden, Mademoiselle de La Chaux learned Hebrew; and while her lover was resting, she would spend part of every night translating extracts from Hebrew writers. Then the time came to go through the Greek authors. Mademoiselle de La Chaux hastened to perfect her knowledge of this language, of which she already possessed a smattering: and while Gardeil slept she was busy translating and copying out passages from Xenophon and Thucydides. To her knowledge of Greek and Hebrew she added that of Italian and English. She mastered English well enough to be able to translate into French Hume's first metaphysical essays, a work in which the difficulties of the language were enormously increased by those of the subject-matter. When her studies had exhausted her strength, she amused herself by copying music. When she felt afraid her lover was becoming bored, she would sing. I'm not exaggerating, as Monsieur Le Camus can tell you – the physician who consoled her in her difficulties and helped her in her need, who rendered her service on countless occasions, who attended her in the attic to which her poverty had condemned her, and who closed her eyes when she died. But I forgot to mention one of her first misfortunes – the persecution she suffered at the hands of a family horrified by a scandalous public relationship. They employed both truth and falsehood in an abominable attempt to restrict her liberty. Her parents and the priesthood pursued her from one district to another, from one house to another, and for several years forced her to live in hiding and alone. She spent her days working for Gardeil. We would go and see her at night; and in her lover's presence all her grief and anxiety would disappear.'

'What! Young, faint-hearted and sensitive, in the midst of so many difficulties she could still be happy?'

'Happy? Yes, she only stopped being happy when Gardeil was ungrateful.'

'But it's impossible that ingratitude should have been the reward for so many rare qualities, so many tokens of love, so many sacrifices of all sorts!'

'You are mistaken: Gardeil was ingratitude personified. One day, Mademoiselle de La Chaux found herself alone in the world, without honour, without fortune and without friends. No, I'm exaggerating: I stood by her for a while, and Doctor Le Camus always.'

'Oh, men, men!'

'Who are you talking about?'

'About Gardeil.'

'You're looking at his bad side and forgetting his good qualities. On that day of sorrow and despair she came running to see me. It was morning. She was as pale as death. She had learned her fate only the night before, yet she presented a picture of long-borne suffering. She was not crying, but you could see that she had cried a great deal. She threw herself into an armchair; she didn't speak; she couldn't speak. She stretched out her arms to me and at the same time uttered a cry. "What's the matter?" I asked her. "Is he dead?" "It's worse than that: he doesn't love me any more; he's abandoning me . . ."'

'Go on.'

'I can't! I can see her and hear her, and my eyes fill with tears. "He doesn't love you any more?" "'No." "He's abandoning you?" "Yes! After all I've done! . . . Monsieur, I can't think properly. Have pity on me; don't leave me . . . whatever you do, don't leave me . . ." As she said this, she seized my arm, gripping it tightly as if there were somebody there who was threatening to tear her away and carry her off . . . "Don't be afraid, Mademoiselle." "I'm afraid only of myself." "What can I do for you?" "First of all, save me from myself . . . He doesn't love me any more! I weary him! I irritate him! I bore him! He hates me! He's abandoning me! He's leaving me! He's leaving me!" This repeated phrase was followed by a profound silence, and this silence by bursts of convulsive laughter a thousand times more terrifying than the accents of despair or the death rattle. Next came tears, cries, inarticulate words, eyes raised towards heaven, trembling lips, a torrent of grief which had to be allowed to take its course. This I did; and I only began to appeal to her reason when I saw that her spirit was broken and stunned.

'Then I began speaking again: "He hates you and he's leaving you? Who told you so?" "He did." "Come now, Mademoiselle, have a little hope and courage. He's no monster . . ." "You don't know him; but you will. He's a monster such as don't exist, such as never existed before." "I can't believe that." "You'll see." "Does he love somebody else?" "No." "Are you sure you've given him no grounds for suspicion or complaint?" "None, none." 'What's the trouble, then?' "My uselessness: I have nothing left, I'm no good for anything any more. His ambition: he has always been ambitious. The loss of my health and my charms: I've suffered so much and worked so hard. Boredom, disgust." "People can stop being lovers and remain friends." "I've become an unbearable nuisance in his eyes; my presence irritates him, and the sight of me distresses and wounds him. If you only knew what he said to me! Yes, Monsieur, he told me that if he were condemned to spend twenty-four hours with me, he would throw himself out of the window." "But this dislike didn't arise all of a sudden." "How do I know? He's so undemonstrative, indifferent and cold by nature! It's so difficult to decipher souls like that, and one is so reluctant to read one's own death warrant! He read it out to me, and so callously!" "I can't understand it." "I have a favour to ask of you, and – that's why I came. Will you grant it me?" "Whatever it may be." "Listen. He respects you, you know how much he owes to me. Perhaps he will be embarrassed to show himself to you under his true colours. No, I don't think he has either the impudence or the courage to do that. I'm only a woman, and you're a man. A man who is tender, honest and fair inspires respect. You will inspire respect in him. Give me your arm, and don't refuse me the favour of accompanying me to his house. I want to speak to him in front of you. Who knows what effect my sorrow and your presence may have on him? Will you come with me?" "Gladly." "Then let's go . . ."'

'I was very much afraid that her sorrow and her presence would have no effect whatever. Disgust! Disgust is a terrible thing in love, especially disgust for a woman!

'I sent for a chair, for she was scarcely in a fit state to walk. We arrived at Gardeil's house, that big new house which is the only one on the right in the Rue Sainte-Hyacinthe, as you come from the Place Saint-Michel. There the porters stopped; they opened the door. I waited. She didn't come out. I drew near and saw a woman trembling uncontrollably from head to foot; her teeth were chattering as if she had a feverish chill; her knees were knocking together. "Just a moment, Monsieur; I beg your pardon; I can't . . . What am I going to do there? I've disturbed your work for nothing. I'm sorry; I apologize." I held out my arm to her all the same. She took it and tried to get up; she couldn't. "Just a moment more," she said. "I'm upsetting

you; you're distressed over my condition ..." Finally she overcame her fears
to a certain extent; and as she got out of the sedan chair she added in an
undertone: "I must go in; I must see him. Who knows? Perhaps I'll die in
there ..."

'Now we had crossed the courtyard; now we were at the door of the
apartment; now we were in Gardeil's study. He was at his desk, wearing a
dressing gown and a nightcap. He greeted me with a wave of the hand
and went on with the work he had begun. Eventually he came over to me
and said: "You must admit, Monsieur, that women are terribly tiresome. I
humbly apologize to you for Mademoiselle's silliness." Then, turning to
the poor creature, who was more dead than alive, he said: "Mademoiselle,
what do you want from me now? It seems to me that after the clear, precise way in which I explained myself, everything should be over between
us. I told you I no longer loved you; I told you this when the two of us
were alone together; apparently you now wish me to repeat it in front of
Monsieur. Well, Mademoiselle, I no longer love you. Love for you is a
feeling which has died in my heart; I may add, if it is any consolation, that
so is love for any other woman." "But tell me why you don't love me any
more." "I don't know. All I know is that I began without knowing why,
that I stopped without knowing why, and that I feel sure that this passion
can never return. It was a fever I contracted, and of which I believe I can
congratulate myself on being completely cured." "What have I done
wrong?" "Nothing." "Have you by any chance some unspoken reproach to
level at my conduct?" "None whatever; you were the most faithful, honest,
affectionate woman any man could desire." "Did I neglect something it
was in my power to do?" "Nothing." "Didn't I sacrifice my parents for your
sake?" "That is so." "My fortune?" "I'm afraid so." "My health?" "Possibly."
"My honour, my reputation, my peace of mind?" "Whatever you like." "And
you find me hateful!" "That's a hard thing to say, and a hard thing to hear,
but seeing that it's the truth, there's no denying it." "I'm hateful to him ...
I can feel I am, yet I don't think any more highly of myself for that ...
Hateful! ... Oh, heavens!"

'With these words a deathly pallor spread over her face; her lips lost
their colour; the drops of cold sweat which formed on her cheeks mingled
with the tears trickling down from her closed eyes; her head fell on to the
back of her armchair; she clenched her teeth; all her limbs trembled, and

this trembling was followed by a fainting fit which struck me as the fulfilment of the wish she had expressed on the threshold of that house. Seeing how long her faint was lasting, I became really alarmed. I took off her mantlet, undid the laces of her dress, loosened those of her petticoats, and threw a few drops of cold water on her face. Her eyes opened a little way, and a muffled murmur came from her throat; she wanted to say: "He finds me hateful," but she pronounced only the final syllable of the word, and then uttered a shrill cry. Her eyelids drooped and she fainted away again.

'Gardeil, coldly sitting in his armchair, his elbow resting on the table and his head in his hand, gazed at her without emotion and left me to look after her. I said to him several times: "But, Monsieur, she's dying . . . We ought to send for help." He replied with a smile and a shrug of the shoulders: "Women are tough; they don't die for a little thing like this. It's nothing; it will pass. You don't know them; they can do whatever they like with their bodies . . ." "She's dying, I tell you." Her body did indeed appear to have no strength or life in it; it was slipping out of the armchair, and she would have fallen on the floor to one side or the other if I had not held her. Meanwhile Gardeil had stood up abruptly; and walking up and down his apartment he said in an impatient, irritable voice: "I could easily have done without this depressing scene; but at least I hope it will be the last. What the devil does this creature want? I was in love with her once; if I beat my head against the wall I couldn't change that one way or the other. I no longer love her; she knows that now, or she'll never know it. There's nothing more to say . . ." "Yes, there is, Monsieur. What! Do you think a self-respecting man can deprive a woman of everything she has and then leave her?" "What do you expect me to do? I'm as poor as she is." "What do I expect you to do? Why, join her in the poverty to which you have reduced her." "That's easy to say. She would be no better off, and I would be much worse off." "Would you behave like this towards a friend who had sacrificed everything for your sake?" "A friend! A friend! I haven't much faith in friends; and this experience has taught me to have none at all in passion. I'm sorry I didn't realize that earlier." "But is it fair that this unfortunate woman should suffer because of an error of your heart?" "And what tells you that in another month or another day I wouldn't have suffered just as cruelly because of an error of hers?" "What tells me? Everything she's done for you, and the condition in which you see her." "What she's done for me? . . . Why, that debt has been more than repaid by the time I've wasted on her." "Oh, Monsieur Gardeil, how can you compare your time with all the priceless things you've taken from her?" "I've achieved nothing and I am nothing. I'm thirty years old; it's high time I began thinking of myself and taking all that nonsense for what it's worth . . ."

'In the meantime the poor woman had partly come to. Hearing these last words, she said somewhat heatedly: "What was that he said about wasting his time? I've learned four languages to lighten the burden of his work; I've read a thousand books; I've written, translated and copied night and day; I've worn myself out, ruined my eyesight, made myself sick with overwork, and caught a tiresome disease of which I may never be cured. He doesn't dare admit the cause of his disgust; but I'll show you what it is."

'She promptly tore off her shawl and slipped one arm out of her dress, baring her shoulder; and showing me an erysipelatous patch on her skin, she said: "This is the reason for his change of heart; this is the result of the nights I've stayed up. He would arrive in the morning with his parchment scrolls. 'Monsieur d'Hérouville,' he would tell me, 'is in a great hurry to know what these contain; this job needs to be done by tomorrow,' and it was . . ."

'At that moment we heard the sound of footsteps approaching the door; it was a servant who announced the arrival of Monsieur d'Hérouville. Gardeil turned pale. I urged Mademoiselle de La Chaux to rearrange her dress and withdraw. "No," she said. "No; I'm staying. I want to unmask this scoundrel. I shall wait for Monsieur d'Hérouville and talk to him." "And what good will that do?" "None," she replied; "you are right." "Tomorrow you would regret it. Leave him with all his wrongs: that's a vengeance which is worthy of you." "But is it worthy of him? Can't you see that that man is only . . . Let's go, Monsieur, let's go quickly; for I can't answer for what I would do or say . . ." In the twinkling of an eye Mademoiselle de La Chaux repaired the disorder of her clothing caused by this scene and shot like an arrow out of Gardeil's study. I followed her and heard the door slammed behind us. I later learned that her description was given to the doorman.

'I took her to her apartment, where I found Doctor Le Camus waiting for us. The passion which he had conceived for that girl differed little from that which she felt for Gardeil. I gave him an account of our call; and despite the signs he gave of anger, sorrow and indignation . . .'

'It was not too difficult to tell from his face that he was not too displeased by your lack of success.'

'True.'

'That's the way men are. They can't be better than that.'

'Her break with Gardeil was followed by a violent illness, and while it lasted, the good, honest, tender, sensitive doctor looked after her better than he would have looked after the greatest lady in France. He came to see her three or four times a day. As long as she was in danger, he slept in her room on a campbed. An illness is a great blessing in a time of great unhappiness.'

'By making us think about ourselves, it banishes the memory of others. Besides, it provides an excuse for feeling sorry for ourselves without indiscretion and without restraint.'

'That observation, though perfectly true, could not be applied to Mademoiselle de La Chaux . . . During her convalescence, we decided how she should spend her time. She had intelligence, imagination, taste and knowledge – more than enough to gain admission to the Académie des Inscriptions. She had heard us discussing metaphysics so often that the most abstract subjects had become familiar to her; and her first attempt in the sphere of literature was a translation of Hume's *Essays concerning Human Understanding*. I went over it, and to tell the truth, she had left me very little to correct. This translation was published in Holland and favourably received by the public. My *Letter on the Deaf and Dumb* appeared at almost the same time. A few shrewd objections which she raised gave rise to a supplement which I dedicated to her. This supplement is not the worst thing I've done.

'Mademoiselle de La Chaux's gaiety had returned to some extent. Now and then the doctor would invite us for a meal, and these dinners were far from melancholy. Ever since Gardeil had left her, the doctor's passion had increased by leaps and bounds. One day, at the dinner-table, over dessert, he expressed his love with all the honesty, sensitivity and naivety of a child and all the subtlety of a man of wit. She replied with a frankness which I found utterly charming but which others may find displeasing: "Doctor, it would be impossible for me to hold you in greater esteem than I do now.

I am overwhelmed by the favours you have done me; and I would be more
despicable than the monster of the Rue Hyacinthe if I were not filled with
the deepest gratitude. Your turn of mind could not please me more than
it does. You speak to me of your passion with such delicacy and grace that
I do believe I should be sorry if you never spoke to me of it again. The
very idea of losing your company or being deprived of your friendship
would be enough to make me unhappy. You are a good man if ever there
was one. You have an incomparably kind and gentle character. I don't think
that a human heart could fall into better hands. I preach to mine in your
favour from morning till night; but it's no use preaching when there's no
desire for reform, and I make no progress. In the meantime you suffer, and
that causes me cruel pain. I know nobody worthier than you of the happiness you seek, and there is nothing I would not do to make you happy.
Nothing at all, without exception. Why, Doctor, I would even ... yes, I
would even sleep ... I would go as far as that. Do you want to sleep with
me? You have only to say the word. That is all I can do for you; but you
want to be loved, and that is what I could never do."

'The doctor listened to her, took her hand, kissed it, and moistened it
with his tears. As for me, I didn't know whether to laugh or cry.

'Mademoiselle de La Chaux knew the doctor well, and when I said to
her the next day: "Mademoiselle, what if the doctor had taken you at your
word?" she replied: "I would have kept my promise; but that couldn't have
happened; my offer was not the sort a man like him could accept ..."
"Why not? It seems to me that if I had been in the doctor's place, I would
have hoped the rest would come later." "Yes; but if you had been in the
doctor's place, Mademoiselle de La Chaux would not have made you the
same offer."

'The translation of Hume hadn't brought her much money. The Dutch
will print whatever you like, provided they don't have to pay anything.'

'Luckily for us; for with the restrictions placed on free thought here, if
they ever took it into their heads to pay authors, they would attract the
entire publishing business to their country.'

'We advised her to write something light which would bring her less
honour but more profit. She worked on it for four or five months, and
then brought me a little historical novel, entitled *The Three Favourites*. It
was subtle, interesting, and written in a delicate style; but, without her

realizing it, for she was incapable of any malice, it was sprinkled with remarks applicable to the King's mistress, the Marquise de Pompadour; and I did not conceal the fact that whatever sacrifice she made, either by softening or by deleting these passages, it was almost impossible for her book to appear without compromising her, and that the annoyance of spoiling something good would not safeguard her against other vexations.

'She appreciated the soundness of my observations and was all the more distressed by them. The good doctor anticipated all her needs; but she accepted his benevolence the more reluctantly in that she felt less disposed to show the sort of gratitude he might have hoped for. Besides, the doctor was not rich at that time; and he did not seem likely to become so. Now and then she would take her manuscript out of her portfolio and say to me sadly: "Oh well, there seems to be nothing to be done with it; it will have to stay there." I gave her a strange piece of advice, which was to send the work as it was, without softening it or altering it in any way, to Madame de Pompadour herself, with a brief letter explaining why she was sending it. She liked this idea, and wrote a letter which was charming in every respect, but above all in a certain ring of truth which was impossible to resist. Two or three months passed without her hearing a word; and she had assumed that her approach had been fruitless when a man wearing the Cross of Saint Louis called on her with an answer from the Marquise. In this message her manuscript was given the praise it deserved; she was thanked for her sacrifice; the passages applicable to the Marquise were accepted and no offence taken at them and the author was invited to come to Versailles, where she would find a woman who was both grateful and prepared to render her such services as lay in her power. As the messenger was leaving Mademoiselle de La Chaux's apartment, he discreetly left a rouleau of fifty louis on the mantelpiece.

'The doctor and I urged her to take advantage of Madame de Pompadour's benevolence; but we were dealing with a girl whose humility and timidity equalled her merit. How could she present herself at Versailles in her rags? The doctor immediately removed this difficulty. After the question of clothes there were other excuses, and then others. The journey to Versailles was put off from day to day until it was almost unseemly to go. Some time had already passed since we had last mentioned it to her when the same messenger returned, with a second letter making the kindest reproaches and another gift equal to the first offered with the same tact. This generous act on Madame de Pompadour's part has never been made public. I mentioned it one day to Monsieur Collin, her confidential agent and the man who distributed her secret favours. He did not know about it; and I like to think that this is not the only act of generosity her tomb conceals.

'It was thus that Mademoiselle de La Chaux twice missed the opportunity of extricating herself from her poverty.

'Later on, she went to live on the outskirts of the city, and I completely lost touch with her. All I know about the rest of her life is that it was nothing but a tissue of grief, illness and poverty. Her family stubbornly closed their doors against her, and it was in vain that she solicited the help of those pious individuals who had persecuted her so zealously.'

'Those are the rules of the game.'

'The doctor didn't abandon her. She died in poverty, in an attic room, while the little tiger of the Rue Hyacinthe, the only lover she had ever had, was practising medicine at Montpellier or Toulouse and, in the midst of the greatest affluence, enjoying a well-deserved reputation as a clever man and an undeserved reputation as an honourable man.'

'But that too is more or less in accordance with the rules. If there exists a good and honourable Tanié, then it's to a Reymer that Providence sends him; if there is a good and honourable de La Chaux, then she falls prey to a Gardeil, so that everything should turn out for the best.'

You may perhaps tell me that I am being too hasty in pronouncing a final judgement on a man's character on the basis of a single act; that such a severe rule would so reduce the number of decent people as to leave fewer of them on earth than the Christian Gospel allows into Heaven; that a man can be inconstant in love, and even pride himself on having few scruples about women, without being devoid of honour and integrity; that nobody can either stop a passion which has been kindled or prolong one which has died; and that there are already enough men walking about who deserve to be called scoundrels without inventing imaginary crimes which would increase their number *ad infinitum*. You may ask me if I have never betrayed, deceived or abandoned a woman without cause. If I agree to answer these questions, I could not do so without provoking a retort and we should become embroiled in an argument which would not finish until the Last Judgement. But examine your own conscience, you the apologist of deceitful, unfaithful men, and tell me if you would like the doctor from Toulouse as your friend ... You hesitate? Enough said, and with that, I beg God to keep under his holy protection any woman to whom you take it into your head to pay your respects.

Translated by Edward Marielle

MARQUIS DE SADE

Augustine de Villeblanche

'Of all the freaks of Nature,' said Mademoiselle de Villeblanche, whom we shall have occasion to discuss in a moment, speaking one day to one of her best friends, 'the one which has evoked the most comment and seemed most curious to those pseudo-philosophers who insist on analysing everything without ever understanding anything, is that peculiar penchant which women with a certain constitution or a certain temperament conceive for persons of their own sex. Although, long before the immortal Sappho and since her time, there has not been a single country in the world or a single city which has not offered examples of women with this penchant, and although, faced with such strong evidence, it would seem more reasonable to accuse Nature of peculiarity than these women of a crime against Nature, society has never ceased to condemn them. Indeed, if it were not for the imperious influence our sex has always exercised, who knows if some legislators or monarchs might not have taken it into their heads to draw up capital laws against these poor, sensitive creatures, such as they promulgated against those men who, built on the same singular pattern, believed that they could be sufficient unto themselves, and fancied that the mingling of the sexes, while very useful for the purpose of propagation, might well not be as essential to the pursuit of pleasure.

'Heaven forbid that we should take sides in this matter,' continued the beautiful Augustine de Villeblanche, blowing kisses to her woman friend which nonetheless seemed just a little suspicious; 'but instead of resorting to contempt, irony, or the stake – all weapons which have completely lost their edge nowadays – would it not be far simpler, in respect of an action so utterly unimportant to society, so immaterial to God, and perhaps more useful than people think to Nature, to let everyone do as he or she pleases?

'What is there to fear from this perversion? Any truly wise person must see that it can prevent greater depravities, while no one will ever convince me that it can lead to any dangerous errors . . . Heavens above, are people afraid that the whims of these individuals of one sex or the other might bring the world to an end, that they might be putting the precious human race in peril, and that their so-called crime might annihilate it through the failure to aid its increase? If they would only think, they would see that all these imaginary losses are a matter of complete indifference to Nature, and that not only does she not condemn them, but she shows us by a thousand examples that she wants them; if these losses irritated her and progeniture was so important to her, why should a woman be able to serve her purpose only a third of her life, and why should half the creatures she produces leave her hands feeling hostile to the progeniture she nonetheless demands? To put it better, she allows the species to multiply but she does not demand it, and in the certainty that there will always be more individuals than she needs, she has no reason to thwart the penchants of those who are not accustomed to propagation and are reluctant to conform to it. Oh, let us allow that good mother to have her way; let us remember that her resources are vast, that nothing we do offends her, and that it lies outside our power to commit a crime against her laws.'

Mademoiselle Augustine de Villeblanche, a sample of whose logic we have just seen, finding herself her own mistress at the age of twenty, with an income of thirty thousand livres at her disposal, had decided never to marry; she was well born if not high born, the daughter of a man who had made his fortune in India, had left no other children, and had died without being able to persuade her to wed. We must not shut our eyes to the fact that the sort of caprice which Augustine had just defended played a large part in the distaste she displayed for marriage. Whether it was as a result of advice, upbringing, physical constitution or hot blood (she was born in Madras), natural inspiration or anything else, Mademoiselle de Villeblanche hated men; utterly addicted to what chaste ears understand by the word sapphism, she found no pleasure save in the company of her sex, and recouped herself only with the Graces for the contempt she felt for Love.

Augustine was a real loss to the male sex: tall and beautiful, with magnificent brown hair, a rather Roman nose, superb teeth, wonderfully lively, expressive eyes, a marvellously white, delicate skin, and altogether a sort of piquant charm. There can be no doubt that, seeing her so well fitted to give love and so determined not to receive it, a great many men could easily give vent to countless sarcastic remarks about a penchant simple enough in itself, but which, depriving the altars of Paphos of one of the earthly creatures best fitted to serve them, was bound to anger the votaries of the temple of Venus. Mademoiselle de Villeblanche laughed heartily at all these reproaches and all these gibes, without indulging any the less in her caprices.

'The worst of all follies,' she used to say, 'is to blush for the penchants we have received from Nature; and to make fun of a person with unusual tastes is just as barbarous as it would be to jeer at a man or a woman born one-eyed or lame, but you have as much chance of convincing fools of these reasonable principles as of stopping the stars in their courses. There is a sort of pleasure for a man's pride in making fun of faults he does not have himself, and such pleasures are so attractive to men and especially to fools that it is extremely rare to see them give them up ... Besides, it gives rise to epigrams, cold witticisms, mediocre puns, and for society – in other words for a collection of creatures brought together by boredom and modified by stupidity – it is infinitely pleasant to talk for two or three hours without saying anything, infinitely delightful to shine at other people's expense and to announce by condemning a vice that one is a long way from having it. It is a sort of tribute one silently pays oneself; at that price one is even prepared to join with others in a cabal to crush the individual whose crime is not to think like the common herd, and one goes home preening oneself on the wit one has shown, when in fact such behaviour has afforded proof of nothing but priggishness and stupidity.'

That was how Mademoiselle de Villeblanche thought; and quite determined to accept no restraint, ignoring criticism, rich enough to be self-sufficient, living above her reputation, aiming sybaritically at a life of pleasure and not at a celestial bliss in which she had little belief, still less at an immortality too chimerical for her senses, and surrounded by a small circle of like-minded women, dear Augustine innocently indulged in all the pleasures that delighted her. She had had a great many suitors, but they had all been so ill-treated that the male sex was finally on the point of giving up the attempt to conquer her when a young man called

Franville, of almost the same social station and at least as rich as her, falling madly in love with her, was not only undeterred by her coldness but actually resolved in all seriousness not to raise the siege until she had been conquered. He spoke of his intention to his friends, was laughed at by them, insisted that he would succeed, was challenged to do so, and accepted the challenge. Franville was two years younger than Mademoiselle de Villeblanche, was still practically beardless, and had a very pretty figure, delicate features and the loveliest hair in the world; when he was dressed as a girl, this costume suited him so well that he always took in both sexes, and received so many unambiguous declarations of love, some made in error and others with complete assurance, that on one and the same day he could have played Antinous to some Adrian or Adonis to some Psyche. It was with this costume that Franville decided to seduce Mademoiselle de Villeblanche; we shall see how he set about doing so.

One of Augustine's greatest pleasures was dressing as a man during Carnival time, and attending every ball in this disguise in such conformity with her tastes. Franville, who had a watch kept on her movements, and who had hitherto taken the precaution of showing himself very rarely to her, learned one day that the woman he loved was due to go that very evening to a ball given by associates of the Opera, to which any mummer would be admitted, and that following that charming girl's custom, she was to attend in the uniform of a captain of dragoons. He for his part disguised himself as a woman, dressed and adorned himself with all possible care and elegance, put on a great deal of rouge and no mask, and accompanied by a sister of his who was much less attractive than himself, went in this accoutrement to the ball, where the delightful Augustine went only in search of amorous adventure.

Franville had not gone round the ballroom three times before he was singled out by Augustine's discerning eyes.

'Who is that beautiful girl?' Mademoiselle de Villeblanche asked the friend accompanying her. 'I cannot remember having seen her anywhere before. But how can such a delightful creature have escaped our notice?'

These words were no sooner spoken than Augustine did everything she could to engage in conversation with the fake Mademoiselle de Franville, who at first fled, turned, twisted and escaped, all in order to make himself more desirable; finally he was accosted and some commonplace exchanges initiated a conversation which gradually became more interesting.

'The heat in the ballroom is terrible,' said Mademoiselle de Villeblanche. 'Let us leave our companions together and go find a little air in the rooms set aside for cards and refreshment.'

'Oh, Monsieur,' said Franville to Mademoiselle de Villeblanche, whom he went on pretending to take for a man; 'I really daren't. I am here with only my sister, but I know that my mother is coming with the husband intended for me, and if they were to see me with you, there would be such a fuss . . .'

'Come, come, one must rise above all these childish fears . . . How old are you, my angel?'

'Eighteen, Monsieur.'

'Well, I can assure you that at eighteen one has acquired the right to do anything one likes . . . Come now, follow me and have no fear . . .'

Franville followed obediently.

'What a charming creature,' Augustine went on, leading the person she still took for a girl towards the rooms adjoining the ballroom; 'what, are you really going to be married? . . . How I pity you! . . . And who is this individual who is destined for you? Some tiresome bore, I'll be bound . . . Oh, how lucky the man is going to be, and how I should like to be in his place! Would you agree to marry me, heavenly creature? Tell me frankly.'

'Alas, Monsieur, you know very well that when one is young one cannot obey the movements of the heart.'

'But spurn him, that dreadful man; we shall become better acquainted, and if we suit each other, why should we not come to an arrangement? I for my part, thank heavens, have no need of any sort of permission. Although I am only twenty, I can do what I wish with my fortune, and if you could influence your parents in my favour, perhaps we could be joined by eternal bonds within a week.'

While talking they had left the ballroom and the cunning Augustine, who had not led away her prey in order to whisper sweet nothings, had been careful to take Franville into a very out-of-the-way room which she never failed to hire from the organizer of the ball.

'Heavens above!' exclaimed Franville, when Augustine locked the door of this room and clasped him in her arms. 'What are you doing? . . . Alone with you, Monsieur, in such a lonely spot . . . Let me go! Let me go, I beg you, or I shall call for help at once!'

'I am going to deprive you of the power to do so, sweet angel,' said Augustine, pressing her beautiful lips on Franville's mouth. 'Cry out now, cry out if you can, and your pure, rose-scented breath will only kindle the fire in my heart the sooner.'

Franville did not put up a very strenuous resistance: it is difficult to be angry when one is being tenderly kissed for the first time by the woman one adores. Encouraged, Augustine attacked more strongly, with that vehemence shown only by delightful women carried away by passion. Soon her hands began to stray, and Franville, playing a woman giving way, let his own hands wander. Clothes were disarranged and fingers darted almost simultaneously where each expected to find what he desired.

Then all of a sudden Franville changed his role.

'Heavens above!' he exclaimed. 'You are just a woman!'

'Horrible creature!' cried Augustine, putting her hand on things whose condition could leave her under no illusion. 'Have I gone to all this trouble just to find a dreadful man? How unlucky I am!'

'No unluckier than myself,' said Franville, rearranging his clothing and displaying the most profound contempt. 'I use a disguise calculated to attract men, I love them and seek them out, and all I meet is a whore.'

'Oh, no, not a whore,' said Augustine tartly. 'I have never been that at any time in my life. A woman who loathes men cannot be called by that name . . .'

'What! You are a woman and you hate men?'

'Yes, just as you are a man and you loathe women.'

'There is no denying that the encounter is unique.'

'It is a sad encounter for me,' said Augustine with every sign of extreme irritation.

'I assure you, Mademoiselle, that it is even more annoying for me,' retorted Franville. 'Now I am polluted for three weeks. In our order, you know, we take a vow never to touch a woman.'

'It seems to me that there can be nothing shameful about touching one like me.'

'Upon my word, my beauty,' Franville continued, 'I can see no good reason for making such an exception, and I cannot agree that a vice must count as another merit for you.'

'A vice? But is it for you to reproach me with mine when you have vices just as infamous?'

'Look,' said Franville, 'let us not quarrel; we are evenly matched. The simplest thing would be for us to part and never see each other again.'

With these words Franville made as if to leave the room.

'Just a minute,' said Augustine, preventing him from opening the door. 'I wager you are going to tell everyone of our adventure.'

'I may perhaps amuse myself by doing so.'

'Well, what does that matter to me, anyway? I do not care what people say, thank goodness. So go, Monsieur, go and tell them whatever you like . . .'

But stopping him once more, she added with a smile:

'This was an extraordinary affair, you know: both of us were mistaken.'

'Oh, the mistake was far more cruel,' said Franville, 'for people with my tastes than for persons with yours . . . and that void fills us with repugnance . . .'

'Believe me, my dear fellow, what you offer us disgusts us every bit as much. Come now, our repugnance is equal on both sides, but it cannot be denied that the situation is highly amusing . . . Are you going back to the ball?'

'I don't know.'

'For my part I am not going back,' said Augustine. 'You have made me feel things . . . Such unpleasantness! . . . I am going to retire to bed.'

'Very well.'

'But it is too much to expect him to escort me home, I suppose. I live only a stone's throw away, my carriage is not here, and he is going to leave me where I am.'

'No, I shall gladly accompany you,' said Franville. 'Our tastes do not prevent us from being polite . . . Would you like my hand? . . . Here it is.'

'Remember that I am only accepting your company because I can find no better.'

'You may rest assured that for my part I am only offering you my company out of courtesy.'

When they reached the door of Augustine's house, Franville prepared to take his leave.

'You are really delightful,' said Mademoiselle de Villeblanche. 'Now you are going to leave me in the street.'

'I beg your pardon,' said Franville. 'I did not dare . . .'

'Oh, how boorish men are who do not care for women!'

'The truth of the matter,' said Franville, nonetheless giving Mademoiselle de Villeblanche his arm as far as her apartment, 'the truth of the matter, Mademoiselle, is that I would like to hurry back to the ball and try to repair my stupid error.'

'Your stupid error? So you are very annoyed at having found me?'

'I would not say that, but is it not true that both of us could have done infinitely better?'

'Yes, you are right,' said Augustine, finally entering her apartment; 'you are right, Monsieur, especially about me . . . for I very much fear that this baneful encounter may cost me my happiness.'

'What! Do you mean you are not absolutely sure of your feelings?'

'I was yesterday.'

'Oh, you are not abiding by your maxims.'

'I abide by nothing, and you are putting me out of patience.'

'Well, I am going, Mademoiselle, I am going . . . Heaven forbid that I should trouble you any longer.'

'No, stay. That is an order. Can you bring yourself to obey a woman once in your life?'

'As I have already told you,' said Franville, obligingly sitting down, 'there is nothing I would not do out of politeness.'

'Do you realize it is a terrible thing at your age to have such perverse tastes?'

'Do you think it is very decent to have such singular tastes as yours?'

'Oh, that is quite another matter. In our case, it is modesty and restraint; it is even pride if you wish; it is fear of surrendering to a sex which never seduces us except to master us . . . However, the senses call, and we give them satisfaction among ourselves; if we succeed in concealing what we do, the result is an appearance of virtue which is often convincing, so that Nature is content, decency is preserved and morality is not outraged.'

'That is what I should call a fine collection of sophistries; looking at things like that, one could justify anything. And what have you just said that we could not likewise put forward in our favour?'

'Nonsense! With very different prejudices you cannot feel the same fears. Your victory lies in our defeat. The more conquests you obtain, the greater your glory, and you cannot resist the feelings we arouse in you except by vice or depravity.'

'I do believe you are going to convert me.'

'I should like to.'

'What would you gain by doing so, as long as you yourself remain in error?'

'My sex will be under an obligation to me, and as I love women, I am happy to work for them.'

'If the miracle took place, its effects would not be as general as you seem to think. I would not like to be converted for more than one woman at the very most ... as an experiment.'

'That is an honest principle.'

'What is quite certain is that it is unreasonable to make up one's mind before trying everything.'

'What! You have never known a woman?'

'Never. And what about you? Is your innocence by any chance equally untouched?'

'My innocence? No ... The women we know are so adroit and jealous that they leave us nothing ... But I have never known a man.'

'And you stand by your vow?'

'Yes, I never want to know a man, or only a man as singular as myself.'

'I am terribly sorry not to have taken the same vow.'

'I do not believe it is possible to show greater impertinence.'

With these words Mademoiselle de Villeblanche stood up and told Franville he was at liberty to retire. As cool-headed as ever, our young lover made a deep curtsey and prepared to leave.

'Are you going back to the ball?' Mademoiselle de Villeblanche asked him curtly, looking at him with an irritation mingled with the most ardent love.

'Why, yes, as I think I told you.'

'So you are incapable of the sacrifice I have made for you?'

'What! You have made some sacrifice for me?'

'I came home only to see nothing more after suffering the misfortune of meeting you.'

'The misfortune?'

'It is you who force me to use that term. It depends entirely on you whether I use a very different one.'

'And how would you reconcile that with your tastes?'

'There is nothing one would not abandon for the person one loves!'

'Granted, but it would be impossible for you to love me.'

'I agree, if you were to cling to your dreadful habits.'

'And if I gave them up?'

'I would immediately sacrifice mine on the altars of love ... Oh, treacherous creature,' said a tearful Augustine, sinking into an armchair, 'how wounding to my vanity is that admission you have just extorted from me!'

'I have won from the most beautiful lips in the world the most flattering admission I could ever hope to hear,' said Franville, throwing himself at Augustine's feet. 'Oh, dearest object of my tender devotion, I implore you not to punish me for the pretence I now confess; I beg for mercy at your feet, and I shall stay here until you forgive me. You see before you, Mademoiselle, the most constant and passionate of lovers; I considered this ruse to be necessary in order to conquer a heart whose powers of resistance were known to me. If I have succeeded, beautiful Augustine, will you refuse a virtuous love what you deigned to promise the guilty lover ... for you thought of me as guilty ... Oh, how could you imagine that an impure passion could exist in the soul of the man who was never set aflame except by you?'

'Traitor, you tricked me ... But I forgive you. However, you will have nothing to give up for me, you deceiver, which is unflattering to my pride. Well, never mind, I for my part give up everything for you ... To please you, I joyfully renounce errors into which vanity leads us almost as often as our tastes. I can feel that Nature has won the day – Nature which I was stifling with vices which I now detest with my whole soul. No one can resist her rule: she created us only for you, and made you only for us. Let us obey her laws; it is through the instrument of love that she reminds me of them today, and I shall hold them all the more sacred on that account. Here is my hand, Monsieur: I believe you to be a man of honour, worthy to be my suitor. If I have lost your esteem for a moment, perhaps by means of care and tenderness I shall be able to repair my wrongs and force you to recognize that those of the imagination do not always degrade a high-born soul.'

Franville, with all his desires fulfilled, shedding tears of joy on to the beautiful hands he held clasped in his, stood up and threw himself into the arms which were opened to receive him.

'This is the happiest day in my life!' he exclaimed. 'Is there anything to compare with my victory? I have brought back to the path of virtue the heart over which I shall reign for ever.'

Again and again Franville kissed the heavenly object of his love before taking his leave. The next day he informed all his friends of his good fortune. Mademoiselle de Villeblanche was too good a match for his parents to withhold their consent, and he married her the same week. Their marriage was distinguished by tenderness and trust, the greatest restraint and the strictest modesty; and while making himself the happiest of men, he was adroit enough to turn the most dissolute of girls into the most virtuous and respectable of women.

Translated by Edward Marielle

ISABELLE DE CHARRIÈRE

The Nobleman
A Moral Tale

'We do not always follow in our ancestors' footsteps, nor in our fathers.'

La Fontaine

In one of the provinces of France, there stands a very ancient castle, inhabited by an old offshoot of an even more ancient family. The Baron d'Arnonville was always alive to the merit of this antiquity, and he was right to be, for he lacked much else in the way of merit, and his castle would have been in a better state had it been a little more modern. One of the towers had subsided into part of the moat, and in the rest there was nothing other than a little muddy water, with frogs instead of fish. The family ate frugally, but the antlers of stags his forefathers had killed in times past still reigned over the dining room. The baron never forgot the meat days when he had the right to hunt, nor the fast days when he had the right to fish, and, content with these rights, he ungrudgingly allowed lowly financiers to eat pheasant and carp without ever feeling a tinge of envy. He spent his modest revenue on pursuing a case that concerned his right to hang people on his lands. It never occurred to him that there might be better uses to which he could put his wealth, nor that he might leave his children something better than high and low jurisdiction. Any remaining money he spent on renewing the coats of arms that bordered all the ceilings and on restoring the portraits of his ancestors.

The Baroness d'Arnonville had died long before, and had left him one son and a daughter, whose name was Julie. The young lord had every right to feel aggrieved at the portion nature and education had bestowed on him, and yet he did not complain. Content with the name of d'Arnonville, and with the knowledge of his family tree, he did without talents or know-ledge. He went hunting sometimes, and ate his game with the girls from the local inn; he drank a good deal, and gambled every evening with his servant. He was disagreeable to look at, and good eyes would have been needed to detect in his face those features that according to some people are the infallible mark of illustrious birth. Julie, on the other hand, had beauty, grace and wit. Her father had made her read some treatises about heraldry that were not at all to her taste, and she had read some novels that she liked much more. She had been to stay with a lady related to her in the capital of the province, and had acquired some knowledge of the world: not much is needed to give polish to someone with a penetrating mind and a good heart.

An artist who was giving a new layer of paint to her ancestors and their coats of arms taught her to draw; she painted landscapes and embroidered flowers; she worked with skill, sang with taste, and as her face and figure needed neither art nor improvement, she always looked very well dressed. She was exceedingly lively and cheerful, although affectionate too, and every so often jokes about the nobility did slip out; but the respect and fondness she had for her father always kept them in check. Her father loved her too, but he would have preferred her to embroider coats of arms rather than flowers, and to study the crumbling scrolls of parchment that recorded the family titles instead of *Télémaque* and *Gil Blas*. He was angry to see that in her bedroom the modern prints were close to the window, while the old portraits were relegated to a dark corner; and he had often chastised her for preferring a young and amiable bourgeoise from nearby to some young lady as ugly and sullen as she was noble, who happened to be staying in the neighbourhood. He would have preferred her never to yield precedence to anything other than good proof of ancient titles, but Julie never did consult the documents of entitlement; she always yielded to age, and would have preferred to be mistaken for a common woman than supposed arrogant. Out of sheer absent-mindedness, she would have assumed precedence over a princess; out of indifference and politeness, she would have let the whole world go ahead of her. Whenever the Baron d'Arnonville wanted to dissuade his children from doing something he disapproved of, he would say, 'This is not appropriate for a person of your rank; it does not befit your noble birth.' He never deigned to use anything so low as an argument to make them do anything at all, not thinking that anything other than perfect uselessness was worthy of high birth nor that it was beneath them to be good for nothing.

Julie didn't want to be too clever, and that was what was so appealing about the cleverness she did have. She didn't know much, but it was clear that this was only because of the absence of any opportunity to learn; her ignorance didn't seem like stupidity. Her lively, sweet and laughing physiognomy attracted everyone who saw her, and her gracious manner confirmed the initial bias in her favour that her physiognomy had created. If she had affected an air of grandeur and reserve, people would have taken as many steps backward as her manner in fact encouraged them to take forward. We wish primarily to please the person who pleases us: if that person does not greet us with warmth, we are mortified; we turn against them and call them disdainful, when perhaps it was merely a bad habit on their part. And yet, often, they will have lost us for ever.

Julie had greatly pleased a lady from Paris who had seen her at the home of the relation I have already mentioned, and this lady invited her to come and spend some time in the country. Julie obtained permission from her father; he advised her to remember what she was, and she departed. This lady was very rich; she had an only son who was nonetheless very agreeable and well brought up. He was very good-looking; Julie was beautiful: they pleased each other at first sight, and to begin with they didn't think either to mention it or to hide it. Bit by bit they came to an understanding, and they found each other even more agreeable once they knew that each was liked by the other – in company, at table, on walks, Valaincourt would often whisper riddles and sweet nothings to Julie; but once they were alone, and he could have said everything, he said not a word. She was surprised, but happy nonetheless; she had read or she had divined that love is timid and tender where it burns strongest; although no speeches gave her such pleasure as those of her lover, she loved his silence even better. Valaincourt had, apart from the reasons that Julie sensed, a motive to keep quiet that she did not know about. She had seen that he had big eyes, fair hair, beautiful teeth; she found that he had much sweetness, wit and generosity; she had noticed order, decency and wealth in his house; but she had forgotten to ask which of his ancestors had been ennobled. Unfortunately it was his father who, after meritorious service and great virtue, had earned this distinction. Wise men opine that when nobility is acquired in this way, the newest creations are the best; that the first noble in a family deserves the greatest glory for the title that he has founded; that the second is better than the twentieth, and that it was more likely that Valaincourt resembled his father, than Julie her ancestor of thirty generations back. But the wise are not competent judges of the work of prejudice. Valaincourt was aware of the prejudice and he knew how far Julie's father carried it. The time for her departure approached; both were distressed, and were the fonder for it. As each retired to bed they found themselves alone in an unlit corridor. Valaincourt took Julie's hand, and kissed it more fervently than he had ever done before; for he had kissed it before, and for some days already Julie had been removing her gloves whenever she thought she was going to need to give her hand to Valaincourt. On the following day Julie made sure she was in the corridor; there was light, and Valaincourt extinguished it and gave her a tender kiss, and then another. Julie wanted to return them . . . fortunately it was the last evening . . . the next day Julie left.

All the while she had been with Valaincourt she had never thought of anything other than the pleasure of seeing and hearing him. When she could no longer see him, she felt the pain of being separated from him; she thought of ways to see him again, and to keep on seeing him for ever. I don't know what else she felt and thought about, but happily the young man for his part was thinking the same things.

One day when she was alone at home, busy with her embroidery, he came in. She remembered the corridor, and blushed; Valaincourt seemed not to remember it, so respectful was his manner of approaching her. With a woman one respects, and who has a modest air, a man almost doubts the favours he has received from her. Valaincourt could not believe that his lips had dared touch the face of this divinity. After the first compliments had been exchanged, he fell back, silent. Julie never supposed it was her manner that was responsible for keeping him at a distance; she thought that he had seen enough of her not to be quite so timid any more, and thinking he must perceive a part of what she was feeling, grew vexed at his silence. 'In his place,' said she to herself, 'I do believe that I would speak.' At the same time she rose to ring the bell and, as the footman was coming into the room, said to Valaincourt, 'How polite you are, sir, to come so far, seeing as you have nothing to say to me. Bring the coffee, and if my father is at home, please ask him to come and have some.'

'Oh! Mademoiselle,' replied Valaincourt, 'how difficult it is to speak when one thinks that all your happiness or our misery depends on what one is about to say . . . what if I set about it the wrong way . . . Oh! Good God! What if I fail to utter the right words . . . ! Julie, adorable Julie, tell me . . . what must I say? What speeches, what reasons, what assurances could ever convince you to give yourself to me?'

'Ah! Valaincourt . . . !' said Julie with a look and a sigh that promised everything, that replied yes to everything he would have liked to say.

Valaincourt, who understood that look and sigh, asked for nothing more; beside himself, he takes her hands and ecstatically kisses them; he even dares – he dares in broad daylight – to press his mouth on hers. The father might have come in right then, but they weren't thinking about that; what could they have foreseen, what could they have feared in their delirium? It didn't last long, however; Julie became alarmed at the ardour of her lover, and at her own willingness.

'Let go, let me go,' she said. 'Valaincourt, we forget ourselves.'

At that moment they heard a noise, and hurried to sit back down. Julie bowed her head over her work to conceal her confusion; the young man went up to Monsieur d'Arnonville with an air of submission that seemed to predispose him in his favour.

'I have taken, monsieur, the liberty of coming to see mademoiselle, your daughter, to whom my good fortune has introduced me.'

'Had you never seen my chateau?'

'No, monsieur; I had never had any pretext to dare to come and pay you my respects.'

'It is very worthy of being seen,' said the old lord. 'A Baron d'Arnonville whose great-great-great-grandfather had been knighted under Clovis had it built in 624. We should not wonder at his having had it built as large as it now is; in that time the nobility was respected as it should be; it was rich and powerful; it was also much purer and much less prevalent than nowadays. At present it is an ordinary recompense; nothing is more common, and I set little store by those little nobles without ancestors –'

'We are stuffed with ancestors from attic to cellar,' said Julie.

'And most of the ancient families,' continued the baron, 'have polluted themselves through misalliance. There are very few families, I dare assert, which have maintained themselves in all their purity; and I therefore hope that my children –'

'It is doubtless,' interrupted the young man, able to contain himself no longer, 'it is doubtless a satisfaction and an extra reason to be virtuous when one finds examples of virtue and love of one's country in one's ancestors. When one joins a great name to great merit, and instead of vanity –'

'As you have never seen the chateau, you have never seen the portraits. I must show them to you; it could only be useful for your study of history. Sir, would you like to follow me?'

'Will mademoiselle be coming with us?' said Valaincourt unhappily.

"No,' replied Julie, laughing. 'I have lived long enough with my grandfathers, and I know them well.'

Julie stayed at her work, or rather at her daydreaming. Lord! How agreeable it was. Never had a moment of solitude been more delicious for her. But how wretched Valaincourt was! The baron, well disposed towards him, spared him not one portrait, not one coat of arms, not one anecdote, and each portrait, each coat of arms confronted him with thoughts that pierced poor Valaincourt's heart. It is not that he was mortified by such a ridiculous display; he would not have had his nobility conferred by King Ninus himself if he'd had to be as vain and as mad as the Baron d'Arnonville – but Julie! Finally they arrived at her bedchamber, and he trembled.

While the father was getting tangled up in the history of the first ancestor to be transmitted to posterity on the end of a paintbrush, Valaincourt's eyes wandered over the creations of the daughter's taste. On a table he saw one landscape she had finished, one she had started, and among the brushes and paints he saw a little Catechism, Segrais, Racine and Gil Blas. He saw the beautiful prints she preferred over old portraits, he saw the flowers ... but he stopped saying anything once he had espied the portrait of Julie. It was drawn in miniature; it looked like her. Valaincourt no longer thought about anything other than getting the father to look somewhere else.

'Who is that respectable man,' he said, 'who is there, sir, behind you?'

The baron turned round. 'That's the one I was telling you so much about; didn't you hear me?'

'Ah! Sir, I apologize; I do remember it.'

Valaincourt had the portrait, and desired nothing more; but seeing that the father was starting again, he also took the pretty landscape he liked. Finally they left the bedchamber. 'It is there,' said Valaincourt under his breath, 'it is there that live, that repose so many charms!'

'It is there,' said the baron, 'that my most ancient portraits are kept; we are finishing our tour with what is most curious – I kept it for last as a special treat.'

'How right you are, sir,' said Valaincourt, who smiled despite his distress. 'There is nothing more precious than the pictures in that room.' And although he thanked him with every sign of the liveliest gratitude, despair was in his heart.

'Is it not true,' said Julie when they rejoined her, 'that I am rich in grandfathers? My grandmothers are not beautiful, but they are ancient. I count on having myself painted many times; beautiful or ugly, in three hundred years my portrait will be worth its weight in gold.'

'Ah! Mademoiselle,' said Valaincourt, 'your portrait will never be as dear, as precious as it is today. Then, vanity may venerate it, but today love adores it.'

'Have you seen it, monsieur?'

'Yes, mademoiselle, you will see that I have seen it as I should see it; I also saw your books, and your landscapes –'

'Were you not vastly entertained to see my ancestors?'

'No, mademoiselle; I only looked at what related to you.'

All this was said in hushed tones. Julie smiled, and Valaincourt was relieved to see that the daughter did not have the same respect for antiquity as her father. It was late; Valaincourt said his good-byes and left.

'Is that young man your lover?' the baron asked his daughter.

'I believe so, Father.'

'Is he thinking of marrying you?'

'Yes, Father.'

'Is he a gentleman?'

Julie had no idea, but supposed so, and again said yes.

'Of an old family?'

'Yes, Father.'

'Where does their nobility derive from?'

'From Renaud de Montauban,' replied Julie, more out of playfulness than for politics.

'What? Daughter, from Renaud de Montauban! My God, how lucky you would be! What joy for me to see you married so well!'

And so saying, he embraced her with such tenderness that she was disconcerted. She was sorry that she had deceived him over something that seemed so important to him, and was fearful what the consequences of her joking might be, should it come to light. She was also exasperated by the extent of her father's folly, and all these feelings together agitated her so much that she was obliged to withdraw. She sat down in her bed-chamber, arms leaning on her dressing table, head bowed in her hands.

'My father does not ask,' said she, 'whether he is virtuous, wise, or whether he has a good heart; he asks whether his family is ancient . . . on that assurance, he gives me to him . . . Ah! If Valaincourt turned out not to be so noble, he would not give me his permission! He would be even more rigid because of my deceit. Good God, how imprudent! Good God, how wrong I was!'

She pondered this sadness for a while longer; then, getting up and pacing round the room, she wanted to look at the landscape that Valaincourt had been talking about to distract herself. Unable to find it anywhere, she turned to her portrait; then she understood what Valaincourt had wanted to tell her. The theft diverted as much as it moved her; she imagined her father on one side saying, 'This is Jean-François-Alexandre d'Arnonville,' while Valaincourt was thinking, 'Here is Julie d'Arnonville; I must carry her off.' When a young girl sees that she is tenderly loved by her lover, her griefs are easily softened; deep joy easily lifts the heart. Julie thought that if Valaincourt was not descended from Renaud, he was probably descended from someone; that she would be able to make her trick look like a mistake; that moreover it wasn't impossible that some use could still be made of it; that she should warn Valaincourt, and work on his genealogy with him.

'If reasonable motives don't touch my father,' she thought, 'am I not allowed to trick him a bit? Should we be the victims of such ridiculous prejudice?'

This rather relaxed morality suited her, and she looked no further. It occurred to her to write to Valaincourt to warn him. She took her inkstand, pens and paper; she imagined how she would get the letter to him; and I would swear to it that she would have written something if only she could have been happy with her style and spelling, but Julie quickly passed over her true motives for not writing; she persuaded herself that the whole panoply of prudence, reserve, modesty and respect for decorum was what was stopping her, and she congratulated herself on virtues that she did not possess.

Julie was called down to supper. Her father had already imparted her hopes to the young baron; they could barely contain themselves in front of the servants. Hardly had these been dismissed before they were drinking to the health of Renaud's descendant; but Julie, unable to bear the sight of their joy, withdrew once more, equally ashamed of her mistake and of their foolishness. Alone in her room, she started to cry. Love, repentance, fear and hope mingled in her heart and oppressed it. When a young person is agitated by different feelings that she can no longer disentangle, her way out will be to cry. By the time Julie stopped crying, the chaos that had seemed so overwhelming had almost dissipated; soon there was nothing left but the idea of her lover. She saw him as she had seen him when they met for the very first time. She remembered his marks of tenderness; she reproached herself for responding to them too much for decency and not enough for love; she remembered kisses, and who knows if she did not wish to receive them again? Finally, she got into her bed, and on doing so, she reflected that a very long time had passed since she'd last seen it. 'Was it only this morning,' said she, 'that I got up? Was it only this afternoon that Valaincourt came?' No day had ever seemed longer to her, because no day of hers had ever been so filled with such different and interesting sensations. She could not comprehend how it was possible for her to have felt and thought so many things, of having had such joy and such grief in such a short amount of time. Julie is not the only one to whom time seems much longer in the rapid succession of varied impressions than in the languor of inaction. Julie fell asleep in spite of her tender feelings; her dreams held no disturbing omens. The following day no presentiments came to trouble her; she spent the morning painting in her room. Her father was dining at the neighbouring chateau, her brother was hunting, and so she was alone. Many times did she wish that Valaincourt would come and interrupt her solitude, and take advantage of moments that were slipping away for nothing! Having started to read on a bench in the avenue, she finally saw him approaching, but he was with her father. He had spent half the night looking at the portrait of his mistress, and half the day too, but he wanted to see his mistress herself again; he first set out after dinner, and met Monsieur d'Arnonville on his way home. The baron wasted no time before speaking of the thing that alone occupied his heart.

'I have learned, monsieur,' he said, after having bowed to him many times, 'I have learned that you have fallen in love with my daughter, and that you were hoping to marry her.'

Valaincourt was stunned by this opening and his only reply was a deep bow. Surprise and anxiety were painted on his face, and kept him silent. 'My fate will be decided,' he said to himself. 'Good God, what will he say?' This eagerness to discuss his love announced either happiness or extraordinary unhappiness. He hardly dared listen.

'I have long been decided, monsieur,' continued the baron with a gracious air, 'only to give my daughter to a man of illustrious birth: the d'Arnonvilles would dishonour no family; they can aspire to anything. My ancestors –'

'Ah! monsieur,' cried Valaincourt, imprudent and in love, 'I know how superior to me you are. I know that I am not worthy to be allied to you, but if the most tender, respectful love, the keenest desire to make your daughter happy could stand in lieu of an older line; if honour, probity, my devotion to you . . .'

By this time Julie had reached them, she had heard what Valaincourt was saying, and her confusion explained all this mystery. Valaincourt was looking in the opposite direction and hadn't yet seen Julie, but the father was not listening to Valaincourt any more. He threw her a look that made her crumple at his feet. Valaincourt, interrupted by these actions, watched the daughter and the father without being able to understand what was causing this touching scene; he didn't know what to think or what to say. Julie, eyes bowed to the ground, allowed her tears to flow, and said nothing. The furious father was unable to speak. Finally he recovered it:

'Daughter unworthy of me and of my forefathers,' said he, 'have you been trying to deceive your father; is everything you said about the birth of your lover nothing other than a fiction?'

'Oh, Father!' Julie replied. 'I am guilty, but ... but I was in love with Valaincourt.'

'What, Julie, have I betrayed you?' Valaincourt cried. 'I should have guessed, I should have kept quiet ... Oh! It is for my sake that you have done this, and I'm the one who is betraying you! Monsieur,' he continued, falling to his knees next to Julie. 'Monsieur, forgive an error that love made her commit, and which we therefore share. Allow me to love your daughter; her graces, her wit, the beauty of her soul as well as her birth raise her high above me. She deserves a throne ... but no king could be more ardent; she would never find more love in his heart than in mine; never will her perfections be more adored ... Again, allow me to love her and see her, and see you, and let your own judgement decide my fate.'

'Renaud de Montauban!' said the father, without seeming to have heard him. 'How long has your family been titled?'

Valaincourt did not reply.

'Tell him,' said Julie. 'Be more honest and open than I was.'

'Thirty-five years.'

'Thirty-five years! And you want me to give you my daughter! Go, mademoiselle; go and weep for your shame, and do not reappear before me. And you, monsieur, let us see you here no longer. Remove yourself from my sight this instant,' he told Julie, who was still on her knees and weeping, 'I can hardly believe you could have forgotten your origin to this extent! You do not deserve to be born to the rank you have!'

'No doubt,' said Valaincourt, helping Julie to get up, 'she did not deserve to be born to a father like you.'

He would have said more had a look from Julie not imposed silence on him, and as she went along the path towards the chateau, the desperate lover went away from it, cursing his fate, and nobility too. As for the Baron d'Arnonville, he was so outraged, so indignant, and in such a passion that he was unable to walk, so he sank down on the same bench Julie had been so peacefully occupying a few moments before, reading and dreaming. Having ordered a labourer who was working in the garden to fetch the housekeeper, he told her what had happened in a few words, and instructed her to make sure that Julie could not get out of her room or receive news from or about her lover. This old woman, whose name was Mademoiselle du Tour, was practically one of the chateau archives in her own right, and having neither heard nor seen anything other than the follies of her masters from her earliest infancy, was almost as passionate on the subject of nobility as the baron. Sharing his resentment with all her heart, she ran off to lock up and harangue her young mistress. Julie, although sweet-natured, was infuriated by this harsh treatment, and as the old woman, having once explained what she had been sent to do, commenced with the words 'For a young lady of your rank ...' Julie said, 'Be silent! I have heard enough of this nonsense! Lock me up, but leave.'

For two days Julie refused to listen or answer; she ate little, slept not at all, and cried a great deal. The baron, left alone on the bench, said to himself: 'How could a minor aristocrat of recent date presume to ally himself to me? How could my daughter listen to him? On the one hand, what boldness! On the other, what cowardice!' He said this all alone until nightfall, then he said it to his son, he said it all night long in his dreams, and the next day while touring the portraits, he thought they were reproaching him, full of indignation. On the third day, the wind knocked down part of the dovecote, and the weather vane engraved with the Arnonville coat of arms toppled from the top of the tower into a muddy ditch in front of his eyes, and his mind was seized with the most piercing fear. He went to bed, his imagination struck by these terrifying omens, and hardly had sleep scattered its sweet poppies over him than he saw the spirits of his ancestors armed from top to toe approaching his bed, looking outraged. The baron awoke with a start and asked them to appear to his daughter, but the antique shades entirely failed to do so. Julie had received a note from Valaincourt that evening, and slept peacefully; her dreams were the work of love and hope. Valaincourt had approached the gardener's little daughter about the note; Julie had always been very kind to her and she was devoted to her mistress. This girl willingly took on the commission, and asked the old jaileress if she might herself take Julie some fruit. Mademoiselle du Tour was not fundamentally unkind, and Julie's grief was beginning to inspire her with pity, so she said yes, and after the young girl had chatted with Julie for a while she whispered to her that at the bottom of the basket of fruit she would find a letter. No sooner was Julie alone than she opened it, and this is what she read:

Beautiful, sweet Julie, since you know what love is, there's no need to tell you what I feel, and what I suffer, and moreover, how could my pen ever express it? My aim is to assure you that there is nothing I will not undertake, nothing that I will not hazard to rescue you from the cruel grip which keeps us apart. Are you capable of not agreeing with me, Julie? Can you submit to such ridiculous prejudice? If I ever thought . . . if I thought that you could ever repent an instant, if you might be less happy . . . God be my witness that I would give up all my happiness to spare you a single regret . . . Tell me, mademoiselle, do you fear regrets? My birth . . . excuse me, Julie, you love me, and I dare suspect your heart? Would you judge as unworthy of your hand he whom you do not judge unworthy of your affection? Is it not for me that you suffer . . . ? Trust in my love, charming Julie; we will not suffer long.

Julie believed him without really knowing why. She read and reread the charming note, and on reading it, hope and even cheerfulness were reborn in her heart. She ate, she slept; and next day she picked up her work again and her painting. Mademoiselle du Tour found her as sweet and courteous as she had ever been, and she finally had the pleasure of haranguing her without being interrupted. The following day the little girl came back with her basket while Mademoiselle du Tour was just saying: 'Given your birth you can aspire to the highest in the land.'

'That may well be,' replied Julie, smiling.

Mademoiselle du Tour, ignorant of the secret power of the basket, thought Julie's cheerfulness was the proof of what she had experienced herself in previous times – that is, that there is no better consolation for the loss of one lover than to have another one. She therefore carried on, saying: 'Your husband will be a great lord; you will have a great chateau, and you will be very happy.'

'That may well be,' said Julie, smiling even more sweetly.

Mademoiselle du Tour, believing that she'd made great progress, congratulated herself and went out to tell the baron that he needed only leave it all to her, and within two days, Julie would have forgotten her lover. But she couldn't find anyone to tell about her skill and delight. The baron had gone out to distract himself, and had left word that he wouldn't be back until the following day. Julie quickly took advantage of the housekeeper's absence to read Valaincourt's latest letter. He told her that he'd examined everything and judged that her escape would be easy; that her window was low, that this part of the moat was almost filled in; that he would wait for her in the avenue at dusk, and that a swift carriage would convey them before daybreak to a town quite far off, where they would swear inviolable love to each other at the foot of the altar.

'I no longer doubt my happiness,' he continued, 'since it depends on you, dear Julie; that would be to insult you. Love gives you to me; its rights are sacred. At midnight, when the moon begins to break through the shadows, leave the sad prison where barbarous prejudice keeps you locked up, and let love guide you to the arms of your lover. I ask for no reply; you told me that you loved me, and that was to promise me everything. Till midnight, Julie … what moments, what pleasures!'

Julie let the letter fall, and stayed quite still for a while. A completely new feeling, part surprise, part joy, suspended her thoughts entirely for some time. An elopement! That very evening! Leaving the house of her father, and giving herself to Valaincourt! Julie finally moved, and without admitting her intentions, opened the window, and in fact looked around to see how easy it would be to get out. Seeing that that side of things was not at all impossible, she picked up the letter and read it again. 'It is true,' she said, 'that the prejudice which keeps me here is as barbaric as it is absurd. It is true that I told him I love him. Valaincourt does not doubt my consent – that would be, says he, to insult me. I am his; he will wait for me …'

Is not the identical tone of authority that is so hateful in a husband compelling in a lover? With the same skill that we evade the rights of one because we hate them, we extend the rights of another because we love them. We don't want our freedom when it comes to employing it against our will. If Valaincourt had pleaded, had asked for her consent, as if doubting whether he'd obtain it, perhaps Julie would not have dared to give in; but Valaincourt demanded, and Julie did not think she could disobey. Valaincourt would no doubt have been hard pressed to explain what these sacred rights of love that he claimed with such assurance actually were. But Julie asked for no explanation, no proof; she believed his word, and she thought she was decided not so much by his passion as by a certain inviolable duty, which she nonetheless did not understand.

There she stands, almost resolved to go ahead, weeping tears over the father she is abandoning and the home in which she was born, and which she is going to leave; but she thinks about her lover, and her tears dry up. 'So I will be,' she bursts out, 'so I will be his, for ever!' Then she goes back to the window, and looking at it more carefully, she sees that at precisely the place where she'd have to climb down, there is a hole, filled with that day's fresh rainfall. She would need to fill that hole in; what should she use? Julie looks around her, and seeing the portraits of her forefathers, says to them, 'You will do me at least this favour,' and, laughing, she immediately jumps on to a chair to take Jean-François d'Arnonville down off the wall. As she is holding him, still up on the chair, Mademoiselle du Tour comes in –

'What are you doing, mademoiselle?'

'Dear lady . . . dear lady . . . am I not right to send this portrait off to the painter for restoration? If I am to be married, as you believe, to a lord from an old chateau, I would like to be able to take the first baron of the family there.'

Mademoiselle du Tour, as we will not be surprised to hear, did not disapprove of this idea, and took the opportunity to make a very long speech about the nothingness of the pleasures of love, and the solidity of the advantages of the nobility. Julie, unconquerably merry and playful, wanted to know whether this fair dame had ever experienced this thing she scorned and du Tour told her that had her lover been cook's boy to a duke, she would have listened to him, but he was only cook's boy to a count.

Once the housekeeper had departed, Julie made a parcel of her most precious belongings, and as the day was drawing in, started to get ready for her escape. Grandpa was hurled into the mud, and he, not being sufficient, was followed by a second, and then a third. Julie had never thought her ancestors could be so useful. This new use amused her; and yet she was very agitated, and if on the one hand her heart was in ecstasies at the hope of belonging to her lover, it was also bleeding for her father. Ah! How powerful the principles of a good education would have been over a naturally virtuous soul, as yet uncertain of itself! But the arguments in favour of duty, which the father had always used, were even less solid than those of the lover in favour of love.

The little girl came to fetch her basket. Not knowing what was in the letters she had carried, and believing a reply from Julie would give great pleasure to Valaincourt, she asked if her mistress had any orders to give her. Julie hesitated; now was the moment to destroy Valaincourt's hopes. Her face turned white, then red. 'There is no reply,' she said to the gardener's daughter, as she gave her a coin.

At eight o clock, her brother came to see her for the first time. After a couple of not very delicate jokes, he told her he had condescended to play a game that he was good at with some little upstart who didn't understand it at all; and that he was so charmed to be duping someone so easily, that he had played all day long, and won a considerable sum. We are never harsher on those faults of which we feel we are completely incapable than when we feel guilty about something else. Julie told him that what he had done was absolutely disgraceful and shameful; he made some contemptuous reply, and left. 'I will soon be far away from this delightful nobility,' said she. 'It is probably with someone like him that I would be condemned to spend the rest of my life; moreover, if his lineage was good I would be thought only too lucky. Oh well! May these great lords enter the Order of Malta as is their right. Valaincourt does not prevent them – I think he is happy for them to have both honour and vows – but my heart and hand have nothing in common with the Maltese cross.'

She carried on getting ready for her departure until the housekeeper came to take her to supper. She went to bed straight afterwards so that no one would be suspicious. Once everyone was asleep, from the young baron to his best friends the hunting dogs, she got up. She dressed quickly, without taking too much care, without light and thus also without a mirror; she thought that at night, by the feeble light of the moon, Valaincourt would not be spending too much time contemplating her attire.

The moon appears, the window opens, midnight sounds, Julie throws her parcel out, climbs up on the windowsill, comes back down into the room, climbs up again. Something is holding her back; she thinks she can hear her father, but what can he say to hold her back? He speaks to her of her name, her birth, of the honour of her origin, which it is her duty to uphold. Julie finds that none of this makes any difference, and that there is no reason why she shouldn't be any less unhappy than her maid, who apparently had permission to go off and elope as she pleased. Love presents her with less feeble reasons, decides her, and Julie jumps down lightly onto the face of one of her ancestors, who rends and snaps beneath her feet. The noise awakens the housekeeper, who sleeps not far from there, but supposing that it was one of those spirits that frequently honour ancient chateaus with their visits, she is content to mutter a Hail Mary and bury herself deeper in her pillows, and this time the ghosts are useful for once.

Julie advances across the ruins and goes into the courtyard. A dog wakes up but doesn't betray the kind mistress who has stroked him so often. She wants to go out by a little door, which unfortunately is locked – trembling, she retraces her steps. 'God! What will become of me,' says she, 'if I can't find a way of getting out?' A little old wall prevents her; she tries to climb up on it. The bricks have been joined together for so long that they come apart without difficulty. She's already in the avenue; now she's with her lover . . . Let us not worry ourselves about what became of them.

The next day, when the frightful news was brought to the old baron, he fainted. Coming back to his senses after a good while, and many medicaments, he said in languishing tones: 'A nobleman of recent creation! Oh my ancestors! Oh my blood! Eternal opprobrium!' It was feared that he would die of pain. In vain did a reasonable man who happened to be there represent to him that nobility is a prejudice about worth, and that recognized worth, such as Valaincourt's, had no need of prejudice; that it is impossible to lay claim to someone else's worth, and that even if it were possible, a nobleman would not often be found with more than anyone else; that the emperor who conferred the titles in the first place may well have been a dishonest man or an idiot . . . This blasphemous speech was followed by an even longer fainting fit than the first one. I think that that would have been the end of the baron had a very consolatory letter not called him back to life. Fate compensated him for the acquisition of a rich, handsome and generally agreeable son-in-law by offering him the most disagreeable daughter-in-law imaginable. He accepted this compensation with joy; he offered up thanks to Heaven, and admired the wisdom of Providence, which dispenses good and evil in equal measure. It goes without saying that the young lady was thoroughly noble; not her portrait but her family tree was sent, and it was such that the father did not hesitate. The son had heard it said that she had a squint and a hunchback; but the honour of uniting his arms and quarters to hers encouraged him to overlook all the rest. In any case he counted on consoling himself with less noble and less ugly creatures, and had too much greatness of soul to think that it was obligatory to love the person one marries. The marriage was therefore rapidly concluded. Julie, having heard the news, found out when the wedding day was to be. At the end of the meal, Daddy d'Arnonville, reliving the vigour of his young days, drank twenty bumpers to the excellence of the union. Once the wine had started mixing old and new nobility in his head, Valaincourt and Julie entered the room, and threw themselves at his feet. Having lost a part of what he called his reason, he felt nothing but tenderness, and forgave them. Julie was happy, and her sons were not knights, not one of them.

Translated by Caroline Warman

VIVANT DENON

No Tomorrow

'The letter killeth, but the spirit giveth life.'

2 Corinthians 3:6

I was desperately in love with the Comtesse de—; I was twenty years old and I was naive. She deceived me, I got angry, she left me. I was naive, I missed her. I was twenty years old, she forgave me, and, because I was twenty years old, because I was naive – still deceived, but no longer abandoned – I thought myself to be the best-loved lover, and therefore the happiest of men. She was a friend of Madame de T—, who seemed to have some designs on me yet did not wish to compromise her dignity. As we shall see, Madame de T— possessed certain principles of decency to which she was scrupulously attached.

One day while waiting for the Countess in her opera box, I heard someone calling from the adjacent box. Was it not the decent Madame de T— again? 'What! So early?' she said to me. 'And with nothing to do! Come over here and join me.'

I had no idea just how fantastic and extraordinary this meeting would turn out to be. A woman's imagination moves quite quickly, and at this very moment Madame de T—'s imagination was singularly inspired.

'I shall spare you the ridicule of such solitude,' she said. 'And since you are here, you must . . . Yes, it's an excellent idea. A divine hand must have led you here. You don't by any chance have plans for this evening? I warn you, they would be pointless. No questions, don't try to resist . . . Call my servants. You are just charming.'

I bowed low, she hurried me into her box, I obeyed.

'Go to Monsieur's house,' she told a servant, 'and let them know he won't be back this evening . . .' She then whispered in his ear and dismissed him. I tried to venture a few words, the opera began, she hushed me. We listened, or pretended to listen. The first act had scarcely ended when the same servant returned with a note for Madame de T— telling her everything was ready. She smiled, asked for my hand, went down to the street, and invited me into her carriage. We were already outside the city before I could find out what she intended to do with me.

Every time I ventured a question, she responded with a burst of laughter. Had I not been so aware that she was a passionate woman, that she was currently involved, and that she could not help knowing that I knew this, I would have been tempted to think myself a quite fortunate fellow. She also knew the state of my heart, for, as I've already said, the Comtesse de— was a close friend of Madame de T—. I therefore refrained from any presumptuous ideas, and I waited to see what would happen. We changed horses and started off again with lightning speed. Suddenly, this all seemed more serious to me. I urged her to tell me where this game would lead me.

'It will lead you to a very beautiful place. Just guess where. Oh, you'll never guess . . . My husband's house. Do you know him?'

'Not at all.'

'I think you'll like him: we're to be reconciled. Negotiations have been going on for six months now, and we have been corresponding with each other for one month. Don't you find it quite obliging of me to go and visit him?'

'Absolutely. But please tell me – what will I do there? How can I be of use in all of this?'

'That's my business. I was afraid a tête-à-tête with him would be boring. You're agreeable, and I'm very glad to have you with me.'

'Strange that you would choose the day of your reconciliation to introduce me. You would have me believe I'm of little consequence. Add to this the natural awkwardness of a first meeting. Honestly, I can see nothing pleasant for any of us in what you intend.'

'Oh, no moralizing, I beg you. You're missing the point of your task. You're supposed to entertain me and amuse me, not preach to me.'

I saw she was quite determined, so I gave in. I began to laugh at the role I was playing, and we became very cheerful.

We changed horses a second time. Night's mysterious orb illuminated a pure sky and spread a voluptuous half-light. We were approaching the place where our tête-à-tête would come to an end. From time to time I was asked to admire the beauty of the landscape, the calm of the night, the moving silence of nature. In order to enjoy all this together, we naturally had to lean towards the same window; the lurching of the carriage caused Madame de T—'s face to touch mine. At an unexpected jolt, she grasped my hand; and I, by the purest chance, caught hold of her in my arms. I don't know what we were trying to do in this position, but what is certain is that my vision dimmed when she let go of me abruptly and threw herself back deep into the depths of the carriage.

'Do you intend,' she said after a rather profound reverie, 'to convince me of my imprudence in your regard?'

The question disconcerted me. 'Intend . . . with you . . . I wouldn't dream of it! You would see through me too easily. But mere chance, a surprise . . . that can be forgiven.'

'It seems that you have been counting on it.'

We had come to this point almost without noticing that we were entering the chateau's forecourt. Everything was brightly lit, everything proclaimed joy, except for the master's face, which stubbornly refused to show any such sign. His languid manner indicated that he felt the need to reconcile for no other than family reasons. Propriety, however, brought Monsieur de T— to the carriage door. I was introduced, he gave me his hand, and I followed, musing over my role, past, present and to come. I passed through rooms decorated with as much taste as magnificence. The master of the house was particularly attuned to all the refinements of luxury, for he was endeavouring to replenish the resources of his worn-out body with images of sensual pleasure. Not knowing what to say, I took refuge in admiration. The goddess eagerly did the honours of the temple, and received my compliments very graciously.

'What you see is nothing; I must take you to Monsieur's apartment.'

'Madame, I had it torn down five years ago.'

'But, of course!' she said.

At supper didn't she take it upon herself to offer Normandy veal to Monsieur? And Monsieur said to her, 'For the past three years I've been on a milk diet.'

'But, of course!' she said again.

Try to picture a conversation between three creatures so surprised to find themselves together!

Supper came to an end. I imagined we would go to bed early, but I was right only in the case of the husband. As we entered the drawing room he said, 'I am grateful to you, Madame, for the foresight you showed in bringing Monsieur with you. In judging that I would be a poor resource for the evening you judged well, because I will be retiring now.' Then, turning to me, he added in an ironic tone, 'Monsieur will please forgive me, and do convey my apologies to Madame.' He left us.

We looked at each other, and as a distraction from our thoughts, Madame de T— suggested we take a stroll on the terrace while waiting for the servants to have their supper. The night was superb; it revealed things in glimpses, and seemed only to veil them so as to give free rein to the imagination. The chateau as well as the gardens, resting against a mountainside, descended in terraces to the banks of the Seine, whose many loops formed small, picturesque, rustic islands that created different views and enhanced the charm of this lovely spot.

We walked first on the longest of these terraces: it was thickly planted with large trees. We had recovered from the unpleasant banter we had just endured, and as we walked she entrusted me with a few confidences. One confidence attracts another, and as I, in turn, confided in her, our confidences became ever more intimate and interesting. We had been walking for a long time. She had at first given me her arm, then that arm somehow or other entwined itself around me, while mine bore her up and prevented her, almost, from touching the ground. This position was pleasant but eventually tiring, and we still had many things to say to each other. A grassy bank appeared before us; we sat down on it without changing position, and in this posture we began to sing the praises of trust, its charm, its sweetness.

'Oh,' she said to me, 'who can enjoy this more than we, and with less apprehension? I am all too aware of how loyal you are to the attachment I know about to fear anything from you.'

Perhaps she wanted me to contradict her, but I did nothing of the sort. We therefore persuaded each other that it was impossible that we could ever be anything other than what we were to each other then.

'Yet I was afraid,' I said, 'that the incident in the carriage might have scared you.'

'I'm not so easily alarmed.'

'Yet I fear it may have left a few clouds.'

'What will it take to reassure you?'

'You can't guess?'

'I would like to have it explained to me.'

'I need to be sure you forgive me.'

'And for that, I would have to . . .'

'Grant me, here, the kiss that chance . . .'

'Very well, you would be too proud of yourself if I refused. Your vanity would convince you I was afraid.'

She wanted to forestall my illusions, and so I received the kiss.

Kisses are like confidences: they attract each other, they accelerate each other, they excite each other. In fact, I had barely received the first kiss when a second followed on its heels, and then another: their pace quickened, interrupting and then replacing the conversation. Soon they scarcely left us time to sigh. Silence fell all around us. We heard it (for one sometimes hears silence), and we were frightened. We stood up without saying a word and began to walk again.

'We must go back in,' she said. 'The evening air isn't good for us.'

'I don't think it's so dangerous for you,' I answered.

'True, I'm less susceptible than certain other women, but no matter – let's go back in.'

'Out of consideration for me, no doubt . . . You want to protect me from the dangerous impressions this walk might make . . . and the consequences that might ensue for me alone.'

'You attribute considerable delicacy to my motives. I'm quite happy to have it that way – but let's go back in, I insist.' (Awkward remarks of this sort are inevitably exchanged by two people who are trying as best they can to say something quite different from what they want to say.)

She forced me to head back towards the chateau.

I don't know – at least I didn't know then – if by this decision she was acting contrary to her own desires, if she had firmly made up her mind, or if she shared the disappointment I felt at watching a scene that had begun so nicely end this way. In any case, as if by a common instinct, we slowed our steps and walked along sadly, discontented with each other and ourselves. We didn't know who or what to blame. Neither of us had any right to ask or demand anything; we couldn't even resort to reproach. How a quarrel would have soothed us! But what should we have quarrelled about? Yet we were nearly back at the house, silently occupied with avoiding the restraint we had so clumsily imposed on ourselves.

We had just reached the door when Madame de T— spoke at last: 'I'm not very pleased with you ... After I have shown such trust in you, it is unfair ... so unfair ... not to grant me any! Have you said even one word about the Countess since we've been together? Even though it is so pleasant to talk about someone you love! And you can't doubt that I would have listened to you with great interest. It is certainly the least I could do for you after having deprived you of her company.'

'Don't I have the same reproach to make to you, and wouldn't you have avoided many problems if instead of making me the confidant of a reconciliation with a husband, you had spoken to me about a more appropriate choice – a choice ...'

'Stop at once ... Remember that the slightest suspicion will hurt a woman. If you know anything at all about women, you know that you have to wait for their confidences. But let's come back to you – what is going on with your friend? Is she making you quite happy? Oh, I fear the contrary, and this distresses me, because I take such a tender interest in you! Yes, Monsieur, I am interested ... more than you may think, perhaps.'

'Now really, Madame, why believe the gossip people enjoy spreading and exaggerating?"

'Don't try to pretend. I know everything about you that can be known. The Countess is not as mysterious as you. Women like her are generous with the secrets of their worshippers, especially when a discreet cast of mind like yours might deprive them of their triumphs. I do not in the least accuse her of being coquettish, but a prude has just as much vanity as a coquette. Tell me frankly: Are you not often the victim of her strange whims? Come now, tell me.'

'But Madame, you wanted to go back in ... and the air ...'

'It has changed.'

She had taken my arm again and we resumed our walk without my noticing the path we were following. What she had just hinted at about the lover I knew she had, what she was telling me about the mistress she knew I had, this whole trip, the scene in the carriage, the scene on the grassy bank, the time of night – all of it disturbed me: I was by turns overcome with vanity or desire, and then returned to myself by reflection. Besides, I was too moved to realize what I was experiencing. While I was prey to such confused emotions, she continued to talk, still about the Countess. My silence seemed to confirm everything she chose to say. Yet several biting remarks she let slip brought me back to myself.

'How cunning she is!' she said. 'How graceful! Treachery in her mouth appears as wit; an infidelity seems an act of reason, a sacrifice to decency. She never forgets herself, is always pleasant, rarely tender, and never true; flighty by nature, a prude by design; lively, cautious, artful, distracted, sensitive, clever, coquettish and philosophical: she's a Proteus of forms, she charms with her manners – she attracts, she eludes. How many roles I've seen her play! Between you and me, how many dupes surround her! How she has mocked the Baron! ... How many tricks she has played on the Marquis! When she took up with you, it was to regain her hold over two overly imprudent rivals who were about to expose her. She had accommodated them too much, they had had time to observe her; eventually, they would have caused a scandal. But she brought you on to the scene, gave them a hint of your attentions, led them to pursue her anew, drove you to despair, pitied you, consoled you – and all four of you were content. Oh, what power an artful woman has over you! And how happy she is when, in this game, she feigns everything and invests nothing of her own!' Madame de T— accompanied this last pronouncement with a very meaningful sigh. It was a masterful manoeuvre.

I felt that a blindfold had just been lifted from my eyes, and I didn't see the new one with which it was replaced. My lover appeared to be the falsest of all women, and I believed to have found a sensitive soul. I sighed too, without knowing for whom I sighed, without distinguishing whether it had been born of regret or hope. She seemed sorry to have distressed me, and to have let herself get too carried away in painting a portrait that could seem questionable, since it had been painted by a woman.

I could not make sense of what I was hearing. Once again, we were heading down the great path of sentiment, and from this vantage point it was impossible to foresee where our steps would lead. In the midst of our metaphysical discussions, she pointed out to me, at the far end of a terrace, a pavilion that had witnessed the sweetest of moments. She described its location and furnishings to me in detail. What a pity she didn't have the key to it! Still chatting, we approached the pavilion. It had been left open; all it lacked now was some daylight. But darkness lent it a certain charm of its own. And besides, I knew the charm of the object that would soon adorn it.

We trembled as we entered. This was love's sanctuary. It took possession of us: our knees buckled, our weakening arms intertwined, and, unable to hold each other up, we sank down on to a sofa that occupied a corner of the temple. The moon was setting, and its last rays soon lifted the veil of a modesty that was, I think, becoming rather tiresome. Everything grew confused in the shadows. The hand that tried to push me away felt my heart beating. Madame de T— was trying to move away from me but kept coming back all the more tender. Our souls met and multiplied; another was born each time we kissed.

Though it became less tumultuous, the intoxication of our senses did not yet allow us the use of our voices. We conversed in silence through the language of thought. Madame de T— took refuge in my arms, hid her head in my breast, sighed, and became calm beneath my caresses: she reprimanded and consoled herself in one breath, and she asked for love in return for everything that love had just stolen away from her.

The same love that had frightened her a moment before comforted her the next. If it is true that lovers want to give what they have allowed to be taken, it is also true that they receive what they have stolen. And both parties hasten to obtain a second victory in order to secure their conquest.

All this had been a little abrupt. We realized our error and returned more leisurely to what we had passed over in haste. When lovers are too ardent, they are less refined. Racing towards climax, they overlook the preliminary pleasures: they tear at a knot, shred a piece of gauze. Lust leaves its traces everywhere, and soon the idol resembles a victim.

Calmer, we found the air purer, cooler. Earlier, we had not heard how the river, its wavelets bathing the walls of the summer house, interrupted the night's silence with a gentle murmur that seemed in harmony with the wild beating of our hearts. The darkness did not allow us to distinguish any objects, but through the transparent veil of a beautiful summer night our imaginations transformed an island that lay before our retreat into an enchanted spot. The river now swarmed with cupids who frolicked in the ripples. Never were the forests of Gnide as peopled with lovers as the far bank of our river. For us, nature housed only happy couples, and none was happier than we. We would have rivalled Amor and Psyche. I was as young as he; I found Madame de T— as charming as she. In her greater abandon, she seemed all the more ravishing. Every passing moment revealed something more beautiful. The torch of love illuminated it in my mind's eye, and the most reliable of the senses confirmed my happiness. When fear disappears, caresses seek out caresses: they call out all the more tenderly to one another. Lovers no longer want their favours stolen. If they defer, it is from refinement. Their refusal is half-hearted, and only another sign of tender care. They desire, but would prefer not to – the compliment alone is pleasing ... Desire flatters ... It uplifts the soul ... They adore ... They will never yield ... They surrender.

'Oh,' she said in a heavenly voice, 'let us leave this dangerous place; our desires keep multiplying here, and we haven't the strength to resist them.' She led me out.

We moved away regretfully. She looked back often. A divine flame seemed to burn in the courtyard.

'You have made this house sacred for me,' she said. 'Who will ever be able to please me here as you have? You truly know how to love! How fortunate she is!'

'Who do you mean?' I cried out in surprise. 'If I bring you happiness, what other creature in the world could you possibly envy?'

We passed before the grassy bank and stopped there involuntarily, with silent emotion.

'Such an immense distance lies between this spot and the summer house we just left!' she said. 'My soul is so full of happiness I can barely remember that I was capable of resisting you.'

'Well,' I said to her, 'am I here to witness the breaking of the magic spell that so filled my imagination back there? Will this spot always be fatal to me?'

'Can there be any such place, as long as I am with you?'

'Yes, it seems so, since I am just as unhappy here as I was happy there.

Love demands multiple tokens: it thinks it hasn't won anything as long as something is still left to be won.'

'Again . . . No, I can't allow it . . . No, never . . .' And after a long silence: 'Oh, but you do know how to love me!'

I beg the reader to remember that I was twenty years old. Meanwhile, the conversation changed its course: it became less serious. We even dared to jest about the pleasures of love, distinguishing moral pleasures from others, reducing them to their simplest forms, and proving that love's favours were nothing more than pleasure; that there was no such thing as a commitment (philosophically speaking) except for those commitments contracted with the public, when we allow it to discover our secrets, and when we agree to share in some indiscretions.

'What a delicious night we've just spent,' she said, 'all because of the attraction of pleasure, our guide and our excuse! I suppose if for some reason we were forced to separate tomorrow, our happiness, unknown to all of nature, would not leave us bound by any tie . . . a few regrets maybe, compensated by pleasant memories . . . And besides, we have had our pleasure, in fact, pleasure, without all the delays, the bother, and the tyranny of courteous behaviour.'

We are such *machines* (and I blush at the idea) that, instead of all the delicacy that tormented me before the scene which just took place, I found myself at least half to blame for the boldness of her principles; I found them sublime, and I felt a strong disposition for the love of freedom.

'What a beautiful night!' she said, 'what beautiful grounds! It has been eight years since I left them, but they have lost none of their charm. Now they have even recovered all the charms of novelty. We will never forget that pavilion, will we? There is an even more charming room in the chateau – but I can't show you anything. You're like a child who wants to touch everything, and who breaks everything he touches.'

Prompted by a violent feeling of curiosity I promised to be only what she would want me to be. I protested that I had become very reasonable. But she quickly changed the subject.

'This night would seem completely delightful if I weren't reproaching myself for one thing,' she said. 'I'm angry, really angry, about what I said to you about the Countess. I don't mean to complain about you. Novelty is exciting. You found me agreeable, and I choose to believe that you were in good faith; but trying to undo the sway of habit is a weary task, and I hardly know how to set about it. Besides, I've exhausted all the resources a heart possesses to bind you. What could you still hope for from me now? What could you still desire? And if a woman leaves a man with nothing to desire or to hope, what will become of her? I have given you everything I could; perhaps one day you will forgive me for the pleasures that, once the moment of intoxication has passed, return you to the severity of your judgement.

'By the way, what did you think of my husband? Rather sullen, isn't he? His diet is not very agreeable. I don't think he looked upon you with much equanimity. Our friendship would soon begin to seem suspect to him. So you shouldn't prolong this first trip: he'll become bad-tempered if you do. As soon as anyone comes, and no doubt someone will come ... Besides, you also have your own discretion to preserve ... Do you remember how Monsieur looked this evening when he left us? ...'

She saw the impression these last words made on me, and immediately added: 'He was more light-hearted when he was so carefully arranging the little room I mentioned to you a short time ago. That was before my marriage. It is attached to my apartment. It has never been for me anything more than evidence of ... the artificial resources Monsieur de T— needed to strengthen his affections, and of how little I was able to stimulate his soul.'

Thus she gradually aroused my curiosity about that little room. 'It is attached to your apartment,' I said to her. 'How delightful it would be to go there and avenge your insulted charms! To pay them the homage they deserve and of which they have been robbed.'

She liked this tone better.

'Oh!' I said to her, 'if only I were to be chosen as the principal actor in that revenge, if only the pleasure of that moment could make you forget, and make up for, the boredom of conjugal routine –'

'If you promise to be good,' she said, interrupting me.

I must confess that I didn't feel all the fervour, all the devotion necessary for visiting this new temple – but I was very curious. It was no longer Madame de T— whom I desired, it was the little room.

We had come back inside. The lamps in the stairwells and hallways had been extinguished; we were wandering through a labyrinth. Even the mistress of the chateau had forgotten the way. At last we arrived at the door of her apartment, the apartment housing that vaunted chamber.

'What are you going to do with me?' I asked. 'What is going to happen to me? Are you going to send me off alone in this darkness? Are you going to expose me to the risk of making a noise, of revealing us, of betraying us, of ruining you?'

This argument seemed irreproachable to her. 'Then you promise me . . .'

'Anything . . . anything you like.'

She accepted my oath. We gently opened the door. We saw two women sleeping, one young, one older. The latter, the trusted one, was the one she awoke. Madame de T— whispered something to her, and I soon saw her leave through a secret door cleverly fashioned in a panel of the wainscoting. I offered to perform the duties of the woman who was still asleep. Madame de T— accepted my services, and she rid herself of all superfluous ornaments. A single ribbon bound up her hair, which escaped in flowing curls; to this she added only a rose I had plucked in the garden and was still absent-mindedly holding; a loose dressing gown replaced all her other clothing. There wasn't a single knot in this whole outfit; I found Madame de T— more beautiful than ever. A little fatigue made her eyelids heavy and lent her gaze a more interesting languor, a gentler expression. The colour of her lips, more vivid than usual, set off the enamel of her teeth, and made her smile more voluptuous; red blushes scattered here and there set off the whiteness of her complexion and attested to its delicacy. These traces of pleasure reminded me of its sway. In truth, she seemed even more attractive to me than my imagination had painted her in our sweetest moments. The panel opened again and the discreet confidante disappeared.

As we were about to enter the chamber, she stopped me. 'Remember,' she said gravely, 'you are supposed never to have seen, never even suspected, the sanctuary you're about to enter. No careless mistakes; I'm not worried about the rest.' Discretion is the most important of the virtues; we owe it many moments of happiness.

All this was like an initiation rite. She led me by the hand across a small, dark corridor. My heart was pounding as though I were a young proselyte being put to the test before the celebration of the great mysteries . . .

'But your Countess . . .' she said, stopping. I was about to reply when the doors opened; my answer was interrupted by admiration. I was astonished, delighted, I no longer know what became of me, and I began in good faith to believe in magic. The door closed again, and I could no longer tell from whence I had entered. All I could see now was a seamless, bird's view of a grove of trees which seemed to stand and rest on nothing. In truth, I found myself in a vast cage of mirrors on which images were so artistically painted that they produced the illusion of all the objects they represented. There was no visible light inside the room; a soft, celestial glow entered, depending on the need each object had to be more or less perceived; incense burners exhaled delicious perfumes; intertwined ciphers and ornamental motifs hid from the eyes the flames of the lamps that magically illuminated this place of delights. The side where we had come in showed latticed porticoes ornamented with flowers, and arbours in each recess. On another side was a statue of Amor handing out crowns of flowers, and before the statue an altar on which shone a flame, and at the base of this altar a cup, crowns of flowers and garlands; a temple of lighthearted design completed the decor of this side. Opposite was a dark grotto, the god of mystery watching over the entrance, and the floor, covered with a plush carpet, imitated grass. On the ceiling, mythological figures were hanging garlands; and on the side opposite the porticoes was a canopy under which were piles of pillows with a baldachin upheld by cupids.

It was here that the queen of this place nonchalantly threw herself down. I fell at her feet, she leaned towards me, she held out her arms to me, and in that instant, because the couple we formed was repeated in its every angle, I saw that island entirely populated by happy lovers.

Desires are reproduced through their images. 'Will you leave my head uncrowned?' I asked her. 'So close to the throne, will I have to endure hardship? Will you reject me?'

'And your vows?' she answered, rising.

'I was a mortal when I made them, but now you have made me a god: my only vow is to adore you.'

'Come,' she said, 'the shadow of mystery must hide my weakness. Come . . .'

At the same time, she went over to the grotto. Scarcely had we passed through the entrance when some sort of cleverly contrived spring caught hold of us and, carried by its movement, we fell gently on our backs on a mound of cushions. Both darkness and silence reigned in this new sanctuary. Our sighs replaced language. More tender, more numerous, more ardent, they expressed our sensations, they marked their progression; and the last sigh of all, suspended for a time, warned us that we would have to offer thanks to Love. She took a crown and set it on my head, and, barely raising her beautiful eyes, damp with lust, she said to me, 'Well, then! Will you ever love the Countess as much as you love me?' I was about to answer when the confidante rushed in and said to me, 'Leave quickly. It's broad daylight. People are already stirring in the chateau.'

Everything vanished as quickly as a dream is destroyed when one awakens, and I found myself in the corridor before I was able to come to my senses. I tried to find my chambers, but where was I to look? Any inquiry would give me away, any wrong turn an indiscretion. The most prudent choice seemed to be to go down into the garden, where I resolved to stay until I could come back in as if I had been out for a morning walk.

The coolness and the pure air of that moment gradually calmed my imagination and drove the sense of magic from it. Instead of an enchanted nature, I saw only an innocent nature. Truth returned to my soul, my thoughts came to me without disturbance and followed one another in an orderly way; at last I could breathe again. I had nothing more pressing to do at that moment than ask myself if I was the lover of the woman I had just left, and I was quite surprised to discover that I didn't know how to answer. Who could have told me yesterday at the opera that I might ever ask myself such a question? I, who thought I knew that she was desperately in love, and had been for two years, with the Marquis de—, I, who thought I was so smitten with the Countess that it would be impossible for me to be unfaithful to her! What! Yesterday! Madame de T— . . . Was it really true? Had she broken with the Marquis? Had she chosen me to succeed him, or only to punish him? What an adventure! What a night! I didn't know if I was still dreaming. I doubted it, then I was convinced, persuaded, and then I didn't believe anything any more. As I was drifting amid these uncertainties, I heard a noise near me: I lifted my eyes, rubbed them, and couldn't believe what I saw. It was . . . none other than the Marquis.

'You didn't expect me so early in the morning, did you? Now, how did it go?'

'You knew I was here?' I asked him.

'Yes, of course. I was told yesterday just as you were leaving. Did you play your part well? Did her husband find your arrival quite ridiculous? When is she sending you back? I've taken care of everything; I'm bringing you a fine carriage which will be at your disposal – I owe you a favour. Madame de T— needed a squire, and you served as one for her, you entertained her on the way here; that was all she wanted. My gratitude . . .'

'Oh, no, no! I'm happy to be of service; and in this case Madame de T— might tell you I've been zealous above and beyond the powers of gratitude.'

He had just solved yesterday's mystery, and given me a key to the rest. I instantly sensed what my new role was. Every word fell into place.

'Why did you come so early?' I asked. 'It seems to me it would have been more prudent . . .'

'Everything has been arranged; it will look as if I have come here by chance. I'm supposed to be returning from a neighbouring estate. Didn't Madame de T— tell you? I'm cross with her for not trusting you, after all you have done for us.'

'No doubt she had her reasons; and perhaps if she had said something, I wouldn't have played my part so well.'

'Well, was it pleasant, my friend? Tell me the details . . . tell me now.'

'Ah! . . . Just a minute. I didn't know that all of this was mere play-acting; and even though I am involved in the play . . .'

'You didn't have the best part.'

'Oh, don't worry; for a good actor, there are no bad parts.'

'Of course – and you came off well?'

'Wonderfully well.'

'And Madame de T—?'

'Sublime. She can play any type.'

'Can you imagine pinning that woman down? It gave me some trouble; but I have moulded her character to the point where there is perhaps no other woman in Paris whose faithfulness can be relied upon so completely.'

'Excellent!'

'That's my special talent. All her inconstancy was mere frivolity, a disorder of the imagination; it all came down to capturing her soul.'

'Yes, absolutely.'

'Isn't that so? You have no idea how attached she is to me. The fact is, she's charming, as you'll agree. Between you and me, I know of only one failing in her, which is that nature, though it gave her everything, refused her that divine flame which is the highest blessing. She inspires everything, causing all sorts of feelings, and yet she herself feels nothing. She's made of stone.'

'Is she? I wouldn't have guessed . . . But, I must say, you seem to know this woman as well as if you were her husband: really, one could easily be deceived. And if I hadn't dined yesterday with the man himself . . .'

'Speaking of which, did he put on a good show?'

'Never was anyone more a husband.'

'Oh, what a fine adventure! But I fear you're not laughing about it enough for my taste. Don't you see just how comical your role is? You must agree that the theatre of the world presents strange opportunities – that it has some very amusing scenes. Let's go in, I'm eager to have a good laugh with Madame de T—. She must be awake by now. I said I would be here early. In all decency, we should begin with the husband. Let's go to your room, I want to put on a little more powder . . . So, did he really take you for a lover?'

'You'll be able to judge my success by the reception he gives me. It's nine o'clock – Let's go straight to Monsieur.' I wanted to avoid my chambers, and with good reason. On our way, however, we happened upon them quite by chance. Through the door, which had been left open, we saw my valet sleeping in an armchair; a candle was dying next to him. Awakening at our noise, he thoughtlessly offered my dressing gown to the Marquis, chiding him for the hour at which he was coming in. I was nervous, but the Marquis was so predisposed to be duped that he saw nothing in this but a dreamer giving him cause for laughter. I gave orders for my departure to my valet, who didn't know what all this meant, and we went in to see Monsieur. One can well imagine who received the welcome; of course, it wasn't I. My friend was warmly encouraged to stay for a while. Monsieur resolved to take him to see Madame, with the hope that she would persuade him. As for me, he dared not, he said, propose the same, for he found me so exhausted, he could not doubt but that the country air was truly fatal for me. Consequently, he advised me to return to town. The Marquis offered me his carriage, and I accepted. Everything was going perfectly, and we were all pleased. Nevertheless, I wanted to see Madame de T— again; it was a pleasure I couldn't deny myself. My impatience was shared by my friend, who couldn't understand my sleepiness, and who was quite far from guessing its cause. As we left Monsieur de T—'s apartment, he said, 'Isn't he quite amazing? If he had been fed his lines, could he have said them any better? In truth, he's a real gentleman; and, all things considered, I'm very pleased to see him reconciled with his wife. He'll run a good household; and you'll agree that, to do it honour, he couldn't make a better choice than his wife.' No one could have agreed more than I. 'Yet however agreeable that man might be, my dear, not another word; secrecy is more essential than ever. I'll let Madame de T— know that her secret couldn't be in better hands.'

'Believe me, my friend, she trusts me; and as you'll see she loses no sleep over this.'

'Oh, everyone would agree that you are unrivalled in putting a woman to sleep.'

'Or a husband, my friend, or even a lover, if need be.'

We were at last told we could go to Madame de T—, and we entered.

'Here, Madame,' said our chatterbox as he entered, 'are your two best friends.'

'I was afraid,' Madame de T— said to me, 'that you might have left before I woke up, and I am grateful to you for having sensed the sorrow that this would have caused me.' She examined us both, but she was soon reassured by the confidence of the Marquis, who continued to tease me. She laughed about it with me as much as was necessary to console me, and without lowering herself in my esteem. She spoke tenderly to him, and honestly and decently to me; bantering with him, she did not tease me.

'Madame,' said the Marquis, 'he finished his part just as well as he began it.'

She responded gravely, 'I was sure Monsieur would perform brilliantly any role one might entrust to him.'

He told her what had just happened in her husband's room. She looked at me, commended me, and did not laugh.

'As for me,' said the Marquis, who evidently could not stop himself, 'I'm delighted with all this: we've made ourselves a friend, here, Madame. I will say it again, our gratitude . . .'

'Come, Monsieur,' said Madame de T—, 'let's speak no more of it, and simply trust that I feel everything I should feel towards Monsieur.'

Monsieur de T— was announced, and we found ourselves all together. Monsieur de T— had ridiculed and then dismissed me; my friend the Marquis was duping the husband and mocking me; and I was paying him back in kind, all the while admiring Madame de T—, who was making fools of us all, without losing her dignity.

After enjoying this scene for a few moments, I felt the time had come for my departure. I withdrew, and Madame de T— followed, pretending she had an errand for me.

'Goodbye, Monsieur; I owe you so many pleasures; but I have paid you with a beautiful dream. Now, your love summons you to return; the object of that love is worthy of it. If I've stolen a few moments of bliss from her, I return you more tender, more attentive, and more sensitive.

'Goodbye, again. You are so charming . . . Don't give the Countess cause to quarrel with me.' She shook my hand and left.

I stepped into the carriage awaiting me. I looked hard for the moral of this whole adventure . . . and found none.

Translated by Andrew Brown

CHARLES NODIER

Jean-François les Bas-bleus

The fantastic is a little out of fashion these days, and that is no bad thing. The imagination all too readily takes advantage of ready resources; and in any case, not everyone is capable of the truly fantastic. The first essential condition for writing a good fantastic story is to believe in it with conviction, and no one believes in something one has invented oneself. Before long a combination of overly contrived effects, an excessively recondite playfulness of thought, a remark of clumsy wit, comes along to give away the scepticism in the storyteller's tale, and the illusion is shattered. It's the player of thimblerig who has let his peas roll out, or the stagehand who has let his strings show. Everything vanishes at once, as it does behind the dull and disenchanting curtain of shadow plays. You have seen what you have seen. The necromancer, stripped of his beard and his pointed hat, commends himself to you when you pay him a visit, if you are satisfied, and he will hardly put you straight lest you be of my taste, for there is nothing more foolish than an illusion which has ended. Send him your acquaintances. That is all you owe him.

I shall never in my life write a fantastic tale, be sure of that, unless I have as sincere a belief in it as I have in the most commonplace notions of my memory, or in the most mundane facts of my existence, and I do not think I owe anything in this regard in terms of intelligence or reason to those *freethinkers* who absolutely refute the fantastic. I differ from them, in truth, by my particular way of seeing, feeling and judging, but they differ therefore from me too, and I do not think myself obliged, by the absence of any public and recognized body, to submit the intimate perceptions of my senses and my conscience to the whim of a rebellious authority which perhaps has no other motive to contest than a presumptuous ignorance. America was a world of the fantastic before Christopher Columbus.

Bring me a man without education, but sure of himself as all fools are, who has by accident a speck of iron in his eye: 'My friend,' I would say to him, 'there is, on Mount Sipylus, in Asia Minor (it's very far from here), an extraordinary stone which would heal your ailing and inflamed eye on the spot, if you could see it up close. It's something utterly mysterious, and which defies explanation, if it is not because God has permitted it to be so; but only this stone can bring you relief.'

'You're having me on,' he would reply in anger, 'with your stone from Mount Sipylus! Old wives' tales! A charlatan's feeble excuse of a joke . . . !'

I had taken this man for a fool. He is already more than half a philosopher.

'As luck would have it,' I would thus reply, 'when I was on my distant travels I had a fragment of that stone set in the bezel of the ring I have here, and we are able to test its power.'

I would then bring the stone of Mount Sipylus close to that painful spot, and the foreign body would fly towards it, for the stone of Mount Sipylus is a magnet. Magnets have fantastic properties for those who have not tried them. The same goes for a thousand other natural forces known to a small number of men, and an infinite multitude of still more occult wonders known to no one.

After all that, Madame, I am ready, if it is of the slightest interest to you at all, to tell you a fantastic story in which I promise to add nothing of my own. It will be for you to judge as you please.

In 1793, there lived in Besançon an idiot, a monomaniac, a madman, whom those of my compatriots who have had the fortune or misfortune to live as long as I have all remember as well as I do. He was called Jean-François Touvet, but far more commonly, in the impudent language of schoolboys and rogues, Jean-François *les Bas-bleus*, because he never wore stockings in any other colour. He was a young man of twenty-four or twenty-five, if I am not mistaken, with a high and neat waist, and the most noble physiognomy one could possibly imagine. His unpowdered bushy black hair, swept back from his brow, his eyebrows, thick, curly and very lively, his big eyes, full of gentleness and a tenderness of expression which alone softened a certain air of gravity, the symmetry of his fine features, the almost celestial kindness of his smile, formed a whole worthy of inspiring affection and respect even in that uncouth rabble that makes a laughing stock of the most touching of man's infirmities: 'That's Jean-François *les Bas-bleus*,' they would say, elbowing each other, 'from a respectable family of old Comtois stock, who has never spoken ill of nor hurt anyone, and who, they say, went mad from being a scholar. One has to let him go quietly on his way not to make him any more ill.'

And Jean-François *les Bas-bleus* passed by indeed without paying attention to anything; for that eye which is beyond my powers to describe was never fixed on the horizon, but always aimed at the sky, with which this aforementioned gentleman (he was a visionary) seemed to maintain a secret conversation, discernible only by the perpetual movement of his lips.

The costume worn by this poor devil was, however, of a kind to amuse passers-by and above all strangers to the region. Jean-François was the son of an honourable tailor of the Rue d'Anvers, who had spared nothing on his education because of the high hopes he had inspired, and because his teachers were taking great pride in making a priest of him, sure that the brilliance of his sermons would lead him one day to the bishopric. He had indeed been at the top of all his classes, and the learned Abbé Barbélenet, the sage Quintilian of our fathers, kept himself regularly informed, in his exile, of the progress of his favourite pupil; but there was little to cheer him, for there seemed to be nothing left of the man of genius in the state of degradation and disdain into which Jean-François *les Bas-bleus* had fallen. The old tailor, who had several other children, had thus by necessity cut back on Jean-François' upkeep, and although he ensured his son was meticulous in his cleanliness, he only dressed him now with a few haphazard clothes which his work gave him the opportunity to acquire cheaply, or with hand-me-downs from his younger brothers, repaired to this end. There was something mournfully burlesque about this manner of get-up, so poorly adapted to his great size, which squeezed him into a sort of sheath ready to split apart, and which left more than half his forearm sticking out of the tight sleeves of his green tail-coat. His breeches, utterly glued to his thighs, neatly but pointlessly tight, met with great difficulty at the knee those blue stockings which had earned Jean-François his popular nickname. As for his three-cornered hat, decidedly ridiculous headgear for anyone, the shape it had been given by its maker and the manner in which Jean-François wore it combined on that poetic and majestic head to create an absurd nonsense. If I were to live for a thousand years I should never forget either the grotesque appearance nor the singular placement of Jean-François *les Bas-bleus'* little three-cornered hat.

One of the most remarkable peculiarities of this fine young man's madness, is that it was only discernible in conversations of no importance, during which the mind applies itself to familiar things. If one approached him to talk about the rain, the good weather, the show, the newspaper, the talk of the town, the state of affairs in the country, he listened attentively and replied politely; but the words which flooded to his lips rushed so tumultuously that they were all mixed up before the end of the first phrase in some inextricable gibberish, from which he could not disentangle his thought. He continued nonetheless, increasingly unintelligibly, and increasingly replacing the natural and logical phrase of the simple man with the babbling of a child who does not know the value of words, or the drivel of an old man who has forgotten it.

And so we would laugh; and Jean-François would fall silent, without anger, and perhaps without interest, raising his big and beautiful dark eyes to the sky, as if looking for more worthy inspiration from the realm on which he had focused all his ideas and all his feelings.

It was a different matter when the conversation involved a moral and scientific question of some interest. Then the rays – so divergent, so scattered – of this ailing intelligence would suddenly converge into a beam, like those of the sun in Archimedes' lens, and lent such brilliance to his words, that one is entitled to wonder whether Jean-François had ever been more learned, more lucid and more persuasive in the complete possession of his wits. The most difficult problems in the exact sciences, which he had studied in particular depth, were now child's play, and the solution launched itself so rapidly from his mind to his mouth, that one would have taken it much less as a result of reflection and calculation than as that of a mechanical operation, subject to the pressing of a key or the action of a coiled spring. It seemed to those listening to him then (and who were worthy of listening to him) that sacrificing the practical benefit of being able to easily articulate vulgar ideas in vulgar language was not too high a price to pay for such elevated powers; but it is the vulgar who judge, and the man in question was for them just an idiot in blue stockings, incapable of having a conversation even with common people. This was true.

As the Rue d'Anvers almost reached as far as my school, there was never a day when I did not pass through it at least four times to go there and back, but it was only in the middle part of the day, and on the milder days of the year blessed with a little sunshine, that I was sure to find Jean-François there, sat on a little stool, outside his father's door, and, more often than not, already trapped within a circle of silly schoolboys enjoying the extravagance of his motley phrases. I would be forewarned of this scene from afar by his listeners' peals of laughter, and when I arrived, my dictionaries tied together under my arm, I sometimes had a little trouble clearing a path to him; but I always felt a fresh pleasure when I did, because I thought I had discovered, child that I was, the secret to his double life, and because I was determined to seek further confirmation of this theory with each new experiment.

On a rather murky evening in early autumn, with the weather readying itself for a storm, the Rue d'Anvers, which as it happens is a quiet street, seemed utterly deserted with the exception of one man. There was Jean-François, sitting still with his eyes to the heavens as usual. No one had taken his stool yet. I approached quietly not to distract him; and, leaning into his ear when it appeared he had heard me:

'Here you are all alone!' I said to him without thinking, for I did not usually approach him other than to discuss the aorist, or logarithms, or the hypotenuse, or tropes, and a few other problems from my joint studies. And then I bit my lip with regret at the thought of this inane reflection, which brought him back down from the highest heavens to earth, and brought on his usual muddle, which I could never hear without a violent pang of anguish.

'Alone!' Jean-François replied, grabbing me by the arm. 'Only the madman is alone, and only the blind man cannot see, and only the paralytic has unsteady legs that cannot press down and stand firm on the ground . . .'

'There we are,' I thought to myself, as he continued to speak in obscure phrases which I dearly wish I could recall, for they may have made more sense than I imagined at the time. 'Poor Jean-François is off, but I'll stop him sure enough. I know the wand which frees him from those spells.'

'It is indeed possible,' I exclaimed, 'that the planets are inhabited, as Monsieur de Fontenelle believed, and that you are engaged in a secret exchange with their inhabitants, like Monsieur le Comte de Gabalis.' I broke off with pride, having deployed such magnificent erudition.

Jean-François smiled, looked at me with that gentle gaze of his, and said to me: 'Do you know what a planet is?'

'I suppose it is a world which more or less resembles ours.'

'And do you know what a world is?'

'A vast body which completes certain revolutions in space with regularity.'

'And space – have you ever wondered what it might be?'

'Wait, wait,' I replied. 'I have to remember our definitions . . . Space? A subtle and infinite realm in which the stars and world move.'

'If you say so. And what are the stars and worlds relative to space?'

'Probably wretched atoms, which vanish within it like dust in the air.'

'And the matter of these stars and worlds, what do you think it is in relation to the subtle matter which fills space?'

'What do you want me to tell you in reply? . . . There are no words to compare such crude bodies with such a pure element.'

'That's the spirit! And you would conclude, child, that God the Creator of all things, who gave these crude bodies inhabitants – imperfect ones no doubt, but nonetheless driven, as the two of us are, by the need of a better life, had left space uninhabited?'

'I would not conclude that!' I replied passionately. 'And I even think that much as we are superior in the subtlety of our construction to that matter to which we are tied, its inhabitants must also be superior to the subtle matter which surrounds them. But how could I know them?'

'By learning to see them,' replied Jean-François, whose hand was pushing me back with the utmost gentleness.

At the same instant, his head fell against the back of his three-legged stool; his gaze resumed its fixed stare, and his lips their movement.

I discreetly headed off. I was barely a few steps away when I heard his father and mother behind me urging him to come inside as the sky was looking menacing. He submitted as ever to their every entreaty; but his return to the real world was always accompanied by that flood of incoherent words which provided the local boors with the object of their usual entertainment.

I went on my way, asking myself if it could be possible that Jean-François had two souls, one which belonged to the crude world in which we live, and the other which purified itself in the subtle space he believed he penetrated through thought. I became a little entangled in this theory, and would become more entangled in it still.

I arrived in this state at my father's, more preoccupied, and above all differently preoccupied than would have been the case had the string of my kite snapped in my hands, or had my extravagantly thrown tennis ball landed in Monsieur de Grobois' garden on the Rue des Cordeliers. My father asked me what had stirred such emotions, and I have never lied to him.

'I thought,' he said, 'that all those daydreams (for I had repeated without forgetting a word my conversation with Jean-François *les Bas-bleus*) had been buried for ever, along with the books of Swedenborg and Saint-Martin, in the grave of my old friend Cazotte; but it seems that this young man, who has spent a few days in Paris, is full of the same extravagances. As for the rest, there is a certain refinement of observation in the ideas his double language suggested to you, and the explanation you found for it asks only to be reduced to its true expression. The faculties of intelligence are not so indivisible that an infirmity of the mind and the body cannot afflict them separately. In this way the alteration of the mind which poor Jean-François exhibits in the most common operations of his judgement may well have not yet spread to the properties of his memory, and this is why he replies appropriately when he is asked about things he learned slowly and retained with difficulty, whereas he makes no sense on all those which land unexpectedly on his senses, and regarding which he never had any need to arm himself with any exact formula. I would be amazed if such a thing may not be observed in the majority of madmen; but I do not know if you have understood me.'

'I think I have understood you, my father, and I could recite your own words back to you in forty years.'

'That is more than I want from you,' he replied as he embraced me. 'In a few years from now, you will be sufficiently informed by more serious studies against illusions that only take hold of feeble souls or sickly intellects. Remember only, as you are so sure of your memories, there is nothing simpler than notions which come close to the truth, and nothing more specious than those which stray from it.'

'It is true,' I thought, as I retired early, 'that the *Thousand and One Nights* are immeasurably more appealing than Bézout's first volume, and who has been able to believe in the *Thousand and One Nights*?'

The storm rumbled on. It was so beautiful that I could not help but open my pretty window looking out onto the Rue Neuve, opposite that elegant fountain with which my grandfather, an architect, had graced the town, and which was adorned by a bronze siren that often, according to my enchanted imagination, mingled poetic songs with the murmur of its waters. I kept following with my eye all those meteors of fire in the clouds, crashing into each other with a force to shake all worlds. – And sometimes, when the blazing curtain was rent by a clap of thunder, my gaze – quicker than the lightning – plunged into the infinite heavens which opened up above, and which seemed to me more pure and tranquil than a fine spring sky.

'Ah!' I said to myself then, 'if the vast plains of space only had inhabitants, how pleasant it would be to rest with them there from all the tempests on earth! What unadulterated peace one would taste in that crystal-clear realm which is never disturbed, which is never deprived of sunlight, and which laughs, luminous and peaceful, above our hurricanes as it does above our miseries. No, delightful valleys of the sky!' I cried out, weeping copiously, 'God did not create you to remain deserts, and I will roam you one day, arm in arm with my father!'

My conversation with Jean-François had left an impression that terrified me from time to time; nature, however, lit my way, as if my fondness for her had brought forth in the most unfeeling beings some spark of divinity. If I had been more learned, I would have understood pantheism. I was inventing it.

But I obeyed my father's advice; I even avoided conversing with Jean-François *les Bas-bleus*, or only approached him when he was losing his way in one of those endless sentences which seemed to have no other purpose than to defy logic and exhaust the dictionary. As for Jean-François *les Bas-bleus*, he did not recognize me, or did not show in any way that he distinguished between me and the other schoolboys of my age, even though I had been the only one to steer him back, when it suited me, to coherent conversations and reasonable definitions.

It had barely been a month since my exchange with the visionary, and this time, I am perfectly sure of the date. It was the very day the school year started, after six weeks of holiday running from the 1st of September, and thus 16 October 1793. It was almost midday and I was returning from school more cheerfully than I had gone there, with two of my friends who took the same route to return to their parents' homes, and who were studying more or less the same subjects as me, but had left me far behind. They are both still alive, and I would name them without fear of being contradicted, if their names, honoured with deserved renown, could be ventured without impropriety in a tale which demands only the requisite plausibility of a tall tale, and which in the final analysis I do not offer in any other spirit.

Upon reaching the crossroads where we would separate to go our own ways, we were struck all at once by the contemplative demeanour of Jean-François *les Bas-bleus*, who had stopped like a statue in the very middle of the square, motionless, arms folded, with a mournfully pensive look, his eyes imperturbably fixed on an elevated point of the western horizon. A few bystanders had gathered little by little around him and searched in vain for the extraordinary object which seemed to be absorbing his attention.

'So what is he looking at up there?' they asked among themselves. 'A passing flight of rare birds – an ascending balloon?'

'I will tell you,' I replied, while I cleared a path to my left and right in the crowd with my elbows. 'Tell us about it, Jean-François,' I continued, 'what have you seen again this morning in the subtle matter of space in which all worlds move.'

'Don't you know as well as I?' he answered, stretching out his arm and tracing with his fingertip a long circular segment from the horizon to the zenith. 'Follow these bloodstains with your eyes, and you will see Marie-Antoinette, Queen of France, rising in the sky.'

The curious onlookers then dispersed, shrugging their shoulders, because they had concluded from his reply that he was mad, and I headed off on my way, surprised only that Jean-François *les Bas-bleus* had so correctly landed on the name of the last of our queens, that particular detail falling within the category of true facts which he had forgotten.

My father used to gather two or three friends for dinner at the start of every fortnight. One of his guests, who was a stranger to the town, kept him waiting for quite a long time.

'I am sorry,' he said as he took his place. 'The rumour had spread, according to some private letters, that the unfortunate Marie-Antoinette was going to be put on trial, and I made myself a little late waiting for the 13 October post to arrive. The gazettes say nothing about it.'

'Marie-Antoinette, Queen of France,' I said with confidence, 'died this morning on the scaffold a few minutes before midday, as I was returning from college.'

'Oh my God!' my father exclaimed. 'Who could have told you such a thing?'

I became flustered, and blushed – I had said too much to stay silent now.

I replied, trembling: 'It was Jean-François *les Bas-bleus*.'

I did not risk raising my gaze towards my father. His extreme indulgence towards me did not reassure me when it came to his displeasure at my blunder.

'Jean-François *les Bas-bleus*?' he said, laughing. 'Thankfully we can rest easy about any news coming from that source. That cruel and futile cowardice will not be committed.'

'So who,' my father's friend resumed, 'is this Jean-François *les Bas-bleus*, who announces events at a distance of a hundred leagues, at the moment he believes them to be taking place? A sleepwalker, a convulsive, a disciple of Mesmer or Cagliostro?'

'Something of that sort,' my father answered, 'but moreover worthy of interest; an honest visionary, an inoffensive maniac, a poor madman who is as pitied as he deserved to be loved. From an honourable – but not well-off – family of honest artisans, he had been their great hope and he promised much. My first year on the bench in a little magistrature was the last year of his studies; my arms grew tired from awarding him all those prizes, and the variety of his successes added to their worth, for one would have said it cost him little to open all the doors of human intelligence. The courtroom almost collapsed from the sound of the applause when he came at last to receive a prize without which all the others count for nothing, for honourable conduct and the virtues of an exemplary youth. There was not a father there who would not have been proud to count him among his children, no wealthy gentleman, so it seemed, who would not have been delighted to call him his son-in-law. I will not mention the young girls, who quite naturally must have been taken with his angelic beauty and his auspicious age of around eighteen to twenty. And that was what did for him there; not that his modesty allowed itself to be lured by the seductions of a conquest, but by the understandable results of the impression he had made. You have heard of the beautiful Madame de Sainte-A—. She was in Franche-Comté – where her family has left so many memories and where her sisters settled down – at the time. She was looking for a tutor for her son, aged twelve at the most, and the acclaim which had just attached itself to Jean-François' humble name determined her choice in his favour. It was, four or five years ago, the beginning of an honourable career for a young man who had made the most of his studies, and who had not been led astray by wild ambitions. Unfortunately (but from hereon in what I will say is based only on incomplete information), the beautiful lady who had so rewarded Jean-François was also mother to a daughter, and this daughter was delightful. Jean-François could not see her without falling in love with her; however, mindful of the impossibility of rising through the ranks as far as her, he seems to have tried to distract himself from a passion that was invincible, and which only gave itself away in the first moments of his illness, as he gave himself to studies dangerous to reason, to dreams of occult sciences and to visions of exalted spiritualism; he became utterly mad, and sent away from Corbeil, the residence of his patrons, with all the care his condition demanded, no glimmer of light has penetrated the darkness of his mind since his return to his family. So you can see that one cannot set much store by his reports, and that we have no reason to be alarmed by them.'

Yet we learned the next day that the queen was on trial, and two days later, that she was no longer alive.

My father feared the impression that the closeness of this extraordinary catastrophe to that prediction would make on me. He spared no effort to convince me that chance was abundant in such coincidences (and he cited twenty examples), which only ignorant credulity adopted as arguments, with both philosophy and religion abstaining from their use.

I left a few weeks later for Strasbourg, where I was to begin further studies. That time was less than propitious to the doctrines of spiritualists, and I easily forgot Jean-François in the midst of the daily turmoil that was tormenting society then.

Circumstances brought me back home in the spring. One morning (it was, I believe, the 3rd Messidor), I had entered my father's bedroom to embrace him, as I always did, before setting out on my daily excursion in search of plants and butterflies.

'Let us not pity poor Jean-François any more for having lost his wits,' he told me, as he showed me the newspaper. 'Better for him to be mad than to learn of the tragic death of his benefactress, his pupil, and the young lady said to be the main cause of his mind's derangement. Those innocent creatures have also fallen under the executioner's hand.'

'Can it be true?' I exclaimed ... 'Alas! I had not said anything to you about Jean-François, because I know you fear I may be influenced by certain mysterious ideas he shared with me ... But he's dead!'

'He's dead?' my father replied sharply. 'Since when?'

'Three days ago, the 29th Prairial. He had been stock still, since that morning, in the middle of the square, at the very place I found him, at the time of the queen's death. Lots of people were gathered around him as usual, even though he was maintaining the deepest silence, for he was too preoccupied to be distracted by any questions. At four o'clock, finally, his attention seemed to intensify. A few minutes later, he raised his arms to the sky with a strange expression of enthusiasm or sorrow, took a few steps as he said the names of those people you just mentioned, let out a cry and fell. People pressed around him, and tried to lift him up, but it was no good. He was dead.'

'The 29th Prairial, at a few minutes past four o' clock?' my father asked as he looked at his newspaper. 'The very hour and day ...!'

'Listen,' he continued after a moment's reflection, his eyes fixed on mine, 'do not refuse what I am about to ask you! – If ever you tell this story, when you are a man, do not present it as true, because it will expose you to ridicule.'

'Are there reasons which may dispense a man from openly publishing something he knows is the truth?' I respectfully countered.

'There is one which is worth all the rest put together,' said my father, shaking his head. 'The truth is useless.'

Translated by Will McMorran

STENDHAL

Vanina Vanini;
or, Particulars concerning the latest Cell of the
Carbonari to be eradicated in the Papal States

It was a spring evening in the year 182*. All Rome seethed with excitement. The famous banker, the Duke de B—, was giving a ball at his new residence in the Piazza Venezia. All the splendour produced by the arts of Italy and the luxury of Paris and London had been brought together to embellish his palazzo. The throng was immense. The fair-haired, demure beauties of noble England had fought for the honour of being present at the ball: they arrived in large numbers. The handsomest ladies of Rome vied with them in beauty. A young woman whose flashing eyes and jet-black hair proclaimed her a daughter of Rome made her entrance on her father's arm: all eyes were on her. Her every movement radiated uncommon pride.

As they went in, foreigners were seen to be forcibly struck by the magnificence of the ball. 'None of the festivities of any of the kings of Europe,' they said, 'come near to matching this.'

Kings do not have palaces designed by Roman architects and they are also obliged to invite the great ladies of their courts. The Duke de B— never invited any save pretty women and that evening he had been fortunate with his invitations. The men were dazzled. Among so many striking women an argument arose as to which was the most beautiful. The verdict remained unsettled for some time but eventually Princess Vanina Vanini, she of the black hair and blazing eyes, was proclaimed Queen of the Ball. At once the foreign gentlemen and the youth of Rome forsook all other rooms and crowded into the salon where she was.

Her father, Prince Asdrubale Vanini, had insisted that she should dance first with two or three of Germany's royal sovereigns. She then accepted invitations from several handsome, very aristocratic Englishmen but their starched manners bored her. She seemed to find more enjoyment in teasing young Livio Savelli, who was visibly besotted with her. He was the most brilliant young man in Rome and moreover he too was a prince. But if you had offered him a novel to read, he would have tossed it away after twenty pages saying that it made his head ache. That was, in Vanina's eyes, not an advantage.

Around midnight, a rumour spread through the ball and produced a considerable effect. A young *carbonaro* who was being held captive in the fortress of Sant'Angelo had escaped that very evening by means of a disguise and, with a startling piece of romantic bravado, had reached the outer guardroom where he had fallen on its occupants with a dagger. But he himself had been wounded, the myrmidons of the law had chased him through the streets and there was every chance that he would be retaken.

While this story was doing the rounds, Don Livio Savelli, dazzled by the loveliness and sensational success of Vanina, with whom he had just danced, and almost maddened by love, asked her as he led her back to her place:

'Tell me, I beg you, what sort of man could ever please you?'

'This young *carbonaro* who has just escaped,' replied Vanina. 'At least he has done more than simply go to the bother of getting himself born.'

Prince Asdrubale came up to his daughter. He was a rich man who for twenty years had not discussed his finances with his steward, who lent him back his own money at a very high rate of interest. If you met him in the street, you would take him for an elderly actor. You would not notice that his hands were primed with five or six enormous rings each set with very large diamonds. Both his sons had become Jesuits and subsequently died mad. He had forgotten them long ago but was exasperated by the fact that his only daughter, Vanina, had no wish to marry. She was already nineteen years of age and had refused proposals from the most illustrious suitors. What was her reason for doing so? The same given by Sylla for abdicating: *contempt for the people of Rome.*

The day after the ball, Vanina observed her father, normally the most lax and casual of men who all his life had never bothered with keys, in the process of cautiously locking the door to a small staircase which led to an apartment situated on the third floor of the palazzo. This apartment had windows which overlooked a terrace planted with orange trees. Vanina went into Rome and paid a number of social calls. When she returned, the main gate to the palazzo was blocked by the preparations for a firework display so her carriage used a rear entrance. Vanina happened to look up and to her surprise saw that one of the windows of the apartment which her father had so carefully locked up was open. She dismissed her companion, made her way up to the eaves of the house, and after a thorough search succeeded in finding a small, barred window which overlooked the terrace with the orange trees. The open window which she had noticed was now only feet from her. Obviously the room was occupied: but by whom? The next day, Vanina managed to get hold of the key to a small door which admitted her to the orange-tree terrace.

Furtively, she crept towards the window which was still open, her approach hidden by a Venetian blind. Inside the room was a bed and there was someone in it. Her first instinct was to go away, but then she saw a woman's dress on the back of a chair. Looking more closely at the figure in the bed, she made out someone with fair hair who seemed very young. She had no doubt in her own mind that it was a woman. There were blood stains on the dress draped over the chair. There was also blood on a pair of women's shoes which stood on a table. The figure stirred and Vanina saw that she was wounded. A wide bloodstained dressing covered her bosom. It was tied in place with ribbons and was clearly not the work of a doctor.

Vanina observed that every day around four o'clock, her father locked himself in his rooms and then went up to see this woman. He would come down again soon afterwards, climb into his carriage, and drive off to call on Countess Vitteleschi.

The moment he left, Vanina climbed up to the terrace from which she could see the unknown occupant. Her sympathies were fervently roused by the plight of the unfortunate young woman. She wondered what had happened to her. The bloodstained dress thrown over the chair had slits in it which seemed to have been made by a dagger. Vanina was able to count them. One day, she had a clearer view of the woman: her blue eyes were staring out at the sky and she seemed to be praying. Soon, the eyes filled with tears. With difficulty, the Princess bit back an urge to speak to her. The next day, Vanina was bolder and hid on the terrace before her father arrived. She saw Don Asdrubale come in through the door. He was carrying a small basket containing provisions. The Prince seemed worried and said very little. He spoke in a whisper so that, although the window was open, Vanina could not make out what he said. He left again almost immediately.

'Poor creature! She must have made terrible enemies,' she said to herself, 'to make my father, usually so easy-going by nature, reluctant to confide in anyone and willing to climb a hundred and twenty steps every day.'

One evening, as Vanina was poking her head round the woman's window, she suddenly found herself staring into a pair of eyes and the secret was let out of its bag. Vanina fell to her knees and cried out:

'I am your friend! I will do anything to help you!'

The unknown woman beckoned to her to come in.

'I owe you a profound apology,' exclaimed Vanina. 'You must be thoroughly offended by my stupid curiosity. I swear to keep your secret and, if you ask, I shall never come here again.'

'Whose heart would not rejoice to see you?' said the woman. 'Do you live here?'

'Of course,' said Vanina. 'I see you do not know who I am. I am Vanina, daughter of Don Asdrubale.'

The woman looked at her in amazement, blushed profusely, and added:

'May I hope that you will come to see me every day? But I would prefer if the Prince knew nothing of your visits.'

Vanina's heart raced. The woman's manner seemed to her to breathe refinement and distinction. No doubt the poor creature had offended some powerful man. Perhaps she had killed her lover in a fit of jealousy! Vanina could not believe that her predicament was due to some ordinary cause. The woman told her she had received a wound in the shoulder which had gone deep into her chest and caused her considerable pain. She could often taste blood in her mouth.

'And you have not been attended by a doctor!' exclaimed Vanina.

'You know that in Rome,' said the woman, 'doctors must provide a detailed report of any wounds they treat to the police. The Prince himself was kind enough to bind up my wounds with the dressing that you see.'

The woman avoided dwelling on her injuries with infinite good grace and tact. Vanina's affection for her was unbounded. Yet one thing surprised

Vanina extremely: in the middle of what seemed a very earnest conversation, the young woman clearly had great difficulty in suppressing a sudden urge to laugh.

'I should very much like,' said Vanina, 'to know your name.'

'My name is Clémentine.'

'Very well, dearest Clémentine, I shall come to see you tomorrow, at five.'

The next day, Vanina found her new friend feeling very ill.

'I want to send for a doctor for you,' said Vanina as she embraced her.

'I'd rather die,' said the woman. 'I have no wish to compromise those who have helped me.'

'The doctor who attends Monsignor Savelli-Catanzara, the governor of Rome, is the son of one of our servants,' Vanina continued eagerly. 'He is absolutely devoted to us and, given his position, fears no one. My father underestimates his loyalty. I shall go and send for him.'

'I refuse to see a doctor,' said the woman with a brusqueness which took Vanina aback. 'Keep coming to see me. If it please God to call me to him, I shall die happy in your arms.'

The next day, the woman's condition had deteriorated further.

'If you love me,' said Vanina as she left her, 'you will see a doctor.'

'If one comes, my happiness will vanish.'

'I am going to send for him,' said Vanina firmly.

Without speaking, the woman detained her and took her hand which she covered with kisses. There was a long silence. There were tears in the woman's eyes. Finally, she released Vanina's hand and, looking as tragic as though she were about to be led away to the scaffold, said:

'I have an admission to make. The day before yesterday, I lied when I told you my name was Clémentine. I am in fact a wretched *carbonaro* . . .'

Startled, Vanina pushed her chair back and stood up.

'I feel,' said the *carbonaro*, 'that my admission will snatch from me the only good thing which binds me to life. But in deceiving you I dishonour myself. My name is Pietro Missirilli and I am nineteen. My father is a poor doctor at Sant'Angelo-in-Vado and I am a *carbonaro*. There was a surprise attack on our organization. I was brought in chains from the Romagna to Rome and was thrown into a cell where a lamp was kept burning night and day: there I remained for thirteen months. A charitable soul conceived a plan of escape for me. I was dressed in women's clothes. As I was leaving the prison and walking past the guards at the last gate, one of them cursed the *carbonari*. I punched him. I assure you that it was no empty gesture of bravado, merely an unthinking reflex. For my imprudence, I was chased in the dark through the streets of Rome. Wounded by several bayonet thrusts and growing weak, I climbed the steps of a house whose door stood open. I could hear the soldiers coming after me. I found my way into a garden and collapsed several paces from a lady who was strolling there.'

'It was Countess Vitteleschi, my father's friend!' said Vanina.

'How do you know this? Did she tell you?' exclaimed Missirilli. 'But no matter. That lady, whose name must never be spoken, saved my life. At the moment when the soldiers swept into her house to arrest me, your father was driving me away from it in his carriage. I feel very ill. For several days now the bayonet wound in my shoulder has been making it difficult for me to breathe. My days are numbered and I shall die in despair because I shall see you no more!'

Vanina had listened with impatience. Then she rushed out of the room. Missirilli had seen no pity in those lustrous eyes, merely the reflection of a haughty character which had just been offended.

Night had just fallen when a doctor appeared. He was alone. Missirilli was in the depths of despair, for he feared he would never see Vanina again. He plied the doctor with questions, but the man bled him and did not reply. The same silence was observed in the days which followed. Pietro's eyes remained fixed on the terrace window through which Vanina usually came. He felt very unhappy. Once, about midnight, he thought he saw someone in the shadow which lay across the terrace. Was it Vanina?

Vanina came each night and pressed her cheek against the young *carbonaro*'s window-pane.

'If I speak to him,' she told herself, 'I am lost! No! I must never see him again!'

Now that this was decided, she remembered, against her better judgement, the feelings of friendship she had conceived for the young man when she had been foolish enough to believe he was a woman. They had been so close, so easy together and yet now she would have to blot him from her mind! In calmer mood, Vanina felt afraid of the change which had come about in her ideas. Ever since Missirilli had identified himself, everything that she normally thought had, so to speak, furred over and become very distant.

Before a week had gone by, Vanina, pale and trembling, appeared in the young *carbonaro*'s room with the doctor. She came to tell him that he must try to persuade the Prince to allow a servant to take over his ministrations. She stayed for moments only. But a few days later, she returned with the doctor, as part of her human duty. One evening, although Missirilli was much better and Vanina could no longer use fears for his life as her excuse, she was bold enough to come alone. When he saw her, Missirilli was overjoyed but told himself he must hide his feelings; above all, he knew that he should not depart from the dignity which so becomes a man. Vanina, who had come to his room with her cheeks flushed red, fearing he might speak of love, was quite disconcerted by the noble, devoted but hardly tender declarations of friendship with which he received her. She left. He made no attempt to detain her.

A few days later, when she returned, she met with the same behaviour, the same assurance of respectful devotion and undying gratitude. Far from having to think how she might apply a brake to the young *carbonaro*'s incandescent passion, Vanina wondered if she was the only one to be in love. She who until that moment had been so proud, was now all too bitterly aware of the extent of her infatuation. She feigned cheerfulness, even cool indifference, came less often but could not bring herself to stop seeing her young patient altogether.

Missirilli, consumed by love but aware both of his undistinguished birth and the urgings of his personal honour, had vowed he would not stoop to speaking of love unless Vanina went a whole week without coming to visit him. The young Princess's pride fought him every inch of the way.

'So be it!' she told herself in the end. 'If I see him, it shall be for me, to please myself. I shall never admit to his face what feelings he has aroused in me.'

She paid Missirilli long visits. He spoke to her as he would have done had there been a score of people present. One evening, after a day spent hating him and vowing to be even colder and more unbending to him than usual, she said she loved him. Soon, she was in no position to refuse him anything.

If Vanina's folly was extreme, it must also be said that she was blissfully happy. Missirilli stopped thinking of the dignity which so becomes a man. He loved her as a man loves for the first time when he is nineteen and Italian. He conscientiously observed the proper protocol of true love even to the point of admitting to his proud Princess the stratagem he had used to make her love him. He was amazed by how excessively happy he was. Four months passed quickly.

One day the doctor declared that his patient was free to go.

'What shall I do?' thought Missirilli. 'Shall I stay hiding in the house of one of the most beautiful women in Rome? If I do, the vile tyrants who kept me locked up for thirteen months and never let me once see the light of day will think they have won! Italy, you are lost if your sons desert you for such flimsy reasons!'

Vanina never doubted that Pietro's greatest happiness was to remain by her side for ever. Certainly he appeared blissfully happy. Yet something General Bonaparte once said reverberated unpleasantly in the young man's soul and dictated the way he behaved with women. In 1796, as Bonaparte was leaving Brescia, the city fathers who escorted him to the city gate told him that its inhabitants loved liberty more than all other Italians.

'Quite,' he replied, 'they like nothing better than talking about it to their mistresses.'

Missirilli said to Vanina, in a somewhat strained voice:

'As soon as it's dark, I must leave.'

'Take good care to be back before daybreak. I shall be waiting for you.'

'At daybreak I shall be several miles from Rome.'

'I see,' said Vanina. 'And where will you be going?'

'To the Romagna, to avenge myself.'

'Since I am so rich,' Vanina went on calmly, 'I trust you will at least allow me to provide you with weapons and money.'

Missirilli looked at her without blinking for several moments and then, clasping her to him:

'Soul of my life,' he cried, 'when I am with you I forget all else, even my duty. But heed your noble heart and you will understand me.'

Vanina wept copiously and it was agreed that he would not leave that day, nor the next, but the day after.

'Pietro,' she said on the morrow, 'you have often told me that a man in the public eye – a Roman prince let's say – with vast wealth to command, would be well placed to render the greatest service to the cause of liberty if ever the attention of Austria were to be deflected from us by some great war elsewhere.'

'That is so,' said Pietro in surprise.

'Well then! You are brave and all you lack is a high position. I offer you my hand and an income of two hundred thousand livres. As to persuading my father to give his consent, you may leave that to me.'

Pietro fell at her knees. Vanina was radiant with joy.

'I love you passionately,' said he. 'But I am an unworthy servant of my country. The more wretched Italy is, the more loyal I must be. To obtain the consent of Don Asdrubale, I would be forced for years to play a shabby role. Vanina, I refuse your proposal.'

Missirilli hastened to commit himself by these words, for he felt his resolve melting away.

'My tragedy,' he exclaimed, 'is that I love you more than life and that for me to leave Rome is the most agonizing of tortures. Oh! Why has not Italy been freed from the yoke of the barbarians? How happy I should be if I could sail away with you and live in America!'

An icy hand clutched at Vanina's heart. Hearing him refuse her offer had shaken her pride. But soon she threw herself into Missirilli's arms.

'I never saw you more adorable than you are at this moment!' she cried. 'You are my little country doctor and I am yours for ever. You have the greatness of our ancient Romans!'

All thoughts of the future, every dismal consideration urged by common sense vanished: it was a moment of perfect love. When they became rational again:

'I shall reach the Romagna almost as soon as you,' said Vanina. 'I shall arrange to take the waters at Poretta. I will stay at the fortress we have at San Nicolo, near Forli . . .'

'There I shall spend the whole of my life with you!' cried Missirilli.

'Henceforth my fate shall be to flinch from nothing,' Vanina went on with a sigh. 'I shall be ruined on your account, but no matter . . . Could you love a woman who has lost her honour?'

'Are you not my woman, my wife,' said Missirilli, 'a wife who shall be worshipped for all eternity? I will love you, 'I shall protect you.'

Vanina had social obligations which she could not neglect. As soon as she had left him, Missirilli began to find his behaviour barbaric.

'What is a man's *country*?' he asked himself. 'It is not a person to whom we owe a debt of gratitude for some benefit received, who might feel disappointed and curse us if we fail to discharge it. A man's *country* and his *freedom* are like his coat, a thing useful to him which in truth he must buy if his father has not bequeathed it to him. So I love my country and freedom because they are things which are useful to me. If I care nothing for them, or if they serve no more purpose than an overcoat in August, what is gained by buying them, and at so high a price? Vanina is so beautiful! She is a person of quite extraordinary spirit! Other men will try to please her; she will forget me. What woman ever had just one lover? All these Roman princes, whom I despise as citizens, have so many advantages over me! How can they not be irresistible? Oh! If I leave now, she will forget me and I shall lose her for ever!'

Vanina came to see him in the middle of the night. He told her about the uncertainty into which he had been plunged and, because he loved her, about the debate he had conducted on the great subject of 'my country'. Vanina was delighted.

'If he had to make a simple choice, one way or the other, between his country and me,' she told herself, 'I would win.'

The clock of the nearby church struck three. The time had come for the last farewell. Pietro tore himself from her loving arms and was already going down the narrow staircase when Vanina, choking back her tears, said with a smile:

'If you'd been nursed by some poor country woman, would you leave without some acknowledgement? Wouldn't you try to pay her? The future is uncertain, you will be travelling through enemy country: give me three days as my recompense, as though I were that poor woman, to repay me for my trouble.'

Missirilli stayed.

Eventually, he left Rome. Using a passport bought from a foreign embassy, he returned to his family. He was greeted with joy, for he had been given up for dead. His friends wanted to give him a rousing welcome by shooting a couple of *carabinieri* (as officers of the law are called in the Papal States).

'We must avoid the unnecessary killing of any Italian who can use a gun,' said Missirilli. 'Our country, unlike fortunate England, is not an island. What we lack are soldiers to resist the encroachments of the kings of Europe.'

A little while later, Missirilli, hard pressed by the *carabinieri*, killed two of them with pistols which Vanina had given him. A price was put on his head.

There was no sign of Vanina in the Romagna. Missirilli thought he had been forgotten. His vanity was hurt. He began to give much thought to the difference in rank which separated him from his mistress. In a moment of tender regret for his past happiness, it entered his head to return to Rome to see what Vanina was doing. This extravagant idea was about to get the better of what he believed was his duty when one evening the angelus rang from a mountain church in the oddest manner, as though the bell-ringer's mind was not on his task. It was the signal for a meeting of the cell of the *carbonari* to which Missirilli had been affiliated when he had arrived back in the Romagna. That night, all its members gathered in a certain hut in the woods occupied by two hermits who, drowsy with opium, were quite unaware of the use to which their little house was being put. When Missirilli arrived, feeling very dejected, he learned that the cell's leader had been arrested and that he, though a young man just turned twenty, was about to be elected leader of a cell which included men aged fifty and more who had been party to conspiracies ever since Murat's expedition in 1815. When he received this unexpected honour, Pietro felt his heart beat faster. The moment he was alone, he made up his mind that he would think no more of the girl from Rome who had forgotten him but devote his every thought to the task of *delivering Italy from the barbarian*.

Two days later, Missirilli discovered, in the list of arrivals and departures which was sent to him as leader of the cell, that Princess Vanina had just reached her fortress at San Nicolo. Reading her name aroused more anxiety than pleasure in his heart. He tried in vain to convince himself that his country came first by denying an urge to ride like the wind to the fortress at San Nicolo that same evening. But the thought of Vanina, whom he was neglecting, prevented him from carrying out his duties efficiently and he saw her the next day: she loved him as she had loved him in Rome. Her father, anxious to find a husband for her, had delayed his departure. She had brought two thousand sequins for him. This unexpected windfall proved extremely useful in raising Missirilli's standing as the group's new leader. Daggers were ordered from Corfu; a hold was acquired over the private secretary of the Legate who was entrusted with the task of hunting down the *carbonari*; a list was obtained of the names of priests who spied for the government.

It was at this time that arrangements were completed for one of the least absurd conspiracies ever mounted in strife-torn Italy. I shall not enter into superfluous detail. I will limit myself to observing that had the enterprise proved successful, Missirilli could have claimed, with every justification, a large share of the glory. Through his work, several thousand insurgents would have risen up when the signal was given and would have waited, fully armed, for their most senior chiefs to arrive. The decisive moment was drawing near when, as invariably happens, the plot was halted by the arrest of its leaders.

Vanina had been in the Romagna for only a short time when she thought it likely that love of country would make her *inamorato* forget every other kind of love. Her pride was offended. She tried to reason with herself, but to no avail. A black cloud of melancholy descended on her: she was surprised to find herself cursing liberty. One day, when she had come to Forli to see Missirilli, she was unable to control her feelings, which until then her pride had kept well in check.

'Be honest,' she told him, 'you love me like a husband. That is not what I deserve.'

Soon her tears were flowing, but they were tears of shame for allowing herself to descend to the level of common fault-finding. Missirilli reacted to them like a man who had more important things on his mind. Suddenly it struck Vanina that she should leave him and return to Rome. She felt a cruel pleasure in punishing herself for the weakness which had prompted her to say what she had. After a brief silence, she saw clearly what was to be done. She would be, in her own eyes, unworthy of Missirilli if she did not leave him. She thought with pleasure how surprised, how heart-broken he would be when he looked for her and could not find her. But then the realization that she had failed to win the love of a man for whom she had committed so many follies filled her with warmer feelings. She broke her silence and did her utmost to extract a tender, loving word from him. He said a few affectionate things but his thoughts were elsewhere and it was in an altogether more passionate voice that he spoke of his political plans, exclaiming tragically:

'Ah! If this present business fails, if the government gets wind of it again, I shall give up the game!'

Vanina froze. For the past hour, she had believed she was seeing her lover for the last time. What he had just said planted a fateful idea in her mind. She told herself:

'The *carbonari* have got several thousand sequins out of me. No one can doubt my enthusiasm for their plottings.'

Vanina cut short her musings and said to Pietro:

'Would you like to spend twenty-four hours with me at the fortress at San Nicolo? The meeting tonight does not call for you to be there. Then tomorrow morning, at San Nicolo, we shall go for a long walk – it will calm your mind and help you regain the composure you will need to see you through this testing time.'

Pietro agreed.

Vanina left him to make the arrangements for the journey. As usual, she locked the door of the room in which she had hidden him.

She hurried off to find one of her maids who had left her service to get married and had opened a small shop at Forli. When she arrived, she took a prayerbook she had got from her room and, in the margin, scribbled down the exact location where the meeting of the *carbonari* was due to be held that very night. She concluded her denunciation with these words: 'This cell has nineteen members. Their names and addresses are as follows.' When she had written out the list, which was complete with the exception of one name, that of Missirilli, which she omitted, she said to the woman, whom she trusted completely:

'Take this book to the Cardinal-Legate. He is to read what is written in it and then return it to you. Here are ten sequins. If he ever mentions your name, you will surely die. But you will save my life if you persuade the Legate to read the page I have just written.'

Everything went smoothly. The Legate lived in a state of such terror that he did not behave like the aristocrat that he was. He agreed to see the common woman who asked to speak to him and allowed her to appear with her face masked, but only on condition that her hands were tied. In this state she was ushered into the presence of the great man, whom she found safely ensconced behind an immense table covered in green baize.

The Legate read the page in the prayerbook, holding it at arm's length, fearing that it might be the carrier of some subtle poison. He gave it back to the woman and did not order her to be followed. In less than forty minutes after leaving her lover, Vanina, who waited until her former maid was safely returned, rejoined Missirilli believing that henceforth he was hers alone. She told him that there was great activity in the town: patrols of *carabinieri* had been seen in streets where they never normally went.

'If you want my opinion,' she said, 'we should leave for San Nicolo without wasting another moment.'

Missirilli agreed. They set out on foot for the young Princess's carriage which, together with the lady who attended her, a discreet, handsomely paid confidante, stood waiting for them half a league outside the town.

On reaching the fortress of San Nicolo, Vanina, greatly troubled by the unwonted step she had taken, became even more attentive and affectionate. But even as she told him how much she loved him, she had the feeling that she was acting a part in a play. The evening before, as she betrayed him, she had felt no remorse. But now, as she folded her lover in her arms, she thought:

'There is a word that someone might say to him, and once that word is spoken, at that instant and for ever after, he will hate me.'

In the middle of the night, one of Vanina's servants burst into her room. The man was a *carbonaro*, although she had never suspected it: clearly, there were things which Missirilli kept from her, even small things like this. She trembled. The man had come to warn Missirilli that during the night the houses of nineteen *carbonari* at Forli had been surrounded and they had been arrested as they returned from the meeting. Despite being ambushed, nine had escaped. The *carabinieri* had marched the ten captives to the citadel's prison. As they were going in, one had leapt into the well, which was very deep, and had been killed.

Vanina turned deathly pale. Fortunately, Pietro did not notice. Had he done so, he would have seen the guilt in her eyes.

'At present,' the servant went on, 'the garrison at Forli is lined up in every street. Each soldier is close enough to the next man to be able to speak to him. Nobody can cross from one pavement to the other except at points where an officer has been posted.'

When the man had gone, Pietro thought for a brief instant and then said:

'There's nothing to be done for the moment.'

Vanina thought she would die. She trembled every time her lover looked at her.

'What on earth has got into you?' he asked.

Then his thoughts reverted to other matters and he turned his eyes away. At about noon, she ventured to say:

'So that's another cell that's been discovered. I imagine you'll have to lie low for some time.'

'Oh, very low!' answered Missirilli with a smile which made her blood run cold.

She went out to pay an unavoidable call on the priest of the village of San Nicolo who was, perhaps, a Jesuit spy. When she got back for dinner at seven, she found no one in the little room where her lover had been hiding. Beside herself, she ran all over the house looking for him. He was not there. She returned in despair to his room and it was only then that she saw the note. It said:

I am going to the Legate to give myself up. I have lost hope in our cause: heaven is against us. Who betrayed us? Probably the swine who threw himself down the well. Since my life is of no use to hapless Italy, I do not want my comrades, when they realize that I alone was not arrested, to think that I was the man who sold them out. Farewell. If you love me, avenge me! Kill, exterminate the scoundrel who betrayed us, even if the traitor should prove to be my father.

Vanina collapsed on to a chair, barely conscious and overcome by the most terrible gloom. She could not speak. Her eyes were dry and inflamed. Finally she fell to her knees:

'Oh God on high,' she cried, 'hear the vow I now make. Yes, I shall punish the traitor. But first, Pietro must be freed!'

Within the hour, she was on her way to Rome. For some time, her father had been urging her to return. He had arranged her marriage with Prince Livio Savelli. The moment she got back, he broached the subject nervously. To his amazement, she consented at once. That same evening, in the house of Countess Vitteleschi, her father, in more or less official terms, presented Don Livio to her. She conversed with him at length. He was the most elegant young man and owned the finest horses. But although he was generally credited with great wit, his character was considered so frivolous that the government believed him to be quite harmless. Vanina thought that if she first turned his head, she could convert him into a useful pawn. Since he was the nephew of Monsignor Savelli-Catanzara, governor of Rome and Minister of Police, she assumed that government spies would not dare watch his movements.

For several days, Vanina showered the amiable Don Livio with attentions. Then she told him he would never be her husband. His mind, she said, was too frivolous.

'If you were not such a boy,' she said, 'your uncle's agents would have no secrets from you. For instance, what is being done about the *carbonari* who were arrested the other day at Forli?'

Two days later, Don Livio called to inform her that all the *carbonari* arrested at Forli had escaped. She fixed her large black eyes on him, treated him to a bitter smile of the deepest contempt, and would not speak to him for the rest of the evening. Two days later, Don Livio returned and blushingly admitted that he had, at first, been misled:

'But,' he said, 'I have managed to get hold of a key to my uncle's study. Among his papers I found one which said that a *congregation*, or committee, of the foremost cardinals and prelates is to meet in the greatest secrecy to decide whether it would be better to try the *carbonari* in Ravenna or Rome. The nine captured at Forli and their leader, a man named Missirilli who was stupid enough to give himself up, are currently being held in the fortress at San Leo.'

When she heard the word 'stupid', Vanina nipped him as hard as she could.

'I would very much like,' she said, 'to see those official papers for myself and break into your uncle's study with you. I expect you read them wrongly.'

When he heard this, Don Livio quailed. What Vanina was asking was virtually impossible. But her determined spirit gave wings to his love. A few days later, Vanina, disguised as a man, wearing a becoming suit in the livery of the Savelli household, spent half an hour reading through the most secret papers of the Minister of Police. She felt a thrill of joy when she came across the daily reports on the prisoner Pietro Missirilli. Her hands shook as she held the paper and she felt a little faint. As they left the palazzo of Rome's governor, she allowed Don Livio to kiss her.

'You have made a commendable start,' she told him, 'on the tests I have decided to set you.'

When he heard this, the young Prince would have burned down the Vatican to please Vanina.

That evening, there was a ball given by the French ambassador. She danced a great deal and almost exclusively with him. Don Livio was drunk with happiness. But he had to be prevented from thinking.

'Really! My father sometimes behaves in the most infuriating way,' she said to him one day. 'This morning, he dismissed two of his servants. They came to me in tears. One wanted me to find him a position in the household of your uncle, the governor of Rome. The other, who used to be an artilleryman under the French, would like me to get him something at the fortress of Sant'Angelo.'

'They can both enter my service,' the young Prince said eagerly.

'Is that what I asked you?' Vanina answered haughtily. 'Do I have to repeat the exact request which those two poor men made to me? They must have what they asked for, not some second best.'

It proved an impossible task. Monsignor Cantazara was anything but careless and never allowed anyone he did not know personally to enter his household.

Living a life apparently filled with every imaginable pleasure, Vanina, gnawed by remorse, was very unhappy. She found the slow pace of events worse than torture. Her father's steward had produced money for her. Should she leave home, travel to the Romagna, and try to find a way of helping her lover to escape? Although the plan was quite irrational, she was about to carry it out when chance smiled on her.

'The ten *carbonari* belonging to Missirilli's cell are about to be transferred to Rome, but they are to be executed in the Romagna after sentence is passed. My uncle received notification to that effect from the Pope this very evening. Only you and I in all Rome know about this. Are you satisfied?'

'You are growing up,' replied Vanina. 'You may give me a portrait of yourself as a present.'

The day before Missirilli was due to arrive in Rome, Vanina found an excuse for visiting Città-Castellana. It is in this town's gaol that *carbonari* spend the night when they are being transferred from the Romagna to Rome. She saw Missirilli the next morning as he was being led out of the prison. He was in chains and rode by himself in an open cart. She thought he looked pale but did not appear down-hearted. An old woman threw him a bunch of violets. Missirilli smiled as he thanked her.

Now that Vanina had seen her lover again, her ideas quickened once more and she was filled with renewed courage. Some considerable time previously, she had succeeded in obtaining a handsome preferment for the abbé Cari, now almoner at the fortress of Sant'Angelo where her lover was about to be locked up. She had taken this good priest as her confessor. It is no small matter in Rome to act as confessor to a princess who happens to be the governor's niece.

The trial of the Forli *carbonari* did not last long. As revenge for their presence in Rome, an affront they could not prevent, the extreme conservative party arranged for the committee appointed to judge the rebels to be packed with the most ambitious clerics. The committee was chaired by the Minister of Police.

The law against the *carbonari* is unambiguous. The men from Forli had nothing to hope for. Even so, they fought for their lives using every possible line of defence. Their judges not only condemned them all to death but several recommended they be put to the most appalling torture, have a hand cut off and so forth. The Minister of Police, whose fortune was already made (for when a man relinquishes that office a cardinal's hat awaits him), had no need of amputated hands. When he conveyed the verdict to the Pope, he succeeded in having the sentence of all the prisoners commuted to a few years in prison. Pietro Missirilli was the only exception. The Minister considered this young man to be a dangerous fanatic and, besides, he had also been given a death sentence for the murder of the two *carabinieri*, as we have already mentioned. Vanina read the verdict and the commuted sentence only moments after the Minister had returned from seeing the Pope.

The next day, Monsignor Catanzara returned to his palazzo around midnight. His valet was nowhere to be found. The Minister, very puzzled, rang several times and eventually an aged, extremely stupid servant appeared. The Minister, losing patience, decided he would undress himself. He locked his door. As it was very warm, he took off his coat and tossed it in a heap on a chair. The coat, thrown too vigorously, sailed over the back of the chair and struck the muslin curtain at the window where it revealed the outline of a man. The Minister sprang to his bedside and reached for a pistol. As he was making his way back to the window, a young man, wearing his livery, advanced towards him, also holding a pistol. When he saw this, the Minister raised his pistol and squinted down the barrel. He was about to fire when the young man laughed and said:

'Oh, Monsignor! Don't you recognize Vanina Vanini?'

'What is the meaning of this tasteless jest?' replied the Minister furiously.

'Let us think calmly,' the young woman said. 'To begin with, your pistol is not loaded.'

The startled Minister checked and saw that it was so. Then he reached for a dagger from a pocket of his waistcoat.*

With a firm but charming gesture, Vanina said:

'Shall we take a seat, Monsignor?'

She sat down calmly on a sofa.

'May I take it you are alone?'

---

* A Roman prelate would doubtless be unable to lead a body of troops with dash and flair, as happened several times with a general who was Minister of Police in Paris at the time of the Mallet affair. But he would never let himself be so easily cornered in his own house. He would be much too afraid of being the butt of his colleagues' jokes. A Roman who knows that he is hated never walks abroad without being well armed. It has not been thought necessary to point out several other differences in the way people behave and speak in Paris and in Rome. Far from wishing to minimize these differences, we have chosen to write them boldly. The Romans who are sketched here do not have the honour of being French.

'Quite alone, you have my word on it,' replied Vanina.

But the Minister insisted on seeing for himself. He walked round the room and looked everywhere. Then he sat down on a chair three paces from Vanina.

'What would I gain,' she said calmly and sweetly, 'by making an attempt on the life of a moderate man who would only be replaced by some weak-minded hothead quite capable of ruining himself and taking others down with him?'

'So what is it you want?' said the Minister tetchily. 'I do not care for this little drama and have no wish to prolong it.'

'What I am about to say,' Vanina went on imperiously, suddenly forgetting her gracious manner, 'concerns you more than it does me. The life of the *carbonaro* Missirilli is to be spared. If he is executed, you will survive him by no more than one week. I have no personal interest in this matter. I have committed what you choose to call an act of folly first, for my own amusement, and second, as a favour for a friend of mine, a lady. What I wanted,' she went on, reverting to the drawing-room manner, 'was to lend a helping hand to an extremely able man who will soon be my uncle and will in all likelihood carry the fortunes of his family to the highest pinnacle.'

The Minister stopped looking angry. Vanina's beauty was doubtless a factor which contributed to this rapid change. Few in Rome were unaware of Monsignor Catanzara's liking for pretty women and, disguised as a footman of the Savelli household, in smooth silk stockings, red waistcoat, that short sky-blue coat with silver facings, and with a pistol in her hand, Vanina was irresistible.

'So you are to be my niece,' said the Minister, barely repressing a laugh. 'You realize that you are doing a very foolish thing – and I doubt very much that it will be the last.'

'I hope that a man as wise as you,' answered Vanina, 'will keep my guilty secret, especially from Don Livio. And to encourage you to do so, dearest uncle, if you grant me the life of the man who so interests my friend, I shall give you a kiss.'

By continuing to maintain the conversation on this level of semi-serious banter, which Roman ladies adopt to further their gravest interests, Vanina succeeded in giving the conversation, which she had begun with a pistol in one hand, the tone of a social call paid by the young Princess Savelli on her uncle, the governor of Rome.

Soon Monsignor Catanzara, imperiously dispelling any impression that he could be forced to act through fear, began acquainting his niece with all the difficulties he would face if he tried to save Missirilli's life. As he spoke, the Minister walked around his study with Vanina. He reached for a carafe of lemonade which stood on the mantelpiece and filled a crystal glass. As he was about to raise it to his lips, Vanina took it from him and, after toying with it for some time, dropped it, accidentally it seemed, into the garden. A moment later, the Minister chose a chocolate drop from a box. Vanina snatched it out of his hand and said with a laugh:

'You should take more care. Everything is poisoned here. For there are people who want you dead. But I have arranged for the life of my future uncle to be spared so that I do not have to enter the Savelli family absolutely empty-handed.'

Monsignor Catanzara, startled out of his wits, thanked his niece and held out high hopes of Missirilli's continuing existence.

'Then our business is concluded!' exclaimed Vanina. 'And to seal it, here is your reward,' she said and she kissed him.

The Minister accepted his reward.

'But let me make one thing clear, Vanina, my dear,' he added. 'I hate bloodshed. Besides, I am still young though I probably seem very old to you and I live in times when blood that is spilt today may leave stains which will appear tomorrow.'

Two o'clock was striking when Monsignor Catanzara escorted Vanina to a side gate of his garden.

Two days later, as the Minister, feeling none too sure of how to frame the request he was about to make, was being shown into the presence of the Pope, His Holiness said:

'Before we begin, I have a favour to ask of you. One of the *carbonari* from Forli has been sentenced to death. The thought of it is preventing me from sleeping. The man's life must be spared.'

The Minister, seeing that the Pontiff's mind was made up, raised many objections but in the end drafted a decree, or *motu proprio*, which the Pope signed, although it was contrary to custom.

Vanina had thought that she might obtain a pardon for her lover but feared that someone would try to poison him. The previous evening, the abbé Cari had brought Missirilli several packets of ship's biscuit with instructions that he was not to touch any food provided by the State.

Vanina subsequently learned that the Forli *carbonari* were to be transferred to the fortress at San Leo and wanted to see Missirilli as he passed through Città-Castellana. She reached the town twenty-four hours before the prisoners. There she found the abbé Cari who had arrived several days previously. He had persuaded the gaoler to allow Missirilli to attend mass, at midnight, in the prison chapel. But he obtained even more: provided Missirilli allowed his arms and legs to be chained, the gaoler would withdraw to the chapel door, so that he could still see the prisoner for whom he was responsible, but not hear what he said.

The day which would decide Vanina's fate finally dawned. Early in the morning, she took up her station in the prison chapel. Who can say what troubled thoughts ran through her mind during the long hours of waiting? Did Missirilli love her enough to forgive her? She had betrayed his cell but had saved his life. When reason gained the upper hand in her tortured mind, Vanina hoped that he would agree to leave Italy with her: if she had sinned, love had driven her to it. Four o'clock was striking when, in the distance, she heard the clatter of the horses of the *carabinieri* in the cobbled streets. The sound of every hoof seemed to reverberate in her heart. Soon, she made out the rumble of the carts which transported the prisoners. They halted in the small square outside the prison gate. She saw two *carabinieri* lift Missirilli, who had been placed in a cart by himself and was bound by so many chains that he could not walk unaided.

'At least he is alive!' she told herself, with tears in her eyes. 'They have not poisoned him yet!'

She spent a cruel evening. The altar lamp, set very high and smoking because the gaoler saved money by buying cheap oil, was the only light that pierced the chapel gloom. Vanina's eyes strayed to the tombs of a number of medieval lords who had died in the prison close by. Their effigies looked wild and fierce.

All sounds had grown still long ago. Vanina was absorbed in her black thoughts.

A little after midnight had struck, she thought she heard a faint noise, like the sound of a bat's wings. She stood up, tried to walk, and stumbled half-conscious over the altar rail. At that very moment, two ghostly figures appeared at her side, though she had not heard them approach. It was the gaoler and Missirilli so closely bound in chains that he was, so to speak, swaddled by them. The gaoler opened the window of a lantern which he placed on the altar rail, close to where Vanina lay, so that he would be able to see his prisoner. Then he walked to the back of the church and stood by the door. As soon as he had gone, Vanina flung her arms around Missirilli's neck. She held him close but could feel only his cold, sharp chains. Who put these chains on him? she thought. She took no pleasure in holding him. This disappointment was followed by another which was more distressing by far: Missirilli reacted so icily that she thought for a moment that he knew the secret of her treachery.

'Oh my dear,' he said after a moment's silence, 'I am heartily sorry you love me as you do. I can find no merit in me to explain it. It would be best, believe me, if we reverted to more Christian sentiments and forgot the illusions which once led us astray. I cannot be yours. The awful fate which has dogged my every undertaking is perhaps a consequence of the state of mortal sin in which I live constantly. But even if I invoke the ordinary standards of human judgement, why was I not arrested with my friends that fatal night at Forli? Why, when the danger was greatest, was I not at my post? Why did my absence give credence to the most hurtful suspicions? Because I had another love which was greater than my desire to see Italy free!'

Vanina was bewildered by the shock produced in her by the alteration in Missirilli. Although he did not seem to have lost weight, he looked at least thirty. Vanina attributed the change to the treatment he had suffered in prison. She burst into tears.

'But,' said she, 'the gaolers swore that they would treat you with kindness.'

The truth was that, when faced by the prospect of imminent death, the religious principles which were consistent with his love of Italian freedom had resurfaced in the heart of the young *carbonaro*. Gradually, Vanina realized that the change she noticed in the man she loved was of the spiritual variety and had nothing to do with his physical treatment. Consequently, her unhappiness, which she thought had reached its zenith, soared to new heights.

Missirilli had stopped speaking. Vanina seemed about to choke on her sobs. Then, in a voice not entirely bereft of feeling, he said:

'If I were ever to love anything or anyone on this earth, it would be you, Vanina. But, by the grace of God, I now have only one aim in life. I shall die, either in prison or in attempting to give Italy her liberty!'

There was another silence. It was clear that Vanina could not speak. Missirilli went on:

'Duty is a cruel master, my dear. But if there were not pain to overcome, where would be the heroism? Give me your word that you will never try to see me again.'

Insofar as his chains allowed, he made a small movement with his hand and held out his fingers to Vanina.

'If you will allow a man who once was dear to you to offer a word of advice: be sensible, marry the worthy man whom your father has chosen for you. Never reveal any dangerous secrets to him, but on the other hand never try to see me again. Let us from this day on be strangers to each other. You gave a large sum of money to our country's cause. If ever Italy is delivered from her tyrants, it will be repaid to you out of the public purse.'

Vanina felt utterly crushed. All the time Pietro had spoken to her, the only time his eyes had lit up was when he pronounced the words 'our country's cause'.

Eventually, her pride came to her rescue. She had come provided with diamonds and a set of small files. Without giving Missirilli an answer, she offered them to him.

'I accept because it is my duty,' said he, 'for I must try to escape. But I shall never see you again, this I swear by the new gifts you bring me. Farewell, Vanina. Promise me you will never write or attempt to see me. Leave me free to give my all to Italy. Think of me as though I were dead. Farewell!'

'No,' replied Vanina in a rage. 'I want you to know what I did for love of you!'

And she recounted everything she had done from the time Missirilli had left the fortress at San Nicolo to give himself up to the Legate. When her tale was finished:

'But that is nothing,' she said, 'I did much more and I did it because I loved you.'

Then she told him how she had betrayed him.

'Oh, you monster!' cried Pietro, white with fury, and he lunged at her, attempting to bludgeon her with his chains.

And he would have succeeded too had the gaoler not come running and restrained him.

'Here, take these, I have no wish to be obliged to a monster like you!' Missirilli said to Vanina, and though hampered by his chains, he threw her files and diamonds back at her, then turned and hurried off.

Vanina was left utterly broken. She returned to Rome.

The newspapers report that she has just married Prince Livio Savelli.

Translated by David Coward

MARCELINE DESBORDES-VALMORE

The Unknown Woman

London, 18—

My friend,

On this lonely square, beside the church of St Dunstan, where you have occasionally written to me, I live a life of such unoccupied leisure it often forces me to look beyond myself so as not to fall too soon to reminiscing; but unable to bring myself to go out in the world in search of the hours of forgetting I crave, I try to find them in the exterior objects within my reach: I tear myself away from my solitude, I open my window, I become curious.

My gaze meets no other obstacle but a plane tree that reaches higher than this window, its green reflection extending to the back of my room when the sun casts its rays on to the panelling with the dancing shadow of the foliage. The branches were once too leafless to hide the row of houses I could visit by looking across the street, and I read on a door opposite that was always closed, 'House to let'.

This silent house, consumed with the melancholy of that which serves no purpose on earth, engrossed me all the more for appearing forsaken, like myself. All of a sudden, one fine spring morning, its windows, whose hinges had rusted, opened noisily; busy workmen could be seen passing through the rooms; the perpetual yellowed sign was taken down; everything, in short, told me the deserted dwelling would very soon be inhabited.

Come now, I said, the fate of dereliction is no longer certain. Someone sufficiently bold has just broken the spell on this building that seemed to have had a curse put on it. Or perhaps its owner has banished an oppressor that is only to return again. There are buildings that are set upon a black stone.

A few weeks resolved the matter.

As soon as the house was properly repaired and the smell of paint no longer reached me on the morning and evening breezes, fresh new furniture was brought to the two floors exposed to my inquisitive gaze. The furniture was modest: its elegance consisted solely of its extreme cleanliness. This luxury of the humble told me the new inhabitants of my street were what are called decent but of limited means. This made the little house all the more agreeable to me: I concentrated on it all the interest of my daily inspection and I devoted to it the spirit of inquiry I was trying to acquire.

The next day a young man of pleasing appearance and with animated features came to give his instructions to a servant he brought with him, pointing out, with a combination of tenderness and liveliness, the placing of each piece of furniture, which he examined, full of painstaking satisfaction. As he had both rung and knocked, he was, beyond any possibility of doubt, according to London custom, the master of the house.

He departed after half an hour, and day after day paid the same short visit to his sole and sturdy servant, who listened to him in silence, saying 'yes' merely by redoubling her efforts. Sweeping, scrubbing, polishing the wooden floors, which shone like mirrors; left to herself and queen of her solitude, this woman went up and down, drew water, washed even the pavement, shook the rugs, laid them out on the staircase made white and lustrous once more by her tireless hands. She did not close the shutters before evening, not worrying in the least if the absence of curtains allowed all and sundry to see how her time was so laboriously spent.

I was untroubled about the fate of the house brought back to life. It would be honoured with frequent ablutions, visited by the pure outdoor air; the servant was no idler, and had no fear of cleaning out dark corners; it was safe to set foot there: her presence lent the whole place the grace of auspiciousness. But what could repay such attention? Money? No, goodness, and I believed I had seen it in the face of her master.

Who was this master? Some notary's clerk? Some civil servant? Perhaps a young merchant clerk in a big trading house, whose work regularly took him away? Why did he not live in this house that was now all repaired and delightful? Why were there still no curtains? Why was that bed set in a deep alcove so perfectly in order morning and evening? Those were questions the servant alone could have answered, for her young master had completely disappeared, and no one, apart from this woman, ever came to open the windows to let into the heart of this sanctuary the warm breath of May.

She continued to be vigilant and remove any dust, shuddering to see it adhere to the virgin furniture entrusted to her care, and which she sometimes admired from a distance by way of rewarding herself, as a painter steps back from his work the better to judge it.

In paradise thus with her industrious daydreams, this honest creature seemed to be the *genius loci*, in the absence of the master I had only glimpsed, when suddenly flowers in the window and fluttering curtains announced his return: I was not mistaken. After an absence of about three weeks, I found him one morning in the middle of the prettiest room, seated at a little round table, breakfasting with a woman so young, so demure, so graceful, so white from head to toe, so blushing and so smiling, I needed no one's help to guess she was till yesterday his betrothed. I greeted the newly-weds with a blessing they did not hear. Did the happy couple have any inkling there were more than two people in the universe?

Their delectable meal over, the man rose first, took the hand of his young Eve and led her on a tour of her little Eden, with patient childishness making her stop in front of all the objects he had gathered together to surprise her. Passing in front of the mirror that adorned the mantel, I saw him gently compel her to look in it, with him, in his embrace! That man trembled with joy. His whole being was a caress. As he was much taller than his idol by a whole head in height, he bowed his forehead over the young woman dressed in white, and mingled his black curly hair with the pale blond tresses he adored in the mirror, while pressing them beneath his ardent lips.

She seemed wonderstruck by above all things a painting by Cipriani, which hung over that fireplace of genuine marble, and felt no less astonishment when, raising her rapturous gaze to the ceiling, she saw here and there a few elegant works by Angelica Kauffman. The drawers of a lemonwood cabinet inlaid with ebony were then opened to her admiration.

Her little hands, pure as the virginal net through which they could be seen, her timid and avid little hands buried themselves for a long time in a great many unexpected treasures, for the smile of gratitude remained no less on her half-open mouth than the kiss suddenly snatched by the generous husband's impassioned mouth.

But what seemed to me to excite *her* gratitude to the highest degree, what wrested from her the sweetest cry of joy that could repay happy love, the love that gives, was the sharp-cornered painted mahogany bookcase and its three rows of books, bound for her, emblazoned, I believe, with her name, which I was unable to read. Whatever it was, it was certainly the name of a happy woman.

One by one, all those books were opened, admired, kissed, before being replaced in their interim prison.

Then, like a stern rousing voice, in a deep rumble the clock struck ten. This unexpected summons made the husband start and rush off, while the lengthy chimes of the pendulum clock held before it in deep attention the newly-wed, joining her hands with a pensive and loving fervour. To see her like that, radiant and motionless, was to hear her distinctly blessing him whose solicitude made the hours so beautiful for her!

Eventually, after intrigued admiration of this future regulator of her life, the examination of all the gifts recommenced; whereupon the young woman's innocent delight erupted once more: she thanked the absent individual, laughed and clapped her hands alone; I surmised she was even obliged to sit down to catch her breath a little. Zémire's apartment did not give rise to more enchanting turmoil in the young prisoner of an invisible lover and king!

However, she recovered herself. Roaming round again in her state of excited solitude, she could not resist the need to speak to someone of the wonderful surprises that overwhelmed her. The servant was called; the tour of that nuptial chamber resumed, and happily this woman-child had an assistant, intelligent or not, to encourage the expressions of delight that swelled her heart to tearfulness.

The extreme heat of the summer often caused the curtains to be drawn against the beating sun that I myself sometimes fled for the countryside, where I took with me only my book. It was all right for them: they loved each other!

But alas! For those who languish over a faded past, incapable of trying to create new memories for themselves, so many days are the days when their leisurely life rises up in dissatisfaction and lays bare its asperities, thereby punishing them perhaps for spending it only in pointless regrets! It is strange, then, to realize to what extent the most banal of external objects become powerfully associated with the bitterness of our inaction. The table, on which we have fallen into the habit of writing or of resting our elbows, appears on these abhorrent days unpolished and marred with countless stains we had never noticed before. We notice the least cobweb hanging from the ceiling, this ceiling itself suddenly having become more oppressive and gloomy than usual. The accommodating veil of habit is everywhere drawn back, as if the light for the first time were entering the place where we are alone, alone of our own volition, firmly enchained in our freedom. The window-panes are dull, just like our eyes that close in the face of these silent disenchantments; a subdued and unexpected shock, like the shudder of a collapsing building, sabotages the very setting in which our resigned heartaches are embedded.

This oil stain on a book we have just opened, this letter hidden inside it and the sight of which is a reminder of an insult or a loss, the drawing that was beginning to evolve beneath our patient fingers and that we find folded in four by the misguided consideration of a servant, everything wounds and mortifies us. It is in vain that our daunted minds try to remember departed friends and relatives; far from the celestial spheres to which their souls have returned, we see only their tombs planted in the ground ... Oh! On those days especially my eyes would be more invincibly drawn to that little house of harmony because to me it testified that happiness still found refuge somewhere! This pure ray of light eased my soul. The sight of others' well-being compensated me for that which was no longer mine; for the happiness that comes of order, that resides in order, is a fine thing, it is worthy of God; and that peaceful home always reminded me of this.

Truly! The madonnas of Italy at whose feet burn perpetual lamps, in compassion for all, would not have rekindled in me a more tender devotion, a deeper faith. After meditating on this station, I was capable of waiting and returning to my isolation.

From time to time, during the long days devoted by *her* to needlework, a youthful, equable singing travelled across the intervening space and came to tell me, plunged as I was in my endless regrets: 'I am happy!' just as the bird discreetly settled on a branch of the plane tree would proclaim to all, 'I am happy!'

The song returned to most often by that untrained voice, but one as silvery as the voice of a choirboy, was a bird song I myself had learned long ago from my sister. It struck my soul with one of those charming reminiscences that innocence alone reserves for those who continue to cherish it.

'Why have you not given me the wings of a bird, mother, since I have neither house, nor rank, nor the land of my fathers!

'What would I myself not give to be able to go directly to the rainbow to find out how drops of rain form those three ribbons of harmonious hues!

'What bliss to float above the earth like a living breeze, to pass through the blossoming trees, to rise airily through them and from the very top of their wind-swayed crowns to look down on the fields of ripe wheat and on the silken flax!

'Why have you not given me the wings of a bird, mother, since I have neither house, nor rank, nor the land of my fathers!

'The life of a bird must be a joyous holiday in woodland filled with leaves that speak. There, the bird is as if beneath the green roof of a palace. There, the bird flies from room after room; they are bright and gay, open to the sun, the stars, whose white rays play in the middle of them.

'I would have blessed you, mother! I would have said to God: I bless my mother, for she has given me the wings of a bird!

'It can leave its nest in the forest oak, birds have no need of a home; young and old fly off to wander abroad together; they traverse their blue world in freedom!

'Listen how they amicably call out to each other in the vault of this shady room! Come, come, they seem to say.

'You have never, then, heard birds calling to each other, mother!

'Come, come! Life is beautiful here, where the leaves dance in summer's breath!

'We're coming, we're coming! the others reply. How sweet that life must be, buried deep in a cool tree!

'I say this, for I have seen a bird flying over the dazzling sea skim the froth on the waves and return, wet, to its branch in the sun.

'How happy it is to fly at will, like us in our dreams, on strong and supple wings, through the dawn, to look into the face of the rising sun.

'How happy it is to pierce through boundless space at will, like an arrow, to cut through silver cloud and to sing at the top of its voice in thunder's sanctuary, to spread its feathers in wild joy over the high mountains filled with the voice of the winds!

'Why have you not given me the wings of a bird, mother, since I have neither house, nor rank, nor the land of my fathers!'

So autumn arrived. My chilled plane tree scattered its leaves that were blown away, trampled underfoot by passers-by. Winter kept us all house-bound, each in our own home: they, happy; I, reflective.

Towards evening, I would always know when it was five o'clock from the rapid knocking and the sound of the doorbell.*

More punctual than a watchman, the breathless husband would rejoin the solitary young woman. Then for a long while two figures formed but one, and peopled that undiscovered haven at the same regular intervals. The lamp never shed its light on any other face but those two, shining with happiness at seeing each other again. Heaven kept away the baleful influence of any outsider.

For myself, I read stories. I tried to write my own, and I tore it up, finding that I had only too much of what intelligence remains to me to recall a useless life that does not deserve to be included in the ledger of divine justice: so it is not anything about myself that I have to relate to you here.

A new spring was announced by countless signs of hope and love. My old tree dressed itself in leaves again; first the swollen buds unfolded a matt white velvet, then their colour became bright and gay, and the huge leaf fan began to quiver in the April breeze. The sky turned blue, even over London. The windows of the house, yesterday enveloped in fog, gleamed once more and were red with flowers. But the lady, who reappeared among them, oh! the lady had grown pale; she had become less sure-footed. When she ventured into her little garden that was revived by the sun, she sat there, languishing, bent over her needlework or over a book; then when

* In London, the master of the house knocks and rings at the same time.

her husband was with her, before or after business hours, she walked slowly, leaning on him for a little support. His tenderness increased visibly in relation to her weakness.

It was strange to observe how his anxious love had matured the young man's lively and ebullient air. His cheerful features, a little coarse perhaps, had become serious and thoughtful. Yes, love aids the development of some dispositions, which it elevates, and which, without it, would have remained irresponsible and inferior. I have seen this pure sentiment transform a vague, indecisive and vacuous character into a staunch and constructive spirit. So, to study a true love is to spell out heaven.

Now comes a bright starry August night; a silvery night, a lofty luminous night, more conducive to dreaming than to sleeping; now, contrary to all custom, the door of the house opens several times, three times the sound of the knocker breaks the silence of the street, and inevitably brings me to the window, focal point of my observations of the happy couple.

What do lights rapidly passing through the rooms of the narrow house signify? Why is it that now the master, now the servant, run up and downstairs in such a hurry? Who is that man, a grave and slightly sleepy-looking stranger, welcomed at the door in such a respectful and impatient manner? Admitted, to my great surprise, to the room with the half-drawn, fluttering white curtains, why does he remove his hat and gloves in silence, walk to and fro, consult his watch, sit down, frequently go to the alcove where the glow of a candle flame softened by the alabaster candleholder barely casts any light, then leave at dawn, accompanied out on to the pavement with countless grateful handshakes by the master of the house? My God! What do these nocturnal disturbances mean?

But by degrees the commotion ceases; the comings and goings become more infrequent; a deep tranquillity cradles and sends back to sleep this nest I am more fond of than everything around me. A single faint light, still burning like the last star in the sky, shows that someone is still awake in the midst of this peaceful silence.

The next day, the knocker on the arched door again attracts my attention. The white leather it is wrapped in to deaden the sound at last explains to me that the young woman has just given her husband a child.

Why keep it to myself? I felt at the sight of this an emotion of a kind that was nobler and more tender than curiosity. That day, honestly, I drank alone to the health of all three of them, calling on heaven to look down on this new little soul and its mother, like the child almost invisible to the world.

But the calm that reigned for several days was suddenly disturbed; a subdued agitation became evident; an air of alarm infused hushed activity that I observed with anxiety; as if by infiltration, sadness overcame me. Again, lights came and went; morning and evening, the watering of the flowers was forgotten. The doctor's carriage stopped at the door three times in rapid succession. One Sunday, he left without reappearing the next day. The next day, the stilled servant had thrown her apron over her head. Like two intelligent lights, my gaze lengthened in order to see everything: it saw the covered white bed, the husband, resting motionless on the little round table, his face buried in his hands, trying perhaps to hide a dreadful torment. All of a sudden, a terrible cry, after which the shutters closed; then a dark carriage waited at the threshold. The mystery was revealed: she was dead!

Dead! No historian will ever record her modest grace, her fleeting life, her dutiful end. Her name ... not even I will record it. The simple coffin left quietly; only one person followed it, his eyes on the ground ... One person only? you will say. No matter, she was mourned! I could not help following, bare-headed, at a distance that cortege with no crowd in attendance. She was mourned! The wealthy, the proud, the magnificent sometimes are not accorded so much.

To another mortal creature, loving and fragile too, this woman was the light of his life. What now! Of all love's delightful plans, what remained to this other creature? The right to obtain for *her* a plot of land and to know where the beloved remains were to lie for ever more.

For we all want to know the last refuge of our frail treasure. Whether it be in the humble graveyard on the hill, or beneath the sumptuous vault that houses the great, we want to know. But the vault of heaven opens up in all its beauty to the pure soul that takes wing again! Marble is so heavy, so cold, compared with the grass where the daisy grows from a dust that is lifeless only to our imperfect senses! Hers, at least, sleeps where flowers grow.

There was still the child. The efforts vainly expended on the mother's bed were redirected to the ailing cradle. Other doctors arrived who prescribed expensive medications. The father arranged for an increasing number of visits that he paid for, no doubt, with all that remained to him, and the ruinous care bought for the wife was now bought for the child. A hired wet-nurse transferred her dutiful smiles to the infant, the father gave it everything of his heart that was not in the tomb; for that frail being was a little bit of *her*, in her image, a still visible ray of her interrupted life. He observed with curiosity the poorly little creature on the lap of its rustic nurse, carried it to the window, beneath the grey September sky, in which stood the last plants that were watered to create some shade for her, that angel, and the face of the widowed husband, etched with the indestructible trace of tears, seized me with incredible pity.

It was the same all over again: another month, not even as much as that, and the shutters closed again; another candle burned in the hearth. All of a sudden it was extinguished, and a little white coffin of little weight followed the other. Mother and child were quickly reunited!

After that a rapid change was to be seen in the man. His grief, for a while suppressed by the slender link still keeping it attached to the world, was no longer containable. He collapsed beneath the unbearable burden he ceased trying to drag around.

For hours on end, I would find him leaning against the narrow bookcase, his eyes and body motionless, forgetful of his meal gone cold on the little round table with never more than one place setting. Time and again the patient servant, who had not forsaken him, carried away to be reheated food that was tasteless to this enervated man choked with grief. The willing servant would return in vain, standing ready to serve him at the slightest sign. When he had seen her, he would turn his head aside and dismiss with a wave of his hand that forlorn table setting that reminded him completely *she* was no longer there for him. Then the servant would disappear without his being capable of addressing a single word to her.

Before long this dejected apathy degenerated into an even more frightful state of moral abandon. Useless to others, he deserted himself, unable any longer to sublimate his sorrow into a duty.

One dreary October evening, I saw him, with a sense of some indefinable terror, walk past his door without recognizing it, slowly retrace his steps, hesitate for a long while, then enter the house, brushing against the wall like a wounded night bird, twitching.

In the morning he was gloomy and dispirited, his hair dishevelled, his complexion leaden, greyer than the ashes beneath his clothes that were as neglected as his person. At night a wild and incongruous drunkenness usurped his heartache, which had become mine.

His orgies extended often until morning, with reprobate companions of his sleepless nights; more often, he returned alone, staggering, stupid, his head bowed, before the dying light of the pale autumn sun hid him from my sight. Then lying, incapable, stretched out in front of his window opened to the fog, he would fall asleep in his loneliness and despairing lassitude. At intervals, however, he became again pensive, remorseful perhaps. During these hours of lucidity, he would turn a fixed, mournful and quietly sad gaze on the dried flowers that had once brightened up the shared home. What then did he think of his hopes, now withered like the garden plants, and of those happy times that like *her* were now gone. And what did he think of *her*? What! Her saintly patience, her true charm, her deep love did not raise in him a love of virtue? Why did he not, in the horrible insensibility in which he allowed himself to wallow, get down on his knees and invoke her chaste apparition? Good God! What had become now of his liveliness, the clearness and intelligence of his brow, his manly courage? Was his career then about to founder having only just begun? Did not the world offer everywhere the same attractions as before? Everything was in order, everything was just as it used to be in the universe, with the exception of one joy: Ah! The fact is, that one joy was in itself his every joy; it was like a magic mirror that had reflected his heart full of emotions, full of countless enchantments, and that mirror was broken. I knew that for two years he had walked even in his dreams on a sun-drenched shore, and now that sun was extinct. Yes, I understood that man; I admitted he was most reprehensible; but I felt he was most unhappy.

Illness consumed his body, because he was in a state of despair. He turned in on himself, shrivelled up like a scorched plant. Old before his time, he would only have languished, stupefied and paralysed, if death, this time his friend, had not suddenly carried him off and taken him away from his miseries.

He, too, I saw leave the house for the last time, like his wife and child. The same signs of mourning alerted me: the closed shutters during the day; the wavering light that then went out; the still silence, then the dark carriage, the servant who followed it, head bowed, quiet and pale, never to reappear.

Everything was sold . . . for whom? I bought the pendulum clock *that had chimed such beautiful hours for them*! And I keep the clock for ever stopped.

A few weeks later the busy workmen were back; they went through the empty house singing. The rooms were papered, cheered up with new paintings; the same sign that eighteen months earlier hung outside with the words 'To Let' on it reappeared on the wall. It was as if the past had returned to that previous moment in time, and the interval between was but a dream.

Anyway, it pained me. 'And is that all?' you will say. Yes, that is all. I could have crowned my story with a sweeter or more gripping ending: with reality there is no choice. I do not hope to draw from it some profitable lesson for others, I shall keep that for myself, for you are past schooling in the courage to flee or vanquish passions. Your heart, if it is sensitive, is at least protected by precepts of bronze: you do not set too much store by happiness or sorrow. You will not place all hope in a woman or a frail child. You know the breath of the east wind can blow it away like dust, and grieving for that precious dust, pining away because it is lost, is at best useless, if not immoral and cowardly: you, my wise friend, know all this. I myself am trying to learn it.

Translated by Christine Donougher

HONORÉ DE BALZAC

A Passion in the Desert

'The whole show is dreadful,' she cried coming out of the menagerie of Monsieur Martin. She had just been looking at that daring speculator 'working with his hyena' – to speak in the style of the programme.

'By what means,' she continued, 'can he have tamed these animals to such a point as to be certain of their affection for –'

'What seems to you a problem,' said I, interrupting, 'is really quite natural.'

'Oh!' she cried, letting an incredulous smile wander over her lips.

'You think that beasts are wholly without passions?' I asked her. 'Quite the reverse; we can communicate to them all the vices arising in our own state of civilization.'

She looked at me with an air of astonishment.

'But,' I continued, 'the first time I saw Monsieur Martin, I admit, like you, I did give vent to an exclamation of surprise. I found myself next to an old soldier with the right leg amputated, who had come in with me. His face had struck me. He had one of those heroic heads, stamped with the seal of warfare, and on which the battles of Napoleon are written. Besides, he had that frank, good-humoured expression which always impresses me favourably. He was without doubt one of those troopers who are surprised at nothing, who find matter for laughter in the contortions of a dying comrade, who bury or plunder him quite light-heartedly, who stand intrepidly in the way of bullets; – in fact, one of those men who waste no time in deliberation, and would not hesitate to make friends with the devil himself. After looking very attentively at the proprietor of the menagerie getting out of his box, my companion pursed up his lips with an air of mockery and contempt, with that peculiar and expressive twist

174

which superior people assume to show they are not taken in. Then, when I was expatiating on the courage of Monsieur Martin, he smiled, shook his head knowingly, and said, 'Well known.'

'How "well known"?' I said. 'If you would only explain me the mystery, I should be vastly obliged.'

'After a few minutes, during which we made acquaintance, we went to dine at the first restaurateur's whose shop caught our eye. At dessert a bottle of champagne completely refreshed and brightened up the memories of this odd old soldier. He told me his story, and I saw that he was right when he exclaimed, "Well known."'

When she got home, she teased me to that extent, was so charming, and made so many promises, that I consented to communicate to her the confidences of the old soldier. Next day she received the following episode of an epic which one might call 'The French in Egypt'.

During the expedition in Upper Egypt under General Desaix, a Provençal soldier fell into the hands of the Maugrabins, and was taken by these Arabs into the deserts beyond the falls of the Nile.

In order to place a sufficient distance between themselves and the French army, the Maugrabins made forced marches, and only halted when night was upon them. They camped round a well overshadowed by palm trees under which they had previously concealed a store of provisions. Not surmising that the notion of flight would occur to their prisoner, they contented themselves with binding his hands, and after eating a few dates, and giving provender to their horses, went to sleep.

When the brave Provençal saw that his enemies were no longer watching him, he made use of his teeth to steal a scimiter, fixed the blade between his knees, and cut the cords which prevented him from using his hands; in a moment he was free. He at once seized a rifle and a dagger, then taking the precautions to provide himself with a sack of dried dates, oats, and powder and shot, and to fasten a scimiter to his waist, he leaped on to a horse, and spurred on vigorously in the direction where he thought to find the French army. So impatient was he to see a bivouac again that he pressed on the already tired courser at such speed, that its flanks were lacerated with his spurs, and at last the poor animal died, leaving the Frenchman alone in the desert. After walking some time in the sand with all the courage of an escaped convict, the soldier was obliged to stop, as the day had already ended. In spite of the beauty of an Oriental sky at night, he felt he had not strength enough to go on. Fortunately he had been able to find a small hill, on the summit of which a few palm trees shot up into the air; it was their verdure seen from afar which had brought hope and consolation to his heart. His fatigue was so great that he lay down upon a rock of granite, capriciously cut out like a camp-bed; there he fell asleep without taking any precaution to defend himself while he slept. He had made the sacrifice of his life. His last thought was one of regret. He repented having left the Maugrabins, whose nomadic life seemed to smile upon him now that he was far from them and without help. He was awakened by the sun, whose pitiless rays fell with all their force on the granite and produced an intolerable heat – for he had had the stupidity to place himself adversely to the shadow thrown by the verdant majestic heads of the palm trees. He looked at the solitary trees and shuddered – they reminded him of the graceful shafts crowned with foliage which characterize the Saracen columns in the cathedral of Arles.

But when, after counting the palm trees, he cast his eyes around him, the most horrible despair was infused into his soul. Before him stretched an ocean without limit. The dark sand of the desert spread further than eye could reach in every direction, and glittered like steel struck with bright light. It might have been a sea of looking-glass, or lakes melted together in a mirror. A fiery vapour carried up in surging waves made a perpetual whirlwind over the quivering land. The sky was lit with an Oriental splendour of insupportable purity, leaving naught for the imagination to desire. Heaven and earth were on fire.

The silence was awful in its wild and terrible majesty. Infinity, immensity, closed in upon the soul from every side. Not a cloud in the sky, not a breath in the air, not a flaw on the bosom of the sand, ever moving in diminutive waves; the horizon ended as at sea on a clear day, with one line of light, definite as the cut of a sword.

The Provençal threw his arms round the trunk of one of the palm trees, as though it were the body of a friend, and then, in the shelter of the thin, straight shadow that the palm cast upon the granite, he wept. Then sitting down he remained as he was, contemplating with profound sadness the implacable scene, which was all he had to look upon. He cried aloud, to measure the solitude. His voice, lost in the hollows of the hill, sounded faintly, and aroused no echo – the echo was in his own heart. The Provençal was twenty-two years old: – he loaded his carbine.

'There'll be time enough,' he said to himself, laying on the ground the weapon which alone could bring him deliverance.

Viewing alternately the dark expanse of the desert and the blue expanse of the sky, the soldier dreamed of France – he smelled with delight the gutters of Paris – he remembered the towns through which he had passed, the faces of his comrades, the most minute details of his life. His Southern fancy soon showed him the stones of his beloved Provence, in the play of the heat which undulated above the wide expanse of the desert. Realizing the danger of this cruel mirage, he went down the opposite side of the hill to that by which he had come up the day before. The remains of a rug showed that this place of refuge had at one time been inhabited; at a short distance he saw some palm trees full of dates. Then the instinct which binds us to life awoke again in his heart. He hoped to live long enough to await the passing of some Maugrabins, or perhaps he might hear the sound of cannon; for at this time Bonaparte was traversing Egypt.

This thought gave him new life. The palm tree seemed to bend with the weight of the ripe fruit. He shook some of it down. When he tasted this unhoped-for manna, he felt sure that the palms had been cultivated by a former inhabitant – the savoury, fresh meat of the dates was proof of the care of his predecessor. He passed suddenly from dark despair to an almost insane joy. He went up again to the top of the hill, and spent the rest of the day in cutting down one of the sterile palm trees, which the night before had served him for shelter. A vague memory made him think of the animals of the desert; and in case they might come to drink at the spring, visible from the base of the rocks but lost further down, he resolved to guard himself from their visits by placing a barrier at the entrance of his hermitage.

In spite of his diligence, and the strength which the fear of being devoured asleep gave him, he was unable to cut the palm in pieces, though he succeeded in cutting it down. At eventide the king of the desert fell; the sound of its fall resounded far and wide, like a sigh in the solitude; the soldier shuddered as though he had heard some voice predicting woe.

But like an heir who does not long bewail a deceased relative, he tore off from this beautiful tree the tall broad green leaves which are its poetic adornment, and used them to mend the mat on which he was to sleep.

Fatigued by the heat and his work, he fell asleep under the red curtains of his wet cave.

In the middle of the night his sleep was troubled by an extraordinary noise; he sat up, and the deep silence around allowed him to distinguish the alternative accents of a respiration whose savage energy could not belong to a human creature.

A profound terror, increased still further by the darkness, the silence, and his waking images, froze his heart within him. He almost felt his hair stand on end, when by straining his eyes to their utmost he perceived through the shadow two faint yellow lights. At first he attributed these lights to the reflections of his own pupils, but soon the vivid brilliance of the night aided him gradually to distinguish the objects around him in the cave, and he beheld a huge animal lying but two steps from him. Was it a lion, a tiger, or a crocodile?

The Provençal was not sufficiently educated to know under what species his enemy ought to be classed; but his fright was all the greater, as his ignorance led him to imagine all terrors at once; he endured a cruel torture, noting every variation of the breathing close to him without daring to make the slightest movement. An odour, pungent like that of a fox, but more penetrating, more profound, – so to speak, – filled the cave, and when the Provençal became sensible of this, his terror reached its height, for he could no longer doubt the proximity of a terrible companion, whose royal dwelling served him for a shelter.

Presently the reflection of the moon descending on the horizon lit up the den, rendering gradually visible and resplendent the spotted skin of a panther.

This lion of Egypt slept, curled up like a big dog, the peaceful possessor of a sumptuous niche at the gate of an hotel; its eyes opened for a moment and closed again; its face was turned towards the man. A thousand confused thoughts passed through the Frenchman's mind; first he thought of killing it with a bullet from his gun, but he saw there was not enough distance between them for him to take proper aim – the shot would miss the mark. And if it were to wake! – the thought made his limbs rigid. He listened to his own heart beating in the midst of the silence, and cursed the too violent pulsations which the flow of blood brought on, fearing to disturb that sleep which allowed him time to think of some means of escape.

Twice he placed his hand on his scimiter, intending to cut off the head of his enemy; but the difficulty of cutting the stiff short hair compelled him to abandon this daring project. To miss would be to die for CER-TAIN, he thought; he preferred the chances of fair fight, and made up his mind to wait till morning; the morning did not leave him long to wait.

He could now examine the panther at ease; its muzzle was smeared with blood.

'She's had a good dinner,' he thought, without troubling himself as to whether her feast might have been on human flesh. 'She won't be hungry when she gets up.'

It was a female. The fur on her belly and flanks was glistening white; many small marks like velvet formed beautiful bracelets round her feet; her sinuous tail was also white, ending with black rings; the overpart of her dress, yellow like burnished gold, very lissome and soft, had the characteristic blotches in the form of rosettes, which distinguish the panther from every other feline species.

This tranquil and formidable hostess snored in an attitude as graceful as that of a cat lying on a cushion. Her bloodstained paws, nervous and well armed, were stretched out before her face, which rested upon them, and from which radiated her straight slender whiskers, like threads of silver.

If she had been like that in a cage, the Provençal would doubtless have admired the grace of the animal, and the vigorous contrasts of vivid colour which gave her robe an imperial splendor; but just then his sight was troubled by her sinister appearance.

The presence of the panther, even asleep, could not fail to produce the effect which the magnetic eyes of the serpent are said to have on the nightingale.

For a moment the courage of the soldier began to fail before this danger, though no doubt it would have risen at the mouth of a cannon charged with shell. Nevertheless, a bold thought brought daylight to his soul and sealed up the source of the cold sweat which sprang forth on his brow. Like men driven to bay, who defy death and offer their body to the smiter, so he, seeing in this merely a tragic episode, resolved to play his part with honour to the last.

'The day before yesterday the Arabs would have killed me, perhaps,' he said; so considering himself as good as dead already, he waited bravely, with excited curiosity, the awakening of his enemy.

When the sun appeared, the panther suddenly opened her eyes; then she put out her paws with energy, as if to stretch them and get rid of cramp. At last she yawned, showing the formidable apparatus of her teeth and pointed tongue, rough as a file.

'A regular little mistress,' thought the Frenchman, seeing her roll herself about so softly and coquettishly. She licked off the blood which stained her paws and muzzle, and scratched her head with reiterated gestures full of prettiness. 'All right, make a little toilet,' the Frenchman said to himself, beginning to recover his gaiety with his courage; 'we'll say good morning to each other presently;' and he seized the small, short dagger which he had taken from the Maugrabins.

At this moment the panther turned her head towards the man and looked at him fixedly without moving. The rigidity of her metallic eyes and their insupportable lustre made him shudder, especially when the animal walked towards him. But he looked at her caressingly, staring into her eyes in order to magnetize her, and let her come quite close to him; then with a movement both gentle and amorous, as though he were caressing the most beautiful of women, he passed his hand over her whole body, from the head to the tail, scratching the flexible vertebrae which divided the panther's yellow back. The animal waved her tail voluptuously, and her eyes grew gentle; and when for the third time the Frenchman accomplished this interesting flattery, she gave forth one of those purrings by which cats express their pleasure; but this murmur issued from a throat so powerful and so deep that it resounded through the cave like the last vibrations of an organ in a church. The man, understanding the importance of his caresses, redoubled them in such a way as to surprise and stupefy his imperious courtesan. When he felt sure of having extinguished the ferocity of his capricious companion, whose hunger had so fortunately been satisfied the day before, he got up to go out of the cave; the panther let him go out, but when he had reached the summit of the hill she sprang with the lightness of a sparrow hopping from twig to twig, and rubbed herself against his legs, putting up her back after the manner of all the race of cats. Then regarding her guest with eyes whose glare had softened a little, she gave vent to that wild cry which naturalists compare to the grating of a saw.

'She is exacting,' said the Frenchman, smilingly.

He was bold enough to play with her ears; he caressed her belly and scratched her head as hard as he could. When he saw that he was successful, he tickled her skull with the point of his dagger, watching for the right moment to kill her, but the hardness of her bones made him tremble for his success.

The sultana of the desert showed herself gracious to her slave; she lifted her head, stretched out her neck and manifested her delight by the tranquillity of her attitude. It suddenly occurred to the soldier that to kill this savage princess with one blow he must poniard her in the throat.

He raised the blade, when the panther, satisfied no doubt, laid herself gracefully at his feet, and cast up at him glances in which, in spite of their natural fierceness, was mingled confusedly a kind of good will. The poor Provençal ate his dates, leaning against one of the palm trees, and casting his eyes alternately on the desert in quest of some liberator and on his terrible companion to watch her uncertain clemency.

The panther looked at the place where the date stones fell, and every time that he threw one down her eyes expressed an incredible mistrust.

She examined the man with an almost commercial prudence. However, this examination was favourable to him, for when he had finished his meagre meal she licked his boots with her powerful rough tongue, brushing off with marvellous skill the dust gathered in the creases.

'Ah, but when she's really hungry!' thought the Frenchman. In spite of the shudder this thought caused him, the soldier began to measure curiously the proportions of the panther, certainly one of the most splendid specimens of its race. She was three feet high and four feet long without counting her tail; this powerful weapon, rounded like a cudgel, was nearly three feet long. The head, large as that of a lioness, was distinguished by a rare expression of refinement. The cold cruelty of a tiger was dominant, it was true, but there was also a vague resemblance to the face of a sensual woman. Indeed, the face of this solitary queen had something of the gaiety of a drunken Nero: she had satiated herself with blood, and she wanted to play.

The soldier tried if he might walk up and down, and the panther left him free, contenting herself with following him with her eyes, less like a faithful dog than a big Angora cat, observing everything and every movement of her master.

When he looked around, he saw, by the spring, the remains of his horse; the panther had dragged the carcass all that way; about two thirds of it had been devoured already. The sight reassured him.

It was easy to explain the panther's absence, and the respect she had had for him while he slept. The first piece of good luck emboldened him to tempt the future, and he conceived the wild hope of continuing on good terms with the panther during the entire day, neglecting no means of taming her, and remaining in her good graces.

He returned to her, and had the unspeakable joy of seeing her wag her tail with an almost imperceptible movement at his approach. He sat down then, without fear, by her side, and they began to play together; he took her paws and muzzle, pulled her ears, rolled her over on her back, stroked her warm, delicate flanks. She let him do whatever he liked, and when he began to stroke the hair on her feet she drew her claws in carefully.

The man, keeping the dagger in one hand, thought to plunge it into the belly of the too confiding panther, but he was afraid that he would be immediately strangled in her last convulsive struggle; besides, he felt in his heart a sort of remorse which bid him respect a creature that had done him no harm. He seemed to have found a friend, in a boundless desert; half unconsciously he thought of his first sweetheart, whom he had nicknamed 'Mignonne' by way of contrast, because she was so atrociously jealous that all the time of their love he was in fear of the knife with which she had always threatened him.

This memory of his early days suggested to him the idea of making the young panther answer to this name, now that he began to admire with less terror her swiftness, suppleness and softness. Towards the end of the day he had familiarized himself with his perilous position; he now almost liked the painfulness of it. At last his companion had got into the habit of looking up at him whenever he cried in a falsetto voice, 'Mignonne'.

At the setting of the sun Mignonne gave, several times running, a profound melancholy cry. 'She's been well brought up,' said the light-hearted soldier; 'she says her prayers.' But this mental joke only occurred to him when he noticed what a pacific attitude his companion remained in. 'Come, ma petite blonde, I'll let you go to bed first,' he said to her, counting on the activity of his own legs to run away as quickly as possible, directly she was asleep, and seek another shelter for the night.

The soldier waited with impatience the hour of his flight, and when it had arrived he walked vigorously in the direction of the Nile; but hardly had he made a quarter of a league in the sand when he heard the panther bounding after him, crying with that saw-like cry more dreadful even than the sound of her leaping.

'Ah!' he said, 'then she's taken a fancy to me, she has never met anyone before, and it is really quite flattering to have her first love.' That instant the man fell into one of those movable quicksands so terrible to travellers and from which it is impossible to save oneself. Feeling himself caught, he gave a shriek of alarm; the panther seized him with her teeth by the collar, and, springing vigorously backwards, drew him as if by magic out of the whirling sand.

'Ah, Mignonne!' cried the soldier, caressing her enthusiastically; 'we're bound together for life and death but no jokes, mind!' and he retraced his steps.

From that time the desert seemed inhabited. It contained a being to whom the man could talk, and whose ferocity was rendered gentle by him, though he could not explain to himself the reason for their strange friendship. Great as was the soldier's desire to stay upon guard, he slept.

On awakening he could not find Mignonne; he mounted the hill, and in the distance saw her springing towards him after the habit of these animals, who cannot run on account of the extreme flexibility of the vertebral column. Mignonne arrived, her jaws covered with blood; she received the wonted caress of her companion, showing with much purring how happy it made her. Her eyes, full of languor, turned still more gently than the day before towards the Provençal, who talked to her as one would to a tame animal.

'Ah! mademoiselle, you are a nice girl, aren't you? Just look at that! So we like to be made much of, don't we? Aren't you ashamed of yourself? So you have been eating some Arab or other, have you? That doesn't matter. They're animals just the same as you are; but don't you take to eating Frenchmen, or I shan't like you any longer.'

She played like a dog with its master, letting herself be rolled over, knocked about and stroked, alternately; sometimes she herself would provoke the soldier, putting up her paw with a soliciting gesture.

Some days passed in this manner. This companionship permitted the Provençal to appreciate the sublime beauty of the desert; now that he had a living thing to think about, alternations of fear and quiet, and plenty to eat, his mind became filled with contrast and his life began to be diversified.

Solitude revealed to him all her secrets, and enveloped him in her delights. He discovered in the rising and setting of the sun sights unknown to the world. He knew what it was to tremble when he heard over his head the hiss of a bird's wing, so rarely did they pass, or when he saw the clouds, changing and many coloured travellers, melt one into another. He studied in the night-time the effect of the moon upon the ocean of sand, where the simoom made waves swift of movement and rapid in their change. He lived the life of the Eastern day, marvelling at its wonderful pomp; then, after having revelled in the sight of a hurricane over the plain where the whirling sands made red, dry mists and death-bearing clouds, he would welcome the night with joy, for then fell the healthful freshness of the stars, and he listened to imaginary music in the skies. Then solitude taught him to unroll the treasures of dreams. He passed whole hours in remembering mere nothings, and comparing his present life with his past.

At last he grew passionately fond of the panther; for some sort of affection was a necessity.

Whether it was that his will powerfully projected had modified the character of his companion, or whether, because she found abundant food in her predatory excursions in the desert, she respected the man's life, he began to fear for it no longer, seeing her so well tamed.

He devoted the greater part of his time to sleep, but he was obliged to watch like a spider in its web that the moment of his deliverance might not escape him, if anyone should pass the line marked by the horizon. He had sacrificed his shirt to make a flag with, which he hung at the top of a palm tree, whose foliage he had torn off. Taught by necessity, he found the means of keeping it spread out, by fastening it with little sticks; for the wind might not be blowing at the moment when the passing traveller was looking through the desert.

It was during the long hours, when he had abandoned hope, that he amused himself with the panther. He had come to learn the different inflections of her voice, the expressions of her eyes; he had studied the capricious patterns of all the rosettes which marked the gold of her robe. Mignonne was not even angry when he took hold of the tuft at the end of her tail to count her rings, those graceful ornaments which glittered in the sun like jewellery. It gave him pleasure to contemplate the supple, fine outlines of her form, the whiteness of her belly, the graceful pose of her head. But it was especially when she was playing that he felt most pleasure in looking at her; the agility and youthful lightness of her movements were a continual surprise to him; he wondered at the supple way in which she jumped and climbed, washed herself and arranged her fur, crouched down and prepared to spring. However rapid her spring might be, however slippery the stone she was on, she would always stop short at the word 'Mignonne'.

One day, in a bright midday sun, an enormous bird coursed through the air. The man left his panther to look at his new guest; but after waiting a moment the deserted sultana growled deeply.

'My goodness! I do believe she's jealous,' he cried, seeing her eyes become hard again; 'the soul of Virginie has passed into her body; that's certain.'

The eagle disappeared into the air, while the soldier admired the curved contour of the panther.

But there was such youth and grace in her form! She was beautiful as a woman! The blond fur of her robe mingled well with the delicate tints of faint white which marked her flanks.

The profuse light cast down by the sun made this living gold, these russet markings burn in a way to give them an indefinable attraction.

The man and the panther looked at one another with a look full of meaning; the coquette quivered when she felt her friend stroke her head; her eyes flashed like lightning – then she shut them tightly.

'She has a soul,' he said, looking at the stillness of this queen of the sands, golden like them, white like them, solitary and burning like them.

'Well,' she said, 'I have read your plea in favour of beasts; but how did two so well adapted to understand each other end?'

'Ah, well! you see, they ended as all great passions do end – by a misunderstanding. For some reason one suspects the other of treason; they don't come to an explanation through pride, and quarrel and part from sheer obstinacy.'

'Yet sometimes at the best moments a single word or a look is enough – but anyhow go on with your story.'

'It's horribly difficult, but you will understand, after what the old villain told me over his champagne. He said – "I don't know if I hurt her, but she turned round, as if enraged, and with her sharp teeth caught hold of my leg – gently, I daresay; but I, thinking she would devour me, plunged my dagger into her throat. She rolled over, giving a cry that froze my heart; and I saw her dying, still looking at me without anger. I would have given all the world – my cross even, which I had not got then – to have brought her to life again. It was as though I had murdered a real person; and the soldiers who had seen my flag, and were come to my assistance, found me in tears.

'"Well sir," he said, after a moment of silence, "since then I have been in war in Germany, in Spain, in Russia, in France; I've certainly carried my carcass about a good deal, but never have I seen anything like the desert. Ah! yes, it is very beautiful!"

'"What did you feel there?" I asked him.

'"Oh! That can't be described, young man! Besides, I am not always regretting my palm trees and my panther. I should have to be very melancholy for that. In the desert, you see, there is everything and nothing."

'"Yes, but explain –"

'"Well," he said, with an impatient gesture, "it is God without mankind."'

Translated by Ernest Dowson

ALEXANDRE DUMAS

A Dead Man's Story Told by Himself

One December evening there were three of us in an artist's studio. It was cold and dark with the continuous and monotonous sound of the wind beating against the window-panes.

The studio was vast and feebly lit by the glow of a stove around which we were gathered.

Although we were all young and light-hearted, the conversation had nevertheless taken on a reflection of that gloomy evening, and our cheerful exchanges were soon exhausted.

One of us kept agitating a lovely blue flame on the punchbowl that cast an uncanny light on all the surrounding objects. The large sketches, the Christs, the bacchantes, the madonnas seemed to move and dance against the walls like great cadavers sharing the same greenish tint. This huge room, radiant during the day with the painter's creations, studded with his dreams, had taken on that evening, in the darkness, a strange character.

Every time the silver spoon dropped back into the bowl full of the flaming liquor, objects appeared on the walls in strange forms, in extraordinary hues, from white-bearded old prophets to those caricatures that people the walls of studios, and that looked like an army of demons such as you see when dreaming, or as grouped by Goya. Finally, the chill misty quietness outdoors complemented the fantastical within.

Add to this that every time we glimpsed each other in that momentary brightness, we had grey-green faces, staring eyes glittering like carbuncles, pale lips and hollow cheeks. But most dreadful of all was a plaster mask, a cast taken of one of our friends who had died a while ago: the mask, hanging by the window, was caught in three-quarters profile by the light reflected from the punch, which gave it a peculiarly mocking look.

Everyone has, like us, experienced the effect of vast shadowy rooms, as rendered by Hoffmann, as painted by Rembrandt; everyone has experienced at least once those groundless fears, those fits of feverishness at the sight of objects to which the pallid moonbeam or the wavering light of a lamp lend a mysterious form; everyone has found himself in a big dark room, at a friend's side, listening to some improbable tale, feeling that secret terror which might instantly be arrested by lighting a lamp or talking about something else: which we refrain from doing, so great is the need of our poor hearts for emotions, whether they be true or false.

Well, that evening, as we have said, there were three of us. The conversation, which never follows a straight line to reach its destination, had been through all the phases of our musings – these being the musings of twenty-year-olds: now as vaporous as the smoke from our cigarettes, now as cheerful as the flame on the punch, now as gloomy as the smile on that plaster mask.

We had reached the stage of not saying anything at all. The cigars, which traced the movement of heads and hands, glowed like three rings of light flitting about in the gloom.

It was clear that the first to open his mouth and disturb the silence, even with a joke, would give the other two a momentary fright, so immersed were we, individually, in our own uneasy reverie.

'Henri,' said he who was tending the punch, addressing the painter, 'have you read Hoffmann?'

'I have indeed!' replied Henri.

'And what do you think of his work?'

'I think it's just marvellous, and all the more so because the person who wrote it evidently believed in what he was writing. And I know that, as far as I'm concerned, when reading it in the evening, I often went to bed without closing my book and without daring to look behind me.'

'So you have a liking for the supernatural?'

'Very much so.'

'And you?' he said, turning to me.

'I too.'

'Well then! I'm going to tell you a tale of the supernatural, something that happened to me.'

'We were bound to come to it in the end. Go on then, tell the story.'

'It's a story that actually happened to you?'

'My own personal experience.'

'Well, go on, tell us! I'm prepared to believe anything today.'

'Especially as I'm the hero of it, I assure you, on my honour.'

'Well, get on with it! We're listening.'

He dropped the spoon into the bowl. The flame gradually died out, and we were left in total darkness, with only our legs catching the light from the fire in the stove.

He began.

'One evening, about a year ago, the weather was exactly the same as today, the same cold, the same rain, the same dreariness. I had a great many patients, and having made my last call, instead of dropping by Les Italiens, as I usually do, I took a cab home. I lived in one of the quietest streets in the Faubourg Saint-Germain. I was very tired and I was very soon in bed. I put out my lamp, and for a while I amused myself by watching the fire that was burning in my room throw great dancing shadows on the curtain round my bed. Then at last my eyes closed and I fell asleep.

'I had been asleep for about an hour when I felt a hand shaking me vigorously. I woke with a start, like a man who had been hoping for a long sleep, and I was surprised to see my nocturnal visitor. It was my servant.

'"Sir," he said, "quickly, get up, someone's come to fetch you for a young woman who's dying."

'"And where does this young woman live?" I asked.

'"Almost opposite; and what's more, the person who came asking for you is here to take you there."

'I got up and hurriedly dressed, thinking the hour and the circumstances would excuse my attire. I picked up my lancet and followed the man who had been sent to fetch me.

'It was pouring with rain.

'Fortunately, I had only to cross the street, and I was immediately at the home of the person needing my attention. She lived in a grand patrician townhouse. I crossed a large courtyard, climbed a few steps to the front door, passed through a hall where servants awaited me; I was shown upstairs and soon found myself in the patient's bedroom. It was a large room entirely furnished with old black carved wooden furniture. A woman led me into this room, and no one followed us in. I went straight over to a big four-poster bed hung with an antique luxurious silk fabric, and I saw on the pillow the most ravishing madonna's face Raphael had ever imagined. She had golden hair, like the flowing waters of the Pactolus, spread around a face of angelic form. Her eyes were half-closed, her lips parted, revealing a double row of pearls. Her neck was of a dazzling whiteness and perfectly contoured; her nightshirt was unfastened, revealing a breast of such beauty St Anthony would have been tempted; and when I took her hand, I recalled those white arms Homer gives Juno. In short, this woman was the epitome of the Christian angel and the pagan goddess. Everything about her revealed a purity of soul and an ardour of the senses. She might have posed as a model either for the Holy Virgin or for a lascivious bacchante, instilled folly in a wise man and faith in an atheist. And when I came near her I smelled through the heat of her feverishness that mysterious perfume, comprising every floral perfume, that emanates from woman.

'I stood there, forgetting what had brought me, staring as though at a revelation, and finding nothing comparable in my memories or my dreams, when she turned her head towards me, opened her big blue eyes and said, "I feel great pain."

'Yet there was almost nothing wrong with her. A bleeding and she was saved. I picked up my lancet; but as I was about to touch that arm – so white and so beautiful – my hand trembled. However, the doctor triumphed over the man. As soon as I opened a vein, blood as pure as liquid coral flowed from it, and she fainted.

'I did not want to leave her now. I stayed with her. I felt a secret happiness in holding the life of this woman in my hands. I staunched the blood, she gradually opened her eyes again, and gazing at me with one of those looks that spell damnation or salvation, "Thank you," she said, "the pain has eased a little."

'There was so much sensual pleasure, love and passion about her, I was rooted to the spot, counting each beat of my heart by the beating of hers, listening to her still slightly feverish breathing, and telling myself that if there was anything of heaven on this earth, it must be the love of this woman.

'She fell asleep.

'I was virtually kneeling on the steps of her bed, like a priest at the altar. An alabaster lamp hanging from the ceiling cast a beguiling light on every object. I was alone with her. The woman who brought me there had gone to convey the news that her mistress was recovering and had no further need of anyone. Indeed, her mistress lay there, as calm and beautiful as an angel that had fallen asleep while praying. As for me, I was out of my mind . . .

'Yet I could not stay in that room all night. So I in turn left quietly, so as not to wake her. I prescribed some treatments as I left and said that I would return the next day.

'Back at home, I stayed awake with the memory of her. I realized the love of that woman must be an eternal enchantment forged of dreams and passion; that she must be as demure as a saint and as passionate as a courtesan; I imagined she must hide from the world all the treasures of her beauty, and to her lover she must yield her naked self wholly. Anyway, the idea of her set my night ablaze, and when daylight came I was madly in love with her.

'However, after the crazed thoughts of a restless night came serious deliberations: I told myself that perhaps an insuperable abyss separated me from this woman, that she was too beautiful not to have a lover; that he must be too dearly loved for her to forget him, and without knowing him I began to hate this man to whom God had given enough happiness in this world to enable him to suffer without a murmur an eternity of pain.

'I was impatient for the moment when I could present myself at her house, and the interval I spent waiting seemed like a century.

'At last the time came and I went out.

'When I arrived, I was shown into a boudoir of exquisite taste, terrifically rococo, overwhelmingly pompadour in style. She was alone, and reading. A voluminous black velvet gown completely enveloped her, leaving uncovered, as with Perugino's virgins, only her hands and her head. She held coquettishly in a scarf the arm I had bled, warming before the fire her two little feet that did not look as if they were made to walk on this earth. In a word, this woman was so utterly beautiful God might have given her to the world as an artist's impression of his angels.

'She held out her hand and made me sit beside her.

'"Up so soon, madame," I said, "you are unwise."

'"No, I'm strong," she said, smiling. "I slept very well, and besides I was not ill."

'"Yet you said you were in pain."

'"More in thought than in body," she said with a sigh.

'"Something saddens you, madame?"

'"Oh, deeply! Fortunately, God is also a physician, and he has found the universal panacea: oblivion."

'"But some sorrows are fatal," I said.

'"Well, death or oblivion, are they not the same thing? One is the tomb of the body, the other the tomb of the heart, that is all."

'"But you, madame," I said, "how can you be suffering heartache? You are too far aloft for it to reach you, and sorrows must pass beneath your feet like clouds beneath the feet of God. For us, storms; for you, serenity!"

'"That's where you're mistaken," she went on, "and that's what proves all your science stops there, at the heart."

'"Well then!" I said. "Try to forget, madame! God sometimes allows happiness to succeed a sorrow, a smile to follow tears, it's true. And when the heart of the person He is putting to the test is too empty to refill itself alone, when the wound is too deep to close without help, He sends into the path of the soul He wishes to console another soul who understands it. For He knows that suffering is lessened if two suffer together; and there comes a time when the empty heart fills again and when the wound heals."

'"And what is the balm, doctor," she said, "with which you would treat such a wound?"

'"That depends on the patient," I replied; "for some I would recommend faith; for others, I would recommend love."

'"You are right," she said; "they are the soul's two sisters of charity."

'There was rather a lengthy silence during which I admired that divine face, with the half-light that filtered through the silk curtains casting delightful hues upon it, and that lovely golden hair, not loosened like the day before but smoothed over her temples and coiled at the back of her head.

'The conversation had from the very start taken this melancholy turn. And with her triple crown of beauty, passion and suffering this woman appeared to me even more radiant than the first time. For God's finishing touch was martyrdom, and he to whom she would give her soul had to accept the twofold doubly sacred mission of making her forget the past and be hopeful of the future.

'So there I remained before her, not frantic as I had been the previous day in the face of her fever, but self-composed in the face of her resignation. If she had given herself to me at that moment, I would have fallen at her feet, I would have taken her hands, and I would have wept with her as with a sister, respecting the angel, consoling the woman.

'But what was this heartache that needed forgetting, that had inflicted this still-bleeding wound, that is what I did not know, that is what I had to guess, for there was already intimacy enough between doctor and patient for her to admit to heartache, but there was not yet enough for her to tell me the cause of it. Nothing around her could give me any indication: no one had come to her bedside the previous day, feeling concerned about her; no one turned up to see her the next day. This heartache must therefore already be in the past and only reflected in the present.

'"Doctor," she said, suddenly emerging from her reverie, "will I soon be able to dance?"

'"Yes, madame," I said, a little surprised by this transition.

'"Because I have to host a long-awaited ball," she said. "You will come, won't you? You must have a very poor opinion of my heartache, which, while making me pine during the day, doesn't stop me from dancing at night. The thing is, you see, there are sorrows that have to be buried in the bottom of one's heart so that the world should learn nothing of them. There are tortures that have to be masked with a smile, so that no one should suspect them. And I want to keep to myself what I suffer, as another would keep to himself his joy. This world, which is jealous of me and envious at the sight of my beauty, believes me to be happy, and that is a belief of which I do not want to disabuse it. That is why I dance, maybe to weep the day after, but to weep alone."

'She held out her hand with an indefinable expression of candour and sadness, and said, "You will come again soon, won't you?"

'I raised her hand to my lips, and I left.

'I arrived home dull-witted.

'From my window I could see hers. I spent the whole day watching those windows, the whole day they were dark and silent. I forgot everything for that woman. I did not sleep, I did not eat. That evening I was feverish, the next morning delirious, and the following evening I was dead.'

'Dead!' we cried.

'Dead,' our friend repeated in a tone of conviction impossible to convey, 'as dead as Fabien whose mask this is.'

'Go on,' I said.

The rain still beat against the window-panes. We put more wood in the stove whose bright red flame cast a little light in the darkness into which the studio disappeared.

He resumed.

'From that moment, I felt nothing but a cold shock. No doubt that was when I was put into the grave.

'I do not know for how long I was buried, when I vaguely heard a voice calling me by name. I trembled with cold, unable to reply. A few moments later the voice called me again. I strove to speak, but my lips, as they moved, felt the shroud that covered me from head to foot. Yet I managed feebly to articulate these words: "Who calls?"

'"I," someone replied.

'"Who are you?"

'"I."

'And the voice grew fainter as if lost in the wind, or as if it had been just a fleeting rustle of leaves.

'Yet a third time I heard my name, but this time the name seemed to pass from branch to branch, so much so the whole cemetery sullenly repeated it, and I heard the sound of wings, as if this name, suddenly spoken in the silence, had made a whole flock of nightbirds take flight.

'My hands went to my face as if moved by mysterious forces. I silently put aside the shroud with which I was covered, and I tried to see. I felt as if I was waking from a long sleep. I was cold.

'I will always remember the grim horror surrounding me. The trees were leafless and their gaunt branches lugubriously twisted, like great skeletons. A moonbeam breaking through long black clouds shed its wan light before me on white tombs that stood against the horizon like a celestial staircase and all those vague voices of the dark that presided over my awakening were full of mystery and terror.

'I turned my head and sought the person who had called me. He was sitting beside my tomb, watching my movements, his head resting on his hands, with a strange smile, a dreadful look in his eye.

'I was scared.

'"Who are you?" I asked, gathering all my strength. "Why have you woken me?"

'"To do you a favour," he replied.

'"Where am I?"

'"In the cemetery."

'"Who are you?"

'"A friend."

'"Leave me to sleep."

'"Listen," he said, "do you remember the earth?"

'"No."

'"You regret nothing?"

'"No."

'"How long have you been sleeping?"

'"I don't know.'

'"I'll tell you how long. You've been dead two days, and your last word was a woman's name instead of that of the Lord. So your body would belong to Satan, if Satan wanted to take it. Do you understand?"

'"Yes."

'"Do you want to live?"

'"Are you Satan?"

'"Satan or not, do you want to live?"

'"Alone?"

'"No, you will see her again."

'"When?"

'"This evening."

'"Where?"

'"At her home."

'"I accept," I said, struggling to get up. "Your conditions?"

'"I make none," replied Satan. "Do you think I'm not capable of doing good from time to time? This evening she is hosting a ball, and I'm taking you there."

'"Let's go, then."

'"Let's go."

'Satan offered me his hand and I found myself upright.

'To describe what I felt would be impossible. A terrible coldness chilled my limbs, that is all I can say.

'"Now," continued Satan, "follow me. You understand, I won't take you out through the main gate, the caretaker would not let you pass, my dear fellow. Once in here, there is no getting out again. So follow me: we are going to your place first, where you will dress, for you cannot go to the ball in what you are wearing now, especially as it is not a masked ball. But wrap up well in your shroud, for the nights are chilly and you might be cold."

'Satan began to laugh the way Satan does, and I continued walking beside him.

'"I am sure," he went on, "that despite the service I am rendering you, you do not yet like me. That is what you men are like, ungrateful towards your friends. Not that I disapprove of ingratitude: it's a vice I invented, and it's one of the most widespread. But I would like to see you less sad at least. It's the only acknowledgement I ask of you."

'I was still following, white and cold as a marble statue set in motion by a hidden spring mechanism. But audible, during moments of silence, would have been my teeth chattering in response to an icy chill, and the bones in my limbs cracking at every step.

'"Will we be there soon?" I said with some effort.

'"Impatient, eh?" said Satan. "She's very beautiful, then?"

'"An angel."

'"Ah! my dear fellow," he replied laughing, "you have to admit, there's a want of tact in what you say. You just spoke to me of an angel, to me, who has been one, and bear in mind no angel would do for you what I am doing today. Yet I forgive you. Some allowance must be made for a man who has been dead for two days. Besides, as I told you, I'm feeling very cheerful this evening. Things have happened in the world today that delight me. I thought men had degenerated, I thought they had become virtuous some time ago, but no, they are still the same, just as I created them. Well, my dear fellow, rarely have I seen days like today: since yesterday evening I have had six hundred and twenty-two suicides in Europe alone, with more young people among them than old, which is a waste because they die childless; two thousand two hundred and forty-three murders, again in Europe alone. In other parts of the world, I have given up counting: there, I am like those rich capitalists, I cannot put a figure on my fortune. Two million six hundred and twenty-three thousand nine hundred and seventy-five new cases of adultery – not so surprising with the number of balls there are; twelve hundred judges who have sold themselves – usually I have more. But what gives me most pleasure are the twenty-seven young girls, the eldest under the age of eighteen, who died blaspheming God. Add them together, my dear fellow, that makes a haul of around two million six hundred and twenty-eight thousand souls in Europe alone. That is not counting cases of incest, counterfeit and rape: those are the small change. So, taking as an average three million souls a day who damn themselves to perdition, you can work out how long it will be before the whole world is mine. I shall be forced to purchase paradise from God in order to expand hell.'

'"I understand your cheerfulness," I murmured, quickening my pace.

'"You say that," Satan said, "in a gloomy and doubtful way. Are you then afraid of me because you see me face to face? Am I then so repellent? Let's consider this a little, please: what would become of the world without me, a world that had sentiments derived from heaven, and not passions derived from me? But the world would die of boredom, my dear fellow! Who invented gold? I did. Gambling? I did. Love? I did; Affairs? Again, it was I. And I do not understand men, who seem so set against me. Your poets, for example, who talk of pure love, do they not understand that by portraying love that saves, they inspire passion that dooms. For, thanks to me, what you are always seeking is not the Virgin-like woman, it is the Eve-like sinner. And you yourself, at this very moment, you whom I have just helped out of a tomb, you who still have the coldness of a corpse and the pallor of a dead man, it is not a pure love you are going to seek from the woman I am taking you to, it is a night of sensual pleasure. You can see very well that wickedness survives death, and that if man had the choice, he would prefer the eternity of passion to the eternity of happiness, and the proof is, that for a few years of passion on earth, he forfeits the eternity of happiness in heaven."

'"We will be there soon?" I said, for the horizon kept receding and we walked without making any progress.

'"Ever impatient," replied Satan, "and yet I am doing my best to take the shortest way possible. You understand I cannot go through the gate, there is a big cross over it, and the cross for me is customs control. As I usually travel with things that are not allowed, I would be stopped, I would be forced to cross myself, and I might readily commit a crime, but I would not commit a sacrilege. And besides, as I have already told you, you would not be allowed to leave. You think a person dies, he is buried, and one fine day he can go off without a word. You're mistaken, my dear fellow: without me, you would have had to wait until the resurrection to life everlasting, which would have been a long wait.

'"So follow me, and don't worry, we'll get there. I promised you a ball, a ball you shall have: I keep my promises and my signature is known to be binding."

'There was in all this banter from my sinister companion something baneful that chilled me. All I have just told you, I seem to hear it still.

'We walked on for a while, then at last we came to a wall with tombs piled before it forming a staircase. Satan stepped on to the first and, unusually for him, walked on the sacred stones, until he reached the top of the wall.

'I hesitated to follow the same route, I was afraid.

'He held out his hand, saying, "There's no danger. You can step on them, they are acquaintances of mine."

'When I reached him, he said, "Would you like me to show you what is happening in Paris?"

'"No, let's keep walking."

'"Very well, since you're in such a hurry."

'We jumped down from the wall on to the ground.

'The moon, under Satan's gaze, had hidden itself like a young girl under an impudent gaze. The night was cold, all doors were closed, all windows dark, all streets silent. It seemed as if no one for a long time had trodden the ground on which we walked: everything around us had a look of doom about it. As though, when daylight came, no one would open the doors, no head would appear in the windows, no footstep would disturb the silence. I felt I was walking through a town that had been dead for centuries and rediscovered during excavations. In short, the town seemed to have lost its inhabitants to the cemetery. We walked on without hearing a sound, without encountering a shadow. It was a long way through this terrifyingly quiet and peaceful town: at last we arrived at our house.

'"Do you recognize where you are?" said Satan.

'"Yes," I replied sullenly, "let's go inside."

'"Wait, I have to open the door. It was also I who invented breaking and entering: I have a second key to every door, except that of paradise, however."

'We entered.

'The quiet outside continued within: it was horrible.

'I thought I was dreaming. I could no longer breathe. Imagine re-entering the room where you died two days earlier, finding everything as it was during your illness, only stamped with that sombreness that death imparts, seeing again all the objects tidied up as if nevermore to be touched by you. The only moving thing I had seen since leaving the cemetery was my large pendulum clock a human being had died beside, and which continued to count the hours of my eternity as it had counted the hours of my life.

'I went to the fireplace. I lit a candle to assure myself of reality, for everything around me appeared through a pale and fantastic light that gave me as it were an interior view.

'Everything was real: this was indeed my room. I saw the portrait of my mother, still smiling at me. I opened the books I was reading a few days before my death. Only the bed now had no sheets on it, and there were seals everywhere.

'As for Satan, he had sat down at the far end of the room, and was reading with close attention *The Lives of the Saints*.

'At that moment I passed in front of a big mirror and I saw myself in my strange outfit, covered in a shroud, looking pale, with lacklustre eyes. I was uncertain about this life an unknown power gave back to me, and I put my hand on my heart.

'My heart was not beating.

'I raised my hand to my brow: my brow like my chest was cold, the pulse stilled like my heart. And yet I recognized everything I had left behind, so nothing in me was alive but my mind and my eyes.

'What was even more horrible, I could not tear my gaze away from that mirror, which reflected back to me my grim, cold, dead image. Every movement of my lips was reflected as the hideous smile of a corpse. I could not stir, I could not cry out.

'The clock made that muffled and lugubrious rumbling sound that precedes the chiming of old pendulum clocks, and struck two. Then all became quiet again.

'A few moments later, a nearby church chimed in turn, then another, then yet another.

'In a corner of the mirror I saw Satan, who had fallen asleep over *The Lives of the Saints*.

'I managed to turn round. There was a mirror opposite the one I was looking at, so I saw myself repeated thousands of times, with the pale light of a single candle in that vast room.

'My fear reached a peak. I cried out.

'Satan awoke.

'"And with this," he said, showing me the book, "men are expected to be made virtuous! It's so boring I fell asleep, I who have stayed awake for six thousand years. Aren't you ready yet?"

'"Yes," I said mechanically, "here I am."

'"Hurry up," replied Satan, "break the seals, take your clothes and most importantly some gold, a lot of gold. Leave your drawers open and tomorrow the judicial system will contrive to condemn some other poor devil for breaking the seals – that will be my little treat."

'I dressed. From time to time I touched my brow and my chest: both were cold.

'When I was ready I looked at Satan.

'"We're going to see her?" I said.

'"In five minutes."

'"And tomorrow?"

'"Tomorrow," he said, '"you will resume your ordinary life. I don't do things by halves."

'"With no conditions?"

'"With no conditions."

'"Let's go," I said.

'"Follow me."

'We went downstairs.

'A few moments later we were in front of the house to which I had been summoned four days earlier.

'We climbed the steps.

'I recognized the steps, the entrance hall, the antechamber. The approaches to the salon were full of people. It was a dazzling array of lights, flowers, gemstones and women.

'People were dancing.

'At the sight of this pleasure I believed in my resurrection.

'I leant towards Satan, who had not left my side, and whispered in his ear. "Where is she?" I said.

'"In her boudoir."

'I waited until the contra dance was over. I crossed the room. The mirrors with lighted candles reflected my pale and sombre image. I saw the smile that had chilled me earlier, but this was no longer a place of solitude, it was a social gathering; this was no longer the cemetery, it was a ball; this was no longer the grave, it was the setting for love. I let this go to my head and forgot for a moment from whence I came, thinking only of her for whom I came.

'On reaching the door to the boudoir, I saw her. She was more beautiful than beauty, more chaste than religious faith. I halted momentarily as if in ecstasy. She was dressed in a gown of dazzling white, her shoulders and arms bare. I saw again, in imagination rather than reality, a little red dot where I had bled her. When I appeared, she was surrounded by young men to whom she was barely listening. She nonchalantly raised her lovely eyes, so full of sensuality, noticed me, seemed to hesitate in recognizing me, then, giving me a charming smile, she left everyone and came to me.

'"You see, I am strong," she said.

'The orchestra struck up.

'"And to prove it to you," she went on, taking my arm, "we are going to waltz together."

'She said a few words to someone passing by. I saw Satan near me.

'"You kept your word," I said to him. "Thank you. But I must have this woman this very night."

'"You will," said Satan, "but wipe your face, you have a worm on your cheek."

'And he disappeared, leaving me even more chilled than before. As if to restore myself to life, I gripped the arm of the woman I came from the depths of the tomb to seek, and I drew her into the salon.

'It was one of those exhilarating waltzes where all those around us disappear, where you exist only for each other, where hands are locked together, the breath of each mingles with that of the other, you are breast to breast. I waltzed with my eyes fixed on hers, and her gaze, which smiled on me eternally, seemed to say, "If you knew the wealth of love and passion I would give to my lover! If you knew what voluptuousness there is in my caresses, what ardour in my kisses! To the man who would love me, all the beauties of my body, all the thoughts of my soul, for I am young, I am loving, I am beautiful!"

'And the waltz swept us up in its swift sensual whirl.

'This went on for a long time. When the music stopped, we were the only ones still waltzing.

'She fell on my arm, her breast heaving, supple as a serpent, and looked up at me with those big eyes that seemed to say the words her mouth did not: "I love you!"

'I drew her into the boudoir, where we were alone. The salons were emptying.

'She dropped on to a loveseat, half-closing her eyes with exhaustion, as if in the embrace of love.

'I leant over her and said to her in a low voice, "If you knew how much I love you!"

'"I know," she said, "and I love you too."

'It was enough to drive a man crazy.

'"I would give my life," I said, "for an hour of love with you, and my soul for a night."

'"Listen," she said, opening a door hidden in the paper-covered wall, "in a moment we shall be alone. Wait for me."

'She gave me a gentle push, and I found myself alone in her bedroom, lit as before by the alabaster lamp.

'Everything in the room had an aura of mysterious voluptuousness impossible to describe. I sat by the fire, for I was cold; I looked at myself in the mirror, I was as pale as ever. I heard the carriages leaving one by one. Then, when the last had gone, there was a mournful and solemn silence. Gradually my terrors returned. I dared not look round. I felt cold. I was surprised she did not come. I counted the minutes, and I heard no sound. I had my elbows on my knees and my head in my hands.

'Then I began to think of my mother, my mother who at that moment was mourning her dead son, my mother to whom I meant everything in life, and to whom I had not until now given any thought whatsoever. All the days of my childhood passed before my eyes like a happy dream. I saw that whenever I had a wound to dress, a pain to allay, it was always my mother to whom I turned. Perhaps, as I was preparing for a night of love, she was preparing for a lonely, silent night of sleeplessness, with objects that reminded her of me, or with only the memory of me as she kept vigil. This was a dreadful thought. I felt remorseful. The tears came to my eyes. I stood up. As I looked in the mirror I saw behind me a pale white shadow, staring at me.

'I turned round. It was my lovely mistress.

'Fortunately my heart was not beating, for with this intensifying succession of emotions it would surely have ruptured.

'All was silent, outside as within.

'She drew me to her and soon I forgot everything. It was a night impossible to relate, with unknown carnal delights, with pleasurings such as came close to pain. In my dreams of love, I encountered nothing to match this woman I held in my arms, ardent as a Messaline, chaste as a madonna, lithe as a tigress, with kisses that burned the lips, with words that set the heart on fire. She had in her something so powerfully attractive there were moments when I was afraid of her.

'At last the lamp began to pale as day began to break.

'"Listen," this woman said to me, "you must leave. It is getting light, you cannot stay here, but this evening, at the first hour of darkness, I shall be expecting you, yes?"

'I felt her lips on mine one last time. She tightly squeezed my hands, and I left.

'There was still the same quiet outside.

'I walked like a madman, hardly believing in my life, with not the least thought of going to my mother's or of returning home, that woman so encompassed my heart.

'I know of only one thing more desirable than a first night spent with one's mistress; that is, a second night.

'Day had dawned, sad, gloomy, cold. I walked aimlessly in the deserted and desolate countryside, awaiting nightfall.

'Nightfall came early.

'I raced to the house where the ball was held.

'As I was crossing the threshold, I saw a pale and decrepit old man descending the steps.

'"Where are you going, sir?" said the caretaker.

'"To call on Madame de P—," I said.

'"Madame de P—," he said, looking at me in astonishment. And pointing to the old man, "That gentleman is the person who lives in this house now. She died two months ago."

'I gave a cry and fell backwards.'

'And then?' I said to the storyteller.

'Then?' he said, revelling in our attention and weighing his words. 'Then I woke, for it was all nothing but a dream.'

Translated by Christine Donougher

VICTOR HUGO

Claude Gueux

Note from the First Edition

The letter below, of which the original is kept in the offices of the *Revue de Paris*, is of such great credit to its author we reproduce it here. It is now included in all reprints of 'Claude Gueux'.

Dunkerque, 30 July 1834

To the Editor of the Revue de Paris

Dear Sir

Claude Gueux, by Victor Hugo, included in your delivery of the 6th inst., teaches a great lesson. Help me, I beg you, to share it.

Kindly do me the favour, if you please, of printing at my expense as many copies as there are Deputies in France, and send a copy correctly addressed to each one of them.

Yours faithfully
CHARLES CARLIER
Bookseller

Seven or eight years ago, a man named Claude Gueux, a poor labourer, lived in Paris. He had a young woman who was his mistress living with him, and a child by that young woman. I tell things as they are, leaving the reader to gather up any morals the facts may leave in their wake. This labourer was able, skilful, intelligent, very ill served by education, very well served by nature, being unable to read and able to think. One winter, he was out of work. No fire or bread in the garret. The man, the young woman and the child were cold and hungry. The man stole. I do not know what he stole, I do not know where he stole. What I do know is, the theft resulted in three days of bread and a fire in the hearth for the woman and child, and five years of prison for the man.

The man was sent to do his time at Clairvaux prison. Clairvaux: an abbey turned into a jail, a monastic cell turned into a prison cell, an altar turned into a pillory. When we speak of progress, that is how some people understand it and implement it. That is the reality they give to our word.

To continue.

Having got there, he was put in a punishment cell at night, and in the workshop during the day. It is not the workshop I condemn.

Claude Gueux, once an honest labourer, now a thief, was a dignified and serious figure. He had a high forehead, already lined though he was still young, a few grey hairs in the tufty black, kind deeply sunken eyes beneath a well-defined arch of the eyebrows, flared nostrils, a prominent chin, a disdainful lip. It was a fine head. We will see what society did to it.

He seldom spoke and was restrained in his movements. There was something imperious about his entire person that commanded obedience and he had a pensive air that was serious rather than long-suffering. Yet he had certainly suffered.

In the jail where Claude Gueux was incarcerated, there was a director of workshops, a special type of prison administrator, who is something of a warder and an employer at the same time, who simultaneously issues a command to the labourer and a threat to the prisoner, who puts a tool in your hands and irons on your feet. This one was himself a particular variety of the type, a short tyrannical man, a slave to his own ideas, always with a tight grip on his authority; moreover, on occasion, a good companion, expansive, even jovial and pleasantly teasing; harsh rather than firm; reasoning with no one, not even himself; a good father, a good husband no doubt, which is a duty and not a virtue; in a word, not wicked but bad. He was one of those men who have nothing vibrant or flexible about them, who are composed of inert molecules, who do not reverberate with the shock of any idea, or from contact with any feeling, who have cold rages, grim hatreds, emotionless outbursts, who become inflamed without warmth, whose heat capacity is nil and who often seem to be made of wood. They blaze at one end and are cold at the other. This man's main character line, the line running diagonally through him, was tenacity. He was proud of being tenacious, and compared himself to Napoleon. This is just an optical illusion. There are many people who are fooled by it and who, at a certain distance, mistake tenacity for will, and a candle for a star. So when this man had once set what he called his will on something absurd, he pursued this absurd thing, stiff-necked, through any obstacle, to the bitter end. Stubbornness without intelligence is folly welded to stupidity, serving to extend it. It goes a long way. In general, when a private or public catastrophe befalls us, if we examine, from the wreckage lying on the ground, how it was put together, we almost always find that it was blindly constructed by a mediocre and obstinate man who had confidence in himself and admired himself. There are throughout the world many of these pig-headed little agents of fate who believe themselves to be Providence.

So that is what the director of workshops of the central prison of Clairvaux was. That is what constituted the flint with which society struck prisoners every day to get sparks out of them.

The spark that such flints extract from such stones often ignite conflagrations.

We have said that having arrived at Clairvaux, Claude Gueux was given a workshop number and assigned to a task. The workshop director got to know him, recognized him as a good worker, and treated him well. Indeed, it seems that one day, being in a good mood, and seeing Claude Gueux looking extremely sad, for the man was always thinking of the companion he called his wife, the director told the prisoner, by way of joking and passing the time, and also to console him, that the poor woman had become a prostitute. Claude coldly asked what had become of the child. No one knew.

After a few months, Claude became acclimatized to the prison atmosphere and seemed not to think about anything any more. A kind of severe serenity, which was in his nature, had reasserted itself. After about the same length of time, Claude had acquired a peculiar influence over all his companions. As if by a kind of tacit agreement, and without anyone knowing why, not even him, all these men consulted him, listened to him, admired him and imitated him, which is the highest form of admiration. It was no ordinary acclaim to be obeyed by all those by nature disobedient men. This ascendancy had come to him without his having given it any thought. It came from the look he had in his eyes. The eye of a man is a window through which may be seen the thoughts that come and go in his mind.

Put a man who has ideas among men who have none, after a certain length of time, and by a law of irresistible attraction, all the tenebrous minds will gravitate, humbly and with adoration, round the radiant mind. There are men who are iron and men who are magnets. Claude was a magnet.

So in less than three months Claude had become the soul, the law and order of the workshop. All those needles turned on his dial face. He must have wondered himself at times whether he was king or prisoner. He was a kind of captive pope among his cardinals.

And, in a completely natural reaction, operating to similar effect in every circumstance, loved by the prisoners, he was hated by the jailers. It is always so. Popularity never goes without dislike. The love of slaves is always matched by the hatred of masters.

Claude Gueux was a big eater. It was a peculiarity of his constitution. His stomach was made in such a way that the daily fare of two ordinary men was barely enough to satisfy him. Monsieur de Cotadilla had such an appetite and joked about it. But what is a matter of mirth for a duke, a Spanish grandee who has five hundred thousand sheep, is a burden to a labourer and a hardship to a prisoner.

Free in his garret, Claude Gueux worked all day, earned his four pounds of bread and ate it. Claude Gueux in prison worked all day and invariably received for his pains one and a half pounds of bread and four ounces of meat. The ration is uncompromising. So Claude was usually hungry in Clairvaux prison.

He was hungry, that was all. He did not talk about it. Such was his nature.

One day, Claude had just devoured his meagre pittance and had resumed his occupation, thinking to stave off hunger with work. The other prisoners were happily eating. A puny, pallid, wan young man came and stood beside him. He was holding in hand his ration, which he had not yet touched, and a knife. He remained standing there, next to Claude, looking as if he wanted to talk to him and dared not. This man, and his bread, and his meat, disturbed Claude.

'What do you want?' he said curtly at last.

'A favour of you,' the young man said timidly.

'What?' said Claude.

'Help me to eat this. It's too much for me.'

A tear welled in Claude's proud eye. He took the knife, divided the young man's ration equally in two, took one half and began to eat it.

'Thank you,' said the young man. 'If you want, we'll share like this every day.'

'What's your name?' said Claude Gueux.

'Albin.'

'Why are you here?' said Claude.

'For stealing.'

'Me too.' said Claude.

So they shared like this every day. Claude Gueux was thirty-six years old and sometimes looked fifty, so grave was his usual line of thought. Albin was twenty and he would have passed for seventeen, such innocence was there still in this thief's eyes. A close friendship developed between these two men, a friendship as between father and son rather than between two brothers. Albin was still almost a child; already Claude was almost an old man.

They worked in the same workshop, they slept beneath the same corner-stone, they took exercise in the same yard, they ate of the same loaf. Each of the two friends meant all the world to the other. They seemed to be happy.

We have already spoken of the director of the workshops. This man, hated by the prisoners, was often obliged, in order to get them to obey him, to seek the help of Claude Gueux, whom they loved. On more than one occasion, when he had acted to prevent a rebellion or a disturbance, Claude Gueux's unaccredited authority had lent invaluable support to the director's official authority. Indeed, to contain the prisoners ten words from Claude were worth ten policemen. Claude had frequently helped out the director in this way. So the director cordially detested him. He was jealous of this thief. Deep in his heart he had a secret, envious, implacable hatred of Claude, the hatred of a lawful sovereign for a sovereign de facto, of temporal power for spiritual power.

These hatreds are the worst.

Claude was very fond of Albin, and he gave no thought to the director.

One day, one morning, when the turnkeys were transferring the prisoners two by two from their dormitory to the workshop, a warder summoned Albin who was paired with Claude, and told him the director wanted to see him.

'What does he want with you?' said Claude.

'I don't know,' said Albin.

The warder led Albin away.

The morning went by, Albin did not return to the workshop. When the meal break came, Claude thought he would find Albin in the yard. Albin was not in the yard.

The prisoners returned to the workshop, Albin did not reappear in the workshop. So the day passed. In the evening, when the prisoners were taken back to their dormitory, Claude looked round for Albin, and did not see him there. At that moment he seemed greatly distressed, for he addressed a warder, something he never did.

'Is Albin ill?' he said.

'No,' replied the warder.

'How is it, then,' Claude continued, 'that he hasn't reappeared today?'

'Ah!' said the turnkey casually. 'He's been moved to a different section.'

The witnesses who later testified to these facts remarked that at this response from the turnkey Claude's hand, in which he held a lighted candle, trembled slightly.

He spoke again calmly. 'Who gave that order?'

The warder replied: 'Monsieur D.'

The director of workshops was called Monsieur D.

The following day went by just like the one before, without Albin.

In the evening, when the working day ended, the director, Monsieur D, came into the workshop on his usual round. As soon as Claude saw him, he removed his thick woollen cap, buttoned up his grey jacket, the pitiful livery of Clairvaux, for it is a tenet in prisons that a respectfully buttoned-up jacket creates a favourable impression on superiors, and he stood, cap in hand, at the end of his workbench waiting for the director to come by. The director walked past.

'Sir!' said Claude.

The director stopped and half turned towards him.

'Sir,' said Claude, 'is it true that Albin has been moved to a different section?'

'Yes,' replied the director.

'Sir,' Claude continued, 'I need Albin to survive.' He added, 'You know I don't have enough to eat with the regular ration, and that Albin shared his bread with me.'

'That was his business,' said the director.

'Sir, would there not be some way of arranging for Albin to be put back in the same section as me?'

'Impossible. The decision's been made.'

'By whom?'

'By me.'

'Sir,' Claude went on, 'this is a matter of life or death to me, and it depends on you.'

'I never go back on my decisions.'

'Sir, have I done you anything to upset you?

'Nothing.'

'In that case,' said Claude, 'why are you separating me from Albin?'

'Because,' said the director.

Having given this explanation, the director walked away.

Claude bowed his head and did not reply. Poor caged lion whose dog had been taken away from him!

We are obliged to say the pain of this separation did not have any effect on the prisoner's somewhat pathological voracity. Indeed nothing was perceptibly changed in him. He did not mention Albin to any of his fellow prisoners. He walked alone in the yard during breaks, and he was hungry. That is all.

However, those who knew him well noticed something dark and gloomy in the expression on his face that intensified day by day. Otherwise, he was calmer than ever.

Several men tried to share their rations with him, he refused with a smile.

Every evening, since the director had given his explanation, Claude did a crazy kind of thing that was surprising in such a sensible man. Whenever the director, coming by at a fixed time on his usual round, walked past Claude's workbench, Claude would look up and stare at him, then address him in a tone full of anguish and anger, that was in the nature of both entreaty and threat, these two words only: 'And Albin?' The director would pretend not to hear or would walk away shrugging his shoulders.

That man was wrong to shrug his shoulders, for it was obvious to all the witnesses of these strange scenes that Claude Gueux was inwardly set upon something. The whole prison waited anxiously on the result of this battle between one man's tenacity and another's resolve.

It has been established that Claude once said to the director, 'Listen, sir, give me back my friend. You would do well to do so, I assure you. Mark my words.'

Another time, a Sunday, while he was out in the yard where he had been sitting on a stone motionless for several hours, in the same position, with his elbows on his knees and his forehead in his hands, the prisoner Faillette approached him and called out, laughing, 'What the devil are you doing there, Claude?'

Claude slowly raised his stern face and said, 'I'm passing judgement on someone.'

Finally one evening, 25 October 1831, as the director was doing his round, Claude noisily crushed under his foot a watch glass he had found that morning in a corridor. The director asked what that noise was.

'It's nothing,' said Claude, 'it was me. Sir, give me back my friend.'

'Impossible,' said the master.

'Yet needs must,' said Claude in a low firm voice. And looking the director in the face, he added, 'Think on it. It's the 25th of October today. I'm giving you until the 4th of November.'

A warder pointed out to Monsieur D that Claude was threatening him, and this called for punishment.

'No, no punishment,' said the director with a disdainful smile. 'You have to be kind to these people!'

The next day, the prisoner Pernot approached Claude, who was walking by himself, lost in thought, leaving the other prisoners to cavort in a little patch of sunshine on the other side of the yard.

'Well now, Claude, what are you thinking about? You look sad.'

'I'm afraid,' said Claude, 'something bad is soon going to happen to that good Monsieur D.'

There are nine full days between the 25th of October and the 4th of November. Claude did not let one day go by without solemnly warning the director of the more and more grievous state in which Albin's disappearance put him. Tired of this, the director once had him put in the punishment cell for twenty-four hours, because his entreaty sounded too much like a warning. That is all Claude managed to obtain.

The 4th of November arrived. That day Claude woke with a serene expression on his face not been seen since the day when Monsieur D's decision had separated him from his friend. When he got up, he rummaged in a kind of deal wood box at the foot of his bed, containing his few tattered clothes. He pulled out a pair of dressmaking scissors. These, together with an odd volume of *Émile*, were all that was left to him of the woman he had loved, of the mother of his child, of his happy little family of times past. Two items that were no good at all to Claude: the scissors could only be of use to a woman, the book to an educated person. Claude could neither sew nor read.

As he was crossing the old degraded and whitewashed cloister that served as a covered walk in winter, he approached the prisoner Ferrari, who was gazing intently at the enormous bars over a window. Claude held in his hand the small pair of scissors. He showed them to Ferrari, saying, 'This evening I shall cut through those bars with these scissors.'

Ferrari, in disbelief, began to laugh, and so did Claude.

That morning he worked more zealously than usual. Never had he worked so quickly and so well. He seemed to attach particular importance to finishing off that morning a straw hat he had been paid for in advance by an honest citizen of Troyes, Monsieur Bressier.

A little before midday, he made some excuse to go down to the carpenters' workshop on the ground floor, the floor below where he worked. Claude was as much liked there as he was elsewhere, but he rarely entered it. So:

'Hey! Claude's here!'

He was surrounded and given an enthusiastic welcome. Claude glanced round the room. Not one of the guards was present.

'Who has an axe to lend me?' he said.

'What for?' he was asked.

He replied, 'It's for killing the director of workshops this evening.'

He was offered several axes to choose from. He took the smallest, which was very sharp, hid it in his trousers, and left. There were twenty-seven prisoners there. He had not told them to keep quiet about it. They all did so.

They did not even talk about it among themselves.

Every man, individually, waited for what would happen. It was a terrible, straightforward and simple matter. No complication possible. Claude could be neither advised nor denounced.

An hour later he approached a young prisoner of sixteen who was yawning in the walkway, and advised him to learn to read. At that moment the convict Faillette drew close to Claude and asked what the devil he was hiding in his trousers.

Claude said, 'It's a hatchet for killing Monsieur D this evening.' He added, 'Does it show?'

'A bit,' said Faillette.

The rest of the day passed as usual. At seven o'clock in the evening the prisoners were locked up, each section in the workshop to which it was assigned, and the guards left the work rooms, which apparently is normal procedure, to return only after the director's round.

Claude Gueux was therefore locked in his workshop like the others, with his fellow workers.

There then occurred in that workshop an extraordinary scene, a scene neither without majesty nor without terror, the only one of its kind of which there is any historical record.

As has been established by the judicial investigation that has taken place since, there were eighty-two thieves in that workshop, including Claude.

Once the guards had left them on their own, Claude climbed on to his workbench and announced to the entire assembly that he had something to say. Silence fell.

Then Claude raised his voice and said, 'You know that Albin was my brother. I don't get enough of what they give me to eat here. Even buying nothing but bread with the little I earn, there would not be enough. Albin shared his ration with me. I loved him at first because he fed me, then because he loved me. The director, Monsieur D, separated us. It did him no harm that we should be together, but he is a wicked man who gets pleasure from inflicting torment. I asked him to return Albin. You saw, he refused. I gave him until the 4th of November to give Albin back to me. He put me in the punishment cell for saying that. During that time, I passed judgement on him and I have condemned him to death. Today is the 4th of November. In two hours' time he will come by on his round. I warn you, I am going to kill him. Have you anything to say about that?'

They all remained silent.

Claude continued. He spoke, apparently, with remarkable eloquence, which incidentally was natural to him. He declared he was well aware he was going to commit a violent deed, but he did not think it was wrong of him to do so. He called on the consciences of the eighty-one thieves listening to him to bear witness:

that he was in dire straits;

that the need to take the law into your own hands was a dead end you sometimes found yourself committed to pursuing;

that in truth he could not take the director's life without giving up his own, but he considered it worthwhile to give his life for a just cause;

that he had thought long and hard about it, and about nothing else, for the last two months;

that he genuinely thought he was not allowing himself to be carried away by resentment, but if such were the case, he begged to be told;

that he honestly submitted his reasons to the just men listening to him;

that he was therefore going to kill Monsieur D, but if anyone had any objection to raise, he was ready to listen.

Only one voice spoke up and said that before killing the director Claude should try one last time to speak to him and to persuade him to change his mind.

'That is fair,' said Claude, 'and I will do so.'

Eight o'clock struck by the big clock. The director was due to come by at nine.

Once this strange supreme court of appeal had as it were ratified the sentence he had passed, Claude regained all his serenity. He laid on a table everything he possessed by way of linen and clothes, the prisoner's poor remains, and summoning one by one those who were his fondest companions after Albin, he distributed everything among them. He kept only the small pair of scissors.

Then he embraced them all. A few wept. At these, he smiled.

There were, during that last hour, moments when he spoke with such equanimity and even cheerfulness that several of his friends inwardly hoped, as they later stated, he would perhaps give up his resolution. He even amused himself once by blowing out with the air from his nostril one of the few candles that lit the workshop, for he had some bad habits that intruded on his natural dignity more often than they should have done.

Nothing could prevent that former street urchin from occasionally smelling of the Paris gutter.

He noticed a young prisoner who looked pale, staring at him, and trembling, no doubt in the expectation of what he was going to see.

'Come now, young man, be brave!' Claude said to him gently. 'It will only be a matter of a moment.'

When he had distributed all his ragged clothes, said his goodbyes, shaken everyone's hand, he interrupted several anxious conversations going on here and there in dark corners of the workshop and ordered everyone back to work. They all obeyed in silence.

The workshop where this took place was an oblong room, a long parallelogram with windows in the two elongated sides and two doors, one at each end, facing each other. The machines were lined up on either side by the windows, the benches set at right angles to the wall and the empty space between the two rows of machines formed a kind of long aisle leading, in a straight line from one door to the other, right across the room. It was this long, rather narrow passageway the director had to walk through as he carried out his inspection. He had to enter from the south door and leave by the north door, having checked over the workers to left and right. Usually he passed through quite quickly and without stopping.

Claude had returned to his bench, and continued working as Jacques Clément might have continued praying.

Everyone was waiting. It was getting nearer the time. All of a sudden the sound of a bell was heard.

Claude said, 'It's a quarter to.'

Then he rose, solemnly walked across part of the room, and went to lean on the corner of the first machine on the left, right next to the entrance. His face was perfectly calm and benign.

Nine o'clock struck. The door opened. The director entered.

At that moment a silence, as of statues, fell on the workshop.

The director was alone as usual.

He came in with that jovial, self-satisfied and intransigent look on his face, did not see Claude who was standing to the left of the door with his right hand hidden in his trousers, and swiftly walked past the first machines, shaking his head, muttering and casting a casual glance here and there, without noticing all eyes around him were fixed on a terrible thought.

All of a sudden he turned round abruptly, surprised to hear a footstep behind him. It was Claude, who had been following him in silence for a few moments.

'What are you doing there?' said the director. 'Why aren't you at your bench?'

For a man is no longer a man in that place, he is a dog, and treated as such.

Claude Gueux replied respectfully. 'I need to talk to you, sir.'

'About what?'

'About Albin.'

'Again!' said the director.

'Still!' said Claude.

'What?' replied the director, walking on. 'Twenty-four hours of the punishment cell wasn't enough for you, then?'

Claude answered while continuing to follow him. 'Sir, give me back my friend.'

'Impossible!'

'Sir,' said Claude in a voice that would have softened the devil, 'I beg you, put Albin back with me, you'll see how well I shall work. To you who are free, it makes no difference, you don't know what a friend is; but I have only the four walls of my prison. You can come and go. I have only Albin. Give him back to me. Albin provided me with food, as you well know. It would cost you only the trouble of saying yes. What difference does it make to you whether a man called Claude Gueux and another called Albin are in the same room? For it is no more complicated than that. Sir, my good sir, I beg you, truly, in the name of heaven!'

Claude had probably never said so much at any one time to any prison guard. After this exertion, he waited, exhausted.

The director responded with a gesture of impatience. 'Impossible. There's no more to be said. Now, don't mention it to me again. You're annoying me.'

And as he was in a hurry, he quickened his pace. Claude too. Talking to each other in this way, they had both reached the exit door. The eighty thieves watched and listened with bated breath.

Claude gently touched the director's arm.

'But at least let me know why I am condemned to death. Tell me why you have separated him from me.'

'I've already told you,' replied the director, 'because.'

And turning his back on Claude, he reached out his hand for the latch on the door.

At the director's response, Claude had taken a step back. The eighty statues who were there saw his right hand appear from his trousers holding the axe. This hand rose and before the director could utter a cry, three blows of the axe, terrible to relate, all three delivered in the same cleft, had split open his skull. As he fell backwards a fourth blow gashed his face. Then, as unleashed fury does not stop short, Claude Gueux gouged his right thigh with a pointless fifth blow. The director was dead.

Then Claude threw down the axe and cried, 'Now for the other!' The other was himself. He was seen to draw from his jacket the small pair of scissors that had belonged to his 'wife', and without anyone thinking to prevent him, he plunged them into his breast. The wool was thin, his breast deep. He delved in his breast at length and more than a dozen times shouting, 'Heart of one who is damned, shall I not find you!' And at last, covered in his own blood, he fell in a faint on the dead man.

Which of the two was the victim of the other?

When Claude regained consciousness, he was in a bed, covered with linen and bandages, the object of care and attention. He had Sisters of Charity at his bedside and also an investigating magistrate who was compiling a report and who asked him with considerable interest, 'How are you?'

He had lost a great deal of blood, but the scissors he had with touching superstition used to strike himself had done their job badly. None of the blows he had inflicted on himself was dangerous. The only blows fatal for him were those he had inflicted on Monsieur D.

The interrogation began. He was asked if it was he who had killed the director of workshops of Clairvaux prison. He replied, 'Yes.' He was asked why. He replied, 'Because.'

However, at a certain point, his wounds became infected. He was taken with a bad fever of which he almost died.

November, December, January and February passed, in nursing and in preparations. Doctors and magistrates gathered round Claude; the former mended his wounds, the latter erected his scaffold.

Let us be brief. On 16 March 1832, having fully recovered, he appeared before the court of assizes at Troyes. As large a crowd as ever the town could muster was there.

Claude demonstrated the right attitude towards the court. He had shaved with care, he was bare-headed, he wore that drab uniform of Clairvaux prisoners, of two different shades of grey.

The crown prosecutor had packed the courtroom with all the bayonettes in the district, 'in order,' he told the hearing, 'to contain all the villains who were to appear as witnesses in this affair.'

When it came to opening the proceedings an exceptional difficulty arose. Not one of the witnesses to the events of the 4th of November wanted to testify against Claude. The presiding judge threatened them with his discretionary power. This was to no avail. Claude then ordered them to testify. Every tongue was loosened. They stated what they had seen.

Claude listened to them with close attention. When one of them, through forgetfulness, or out of affection for Claude, omitted some facts that weighed against the accused, Claude re-established them. From testimony to testimony, the series of facts we have just laid out was disclosed before the court.

There was a moment when the women present wept. The court bailiff summoned the prisoner Albin. It was his turn to testify. He entered unsteadily. He was sobbing. The police could not prevent him from going and falling into Claude's arms. Claude held him and said with a smile to the crown prosecutor, 'This is a villain who shares his bread with those who are hungry.' Then he kissed Albin's hand.

Having exhausted the list of witnesses, the crown prosecutor rose and spoke in these terms: 'Gentlemen of the jury, society would be shaken to its foundations if the state did not prosecute great criminals like the one who, etc.'

After this memorable speech, Claude's lawyer spoke. The case for the prosecution and the case for the defence, each in turn, followed the pattern they usually do in this kind of arena that is called a criminal trial.

Claude did not believe everything had been said. He in turn rose. He spoke in such a way that an intelligent person attending that hearing was left amazed by it.

It seemed this poor labourer was in the nature of an orator rather than a murderer. He stood to speak, in a voice that carried and was well controlled, with a clear, honest and resolute look in his eye, adopting a stance that was almost always the same, but full of authority. He told things as they were, simply, seriously, without exaggeration or attenuation, admitted to everything, faced up to article 296, and laid his head under it. He had moments of truly remarkable eloquence that stirred the crowd, and where what he had just said was repeated in whispers among the audience.

This caused a murmur during which Claude would catch his breath, casting a proud glance over those attending the trial.

At times, this man who could not read was restrained, polite, decorous, like an educated man, then, at other moments, modest, measured, attentive, going step by step through the contentious part of his argument, respectful towards the judges. Only once did he give way to an outburst of anger. The crown prosecutor had established in the speech we have cited in its entirety that Claude Gueux had murdered the director of workshops without assault or violence on the director's part, consequently without provocation.

'What!' cried Claude. 'I was not provoked! Ah, yes, indeed, that is true, I understand you. A drunken man thumps me, I kill him, I've been provoked, you spare me, you sentence me to hard labour. But a man who is not drunk and is in full possession of his senses oppresses me for four years, humiliates for four years, goads me with a pinprick in some unexpected place every day, every hour, every minute, for four years! I had a wife for whom I stole, he tortures me with that wife. I had a child for whom I stole, he tortures me with that child. I haven't enough bread, a friend gives me some, he takes away my friend and my bread. I ask for my friend back, he puts me in the punishment cell. I address him, a police informer, respectfully, he treats me with incivility. I tell him I am suffering, he tells me I am annoying him. So what do you expect me to do? I kill him. That's right, I am a monster, I killed that man, I was not provoked, you cut off my head. Do what you will.'

A sublime intervention, in our opinion, that suddenly raised, over and above the system of physical provocation, on which rests the ill-proportioned scaffold of attenuating circumstances, an entire theory of moral provocation, overlooked by the law.

The cases for and against having been made, the presiding judge then delivered his impartial and illuminating summing-up. It amounted to this. A reprehensible life. A monster indeed. Claude Gueux had begun by living in sin with a prostitute, then he had stolen, then he had killed. All this was true.

As he was about to send the members of the jury to their deliberation room, the presiding judge asked the accused if he had anything to say about the questions the jury had been asked to consider.

'Very little,' said Claude. 'Yet there is this. I am a thief and a murderer. I have stolen and killed. But why did I steal? Why did I kill? Ask these two questions alongside the others, gentlemen of the jury.'

After a quarter of an hour's deliberation, the twelve citizens of Champagne appointed gentlemen of the jury delivered their verdict. Claude Gueux was condemned to death.

There is no doubt that from the very opening of the trial, several of them had noticed the name of the accused was Gueux, which had made a deep impression on them.*

The judgement was read out to Claude. All he said was, 'Fair enough. But why did this man steal? Why did this man kill? Those are two questions they have not answered.'

Back in prison, he was cheerful at supper and said, 'That's thirty-six years clocked up!'

---

* Translator's note: *gueux* meaning 'beggar'

He did not want to take his case to the court of appeal. One of the nuns who had nursed him came in tears begging him to do so. For her sake, he appealed. It seems he resisted until the very last moment, because when he signed his application in the court of appeal register the legal time limit of three days had expired by a few minutes.

The poor grateful woman gave him five francs. He took the money and thanked her.

While his appeal was pending, the prisoners at Troyes all did what they could to offer him a chance of escape. He refused.

Through the air vent into his cell the inmates threw in succession a nail, a piece of wire and a bucket handle. Each of these three tools would have been sufficient, to a man as intelligent as Claude, to file through his chains. He handed over to the warder the handle, the wire and the nail.

On 8 June 1832, seven months and four days after the event, expiation came, *pede claudo*, as can be seen. That day, at seven in the morning, the court clerk entered Claude's cell, and told him he had no more than an hour to live.

His appeal had been rejected.

'Well,' said Claude coldly, 'I slept well last night, having no idea I would sleep even better tonight.'

It seems the words of strong men must always acquire a certain grandeur from the approach of death.

The priest arrived, then the executioner. Claude was humble with the priest, meek with the other. He refused neither his soul nor his body.

He retained a perfect independence of mind. While his hair was being cut, someone in a corner of the cell spoke of the cholera threat to Troyes at that time.

'For myself,' said Claude with a smile, 'I have no fear of cholera.'

And he listened to the priest with the utmost attention, berating himself a great deal and regretting that he had not been instructed in religion.

At his request the scissors with which he had stabbed himself were returned to him. They had a blade missing, which had broken in his chest. He asked the prison guard to convey these scissors to Albin on his behalf. He also said he wanted to add to this legacy the ration of bread he should have eaten that day.

He asked those who tied his hands to put in his right hand the five-franc coin the nun had given him, which was the only thing he had left.

At a quarter to eight, he left the prison, with the whole grim entourage that ordinarily accompanies condemned prisoners. He was on foot, pale, his eyes fixed on the priest's crucifix, but walking steadily.

That day had been chosen for the execution because it was a market day, so there would be as many as possible watching as he went by. For apparently there are still half-savage towns in France where, when society kills a man, it gloats on it.

He climbed the scaffold solemnly, his eye still fixed on Christ's gibbet. He wanted to kiss the priest, then the executioner, thanking the one, pardoning the other. According to one report the executioner gently pushed him away. When the assistant bound him to the hideous contraption, Claude signalled to the priest to take the five-franc coin he held in his right hand, and said to him, 'For the poor.'

As eight o'clock was striking just at that moment, the noise from the belfry drowned his voice and the confessor told him he could not hear. Claude waited for the interval between two strokes and quietly repeated, 'For the poor.'

The eighth stroke had not yet sounded when this noble and intelligent head had fallen.

What a wonderful effect public executions have! That same day, the guillotine still unwashed and standing there among them, the people in the market rioted over some matter of taxation and almost murdered an employee of the municipal tax office. What gentle folk these laws create!

We believed it to be our duty to recount in detail the story of Claude Gueux because in our opinion every paragraph of this story might serve as a chapter heading for a book in which the great nineteenth-century problem of the people would be resolved.

In this significant life there are two main phases: before the fall, and after the fall; and within these two phases, two questions: the question of education, and the question of penal sanctions; and between these two questions, society as a whole.

This man was certainly of good disposition, good constitution, good potential. What then did he lack? Reflect on it.

Herein lies the great problem of proportion to which the solution, yet to be found, will lead to universal equilibrium: whereby society should always do as much for the individual as nature. Look at Claude Gueux. Sound of heart and mind, undoubtedly. But fate puts him in a society so badly organized, he ends up by stealing. Society puts him in a prison so badly organized, he ends up by killing.

Who is really guilty?

Is it him?

Is it us?

Harsh questions, painful questions, that at this time importune all intelligent minds, that tug at the coat-tails of all of us, such as we are, and that will one day so completely bar our way we shall have to face up to them and find out what they want of us.

He who writes these lines will soon perhaps try to explain how he understands them.

When you are in the presence of such facts, when you reflect how these questions press themselves upon us, you wonder what those who govern are thinking about if they are not thinking about this.

The Chambers of government are seriously occupied every year. It is no doubt very important to reduce sinecures and trim the budget. It is very important to pass laws that require me to go, dressed up as a soldier, and patriotically mount guard at the gate of Monsieur le Comte de Lobau, whom I do not know and do not wish to know; or that compel me to parade on Marigny Square, subject to the good pleasure of my greengrocer's will, he having been appointed my officer.*

It is important, deputies or ministers, to grind down and pull to bits in totally abortive discussions everything about this country and all its ideas. It is essential, for instance, to put in the dock and interrogate and cross-question in full cry, without knowing what you are talking about, the art of the nineteenth century, that noble and austere defendant that does not deign to reply, and does well not to. It is expedient to spend your time, rulers and legislators, in lectures about the classical that make schoolmasters

---

* It goes without saying it is not our intent here to attack the municipal patrol, a useful thing, that protects our streets, houses and homes; but only the parade, the pompom, the vainglory and military hoo-ha, ridiculous things, that serve only to turn the citizen into a parody of a soldier.

outside the city shrug their shoulders. It is useful to declare it is modern drama that invented incest, adultery, patricide, infanticide and poisoning, and to prove thereby you are unfamiliar with Phaedra, Jocasta, Oedipus, Medea, Rodogune. It is indispensable that the political orators of this country should for three whole days, in the context of the budget, put up a fight, against whom no one knows, in defence of Corneille and Racine, and take advantage of this literary occasion to outdo each other in plunging deep into the ravine of terrible mistakes of French grammar.

All this is important. However, we believe there could be things of even greater importance.

What would the Chamber say, in the midst of the futile squabbles that so often lead to the government being caught out by the opposition and the opposition by the government, if, all of a sudden, from the benches in the Chamber or in the public gallery, what does it matter which, someone got up and spoke these serious words:

'Silence, whoever you are, you who are speaking here, silence! You think you are addressing the issue, you are not.

'The issue is this: the judicial system, barely a year ago, in Pamiers, hacked a man to death with a pocket knife. In Dijon, it has just torn off a woman's head. In Paris, it is carrying out executions at the Barrière Saint-Jacques in secret.

'This is the issue. Occupy yourselves with this.

'You can argue among yourselves afterwards whether the National Guard should have white or yellow buttons, and whether "confidence" is a finer thing than "certainty".

'Gentlemen of the centres, gentlemen of the left or the right, the mass of people are suffering. Whether you call it republic or whether you call it monarchy, the people are suffering, this is a fact.

'The people are hungry, the people are cold. Poverty drives them to crime or to vice, depending on their sex. Have pity on the people, from whom prison takes their sons and the brothel takes their daughters. You have too many convicts, you have too many prostitutes.

'What do these two cancers prove?

'That the body politic has blood poisoning.

'There you are, gathered in consultation at the patient's bedside: treat the illness.

'This illness, you are treating badly. Study it better. The laws you make, when you make any, are no more than palliatives and expedients. Half your legislation is routine, the other half empiricism.

'Branding was a cauterization that made the wound gangrenous. What an insane penalty that stamped the crime on the criminal and shackled them together! Making them two friends, two inseparable companions!

'Penal servitude is an absurd vesicatory that allows almost all the bad blood it extracts to be reabsorbed, not without having poisoned it even more.

'Now, branding, penal servitude, the death penalty are three things that go together. You have abolished branding. If you are logical, abolish the rest.

'The branding iron, the shackles and the guillotine were three parts of a syllogism. You have removed the branding iron. The shackles and the guillotine no longer make any sense. Farinacci was terrible; but he was not absurd.

'Dismantle this rickety old ladder of crime and punishment, and remake it. Remake your penal system, remake your codes, remake your prisons, remake your judges. Bring the laws back in line with moral decency.

'Gentlemen, too many heads are cut off every year in France. Since you are in the process of making economies, make some there.

'Since you are keen to make cut-backs, cut back on the executioner. With the salaries of your eighty executioners, you will pay for six hundred schoolmasters.

'Think of the mass of people. Schools for the children, workshops for the men.

'Do you know, France is one of the countries of Europe with the smallest proportion of the native population that can read! What! Switzerland can read, Belgium can read, Denmark can read, Greece can read, Ireland can read, and France cannot read? This is a disgrace.

'Go into the prisons. Have all the convicts gather round you. Examine one by one all these men made outcasts by human law. Calculate the angle of all these profiles, feel all these skulls. Under the skin each of these fallen men has his bestial type. In every one of them there seems to be a point of intersection between this or that animal species and humankind. Here is the lynx, here is the cat, here is the monkey, here is the vulture, here is the hyena. Now, for these poor ill-shaped heads, nature is doubtless the first to blame, and education the second.

'Nature made a bad preliminary model, education worked on that model badly. Turn your attention in that direction. A good education for the people. Do your best to develop these unfortunate heads, so the intelligence within them might increase.

'Nations have well-shaped or ill-shaped skulls depending on their institutions.

'Rome and Greece had high foreheads. Open the facial angle of the people as much as you can.

'When France is able to read, do not leave directionless that intelligence you will have developed. That would be another disorder. Ignorance is still better than ill-guided knowledge.

'No. Remember, there is a book more philosophical than *Le Compère Mathieu*, more popular than *Le Constitutionnel*, more eternal than the Charter of 1830. That book is Holy Scripture. And here a word of explanation.

Whatever you do, the fate of the masses, the multitude, the majority will always be relatively poor and miserable and unfortunate. To them falls the hard work, the loads to push, the loads to drag, the loads to carry.

'Look at this balance: all the pleasures in the rich man's pan, all the miseries in the poor man's pan. Are not the two parts unequal? Must not the balance inevitably tip to one side, and the state with it?

'And now in the poor man's lot, in the pan of miseries, throw the certainty of a heavenly future, throw the aspiration to eternal happiness, throw paradise, a magnificent counterweight! You restore the balance. The poor man's share is as rich as the rich man's.

'This is something Jesus knew, and he knew more about this than Voltaire.

'Give to the people, who labour and suffer, give to the people, for whom this world is harsh, the belief there is a better world made for them.

'They will be quiet, they will be patient. Patience is made of hope.

'Sow the villages, then, with the gospels. One bible to every cottage. Let every book and every field between them produce a virtuous worker.

'The man of the people's head, that is the issue. This head is full of useful seed. To enable it to mature and fulfil its potential, use what is most illuminating and most steeped in virtue.

'He who has been a highway murderer, if better guided might have been the city's most excellent servant.

'This man of the people's head, cultivate it, weed it, water it, fertilize it, enlighten it, instruct it, use it. You will not need to cut it off.

Translated by Christine Donougher

PROSPER MÉRIMÉE

The Venus of Ille

"Ἵλεως ἦν δ' ἐγώ, ἔστω. ὁ ἀνδριὰς
καὶ ἤπιος, οὕτως ἀνδρεῖος ὤν.'

ΛΟΥΚΙΑΝΟΥ ΦΙΛΟΨΕΥΔΗΣ

I was descending the final slope of Mount Canigou, and although the sun
had already set, on the plain I could make out the houses of the little town
of Ille, which was my destination.

'I don't suppose you know where Monsieur de Peyrehorade lives?'
I asked the Catalan who had been acting as my guide since the
previous day.

'Why, of course I do!' he exclaimed. 'I know his house as well as I know
my own. If it weren't so dark I'd point it out to you. It's the finest house
in Ille. He's a rich man, is Monsieur de Peyrehorade, and he's marrying
his son to a girl who's wealthier still.'

'And is this marriage to take place soon?' I asked him.

'Soon! I daresay they've already hired the musicians for the wedding
feast. Perhaps this evening, or tomorrow or the day after, I couldn't say.
The wedding's taking place at Puygarrig, because it's Mademoiselle de
Puygarrig that young Monsieur de Peyrehorade is marrying. Oh yes, it
will be a grand occasion!'

I had been given an introduction to Monsieur de Peyrehorade by my
friend Monsieur de P—. He was, my friend had told me, a most erudite
antiquary, and infinitely obliging. He would be delighted to show me all
the ruins for ten leagues around. I had been counting on him to give me
a conducted tour of the country around Ille, which I knew to be rich in

ancient and medieval monuments. This marriage, which I was now hearing of for the first time, looked like upsetting all my plans.

I'm going to be in everybody's way, I said to myself. But I was expected; now that my arrival had been announced by Monsieur de P—, I would have to present myself.

'I'll bet you, sir,' my guide said to me as we came onto the plain, 'I'll bet you a cigar I can guess what you're going to do at Monsieur de Peyrehorade's.'

'Why, that's not very hard to guess,' I said, offering him a cigar. 'At this time of day, after a six-league trek over Mount Canigou, supper is the main item on the agenda.'

'Yes, but what about tomorrow? – Come on, I'll lay odds you've come to Ille to see the idol. I guessed as much when I saw you drawing those pictures of the saints at Serrabona.'

'Idol! What idol?' The word had aroused my curiosity.

'Why, didn't they tell you in Perpignan how Monsieur de Peyrehorade came to unearth an idol?'

'An earthen idol? Do you mean a terracotta statue, one made out of clay?'

'No, no, a real copper one. It must be worth a packet, weighs as much as a church bell. We found her deep in the ground, at the foot of an olive tree.'

'Were you present at the discovery, then?'

'Yes, sir. A fortnight ago, Monsieur de Peyrehorade told us, me and Jean Coll, to grub out an old olive tree which had caught the frost last year, for it was a hard winter, you know. So there was Jean Coll going at it for all he was worth, takes a swing with his pick, and I heard this "dong", as if he'd struck a bell. "What's that?" I says. So we dug and dug, and gradually this black hand appears, like a dead man's hand reaching up out of the ground. So then I got frightened, I went off to monsieur, and I said to him: "Dead men, master, under the olive tree. Better call the priest!" "What dead men?" he says to me. He came, took one look at the hand, and exclaimed, "An antiquity, an antiquity!" Anyone would have thought he'd found treasure. And there he was, digging away with the pick and with his hands, working almost as hard as the two of us put together.'

'And what did you eventually find?'

'A great black woman, more than half naked, begging your pardon, sir; solid copper, and Monsieur de Peyrehorade told us it was an idol from pagan times – you know, from the time of Charlemagne!'

'I see. Some bronze Virgin plundered from a convent.'

'A Virgin? Oh, dear me, no! I'd soon have recognized it if it had been a Virgin. It's an idol, I tell you – you can tell from the look of her. She looks at you with these big white eyes of hers . . . it's as if she was staring at you. You can't look her in the eyes.'

'White eyes? No doubt they are embedded in the bronze. It sounds as if it may be a Roman statue.'

'Roman, that's it! Monsieur de Peyrehorade says it's a Roman lady. Ah! I can see you're a scholar like him!'

'Is it intact, in a good state of preservation?'

'Oh, there's nothing missing, sir! It's a lovely bit of work, even better than the painted plaster bust of Louis-Philippe in the town hall. All the same, I don't like the look of her. She looks vicious . . . and what's more, she is, too.'

'Vicious? Has she done you any harm?'

'Not me exactly. But let me tell you. We was trying for all we was worth to get her upright, Monsieur de Peyrehorade too, he was pulling on the rope as well, though he's got no more strength than a chicken, bless him! After a lot of heaving we got her upright. I was picking up a bit of tile to wedge her with when, crash! down she went flat on her back again. "Watch out!" I said. Not quick enough, though, because Jean Coll didn't have time to get his leg out of the way.'

'And was he hurt?'

'Why, his poor leg was snapped clean through like a vine-prop. Poor lad, when I saw what had happened I was livid. I was all set to smash up the idol with my pick, but Monsieur de Peyrehorade held me back. He gave Jean Coll some money, but all the same he's still in bed a fortnight after it happened, and the doctor says he'll never walk as well on that leg as on the other. It's a shame, he was our best runner and, apart from Monsieur de Peyrehorade's son, the best *pelota* player. Young master Alphonse was proper upset about it, because Coll and him, they used to play against one another. What a sight it was to see them returning the balls – thump! thump! they never touched the ground.'

Discoursing in this vein we entered Ille, and I soon found myself in the company of Monsieur de Peyrehorade. He was a little old man, still hale and hearty, powdered, red-nosed, and with a jovial, bantering manner. Before he had even had time to read Monsieur de P—'s letter, he had sat me down at a generously spread table and had introduced me to his wife and son as a distinguished archaeologist who was destined to rescue Roussillon from the oblivion to which scientific indifference had condemned it.

While tucking in with zest, for nothing whets the appetite better than the keen mountain air, I was studying my hosts. I have already said a word about Monsieur de Peyrehorade. I should add that he was vivacity personified. He was constantly talking, eating, getting up, running to his library, bringing me books, showing me etchings, pouring me wine; he was never still for two minutes. His wife, who was rather too plump, like most Catalan women over the age of forty, struck me as an out-and-out provincial, totally absorbed in running her household. Although there was enough supper for at least six people, she ran to the kitchen, ordered pigeons to be killed and maize cakes fried, and opened I don't know how many pots of preserves. In a moment the table was laden with dishes and bottles, and I should certainly have died of indigestion if I had so much as tasted everything I was offered. However, with each dish I refused there were renewed apologies. They were afraid I should not be comfortable in Ille. Resources are so limited in the provinces, and Parisians are so hard to please!

Amid his parents' comings and goings, Monsieur Alphonse de Peyrehorade sat motionless like a Roman *Terminus*. He was a tall young man of twenty-six, whose features were fine and regular but somewhat expressionless. His athletic figure and build certainly bore out the reputation he enjoyed locally of being an indefatigable *pelota* player. That evening he was dressed elegantly, exactly in the style illustrated in the latest number of the *Journal des modes*. But he seemed to me to be inconvenienced by his clothes; he was as stiff as a peg in his velvet collar, and moved his whole body as he turned. His large, sunburned hands and short nails contrasted strangely with his attire: they were the hands of a ploughman emerging from the sleeves of a dandy. Furthermore, although he scrutinized me keenly on account of my Parisian credentials, he spoke to me only once in the course of the evening, and that was to ask me where I had bought my watch chain.

'Well now, my dear guest,' Monsieur de Peyrehorade said to me as supper drew to an end, 'I have you at my mercy. You are in my house, and I'll not let you go until you've seen all the curiosities our mountains have to offer. You must get to know our Roussillon, and you must do it justice. You can't imagine how much there is to show you. Phoenician, Celtic, Roman, Arab and Byzantine monuments – you will see everything from the cedar tree to the hyssop. I shall take you everywhere, and I shall not spare you a single brick.'

A fit of coughing obliged him to break off. I took this opportunity to tell him that I should be sorry to inconvenience him at a time of such significance for his family. If he would be so good as to give me the benefit of his excellent advice on what excursions I should make, then, without putting him to the trouble of accompanying me, I should be able . . .

'Ah! You're referring to that boy's wedding,' he exclaimed, interrupting me. 'A mere trifle. It will be all over two days hence. You shall celebrate with us, as one of the family. The bride-to-be is in mourning for an aunt who died leaving her all her money, so there will be no reception, no ball. A pity, you'd have been able to see our Catalan girls dancing. They are pretty, and perhaps you would have felt like taking a leaf out of Alphonse's book. One marriage, they say, leads to another . . . On Saturday, once the young couple are married, I shall be free, and we'll begin our excursions. I must ask your pardon for inflicting a provincial wedding on you. For a Parisian, bored with parties . . . and a wedding without a ball, at that! However, you will see a bride . . . What shall I say? – you will be delighted with her. But then you are a serious-minded man, you're not interested in women any more. I've got better things to show you. Wait till you see the fine surprise I've got up my sleeve to show you tomorrow.'

'Upon my word,' I said, 'it's not easy to have a treasure in one's house without everyone getting to hear about it. I think I can guess the surprise you have in store for me. But if it's your statue we're talking about, the description my guide gave me of it has only served to arouse my curiosity and to predispose me to admire it'

'Ah! He told you about the idol – for that's what they call my beautiful Venus Tur . . . – but I shan't say another word. Tomorrow you shall see her in daylight, and then you can tell me whether I am justified in considering her a masterpiece. To be sure, you couldn't have arrived at a better moment! There are some inscriptions which, ignorant as I am, I have interpreted to the best of my ability. But perhaps you, a scholar from Paris, will laugh at my interpretation, for the fact is, I have written a monograph. I, your humble servant, an elderly provincial antiquary, have put pen to paper . . . I want to make the presses groan. If you would be so good as to read and amend what I have written, I might hope . . . For example, I am very curious to know how you will construe this inscription on the pedestal: *CAVE* . . . – but I shall ask you nothing yet! Tomorrow, tomorrow! Not another word about the Venus today!'

'You are right not to keep going on about your idol, Peyrehorade,' said his wife. 'Can't you see you are preventing monsieur from eating? Why, he has seen much more beautiful statues than yours in Paris. At the Tuileries there are dozens of them, bronze ones, too.'

'Such is the ignorance, the blessed ignorance of the provinces!' Monsieur de Peyrehorade interrupted. 'Fancy comparing a marvel of antiquity with Coustou's lifeless figures!'

> With what irreverence
> My wife doth speak of the gods!

'Do you know, my wife wanted me to melt down my statue to make a bell for our church. She would have been the sponsor, you see. A masterpiece by Myron, sir!'

'Masterpiece? Masterpiece? A fine masterpiece she is, breaking a man's leg!'

'I tell you, my dear,' said Monsieur de Peyrehorade resolutely, extending towards her a right leg clad in shot silk, 'if my Venus had broken this leg of mine, I would not regret it.'

'Good heavens, Peyrehorade, how can you say such a thing! Fortunately the man is recovering . . . Even so, I can't bring myself to look at a statue that does such wicked things. Poor Jean Coll!'

'Wounded by Venus, sir,' said Monsieur de Peyrehorade with a hearty laugh. 'Wounded by Venus, and the rascal complains.

Veneris nec praemia noris.

'Which of us has not been wounded by Venus?'

Monsieur Alphonse, whose French was better than his Latin, gave a knowing wink, and looked at me as if to say: 'And you, Parisian, do you understand?'

Supper finished. It was an hour since I had eaten anything. I was tired, and I could not manage to stifle my frequent yawns. Madame de Peyrehorade was the first to notice the fact, and observed that it was time to go to bed. At this they again began to apologize for the poor accommodation I was going to have. It would not be like Paris. There are so few comforts in the provinces. I must show indulgence towards the people of Roussillon. In vain did I protest that after a journey through the mountains I would be delighted with a heap of straw for a bed; they continued to beg me to forgive poor countryfolk if they did not treat me as well as they would have wished. At last I went up to the room that had been prepared for me, accompanied by Monsieur de Peyrehorade. The staircase, whose upper flight was of wood, ended in a corridor extending to either side, with several bedrooms opening onto it.

'To your right,' my host said to me, 'are the rooms I am setting apart for the future Madame Alphonse. Your bedroom is at the end of the other corridor. Of course,' he added, doing his best to sound discreet, 'you realize that newlyweds must have privacy. You are at one end of the house, they are at the other.'

We entered a well-appointed bedroom, in which the first object that caught my eye was a bed seven feet long, six feet wide, and so high that one needed a stepladder to hoist oneself into it. After showing me where to find the bell, checking for himself that the sugar bowl was full and that the flasks of eau de cologne had been duly placed on the washstand, and asking me several times if I needed anything, my host wished me goodnight and left me alone.

The windows were shut. Before undressing I opened one of them so as to breathe in the fresh night air which, after that long supper, seemed delicious. Opposite lay Mount Canigou, a magnificent sight in any weather, but which that evening, by the light of a resplendent moon, seemed to me the most beautiful mountain in the world. I stood for a few minutes contemplating its marvellous outline, and was about to close my window when, lowering my eyes, I noticed the statue on a pedestal about a hundred yards from the house. It stood at one corner of a quick-set hedge separating a little garden from a large square of perfectly level ground which, I later learned, was the town *pelota* court. This ground, which was the property of Monsieur de Peyrehorade, had been made over by him to the community, in response to insistent demands by his son.

At that distance it was hard for me to make out the appearance of the statue; I could only judge its height, which seemed to me to be around six feet. At that moment two local lads were crossing the *pelota* court, quite near the hedge, whistling the pretty Roussillon tune *Montagnes régalades*. They stopped to look at the statue; one of them even addressed it in a loud voice. He spoke in Catalan, but I had been in Roussillon long enough to be able to get the gist of what he said.

'So there you are, you hussy!' (the Catalan term was stronger). 'There you are!' he said. 'So it's you that broke Jean Coll's leg! If you were mine I'd break your neck.'

'Huh! What with?' said the other. 'She's made of copper, and it's so hard that Étienne broke his file trying to cut into her. It's copper from pagan times, and harder than I don't know what.'

'If I had my cold chisel' (apparently he was a locksmith's apprentice) 'I'd soon gouge those big white eyes out for her, like prising almonds out of their shells. There's more than a hundred sous' worth of silver in them.'

They began to walk away.

'I must just say goodnight to the idol,' said the taller of the two apprentices, stopping suddenly.

He bent down, and doubtless picked up a stone. I could see him straighten an arm, then throw something, and immediately the bronze emitted a resonant note. At the same moment the apprentice put his hand to his head and uttered a cry of pain.

'She threw it back at me!' he exclaimed.

And the two young lads took to their heels. Evidently the stone had rebounded off the metal and punished the rascal for this act of sacrilege against the goddess.

I shut the window, laughing heartily.

'Another vandal punished by Venus. May all destroyers of our ancient monuments get their heads broken in the same way!' On this charitable thought, I fell asleep.

It was broad daylight when I woke. At one side of my bed stood Monsieur de Peyrehorade, in his dressing gown; at the other, a servant sent by his wife, holding a cup of chocolate in his hand.

'Come on, Parisian, up we get! How lazy they are in the capital!' my host was saying as I dressed hastily. 'Eight o'clock and still in bed. I've been up since six. This is the third time I've come upstairs. I tiptoed to your door: nothing stirring, no sign of life. It's not good for you to sleep so much at your age. And you haven't even seen my Venus yet! Quick, drink this cup of Barcelona chocolate, it's real contraband . . . You won't get chocolate like that in Paris. Get your strength up, for once you are standing before my Venus we won't be able to tear you away.'

In five minutes I was ready: that is to say, half-shaved, ill-buttoned, and burned by the scalding chocolate I had gulped down. I went down into the garden and found myself looking at a splendid statue.

It was indeed a Venus, and a marvellously beautiful one. The upper part of her body was naked, as was customary among the ancients when depicting great divinities. Her right hand was raised to the level of her breast, with the palm turned inwards, the thumb and first two fingers extended, and the other two slightly bent. The other hand, held near her hip, supported the drapery that covered the lower part of her body. The attitude of the statue recalled that of the *Mora Player*, which for some reason or other is known as *Germanicus*. Perhaps someone had wanted to portray the goddess playing the game of *mora*.

Be that as it may, nothing could be more perfect than the body of that Venus; nothing softer or more voluptuous than her contours; nothing more elegant or more noble than her drapery. I had been expecting some work of the Lower Empire; what I saw was a masterpiece from the finest period of statuary. What especially struck me was the exquisite truth of the forms, so perfect that one could have thought them moulded from nature, had nature ever produced such models.

The hair, brushed up from the brow, seemed at one time to have been gilded. The head, which was small, like that of almost all Greek statues, was tilted slightly forward. As for the face, it had a strange quality which defies description, and which resembled that of no other ancient statue I can recall. It had none of that calm and severe beauty of the Greek sculptors, who systematically imparted a majestic immobility to every feature. Here, on the contrary, I observed with surprise that the artist had clearly intended to render a mischievousness bordering on the vicious. All the features were contracted slightly: the eyes a little slanting, the mouth turned up at the corners, the nostrils somewhat flared. Disdain, irony, cruelty could be read in that face, which, notwithstanding, was incredibly beautiful. The fact is, the more one looked at that admirable statue, the more one became aware of the distressing truth that such wonderful beauty could go hand in hand with a total absence of feeling.

'If ever there was a model for this statue,' I said to Monsieur de Peyrehorade, 'and I doubt that Heaven ever brought forth such a woman, how I pity her lovers! She must have delighted in letting them die of despair. There is something ferocious in her expression, and yet I have never seen anything so beautiful.'

'*C'est Vénus tout entière à sa proie attachée!*' exclaimed Monsieur de Peyrehorade, satisfied at my enthusiasm.

Her expression of diabolical irony was perhaps heightened by the contrast between the very bright eyes, of inlaid silver, and the blackish-green patina with which time had overlaid the rest of the statue. Those bright eyes produced an illusion of reality, of life. I recalled what my guide had told me, that she made those who looked at her lower their eyes. It was almost true, and I could not help being momentarily angry with myself for feeling ill at ease in the presence of this bronze figure.

'Now that you have admired everything in detail, my dear fellow student of bric-à-brac,' said my host, 'let us hold a learned colloquium. What is your view of this inscription, which you have not yet noticed?'

He was pointing at the base of the statue, on which I read these words:

CAVE AMANTEM

'*Quid dicis, doctissime?*' he asked me, rubbing his hands. 'Let's see if we can agree on the meaning of this *cave amantem*.'

'Well,' I replied, 'there are two possible meanings. One could translate it as: "Beware of him who loves you, mistrust lovers". But I don't know whether, if that were the sense, *cave amantem* would be very good Latin.

Having seen the lady's diabolical expression, I am more inclined to believe that the artist wanted to put the beholder on his guard against this terrible beauty, and I would therefore translate as follows: 'Beware if *she* loves you".'

'Hmm!' said Monsieur de Peyrehorade. 'That's a splendid meaning. But, if you'll forgive me, I prefer the first translation, on which, however, I shall elaborate. You know who was the lover of Venus?'

'She had several.'

'Yes, but the first was Vulcan. Don't you think what is meant is: "Despite all your beauty, your disdainful air, you shall have an ugly, lame blacksmith for a lover"? An object-lesson, sir, for coquettes.'

I could not suppress a smile, so far-fetched did the explanation seem to me.

'Latin is a shocking language for concision,' I observed, to avoid open disagreement with my antiquarian friend; and I stepped back a few paces so as to get a better view of the statue.

'One moment, my dear colleague,' said Monsieur de Peyrehorade, seizing me by the arm to detain me, 'you have not seen everything yet! There is another inscription. Climb onto the pedestal and look on the right arm.' As he spoke he was helping me up.

I clung rather unceremoniously to the neck of the Venus, with whom I was beginning to get on familiar terms. For a moment I even looked her boldly in the face, and from close up I found her even more vicious and even more beautiful. Then I noticed that engraved on the arm were what looked to me like some characters in ancient cursive script. With much recourse to spectacles, I spelled out the following inscription, while Monsieur de Peyrehorade repeated each word as I uttered it, with sounds and gestures of approval. What I read was:

VENERI TVRBVL . . .
EVTYCHES MYRO
IMPERIO FECIT

After the word *TVRBVL* in the first line, it looked to me as if a few letters had been worn away; but *TVRBVL* was perfectly legible.

'Meaning . . . ?' my host asked me, beaming, but with a glint of mischief in his smile, for he was quite sure that *TVRBVL* was going to give me a hard time.

'There's one word that I haven't worked out yet,' I said. 'The rest is easy. 'Eutychus Myron made this offering to Venus at her command.'

'Excellent. But *TVRBVL*, what do you make of that? What is *TVRBVL* ?'

'*TVRBVL* has me baffled. I'm racking my brains to try to find some well-known epithet for Venus that might come to my aid. Let's see, what would you say to *TVRBVLENTA* ? Venus who disturbs, who disrupts . . . As you can see, I am still preoccupied with her vicious expression. *TVRBVLENTA*, that's not too bad an epithet for Venus,' I added modestly, for I was not myself very satisfied with my explanation.

'Venus the turbulent! Venus the reveller! So you think that my Venus is a Venus of the taverns? Not a bit of it, sir, my Venus keeps good company. But now I shall explain *TVRBVL* . . . to you. Promise me one thing: not to reveal my discovery until my paper has been printed. The fact is, you see, I'm rather proud of my find . . . You must leave us poor devils in the provinces a few ears of corn to glean. You Paris scholars are so well off!'

From the top of the pedestal, on which I was still perched, I promised him solemnly that I would never stoop so low as to plagiarize his discovery.

'For *TVRBVL* . . . , sir,' he said, drawing closer and lowering his voice lest anyone other than myself should hear him, 'read *TVRBVLNERAE*.'

'I am none the wiser.'

'Listen carefully. A league from here, at the foot of the mountain, there is a village called Boulternère. The name is a corruption of the Latin word *TVRBVLNERA* – nothing is commoner than these inversions. Boulternère, sir, was a Roman city. I had always suspected as much, but I never had any proof. This is the proof I was seeking. This Venus was the local deity of the city of Boulternère; and the word Boulternère, whose ancient origin I have just demonstrated, proves something more curious still, namely, that before being a Roman city, Boulternère was a Phoenician city!'

He paused for a moment to get his breath and to enjoy my surprise. I managed to suppress a strong inclination to laugh.

'In fact,' he resumed, '*TVRBVLNERA* is pure Phoenician: *TVR*, pronounced *Tour. Tour* and *Sour* are the same word, aren't they? – "Sour" is the Phoenician name for Tyre (there's no need to remind you of the meaning). *BVL* is "Baal"; Bâl, Bel, Bul – minor differences in pronunciation. As for *NERA*, that gave me a bit of trouble. Having failed to find a Phoenician word, I am tempted to believe that it comes from the Greek *νηρός*, humid, marshy. In that case this would be a hybrid word. In order to justify *νηρός*, I will show you at Boulternère how the streams from the mountain form stagnant pools there. On the other hand, the termination *NERA* may have been added much later in honour of Nera Pivesuvia, wife of Tetricus, who may have granted some favour to the city of Turbul. But on account of the pools I prefer the derivation from *νηρός*.'

He took a pinch of snuff with a self-satisfied air.

'But enough of the Phoenicians – let's get back to the inscription. I therefore translate it: "To Venus of Boulternère Myron dedicates at her command this statue, his work".'

I took good care not to criticize his etymology, but I wanted to have a chance to show some proof of my own perceptiveness, and I said: 'Not so fast, sir. Myron dedicated something, but I certainly don't see that it need have been this statue.'

'What!' he exclaimed. 'Wasn't Myron a famous Greek sculptor? The talent must have been handed down in the family; it was one of his descendants who made this statue, nothing could be more certain.'

'But I can see a small hole on the arm,' I replied. 'I think it was for attaching something, a bracelet, for example, that this Myron offered to Venus as an expiatory gift. Myron was an unhappy lover. Venus was angry with him, and he propitiated her by dedicating a gold bracelet to her. Bear in mind that *fecit* is very often used with the meaning of *consecravit*; the terms are synonymous. I could show you more than one example if I had Gruter or Orelli to hand. It's only natural that a lover should dream of Venus, and that he should imagine her to be commanding him to give a gold bracelet to her statue. Myron dedicated a bracelet to her. Then the barbarians, or perhaps some sacrilegious thief . . .'

'Ah! How easy it is to see that you have written novels!' exclaimed my host, reaching out a hand to help me down. 'No, sir, it is a work of the school of Myron. Just look at the workmanship and you will agree.'

Having made it a rule never to persist in contradicting stubborn antiquarians, I lowered my head as if conceding defeat and said: 'It is an admirable piece.'

'Good heavens!' cried Monsieur de Peyrehorade, 'another act of vandalism! Someone has been throwing stones at my statue!'

He had just noticed a white mark a little above the breast of the Venus. I noticed a similar trace of white on the fingers of the right hand. At the time I supposed that they had been grazed by the stone in its flight, or that a fragment had broken off on impact and ricocheted onto the hand. I recounted to my host the insult I had witnessed and the prompt punishment which had been its sequel. He laughed a good deal at this, comparing the apprentice to Diomedes and expressing the wish that, like the Greek hero, he might see all his companions changed into white birds.

The bell for lunch interrupted this classical discussion, and, as on the evening before, I was obliged to eat enough for four. Then some of Monsieur de Peyrehorade's tenant farmers called by, and while he was attending to them his son took me out to see a carriage which he had bought in Toulouse for his fiancée, and for which, needless to say, I expressed admiration. Then I went with him to the stables, where he detained me for half an hour, boasting of his horses, giving me their pedigrees, and recounting to me the prizes they had won at races in the *département*. Finally, by way of a grey mare that he was reserving for her, he brought the conversation round to his bride-to-be.

'We shall see her today,' he said. 'I don't know whether you will find her pretty. You Parisians are hard to please, but everyone here and in Perpignan finds her charming. The best thing about her is that she's got lots of money. Her aunt in Prades left everything to her. Yes, I shall be very happy!'

I was deeply shocked to see a young man seemingly more moved by his bride's dowry than by her beautiful eyes.

'You know all about jewels,' Monsieur Alphonse continued. 'What do you think of this? It's the ring I shall be giving her tomorrow.'

As he spoke he drew from the first phalange of his little finger a large ring encrusted with diamonds, in the form of two interlocked hands – an allusion I found profoundly poetic. It was an ancient piece of workmanship, but I judged that the diamonds were a later addition. Inside the ring, in gothic lettering, were engraved the words *Sempr'ab ti,* that is, 'always with you'.

'It's a pretty ring,' I said. 'But these diamonds that have been added detract from its character somewhat.'

'Oh, it's much finer like that,' he replied with a smile. 'There's twelve hundred francs' worth of diamonds there. My mother gave it to me. It's a family ring, and very old – it dates from the age of chivalry. It used to be my grandmother's, and she had it from her own grandmother. Lord knows when it was made.'

'In Paris,' I said, 'it is customary to give quite a simple ring, usually composed of two different metals, such as gold and platinum. Look, that other ring, the one you've got on that finger, would be most appropriate. This one, with its diamonds and the hands in relief, is so large that you couldn't wear a glove over it.'

'Oh, Madame Alphonse will do as she sees fit. I'm sure she'll always be very pleased to own it – it's nice to have twelve hundred francs on one's finger. That little ring,' he added, looking with an air of satisfaction at the perfectly plain ring he wore on one hand, 'was given to me by a woman in Paris one Mardi Gras. Ah, what a time I had when I was in Paris two years ago! That's the place to enjoy yourself . . .' And he sighed with regret.

We were to dine that day at Puygarrig, with the bride's relatives. We got into a carriage and drove to the chateau, which was about a league and a half from Ille. I was introduced and welcomed as a friend of the family. I shall not speak of the dinner, nor of the conversation that followed, in which I took little part. Monsieur Alphonse, seated next to his bride, spoke one word in her ear every quarter of an hour. As for the bride, she scarcely raised her eyes, and each time that her fiancé spoke to her she blushed modestly but replied without embarrassment.

Mademoiselle de Puygarrig was eighteen years old; her supple and delicate figure contrasted with her robust fiancé's angular form. She was not only beautiful, but captivating. I admired the perfect spontaneity of all her responses; and her air of kindness, not without a tinge of mischief, put me involuntarily in mind of the Venus of my host. Comparing them mentally, I wondered whether the superiority in beauty that one had surely to concede to the statue was not very largely attributable to its tigress-like expression; for energy, even in evil passions, always awakens in us a feeling of astonishment and a kind of instinctive admiration.

'What a pity,' I said to myself on leaving Puygarrig, 'that such a delightful person should be rich, and that her dowry should earn her the attentions of a man so unworthy of her!'

Returning to Ille, and unsure what to say to Madame de Peyrehorade, to whom I felt it proper to address a few words now and then, I exclaimed:

'You are certainly free-thinkers down here in Roussillon! Why, madam, you are celebrating a marriage on a Friday! In Paris we would be more superstitious. No one would dare to get married on that day.'

'Goodness, don't even speak of it!' she said. 'If it had been up to me, we would certainly have chosen another day. But it's what Peyrehorade wanted, and we had to let him have his way. But it distresses me all the same. Suppose there were some misfortune? And there must be a good reason for it, for why else should everyone be afraid of Fridays?'

'Friday,' exclaimed her husband, 'is the day of Venus! A splendid day for a wedding! You see, my dear colleague, I think only of my Venus. Upon my word, it was on her account that I chose a Friday. If you like, tomorrow, before the wedding, we will make her a little sacrifice; we will sacrifice two wood pigeons, and if I knew where to get hold of some incense . . .'

'Shame on you, Peyrehorade!' interrupted his wife, utterly scandalized. 'Burning incense before an idol? That would be an abomination! Whatever would they say about us in the district?'

'At least,' said Monsieur de Peyrehorade, 'you will allow me to place a wreath of roses and lilies on her head:

Manibus date lilia plenis.

'You see, sir, the constitution is mere empty words: we do not enjoy freedom of worship!'

The arrangements for the following day were as follows: everyone was to be ready and dressed for the occasion at ten o'clock prompt. Having drunk our chocolate, we would go by carriage to Puygarrig. The civil ceremony was to take place at the village *mairie*, and the religious service at the chapel in the chateau. Next would come lunch. After lunch we would amuse ourselves as best we could until seven o'clock. At seven o'clock we would return to Ille, to Monsieur de Peyrehorade's house, where the two families were to dine together. The rest would follow as a matter of course:

as there would be no dancing, the intention was to eat as much as possible.

At eight o'clock I was already seated before the Venus, pencil in hand, beginning my twentieth attempt at drawing the statue's head, yet still not managing to capture its expression. Monsieur de Peyrehorade kept hovering around me, giving me advice, repeating to me his Phoenician etymologies; then arranging Bengal roses on the pedestal of the statue and, in tragicomic tones, addressing prayers to it for the couple who were soon to live under his roof. Around nine o'clock he went indoors to see about getting dressed, and at the same moment Monsieur Alphonse appeared, wearing a tight-fitting new dress coat, white gloves, patent leather shoes, chased buttons, and a rose in his buttonhole.

'Will you do a portrait of my wife?' he said to me, leaning over my drawing. 'She is pretty too.'

At that moment a game was beginning on the *pelota* court of which I have spoken; this at once attracted Monsieur Alphonse's attention. And, weary of drawing and despairing of ever rendering that diabolical face, I too soon went over to watch the players. Among them were some Spanish muleteers who had arrived the day before. They were from Aragon and Navarre, and almost all wonderfully skilled at the game. Consequently, though spurred on by the presence and advice of Monsieur Alphonse, the men from Ille were rapidly vanquished by these new champions. The local spectators were dismayed. Monsieur Alphonse looked at his watch; it was still only half past nine. His mother had not yet finished having her hair dressed. He hesitated no longer: he took off his dress coat, asked for a jacket, and challenged the Spaniards. I watched him, smiling and a little surprised.

'The honour of the province must be upheld,' he said.

It was then that I found him truly handsome. He was in the grip of his enthusiasm. His clothes, about which he had been so concerned a moment before, had ceased to matter to him. A few minutes earlier he would have been afraid to turn his head for fear of disarranging his cravat. Now he had no thought for his curled hair or his carefully pleated jabot. And what of his fiancée? Upon my word, if it had been necessary, I believe he would have had the marriage postponed. I watched him hastily don a pair of sandals, roll up his sleeves, and place himself confidently at the head of the defeated side, like Caesar rallying his troops at Dyrrhachium. I leaped over the hedge and placed myself comfortably in the shade of a nettle tree, so as to have a good view of the two camps.

Contrary to general expectation, Monsieur Alphonse missed the first ball; admittedly it came skimming low over the ground, driven with surprising force by an Aragonese who seemed to be the captain of the Spanish team.

He was a man of about forty, lean and sinewy, six feet tall, with an olive complexion that was almost as dark as the bronze of the Venus.

Monsieur Alphonse hurled his racquet to the ground in fury.

'That confounded ring!' he exclaimed. 'It stopped me bending my finger, and made me miss an easy ball.'

Not without difficulty, he removed the diamond ring. I stepped forward to take it, but he forestalled me, ran to the Venus, slipped the ring on to her third finger, and returned to his place at the head of the men from Ille.

He was pale, but calm and determined. From then on he didn't once miscalculate, and the Spaniards were soundly beaten. The spectators' enthusiasm was a fine sight to see: some cheered exuberantly and threw their caps in the air; others shook him by the hand, calling him a credit to the province. Had he repelled an invasion, I doubt that he would have received livelier and more sincere congratulations. The chagrin of the losers added still more to the lustre of his victory.

'We shall play you again, my good fellow,' he said to the Aragonese in a tone of condescension, 'but I shall give you points.'

I could have wished Monsieur Alphonse more modest, and I was quite upset at his rival's humiliation.

The Spanish giant keenly resented this insult. I saw him go pale under his tanned skin. He looked dejectedly at his racquet and clenched his teeth; then, in an undertone, he muttered the words: '*Me lo pagarás.*'

The sound of Monsieur de Peyrehorade's voice cut short his son's triumph; my host was greatly astonished not to find him supervising the preparation of the new carriage, and even more so to see him standing drenched in sweat and with a racquet in his hand. Monsieur Alphonse ran to the house, washed his face and hands, again put on his new coat and patent leather shoes; and five minutes later we were trotting briskly along the road to Puygarrig. Every *pelota* player in the town and a large number of spectators followed us with cries of joy. The sturdy horses that drew us could barely keep ahead of the intrepid Catalans.

We were at Puygarrig, and the procession was about to set off for the *mairie,* when, striking his brow, Monsieur Alphonse whispered to me:

'What a blunder! I've forgotten the ring! It's still on the Venus's finger, devil take her. Whatever you do, don't mention it to my mother. Perhaps she won't notice.'

'You could always send for it,' I said.

'Not a chance. My servant stayed behind in Ille, and I don't trust any of the servants here. Twelve hundred francs' worth of diamonds might be too much of a temptation for some of them. And besides, what would people think of my absent-mindedness? I should seem too ridiculous. They would say I was married to the statue ... Just so long as nobody steals it! Fortunately that rabble are afraid of the idol, they daren't go within an arm's length of it. Oh well, no matter, I've got another ring.'

The two ceremonies, civil and religious, were performed with suitable pomp; and Mademoiselle de Puygarrig received the ring of a Paris milliner, never suspecting that her fiancé was sacrificing a love-token on her behalf. Then we sat down to table, where we drank, ate and even sang, all at great length. I pitied the bride for the outbursts of vulgar mirth to which she was exposed; yet she put a better face on it than I would have expected, and her embarrassment was neither gauche nor affected.

Perhaps courage comes to us in difficult situations.

It was four o'clock when a merciful Heaven saw fit to put an end to lunch. The men went to stroll in the grounds, which were magnificent, or watched the peasant girls of Puygarrig, decked out in their holiday best, dancing on the lawn of the chateau. In this way we filled a few hours. Meanwhile the women were fussing around the bride, who was showing off the wedding presents to them. Then she got changed, and I noticed how she covered her beautiful hair with a bonnet and a plumed hat; for women are in a great hurry to assume at the earliest opportunity the adornments that custom forbids them to wear whilst they are still unmarried.

It was almost eight o'clock when we prepared to leave for Ille. But first there occurred a pathetic scene. Mademoiselle de Puygarrig's aunt, a very old and very devout lady, who was like a mother to her, was not to accompany us to the town. On our departure, she gave her niece a touching lecture on her conjugal obligations, which led to a torrent of tears and interminable embraces. Monsieur de Peyrehorade compared this separation to the rape of the Sabine women. We finally managed to get away, and on the road home we all did our utmost to entertain the bride and bring a smile to her lips; but to no avail.

At Ille, supper was waiting for us – and what a supper! If the vulgar mirth of that morning had shocked me, I was far more shocked by the jokes and double entendres that were now directed particularly at the bride and groom. The groom, who had disappeared for a moment before sitting down to table, was pale and chillingly grave in his manner. He kept taking gulps of old Collioure wine that was almost as strong as brandy. I was seated next to him, and I felt obliged to warn him:

'Take care! They say that wine . . .' I do not remember what stupid remark I made so as to enter into the spirit of the festivities.

He nudged my knee and said to me in a very low voice:

'When we leave the table . . . may I have a word with you?'

His solemn tone surprised me. I looked more closely at him, and I noticed how extraordinarily his features had changed.

'Are you feeling ill?' I asked him.

'No.'

And he resumed his drinking.

Meanwhile, amid cheers and applause, an eleven-year-old child, who had crawled under the table, was showing the company a pretty pink and white ribbon, commonly known as a garter, which he had just removed from the bride's ankle. It was immediately cut into bits and distributed to the young men, each of whom put a piece of it in his buttonhole, in accordance with an age-old custom that still survives in a few ancient families. This caused the bride to blush to the roots of her hair. But her confusion was crowned when, having called for silence, Monsieur de Peyrehorade sang her some verses in Catalan, made up on the spur of the moment, or so he claimed. This is how they went, if I understood them correctly:

'What then is this, my friends? Is the wine I have drunk making me see double, or are there two Venuses here?'

The groom turned his head sharply with a startled look, causing everybody to laugh.

'Yes,' continued Monsieur de Peyrehorade, 'there are two Venuses under my roof. One I found in the ground like a truffle; the other, descended from the skies, has just shared out her girdle among us.'

He meant her garter.

'My son, choose, between the Roman and the Catalan Venus, the one whom you prefer. The rogue has chosen the Catalan Venus, and he has the better of the bargain. The Roman Venus is black, the Catalan Venus is white. The Roman is cold, the Catalan enflames everything that approaches her.'

This ending provoked such acclaim, such clamorous applause, and such uproarious laughter that I thought the ceiling was going to fall about our heads. Around the table there were only three serious faces, those of the bride and groom, and my own. I had a fearful headache; and besides, I don't know why, but a wedding always depresses me. This one, furthermore, disgusted me rather.

When the last couplets had been sung by the deputy mayor – and pretty ribald they were, I must say – we moved into the drawing room to celebrate the departure of the bride, who was soon to be escorted to her chamber, for it was nearly midnight.

Monsieur Alphonse drew me into the embrasure of a window and, averting his eyes, said to me:

'You're going to laugh at me ... but I don't know what's the matter with me. I'm bewitched! The Devil's making off with me!'

The first thought that occurred to me was that he felt threatened by some misfortune of the sort alluded to by Montaigne and by Madame de Sévigné: '*All Love's empire is full of tragic histories*', et cetera. 'I thought misfortunes of that sort only befell men of intelligence,' I said to myself.

'You've drunk too much of that Collioure wine, my dear Monsieur Alphonse,' I said to him. 'I warned you.'

'Yes, no doubt. But there's something far worse than that.'

His voice kept breaking. I thought he was completely drunk.

'You know that ring of mine?' he went on after a silence.

'Well? Has it been taken?'

'No.'

'In that case, have you got it?'

'No. I ... I can't get it off the finger of that damned Venus.'

'So, you didn't pull hard enough!'

'Yes, I did. But the Venus ... has bent her finger.'

He was staring at me wild-eyed, clutching the window hasp to prevent himself from falling.

'A likely story!' I said. 'You pushed the ring on too far. Tomorrow you can get it off with some pliers. But be careful not to damage the statue.'

'No. I tell you the finger of the Venus is bent, curled in. Her fist is clenched, don't you understand? It seems she is my wife, since I've given her my ring. Now she won't give it back.'

I felt a sudden shudder, and for a moment I had gooseflesh. Then he heaved a great sigh that sent a blast of wine fumes in my direction, and all my emotions evaporated.

'The wretch is completely drunk,' I thought.

'You are an antiquarian, sir,' added the bridegroom plaintively. 'You are familiar with these statues. Perhaps there is some spring, some fiendish device I don't know about. Could you go and see?'

'Gladly,' I said. 'Come with me.'

'No, I'd rather you went alone.'

I went out of the drawing room.

The weather had changed during supper, and rain was beginning to fall heavily. I was about to ask for an umbrella when a thought stopped me short. I would be a complete fool, I said to myself, to go out to confirm a drunken man's story. Besides, perhaps he means to play some practical joke on me, to raise a laugh among these good provincials; and the very least I can expect is to get soaked to the skin and catch my death of cold.

From the door I cast a glance at the statue, which was streaming with water, and I went up to my bedroom without returning to the drawing room. I went to bed, but sleep was a long time coming. All the scenes of that day passed through my mind. I thought of that girl, so beautiful and chaste, abandoned to a brutal drunkard. What an odious thing a marriage of convenience is, I said to myself. A mayor dons a tricolour sash, a priest a stole, and lo and behold, the most charming girl in the world is delivered up to the Minotaur! What can two beings who are not in love find to say to one another at such a moment, which two lovers would purchase with their lives? Can a woman ever love a man when once she has seen him acting boorishly? First impressions are never obliterated, and I am certain that Alphonse will richly deserve to be hated.

During my monologue, which I have abridged a good deal, I had heard much to-ing and fro-ing in the house, the sound of doors opening and closing and of carriages leaving; then I thought I could hear on the stairs the light footsteps of several women heading for the other end of the corridor on which my bedroom was situated. No doubt it was the bride being escorted to bed by her entourage. Then I heard people returning downstairs. Madame de Peyrehorade's door closed. 'How distressed and ill at ease that poor girl must feel!' I said to myself. I was tossing and turning in my bed with ill-humour. A bachelor cuts a ridiculous figure in a house where a marriage is being celebrated.

Silence had reigned for some time when it was disturbed by heavy footfalls mounting the stairs. The wooden steps creaked loudly.

'What an oaf!' I exclaimed. 'I'll lay odds he's going to fall downstairs!'

Everything became quiet again. I picked up a book to turn my thoughts to other things. It was a volume of statistics on the *département*, graced with an article by Monsieur de Peyrehorade on the Druidic monuments of the Prades arrondissement. I nodded off on page three.

I slept badly and woke several times. It must have been five in the morning, and I had been awake for more than twenty minutes, when the cock crew. Day was breaking. At that moment I distinctly heard the same heavy footfalls, the same creaking of the stairs that I had heard before falling asleep. This struck me as strange. Yawning, I tried to fathom why Monsieur Alphonse should be getting up so early. I could think of no plausible explanation. I was on the point of closing my eyes again when my attention was once more aroused by strange scufflings, soon joined by the sound of bells being rung and of doors being noisily opened. Then I heard confused shouts.

'My drunken friend must have set fire to something!' I thought as I leaped from my bed.

I dressed hastily and went out into the corridor. From the other end came cries and lamentations, with one piercing voice dominating all the rest: 'My son, my son!' It was clear that some misfortune had befallen Monsieur Alphonse. I ran to the bridal chamber; it was full of people. The first sight that greeted me was the young man, half undressed and sprawled across the bed, the timber frame of which was broken. He was ashen-faced and motionless. His mother was weeping and lamenting by his side. Monsieur de Peyrehorade was bustling about, rubbing his son's temples with eau de cologne and holding smelling-salts to his nose. Alas! his son had been dead for some time. On a couch at the other end of the bedroom lay the bride, in the throes of dreadful convulsions. She was uttering inarticulate cries, and two strong maidservants were having the utmost difficulty in restraining her.

'What in Heaven's name has happened?' I exclaimed.

I approached the bed and lifted the body of the unfortunate young man; it was already stiff and cold. His clenched teeth and blackened features betokened the most dreadful anguish. It was quite apparent that his death had been violent and his last struggle a terrible one. Yet there was no trace of blood on his clothes. I lifted his shirt and saw on his chest a livid imprint that extended to his ribs and back. It was as if he had been squeezed in an iron hoop. I trod on something hard which was lying on the carpet; I bent down and saw the diamond ring.

I hauled Monsieur de Peyrehorade and his wife away to their room; then I had the bride taken there. 'You still have a daughter,' I said to them. 'You owe her your care.' Then I left them alone.

It seemed to me that Monsieur Alphonse had undoubtedly been the victim of murderers who had found a way into the bride's bedroom in the night. Those bruises on the chest, however, and their circular conformation, puzzled me greatly, for they could not have been caused by a stick or an iron bar. Suddenly I remembered having heard that, in Valencia, *bravos* use long leather bags filled with fine sand to strike down those they have been hired to kill. At once I remembered the Aragonese muleteer and his threat; however, I hardly dared think that he would have exacted so terrible a vengeance for a trivial jest.

I was going around the house searching for evidence that it had been broken into, but I found none anywhere. I went into the garden to see whether the murderers might have got in that way; but I found nothing definite. The previous day's rain had in any case made the ground so wet that it would not have retained any distinct traces. I did, however, observe some deep footprints in the ground; there were two sets, running in opposite directions but along the same path, from the corner of the hedge adjoining the *pelota* court to the front door of the house. They might have been the footprints left by Monsieur Alphonse when he went to fetch his ring from the statue's finger. On the other hand, since the hedge was less thick at this point than elsewhere, it might have been here that the murderers had penetrated it. Walking back and forth in front of the statue, I stopped for a moment to gaze at it. This time, I must confess, I could not contemplate without awe its expression of vicious irony; and, with my head still full of the horrible scenes I had just witnessed, I felt as if I were looking at an infernal deity applauding the misfortune which had overtaken this house.

I returned to my room and stayed there until midday. Then I emerged and enquired after my hosts. They were somewhat calmer. Mademoiselle de Puygarrig, or rather Monsieur Alphonse's widow, had regained consciousness. She had even talked to the public prosecutor from Perpignan, who happened to be in Ille on circuit at the time, and that judge had received her deposition. He asked me for mine. I told him all I knew, and did not conceal from him my suspicions regarding the Aragonese muleteer. He ordered the man to be arrested at once.

'Did you learn anything from Madame Alphonse?' I asked the public prosecutor when my deposition had been written and signed.

'The unfortunate lady has gone mad,' he told me with a sad smile. 'Mad! Totally mad! This is her story:

'She had been in bed, she says, for a few minutes, with the bed-curtains drawn, when her bedroom door opened and someone came in. At the time Madame Alphonse was lying at the very edge of the bed with her face turned towards the wall. She did not move, sure that it was her husband. After a moment the bed groaned as if under an enormous weight. She was very frightened, but did not dare turn her head. Five minutes, perhaps ten minutes – she cannot say how long – passed in this way. Then she made an involuntary movement, or else the person in the bed did, and she felt the contact of something as cold as ice – those were her words. She pressed herself closer to the side of the bed, trembling in every limb. A little later, the door opened a second time, and someone came in and said, "Good evening, my little wife." Soon afterwards the curtains were drawn back. She heard a stifled cry. The person who was in the bed beside her sat upright and seemed to reach out their arms. Thereupon she turned her head and saw, so she says, her husband kneeling by the bed with his head on a level with the pillow, in the arms of a sort of greenish giant that was crushing him in a tight embrace. She says – and she repeated it a score of times, poor woman – she says that she recognized – can you guess? – the bronze Venus, Monsieur de Peyrehorade's statue. Ever since it turned up, everyone has been dreaming about it. But to return to this poor crazed woman's story: at this sight she fainted, and she had probably taken leave of her senses several moments before. She is quite unable to say how long she remained in a faint. When she came to, she again saw the ghost, or the statue, as she persists in calling it, motionless, with its legs and the lower part of its body in the bed, its torso and arms extended forwards, and in its arms her husband, quite still. A cock crew. Thereupon the statue got out of bed, dropped the corpse and went out. Madame Alphonse made a grab for the bell pull and the rest you know.'

They brought in the Spaniard. He was calm, and defended himself with great composure and presence of mind. In any case, he did not deny saying the words I had overheard; but he explained them by claiming he had meant nothing more than that, on the following day, when he was rested, he would have defeated his victorious opponent in another game of *pelota*. I remember him adding:

'When he is insulted, a man from Aragon does not wait till the next day to take his revenge. If I had thought that Monsieur Alphonse had meant to insult me, I would have run my knife into his belly there and then.'

They compared his shoes with the footprints in the garden; his shoes were much larger.

Finally the keeper of the inn at which he was staying assured us that the man had spent the whole night rubbing down and administering medicine to one of his mules that was sick.

Besides, the Aragonese was a man of good repute, well known in the region, which he visited every year on business. So he was released, with apologies.

I almost forgot to mention the statement of a servant who had been the last person to see Monsieur Alphonse alive. It was at the moment when he was about to go up to his wife, and he had called this man and asked him anxiously if he knew where I was. The servant replied that he had not seen me. Monsieur Alphonse heaved a sigh and stood in silence for more than a minute. Then he said: 'Oh well, the Devil must have made off with him too!'

I asked this man whether Monsieur Alphonse had had his diamond ring when he spoke to him. The servant hesitated before replying. Finally he said that he thought not, but that in any case he had not paid any attention to the matter. On second thoughts he added, 'If he'd been wearing the ring I'm sure I would have noticed it, since I supposed he had given it to Madame Alphonse.'

Questioning this man, I experienced something of the superstitious terror that Madame Alphonse's statement had spread throughout the household. The prosecutor looked at me, smiling, and I refrained from questioning him further.

A few hours after Monsieur Alphonse's funeral, I prepared to leave Ille. Monsieur de Peyrehorade's carriage was to take me to Perpignan. Despite his weak state, the poor old man wished to accompany me as far as his garden gate. We passed through the garden in silence; he could barely drag himself along, supporting himself on my arm. As we parted, I looked one last time at the Venus. I was confident that, although he did not share the fear and hatred it inspired among one section of his family, my host would wish to be rid of an object which would serve as a constant reminder of a dreadful misfortune. My intention was to urge him to place it in a museum. I was plucking up the courage to broach the subject when Monsieur de Peyrehorade turned his head mechanically in the direction in which he could see me staring. He saw the statue and at once burst into tears. I embraced him, and, not daring to say a single word to him, I got into the carriage.

Since my departure I have not heard that any new light has been shed on this mysterious catastrophe.

Monsieur de Peyrehorade died a few months after his son. In his will he left me his manuscripts, and perhaps I shall have them published one day. I found no trace among them of the monograph concerning the inscriptions on the Venus.

*

P.S. My friend Monsieur de P— has just written from Perpignan, informing me that the statue no longer exists. After her husband's death Madame de Peyrehorade's first concern was to have it melted down and recast into a bell, and in this new shape it serves the church in Ille. But, adds Monsieur de P—, it seems that misfortune dogs those who possess this bronze. Since the bell has been ringing at Ille the vines have frozen twice.

Translated by Nicholas Jotcham

ALOYSIUS BERTRAND

Scarbo

'He looked under the bed, in the chimney, in the cupboard; – Nobody. He could not understand how he had come in, or how he had escaped.'

Hoffmann, *Tales of the Night*

Oh! How often have I heard and seen him, Scarbo, when at midnight the moon shines in the sky like a silver shield on an azure banner strewn with golden bees!

How often have I heard his laugh buzzing in the shadow of my alcove, his fingernail scrape along the silk of the curtains around my bed!

How often have I seen him land on the floor, pirouette on one foot and roll through my bedroom like the spray from a sorceress's wand!

Did I think he had disappeared then? The dwarf grew between the moon and me, like the steeple of a gothic cathedral, a little golden bell wobbling on his pointy cap!

But soon his body began to turn blue, translucent as melting wax, his face becoming pale as the wax of a votive candle – and suddenly his light went out.

Translated by Patrick McGuinness

JULES BARBEY D'AUREVILLY

Don Juan's Crowning Love Affair

'Innocence is the devil's choicest dish.'

(A.)

I

'Is he still alive, then, the old rogue?'

'Dear God! Still alive, yes! – and by God's command, Madame – I added, remembering her piety – of the parish of Sainte-Clotilde, the parish of dukes! – The King is dead! Long live the King! as they used to say under the old monarchy before it was broken, like a set of antique Sèvres porcelain. But Don Juan will survive all democracies, he is a monarch that no one will break.'

'In any case, the devil is immortal!' she said self-approvingly.

'He even ...'

'Who? ... the devil? ...'

'No, Don Juan ... supped, three days ago, at a cabaret ... Guess where? ...'

'At your frightful Maison-d'Or, I suppose ...'

'By no means, Madame! Don Juan no longer sets foot in the place ... there's nothing there piquant enough for the taste of his Highness. The princely Don Juan has always rather resembled the famous monk D'Arnaud de Brescia who, according to the chronicles, lived off nothing but the blood of souls. He likes to pink his champagne with it, and you can't find liquor like that any more among the cabaret *cocottes*!'

'Indeed,' she went on with irony, 'so he supped at the Benedictine Convent, with the ladies . . .'

'Of Perpetual Adoration, yes, Madame! For once he has inspired adoration, the old devil, it does tend to last for ever.'

'For a Catholic I find you full of profanity,' she said slowly, but a little nettled, 'and I beg you to spare me the details of your dissolute suppers, if this is what you intend to impart to me by harping on so about Don Juan.'

'I'm not inventing anything, Madame! The harlots at that particular supper, if harlots they were, are nothing to do with me . . . unfortunately . . .'

'That's enough, Monsieur!'

'Allow me my modesty. They were . . .'

'The *mille e tre*? . . .' she broke in, curious now, altering her manner, almost friendly again.

'Oh! Not all of them, Madame . . . Only a dozen. It's quite enough, really, a respectable number . . .'

'And not quite respectable, either,' she put in.

'Besides, you know as well as I do that you can't fit many people into the boudoir of the Comtesse de Chiffrevas. It has seen great exploits, to be sure, but it *is* a very small boudoir . . .'

'What?' she exclaimed, sounding shocked. 'They had supper in the boudoir? . . .'

'Yes, Madame, in the boudoir. And why not? People have supper on the battlefield. They wanted to give a sumptuous supper to Don Juan, and where better to honour him than in the very theatre of his triumphs, the place where memories bloom in lieu of orange trees. It was a charming idea, both tender and melancholic. This was not the *victims' ball*; it was the *victims' supper*.'

'And Don Juan?' she said, much as Orgon, in the play, says 'And Tartuffe?'

'Don Juan took it all in good heart, and ate an excellent supper,
. . . He, alone, in front of the women!
in the person of someone of your acquaintance . . . none other than the Comte Jules-Amédée-Hector de Ravila de Ravilès.'

'*Him!* It's true, he *is* Don Juan,' she said.

And though she was too old for such daydreams – a pious bigot in beak and claw – she dreamed nevertheless of the Comte Jules-Amédée-Hector – of the ancient and eternal race of Juan, to whom God did not give the world, but allowed the devil to do so instead.

II

What I just recounted to the old Marquise Guy de Ruy was nothing less than the truth. Barely three days earlier, a dozen ladies, hailing from the irreproachably virtuous Faubourg Saint-Germain (let them rest easy, I shall not name names!), all twelve of whom, according to the dowagers of gossip, *had been honoured* (to use the piquant old expression) by the Comte Ravila de Ravilès, took it into their heads to hold a supper for him – *at which he was to be the only male present* – to celebrate . . . what? They didn't say. Giving such a supper was an audacious enterprise; but women, cowardly when alone, become daring in numbers. Probably not one of them would have dared to invite the Comte Jules-Amédée-Hector to a supper *en tête à tête*; but together, and using each other as moral support, they gladly formed a Mesmer chain, bound by magnetic force to the compelling, to the dangerous, Ravila de Ravilès . . .

'What a name!'

'And a most fitting one, Madame . . .'

The Comte de Ravila de Ravilès, who incidentally had always obeyed the directive suggested by his imperious name, was indeed the incarnation in one man of every seducer ever evoked in history or in novels. Even the Marquise Guy de Ruy – who was an old malcontent, with cold, sharp blue eyes, if less cold than her heart, and less sharp than her wit – conceded that in an age when matters concerning women became daily less relevant, then if there *did* exist anyone who resembled Don Juan, it had to be him! Unfortunately, he was the Don of the fifth act. The witty Prince de Ligne never fully accepted the fact that Alcibiades could ever get to be fifty years old. And by the same token, the Comte de Ravila went on acting like Alcibiades. Like the Comte d'Orsay, that dandy cast in the bronze of Michelangelo, who was handsome to the day he died, Ravila had the sort of beauty particular to the race of Don Juan – that mysterious race which does not proceed from father to son, like everyone else, but which occurs here and there, at different intervals, within the families of humanity.

His beauty was the genuine article – insolent, joyous, imperious – in a word, it was *Juanesque*: the adjective says it all and needs no further elaboration; and what is more – had he made a pact with the devil? – he possessed it still ... Only, God had now started to stake his claim – the tiger claws of life had begun to furrow the superb forehead that had been so crowned with roses, and by scores of lips; and on his broad, insolent temples the first white hairs were visible, announcing the imminent arrival of the barbarians, and the end of the Empire ... In truth, he bore them with the imperviousness that comes from pride magnified by potency; but the women who had loved him observed them with melancholy. Who knows? Did they see their own advancing age reflected in his countenance? Alas, for them as well as for him, the hour had come for that terrible supper with the cold and marble-white Commendatore, after which there was nowhere left but hell – the hell of old age, waiting for the one to come! Which is why, perhaps, before they came to share with him the bitterness of that ultimate supper, they thought they would treat him to their own, and it would be a masterpiece.

A masterpiece it was indeed, of taste, delicacy, patrician luxury, of inventiveness and resource; it was to be the most delightful, delicious, generous, captivating, and above all the most original of suppers. Just imagine it! Normally, suppers are made of overflowing high spirits, intent on a good time; but this one was animated by memory, by regret, almost by despair, but despair dressed up, hidden behind smiles and laughter, and determined on this final feast or folly, on this last intoxicating return of youth, oh may it never end! ...

The Amphitryons who gave this unbelievable supper, so contrary to the insipid customs of the class to which they belonged, must have felt rather like Sardanapalus on his pyre, which he heaped with his wives, slaves, horses, jewels, and every luxury he possessed, so they would perish with him. In the same way, these women heaped this blazing supper with every luxury they had. They brought to it everything they had of beauty, wit, resource, ornament, allure, and poured all of it all at once into this supreme conflagration.

The man for whom they draped and enveloped themselves in this final flame was worth more, in their eyes, than all of Asia in the eyes of Sardanapalus. They were more deliciously flirtatious with him than women had ever been with any man, or even with a drawing room full of men; and this flirtatiousness they spiced up with the jealousy which is hidden in society, and which they had no need to hide, for they all knew that this man had been with each one of them, and a shameful secret shared is one no longer ... The only rivalry between them now was, whose epitaph would be graven most deeply upon his heart.

That evening he had the sensuous, sovereign, nonchalant, fastidious manner of a confessor to nuns, or of a sultan. Seated like a king – or the master – at the centre of the table, directly opposite the Comtesse de Chiffrevas, in her peach-tinted boudoir of forbidden fruits, the Comte de Ravila turned his hell-blue eyes – eyes that so many poor creatures had mistaken for the blue of the sky – blazing upon this gorgeous circle of twelve women. Their elegance was touched with genius, and where they sat, around this table loaded with crystal, lighted candles and flowers, they spread before him, from the scarlet of the full rose to the softened amber glow of the grape cluster, every nuance of maturity.

Excluded from this company were the green young things that Byron abhorred, the little misses who smell of tartlet and whose figures are still wispy; here were resplendent and delicious summers, voluptuous autumns, lavish and full-bodied, their dazzling breasts at the full, overflowing the corsetry, with shoulders and arms of every plumpness, but powerful too, with biceps worthy of the Sabines who fought off the Romans, and who were ready to intertwine themselves between the spokes of the chariot of life, and stop it dead.

I spoke of pretty ideas. Among the most charming at this supper was to have it served by chambermaids, so nothing could be said to have interrupted the harmony of a feast at which women were the undisputed sovereigns, since they also served ... His lordship Don Juan – of the Ravila line – could thus plunge his ferocious gaze into a sea of luminous and living flesh, of the kind Rubens plies in his formidable paintings; but he could also plunge his pride into the elixir – be it clear or cloudy – of these hearts. Because at bottom, despite all indications to the contrary, Don Juan is a masterly psychologist! Like the demon himself, he loves souls more even than bodies, and like the infernal slaver that he is, would rather traffic in the former than the latter!

Witty, noble, and while remaining impeccably Faubourg Saint-Germain in tone, so daring were the women that evening they were like the king's pages, when there was a king with pages; they were brilliantly animated, full of incomparable repartee and *brio*. They felt more invincible than they had ever felt, even at their most triumphant. They experienced an unfamiliar power which came from the very core of their beings, and whose existence, until that moment, they had never suspected.

The happiness occasioned by this discovery was a feeling that tripled their sense of being alive; added to this, there was the physical ambience, which always has a decisive impact on the nervous system, the brilliance of the lights, the heady perfume of all the flowers that swooned in the close atmosphere heated by these beautiful creatures, the stirring effect of the wines, the very idea of the supper which had about it a sulphurous piquancy, of the kind the Neapolitan required of his sorbet to make it perfect; add to this the intoxicating thought of being accomplices in this *risqué* little supper – a supper that never descended into the vulgarity of the Regency period; indeed, it remained throughout very much a nineteenth-century, Faubourg Saint-Germain supper, and nothing came loose or undone in those adorable *décolletés*, pressed against hearts that had felt the fire and desired to stoke it even more. In a word, all these things acted together, and strung to the utmost degree the mysterious harp contained within each of these wondrous organisms, as tight as it was possible to string without its breaking, so it produced ineffable octaves and harmonies ... It must have been extraordinary, don't you agree? One of the most vibrant pages of Ravila's memoirs, if he ever gets round to writing them? ... I ask the question, but he alone can write it ... As I explained to the Marquise Guy de Ruy, I was not present at the supper, and if I give these details, and recount the story he told at the end, I am only repeating what de Ravila told me himself; for true to the tradition of the Juan clan, he is indiscreet, and he went to the trouble one evening of telling me everything.

III

By now it was late – or rather, early! It was dawn. Against the ceiling, and concentrated at a certain spot on the pink silk curtains of the boudoir, which were drawn tight closed, an opal-tinted droplet started to grow, like a widening eye, curious to see what was going on in this fiery boudoir. A certain languor had begun to invade these valiant dame Knights of the Round Table, these carousers, who had been so lively only a moment before. It was that moment, familiar at any dinner-party, when the fatigue which comes with the emotion of the evening just passed begins to show, in the chignons coming slightly loose, in the burning cheeks, flushed or grown paler, in the wearied looks from dark-rimmed eyes, and even in the thousand flaring and guttering lights in the candelabra, which are like bouquets of flame whose stalks are sculpted in bronze and gold.

The conversation, which had been carried on in a general and lively fashion, a game of shuttlecock in which everyone had batted back and forth, had become fragmented, and nothing distinct could now be heard above the harmonious hubbub made by all these voices, with their aristocratic accents, warbling together like the dawn chorus at the edge of a wood . . . when one of these voices – a clarion voice – imperious and almost impertinent, just as the voice of a duchess should be – made itself heard above the others, and addressed the following words to the Comte de Ravila, which must have been the logical conclusion to a quiet conversation she had been having with him, and which none of the other chattering ladies had heard:

'Since you are reputed to be the Don Juan of our time, you ought to tell us the story of your greatest conquest, the one that most flattered your pride as a lover of women, and which you consider, in the light of this present moment, to be the crowning love of your life . . .'

This challenge, as much as the voice that delivered it, cut through all the other conversations, and a sudden silence fell.

The voice belonged to the Duchesse de— – I shall leave her disguised behind the asterisks; but some of you may recognize her, when I say that she has the palest of pale hair and complexions, and the blackest eyes beneath her golden brows, in all of the Faubourg Saint-Germain. – She was seated, like one of the just at the right hand of God, directly to the right of the Comte de Ravila, god of this feast, who had left off using his enemies as a footstool; slim and ethereal as an arabesque, she was fairylike in her green velvet dress with its silvery reflections, whose long train wound around her chair, not unlike the serpent's tail that prolonged the charming posterior of Melusina the sea-nymph.

'Now there's an idea!' said the Comtesse de Chiffrevas, eager in her role as hostess to second the motion the Duchesse had put forward. 'Yes, the love you place above all the others, whether inspired, or felt – the one, were it possible, you should most like to live through again.'

'Oh! I should like to live through them all again!' answered Ravila with the unflagging appetite of a Roman emperor, or other replete monsters of the type. And he raised his champagne glass, which was not the crude and pagan cup they have replaced it with, but the tall, thin vessel used by our ancestors, known as the *flûte*, perhaps because of the heavenly melodies it pours into our hearts! – Then, looking round the table, he embraced with his eyes every woman in that magnetic chain. 'And yet,' he went on, setting down his glass before him with a melancholy astonishing for a Nebuchadnezzar like him, who had not yet eaten grass except in the tarragon salads of the Café Anglais – 'and yet it is true, there is *one* feeling one has experienced in all one's life, which shines more strongly in the memory than others, as life advances, and for which one would give up the rest!'

'The diamond in the set,' said the Comtesse de Chiffrevas, dreamily, possibly contemplating the facets of her own.

'... And as legend has it in my country', chimed in the Princesse Jable ... 'which lies at the foot of the Ural Mountains, there is the famous and fabulous diamond that starts off pink, and then turns black, while remaining a diamond, and still more brilliant black than pink ...' She said that with all the strange charm that she has, this Bohemian! For she is a true Bohemian, married for love to the finest prince among the Polish exiles, and as much a princess in her bearing as any born in the palace of the Jagellons.

This was followed by a veritable explosion ... 'Yes!' they all exclaimed. 'Do tell us about it, Comte!' they added with warmth, begging him now, all trembling with curiosity down to the curls at the nape of their necks, and bunching up together shoulder to shoulder, some with cheek in hand, an elbow propped on the table, others leaning back in their chairs, fans in front of their mouths; they challenged him with wide, inquisitive eyes.

'If you absolutely insist . . .' said the Comte, with the nonchalance of a man who knows how much delay exacerbates desire.

'We do, absolutely!' said the Duchesse, fixing – much as a Turkish despot might the blade of his sword – the golden prongs of her dessert fork.

'Then listen,' he concluded, still casually.

They became as one, staring at him with rapt attention. They drank him and devoured him with their eyes. Women always like a love story – but who knows? Perhaps the particular charm here was that the story he was to tell would be their very own . . . They knew he was too well bred and too well versed in social etiquette to name names, and that he would omit certain details that were too compromising; and knowing this made them even more impatient to hear the story. They more than desired to hear it, they placed their hopes in it.

In their vanity, they found themselves rivalling each other, to be the most beautiful memory in the life of a man who must have had so many of them. The old Sultan was once more to throw down the hand-kerchief . . . that no one would pick up – but the one for whom he threw it down would assuredly receive it silently into her heart . . .

And now, in the light of their expectations, this is the little thunderbolt he unleashed on their attentive heads:

IV

'I have often heard it said by the moralists, who are fine connoisseurs of life,' began the Comte de Ravila, 'that our greatest love is not the first, nor the last, as many think, but the second. But in matters of love, everything is true, and everything is false, and in any case, it was not so with me . . . What you have asked of me tonight, ladies, and what I am about to relate dates back to the proudest moment of my youth. I was no longer exactly what they call a 'young man', but I was young, and as an old uncle of mine – a Knight of Malta – used to say of this stage in life, 'I had sown my wild oats'. In my prime, then, I was in full relations, as the Italians put it so charmingly, with a woman who is known to you all and whom you have all admired . . .'

And here, the look which all these women – who were drinking up the words of the old serpent – then exchanged with each other had to be seen to be believed – it was truly indescribable.

'She was a fine woman,' went on Ravila, 'and utterly distinguished, in every sense of the word. She was young, rich, of noble extraction; she was beautiful and spirited, with a broad-minded, artistic intelligence; and she was unaffected – in a way your milieu can produce, when it does . . . In any case, all she desired then was to please me, to play the role of the tenderest of mistresses, and the dearest of friends.

'I was not, I think, the first man she had loved . . . She had been in love before, but not with her husband; this was of the virtuous, platonic, uto-pian type – the kind of love that exercises the heart rather than fills it; the kind that strengthens the heart for the love that almost always follows soon after – the trial run, so to speak, like the white mass, said by young priests practising for when they come to celebrate the true, consecrated mass . . . When I came into her life she was still at the white mass. I was her first true mass, and she celebrated it sumptuously and with full cere-mony, like a cardinal.'

At this remark, the prettiest of pretty smiles went round that table of beautiful expectant mouths, like a concentric ring on the limpid surface of a lake . . . It was swift, but ravishing!

'She was a rare pearl!' the Comte went on. 'Rarely have I seen such genuine goodness, such tender-heartedness, such good instinctive feeling, intact even in passion, which as you know, is not always good . . . I have never encountered less calculation, less prudery and coquettishness – two things often to be found mingled in women, like some material marked with a cat's claw . . . there was nothing of the cat in her . . . Hers was what those blasted scribblers who poison our lives by their style call a simple nature, ornamented by civilization; but she was in possession of all the luxuries, and not one of the little vices that come to seem even more charming than the luxuries . . .'

'Was she brunette?' the Duchesse broke in point-blank, who was grow-ing bored with all this metaphysics.

'Ah! You don't look deep enough!' said Ravila cleverly. 'Yes, she was brunette, brunette to the point of being black as jet, the most luxuriant mirror of ebony I have ever seen shining on the voluptuous curve of a woman's head, but she was fair-complexioned – and it is by the complexion, and not the hair, that you have to judge if a woman is blonde or brunette' – added the great observer, who had not studied women just to paint their portraits. – 'She was a blonde with black hair ...'

All the lovely heads around the table who were blonde of hair only, stirred imperceptibly. For them, clearly, the story had already lost something of its interest.

'She had the sable locks of Night,' went on Ravila, 'but they framed the face of Dawn itself, a face that shone with a rare and radiant freshness that had lost nothing of its bloom despite exposure to years of Parisian nightlife, which burns up so many roses in its candelabra. Hers seemed merely to have been kissed, the pink in her cheeks and lips remaining bright to the point of luminosity. The twofold flush also went well with the ruby frontlet she usually wore – this was the time women did their hair *en ferronnière*, after Leonardo. With her flashing eyes, whose colour was obscured by the flame that issued from them, they made a triangle whose tips were rubies! Slim, but strong, majestic even, she was built to be the wife of a colonel of dragoons – her husband was at that time merely a squadron-leader in the light cavalry – and she enjoyed, despite her pedigree, the rude health of a peasant-girl who drinks in the sun through her skin. She had the ardour that goes with it, too – she imbibed the sun into her soul as well as her veins, she was always present, and always ready ... But here's the strange thing! This powerful and unaffected creature, whose pure, passionate nature was like the blood that fed her beautiful cheeks and gave a pink flush to her arms, was ... would you credit it? awkward in a man's arms ...'

At this some of his listeners lowered their eyes, but raised them again, mischievously ...

'As awkward in love as she was rash in life,' went on Ravila, who did not linger on the tidbit he had just dropped. 'And the man who loved her had repeatedly to instruct her in two things she seemed not to have learned ... never to lose control in a world always hostile and always implacable, and in private, to learn the greatest art of love, which is that of keeping it alive. She loved, certainly; but the art of love was lacking in her . . . In this she was unlike the majority of women, who possess merely the art! Now, to understand and apply the strategies of *The Prince*, you must first be a Borgia. Borgia comes before Machiavelli. One is the poet, the other is the critic. She possessed nothing of the Borgia. She was a good woman, very much in love; and despite her monumental beauty, she remained naive, like the little girl in one of those motifs above a door who, being thirsty, thrusts her hand impulsively into the fountain and stands there abashed, when all the water pours through her fingers . . .

'The co-existence of this awkwardness and shame with the grand woman of passion was actually rather endearing. Few who observed her in society had any inkling of it – they would have seen someone who had love, and even happiness, but they would not suspect that she lacked the art to return it in kind. Only I was not then sufficiently detached to be able to content myself with observing the *artistic effect*, and sometimes this made her anxious, jealous, violent – as one is when in love, and she was that! – But her anxiety, jealousy and violence simply died away in the inexhaustible goodness of her heart, the instant she had or thought that she had hurt someone – she was as inept at causing pain as she was at giving pleasure. Strange lioness, indeed! She thought she possessed claws, but when she tried to bare them, nothing emerged from her magnificent velvet paws. Her scratches were of velvet!'

'Where is all this leading?' said the Comtesse de Chiffrevas to her neighbour – for this couldn't, surely, be the crowning love of Don Juan . . .

None of those sophisticates could conceive of such simplicity!

'And so we enjoyed an intimacy that was sometimes stormy, but never tortured, and in the provincial town known as Paris, it was a mystery to no one . . . The Marquise . . . she was a Marquise . . .'

There were three of them sitting at that table, and they were all brunettes. But they didn't blink. They knew full well he wasn't talking of them . . . The only velvet they shared between them was the down that one of them had on her upper lip – a beautifully modelled lip which at that moment, I could swear, was curled in some disdain.

'. . . And a Marquise three times over, just as pachas can have three tails!' went on Ravila, who was getting into his stride. 'The Marquise was one of those women who cannot hide anything, however they might wish to.

Even her daughter, a girl of thirteen, innocent as she was, recognized only too well the feelings her mother had for me. I wonder, has any poet fathomed what these daughters feel about us, their mothers' lovers? The question goes deep! It is one I pondered frequently, when I caught the little girl looking at me out of her huge dark eyes, a black, spying look, fraught with menace. She was shy, like a wild animal, and usually left the drawing room the moment I entered it, or sat as far away from me as possible, if she was forced to stay . . . she had an almost compulsive horror of my person, that she would try and hide, but it ran so strong in her she could not help herself . . . It came out in tiny details, but I noticed them all. Even the Marquise, who was usually quite unobservant, kept saying: "Take care, my friend. I think my daughter is jealous of you."

'And I did take care, much more so than she.

'But had the little girl been the devil in person, I would still have defied her to see through my game . . . the thing was, her mother's game was perfectly transparent. That flushed face, so often troubled, mirrored her every feeling. Judging by her daughter's hatred of me, I could not help thinking she must have sensed her mother's emotion by catching some look of uncommon tenderness in her expression towards me. The girl was, I might add, a skinny little waif, quite unworthy of the resplendent mould she issued from – even her mother agreed she was ugly, for which she loved her all the more; she was a small scorched topaz . . . or a little bronze mannikin, but with those black eyes . . . sheer sorcery! And after that, she . . .'

At this hiatus he stopped short . . . as if seeking to erase his last remark, as though he had said too much . . . His listeners, however, woke up again; anticipation could be read on all their eager faces, and the Comtesse even hissed between her teeth, expressing their collective relief: 'At last!'

V

'In the early days of my relationship with her mother,' the Comte de Ravila resumed, 'I lavished the kind of fond attention on the girl that we reserve for any child . . . I would bring her bags of sweets, I called her my "little mask", and frequently when I was talking to her mother, I would stroke the plait of hair at her temple, a plait of black, lank hair, with reddish gleams. But "little mask" who had a wide smile for everybody, recoiled from me, frowningly extinguished her smile, and became truly a "little mask" from screwing up her face, the wrinkled mask of some humiliated caryatid that seemed verily to bear the contact of my stroking hand as if she were suffering the weight of a stone cornice.

'Encountering the same sullenness every time, which seemed to spring from hostility, I eventually ignored the little marigold-coloured exotic, that closed up each time I so much as stroked her hair . . . I no longer even spoke to her! "She senses that you are taking me from her," the Marquise would say. "Instinctively, she knows you are depriving her of part of her mother's love." And sometimes, truthful as she was, she would add: "The child is my conscience, and her jealousy, my remorse."

'One day, trying to broach the subject of her aloofness towards me, the Marquise received nothing but the broken, stubborn, facetious answers one extracts painfully, like teeth, from a child who refuses to be drawn – "There's nothing wrong . . . I don't know" – and noting the hardness of the little bronze figure, she stopped asking, and out of lassitude dropped the subject . . .

'I have forgotten to mention that this strange child was very devout, with a kind of Spanish, medieval devotion, dark and superstitious. She would wrap all sorts of scapulars around her skinny body, and plastered over her perfectly flat chest and hung around her sallow neck were stacks of crosses, Blessed Virgins and Holy Ghosts! "Alas, you are an ungodly soul," the Marquise remarked to me, "and you might have scandalized her by something you said. I beg you to watch your tongue when she is present. Don't magnify my faults in the eyes of the child, I already feel so guilty about her!" And when the child's conduct did not alter or soften in any way: "You'll end up hating her," said the Marquise, worried now. "And I shouldn't blame you." But she was mistaken: I felt merely indifference towards the sulky little thing, when she didn't actively irritate me.

'I had become polite with her, as adults do when they dislike each other. I treated her with exaggerated formality, addressing her as "Mademoiselle", to which she would return a glacial "Monsieur". She refused point-blank to do anything to make herself amiable, or to put herself out in the slightest way for me . . . Her mother never succeeded in getting her to show me her drawings, or to play the piano for me. Sometimes I would surprise her, practising a piece with intense concentration, and she would leave off immediately, rise from the piano-stool, and play no more . . .

'Only once, at her mother's insistence (there were guests present), did she sit down at the open instrument, with one of her *martyred* expressions which, I assure you, had nothing gentle about it. She started to play through some piece or other, stumbling horribly, all fingers and thumbs. I was standing in front of the fire, looking at her from an oblique angle. Her back was turned towards me, and with no mirror in front of her she had no way of telling that I was looking at her . . . Suddenly her back (normally she sat with it curved, so that her mother would often say, "If you keep sitting like that, you'll end up with a weak chest") – her back straightened up, as if by gazing at her I had put a bullet through her spine and broken it. Slamming down the piano-lid, which made a fearful racket in falling, she fled the room . . . People went to fetch her back; but that evening no one could induce her to return.

'Well, it appears that the obtusest of men can never be obtuse enough, for there was nothing in the conduct of this sombre child, who interested me so little, to lead me to dwell on the nature of her feelings towards me. Neither did her mother. The latter, who was jealous of every other woman in her salon, was no more jealous of her daughter than I was obtuse about her. The girl's feelings were revealed when the Marquise, who was expansiveness itself in private, and still pale from terror at what she had felt, and now laughing hard at herself for having been so, was imprudent enough to impart to me the cause of it all.'

Like a clever actor, the Comte laid just the right stress on the word *imprudent*, knowing that the entire interest of the story must hang upon that word!

And it worked, apparently, for these twelve beautiful women's faces lit up again with a feeling as intense as that reflected in the faces of cherubim before the throne of God. Is not the curiosity of women as intense as the adoration of the angels? . . . He looked at them, then, with their cherubic faces, shoulders, and so on down – and finding them all ready for what he had to tell them, he resumed quickly and did not stop again:

'Yes indeed, the mere thought of it sent the Marquise into fits of laughter! – as she reported when she told me about it all a little while later;

but she had not always found it funny! – "Imagine the scene," she said to me (I am trying to remember her exact words) – "I was sitting where we are now."

'(It was one of those double-backed couches, known as a *dos-à-dos*, a perfectly designed item of furniture on which to quarrel and make up without moving.)

'"Happily you weren't there when a visitor was announced . . . can you guess who? . . . You'll never guess . . . the priest of Saint-Germain-des-Prés. Do you know him? . . . No, of course you don't, you never go to mass, which is very wicked of you . . . How could you know that this poor old priest is actually a saint, who never sets foot in a lady's house except to beg alms for the poor of the parish or for the church? I thought at first this was why he had come.

'"He prepared my daughter for her First Communion; since that time she communicates regularly, and she has kept him as her confessor. Which is why, since then, I have invited him many times to dinner – all to no avail . . . When he came in, he was extremely agitated. Seeing his features, that were normally so serene, working with such great and undisguised distress, I realized it was not just his shyness, and I could not prevent myself from this unceremonious greeting:

'"'In heaven's name, what is the matter, Father?'

'"'What is wrong, Madame,' he replied, 'is that you see before you the most embarrassed man in all the world. I have been in holy orders for more than fifty years, and I have never been charged with such a delicate mission, or one that I understand less, as this one which concerns you . . .'

'"He sat down, and asked me to make sure that no one interrupted us for as long as our interview lasted. You know how much such formalities tend to frighten me . . . This he noticed.

'"'Madame, do not upset yourself so, you will need all your self-control to hear what I have to say and then explain to me this extraordinary thing, which in truth I cannot bring myself to believe . . . Mademoiselle your daughter, from whom I have just come, is an angel of purity and piety – you know this as well as I. I know her soul. I have held it in my hands since her seventh year, and I am certain that she is mistaken . . . perhaps because of her innocence . . . But this morning she came to tell me in confession that she was – you are not going to believe this any more than I do, Madame, but I must say the word . . . pregnant!'

"'I let out a gasp . . .

"'I gasped just like you, in my confessional this morning,' resumed the priest, 'at this declaration, which she made accompanied by all the signs of the sincerest and most dreadful despair! I know this child through and through. She knows nothing of the world or of sin . . . Of all the girls in my confession, she is certainly the one I would vouch for most readily before God. That is all I can tell you! We priests are the doctors of the soul, and we are charged to deliver them of all their burdens with hands that neither wound nor stain. And so, proceeding with the utmost caution, I asked her, I questioned her, I pressed her, but once the despairing child had uttered the word, and confessed her fault, which she calls a hellish crime (the poor girl thinks she is damned!) – she said nothing more and retreated into a stubborn silence which she would not break except to beg me to come and see you, Madame, to tell you of her crime – "for my mother will have to know," she said, "and I will never have the strength to tell her!"'

"'I listened to the old priest of Saint-Germain-des-Prés, and I scarcely need describe the mixture of astonishment and anguish his words caused me! Like him, and even more than him, I was convinced of the innocence of my daughter; but often the innocent fall, even through their own innocence . . . And what she had said to her confessor was not impossible! . . . She was only thirteen, but she had become a woman, and her precocity had in fact frightened me . . . I was seized with an access of curiosity.

"'I want to know and I shall know everything!' I burst out to the poor old man, who stood before me, patting his hat, speechless with embarrassment. – 'Leave me now, Father. She would not speak to you. But I am sure she will tell me everything . . . I shall drag everything out of her, and then we shall understand what is at present beyond our understanding!'

"'Upon which the priest left – and no sooner had he gone than I went up to my daughter's room, too impatient to ask her to come down and wait for her.

"'I found her before the crucifix above her bed, not kneeling, but prostrated, and pale as death. Her eyes were dry, but red, like eyes that have been crying heavily. I took her in my arms, sat her down next to me, then on my knee, and I told her that I could not believe what her confessor had just told me.

'"But she interrupted me to assure me, with anguish in her voice and expression, that what he had said was indeed true. And then, increasingly alarmed and amazed, I asked her for the name of the man who . . .

'"I did not finish ... What a terrible moment! She buried her head and face in my shoulder ... but I could see the back of her neck, which was burning scarlet, and I could feel her shuddering. And then she became stubbornly silent, as she had with the priest. It was a wall.

'"'It must be someone very unworthy of you, since you seem so ashamed?' I said, trying to provoke her into speaking, since I knew her to be proud.

'"But she stayed silent, her head buried in my shoulder. This went on for what seemed like an eternity, when she said suddenly, without changing position: 'Promise me that you'll forgive me, mother.'

'"I swore that I would, at the risk of perjuring myself a hundred times over; not that I cared a whit! I was boiling over with impatience ... I thought my brain was going to come bursting out of my head ...

'"'In that case, it was Monsieur de Ravila!' she whispered, and stayed where she was, in my arms.

'"Oh, when she said that name, Amédée! I felt I had been punished with a single blow to the heart, for the great misdemeanour of my life. You are a man so terrible where women are concerned, and rack me with so many jealousies, that the horrible 'and why not?' – when one comes to doubt the man one loves – arose in me ... But I had the strength to hide my feelings from the cruel child, who must have sensed that her mother was in love.

'"'Monsieur de Ravila!' I exclaimed, with a voice that I felt must betray me completely – 'but you never even speak to him! – You avoid him' – I was about to add, my anger rising, I could feel it ... 'So you have both betrayed me!' – But I repressed that ... Did I not have to pry out, one by one, every detail of this horrible seduction? ... And so I asked her for them, with a gentleness that nearly killed me, when she herself released me from the vice-like grip, this torture, by saying quite ingenuously:

'"'It was one evening, mother. He was in the big armchair in the corner by the fire, opposite the sofa. He stayed there a long while, then he got up, and I had the misfortune to go and sit in the armchair he had just left. Oh, mother! . . . I felt I had fallen into fire. I wanted to get up, but I couldn't . . . I didn't have the strength! And I felt . . . here, mother, feel here! . . . that what I had . . . was a child! . . .'"'

The Marquise had laughed, said Ravila, when she told him the story; but not one of the twelve women seated round that table dreamed of laughing – and nor did Ravila.

'So there you have it, ladies, believe it or not,' he added, by way of conclusion, 'the crowning love, the most beautiful I have ever inspired in my life!'

He fell silent, and so did his listeners. They were pensive . . . had they understood him?

When Joseph was bound a slave to Potiphar's wife, he was so handsome, says the Koran, that the women he served at table cut their fingers with their knives from looking at him. But the age of Joseph is past, and our preoccupations over dessert are less beguiling.

'What a great ninny that Marquise of yours is, for all her wit, to have told you such a thing!' said the Duchesse, who decided to be cynical, but who still had her golden knife in her hand, and had not used it to cut anything at all.

The Comtesse de Chiffrevas gazed deep into her glass of Rhenish wine, an emerald crystal glass, as mysterious as her reverie.

'And Little Mask?' she inquired.

'Oh, she got married to someone in the provinces – and then she died, very young, before her mother told me this story,' said Ravila.

'That, too . . .' said the Duchesse thoughtfully.

Translated by Stephen Romer

XAVIER FORNERET

A Dream

It's

A dream. – Don't ask me any questions; I'm just describing it as it came to me; see for yourselves. – I thought it was evening. I was in a bedroom and the window was open. The sun was peering in with dying eyes, and seemed to be telling the six upright white sticks that shone up near the ceiling: 'Lights, you will turn pale!' And indeed the sun and the lights were like a diamond set about with rhinestones.

The sun was roaming over a long wooden rectangle, on which there lay a sheet yellow with age and soiled by men. It was also gold over the copper.

The six sticks were six candles.

The long wooden rectangle was a box for a corpse. Around the box, droplets darkened the pavement. It was not blood, but holy water.

God on his silver cross hung his head over the closed box.

Flowers on the box were drying out because of the death that lay beneath them; and despite the sweet breath they exhaled as they died, I smelled an odour of turning flesh, the smell of a marigold in a bouquet of roses.

An old woman was on her knees, praying.

She made the sign of the cross twice over her body and her mouth, which was spitting out Latin and French, said this: 'There's a young woman in there; but what's it to you? I have something else to say to you. Listen: I tear the rings off the withered fingers of the dead, and when I can't tear them off I chop off the fingers. I sell beautiful hair from fair heads. I make myself handkerchiefs out of their *last shirts*. I wear bonnets with stains that are impossible to remove. I live off human death. God may take pity on me, but I don't think he forgives me.'

Only the old woman's lips were speaking in the dead girl's room.

Suddenly I see the coffin roll with a screeching noise,

And the candles light the yellow sheet,

And the old woman falls and her old bones ring out.

The sun disappears.

The room was black and red.

I wake up . . .

It's a quarter to two in the morning. The owl on my windowsill sings of the corpses. Its cry makes me cold all over. Water runs over me. I'm weakening. I go back to sleep.

And I see

Verdigris at the bottom of a vase.

And I see

Lights going off and on like eyes closing and opening.

And I see,

Under a row of green trees, a row of bodies without heads which nonetheless seem to be sticking their tongues out of mouths without teeth.

I reach a vault where the stars skitter about and crash into each other like glass smashing.

And I hear

Iron striking wood, irregular like the rolling of thunder.

And I see

Huge hanging things billowing that look like human skins.

And I smell

An odour that's choking me . . .

Yet I catch my breath and I start to see once more.

A woman approaches me; her heart is on her hand.

A sword goes into and out of the ground around her. The sword seems to have ribbons on it and an eye that's watching.

Suddenly the sword rolls the woman towards me. I'm afraid. I push her away. She turns, and I hear iron striking wood irregularly like rolling thunder.

I can hear the woman hurling fragments of words at me.

And in the air I see

Four men in coats with large hats and big sticks.

A Dream

The woman lunges at them crying 'La Bolivarde! La Bolivarde! La Bolivarde!' I couldn't say why. (I think she meant death.)

Then she disappears inside the four men's coats.

And then I see

A very young girl, with hair rocking back and forth and tears falling, running after the woman, crying out to her and pointing at me: 'But mother, what does he want from you?' 'Nothing more,' the woman replies; 'tell him I AM LEAVING HIM.'

At these words ringing out like a huge church bell, I wake up and see, in the glow of my lamp:

A long shadow without hair, with a violet face, and wide white eyes. It slides and its slides and its steps are like iron striking wood.

And something like a powerful arm tosses me out of my bed.

I run to the window. I open it. The day reveals . . . reveals what? It's light. The owl is still singing, but further away from me.

I look for the spot which the bird has just left.

At that spot, which is still warm, is one of its feathers.

The owl is still singing, but further, further.

And this feather has the same smell that was choking me in my dream.

If all this had any meaning, it wouldn't be a dream.

Translated by Patrick McGuinness

THÉOPHILE GAUTIER

The Mummy's Foot

I had entered, in an idle mood, the shop of one of those curiosity vendors who are called *marchands de bric-à-brac* in that Parisian *argot* which is so perfectly unintelligible elsewhere in France.

You have doubtless glanced occasionally through the windows of some of these shops, which have become so numerous now that it is fashionable to buy antiquated furniture, and that every petty stockbroker thinks he must have his *chambre au moyen âge*.

There is one thing there which clings alike to the shop of the dealer in old iron, the ware-room of the tapestry maker, the laboratory of the chemist, and the studio of the painter: in all those gloomy dens where a furtive daylight filters in through the window-shutters the most manifestly ancient thing is dust. The cobwebs are more authentic than the gimp laces, and the old pear-tree furniture on exhibition is actually younger than the mahogany which arrived but yesterday from America.

The warehouse of my bric-à-brac dealer was a veritable Capharnaum. All ages and all nations seemed to have made their rendezvous there. An Etruscan lamp of red clay stood upon a Boule cabinet, with ebony panels, brightly striped by lines of inlaid brass; a duchess of the court of Louis XV nonchalantly extended her fawn-like feet under a massive table of the time of Louis XIII, with heavy spiral supports of oak, and carven designs of chimeras and foliage intermingled.

Upon the denticulated shelves of several sideboards glittered immense Japanese dishes with red and blue designs relieved by gilded hatching, side by side with enamelled works by Bernard Palissy, representing serpents, frogs and lizards in relief.

From disembowelled cabinets escaped cascades of silver-lustrous

Chinese silks and waves of tinsel, which an oblique sunbeam shot through with luminous beads, while portraits of every era, in frames more or less tarnished, smiled through their yellow varnish.

The striped breastplate of a damascened suit of Milanese armour glittered in one corner; loves and nymphs of porcelain, Chinese grotesques, vases of *céladon* and crackleware, Saxon and old Sèvres cups encumbered the shelves and nooks of the apartment.

The dealer followed me closely through the tortuous way contrived between the piles of furniture, warding off with his hand the hazardous sweep of my coat-skirts, watching my elbows with the uneasy attention of an antiquarian and a usurer.

It was a singular face, that of the merchant; an immense skull, polished like a knee, and surrounded by a thin aureole of white hair, which brought out the clear salmon tint of his complexion all the more strikingly, lent him a false aspect of patriarchal *bonhomie*, counteracted, however, by the scintillation of two little yellow eyes which trembled in their orbits like two louis-d'or upon quicksilver. The curve of his nose presented an aquiline silhouette, which suggested the Oriental or Jewish type. His hands – thin, slender, full of nerves which projected like strings upon the finger-board of a violin, and armed with claws like those on the terminations of bats' wings – shook with senile trembling; but those convulsively agitated hands became firmer than steel pincers or lobsters' claws when they lifted any precious article – an onyx cup, a Venetian glass, or a dish of Bohemian crystal. This strange old man had an aspect so thoroughly rabbinical and cabalistic that he would have been burnt on the mere testimony of his face three centuries ago.

'Will you not buy something from me to-day, sir? Here is a Malay kreese with a blade undulating like flame. Look at those grooves contrived for the blood to run along, those teeth set backward so as to tear out the entrails in withdrawing the weapon. It is a fine character of ferocious arm, and will look well in your collection. This two-handed sword is very beautiful. It is the work of Josepe de la Hera; and this *colichemarde* with its fenestrated guard – what a superb specimen of handicraft!'

'No; I have quite enough weapons and instruments of carnage. I want a small figure, – something which will suit me as a paperweight, for I cannot endure those trumpery bronzes which the stationers sell, and which may be found on everybody's desk.'

The old gnome foraged among his ancient wares, and finally arranged before me some antique bronzes, so-called at least; fragments of malachite, little Hindoo or Chinese idols, a kind of poussah-toys in jade-stone, representing the incarnations of Brahma or Vishnoo, and wonderfully appropriate to the very undivine office of holding papers and letters in place.

I was hesitating between a porcelain dragon, all constellated with warts, its mouth formidable with bristling tusks and ranges of teeth, and an abominable little Mexican fetich, representing the god Vitziliputzili *au naturel*, when I caught sight of a charming foot, which I at first took for a fragment of some antique Venus.

It had those beautiful ruddy and tawny tints that lend to Florentine bronze that warm living look so much preferable to the grey-green aspect of common bronzes, which might easily be mistaken for statues in a state of putrefaction. Satiny gleams played over its rounded forms, doubtless polished by the amorous kisses of twenty centuries, for it seemed a Corinthian bronze, a work of the best era of art, perhaps moulded by Lysippus himself.

'That foot will be my choice,' said to the merchant, who regarded me with an ironical and saturnine air, and held out the object desired that I might examine it more fully.

I was surprised at its lightness. It was not a foot of metal, but in sooth a foot of flesh, an embalmed foot, a mummy's foot. On examining it still more closely the very grain of the skin, and the almost imperceptible lines impressed upon it by the texture of the bandages, became perceptible. The toes were slender and delicate, and terminated by perfectly formed nails, pure and transparent as agates. The great toe, slightly separated from the rest, afforded a happy contrast, in the antique style, to the position of the other toes, and lent it an aerial lightness – the grace of a bird's foot. The sole, scarcely streaked by a few almost imperceptible cross lines, afforded evidence that it had never touched the bare ground, and had only come in contact with the finest matting of Nile rushes and the softest carpets of panther skin.

'Ha, ha, you want the foot of the Princess Hermonthis!' exclaimed the merchant, with a strange giggle, fixing his owlish eyes upon me. 'Ha, ha, ha! For a paperweight! An original idea! – artistic idea! – Old Pharaoh would certainly have been surprised had someone told him that the foot of his adored daughter would be used for a paperweight after he had had a mountain of granite hollowed out as a receptacle for the triple coffin, painted and gilded, covered with hieroglyphics and beautiful paintings of the Judgment of Souls,' continued the queer little merchant, half audibly, as though talking to himself.

'How much will you charge me for this mummy fragment?'

'Ah, the highest price I can get, for it is a superb piece. If I had the match of it you could not have it for less than five hundred francs. The daughter of a Pharaoh! Nothing is more rare.'

'Assuredly that is not a common article, but still, how much do you want? In the first place let me warn you that all my wealth consists of just five louis. I can buy anything that costs five louis, but nothing dearer. You might search my vest pockets and most secret drawers without even find-ing one poor five-franc piece more.'

'Five louis for the foot of the Princess Hermonthis! That is very little, very little indeed. 'Tis an authentic foot,' muttered the merchant, shaking his head, and imparting a peculiar rotary motion to his eyes. 'Well, take it, and I will give you the bandages into the bargain,' he added, wrapping the foot in an ancient damask rag. 'Very fine? Real damask – Indian dam-ask which has never been redyed. It is strong, and yet it is soft,' he mumbled, stroking the frayed tissue with his fingers, through the trade-acquired habit which moved him to praise even an object of such little value that he himself deemed it only worth the giving away.

He poured the gold coins into a sort of medieval alms-purse hanging at his belt, repeating:

'The foot of the Princess Hermonthis to be used for a paperweight!'

Then turning his phosphorescent eyes upon me, he exclaimed in a voice strident as the crying of a cat which has swallowed a fish bone:

'Old Pharaoh will not be well pleased. He loved his daughter, the dear man!'

'You speak as if you were a contemporary of his. You are old enough, goodness knows! but you do not date back to the Pyramids of Egypt,' I answered, laughingly, from the threshold.

I went home, delighted with my acquisition.

With the idea of putting it to profitable use as soon as possible, I placed the foot of the divine Princess Hermonthis upon a heap of papers scribbled over with verses, in themselves an undecipherable mosaic work of erasures; articles freshly begun; letters forgotten, and posted in the table drawer instead of the letter-box, an error to which absent-minded people are peculiarly liable. The effect was charming, *bizarre*, and romantic.

Well satisfied with this embellishment, I went out with the gravity and pride becoming one who feels that he has the ineffable advantage over all the passers-by whom he elbows, of possessing a piece of the Princess Hermonthis, daughter of Pharaoh.

I looked upon all who did not possess, like myself, a paperweight so authentically Egyptian as very ridiculous people, and it seemed to me that the proper occupation of every sensible man should consist in the mere fact of having a mummy's foot upon his desk.

Happily I met some friends, whose presence distracted me in my infatuation with this new acquisition. I went to dinner with them, for I could not very well have dined with myself.

When I came back that evening, with my brain slightly confused by a few glasses of wine, a vague whiff of Oriental perfume delicately titillated my olfactory nerves. The heat of the room had warmed the natron, bitumen and myrrh in which the *paraschistes*, who cut open the bodies of the dead, had bathed the corpse of the princess. It was a perfume at once sweet and penetrating, a perfume that four thousand years had not been able to dissipate.

The Dream of Egypt was Eternity. Her odours have the solidity of granite and endure as long.

I soon drank deeply from the black cup of sleep. For a few hours all remained opaque to me. Oblivion and nothingness inundated me with their sombre waves.

Yet light gradually dawned upon the darkness of my mind. Dreams commenced to touch me softly in their silent flight.

The eyes of my soul were opened, and I beheld my chamber as it actually was. I might have believed myself awake but for a vague consciousness which assured me that I slept, and that something fantastic was about to take place.

The odour of the myrrh had augmented in intensity, and I felt a slight headache, which I very naturally attributed to several glasses of champagne that we had drunk to the unknown gods and our future fortunes.

I peered through my room with a feeling of expectation which I saw nothing to justify. Every article of furniture was in its proper place. The lamp, softly shaded by its globe of ground crystal, burned upon its bracket; the watercolour sketches shone under their Bohemian glass; the curtains hung down languidly; everything wore an aspect of tranquil slumber.

After a few moments, however, all this calm interior appeared to become disturbed. The woodwork cracked stealthily, the ash-covered log suddenly emitted a jet of blue flame, and the discs of the pateras seemed like great metallic eyes, watching, like myself, for the things which were about to happen.

My eyes accidentally fell upon the desk where I had placed the foot of the Princess Hermonthis.

Instead of remaining quiet, as behoved a foot which had been embalmed for four thousand years, it commenced to act in a nervous manner, contracted itself, and leaped over the papers like a startled frog. One would have imagined that it had suddenly been brought into contact with a galvanic battery. I could distinctly hear the dry sound made by its little heel, hard as the hoof of a gazelle.

I became rather discontented with my acquisition, inasmuch as I wished my paperweights to be of a sedentary disposition, and thought it very unnatural that feet should walk about without legs, and I commenced to experience a feeling closely akin to fear.

Suddenly I saw the folds of my bed-curtain stir, and heard a bumping sound, like that caused by some person hopping on one foot across the floor. I must confess I became alternately hot and cold, that I felt a strange wind chill my back, and that my suddenly rising hair caused my nightcap to execute a leap of several yards.

The bed-curtains opened and I beheld the strangest figure imaginable before me.

It was a young girl of a very deep coffee-brown complexion, like the bayadère Amani, and possessing the purest Egyptian type of perfect beauty. Her eyes were almond-shaped and oblique, with eyebrows so black that they seemed blue; her nose was exquisitely chiselled, almost Greek in its delicacy of outline; and she might indeed have been taken for a Corinthian statue of bronze but for the prominence of her cheek-bones and the slightly African fullness of her lips, which compelled one to recognize her as belonging beyond all doubt to the hieroglyphic race which dwelt upon the banks of the Nile.

Her arms, slender and spindle-shaped like those of very young girls, were encircled by a peculiar kind of metal bands and bracelets of glass beads; her hair was all twisted into little cords, and she wore upon her bosom a little idol-figure of green paste, bearing a whip with seven lashes, which proved it to be an image of Isis; her brow was adorned with a shining plate of gold, and a few traces of paint relieved the coppery tint of her cheeks.

As for her costume, it was very odd indeed.

Fancy a *pagne*, or skirt, all formed of little strips of material bedizened with red and black hieroglyphics, stiffened with bitumen, and apparently belonging to a freshly unbandaged mummy.

In one of those sudden flights of thought so common in dreams I heard the hoarse falsetto of the bric-à-brac dealer, repeating like a monotonous refrain the phrase he had uttered in his shop with so enigmatical an intonation:

'Old Pharaoh will not be well pleased. He loved his daughter, the dear man!'

One strange circumstance, which was not at all calculated to restore my equanimity, was that the apparition had but one foot; the other was broken off at the ankle!

She approached the table where the foot was starting and fidgeting about more than ever, and there supported herself upon the edge of the desk. I saw her eyes fill with pearly gleaming tears.

Although she had not as yet spoken, I fully comprehended the thoughts which agitated her. She looked at her foot – for it was indeed her own – with an exquisitely graceful expression of coquettish sadness, but the foot leaped and ran hither and thither, as though impelled on steel springs.

Twice or thrice she extended her hand to seize it, but could not succeed.

Then commenced between the Princess Hermonthis and her foot – which appeared to be endowed with a special life of its own – a very fantastic dialogue in a most ancient Coptic tongue, such as might have been spoken thirty centuries ago in the syrinxes of the land of Ser. Luckily I understood Coptic perfectly well that night.

The Princess Hermonthis cried, in a voice sweet and vibrant as the tones of a crystal bell:

'Well, my dear little foot, you always flee from me, yet I always took good care of you. I bathed you with perfumed water in a bowl of alabaster; I smoothed your heel with pumice-stone mixed with palm-oil; your nails were cut with golden scissors and polished with a hippopotamus tooth; I was careful to select *tatbebs* for you, painted and embroidered and turned up at the toes, which were the envy of all the young girls in Egypt. You wore on your great toe rings bearing the device of the sacred Scarabseus, and you supported one of the lightest bodies that a lazy foot could sustain.'

The foot replied in a pouting and chagrined tone:

'You know well that I do not belong to myself any longer. I have been bought and paid for. The old merchant knew what he was about. He bore you a grudge for having refused to espouse him. This is an ill turn which he has done you. The Arab who violated your royal coffin in the subterranean pits of the necropolis of Thebes was sent thither by him. He desired to prevent you from being present at the reunion of the shadowy nations in the cities below. Have you five pieces of gold for my ransom?'

'Alas, no! My jewels, my rings, my purses of gold and silver were all stolen from me,' answered the Princess Hermonthis with a sob.

'Princess,' I then exclaimed, 'I never retained anybody's foot unjustly. Even though you have not got the five louis which it cost me, I present it to you gladly. I should feel unutterably wretched to think that I were the cause of so amiable a person as the Princess Hermonthis being lame.'

I delivered this discourse in a royally gallant, troubadour tone which must have astonished the beautiful Egyptian girl.

She turned a look of deepest gratitude upon me, and her eyes shone with bluish gleams of light.

She took her foot, which surrendered itself willingly this time, like a woman about to put on her little shoe, and adjusted it to her leg with much skill.

This operation over, she took a few steps about the room, as though to assure herself that she was really no longer lame.

'Ah, how pleased my father will be! He who was so unhappy because of my mutilation, and who from the moment of my birth set a whole nation at work to hollow me out a tomb so deep that he might preserve me intact until that last day when souls must be weighed in the balance of Amenthi! Come with me to my father. He will receive you kindly, for you have given me back my foot.'

I thought this proposition natural enough. I arrayed myself in a dressing gown of large-flowered pattern, which lent me a very Pharaonic aspect, hurriedly put on a pair of Turkish slippers, and informed the Princess Hermonthis that I was ready to follow her.

Before starting, Hermonthis took from her neck the little idol of green paste, and laid it on the scattered sheets of paper which covered the table.

'It is only fair,' she observed, smilingly, 'that I should replace your paperweight.'

She gave me her hand, which felt soft and cold, like the skin of a serpent, and we departed.

We passed for some time with the velocity of an arrow through a fluid and greyish expanse, in which half-formed silhouettes flitted swiftly by us, to right and left.

For an instant we saw only sky and sea.

A few moments later obelisks commenced to tower in the distance; pylons and vast flights of steps guarded by sphinxes became clearly outlined against the horizon.

We had reached our destination.

The princess conducted me to a mountain of rose-coloured granite, in the face of which appeared an opening so narrow and low that it would have been difficult to distinguish it from the fissures in the rock, had not its location been marked by two stelae wrought with sculptures.

Hermonthis kindled a torch and led the way before me.

We traversed corridors hewn through the living rock. Their walls, covered with hieroglyphics and paintings of allegorical processions, might well have occupied thousands of arms for thousands of years in their formation. These corridors of interminable length opened into square chambers, in the midst of which pits had been contrived, through which we descended by cramp-irons or spiral stairways. These pits again conducted us into other chambers, opening into other corridors, likewise decorated with painted sparrowhawks, serpents coiled in circles, the symbols of the *tau* and *pedum* – prodigious works of art which no living eye can ever examine – interminable legends of granite which only the dead have time to read through all eternity.

At last we found ourselves in a hall so vast, so enormous, so immeasurable, that the eye could not reach its limits. Files of monstrous columns stretched far out of sight on every side, between which twinkled livid stars of yellowish flame; points of light which revealed further depths incalculable in the darkness beyond.

The Princess Hermonthis still held my hand, and graciously saluted the mummies of her acquaintance.

My eyes became accustomed to the dim twilight, and objects became discernible.

I beheld the kings of the subterranean races seated upon thrones – grand old men, though dry, withered, wrinkled like parchment, and blackened with naphtha and bitumen – all wearing *pshents* of gold, and breastplates and gorgets glittering with precious stones, their eyes immovably fixed like the eyes of sphinxes, and their long beards whitened by the snow of centuries. Behind them stood their peoples, in the stiff and constrained posture enjoined by Egyptian art, all eternally preserving the attitude prescribed by the hieratic code. Behind these nations, the cats, ibixes, and crocodiles contemporary with them – rendered monstrous of aspect by their swathing bands – mewed, flapped their wings, or extended their jaws in a saurian giggle.

All the Pharaohs were there – Cheops, Chephrenes, Psammetichus, Sesostris, Amenotaph – all the dark rulers of the pyramids and syrinxes. On yet higher thrones sat Chronos and Xixouthros, who was contemporary with the deluge, and Tubal Cain, who reigned before it.

The beard of King Xixouthros had grown seven times around the granite table upon which he leaned, lost in deep reverie, and buried in dreams.

Further back, through a dusty cloud, I beheld dimly the seventy-two pre-adamite kings, with their seventy-two peoples, for ever passed away.

After permitting me to gaze upon this bewildering spectacle a few moments, the Princess Hermonthis presented me to her father Pharaoh, who favoured me with a most gracious nod.

'I have found my foot again! I have found my foot!' cried the princess, clapping her little hands together with every sign of frantic joy. 'It was this gentleman who restored it to me.'

The races of Kemi, the races of Nahasi – all the black, bronzed and copper-coloured nations repeated in chorus:

'The Princess Hermonthis has found her foot again!'

Even Xixouthros himself was visibly affected.

He raised his heavy eyelids, stroked his moustache with his fingers, and turned upon me a glance weighty with centuries.

'By Oms, the dog of Hell, and Tmei, daughter of the Sun and of Truth, this is a brave and worthy lad!' exclaimed Pharaoh, pointing to me with his sceptre, which was terminated with a lotus-flower.

'What recompense do you desire?'

Filled with that daring inspired by dreams in which nothing seems impossible, I asked him for the hand of the Princess Hermonthis. The hand seemed to me a very proper antithetic recompense for the foot.

Pharaoh opened wide his great eyes of glass in astonishment at my witty request.

'What country do you come from, and what is your age?'

'I am a Frenchman, and I am twenty-seven years old, venerable Pharaoh.'

'Twenty-seven years old, and he wishes to espouse the Princess Hermonthis who is thirty centuries old!' cried out at once all the Thrones and all the Circles of Nations.

Only Hermonthis herself did not seem to think my request unreasonable.

'If you were even only two thousand years old,' replied the ancient king, 'I would willingly give you the princess, but the disproportion is too great; and, besides, we must give our daughters husbands who will last well. You do not know how to preserve yourselves any longer. Even those who died only fifteen centuries ago are already no more than a handful of dust. Behold, my flesh is solid as basalt, my bones are bars of steel!

'I will be present on the last day of the world with the same body and the same features which I had during my lifetime. My daughter Hermonthis will last longer than a statue of bronze.

'Then the last particles of your dust will have been scattered abroad by the winds, and even Isis herself, who was able to find the atoms of Osiris, would scarce be able to recompose your being.

'See how vigorous I yet remain, and how mighty is my grasp,' he added, shaking my hand in the English fashion with a strength that buried my rings in the flesh of my fingers.

He squeezed me so hard that I awoke, and found my friend Alfred shaking me by the arm to make me get up.

'Oh, you everlasting sleeper! Must I have you carried out into the middle of the street, and fireworks exploded in your ears? It is afternoon. Don't you recollect your promise to take me with you to see Monsieur Aguado's Spanish pictures?'

'God! I forgot all, all about it,' I answered, dressing myself hurriedly. 'We will go there at once. I have the permit lying there on my desk.'

I started to find it, but fancy my astonishment when I beheld, instead of the mummy's foot I had purchased the evening before, the little green paste idol left in its place by the Princess Hermonthis!

Translated by Lafcadio Hearn

GUSTAVE FLAUBERT

A Simple Heart

I

Madame Aubain's servant Félicité was the envy of the ladies of Pont-l'Évêque for half a century.

She received four pounds a year. For that she was cook and general servant, and did the sewing, washing and ironing; she could bridle a horse, fatten poultry and churn butter – and she remained faithful to her mistress, unamiable as the latter was.

Madame Aubain had married a handsome young man without money who died at the beginning of 1809, leaving her with two small children and a quantity of debts. She then sold all her property except the farms of Toucques and Geffosses, which brought in two hundred pounds a year at most, and left her house in Saint-Melaine for a less expensive one that had belonged to her family and was situated behind the market.

This house had a slate roof and stood between an alley and a lane that went down to the river. There was an unevenness in the levels of the rooms which made you stumble. A narrow hall divided the kitchen from the 'parlour' where Madame Aubain spent her day, sitting in a wicker easy chair by the window. Against the panels, which were painted white, was a row of eight mahogany chairs. On an old piano under the barometer a heap of wooden and cardboard boxes rose like a pyramid. A stuffed armchair stood on either side of the Louis-Quinze chimney-piece, which was in yellow marble with a clock in the middle of it modelled like a temple of Vesta. The whole room was a little musty, as the floor was lower than the garden.

The first floor began with 'Madame's' room: very large, with a pale-flowered wallpaper and a portrait of 'Monsieur' as a dandy of the period. It led to a smaller room, where there were two children's cots without mattresses. Next came the drawing room, which was always shut up and full of furniture covered with sheets. Then there was a corridor leading to a study. The shelves of a large bookcase were respectably lined with books and papers, and its three wings surrounded a broad writing-table in dark wood. The two panels at the end of the room were covered with pen drawings, watercolour landscapes and engravings by Audran, all relics of better days and vanished splendour. Félicité's room on the top floor got its light from a dormer window, which looked over the meadows.

She rose at daybreak to be in time for Mass, and worked till evening without stopping. Then, when dinner was over, the plates and dishes in order, and the door shut fast, she thrust the log under the ashes and went to sleep in front of the hearth with her rosary in her hand. Félicité was the stubbornest of all bargainers; and as for cleanness, the polish on her saucepans was the despair of other servants. Thrifty in all things, she ate slowly, gathering off the table in her fingers the crumbs of her loaf – a twelve-pound loaf expressly baked for her, which lasted for three weeks.

At all times of year she wore a print handkerchief fastened with a pin behind, a bonnet that covered her hair, grey stockings, a red skirt and a bibbed apron – such as hospital nurses wear – over her jacket.

Her face was thin and her voice sharp. At twenty-five she looked like forty. From fifty onwards she seemed of no particular age; and with her silence, straight figure and precise movements she was like a woman made of wood, and going by clockwork.

II

She had had her love story like another.

Her father, a mason, had been killed by falling off some scaffolding. Then her mother died, her sisters scattered, and a farmer took her in and employed her, while she was still quite little, to herd the cows at pasture. She shivered in rags and would lie flat on the ground to drink water from the ponds; she was beaten for nothing, and finally turned out for the theft of a shilling which she did not steal. She went to another farm, where she became dairy-maid; and as she was liked by her employers her companions were jealous of her.

One evening in August (she was then eighteen), they took her to the assembly at Colleville. She was dazed and stupefied in an instant by the noise of the fiddlers, the lights in the trees, the gay medley of dresses, the lace, the gold crosses, and the throng of people jigging all together. While she kept shyly apart, a young man with a well-to-do air, who was leaning on the shaft of a cart and smoking his pipe, came up to ask her to dance. He treated her to cider, coffee and cake, and bought her a silk handkerchief; and then, imagining she had guessed his meaning, offered to see her home. At the edge of a field of oats he pushed her roughly down. She was frightened and began to cry out; and he went off.

On another evening, she was on the Beaumont road. A big hay-wagon was moving slowly along; she wanted to get in front of it, and as she brushed past the wheels she recognized Théodore. He greeted her quite calmly, saying she must excuse it all because it was 'the fault of the drink'. She could not think of any answer and wanted to run away.

He began at once to talk about the harvest and the worthies of the commune, for his father had left Colleville for the farm at Les Écots, so that now he and she were neighbours. 'Ah!' she said. He added that they thought of settling him in life. Well, he was in no hurry; he was waiting for a wife to his fancy. She dropped her head; and then he asked her if she considered marrying. She answered with a smile that it was mean to make fun of her.

'But I am not, I swear!' – and he passed his left hand round her waist. She walked in the support of his embrace; their steps grew slower. The wind was soft, the stars glittered, the huge wagonload of hay swayed in front of them, and dust rose from the dragging steps of the four horses. Then, without a word of command, they turned to the right. He clasped her once more in his arms, and she disappeared into the shadow.

The week after Théodore secured some assignations with her.

They met at the edge of some farmyard, behind a wall, or under a solitary tree. She was not innocent as young ladies are – she had gained knowledge from the animals – but her reason and the instinct of her honour would not let her fall. Her resistance exasperated Théodore's passion; so much so that to satisfy it – or perhaps quite artlessly – he made her an offer of marriage. She was in doubt whether to trust him, but he swore great oaths of fidelity.

Soon he confessed to something troublesome; the year before his parents had bought him a substitute for the army, but any day he might be called up again, and the idea of serving was a terror to him. Félicité took this cowardice of his as a sign of affection, and it redoubled hers. She stole away at night to see him, and when she reached their meeting place Théodore racked her with his anxieties and urgings.

At last he declared that he would go himself to the prefecture for information, and would tell her the outcome on the following Sunday, between eleven and midnight.

When the moment came she sped towards her lover. Instead of him she found one of his friends.

He told her that she would not see Théodore any more. To ensure himself against conscription he had married an old woman, Madame Lehoussais, of Toucques, who was very rich.

There was an uncontrollable outburst of grief. She threw herself on the ground, screamed, called to the God of mercy, and moaned by herself in the fields till daylight came. Then she returned to the farm and announced that she was going to leave; and at the end of the month she received her wages, tied all her small belongings in a handkerchief, and went to Pont-l'Évêque.

In front of the inn there she made inquiries of a woman in a widow's cap, who, as it happened, was just looking for a cook. The girl did not know much, but her willingness seemed so great and her demands so small that Madame Aubain ended by saying:

'Very well, then, I will take you.'

A quarter of an hour afterwards Félicité was installed in her house.

She lived there at first in a tremble, as it were, at 'the style of the house' and the memory of 'Monsieur' floating over it all. Paul and Virginie, the first aged seven and the other hardly four, seemed to her beings of a precious substance; she carried them on her back like a horse; it was a sorrow to her that Madame Aubain would not let her kiss them every minute. And yet she was happy there. Her grief had melted in the pleasantness of things all around.

Every Thursday regular visitors came in for a game of boston, and

Félicité got the cards and foot-warmers ready beforehand. They arrived punctually at eight and left before the stroke of eleven.

On Monday mornings, the dealer who lodged in the covered passage spread out all his old iron on the ground. Then a hum of voices began to fill the town, mingled with the neighing of horses, bleating of lambs, grunting of pigs, and the sharp rattle of carts along the street. About noon, when the market was at its height, a tall, hook-nosed old countryman with his cap pushed back would appear at the door. It was Robelin, the farmer of Geffosses. A little later came Liébard, the farmer from Toucques – short, red and corpulent – in a grey jacket and gaiters shod with spurs.

Both had poultry or cheese to offer their landlady. Félicité was invariably a match for their cunning, and they went away filled with respect for her.

At vague intervals Madame Aubain had a visit from the Marquis de Gremanville, one of her uncles, who had ruined himself by debauchery and now lived at Falaise on his last remaining morsel of land. He invariably came at the luncheon hour, with a dreadful poodle whose paws left all the furniture in a mess. In spite of efforts to show his breeding, which he carried to the point of raising his hat every time he mentioned his 'late father', habit was too strong for him; he poured himself out glass after glass and fired off improper remarks. Félicité edged him politely out of the house – 'You have had enough, Monsieur de Gremanville! Another time!' – and she shut the door on him.

She opened it with pleasure to Monsieur Bourais, who had been a lawyer. His baldness, his white stock, frilled shirt and roomy brown coat, his way of rounding the arm as he took snuff – his whole person, in fact, created that disturbance of mind which overtakes us at the sight of extraordinary men.

As he looked after the property of 'Madame' he remained shut up with her for hours in 'Monsieur's' study, though all the time he was afraid of compromising himself. He respected the magistracy immensely, and had some pretensions to Latin.

To combine instruction and amusement he gave the children a geography book made up of a series of prints. They represented scenes in different parts of the world: cannibals with feathers on their heads, a monkey carrying off a young lady, Bedouins in the desert, the harpooning of a whale, and so on. Paul explained these engravings to Félicité; and that, in fact, was the whole of her literary education. The children's education was undertaken by Guyot, a poor creature employed at the town hall, who was famous for his beautiful hand and sharpened his penknife on his boots.

When the weather was bright, the household set off early for a day at the farm at Geffosses.

Its courtyard was on a slope, with the farmhouse in the middle, and the sea looked like a grey streak in the distance.

Félicité brought slices of cold meat out of her basket, and they breakfasted in a room adjoining the dairy. It was the only surviving fragment of a country house which was now no more. The wallpaper hung in tatters, and quivered in the draughts. Madame Aubain sat with bowed head, overcome by her memories; the children became afraid to speak. 'Why don't you go and play?' she would say, and off they went.

Paul climbed into the barn, caught birds, played at ducks and drakes over the pond, or hammered with his stick on the big casks which boomed like drums. Virginie fed the rabbits or dashed off to pick cornflowers, her quick legs showing their embroidered little drawers.

One autumn evening they went home by the fields. The moon was in its first quarter, lighting part of the sky; and mist floated like a scarf over the windings of the Toucques. Cattle, lying out in the middle of the grass, looked quietly at the four people as they passed. In the third meadow some of them got up and made a half-circle in front of the walkers. 'There's nothing to be afraid of,' said Félicité, as she stroked the nearest on the back with a kind of crooning song; it wheeled round and the others did the same. But when the walkers crossed the next pasture there was a formidable bellow. It was a bull, hidden in the mist. Madame Aubain was about to run. 'No! no! don't go so fast!' They mended their pace, however, and heard a loud breathing behind them, which came nearer. Hoofs thudded on the meadow grass like hammers; why, the bull was galloping now! Félicité turned round, tore up clods of earth with both hands and threw them in its eyes. It lowered its muzzle, waved its horns, and quivered with fury, bellowing terribly. Madame Aubain, now at the end of the pasture with her two little ones, was looking wildly for a place to get over the high bank. Félicité was retreating, still with her face to the bull, keeping up a shower of clods which blinded it, and crying all the time, 'Be quick! Be quick!'

Madame Aubain went down into the ditch, pushed Virginie ahead of her and then Paul, fell several times as she tried to climb the bank, and managed it at last by dint of courage.

The bull had driven Félicité to bay against a rail fence; its slaver was spraying into her face; another second, and it would have gored her. She had just time to slip between two of the rails, and the big animal stopped short in amazement.

This adventure was talked of at Pont-l'Évêque for many a year. Félicité did not pride herself on it in the least, not having the barest suspicion that she had done anything heroic.

Virginie was the sole object of her thoughts, for the child developed a nervous complaint as a result of her fright, and Monsieur Poupart, the doctor, advised sea-bathing at Trouville. It was not a frequented place then. Madame Aubain collected information, consulted Bourais, and made preparations as though for a long journey.

Her luggage started a day in advance, in Liébard's cart. The next day he brought round two horses, one of which had a lady's saddle with a velvet back to it, while a cloak was rolled up to make a kind of seat on the crupper of the other. Madame Aubain rode on that, behind the farmer. Félicité took charge of Virginie, and Paul mounted Monsieur Lechaptois' donkey, lent on condition that great care was taken of it.

The road was so bad that its five miles took two hours. The horses sank in the mud up to their pasterns, and their haunches jerked abruptly in the effort to get out; or else they stumbled in the ruts, and at other moments had to jump. In some places Liébard's mare came suddenly to a halt. He waited patiently until she went on again, talking about the people who had properties along the road, and adding moral reflections to their histories. So it was that as they were in the middle of Toucques, and passed under some windows bowered with nasturtiums, he shrugged his shoulders and said: 'There's a Madame Lehoussais lives there; instead of taking a young man she . . .' Félicité did not hear the rest; the horses were trotting and the donkey galloping. They all turned down a bypath; a gate swung open and two boys appeared; and the party dismounted in front of a manure-heap at the very threshold of the farmhouse door.

When Madame Liébard saw her mistress she gave lavish signs of joy. She served her a luncheon with a sirloin of beef, tripe, black pudding, a fricassee of chicken, sparkling cider, a fruit tart and brandied plums; seasoning it all with compliments to Madame, who seemed in better health; Mademoiselle, who was 'splendid' now; and Monsieur Paul, who had 'filled out' wonderfully. Nor did she forget their deceased grandparents, whom the Liébards had known, as they had been in the service of the family for several generations. The farm, like them, had the stamp of antiquity. The beams on the ceiling were worm-eaten, the walls blackened with smoke, and the window-panes grey with dust. There was an oak dresser laden with every sort of useful article – jugs, plates, pewter bowls, wolf-traps and sheep-shears; and a huge syringe made the children laugh. There was not a tree in the three courtyards without mushrooms growing at the bottom of it or a tuft of mistletoe on its boughs. Several of them had been thrown down by the wind. They had taken root again at the middle; and all were bending under their wealth of apples. The thatched roofs, like brown velvet and of varying thickness, withstood the heaviest squalls. The cart shed, however, was falling into ruin. Madame Aubain said she would see about it, and ordered the animals to be saddled again.

It was another half-hour before they reached Trouville. The little caravan dismounted to pass Écores – it was an overhanging cliff with boats below it – and three minutes later they were at the end of the quay and entered the courtyard of the Golden Lamb, kept by good Madame David.

From the first days of their stay Virginie began to feel less weak, thanks to the change of air and the effect of the sea-baths. These, for want of a bathing-dress, she took in her chemise; and her nurse dressed her afterwards in a coastguard's cabin which was used by the bathers.

In the afternoons they took the donkey and went off beyond Black Rocks, in the direction of Hennequeville. The path climbed at first through gently undulating terrain resembling the green sward of a park, and then reached a plateau where grass fields and arable lay side by side. Hollies rose stiffly out of the briary tangle at the edge of the road; and here and there a great withered tree made zigzags in the blue air with its branches.

They nearly always rested in a meadow, with Deauville on their left, Le Havre on their right, and the open sea in front of them. It glittered in the sunshine, smooth as a mirror and so quiet that its murmur was scarcely to be heard; sparrows chirped out of sight and the immense sky arched over it all. Madame Aubain sat doing her needlework; Virginie plaited rushes by her side; Félicité pulled up lavender, and Paul was bored and anxious to start home.

Other days they crossed the Toucques in a boat and looked for shells. When the tide went out, sea urchins, starfish and jellyfish were left exposed; and the children ran in pursuit of the foam-flakes which scudded in the wind. The sleepy waves broke on the sand and unrolled all along the beach; it stretched away out of sight, bounded on the land side by the dunes which parted it from the Marsh, a wide meadow shaped like an arena. As they came home that way, Trouville, on the hill-slope in the background, grew bigger at every step, and its miscellaneous cluster of houses seemed to break into a gay disorder.

On days when it was too hot they did not leave their room. From the dazzling brilliance outside light fell in streaks between the laths of the blinds. There were no sounds in the village; and on the pavement below not a soul. This silence round them deepened the quietness of things. In the distance, where men were caulking, there was a tap of hammers as they plugged the hulls, and a sluggish breeze wafted up the smell of tar.

The chief amusement was the return of the fishing boats. They began to tack as soon as they had passed the buoys. With their sails hanging at half mast, they drew on with their foresail swelling like a balloon, glided through the splash of the waves, and when they had reached the middle of the harbour suddenly dropped anchor. Then the boats drew up against the quay. The sailors threw quivering fish over the side; a row of carts was waiting, and women in cotton bonnets darted out to take the baskets and give their men a kiss.

One of them came up to Félicité one day, and she entered the lodgings a little later in a state of delight. She had found a sister again – and then Nastasie Barette, 'wife of Leroux', appeared, holding an infant at her breast and another child with her right hand, while on her left was a little cabin boy with his hands on his hips and a cap over his ear.

After a quarter of an hour Madame Aubain sent them off; but they were always to be found hanging about the kitchen, or encountered in the course of a walk. The husband never appeared.

Félicité was seized with affection for them. She bought them a blanket, some shirts and a stove; it was clear that they were making a good thing out of her. Madame Aubain was annoyed by this weakness of hers, and she did not like the liberties taken by the nephew, who said 'thee' and 'thou' to Paul. So as Virginie was coughing and the fine weather gone, she returned to Pont-l'Évêque.

There Monsieur Bourais enlightened her on the choice of a boys' school. The one at Caen was reputed to be the best, and Paul was sent to it. He said his goodbyes bravely, content enough to be going to live in a house where he would have companions.

Madame Aubain resigned herself to her son's absence as a thing that had to be. Virginie thought about it less and less. Félicité missed the noise he made. But she found an occupation to distract her; from Christmas onward she took the little girl to catechism every day.

III

After making a genuflexion at the door she walked up between the double row of chairs under the lofty nave, opened Madame Aubain's pew, sat down, and began to look about her. The choir stalls were filled with the boys on the right and the girls on the left, and the curé stood by the lectern. On a painted window in the apse the Holy Ghost looked down upon the Virgin. Another window showed her on her knees before the child Jesus, and a group carved in wood behind the altar shrine represented St Michael overthrowing the dragon.

The priest began with a sketch of sacred history. The Garden, the Flood, the Tower of Babel, cities in flames, dying nations and overturned idols passed like a dream before her eyes; and the dizzying vision left her with reverence for the Most High and fear of His wrath. Then she wept at the story of the Passion. Why had they crucified Him, when He loved children, fed multitudes, healed the blind, and had willed, in His meekness, to be born among the poor, on the dung-heap of a stable? The sowings, harvests, wine-presses, all the familiar things the Gospel speaks of, were a part of her life. They had been made holy by God's passing; and she loved the lambs more tenderly for her love of the Lamb, and the doves because of the Holy Ghost.

She found it hard to imagine Him in person, for He was not merely a bird, but a flame as well, and a breath at other times. It may be His light, she thought, which flits at night about the edge of the marshes, His breathing which drives on the clouds, His voice which gives harmony to the bells; and she would sit rapt in adoration, enjoying the coolness of the walls and the quiet of the church.

Of doctrines she understood nothing – did not even try to understand. The curé discoursed, the children repeated their lesson, and finally she went to sleep, waking up with a start when their wooden shoes clattered on the flagstones as they left.

It was thus that Félicité, whose religious education had been neglected in her youth, learned the catechism by dint of hearing it; and from that time she copied all Virginie's observances, fasting as she did and confessing with her. On Corpus Christi Day they made a festal altar together.

The First Communion loomed distractingly ahead. She fussed over the shoes, the rosary, the book and gloves; and how she trembled as she helped Virginie's mother to dress her!

All through Mass she was racked with anxiety. She could not see one side of the choir because of Monsieur Bourais; but straight in front of her was the flock of maidens, the white crowns above their hanging veils like a field of snow; and she knew her dear child at a distance by her dainty neck and thoughtful air. The bell tinkled. The heads bowed, and there was silence. As the organ pealed, singers and congregation took up the 'Agnus Dei'; then the procession of the boys began, and after them the girls rose. Walking slowly, with their hands joined in prayer, they went towards the lighted altar, knelt on the first step, received the sacrament one after the other, and came back in the same order to their places. When Virginie's turn came Félicité leaned forward to see her; and with the imaginativeness of deep and tender feeling it seemed to her that she actually was the child; Virginie's face became hers, she was dressed in her clothes, it was her heart beating in her breast. As the moment came to open her mouth she closed her eyes and nearly fainted.

She appeared early in the sacristy next morning to receive communion. She took it with devotion, but it did not give her the same exquisite delight.

Madame Aubain wanted to make her daughter into an accomplished person; and as Guyot could not teach her music or English she decided to place her in the Ursuline Convent at Honfleur as a boarder. The child made no objection. Félicité sighed and thought that Madame lacked feeling. Then she reflected that her mistress might be right; matters of this kind were beyond her.

So one day an old spring-van drew up at the door, and out of it stepped a nun to fetch the young lady. Félicité hoisted the luggage on to the top, admonished the driver, and put six pots of preserves, a dozen pears, and a bunch of violets under the seat.

At the last moment Virginie broke into a fit of sobbing; she threw her arms round her mother, who kissed her on the forehead, saying over and over: 'Come, be brave! Be brave!' The step was raised, and the carriage drove off.

Then Madame Aubain's strength gave way; and in the evening all her friends – the Lormeau family, Madame Lechaptois, the Rochefeuille ladies, Monsieur de Houppeville and Bourais – came in to console her.

To be without her daughter was very painful for her at first. But she heard from Virginie three times a week, wrote to her on the other days, walked in the garden, and so filled up the empty hours.

From sheer habit Félicité went into Virginie's room in the mornings and gazed at the walls. It was boredom to her not to have to comb the child's hair now, lace up her boots, tuck her into bed – and not to see her charming face perpetually and hold her hand when they went out together. In this idle condition she tried making lace. But her fingers were too heavy and broke the threads; she could not attend to anything, she had lost her sleep, and was, in her own words, 'destroyed'.

To 'divert herself' she asked leave to have visits from her nephew Victor.

He arrived on Sundays after Mass, rosy-cheeked, bare-chested, with the scent of the country he had walked through still about him. She laid her table promptly and they had lunch, sitting opposite each other. She ate as little as possible herself to save expense, but stuffed him with food so generously that at last he went to sleep. At the first stroke of vespers she woke him up, brushed his trousers, fastened his tie, and went to church, leaning on his arm with maternal pride.

Victor was always instructed by his parents to get something out of her – a packet of moist sugar, it might be, a cake of soap, spirits, or even money at times. He brought his things for her to mend and she took over the task, only too glad to have a reason for making him come back.

In August his father took him off on a coasting voyage.

It was holiday time, and she was consoled by the arrival of the children. Paul, however, was getting selfish, and Virginie was too old to be addressed as 'thou' any longer; this put a constraint and barrier between them.

Victor went to Morlaix, Dunkirk and Brighton in succession and gave Félicité a present on his return from each voyage. It was a box made of shells the first time, a coffee cup the next, and on the third occasion a large gingerbread man. Victor was growing handsome. He was well made, had a hint of a moustache, good honest eyes, and a small leather hat pushed backwards like a pilot's. He entertained her by telling stories embroidered with nautical terms.

On a Monday, 14 July 1819 (she never forgot the date), he told her that he had signed on for a big voyage and next night but one he would take the Honfleur boat and join his schooner, which was to weigh anchor from Le Havre before long. Perhaps he would be gone two years.

The prospect of this long absence plunged Félicité into deep distress; one more goodbye she must have, and on the Wednesday evening, when Madame's dinner was finished, she put on her clogs and made short work of the twelve miles between Pont-l'Évêque and Honfleur.

When she arrived in front of the Calvary she took the turn to the right instead of the left, got lost in the timber yards, and retraced her steps; some people to whom she spoke advised her to be quick. She went all round the harbour basin, full of ships, and knocked against hawsers; then the ground fell away, lights flashed across each other, and she thought her wits had left her, for she saw horses up in the sky.

Others were neighing by the quayside, frightened at the sea. They were lifted by a tackle and deposited in a boat, where passengers jostled each other among cider casks, cheese baskets and sacks of grain; fowls could be heard clucking, the captain swore; and a cabin boy stood leaning over the bows, indifferent to it all. Félicité, who had not recognized him at first, called 'Victor!' and he raised his head; all at once, as she was darting forward, the gangway was drawn back.

The Honfleur packet, women singing as they hauled it, passed out of harbour. Its framework creaked and the heavy waves whipped its bows. The canvas had swung round, no one could be seen on board now; and on the moon-silvered sea the boat was a black speck which paled gradually, dipped and vanished.

As Félicité passed by the Calvary she had a wish to commend to God what she cherished most, and she stood there praying a long time with her face bathed in tears and her eyes towards the clouds. The town was asleep, coastguards were walking to and fro; and water poured ceaselessly through the holes in the sluice, with the noise of a torrent. The clocks struck two.

The convent parlour would not be open before day. If Félicité were late Madame would most certainly be annoyed; and in spite of her desire to kiss the other child she turned home. The maids at the inn were waking up as she came in to Pont-l'Évêque.

So the poor slip of a boy was going to toss for months and months at sea! She had not been frightened by his previous voyages. From England or Brittany you came back safe enough; but America, the colonies, the islands – these were lost in a dim region at the other end of the world.

Félicité's thoughts from that moment ran entirely on her nephew. On sunny days she was harassed by the idea of thirst; when there was a storm she was afraid of the lightning on his account. As she listened to the wind growling in the chimney or carrying off the slates she pictured him lashed by that same tempest, at the top of a shattered mast, with his body thrown backwards under a sheet of foam; or else (with a reminiscence of the illustrated geography book) he was being eaten by savages, captured in a wood by monkeys, or dying on a desert shore. And never did she mention her anxieties.

Madame Aubain had anxieties of her own, about her daughter. The good sisters found her an affectionate but delicate child. The slightest emotion unnerved her. She had to give up the piano.

Her mother stipulated regular letters from the convent. She lost patience one morning when the postman did not come, and walked to and fro in the parlour from her armchair to the window. It was really amazing; not a word for four days!

To console Madame Aubain by her own example Félicité remarked: 'As for me, Madame, it's six months since I heard ...'

'From whom, pray?'

'Why ... from my nephew,' the servant answered gently.

'Oh! Your nephew!' And Madame Aubain resumed her walk with a shrug of the shoulders, as much as to say: 'I was not thinking of him! And what is more, it's absurd! A scamp of a cabin boy – what does he matter? ... whereas my daughter ... why, just think!'

Félicité, though she had been brought up on harshness, felt indignant with Madame – and then forgot. It seemed the simplest thing in the world to her to lose one's head over the little girl. For her the two children were equally important; a bond in her heart made them one, and their destinies must be the same.

She heard from the chemist that Victor's ship had arrived at Havana. He had read this piece of news in a gazette.

Cigars – they made her imagine Havana as a place where no one does anything but smoke, and there was Victor walking among Negroes in a cloud of tobacco. Could you, she wondered, 'in case you needed to', return by land? What was the distance from Pont-l'Évêque? She questioned Monsieur Bourais to find out.

He reached for his atlas and launched into explanations about longitude; Félicité's consternation provoked a fine pedantic smile. Finally he marked with his pencil a black, imperceptible point in the indentations of an oval spot, and said as he did so, 'Here it is.' She bent over the map; the maze of coloured lines wearied her eyes without conveying anything; and, as Bourais invited her to say what was confusing her, she begged him to show her the house where Victor was living. Bourais threw up his arms, sneezed and laughed immensely: a simplicity like hers was a positive joy. And Félicité did not understand the reason; how could she when she expected, very likely, to see the actual image of her nephew – so stunted was her mind!

A fortnight afterwards Liébard came into the kitchen at market time as usual and handed her a letter from her brother-in-law. As neither of them could read she took it to her mistress.

Madame Aubain, who was counting the stitches in her knitting, put the work down by her side, broke the seal of the letter, started, and said in a low voice, with a look of meaning:

'It is bad news ... that they have to tell you. Your nephew ...'

He was dead. The letter said no more.

Félicité fell on to a chair, leaning her head against the wainscot; and she closed her eyelids, which suddenly flushed pink. Then with bent forehead, hands hanging and fixed eyes, she repeated at intervals:

'Poor little lad! Poor little lad!'

Liébard watched her and heaved sighs. Madame Aubain trembled a little.

She suggested that Félicité should go to see her sister at Trouville. Félicité answered by a gesture that she had no need.

There was a silence. The worthy Liébard thought it was time for them to withdraw.

Then Félicité said:

'They don't care, not they!'

Her head dropped again; and she took up mechanically, from time to time, the long needles on her work table.

Women passed in the yard with a barrow of dripping linen.

As she saw them through the window-panes she remembered her washing; she had put it to soak the day before, today she must wring it out; and she left the room.

Her plank and tub were at the edge of the Toucques. She threw a pile of linen on the bank, rolled up her sleeves and, taking her wooden beater, dealt lusty blows whose sound carried to the neighbouring gardens. The meadows were empty, the river stirred in the wind; and down below long grasses wavered, like the hair of corpses floating in the water. She kept her grief down and was very brave until the evening; but once in her room she surrendered to it utterly, lying stretched on the mattress with her face in the pillow and her hands clenched against her temples.

Much later she heard, from the captain himself, the circumstances of Victor's end. They had bled him too much at the hospital for yellow fever. Four doctors held him at once. He had died instantly, and the chief doctor had said:

'Bah! There goes another!'

His parents had always been brutal with him. She preferred not to see them again; and they made no advances, either because they forgot her or from the callousness of the wretchedly poor.

Virginie began to grow weaker.

Tightness in her chest, coughing, continual fever and veinings on her cheekbones betrayed some deep-seated complaint. Monsieur Poupart had advised a stay in Provence. Madame Aubain determined on it, and would have brought her daughter home at once but for the climate of Pont-l'Évêque.

She made an arrangement with a job-master, and he drove her to the convent every Tuesday. There is a terrace in the garden, with a view over the Seine. Virginie took walks there over the fallen vine leaves, on her mother's arm. A shaft of sunlight through the clouds made her blink sometimes, as she gazed at the sails in the distance and the whole horizon from the castle of Tancarville to the lighthouses at Le Havre. Afterwards they rested in the arbour. Her mother had secured a little cask of excellent Malaga wine; and Virginie, laughing at the idea of getting tipsy, drank a thimbleful of it, no more.

Her strength came back visibly. The autumn glided gently away. Félicité reassured Madame Aubain. But one evening, when she had been out on an errand in the neighbourhood, she found Monsieur Poupart's gig at the door. He was in the hall, and Madame Aubain was tying her bonnet.

'Give me my foot-warmer, purse, gloves! Quicker, come on!'

Virginie had inflammation of the lungs; perhaps it was hopeless.

'Not yet!' said the doctor, and they both got into the carriage under whirling flakes of snow. Night was drawing in and it was very cold.

Félicité rushed into the church to light a taper. Then she ran after the gig, caught up with it in an hour, and jumped lightly in behind. As she held on to the straps a thought came into her mind: 'The courtyard has not been shut up; supposing burglars got in!' And she jumped off.

At dawn next day she presented herself at the doctor's. He had returned home and started for the country again. Then she waited at the inn, thinking that a letter would come by some hand or other. Finally, when it was twilight, she took the Lisieux coach.

The convent was at the end of a steep lane. When she was about half-way up she heard strange sounds – a death-bell tolling. 'It is for someone else,' thought Félicité, and she pulled the knocker violently.

After some minutes she heard the shuffling of slippers, the door opened ajar, and a nun appeared.

The good sister, with an air of compunction, announced: 'She has just passed away.' On the instant the bell of St Leonard's tolled twice as fast.

Félicité went up to the second floor.

From the doorway she saw Virginie stretched on her back, with her hands joined, her mouth open and her head thrown back, beneath a black crucifix that leaned towards her, her ashen face paler than the curtains that hung stiffly around her. Madame Aubain, at the foot of the bed which she clasped with her arms, was choking with sobs of agony. The mother superior stood on the right. Three candlesticks on the chest of drawers made spots of red, and the mist whitened the windows. Some nuns led Madame Aubain away.

For two nights Félicité never left the dead child. She repeated the same prayers, sprinkled holy water over the sheets, then sat down again and watched her. At the end of the first vigil she noticed that the face had grown yellow, the lips turned blue, the nose was sharper, and the eyes sunk in. She kissed them several times, and would not have been immensely surprised if Virginie had opened them again; to minds like hers the supernatural is quite simple. She made the girl's toilette, wrapped her in her shroud, lifted her down into her bier, put a garland on her head, and spread out her hair. It was fair, and extraordinarily long for her age. Félicité cut off a big lock and slipped half of it into her bosom, determined that she should never part with it.

The body was brought back to Pont-l'Évêque, as Madame Aubain intended; she followed the hearse in a closed carriage.

It took another three-quarters of an hour after Mass to reach the cemetery. Paul walked in front, sobbing. Monsieur Bourais was behind, and then came the town's dignitaries, the women wearing black mantles, and Félicité. She thought of her nephew; and because she had not been able to pay these honours to him her grief was doubled, as though the two were being buried together.

Madame Aubain's despair was boundless. It was against God that she first rebelled, thinking it unjust of Him to have taken her daughter from her – she had never done evil and her conscience was so clear! Ah, no! – She ought to have taken Virginie off to the South. Other doctors would have saved her. She accused herself now, wanted to join her child, and broke into cries of distress in the middle of her dreams. One dream haunted her above all. Her husband, dressed as a sailor, had returned from a long voyage, and, shedding tears, announced that he had been ordered to take Virginie away. Then they consulted on how to hide her.

Once she came in from the garden quite upset. A moment ago – and she pointed out the place – father and daughter had appeared to her, standing side by side, and they were doing nothing, just staring at her.

For several months after this she stayed inertly in her room. Félicité lectured her gently; she must live for her son's sake, and for the other, in remembrance of 'her'.

'Her?' answered Madame Aubain, as though she were just waking up. 'Ah, yes! ... yes! ... You do not forget her!' This was an allusion to the cemetery, where she was strictly forbidden to go.

Félicité went there every day.

Precisely at four in the afternoon, she skirted the houses, climbed the hill, opened the gate, and made her way to Virginie's grave. There was a little column of pink marble standing over a stone slab and a garden plot enclosed by chains. The beds were hidden under a coverlet of flowers. She watered their leaves, freshened the gravel, and knelt down to clear the earth. When Madame Aubain was able to come to the grave she felt relief and a sort of consolation.

Then years slipped away, one year like another, and the only notable episodes were the great festivals as they recurred – Easter, the Assumption, All Saints' Day. Only little household incidents marked certain dates and made them memorable years later. In 1825, for instance, two glaziers white-washed the hall; in 1827 a piece of the roof fell into the courtyard and nearly killed a man. In the summer of 1828 it was Madame's turn to offer the consecrated bread; Bourais, about this time, mysteriously absented himself; and one by one old acquaintances passed away: Guyot, Liébard, Madame Lechaptois, Robelin and Uncle Gremanville, who had been paralysed for a long time.

One night the driver of the mail-coach announced the Revolution of July in Pont-l'Évêque. A new sub-prefect was appointed a few days later – Baron de Larsonnière, who had been consul in America, and brought with him, besides his wife, a sister-in-law and three young ladies, quite grown up. They were to be seen about on their lawn, in loose blouses, and they had a Negro servant and a parrot. They paid a call on Madame Aubain, which she did not fail to return. The moment they were spotted in the distance Félicité ran to let her mistress know. But only one thing could really move her – the letters from her son.

Paul's days were spent in a tavern and he was incapable of pursuing a career. She paid his debts, he made new ones; and the sighs that Madame Aubain uttered as she sat knitting by the window reached Félicité at her spinning-wheel in the kitchen.

They took walks together along the espaliered wall, always talking of Virginie and wondering if such and such a thing would have pleased her and what, on some occasion, she would have been likely to say.

All her small belongings filled a cupboard in the two-bedded room. Madame Aubain inspected them as seldom as she could. One summer day she made up her mind to it – and some moths flew out of the cupboard.

Virginie's dresses were hung in a row underneath a shelf, on which there were three dolls, some hoops, a set of toy pots and pans, and the basin that she used. They took out her petticoats as well, and the stockings and handkerchiefs, and laid them out on the two beds before folding them up again. The sunshine lit up these poor things, bringing out their stains and the creases made by the movements of Virginie's body. The air was warm and blue, a blackbird warbled, life seemed bathed in a deep sweetness. They found a little plush hat with thick, chestnut-coloured pile; but it had been eaten all over by moths. Félicité begged it for her own. Their eyes met fixedly and filled with tears; at last the mistress opened her arms, the servant threw herself into them, and they embraced each other, satisfying their grief in a kiss that made them equal.

It was the first time in their lives, Madame Aubain's nature not being expansive. Félicité was as grateful as if she had received a favour, and cherished her mistress from that moment with dog-like devotion and the reverence that would be accorded to a saint.

The kindness of her heart unfolded.

When she heard the drums of a marching regiment in the street she posted herself at the door with a pitcher of cider and asked the soldiers to drink. She nursed cholera patients and protected the Polish refugees; one of these even declared that he wished to marry her. They quarrelled, however; for when she came back from the Angelus one morning she found that he had got into her kitchen and helped himself to a dressed salad which he was quietly eating.

After the Poles came Father Colmiche, an old man who was supposed to have committed atrocities in '93. He lived by the side of the river in the ruins of a pigsty. Little boys watched him through the cracks in the wall, and threw pebbles at him which fell on the pallet where he lay constantly shaken by a catarrh; his hair was very long, his eyes inflamed, and there was a tumour on his arm bigger than his head. She got him some linen and tried to clean up his miserable hole; her dream was to establish him in the bakehouse, without letting him annoy Madame. When the tumour burst she dressed it every day; sometimes she brought him cake, and would put him in the sunshine on a truss of straw. The poor old man, slobbering and trembling, thanked her in his worn-out voice, terrified that he might lose her, and stretched out his hands when he saw her go away. He died; and she had a Mass said for the repose of his soul.

That very day a great happiness befell her; just at dinner-time appeared Madame de Larsonnière's Negro servant, carrying the parrot in its cage, with perch, chain and padlock. A note from the baroness informed Madame Aubain that her husband had been raised to a prefecture and they were departing that evening; she begged her to accept the bird as a memento and mark of her regard.

For a long time the bird had fired Félicité's imagination, because it came from America; and that name reminded her of Victor, so much so that she made inquiries of the servant. She had once gone so far as to say: 'How Madame would enjoy having him!'

The Negro had repeated the remark to his mistress; and as she could not take the bird away with her she chose this way of getting rid of him.

IV

His name was Loulou. His body was green and the tips of his wings rose-pink; his forehead was blue and his throat golden.

But he had the tiresome habits of biting his perch, tearing out his feathers, sprinkling his dirt about, and spattering the water of his tub. He annoyed Madame Aubain, and she gave him to Félicité for good.

She endeavoured to train him; soon he could repeat 'Nice boy! Your servant, sir! Good morning, Marie!' He was placed by the side of the door, and astonished several people by not answering to the name Jacquot, for all parrots are called Jacquot. People compared him to a turkey and a log of wood, and stabbed Félicité to the heart each time. A strange obstinacy on Loulou's part!: as soon as you looked at him he refused to speak.

Nonetheless he was eager for society; for on Sundays, while the Roche-feuille ladies, Monsieur de Houppeville and new familiars – Onfroy the apothecary, Monsieur Varin and Captain Mathieu – were playing their game of cards, he beat the windows with his wings and threw himself about so frantically that they could not hear each other speak.

Bourais' face, undoubtedly, struck him as extremely droll. Directly he saw it he began to laugh – and laugh with all his might. His peals rang through the courtyard and were repeated by the echo; the neighbours came to their windows and laughed too; while Monsieur Bourais, gliding along under the wall to escape the parrot's eye, and hiding his profile with his hat, got to the river and then entered by the garden gate. There was a lack of tenderness in the looks which he darted at the bird.

Loulou had been slapped by the butcher-boy for making so free as to plunge his head into his basket; and since then he was always trying to nip him through his shirt. Fabu threatened to wring his neck, although he was not cruel, for all his tattooed arms and large whiskers. Far from it; he really rather liked the parrot, and in a jovial humour even wanted to teach him to swear. Félicité, who was alarmed by such proceedings, put the bird in the kitchen. His little chain was taken off and he roamed about the house.

His way of going downstairs was to lean on each step with the curve of his beak, raise the right foot, and then the left; and Félicité was afraid that these gymnastics brought on fits of giddiness.

He fell ill and could not talk or eat any longer. There was a growth under his tongue, such as fowls have sometimes. She cured him by tearing the pellicle off with her fingernails. Monsieur Paul was thoughtless enough one day to blow some cigar smoke into his nostrils, and another time when Madame Lormeau was teasing him with the end of her umbrella he snapped at the ferrule. And one day he got lost.

Félicité had put him on the grass to refresh him, and left for a minute, and when she came back – no sign of the parrot! She began by looking for him in the shrubs, by the waterside, and over the roofs, without heeding her mistress's cries of 'Take care, do! You are out of your wits!' Then she investigated all the gardens in Pont-l'Évêque, and stopped the passersby. 'You don't happen to have seen my parrot, by any chance, do you?' And she gave a description of the parrot to those who did not know him. Suddenly, behind the mills at the foot of the hill she thought she could make out something green that fluttered. But on the top of the hill there was nothing. A hawker assured her that he had come across the parrot just before, at Saint-Melaine, in Mother Simon's shop. She rushed there; they had no idea of what she meant. At last she returned home exhausted, with her slippers in shreds and despair in her soul; and as she was sitting in the middle of the garden-seat at Madame's side, telling the whole story of her efforts, a light weight dropped on to her shoulder—it was Loulou! What on earth had he been doing? Exploring the neighbourhood, perhaps!

She had some trouble recovering from this, or rather never did recover. As the result of a chill she had an attack of quinsy, and soon afterwards an earache. Three years later she was deaf; and she spoke very loud, even in church. Though Félicité's sins might have been published in every corner of the diocese without dishonour to her or scandal to anybody, the curé thought it right now to hear her confession in the sacristy only.

Imaginary noises in her head added to her confusion. Her mistress often said to her, 'Heavens! How stupid you are!' 'Yes, Madame,' she replied, and looked about her for something.

Her little circle of ideas grew still narrower; the peal of church-bells and the lowing of cattle ceased to exist for her. All living beings moved as silently as ghosts. One sound only reached her ears now – the parrot's voice.

Loulou, as though to amuse her, reproduced the click-clack of the turnspit, the shrill call of a man selling fish, and the noise of the saw in the joiner's house opposite; when the bell rang he imitated Madame Aubain's 'Félicité! The door! The door!'

They carried on conversations, he endlessly reciting the three phrases in his repertory, to which she replied with words that were just as disconnected but uttered what was in her heart. Loulou was almost a son and a lover to her in her isolated state. He climbed up her fingers, nibbled at her lips, and clung to her kerchief; and when she bent her forehead and shook her head gently to and fro, as nurses do, the great wings of her bonnet and the bird's wings quivered together.

When the clouds massed and the thunder rumbled Loulou broke into cries, perhaps remembering the downpours in his native forests. The streaming rain made him absolutely mad; he fluttered wildly about, dashed up to the ceiling, upset everything, and went out through the window to dabble in the garden; but he was back quickly to perch on one of the fire-dogs and hopped about to dry himself, exhibiting his tail and his beak in turn.

One morning, in the terrible winter of 1837, she put him in front of the fireplace because of the cold. When she returned to him she found him dead in the middle of his cage, his head facing down and his claws caught in the bars. He had died from congestion, no doubt. But Félicité thought he had been poisoned with parsley, and though there was no proof of any kind her suspicions inclined to Fabu.

She wept so piteously that her mistress said to her, 'Well, then have him stuffed!'

She asked advice from the chemist, who had always been kind to the parrot. He wrote to Le Havre, and a person called Fellacher took on the job. But as parcels sometimes got lost in the coach she decided to take the parrot as far as Honfleur herself.

Along the sides of the road were leafless apple-trees, one after the other. Ice covered the ditches. Dogs barked about the farms; and Félicité, with her hands under her cloak, her little black sabots and her basket, walked briskly in the middle of the road.

She crossed the forest, passed High Oak, and reached St Gatien.

A cloud of dust rose behind her, and in it a mail-coach, carried away by the steep hill, rushed down at full gallop like a hurricane. Seeing this woman who would not get out of the way, the driver stood up in front and the postilion shouted too. He could not hold in his four horses, which increased their pace, and the two leaders were grazing her when he forced them to one side of the road with a jerk of the reins. But he was wild with rage, and lifting his arm as he passed at full speed, gave her such a lash from waist to neck with his big whip that she fell on her back.

Her first act, when she recovered consciousness, was to open her basket. Loulou was happily none the worse. She felt a burn in her right cheek, and when she put her hands against it they were red; the blood was flowing.

She sat down on a heap of stones and bound up her face with her handkerchief. Then she ate a crust of bread which she had put in the basket as a precaution, and found a consolation for her wound in gazing at the bird.

When she reached the crest of Ecquemauville she saw the Honfleur lights sparkling in the night sky like a company of stars; beyond, the sea stretched dimly. Then a faintness overtook her and she stopped; her wretched childhood, the disillusion of her first love, her nephew's going away, and Virginie's death all came back to her at once like the waves of an oncoming tide, rose to her throat and choked her.

Afterwards, at the boat, she made a point of speaking to the captain, begging him to take care of the parcel, though she did not tell him what was in it.

Fellacher kept the parrot a long time. He was always promising it for the following week. After six months he announced that a packing-case had been sent, and then nothing more was heard of it. It really seemed as though Loulou was never coming back. 'Ah, they have stolen him!' she thought.

He arrived at last, and looked superb. There he was, erect upon a branch which screwed into a mahogany socket, with a foot in the air and his head on one side, biting a nut which the bird-stuffer – with a taste for impressiveness – had gilded.

Félicité shut him up in her room. It was a place to which few people were admitted, and it held so many religious objects and miscellaneous things that it looked like a chapel and bazaar in one.

A big cupboard impeded you as you opened the door. Opposite the window commanding the garden a little circular one looked into the courtyard; there was a table by the folding bed with a water jug, two combs, and a cube of blue soap in a chipped plate. On the walls hung rosaries, medals, several benign Virgins, and a holy water vessel made out of cocoa nut; on the chest of drawers, which was covered with a cloth like an altar, was the shell box that Victor had given her, and after that a watering can, a toy balloon, exercise books, the illustrated geography, and a pair of young lady's boots; and, fastened by its ribbons to the nail of the looking-glass, hung the little plush hat! Félicité carried observances of this kind so far as to keep one of Monsieur's frock-coats. All the old things Madame Aubain no longer needed she laid hands on for her room. That was why there were artificial flowers along the edge of the chest of drawers and a portrait of the Comte d'Artois in the little window recess.

With the aid of a bracket Loulou was established over the chimney, which jutted into the room. Every morning when she woke up she saw him there in the dawning light, and recalled old days and the smallest details of insignificant acts in a deep quietness which knew no pain.

Unable as she was to communicate with anyone, Félicité lived as insensibly as if she were walking in her sleep. The Corpus Christi processions roused her to life again. Then she went round begging mats and candlesticks from the neighbours to decorate the altar they put up in the street.

In church she was always gazing at the Holy Ghost in the window, and observed that there was something of the parrot in him. The likeness was still clearer, she thought, on a crude colour print representing the baptism of Our Lord. With his purple wings and emerald body the dove was the very image of Loulou.

She bought it, and hung it up instead of the Comte d'Artois, so that she could see them both together in one glance. They were linked in her thoughts; and the parrot was consecrated by his association with the Holy Ghost, which became more vivid to her eye and more intelligible. The Father could not have chosen to express Himself through a dove, for such creatures cannot speak; it must have been one of Loulou's ancestors, surely. And though Félicité looked at the picture while she said her prayers, she swerved a little from time to time towards the parrot.

She wanted to join the Ladies of the Virgin, but Madame Aubain dissuaded her.

And then a momentous event loomed up before them – Paul's marriage.

He had been a solicitor's clerk to begin with, and then tried business, the Customs, the Inland Revenue, and made efforts, even, to get into the Rivers and Forests. By an inspiration from heaven he had suddenly, at thirty-six, discovered his real line – the Registrar's Office. And there he showed such marked capacity that an inspector had offered him his daughter's hand and promised him his influence.

So Paul, grown serious, brought the lady to see his mother.

She sniffed at the ways of Pont-l'Évêque, gave herself great airs, and wounded Félicité's feelings. Madame Aubain was relieved at her departure.

The week after came news of Monsieur Bourais' death in an inn in Lower Brittany. The rumour of suicide was confirmed, and doubts arose as to his honesty. Madame Aubain studied his accounts, and soon found out the whole tale of his misdoings – embezzled arrears, secret sales of wood, forged receipts, etc. Besides that he had an illegitimate child, and 'relations with a person at Dozulé'.

These shameful facts distressed her considerably. In March 1853 she was seized with a pain in the chest; her tongue seemed to be covered with a film, and leeches did not ease her laboured breathing. On the ninth evening of her illness she died, aged just seventy-two.

She passed as being younger, owing to the bands of brown hair which framed her pale, pock-marked face. There were few friends to regret her, for she had a stiffness of manner which kept people at a distance.

But Félicité mourned for her as one seldom mourns for a master. It upset her sense of the world and seemed contrary to the order of things, impossible and monstrous, that Madame should die before her.

Ten days afterwards, which was the time it took to hurry there from Besançon, the heirs arrived. The daughter-in-law ransacked the drawers, chose some furniture, and sold the rest; and then they went back to their registering.

Madame's armchair, her small round table, her foot-warmer and the eight chairs were gone! Yellow patches in the middle of the panels showed where engravings had hung. They had carried off the two little beds and the mattresses, and all Virginie's belongings had disappeared from the cupboard. Félicité went from floor to floor dazed with sorrow.

The next day there was a notice on the door, and the apothecary shouted in her ear that the house was for sale.

She tottered, and was obliged to sit down. What distressed her most of all was to give up her room, so suitable as it was for poor Loulou. She enveloped him in a look of anguish when she was imploring the Holy Ghost, and formed the idolatrous habit of kneeling in front of the parrot to say her prayers. Sometimes the sun shone in at the little window and caught his glass eye, and a great luminous ray shot out of it and put her in an ecstasy.

She had a pension of fifteen pounds a year which her mistress had left her. The garden gave her a supply of vegetables. As for clothes, she had enough to last her to the end of her days, and she economized in candles by going to bed at dusk.

She hardly ever went out, as she did not like passing the dealer's shop, where some of the old furniture was exposed for sale. Since her fit of giddiness she dragged one leg; and as her strength was failing Mother Simon, whose grocery business had collapsed, came every morning to split the wood and pump water for her.

Her eyes grew feeble. The shutters ceased to be thrown open. Years and years passed, and the house was neither let nor sold.

Félicité never asked for repairs because she was afraid of being sent away. The boards on the roof rotted; her bolster was wet for a whole winter. After Easter she spat blood.

Then Mother Simon called in a doctor. Félicité wanted to know what was the matter with her. But she was too deaf to hear, and the only word which reached her was 'pneumonia'. It was a word she knew, and she answered softly 'Ah! Like Madame,' thinking it natural that she should follow her mistress.

The time for the festal shrines was drawing near. The first one was always at the bottom of the hill, the second in front of the post office, and the third towards the middle of the street. There was some rivalry in the matter of this one, and the women of the parish ended by choosing Madame Aubain's courtyard.

Félicité's breathing became more laboured and her fever increased. She was vexed to be doing nothing for the altar. If only she could at least have put something there! Then she thought of the parrot. The neighbours objected that it would not be decent. But the curé gave her permission, which so intensely delighted her that she begged him to accept Loulou, her sole possession, when she died.

From Tuesday to Saturday, the eve of the festival, she coughed more often. By the evening her face had shrivelled, her lips stuck to her gums, and she was vomiting; and at twilight next morning, feeling very low, she sent for a priest.

Three kindly women were round her during the extreme unction. Then she announced that she must speak to Fabu. He arrived in his Sunday clothes, ill at ease in the funereal atmosphere.

'Forgive me,' she said, with an effort to stretch out her arm; 'I thought it was you who had killed him.'

What did she mean by such stories? She suspected him of murder – a man like him! He waxed indignant, and was on the point of making a row.

'There,' said the women, 'she is no longer in her senses, you can see it well enough!'

Félicité spoke to shadows of her own from time to time. The women went away, and Mother Simon had breakfast. A little later she took Loulou and brought him close to Félicité with the words:

'Come, now, say goodbye to him!'

Loulou was not a corpse, but worms had devoured him; one of his wings was broken, and tow was coming out of his stomach. But she was blind now; she kissed him on the forehead and kept him close against her cheek. Mother Simon took him back from her to go and put him on the altar.

V

Summer scents were coming up from the meadows; flies were buzzing; the sun was making the river glitter and heating the slates. Mother Simon came back into the room and slowly fell asleep.

She woke at the noise of bells; people were coming out from vespers. Félicité's delirium subsided. She thought of the procession and saw it as if she were there.

All the schoolchildren, the church singers and the firemen walked on the pavement, while in the middle of the road the verger armed with his halberd and the beadle bearing a large cross advanced in front. Then came the schoolmaster, with an eye on his boys, and the sister, anxious about her little girls; three of the daintiest, each with a head of angelic curls, were scattering rose-petals in the air; the deacon conducted the band with outstretched arms; and two censer-bearers turned back at every step towards the Holy Sacrament, which was borne by the curé, wearing his beautiful chasuble, under a canopy of dark-red velvet held up by four churchwardens. A crowd of people pressed behind, between the white cloths covering the house walls, and they reached the bottom of the hill.

A cold sweat moistened Félicité's temples. Mother Simon sponged her with a piece of linen, saying to herself that one day she would have to go that way.

The hum of the crowd increased, was very loud for an instant, and then became fainter.

A fusillade shook the window-panes. It was the postilions saluting the monstrance. Félicité rolled her eyes and said as audibly as she could: 'Does he look well?' The parrot was weighing on her mind.

Her agony began. A death-rattle that grew more and more convulsed made her sides heave. Bubbles of froth came at the corners of her mouth and her whole body trembled.

Soon the booming of the ophicleides, the high voices of the children and the deep voices of the men were distinguishable. At intervals all was silent, and the tread of feet, deadened by the flowers they walked on, sounded like a flock pattering on grass.

The clergy appeared in the courtyard. Mother Simon clambered on to a chair to reach the little window, and looked straight down at the shrine. Green garlands hung over the altar, which was decked with a flounce of English lace. In the middle was a small frame with relics in it; there were two orange-trees at the corners, and all along stood silver candlesticks and china vases, with sunflowers, lilies, peonies, foxgloves and tufts of hortensia. This heap of blazing colour slanted from the level of the altar to the carpet which went on over the pavement; and some rare objects caught the eye. There was a silver-gilt sugar basin with a crown of violets; pendants of Alençon stone glittered on the moss, and two Chinese screens displayed their landscapes. Loulou was hidden under roses, and showed nothing but his blue forehead, like a plaque of lapis lazuli.

The churchwardens, singers and children took their places round the three sides of the yard. The priest went slowly up the steps, and placed his great, radiant golden sun upon the lace. Everyone knelt down. There was a deep silence; and the censers glided to and fro on the full swing of their chains.

An azure vapour rose up into Félicité's room. Her nostrils met it; she inhaled it sensuously, mystically; and then closed her eyes. Her lips smiled. The beats of her heart lessened one by one, fainter each time and softer, as a fountain peters out, an echo disappears; and when she sighed her last breath she thought she saw an opening in the heavens, and a gigantic parrot hovering above her head.

Translated by Arthur McDowall

CHARLES BAUDELAIRE

Knock Down the Poor!

For fifteen days I kept to my room, surrounding myself with books popular at the time (sixteen or seventeen years ago): I'm referring to books on the art of making people happy and wise and rich in twenty-four hours. I had thus digested – or rather, swallowed – every elucubration of every entrepreneur of public happiness, those who counsel all the poor to become slaves, and those who would rather persuade the poor that they are each and all dethroned kings. It is not surprising that I was in a state somewhere between vertigo and idiocy.

Only it had seemed to me that I felt, hidden at the bottom of my intellect, the obscure germ of an idea superior to all the old wives' formulas I had come across recently in the dictionaries. But it was only the idea of an idea, infinitely vague.

I left my room with a great thirst. A passionate taste for bad reading matter breeds a proportionate need for the air at large and for refreshment.

As I went into a bar, a beggar held out his hat with one of those looks that would throw down thrones if mind moved matter, or if the magnetizers could really ripen grapes.

At the same time, I heard a voice at my ear whispering, a voice I knew well; it was that of a good Angel, or good Demon, one always with me. If Socrates had his good Demon, why could I not have my good Angel, and why could I not have the honour, like Socrates, of my own certificate of madness, signed by the subtle Lélut and the circumspect Baillarger?

There is this difference between Socrates' Demon and mine, that his acted only in restraining, averting, holding back, whereas mine works to counsel, suggest, persuade. Poor Socrates had merely a prohibiting Demon; mine is a great affirmer, a Demon of action, a Demon of combat.

What his voice whispered now was: 'One is equal to another only if he can prove it, and worthy of liberty only if he can win it.'

Immediately I attacked my beggar. With a single blow of my fist I took care of one eye which, in a second, swelled into a ball. I broke one of my fingernails in cracking two of his teeth and, since I didn't feel strong enough – delicately endowed as I am and without experience in boxing – to knock this old guy out quickly – with one hand I grabbed him by the collar and with the other seized his throat and proceeded to bang his head against the wall. I must admit I had already given the place a good look around, verifying that in this deserted suburb I could count on plenty of time outside any police beat.

Afterwards, by a kick in the back sharp enough to break a shoulder blade, having floored this battered sexagenarian, I got hold of a fallen tree branch and belaboured him with the fierce energy of a cook tenderizing a steak.

Then suddenly – O miracle! O joyful philosopher, the excellence of whose theory is verified! – I beheld that antique carcass flip over and rise up with an energy I would never have suspected in a machine so dilapidated and, with a look of hatred that appeared to me *good augury*, the decrepit ruffian threw himself on me, blacked both my eyes, broke four teeth, and with the same old branch fell to beating me nearly to jelly. – By my active medication I had restored to him his pride and his life.

Well I gave him forcible signs that I considered the discussion at an end and, standing up with the satisfaction of a Stoic sophist, I said to him, 'Monsieur, *you are my equal!* Do me the honour of sharing my purse; and remember, if you are really a philanthropist, then you must render to all your colleagues, when they go to begging, the theory that I just had the *pain* of trying out on your back.'

He swore to me that he understood my theory, and would follow my counsels.

Translated by Keith Waldrop

JULES VERNE

A Drama in the Air

In the month of September, 185–, I arrived at Frankfort-am-Maine. My passage through the principal German cities had been brilliantly marked by balloon ascents; but as yet no German had accompanied me in my car, and the fine experiments made at Paris by Messieurs Green, Eugene Godard and Poitevin had not tempted the grave Teutons to essay aerial voyages.

But scarcely had the news of my approaching ascent spread through Frankfurt, than three of the principal citizens begged the favour of being allowed to ascend with me. Two days afterwards we were to start from the Place de la Comédie. I began at once to get my balloon ready. It was of silk, prepared with gutta percha, a substance made impermeable by acids or gasses; and its volume, which was three thousand cubic yards, enabled it to ascend to the loftiest heights.

The day of the ascent was that of the great September fair, which attracts so many people to Frankfort. Lighting gas, of a perfect quality and of great lifting power, had been furnished to me in excellent condition, and at about eleven o'clock the balloon was filled; but only three-quarters filled, – an indispensable precaution, for, as one rises, the atmosphere diminishes in density, and the fluid enclosed within the balloon, acquiring more elasticity, might burst its sides. My calculations had furnished me with exactly the quantity of gas necessary to carry up my companions and myself.

We were to start at noon. The impatient crowd which pressed around the enclosed space, filling the enclosed square, overflowing into the contiguous streets, and covering the houses from the ground floor to the slated gables, presented a striking scene. The high winds of the preceding days had subsided. An oppressive heat fell from the cloudless sky. Scarcely a breath animated the atmosphere. In such weather, one might descend again upon the very spot whence he had risen.

I carried three hundred pounds of ballast in bags; the car, quite round, four feet in diameter, was comfortably arranged; the hempen cords which supported it stretched symmetrically over the upper hemisphere of the balloon; the compass was in place, the barometer suspended in the circle which united the supporting cords, and the anchor carefully put in order. All was now ready for the ascent.

Among those who pressed around the enclosure, I remarked a young man with a pale face and agitated features. The sight of him impressed me. He was an eager spectator of my ascents, whom I had already met in several German cities. With an uneasy air, he closely watched the curious machine, as it lay motionless a few feet above the ground; and he remained silent among those about him.

Twelve o'clock came. The moment had arrived, but my travelling companions did not appear.

I sent to their houses, and learned that one had left for Hamburg, another for Vienna, and the third for London. Their courage had failed them at the moment of undertaking one of those excursions which, thanks to the ability of living aeronauts, are free from all danger. As they formed, in some sort, a part of the programme of the day, the fear had seized them that they might be forced to execute it faithfully, and they had fled far from the scene at the instant when the balloon was being filled. Their courage was evidently the inverse ratio of their speed in decamping.

The multitude, half deceived, showed not a little ill-humour. I did not hesitate to ascend alone. In order to re-establish the equilibrium between the specific gravity of the balloon and the weight which had thus proved wanting, I replaced my companions by more sacks of sand, and got into the car. The twelve men who held the balloon by twelve cords fastened to the equatorial circle, let them slip a little between their fingers, and the balloon rose several feet higher. There was not a breath of wind, and the atmosphere was so leaden that it seemed to forbid the ascent.

'Is everything ready?' I cried.

The men put themselves in readiness. A last glance told me that I might go.

'Attention!'

There was a movement in the crowd, which seemed to be invading the enclosure.

'Let go!'

The balloon rose slowly, but I experienced a shock which threw me to the bottom of the car.

When I got up, I found myself face to face with an unexpected fellow-voyager, – the pale young man.

'Monsieur, I salute you,' said he, with the utmost coolness.

'By what right –'

'Am I here? By the right which the impossibility of your getting rid of me confers.'

I was amazed! His calmness put me out of countenance, and I had nothing to reply. I looked at the intruder, but he took no notice of my astonishment.

'Does my weight disarrange your equilibrium, monsieur?' he asked. 'You will permit me –'

And without waiting for my consent, he relieved the balloon of two bags, which he threw into space.

'Monsieur,' said I, taking the only course now possible, 'you have come; very well, you will remain; but to me alone belongs the management of the balloon.'

'Monsieur,' said he, 'your urbanity is French all over: it comes from my own country. I morally press the hand you refuse me. Make all precautions, and act as seems best to you. I will wait till you have done –'

'For what?'

'To talk with you.'

The barometer had fallen to twenty-six inches. We were nearly six hundred yards above the city; but nothing betrayed the horizontal displacement of the balloon, for the mass of air in which it is enclosed goes forward with it. A sort of confused glow enveloped the objects spread out under us, and unfortunately obscured their outline.

I examined my companion afresh.

He was a man of thirty years, simply clad. The sharpness of his features betrayed an indomitable energy, and he seemed very muscular. Indifferent to the astonishment he created, he remained motionless, trying to distinguish the objects which were vaguely confused below us.

'Miserable mist!' said he, after a few moments.

I did not reply.

'You owe me a grudge?' he went on. 'Bah! I could not pay for my journey, and it was necessary to take you by surprise.'

'Nobody asks you to descend, monsieur!'

'Eh, do you not know, then, that the same thing happened to the Counts of Laurencin and Dampierre, when they ascended at Lyon, on 15 January 1784? A young merchant, named Fontaine, scaled the gallery, at the risk of capsizing the machine. He accomplished the journey, and nobody died of it!'

'Once on the ground, we will have an explanation,' replied I, piqued at the light tone in which he spoke.

'Bah! Do not let us think of our return.'

'Do you think, then, that I shall not hasten to descend?'

'Descend!' said he, in surprise. 'Descend? Let us begin by first ascending.'

And before I could prevent it, two more bags had been thrown over the car, without even having been emptied.

'Monsieur!' cried I, in a rage.

'I know your ability,' replied the unknown quietly, 'and your fine ascents are famous. But if Experience is the sister of Practice, she is also a cousin of Theory, and I have studied the aerial art long. It has got into my head!' he added sadly, falling into a silent reverie.

The balloon, having risen some distance farther, now became stationary. The unknown consulted the barometer, and said, –

'Here we are, at eight hundred yards. Men are like insects. See! I think we should always contemplate them from this height, to judge correctly of their proportions. The Place de la Comédie is transformed into an immense ant-hill. Observe the crowd which is gathered on the quays; and the mountains also get smaller and smaller. We are over the Cathedral. The Main is only a line, cutting the city in two, and the bridge seems a thread thrown between the two banks of the river.'

The atmosphere became somewhat chilly.

'There is nothing I would not do for you, my host,' said the unknown. 'If you are cold, I will take off my coat and lend it to you.'

'Thanks,' said I dryly.

'Bah! Necessity makes law. Give me your hand. I am your fellow countryman; you will learn something in my company, and my conversation will indemnify you for the trouble I have given you.'

I sat down, without replying, at the opposite extremity of the car. The young man had taken a voluminous manuscript from his great-coat. It was an essay on ballooning.

'I possess,' said he, 'the most curious collection of engravings and caricatures extant concerning aerial manias. How people admired and scoffed at the same time at this precious discovery! We are happily no longer in the age in which Montgolfier tried to make artificial clouds with steam, or a gas having electrical properties, produced by the combustion of moist straw and chopped-up wool.'

'Do you wish to depreciate the talent of the inventors?' I asked, for I had resolved to enter into the adventure. 'Was it not good to have proved by experience the possibility of rising in the air?'

'Ah, monsieur, who denies the glory of the first aerial navigators? It required immense courage to rise by means of those frail envelopes which only contained heated air. But I ask you, has the aerial science made great progress since Blanchard's ascensions, that is, since nearly a century ago? Look here, monsieur.'

The unknown took an engraving from his portfolio.

'Here,' said he, 'is the first aerial voyage undertaken by Pilâtre des Rosiers and the Marquis d'Arlandes, four months after the discovery of balloons. Louis XVI refused to consent to the venture, and two men who were condemned to death were the first to attempt the aerial ascent. Pilâtre des Rosiers became indignant at this injustice, and, by means of intrigues, obtained permission to make the experiment. The car, which renders the management easy, had not then been invented, and a circular gallery was placed around the lower and contracted part of the Montgolfier balloon. The two aeronauts must then remain motionless at each extremity of this gallery, for the moist straw which filled it forbade them all motion. A chafing-dish with fire was suspended below the orifice of the balloon; when the aeronauts wished to rise, they threw straw upon this brazier, at the risk of setting fire to the balloon, and the air, more heated, gave it fresh ascending power. The two bold travellers rose, on 21 November 1783, from the Muette Gardens, which the dauphin had put at their disposal. The balloon went up majestically, passed over the Isle of Swans, crossed the Seine at the Conference barrier, and, drifting between the dome of the Invalides and the Military School, approached the Church of Saint Sulpice. Then the aeronauts added to the fire, crossed the Boulevard, and descended beyond the Enfer barrier. As it touched the soil, the balloon collapsed, and for a few moments buried Pilâtre des Rosiers under its folds.'

'Unlucky augury,' I said, interested in the story, which affected me nearly.

'An augury of the catastrophe which was later to cost this unfortunate man his life,' replied the unknown sadly. 'Have you ever experienced anything like it?'

'Never.'

'Bah! Misfortunes sometimes occur unforeshadowed!' added my companion.

He then remained silent.

Meanwhile we were advancing southward, and Frankfort had already passed from beneath us.

'Perhaps we shall have a storm,' said the young man.

'We shall descend before that,' I replied.

'Indeed! It is better to ascend. We shall escape it more surely.'

And two more bags of sand were hurled into space.

The balloon rose rapidly, and stopped at twelve hundred yards. I became colder; and yet the sun's rays, falling upon the surface, expanded the gas within, and gave it a greater ascending force.

'Fear nothing,' said the unknown. 'We have still three thousand five hundred fathoms of breathing air. Besides, do not trouble yourself about what I do.'

I would have risen, but a vigorous hand held me to my seat.

'Your name?' I asked.

'My name? What matters it to you?'

'I demand your name!'

'My name is Erostratus or Empedocles, whichever you choose!'

This reply was far from reassuring.

The unknown, besides, talked with such strange coolness that I anxiously asked myself whom I had to deal with.

'Monsieur,' he continued, 'nothing original has been imagined since the physicist Charles. Four months after the discovery of balloons, this able man had invented the valve, which permits the gas to escape when the balloon is too full, or when you wish to descend; the car, which aids the management of the machine; the netting, which holds the envelope of the balloon, and divides the weight over its whole surface; the ballast, which enables you to ascend, and to choose the place of your landing; the india-rubber coating, which renders the tissue impermeable; the barometer, which shows the height attained. Lastly, Charles used hydrogen, which, fourteen times lighter than air, permits you to penetrate to the highest atmospheric regions, and does not expose you to the dangers of a combustion in the air. On 1 December 1783, three hundred thousand spectators were crowded around the Tuileries. Charles rose, and the soldiers presented arms to him. He travelled nine leagues in the air, conducting his balloon with an ability not surpassed by modern aeronauts. The king awarded him a pension of two thousand livres; for then they encouraged new inventions.'

The unknown now seemed to be under the influence of considerable agitation.

'Monsieur,' he resumed, 'I have studied this, and I am convinced that the first aeronauts guided their balloons. Without speaking of Blanchard, whose assertions may be received with doubt, Guyton-Morveaux, by the aid of oars and rudder, made his machine answer to the helm, and take the direction he determined on. More recently, Monsieur Julien, a watchmaker, made some convincing experiments at the Hippodrome, in Paris; for, by a special mechanism, his aerial apparatus, oblong in form, went visibly against the wind. It occurred to Monsieur Petin to place four hydrogen balloons together; and, by means of sails hung horizontally and partly folded, he hopes to be able to disturb the equilibrium, and, thus inclining the apparatus, to convey it in an oblique direction. They speak, also, of forces to overcome the resistance of currents, – for instance, the screw; but the screw, working on a moveable centre, will give no result. I, monsieur, have discovered the only means of guiding balloons; and no academy has come to my aid, no city has filled up subscriptions for me, no government has thought fit to listen to me! It is infamous!'

The unknown gesticulated fiercely, and the car underwent violent oscillations. I had much trouble in calming him.

Meanwhile the balloon had entered a more rapid current, and we advanced south, at fifteen hundred yards above the earth.

'See, there is Darmstadt,' said my companion, leaning over the car. 'Do you perceive the chateau? Not very distinctly, eh? What would you have? The heat of the storm makes the outline of objects waver, and you must have a skilled eye to recognize localities.'

'Are you certain it is Darmstadt?' I asked.

'I am sure of it. We are now six leagues from Frankfort.'

'Then we must descend.'

'Descend! You would not go down on the steeples,' said the unknown, with a chuckle.

'No, but in the suburbs of the city.'

'Well, let us avoid the steeples!'

So speaking, my companion seized some bags of ballast. I hastened to prevent him; but he overthrew me with one hand, and the unballasted balloon ascended to two thousand yards.

'Rest easy,' said he, 'and do not forget that Brioschi, Biot, Gay-Lussac, Bixio and Barral ascended to still greater heights to make their scientific experiments.'

'Monsieur, we must descend,' I resumed, trying to persuade him by gentleness. 'The storm is gathering around us. It would be more prudent –'

'Bah! We will mount higher than the storm, and then we shall no longer fear it!' cried my companion. 'What is nobler than to overlook the clouds which oppress the earth? Is it not an honour thus to navigate on aerial billows? The greatest men have travelled as we are doing. The Marchioness and Countess de Montalembert, the Countess of Podenas, Mademoiselle la Garde, the Marquis de Montalembert, rose from the Faubourg Saint-Antoine for these unknown regions, and the Duke de Chartres exhibited much skill and presence of mind in his ascent on 15 July 1784. At Lyon, the Counts of Laurencin and Dampierre; at Nantes, Monsieur de Luynes; at Bordeaux, D'Arbelet des Granges; in Italy, the Chevalier Andreani; in our own time, the Duke of Brunswick, – have all left the traces of their glory in the air. To equal these great personages, we must penetrate still higher than they into the celestial depths! To approach the infinite is to comprehend it!'

The rarefaction of the air was fast expanding the hydrogen in the balloon, and I saw its lower part, purposely left empty, swell out, so that it was absolutely necessary to open the valve; but my companion did not seem to intend that I should manage the balloon as I wished. I then resolved to pull the valve cord secretly, as he was excitedly talking; for I feared to guess with whom I had to deal. It would have been too horrible! It was nearly a quarter before one. We had been gone forty minutes from Frankfort; heavy clouds were coming against the wind from the south, and seemed about to burst upon us.

'Have you lost all hope of succeeding in your project?' I asked with anxious interest.

'All hope!' exclaimed the unknown in a low voice. 'Wounded by slights and caricatures, these asses' kicks have finished me! It is the eternal punishment reserved for innovators! Look at these caricatures of all periods, of which my portfolio is full.'

While my companion was fumbling with his papers, I had seized the valve-cord without his perceiving it. I feared, however, that he might hear the hissing noise, like a water course, which the gas makes in escaping.

'How many jokes were made about the Abbé Miolan!' said he. 'He was to go up with Janninet and Bredin. During the filling their balloon caught fire, and the ignorant populace tore it in pieces! Then this caricature of "curious animals" appeared, giving each of them a punning nickname.'

I pulled the valve-cord, and the barometer began to ascend. It was time. Some far-off rumblings were heard in the south.

'Here is another engraving,' resumed the unknown, not suspecting what I was doing. 'It is an immense balloon carrying a ship, strong castles, houses, and so on. The caricaturists did not suspect that their follies would one day become truths. It is complete, this large vessel. On the left is its helm, with the pilot's box; at the prow are pleasure-houses, an immense organ, and a cannon to call the attention of the inhabitants of the earth or the moon; above the poop there are the observatory and the balloon long-boat; in the equatorial circle, the army barrack; on the left, the funnel; then the upper galleries for promenading, sails, pinions; below, the cafés and general storehouse. Observe this pompous announcement: "Invented for the happiness of the human race, this globe will depart at once for the ports of the Levant, and on its return the programme of its voyages to the two poles and the extreme west will be announced. No one need furnish himself with anything; everything is foreseen, and all will prosper. There will be a uniform price for all places of destination, but it will be the same for the most distant countries of our hemisphere – that is to say, a thousand louis for one of any of the said journeys. And it must be confessed that this sum is very moderate, when the speed, comfort and arrangements which will be enjoyed on the balloon are considered – arrangements which are not to be found on land, while on the balloon each passenger may consult his own habits and tastes. This is so true that in the same place some will be dancing, others standing; some will be enjoying delicacies; others fasting. Whoever desires the society of wits may satisfy himself; whoever is stupid may find stupid people to keep him company. Thus pleasure will be the soul of the aerial company." All this provoked laughter; but before long, if I am not cut off, they will see it all realized.'

We were visibly descending. He did not perceive it!

'This kind of "game at balloons",' he resumed, spreading out before me some of the engravings of his valuable collection, 'this game contains the entire history of the aerostatic art. It is used by elevated minds, and is played with dice and counters, with whatever stakes you like, to be paid or received according to where the player arrives.'

'Why,' said I, 'you seem to have studied the science of aerostation profoundly.'

'Yes, monsieur, yes! From Phaethon, Icarus, Architas, I have searched for, examined, learned everything. I could render immense services to the world in this art, if God granted me life. But that will not be!'

'Why?'

'Because my name is Empedocles, or Erostratus.'

Meanwhile, the balloon was happily approaching the earth; but when one is falling, the danger is as great at a hundred feet as at five thousand.

'Do you recall the battle of Fleurus?' resumed my companion, whose face became more and more animated. 'It was at that battle that Contello, by order of the Government, organized a company of balloonists. At the siege of Manbenge, General Jourdan derived so much service from this new method of observation that Contello ascended twice a day with the general himself. The communications between the aeronaut and his agents who held the balloon were made by means of small white, red and yellow flags. Often the gun and cannon shot were directed upon the balloon when he ascended, but without result. When General Jourdan was preparing to invest Charleroi, Contello went into the vicinity, ascended from the plain of Jumet, and continued his observations for seven or eight hours with General Morlot, and this no doubt aided in giving us the victory of Fleurus. General Jourdan publicly acknowledged the help which the aeronautical observations had afforded him. Well, despite the services rendered on that occasion and during the Belgian campaign, the year which had seen the beginning of the military career of balloons saw also its end. The school of Meudon, founded by the Government, was closed by Buonaparte on his return from Egypt. And now, what can you expect from the new-born infant? as Franklin said. The infant was born alive; it should not be stifled!'

The unknown bowed his head in his hands, and reflected for some moments; then raising his head, he said, –

'Despite my prohibition, monsieur, you have opened the valve.'

I dropped the cord.

'Happily,' he resumed, 'we have still three hundred pounds of ballast.'

'What is your purpose?' said I.

'Have you ever crossed the seas?' he asked.

I turned pale.

'It is unfortunate,' he went on, 'that we are being driven towards the Adriatic. That is only a stream; but higher up we may find other currents.'

And, without taking any notice of me, he threw over several bags of sand; then, in a menacing voice, he said, –

'I let you open the valve because the expansion of the gas threatened to burst the balloon; but do not do it again!'

Then he went on as follows: –

'You remember the voyage of Blanchard and Jeffries from Dover to Calais? It was magnificent! On 7 January 1785, there being a north-west wind, their balloon was inflated with gas on the Dover coast. A mistake of equilibrium, just as they were ascending, forced them to throw out their ballast so that they might not go down again, and they only kept thirty pounds. It was too little; for, as the wind did not freshen, they only advanced very slowly towards the French coast. Besides, the permeability

335

of the tissue served to reduce the inflation little by little, and in an hour and a half the aeronauts perceived that they were descending.

'"What shall we do?" said Jeffries.

'"We are only one quarter of the way over," replied Blanchard, "and very low down. On rising, we shall perhaps meet more favourable winds."

'"Let us throw out the rest of the sand."

'The balloon acquired some ascending force, but it soon began to descend again. Towards the middle of the transit the aeronauts threw over their books and tools. A quarter of an hour after, Blanchard said to Jeffries, –

'"The barometer?"

'"It is going up! We are lost, and yet there is the French coast."

'A loud noise was heard.

'"Has the balloon burst?" asked Jeffries.

'"No. The loss of the gas has reduced the inflation of the lower part of the balloon. But we are still descending. We are lost! Out with everything useless!"

'Provisions, oars, and rudder were thrown into the sea. The aeronauts were only one hundred yards high.

'"We are going up again," said the doctor.

'"No. It is the spurt caused by the diminution of the weight, and not a ship in sight, not a bark on the horizon! To the sea with our clothing!"

'The unfortunates stripped themselves, but the balloon continued to descend.

'"Blanchard," said Jeffries, "you should have made this voyage alone; you consented to take me; I will sacrifice myself! I am going to throw myself into the water, and the balloon, relieved of my weight, will mount again."

'"No, no! It is frightful!"

'The balloon became less and less inflated, and as it doubled up its concavity pressed the gas against the sides, and hastened its downward course.

'"Adieu, my friend," said the doctor. "God preserve you!"

'He was about to throw himself over, when Blanchard held him back.

'"There is one more chance," said he. "We can cut the cords which hold the car, and cling to the net! Perhaps the balloon will rise. Let us hold ourselves ready. But – the barometer is going down! The wind is freshening! We are saved!"

'The aeronauts perceived Calais. Their joy was delirious. A few moments more, and they had fallen in the forest of Guines. I do not doubt,' added the unknown, 'that, under similar circumstances, you would have followed Doctor Jeffries' example!'

The clouds rolled in glittering masses beneath us. The balloon threw large shadows on this heap of clouds, and was surrounded as by an aureola. The thunder rumbled below the car. All this was terrifying.

'Let us descend!' I cried.

'Descend, when the sun is up there, waiting for us? Out with more bags!'

And more than fifty pounds of ballast were cast over.

At a height of three thousand five hundred yards we remained stationary.

The unknown talked unceasingly. I was in a state of complete prostration, while he seemed to be in his element.

'With a good wind, we shall go far,' he cried. 'In the Antilles there are currents of air which have a speed of a hundred leagues an hour. When Napoleon was crowned, Garnerin sent up a balloon with coloured lamps, at eleven o'clock at night. The wind was blowing north-north-west. The next morning, at daybreak, the inhabitants of Rome greeted its passage over the dome of St Peter's. We shall go farther and higher!'

I scarcely heard him. Everything whirled around me. An opening appeared in the clouds.

'See that city,' said the unknown. 'It is Spires!'

I leaned over the car and perceived a small blackish mass. It was Spires. The Rhine, which is so large, seemed an unrolled ribbon. The sky was a deep blue over our heads. The birds had long abandoned us, for in that rarefied air they could not have flown. We were alone in space, and I in presence of this unknown!

'It is useless for you to know whither I am leading you,' he said, as he threw the compass among the clouds. 'Ah! A fall is a grand thing! You know that but few victims of ballooning are to be reckoned, from Pilâtre des Rosiers to Lieutenant Gale, and that the accidents have always been the result of imprudence. Pilâtre des Rosiers set out with Romain of Boulogne, on 13 June 1785. To his gas balloon he had affixed a Montgolfier apparatus of hot air, so as to dispense, no doubt, with the necessity of losing gas or throwing out ballast. It was putting a torch under a powder-barrel.

When they had ascended four hundred yards, and were taken by opposing winds, they were driven over the open sea. Pilâtre, in order to descend, essayed to open the valve, but the valve-cord became entangled in the balloon, and tore it so badly that it became empty in an instant. It fell upon the Montgolfier apparatus, overturned it, and dragged down the unfortunates, who were soon shattered to pieces! It is frightful, is it not?'

I could only reply, 'For pity's sake, let us descend!'

The clouds gathered around us on every side, and dreadful detonations, which reverberated in the cavity of the balloon, took place beneath us.

'You provoke me,' cried the unknown, 'and you shall no longer know whether we are rising or falling!'

The barometer went the way of the compass, accompanied by several more bags of sand. We must have been five thousand yards high. Some icicles had already attached themselves to the sides of the car, and a kind of fine snow seemed to penetrate to my very bones. Meanwhile a frightful tempest was raging under us, but we were above it.

'Do not be afraid,' said the unknown. 'It is only the imprudent who are lost. Olivari, who perished at Orleans, rose in a paper "Montgolfier"; his car, suspended below the chafing-dish, and ballasted with combustible materials, caught fire; Olivari fell, and was killed! Mosment rose, at Lille, on a light tray; an oscillation disturbed his equilibrium; Mosment fell, and was killed! Bittorf, at Mannheim, saw his balloon catch fire in the air; and he, too, fell, and was killed! Harris rose in a badly constructed balloon, the valve of which was too large and would not shut; Harris fell, and was killed! Sadler, deprived of ballast by his long sojourn in the air, was dragged over the town of Boston and dashed against the chimneys; Sadler fell, and was killed! Cokling descended with a convex parachute which he pretended to have perfected; Cokling fell, and was killed! Well, I love them, these victims of their own imprudence, and I shall die as they did. Higher! still higher!'

All the phantoms of this necrology passed before my eyes. The rarefaction of the air and the sun's rays added to the expansion of the gas, and the balloon continued to mount. I tried mechanically to open the valve, but the unknown cut the cord several feet above my head. I was lost!

'Did you see Madame Blanchard fall?' said he. 'I saw her; yes, I! I was at Tivoli on 6 July 1819. Madame Blanchard rose in a small-sized balloon, to avoid the expense of filling, and she was forced to entirely inflate it. The gas leaked out below, and left a regular train of hydrogen in its path. She carried with her a sort of pyrotechnic aureola, suspended below her car by a wire, which she was to set off in the air. This she had done many times before. On this day she also carried up a small parachute ballasted by a firework contrivance, that would go off in a shower of silver. She was to start this contrivance after having lighted it with a port-fire made on purpose. She set out; the night was gloomy. At the moment of lighting her fireworks she was so imprudent as to pass the taper under the column of hydrogen which was leaking from the balloon. My eyes were fixed upon her. Suddenly an unexpected gleam lit up the darkness. I thought she was preparing a surprise. The light flashed out, suddenly disappeared and reappeared, and gave the summit of the balloon the shape of an immense jet of ignited gas. This sinister glow shed itself over the Boulevard and the whole Montmartre quarter. Then I saw the unhappy woman rise, try twice to close the appendage of the balloon, so as to put out the fire, then sit down in her car and try to guide her descent; for she did not fall. The combustion of the gas lasted for several minutes. The balloon, becoming gradually less, continued to descend, but it was not a fall. The wind blew from the north-west and drove it towards Paris. There were then some large gardens just by the house No. 16, Rue de Provence. Madame Blanchard essayed to fall there without danger: but the balloon and the car struck on the roof of the house with a light shock. 'Save me!' cried the wretched woman. I got into the street at this moment. The car slid along the roof, and encountered an iron cramp. At this concussion, Madame Blanchard was thrown out of her car and precipitated upon the pavement. She was killed!'

These stories froze me with horror. The unknown was standing with bare head, dishevelled hair, haggard eyes!

There was no longer any illusion possible. I at last recognized the horrible truth. I was in the presence of a madman!

He threw out the rest of the ballast, and we must have now reached a height of at least nine thousand yards. Blood spurted from my nose and mouth!

'Who are nobler than the martyrs of science?' cried the lunatic. 'They are canonized by posterity.'

But I no longer heard him. He looked about him, and, bending down to my ear, muttered, –

'And have you forgotten Zambecarri's catastrophe? Listen. On 7 October 1804, the clouds seemed to lift a little. On the preceding days, the wind and rain had not ceased; but the announced ascension of Zambecarri could not be postponed. His enemies were already bantering him. It was necessary to ascend, to save the science and himself from becoming a public jest. It was at Boulogne. No one helped him to inflate his balloon.

'He rose at midnight, accompanied by Andreoli and Grossetti. The balloon mounted slowly, for it had been perforated by the rain, and the gas was leaking out. The three intrepid aeronauts could only observe the state of the barometer by aid of a dark lantern. Zambecarri had eaten nothing for twenty-four hours. Grossetti was also fasting.

'"My friends," said Zambecarri, "I am overcome by cold, and exhausted. I am dying."

'He fell inanimate in the gallery. It was the same with Grossetti. Andreoli alone remained conscious. After long efforts, he succeeded in reviving Zambecarri.

'"What news? Whither are we going? How is the wind? What time is it?"

'"It is two o'clock."

'"Where is the compass?"

'"Upset!"

'"Great God! The lantern has gone out!"

'"It cannot burn in this rarefied air," said Zambecarri.

'The moon had not risen, and the atmosphere was plunged in murky darkness.

'"I am cold, Andreoli. What shall I do?"

'They slowly descended through a layer of whitish clouds.

'"Sh!" said Andreoli. '"Do you hear?"

'"What?" asked Zambecarri.

'"A strange noise."

'"You are mistaken."

'"No."

'Consider these travellers, in the middle of the night, listening to that unaccountable noise! Are they going to knock against a tower? Are they about to be precipitated on the roofs?

'"Do you hear? One would say it was the noise of the sea."

'"Impossible!"

'"It is the groaning of the waves!"

'"It is true."

'"Light! light!"

'After five fruitless attempts, Andreoli succeeded in obtaining light. It was three o'clock.

'The voice of violent waves was heard. They were almost touching the surface of the sea!

'"We are lost!" cried Zambecarri, seizing a large bag of sand.

'"Help!" cried Andreoli.

'The car touched the water, and the waves came up to their breasts.

'"Throw out the instruments, clothes, money!"

'The aeronauts completely stripped themselves. The balloon, relieved, rose with frightful rapidity. Zambecarri was taken with vomiting. Grossetti bled profusely. The unfortunate men could not speak, so short was their breathing. They were taken with cold, and they were soon crusted over with ice. The moon looked as red as blood.

'After traversing the high regions for a half-hour, the balloon again fell into the sea. It was four in the morning. They were half submerged in the water, and the balloon dragged them along, as if under sail, for several hours.

'At daybreak they found themselves opposite Pesaro, four miles from the coast. They were about to reach it, when a gale blew them back into the open sea. They were lost! The frightened boats fled at their approach. Happily, a more intelligent boatman accosted them, hoisted them on board, and they landed at Ferrada.

'A frightful journey, was it not? But Zambecarri was a brave and energetic man. Scarcely recovered from his sufferings, he resumed his ascensions. During one of them he struck against a tree; his spirit-lamp was broken on his clothes; he was enveloped in fire, his balloon began to catch the flames, and he came down half consumed.

'At last, on 21 September 1812, he made another ascension at Boulogne. The balloon clung to a tree, and his lamp again set it on fire. Zambecarri fell, and was killed! And in presence of these facts, we would still hesitate! No. The higher we go, the more glorious will be our death!'

The balloon being now entirely relieved of ballast and of all it contained, we were carried to an enormous height. It vibrated in the atmosphere. The least noise resounded in the vaults of heaven. Our globe, the only object which caught my view in immensity, seemed ready to be annihilated, and above us the depths of the starry skies were lost in thick darkness.

I saw my companion rise up before me.

'The hour is come!' he said. 'We must die. We are rejected by men. They despise us. Let us crush them!'

'Mercy!' I cried.

'Let us cut these cords! Let this car be abandoned in space. The attractive force will change its direction, and we shall approach the sun!'

Despair galvanized me. I threw myself upon the madman, we struggled together, and a terrible conflict took place. But I was thrown down, and while he held me under his knee, the madman was cutting the cords of the car.

'One!' he cried.

'My God!'

'Two! Three!'

I made a superhuman effort, rose up, and violently repulsed the madman.

'Four!'

The car fell, but I instinctively clung to the cords and hoisted myself into the meshes of the netting.

The madman disappeared in space!

The balloon was raised to an immeasurable height. A horrible cracking was heard. The gas, too much dilated, had burst the balloon. I shut my eyes –

Some instants after, a damp warmth revived me. I was in the midst of clouds on fire. The balloon turned over with dizzy velocity. Taken by the wind, it made a hundred leagues an hour in a horizontal course, the lightning flashing around it.

Meanwhile my fall was not a very rapid one. When I opened my eyes, I saw the country. I was two miles from the sea, and the tempest was driving me violently towards it, when an abrupt shock forced me to loosen my hold. My hands opened, a cord slipped swiftly between my fingers, and I found myself on the solid earth!

It was the cord of the anchor, which, sweeping along the surface of the ground, was caught in a crevice; and my balloon, unballasted for the last time, careered off to lose itself beyond the sea.

When I came to myself, I was in bed in a peasant's cottage, at Harder-wick, a village of La Gueldre, fifteen leagues from Amsterdam, on the shores of the Zuyder-Zee.

A miracle had saved my life, but my voyage had been a series of impru-dences, committed by a lunatic, and I had not been able to prevent them.

May this terrible narrative, though instructing those who read it, not discourage the explorers of the air.

Translated by George M. Towle

VILLIERS DE L'ISLE ADAM

Véra

For Madame la Comtesse d'Osmoy

'The form of the body is more *essential* to it than its substance.'

Modern Physiology

Love is stronger than Death, said Solomon; and it is true that its mysterious power knows no limits.

It was dusk one autumn evening, some years ago, in Paris. A few carriages, with their lamps already lit, were rolling along towards the darkened Faubourg Saint-Germain, returning from the Bois de Boulogne later than the rest. One of them stopped in front of the entrance to a huge mansion surrounded by age-old gardens; the stone shield over the archway bore the arms of the ancient family of the Comtes d'Athol, namely a silver star on a blue ground, with the motto *Pallida Victrix*, under the ermine-lined coronet of a prince. The heavy doors swung open. A man of thirty-five, dressed in mourning, with a deathly pale face, got out of the carriage. On the staircase silent servants raised torches into the air. Without seeing them, he climbed the steps and went into the house. It was the Comte d'Athol.

Reeling slightly, he climbed the white stairs leading to the bedroom where, that very morning, in a velvet coffin, covered in violets and wrapped in folds of batiste, he had laid his pale wife, his lady of joy, Véra, his despair.

Upstairs, the door opened softly over the carpet; he drew the curtain aside.

Everything was where the countess had left it the previous evening. Death had struck swiftly. The night before, his beloved had fainted away in such profound joys, had abandoned herself in such exquisite embraces, that her heart, bursting with delight, had failed her: her moist lips had suddenly turned a mortal purple. She had scarcely had time to give her husband a farewell kiss, smiling wordlessly; then her long lashes had fallen like mourning veils over the splendid darkness of her eyes.

The indescribable day had passed.

About noon, after the horrible ceremony in the family vault, the Comte d'Athol had dismissed his black-clad escort at the cemetery. Then, shutting himself up alone with the dead woman, between the four marble walls, he had pulled to the iron door of the mausoleum. Incense was burning on a tripod before the coffin: a bright crown of lamps shone around the young woman's head.

He had stood there all day, dreaming, conscious of nothing but a tenderness bereft of hope. At six o'clock, as dusk was falling, he had left the sacred spot. After closing the vault, he had pulled the silver key out of the lock, and, standing on tiptoe on the topmost step of the threshold, he had gently tossed it into the tomb. He had thrown it through the trefoil over the door, on to the flagstones inside. Why had he done this? Undoubtedly in response to some mysterious resolution never to return.

And now he stood once more in her death chamber.

The window, draped with huge curtains of cashmere brocaded in gold, was open: the last ray of the evening sun lit up, in its frame of old wood, the large portrait of the dead woman. The count looked around him at the dress thrown on to an armchair the evening before; and at the jewels on the mantelpiece, the pearl necklace, the half-open fan, the heavy bottles of perfumes which she would never breathe again. On the unmade ebony bed with the twisted columns, beside the pillow on which the impression of her divine, beloved head was still visible in the midst of the lace, he caught sight of the bloodstained handkerchief in which her young soul had flown on one wing for a moment; the open piano, holding a piece of music which would never be finished now, the Indian flowers which she had picked in the conservatory and which were withering in old Dresden vases; and, at the foot of the bed, on the black floor, the little Oriental velvet slippers, on which there gleamed a whimsical motto of Véra's, embroidered in pearls: *Qui verra Véra l'aimera.*

His beloved's bare feet had played in them the morning before, kissed at every step by the swansdown lining. And over there, in the shadows, stood the clock, whose spring he had broken so that it should strike no more hours.

So she had gone . . . But where? . . . And why should he go on living? . . . It was impossible, absurd.

And the count gave himself up to his thoughts.

He looked back over the whole of his past life. Six months had elapsed since his marriage. Had it not been abroad, at an embassy ball, that he had seen her for the first time? . . . Yes. That moment was resuscitated very clearly before his eyes. She appeared before him, a radiant vision. That evening their eyes had met, and they had realized, deep in their hearts, that they were of similar natures and destined to love each other for ever.

The discouraging remarks, the watchful smiles, the insinuations – all the obstacles which the world raises to delay the inevitable happiness of those who belong to one another – had vanished in the face of the tranquil confidence in each other which they felt at that very moment.

Véra, weary of the insipid formalities of her circle, had come to see him at the first difficulty which had arisen between them, thus simplifying in august fashion the commonplace exchanges in which the precious substance of time is wasted.

At their first words the futile comments of other people on their score struck them as a flight of night birds disappearing into the darkness. What a smile they exchanged! What an indescribable embrace!

Yet the fact was that their natures were most extraordinary. They were two creatures endowed with wonderful senses, but of a wholly earthly character. Feelings were prolonged in them with an alarming intensity. They forgot themselves in the joy of sensation. On the other hand certain ideas, such as those of the soul, of Infinity, of God Himself, were so to speak hidden from their understanding. The faith of a great number of human beings in things supernatural was simply a source of vague astonishment to them, a closed book to which they paid no attention, not being qualified either to condemn or justify. Consequently, recognizing that the world was foreign to them, they had isolated themselves, as soon as they were married, in this dark old mansion, whose thickly planted gardens deadened the sounds from outside.

Here the two lovers plunged into the ocean of those languid and per verse pleasures in which the spirit mingles with the mysteries of the flesh. They exhausted the violence of desire, the thrill of tender passion. They became the beat of one another's heart. Their minds penetrated their bodies so perfectly that their forms assumed an intellectual character, and their kisses, the meshes of a burning chainmail, bound them together in an ideal fusion, a prolonged ecstasy. But all of a sudden the charm was broken; the terrible accident parted them; their arms untwined. What shadow had taken his dead love from him? Dead? He could not believe that. Did the soul of a cello disappear in the cry of a broken string?

The hours passed.

Through the window he looked at the darkness spreading across the heavens; and Night took on a personality in his eyes. He saw her as a queen walking sadly in exile, and the diamond clip of her mourning tunic, Venus, shone all alone above the trees, lost in the depths of the sky.

'It is Véra,' he thought.

At this name, spoken in an undertone, he started like a man awakening; then, standing up, he looked around him.

The objects in the room were now lit by a hitherto indistinct glow, that of a night light which was tinting the darkness blue, and to which the night sky gave the appearance of another star. It was the incense-scented flame of an iconostasis, a family heirloom of Véra's. The triptych, made of precious old wood, was hanging by its Russian esparto between the mirror and the picture. A quivering gleam of light from the gold inside fell on the necklace, among the jewels on the mantelpiece. The halo of the Madonna, clad in sky-blue garments, shone brightly, tinged with pink by the Byzantine cross whose delicate red outlines, melting in the glow, streaked the gleaming pearls with blood. Ever since childhood Véra had gazed pityingly with her great eyes at the pure, motherly face of the hereditary Madonna, and since by her nature she could give her only a superstitious love, she offered her that sometimes, when she passed, innocent and thoughtful, in front of the night light.

The count, moved to the depths of his soul at this sight by painful memories, stood up, hurriedly blew out the holy light, and, groping in the darkness for a bellrope, gave it a tug.

A servant appeared: an old man dressed in black. He was holding a lamp which he put down in front of the countess's portrait. When he turned round, it was with a shudder of superstitious terror that he saw his master standing smiling as if nothing had happened.

'Raymond,' the count said calmly, 'the countess and I are tired out this evening; you will serve supper about ten o'clock ... Incidentally, we have decided to isolate ourselves even more here, as from tomorrow. None of my servants, except yourself, is to pass the night in the house. You will give each of them three years' wages and tell them to leave. Then you will bar the door and light the candelabra downstairs, in the dining room. You will be able to look after us by yourself. We shall do no entertaining in the future.'

The old man trembled and looked at him attentively.

The count lit a cigar and went down to the gardens.

The servant thought at first that his master's grief, too keen and overwhelming for him to bear, had unhinged his mind. He had known him since childhood, and realized at once that the shock of too sudden an awakening could be fatal to this sleepwalker. His first duty was to keep the secret entrusted to him.

He bowed his head. Was he to give his loyal support to this pious dream ... to obey ... to go on serving *them* without taking Death into account? What a strange idea! Would it last a single night? ... Tomorrow, tomorrow, alas! ... Oh, who could tell? ... Perhaps! ... After all, it was a sacred undertaking. And by what right was he reflecting on it?

He left the bedroom and carried out his orders to the letter; that very evening, the strange existence began.

It was a question of creating an awe-inspiring mirage.

The awkwardness of the first few days quickly disappeared. Raymond, first of all in a daze, then out of a sort of tender deference, made such an effort to be natural that before three weeks had passed he occasionally felt almost taken in himself by his good will. His mental reservations disappeared. Now and then, feeling a kind of giddiness, he had to remind himself that the countess was definitely dead. He was caught up in this funereal game and kept forgetting the reality. Soon he needed more than a moment's thought to convince himself and take hold of himself. He saw that he would end up by abandoning himself entirely to the terrifying magnetism with which the count was gradually imbuing the atmosphere around them; and he was filled with fear, a vague, sweet fear.

D'Athol was in fact living in complete oblivion of his beloved's death. He could not help but feel that she was perpetually present, the young woman's body was so closely linked to his. Sometimes, on sunny days, on a bench in the garden, he would read aloud the poems she loved; sometimes, in the evening, by the fireside, with the two cups of tea on a little table, he would chat with the smiling Illusion whom he could see sitting in the other armchair.

The days, the nights, the weeks flew by. Neither of the two men realized what they were doing. And strange phenomena now started occurring in which it became difficult to distinguish the point at which real and imaginary coincided. A presence was floating in the air; a form was trying to break through, to weave itself on what had become an indefinable space.

D'Athol was living two lives, like a visionary. A pale, gentle face, glimpsed like a flash of lightning between two flickers of an eyelid; a faint chord suddenly struck on the piano; a kiss which closed his lips just as he was about to speak; *feminine* affinities of thought which awoke in him in response to what he said; a division of himself so profound that he could smell, as in a fluid mist, the sweet, heady scent of his beloved beside him; and, at night, between wakefulness and sleep, the sound of whispered words; all these were signs of a negation of Death, raised to a power never known before.

Once D'Athol felt her and saw her so clearly beside him that he took her in his arms: but this movement dispelled her.

'Child!' he murmured with a smile.

And he went back to sleep like a lover playfully rebuffed by his sleepy mistress.

On her birthday, by way of a joke, he placed an immortelle in the bouquet which he tossed on to Véra's pillow.

'Seeing that she thinks she is dead,' he said.

Thanks to the profound and omnipotent determination of Monsieur d'Athol, who, by the sheer power of his love, created the life and presence of his wife in the house, this existence ended up by taking on a sombre, persuasive charm. Raymond himself no longer felt any fear, having gradually become accustomed to these impressions.

A black velvet dress glimpsed round the bend of a path; a laughing voice calling to him from the drawing room; a ring on the bell when he awoke, as in the old days; all this had become familiar to him. It was as if the dead woman were playing at being invisible, like a child. She felt so deeply loved that it was perfectly natural.

A year had passed.

On the evening of the anniversary the count, sitting by the fire in Véra's room, had just finished reading her a Florentine fable: *Callimaco*. He closed the book, and then, pouring himself some tea, he said:

'*Douschka*, do you remember Rose Valley, the banks of the Lahn, the castle of the Four Towers? . . . That story reminded you of them, didn't it?'

He stood up, and saw in the bluish mirror that he was looking paler than usual. He took a pearl bracelet out of a bowl and examined it closely. Had not Véra removed it from her arm just now, before undressing? The pearls were still warm and their orient softened, as if by the warmth of her flesh. And what of the opal in that Siberian necklace, which, like the pearls, loved Véra's beautiful breasts so much that it turned sickly pale in its gold trellis-work when the young woman forgot it for a little while? In the old days the countess used to love the faithful stone because of that . . . This evening the opal was shining as if it had just been taken off, and as if it were still imbued with the dead woman's exquisite magnetism. Putting down the necklace and the precious stone, the count accidentally touched the batiste handkerchief on which the drops of blood were as wet and red as carnations on snow . . . There, on the piano, who had turned the last page of the music she had been playing? And the holy light must have rekindled in the reliquary, for its golden flame was casting a mystic glow over the Madonna's face and closed eyes! And those newly picked Oriental flowers, blossoming in the old Dresden vases – what hand had just placed them there? The room seemed gay and full of life, in a more intense, significant way than usual. But nothing could surprise the count. It seemed so normal to him that he did not even pay any attention when the hour struck on the clock which had been stopped for a year.

Yet this evening anybody would have sworn that the countess was trying in an adorable way to come back into this room which was scented with her presence. She had left so much of herself in it! Everything which had formed her life drew her here. Her charm hung in the air; the prolonged assaults made by her husband's passionate will must have loosened the vague bonds of the invisible around her ...

She was forced to come back. Everything she loved was here.

No doubt she wanted to smile once more at her reflection in this mysterious mirror in which she had so often admired her lily-like face. The sweet creature must have shuddered, over there, among her violets, under the extinguished lamps; the divine creature must have shivered, all alone in the vault, looking at the silver key which had been tossed on to the flagstones. She wanted to come to him, too. And her will dwelt on the idea of incense and isolation. Death is a final circumstance only for those who hope for something from Heaven; but, for her, Death and Heaven and Life were all contained in their embrace. The solitary kiss of her husband attracted her lips in the darkness. And the bygone sound of melodies, the intoxicated words of former times, the materials which covered her body and preserved its perfume, those magic jewels which summoned her to them in their obscure sympathy, and above all the overwhelming, absolute impression of her presence – an impression which objects themselves had come to share in the end – everything was calling her there, and had been drawing her there for so long and so imperceptibly that, finally cured of the sleeping Death, She alone was missing.

Ideas are living creatures; and since the count had hollowed out in the air the shape of his love, that space had to be filled by the only creature which was homogeneous with it, or else the Universe would have collapsed. The impression was created at that moment, final, simple and absolute, that She must be there in the room. He was as calmly certain of this as of his own existence, and all the objects around him were saturated with this conviction. It could be seen in them. And since Véra alone, tangible and visible, was missing, it was essential that she should be there and that the great Dream of Life and Death should open its infinite doors for a moment. Faith extended the road of the resurrection to her tomb. A gay, musical laugh lit up the marriage bed with its joy; the count turned round. And there before his eyes, created out of will and memory, languidly lying with one elbow on the lace pillow, her hand supporting her heavy black tresses, her lips deliciously parted in a smile of paradisiacal delight, beautiful beyond compare, the countess was looking at him with eyes which were still a little drowsy.

'Roger!' she said in a far-away voice.

He came over to her. Their lips met in a divine, oblivious, immortal joy. And they realized then that they were in fact *one and the same being*.

The hours brushed with impassive wings this ecstasy in which, for the first time, earth and heaven were united.

Suddenly the Comte d'Athol gave a start, as if struck by a fatal reminiscence.

'But now I remember!' he said. 'What is the matter with me? You are dead!'

The moment he uttered this last word, the mystic flame of the iconostasis went out. The pale light of morning – a greyish, rainy, commonplace morning – filtered into the room through the gaps between the curtains. The candles turned pale and guttered out, their red wicks giving off an acrid smoke; the fire disappeared under a layer of warm ash; the flowers faded and withered in a few moments, the pendulum of the clock gradually regained its previous immobility. The *conviction* of all the objects vanished abruptly. The opal had died and lost its gleam; the bloodstains had faded too on the batiste next to it; and effacing herself between the desperate arms which were trying in vain to hold her tight, the passionate white vision withdrew into the air and was lost from sight. A farewell sigh, faint but distinct, penetrated to Roger's very soul. The count stood up; he had just realized that he was alone. His dream had dissolved all of a sudden; he had broken the magnetic thread of its radiant texture with a single word. The atmosphere was now that of a death chamber.

Like those glass tears which are illogically shaped and yet so solid that a blow with a mallet on their thick end would not break them, but which shatter immediately into an impalpable dust if the needle-thin tip is broken off, everything had vanished.

'Oh!' he murmured. 'So it's all over! . . . I have lost you! . . . You are all alone! ... What road must I take now to reach you? Show me the path which leads me to you!'

Suddenly, like a reply, a shining object fell with a metallic sound from the marriage bed on to the black fur. A ray of the sinister earthly dawn lit it up ... The lonely man bent down and picked it up; and a sublime smile illumined his face as he recognized this object. It was the key to the tomb.

Translated by Robert Baldick

ÉMILE ZOLA

Death by Advertising

I once knew a very nice young man. He died last year. His life had become a sheer martyrdom. Let me tell you the story of a man killed by advertising. Pierre Landry was born in the Rue Saint-Honoré, near the Central Markets; a paradise for idle loafers. His first reading lessons were given him by his nurse who made him spell out the signs and billposters in the streets. He grew to like those large oblong yellow and blue pieces of paper so conveniently displayed on the walls and later on, as a young lad roaming the streets, he fell in love with some of the posters – the ones printed in enormous characters in queer shapes, on which there is a lot to read. His father, a retired hosier, had completed his son's education by letting him have the advertisement page to read – everyone knows that the large print of the advertisements is easier for children to make out.

At the age of twenty, Pierre Landry was orphaned and found himself quite well-off. He decided to live entirely for his own pleasure and to exploit every aspect of modern progressive civilization for his own personal benefit. His father had been a worker; he was going to relax and enjoy the fantastic luxury of the Golden Age promised him by the advertisements on page four of his paper and on the hoardings. 'What a marvellous age we live in!' he mused. 'An age of enlightenment and benefits without end. Where can you see anything more moving than those men who devote themselves night and day to the happiness of mankind by producing a constant stream of inventions to provide us with a more peaceful and happy life and who are even so generous as to put all these delightful things within reach of the most modest purse? And to think that these benefactors of mankind even take the trouble to draw our attention to all these wonderful things, great and small, tell us where to find them, and even how much we'll have to pay for them! Some of them we really ought to thank on bended knees for being willing even to lose money on our behalf, and others are quite satisfied merely to cover their expenses. They're working purely in the service of mankind, so that we can live richer, peaceful lives. Well, I've already planned how I want to live. I intend to keep up with progress and enjoy all the advantages of the modern world without any further question. I want a blissfully happy life and for that, all I need is to consult the newspapers and posters, night and morning, and do exactly what they tell me. It's an infallible guide to true wisdom, and happiness is guaranteed!'

From then on, Pierre's guideline in life was the advertisements in the papers and on the hoardings. He followed them blindly whenever he had a decision to make and he would never buy or do anything that hadn't been warmly recommended by the publicity men. Every morning he would religiously scan the papers, conscientiously noting down the new discoveries and products. As a result his home became a repository of every crackbrained invention or shoddy article on sale in Paris. Indeed, his basic reasoning was not without logic. By keeping abreast of the times, and choosing the products most enthusiastically praised and recommended in rhapsodic terms by the publicity men, he could claim, with legitimate pride, that he was using the most advanced products of the most highly developed civilization in the world and had thus solved the problem of attaining perfection. However, this was only the theory, and unfortunately the reality became more unpleasant every day. Although everything should have been for the best, in fact it all went from bad to worse and the drama now began which was to make his life a hell on earth.

He had bought a plot of filled-in swampland, into which his house slowly sank. The house itself had been built according to the latest modern principles; when the wind blew, it shook and when rainstorms came, it gently crumbled. The fireplaces, equipped with ingenious smokeless hoods, belched forth asphyxiating fumes; the electric bells remained obstinately silent; the carefully planned modern lavatories turned out to be noisome cesspits; cupboards provided with special mechanical locks would neither open nor shut properly.

In particular, there was a splendid pianola which sounded like a rather inferior hurdy-gurdy, and a burglar-proof and fireproof safe which was quietly removed, bodily, by burglars one fine winter's night. There was also the country cottage that Pierre had bought at Arcueil, which was quite a different story. Here, he experimented with trees cut out of sheet metal and tried cultivating rare plants which, when they grew, looked like rather poor couch grass. His architect-designed water tank, widely advertised, collapsed and he was nearly drowned as well as almost crushed to death.

Amidst all these trials and tribulations, Pierre continued to smile blandly, his faith quite unshaken. On the contrary, his confidence grew stronger. 'Everything isn't yet for the best in the best of all possible worlds,' he said to himself, 'and the most logical way to avoid all these misfortunes is to follow the march of progress even more closely. The reason my water tank collapsed was that my architect wasn't warmly enough recommended. I must find one recommended more strongly. If I watch the newspapers, I'm bound to achieve perfection and perfect happiness.'

Poor Pierre suffered not only in his possessions but in his person.

His clothes would split at the seams as he was walking down the street: he had bought them from firms offering vast discounts on stocks being cleared, either because of stock-taking or a takeover. He would seek out such bargains not through meanness but solely in order to enjoy all the benefits of the modern world.

One day when I met him, he'd gone completely bald. In his tireless pursuit of progress, he had hit on the odd idea of changing the colour of his hair from blond to dark. He'd applied a liquid which made all his hair fall out, to his great delight, since he could now, he claimed, employ a certain hair lotion guaranteed to give him a head of brown hair twice as thick as his previous one. Incidentally, his cheeks and chin were perpetually covered in gashes from the superior modern razors he used. His hats went out of shape after a week's wear and the clever little springs designed to open his umbrella never worked when it was raining.

I won't mention all his patent medicines. He had always been strong and healthy; he became emaciated and short of breath. And now advertising really started to destroy him. Thinking he was ill, he began to try out all the wonder-cures advertised in such glowing terms, and to increase their effectiveness, since he was quite at a loss to distinguish between their conflicting claims, all couched in equally high-flown language, he took all the medicines at once. He also consumed enormous quantities of chocolate, unable to resist the blandishments of the various manufacturers. He used toiletries in great abundance and several times went to have teeth pulled out in order to provide work for numerous philanthropic dentists who swore blind that their extraction would be painless, nearly breaking your jaw in the process.

Advertising attacked his mind as well as his body. He had bought an extendable bookcase into which he crammed all the books recommended in newspaper reviews. He invented a very ingenious classification system: he arranged books according to their order of merit, that is to say, according to the degree of enthusiasm displayed by the reviewers, all subsidized by the publishers. His shelves groaned under the weight of his collection of rubbish recording all the stupidity and corruption of the age. On the back of each volume, Pierre carefully stuck the blurb which had caused him to buy it, so that each time he opened it he knew in advance how he ought to react: he could laugh or weep according to the instructions.

The outcome of all this was to turn him into a moron, although, having become more selective and difficult to please, in the end he bought only those books described as 'outstanding masterpieces', thereby reducing his purchases to some twenty books a week.

We now reach the last act of this harrowing drama. Having heard of a clairvoyante claiming to cure all ills, he rushed round to consult her about his own non-existent diseases. The clairvoyante obligingly offered to restore his youth. All he had to do was to drink a certain liquid and take a bath. Pierre Landry was convinced that such a potion must be the acme of civilization. He swallowed the drug, jumped into his bath and regained his youth to such good effect that two hours later he was discovered there, dead. He had a smile on his lips and the look of ecstasy on his face suggested that he had died worshipping the Great God Advertising. This was no doubt the radical remedy for all ills promised him by the clairvoyante.

Even in death, Pierre Landry remained the humble devotee of advertising. In his will, he had asked to be embalmed in a casket in accordance with a recently patented instant chemical process. At the cemetery, the coffin burst open, tipping his wretched corpse into the mud. He had to be buried higgledy-piggledy with the broken bits of plank. Next winter, the rains rotted the papier mâché of his imitation marble tombstone, and his grave was left an anonymous heap of mouldering refuse.

Translated by Douglas Parmée

STÉPHANE MALLARMÉ

The Pipe

Yesterday, I found my pipe as I looked forward to a long evening of work, fine winter work. Cast aside were my cigarettes with all the childish joys of summer, into the past lit by shining blue leaves of sun, the muslin leaves, and my solemn pipe taken up once more by a serious man who wants to smoke for a long time without being disturbed, the better to work: but I did not expect the surprise this abandoned object had in store for me; hardly had I taken the first puff when I forgot all about the great books I had yet to write, and amazed, tenderly moved, I breathed in the previous winter as it came back to me. I had not touched my faithful friend since my return to France, and all of London – London as I lived it alone, a year ago, appeared before me; first, those dear fogs which muffle our brains and have, over there, a special odour of their own when they seep beneath the casement window. My tobacco smelled of a dark room with leather furniture dusted with coal-ash on which a thin black cat lounged; those great fires! and the maid with her red arms pouring the coals, and the noise of the coal falling out of the iron buckets in the morning – as the postman knocked his solemn double knock, which kept me alive! Through the window I saw once more those sickly trees in the deserted square – I saw the open sea, so often crossed that winter, as I shivered on the deck of a steamer soaked with drizzle and black from smoke – with my poor wandering beloved in her travelling clothes, a long dull dress the colour of dust, a coat clinging damply to her freezing shoulders, one of those straw hats, featherless and almost rib-bonless, that rich ladies throw away when they arrive, so ravaged are they by the sea, and which poor beloveds refurbish for many seasons to come.

Around her neck was tied the terrible handkerchief we wave when saying goodbye for ever.

Translated by Patrick McGuinness

CHARLES CROS

The Cabinet

To Madame Mauté de Fleurville

It required a darting gaze, a sensitive ear, and my attention razor-sharp,

To uncover the mystery of the cabinet, to penetrate behind the lines of marquetry, to reach the imaginary world behind the little mirrors.

But I finally caught sight of the secret celebration, I heard the miniature minuets, I eavesdropped on the complicated intrigues that are plotted inside the cabinet. Opening the panels, we see a sort of drawing room for insects, notice the white, brown and black tiles, with their exaggerated perspective-lines.

A mirror in the middle, a mirror on the right a mirror on the left, like doors in symmetrical stage-plays. But really these mirrors are portals opening on to an imaginary world.

But there is a strange solitude, a tidiness whose purpose is unclear in this deserted drawing room, a pointless luxury for an interior where only the night reigns.

We are fooled by all that. We tell ourselves, 'It's just a cabinet, that's all', and we assume there's nothing behind these mirrors except the reflection of what stands in front of them.

These are manipulations whose source is elsewhere, lies whispered to our rationality in the service of a deliberate agenda, and ignorance in which we are kept by certain interested parties I won't go into.

But I am no longer afraid, I do not care what might come of it, I have no fear of imaginary consequences. When the cabinet is closed, when the ears of ignorant people are blocked by sleep or by external noises, when human thought bears down upon some empirical object:

Then strange scenes unfold in the drawing room of this cabinet; a few tiny, bizarre characters emerge from the little mirrors; certain groups, illuminated by faint lights, begin to move amid the contorted reflections.

From the depths of the marquetry, from behind the *trompe l'œil* colonnades, from the shadows of the illusory corridors in the reverse of the panels,

Dandies from a dream-era swagger by, young women looking for a position in this society of reflections and agèd relatives, potbellied diplomats and blotchy dowagers.

On the polished wooden wall, attached who knows how, the candelabra light up. In the middle of the room, hanging from the non-existent ceiling, a glittering chandelier loaded with pink candles, long and thick as slugs' antennae. In the imaginary chimneys, fires burn like glow-worms.

Who placed these armchairs here, deep as hazelnut shells and ranged in a circle? These tables loaded with intangible refreshments or microscopic gambling chips? These sumptuous curtains, heavy as spider-webs?

But the ball is beginning. The orchestra, apparently composed of May bugs, unleashes its buzzing and whistling of inaudible notes. Young people hold hands and bow to each other.

Maybe a few imaginary kisses are exchanged on the sly, secret smiles hidden behind fans of bluebottle wings, bouquets of dead flowers are exchanged as tokens of indifference reciprocated.

How long does all this last? What conversations arise at these parties? Where does this insubstantial society retire to at the end of the evening?

The Cabinet

We do not know. Because, if we open the cabinet, the lights and the fires are extinguished; the guests, dandies, coquettish girls and agèd parents scatter and disappear, with no care for propriety, into the mirrors, the corridors and the colonnades; the armchairs and the tables and the curtains are gone into thin air.

Only the drawing room remains, empty, silent and clean;

So everyone simply says: 'It's a marquetry cabinet, that's all there is to it', without realizing that as soon as they turn away,

Little mischievous faces emerge from the symmetrical mirrors, from behind the inlaid colonnades, from the depths of the *trompe l'œil* corridors.

And you need a particularly keen eye, quick and meticulous, to catch them out as they float away into these twisted lines, when they hide in the depths of the little mirrors, at the moment when they return inside the unreal hideaways of the polished wood.

Translated by Patrick McGuinness

JULES RENARD

The Image-Hunter

He leaps out of bed bright and early, and leaves only if his conscience is clear, his heart pure, and his body light as a summer shirt. He takes no supplies with him. He will drink the fresh air and breathe in the wholesome smells. He leaves his weapons at home and is content just to open his eyes. His eyes are nets where images are trapped of their own accord.

The first one he catches is the image of the path that reveals its bones of polished stones and the burst veins of its ruts, between two hedges rich with sloes and blackberries.

Next, he captures the image of the river. It is white at the elbows and sleeps under the caresses of the willows. It shimmers when a fish turns, as if a silver coin had been cast into it; then, as soon as the rain comes down, it gets goosebumps.

He pulls up the image of the rippling corn, the tempting alfalfa, the prairies fringed with streams. He snatches in passing the flight of a lark or a goldfinch.

Then he enters the wood. He did not know he had such delicate senses. Quickly permeated with smells, he catches every muffled sound; and, so he can communicate with the trees, his nerves fuse with the veins of the leaves.

Soon, responsive to the point of fainting, he senses too much, he's fizzing over, he's afraid, he leaves the wood and follows, from afar, the peasant millworkers heading back to the village.

Outside, he stares at the sun until his eye explodes, the sun that's setting and undressing on the horizon, casting off its luminous clothes, its scattered clouds.

At last, home once again, his head full, he puts out his lamp and for hours before falling asleep, he counts his images.

Docile, they are reborn at the summons of memory. Each one awakes another, and endlessly their shining parade grows with new arrivals, the way partridges that are hunted and dispersed sing at night, safe from danger, and call out to each other from the hollows and the furrows.

Translated by Patrick McGuinness

JORIS-KARL HUYSMANS

Monsieur Bougran's Retirement

I

Monsieur Bougran gazed in consternation at the imprecise flower pattern on the carpet.

'Yes,' continued the chief clerk, Monsieur Devin, in a benevolent tone, 'yes, my dear colleague, I defended you to the hilt – I tried to get the human-resources department to review its decision, but my efforts failed. As from next month you are being retired, due to infirmities resulting from the exercise of your functions.'

'But I don't have any infirmities, I'm perfectly healthy!'

'No doubt, but a man like you doesn't need me to tell you anything about the legislation on this matter. The law of 9 June 1853 on civil pensions permits, as you well know . . . this interpretation. The decree of 9 November of the same year, which lays down the terms within the service for the execution of the said law, states in one of its articles –'

'Article 30,' said Monsieur Bougran, sighing.

'Just as I was about to say . . . It states that civil servants can be prematurely retired as a result of psychological infirmity, undetectable by men of the medical art.'

Monsieur Bougran had stopped listening. With the gaze of a stunned animal his eyes wandered round the chief clerk's study, which he usually entered on tiptoe, respectfully, as if he were entering a chapel. This dry, cold but familiar room suddenly struck him as sullen and bloated, hostile, with its green matt wallpaper with velvet stripes, its glass-fronted bookshelves painted in oak and full of legal documents, 'collections of administrative acts', all preserved in those bindings special to ministries – bindings in mottled calfskin, with wooden boards and yellow edges – its mantelpiece adorned with a massive clock, two Empire candlesticks, its horsehair sofa, its carpet with roses looking like cabbages, its mahogany table laden with bundles of paper and books, on which was perched a rosette-shaped bell studded with almond-shaped decorations to summon people with, its armchairs with their wheezy springs, its office chair with its cane worn down at the arms by long use into a half-moon shape.

Bored with the interview, Monsieur Devin rose and went to stand with his back to the fire, whose ashes he fanned with the tails of his frock coat.

Monsieur Bougran came back to his senses and very faintly asked, 'Have they chosen my successor, so that I can bring him up to date before I leave?'

'Not as far as I know, so I'll be obliged if you will continue in post until further notice.'

And to hasten Monsieur Bougran's departure, Monsieur Devin left the mantelpiece and advanced slowly towards his employee, who retreated towards the door. There, Monsieur Devin assured him of his deep regret and his profound esteem.

Monsieur Bougran returned to his own office and sank down, like a broken man, on a chair. Then he felt as if he were being suffocated. He put on his hat and went out to get a breath of fresh air. He walked through the streets and, without even knowing where he was, he finally ended up on a bench in a small square.

So it was true: he had been retired at the age of fifty! He, who had been such a devoted employee that he had even sacrificed his Sundays and his holidays so that the work he was responsible for would not suffer any delay. And this was all the gratitude he got for his zeal! He felt a momentary anger, and dreamed of appealing to the Council of State; then, coming down to earth, he told himself, 'I'll lose my case, and it'll cost me dear.' Slowly and calmly he considered all the articles of that law; he examined every trail through that dense prose, tested the gangways thrown across from article to article. At first sight, these paths seemed quite safe, well lit and straight; then, little by little, they would ramify, leading to shadowy turnings, dark dead ends where you suddenly fell flat on your face.

'Yes, the 1853 legislator has laid traps all over the place in this indulgent text. He has foreseen everything,' concluded Monsieur Bougran. 'Hence the case of "redundancy", which is one of those most frequently used to get rid of people; you make the position held by the man in question redundant, then you re-establish it a few days later under a new description, and lo and behold, Bob's your uncle! There are always the physical infirmities contracted in the exercise of your functions and verified by the doctors, who are quick to do what is asked of them – and then there is (and basically this is the simplest method) so-called psychological infirmity, for which there's no need to resort to any practitioner, since a simple report signed by your director and approved by the human-resources manager is enough.

'This system is the most humiliating. To have them judging you senile! It's too much!' groaned Monsieur Bougran.

Then he started to reflect. The minister doubtless had some protégé he needed to find a job for, since there were fewer and fewer employees who really had a right to take retirement. For years there had been swingeing cutbacks in the offices, replacing the older staff, of which he was one of the last remnants, with new blood. And Monsieur Bougran nodded.

'In my time,' he said, 'we were conscientious and full of enthusiasm – now all these little youngsters, recruited from Heaven knows where, have none of the faith we had. They don't go right to the bottom of any business – they don't study any text in detail. All they can think of is getting out of the office, so they bodge their work and can't be bothered to learn the bureaucratic language that the older generation manipulated so adroitly. They all write as if they were just penning personal letters! Even the chief clerks, enlisted for the most part from outside, the flotsam and jetsam of whole series of ministers fallen from power, no longer have that bearing at once friendly and haughty which used to distinguish them from ordinary folk' – and forgetting his own misadventure, in a respectful vision he dwelt on the image of one of his former chief clerks, Monsieur Desrots des Bois, trussed up in his frock coat, his buttonhole concealed by an enormous red disc like the 'STOP!' sign for trains, the temples of his bald head encircled by fluffy down like a chick's, descending the stairs straight-backed, not turning to look at anyone, a portfolio under his arm, en route to see the director.

Every head bowed as he passed. The employees could well believe that this man's importance redounded on them, and they derived a greater sense of self-esteem from it.

At that time, everything was done in due form, and the nuances that had now vanished still existed. In administrative letters, there were different terms used to refer to the petitioners: the full 'Monsieur Dupont' for a person who held an honourable rank in society, plain 'Dupont' for a less distinguished man and 'a certain Dupont' for workers and convicts. And what ingenious devices they used to vary the vocabulary and avoid having to repeat the same words! They would designate the petitioner as 'the postulant', then 'the suppliant', then 'the plaintiff', then 'the applicant'. The prefect would become, in another part of the sentence, 'that high functionary'; the person whose name was the reason for the letter would change into 'this individual' or 'the above-mentioned', or 'the aforesaid'; in referring to itself, the service would sometimes describe itself as 'central' and sometimes as 'superior'; it made lavish use of synonyms, and added, as the envoi to a letter, phrases such as 'find attached, enclosed, herewith'. Protocols ran on and on; the signing-off formulae at the end of letters could take infinitely varying forms, all precisely calculated, on a scale which demanded from the office pianists a rare talent for fingering. In one letter, addressed to the pinnacle of the hierarchy, it was the assurance 'of our deepest and most humble respect'; then, as the degree of respect diminished, for men without ministerial rank it became 'our humble respect', 'our deep respect', 'our great respect', 'our cordial respect', ending up as 'respect' full stop, a respect which cancelled itself out, representing as it did the height of contempt.

Which employee now knew how to manipulate that delicate keyboard to strike the right note at the end of letters, choosing those deferential terms that were sometimes so difficult to determine when it was a matter of replying to people whose status hadn't been foreseen by the imperfectly laid-down dogmas of the protocols! Ah, the copying clerks had lost all sense for the right turn of phrase, and were ignorant of the skilful game of measuring respect out drop by drop! And what did it matter, after all, since for years everything had been falling apart, relapsing into chaos. The time of democratic abominations had come, and the title of 'Excellency' that ministers had once exchanged with each other had disappeared. They wrote from one ministry to another on an equal footing, like shopkeepers or ordinary middle-class folk. Even the favours – those silk ribbons in blue, green or tricolour which used to tie together letters when they consisted of more than two pages – had been replaced by pink string, at five sous a ball!

How commonplace everything had become! What a comedown! 'I never felt at home in that environment devoid of any real dignity or bearing, but . . . but . . . that's not the same as actually wanting to leave . . .' And with a sigh, Monsieur Bougran returned to his own situation and turned his thoughts to his own plight.

In his head he totted up the pro-rata pension he would be entitled to claim: eighteen hundred francs at most. With the small fixed income his father had provided for him, there would be just enough to live on. 'It's true,' he said to himself, 'that my old servant Eulalie and I get by on nothing.'

But much more worrying than his personal resources was the question of how he would manage to kill the time. How could he break away overnight from the habit of being shut up in the same old office room for identical hours each day, and participating in the customary exchange of conversation each morning with his colleagues? True, the talk had not been very varied: it generally concerned the greater or lesser degree of promotion to be expected at the end of the year, as the clerks tried to work out who was due for retirement, and even tried to guess who might die, or imagined illusory perks, deviating from these fascinating subjects only in order to launch out into interminable reflections on the events related in the newspaper. But even this lack of novelty was in such perfect harmony with the monotony of the faces, the flatness of the jokes and, indeed, the uniformity of the office rooms!

Then there had been, after all, some interesting discussions in the office of the chief clerk or his deputy on the best way of swinging this or that piece of business. What would replace those juridical jousts now – those apparent disputes, those cheerful agreements, those welcome quarrels? How could he find anything entertaining enough to make him forget a profession that pierced you to the marrow, possessed you entirely, to the very depths of your being?

And Monsieur Bougran shook his head in despair, telling himself, 'I'm alone, a bachelor, without family, friends or acquaintances. I have no talent to take up any job other than the one that has kept me busy for the past twenty years. I'm too old to start out on a new life.' This realization terrified him.

'Well,' he resumed as he rose to his feet, 'I've still got to go back to my office!' His legs were unsteady. 'I don't feel very well ... What if I went and had a lie-down?' But he forced himself to walk, resolved to die with the harness on his back. He made his way to the ministry and returned to his office.

There he really and truly almost fainted away. He looked around in dismay, tears in his eyes, at this shell which had protected him for so many years – while his colleagues softly entered in single file.

They had been awaiting his return, and their condolences varied with the expression on their faces. The assistant clerk – a tall, gangling fellow with the head of a stork and a few colourless hairs straggling across his pate – shook him fervently by the hand without uttering a word. His demeanour was that of someone consoling the family of a dead man on leaving church while the bier is waiting outside, after the absolution. The copying clerks wagged their heads, demonstrating their official sympathy by repeated bows.

The clerks who drafted the letters – who, being his colleagues, knew him better – tried to think of a few words of comfort.

'Come now, you have to make the best of a bad job – and then, old chap, just think that when it comes down to it, you have neither wife nor children: you could have been retired in much more difficult circumstances, if you'd had a daughter to marry off, for instance – as I do. So you can count yourself as lucky as anyone can be in a similar situation.'

'It's only right to look on the bright side, whatever happens,' said another. 'You're going to be free to take walks – you can live off your income and laze in the sunshine.'

'And you can go and live in the countryside – you'll be in clover!' added a third.

Monsieur Bougran mildly pointed out that he had been born in Paris, that he knew nobody out in the provinces, that he didn't feel he had the strength to go into exile in some hole or other just to save money. All of them continued, nonetheless, to demonstrate to him that, all things considered, he wasn't so very badly off.

And as none of them was of an age to feel threatened by a similar fate, they exhibited a genuine resignation, almost waxing indignant at the sadness shown by Monsieur Bougran.

The finest example of real sympathy and authentic regret was Baptiste, the office boy, Bougran's main assistant. With an air of unctuous consternation, he offered to carry Monsieur Bougran's odds and ends home for him – his old overcoat, his pens, pencils, etc., all his office possessions – intimating that this would be the last time Monsieur Bougran would have the opportunity of giving him a fat tip.

'Come now, gentlemen,' said the chief clerk as he entered the office room. 'The director wants the portfolio ready for five o'clock.'

They all went back to their desks – and, whinnying like an old horse, Monsieur Bougran settled down to work, his mind entirely occupied by the task in hand, hurrying to make up for the time he had wasted indulging in gloomy daydreams on the bench.

II

The first days were quite awful. Waking at the same time as before, he asked himself what was the point of getting up – he continued to lounge in bed, quite contrary to his normal habits, started to feel cold, yawned and finally got dressed. But good Lord! What was he to do to fill his time? On mature reflection, he decided to go for a walk and take a stroll round the Luxembourg Gardens, which were not far from the Rue de Vaugirard, where he lived.

But those immaculately manicured lawns, without a trace of earth or water, that looked as if they were freshly repainted and varnished each morning as soon as the sun rose, those flowers raised erect as if newly blossoming on their wiry stalks, those trees with all the girth of reeds, that whole artificial landscape, planted with ridiculous statues – none of this cheered him. He went to take refuge at the far end of the garden, in the former seedbed over which the buildings of the École de Pharmacie and the Lycée Louis-le-Grand cast their solemn shadows. The verdure here was just as glossily kept and emaciated as elsewhere. The lawns spread out their grass, cropped short and green, the little trees nodded the bored plumes of their heads, but the torture inflicted on the fruit trees, in some of the flower beds, made him halt. These trees no longer had the shape of trees. They were made to extend their branches along wooden laths, or to crawl along wires laid out on the ground; their limbs were twisted into odd shapes as soon as they were born. In this way, acrobatical vegetation was produced, with trunks that bent every which way, as flexible as if they had been made of rubber. They ran along, snaking like adders, rose like conical baskets, mimicked beehives, pyramids, fan shapes, vases of flowers, or a clown's tuft of hair. This garden was a real torture chamber for trees and shrubs. Here, with the help of racks and boots of wickerwork or cast iron, straw contraptions and orthopaedic corsets, gardeners with hernias tried not so much to straighten the curved and twisted limbs as do the bandage makers of humanity, but to do the precise opposite, forcing them into strange shapes, dislocating them and twisting them in accordance with some putative Japanese ideal designed to produce monsters!

But when he had spent some time admiring this way of murdering trees on the pretext of extorting better fruit from them, he wandered up and down, at a loose end, without having even realized that this vegetable-garden surgery represented the most perfect symbol of the civil service that he had known and worked in for years. In office life, as in the Luxembourg Gardens, they went out of their way to take simple things to bits and pieces; they took some administrative legal document whose meaning was clear and precise and immediately, with the help of hazy and long-winded arguments, unprecedented precedents and legal quibbles going back to the Messidors and Ventôses of Revolutionary times, they turned this text into a hopeless muddle, a contorted piece of literature grimacing like an ape, which produced decisions that were the complete opposite of the ones that could have been anticipated.

Then he made his way back up to the terrace of the Luxembourg, where the trees seem less young, less freshly dusted, more true to life. And he walked along between the garden chairs, watching the children make mud pies in the sand with their little buckets, while their mothers enjoyed a natter, shoulder to shoulder, energetically swapping ideas on the best way to cook veal and how to use the leftovers for the next day's lunch.

And, feeling worn out, he returned home, climbed the stairs yawning and received a scolding from his maid Eulalie, who complained that he was turning into a real 'pain in the neck' if he imagined he could come and 'troll around' in her kitchen.

Soon, insomnia was added to his woes. Torn away from its habits, transported into an atmosphere of oppressive sloth, his body no longer functioned properly. His appetite had fled; his nights, which had previously been so peaceful under the blankets, became restless and filled with dark ideas, while in the black silence, one by one, the hours chimed in the distance.

When it rained, he tried spending the days reading, and then, worn out by his insomnia, he fell asleep – and the night that followed these periods of slumber became even longer, even more wakeful. Even when the weather turned nasty, he found he still had to go for a walk to tire his legs out, and he fetched up in the museums – but not a single painting aroused his interest: he did not recognize a single canvas or a single great artist, and he ambled slowly along, his hands behind his back, from frame to frame, his thoughts occupied by the attendants, who were drowsing on their chairs, totting up the pension that they too, as state functionaries, could one day count on.

Tired of colours and white statues, he went for a stroll through the city's covered passages, but he was quickly sent packing. He was observed; the words 'informer', 'copper's nark', 'spy' were heard. Shamefaced, he fled back out into the downpour and rushed to take refuge in his home.

And, more poignant than ever, the memory of his office obsessed him. Seen from afar, the ministry appeared to him as a real paradise. He had quite forgotten the iniquities he had endured, his post as under-chief clerk nabbed by an outsider who had entered the service on the coat tails of a minister, the irritations of a job that was both mechanical and stressful. The darker side of this existence spent polishing his chair with the seat of his pants had evaporated: all that was left was the vision of a nice sedentary life, cosy and warm, made cheery by the conversation of his colleagues, by their awful puns and their third-rate practical jokes.

'There's nothing for it: I must think of something to do,' said Monsieur Bougran to himself glumly. For a few hours he imagined that he could look for a new job that would keep him busy and even bring in a bit of money, but even if there were some shopkeeper prepared to take on a man of his age, he would then have to slave away morning, noon and night, and he would have only a derisory wage, since he wasn't up to doing a real job, in a profession whose secrets and tricks of the trade he was ignorant of.

And it would be such a come-down in the world! ... For, like many government employees, Monsieur Bougran considered himself to be a member of a superior caste, and he despised the people who worked in commerce and banking. He even ranged his peers into hierarchies, judging a ministry employee superior to the employee of a prefecture, just as the latter was, in his eyes, of a higher rank than the petty clerk employed in a town hall.

So what could he turn to? What was he to do? And this nagging question remained unanswered.

For want of anything better, he went back to his office on the pretext of seeing his colleagues, but he was received by them in the way that people who are no longer part of the group are always received: coldly. They enquired indifferently after his health; a few of them pretended to envy him, praised the freedom he enjoyed, the strolls he must be able to indulge in.

Monsieur Bougran smiled, heavy-hearted. One final blow was accidentally inflicted on him. He allowed himself to be dragged over to his old office room. He saw the employee who had replaced him – a complete stripling! He was filled with rage against this successor, who had changed the appearance of the room that Monsieur Bougran loved, shifting the desk, pushing the chairs over into another corner, filing the folders away in different pigeon-holes – the inkpot was now on the left, and the pen holder on the right!

He left feeling completely despondent.

On the way home, suddenly, an idea sprang up and grew in his mind. 'Ah!' he thought. 'Perhaps all's not lost!' And such was his joy that, back home that evening, he ate with a hearty appetite, slept like a log and awoke in the best of humour at first light.

III

The plan that had put him in such a good mood was easy to carry out. At first, Monsieur Bougran did the rounds of the wallpaper shops, purchased several rolls of a horrible milk-chicory-coffee paper that he hung on the walls of the smallest room in his apartment. Then he bought a desk in black-painted pinewood with a row of compartments on top, a little table on which he placed a chipped basin and a piece of marshmallow soap in an old glass, a semicircular cane armchair and two chairs. He had his walls set up with pigeon-holes in white wood, which he filled with green folders with copper clasps; he pinned a calendar over the mantelpiece, from which he had first removed the mirror, and piled boxes of slips on the shelf; he slung a doormat on the floor and a waste-paper basket under his desk, and, stepping back, exclaimed in delight: 'That's it! It's like being there!'

On his desk he set out, methodically, the whole row of his pen holders and pencils – cork pen holders in the shape of a sledgehammer, copper-armoured pen holders sheathed in rosewood, which were good to chew on, and black, blue and red pencils for annotations and cross-references. Then he arranged, just as in bygone days, a porcelain inkwell, encircled with sponges, to the right of his desk blotter, a small bowl full of wood shavings on the left; opposite, a container with a grotesque face – its green velvet lid, bristling with pins, concealing rubber stamps and pink string. Dossiers of yellowish paper were scattered about pretty much everywhere. Over the pigeon-holes were ranged the necessary tomes: Block's *Dictionnaire de l'administration*, the *Civil Code*, the legal reference works, Béquet and Blanche. He found himself back in front of his old desk in his old office room without having budged an inch.

He sat down, radiant, and from that moment on he relived the halcyon days of yore. Every morning he would leave his home, just as he used to, and stepping out like a man eager to arrive on time he would stride down the Boulevard Saint-Germain, stopping halfway towards his former office, then retrace his steps, return home, taking out his watch to check the time as he climbed the stairs, and he would lift the cardboard lid of his inkwell, remove his cuffs, replace them with cuffs in thick Manila paper, of the kind used to cover the dossiers, change his own suit of clothes for the old frock coat he used to wear at the ministry – and *voilà*! He could get down to work!

He would make up questions to be decided, address petitions to himself, reply to them, keep what is called a 'log' by writing in a big thick book the date they were received and sent out. And, once his office hours came to an end, he would take an hour-long stroll, just as in bygone days, through the streets, before returning home for dinner.

He had the good fortune, at first, to dream up a problem of the kind he had enjoyed solving in bygone days – but one more muddled, more chimerical, more outlandishly inane. He slogged long and hard over it, searched through the decisions of the Council of State and the Court of Appeal for the judgements that can be used, as you like, to defend or support this case or that. Happy to wade through the Byzantine complexities of the law, trying to find ridiculous legal details that he could bend this way and that to fit his thesis, he sweated over his papers, starting his minutes or his drafts several times over again from scratch, correcting them in the margin he had left blank, just as his chief clerk had done in former times – never managing, in spite of all this, to satisfy himself, gnawing his pen holder, striking his brow, feeling breathless and opening the window for a breath of fresh air.

He lived like this for a month, then he was seized by a sense of malaise. He would work until five o'clock, but he felt exhausted, dissatisfied, distracted, incapable of seeing things in perspective, his head filled by his dossiers. By now, he was aware of the make-believe he had got caught up in. He had indeed restored the ambience of his former office, of the very room he had worked in. He left the door and window shut, if need be, so it would retain that smell of dust and dried ink that emanates from the rooms in the ministries – but the noise, the conversation, the comings and goings of his colleagues were all missing. Not a soul to talk to. This solitary office was not, when all was said and done, a real office. It was no use his having resumed all his old habits: it just wasn't the same ... Ah! God knows what he would have given to have been able to ring, so as to see the office boy come in and have a chat for a few minutes!

And then ... and then ... other holes were starting to open up in the artificial soil of this slack life. In the morning, as he went through the letters he had sent himself the day before, he knew what the envelopes contained: he recognized his own writing, the format of the envelope in which he had enclosed this or that piece of business, and this destroyed his every illusion! He would at least have needed another person there to write the address, using envelopes that he couldn't recognize!

He was overwhelmed by dejection. He grew so bored that he allowed himself to take a few days off and wandered through the streets.

'Monsieur is looking peaky,' said Eulalie when she looked at her master. And, her hands in her apron pockets, she added, 'I really can't understand anyone working so hard when it doesn't bring any money in!'

He sighed and, when she left, contemplated his face in the mirror. Still, it was true that he looked peaky – and how old he had grown! His eyes, a startled and mournful blue, always opened wide in a fixed stare, were surrounded by wrinkles, and his bushy eyebrows were turning white. His pate was going bald, his side whiskers were all grey – even his clean-shaven mouth had drooped, and was outshone by his prominent chin. His whole podgy little body was sagging, his shoulders stooping; his clothes seemed too big for him now, and looked much shabbier. He saw himself ruined, decrepit, crushed by the weight of the fifty years that he had borne so cheerfully as long as he was working in a real office.

'Monsieur ought to take a purgative,' Eulalie kept saying each time she saw him. 'Monsieur is bored – why doesn't he go fishing? He could bring us back a nice fish to fry from the Seine – it would be a change for him.'

Monsieur Bougran gently shook his head and went out.

One day, a chance stroll led him, without his even noticing, to the Jardin des Plantes, and his gaze was suddenly drawn by an arm waving on the edge of his line of vision. He stopped, pulled himself together and saw one of his former office assistants greeting him.

He brightened up for a moment – almost shouted for joy.

'Huriot,' he said. The other turned round, lifted his cap and shouldered the pipe he was holding.

'Well now, old friend, what's become of you, then?'

'Oh, nothing, Monsieur Bougran, I'm doing odd jobs here and there to save up a few more pennies for my pension – but, saving your presence,

I'm just bumming around, as I'm not much use for anything these days, ever since my legs have stopped working!'

'Listen, Huriot . . . Do you still have one of the uniforms you used to wear in the ministry?'

'Oh yes, Monsieur, I've got an old one I use at home so I can save my best clothes for when I go out.'

'Ah!'

Monsieur Bougran was rapt in a delightful daydream: take him into his service at home, in his office uniform! Every quarter of an hour he would come into his room bringing papers, just as before. And then he'd be able to take care of the dispatches, writing the addresses on the envelopes. It would perhaps be like *real* office life, at long last!

'Listen, my boy, I've got something to tell you,' Monsieur Bougran went on. 'I'll pay you fifty francs a month to come to my place, exactly like the office – *exactly*, do you understand? You won't have all those stairs to go up and come down – but you can go and shave off your beard and grow sideburns like you used to, and wear your uniform again. Does that grab your fancy?'

'Not half!' And, as he hesitated, he screwed up his eyes. 'So, are you going to set up your own company – a bank or something, Monsieur Bougran?'

'No, it's something else. I'll explain when the time comes – meanwhile, here's my address. Make whatever arrangements you need to, but turn up at my place tomorrow, and you can start work.'

And he left him and trotted back home, feeling rejuvenated.

'Good! That's what Monsieur ought to look like every day,' said Eulalie, observing him and wondering what had cropped up into this monotonous life.

He needed to pour out his heart, to express his joy, to talk. He told his maid the story of his encounter, then he stood there, anxious and mute as she gazed sternly at him.

'So this gentleman is going to come here to do nothing but eat up your funds, just like that!' she said drily.

'No, no, Eulalie, he'll have his work to do, and in any case he's a good chap, an old civil servant who knows his job thoroughly.'

'That's not much use! Look, I bet he'll get fifty francs just to sit there twiddling his thumbs, while I get only forty francs a month – and *I* do the housework and the cooking, and take good care of you! . . . It's too much, it really is! . . . No, Monsieur Bougran, it just won't do. You can keep that old office skivvy and get *him* to rub you down with a flannel to ease your rheumatism and some of that ointment that stinks of fresh paint – *I'm* leaving! I'm not going to be treated like this, at my age!'

Monsieur Bougran looked at her, dumbfounded.

'But look here, Eulalie my dear, don't get angry like that. Come on, if you like I'll raise your wages a bit . . .'

'My wages! Oh no, don't think I'd stay for the fifty francs a month you're offering me now. If I want to leave, it's because of the way you're behaving towards me!'

The thought crossed Monsieur Bougran's mind that he hadn't at all offered to give her a wage of fifty francs: he had simply intended to raise her present wage by five francs a month – but faced with the old woman's wrathful countenance as she declared that she was going to leave in spite of everything, he bowed his head and made excuses, trying to soft-talk her with wheedling compliments and get her to stay rather than pack her bags as she was threatening.

'And where will you put him, then? Not in my kitchen, I hope!' said Eulalie – who, having obtained what she wanted, allowed herself to calm down.

'No, in the hallway – you won't need to bother about him, or even see him. As you see, dearie, there was no need to fly off the handle the way you did!'

'I'll fly off the handle, if I want to! And don't you try and tell me what to do!' she cried, getting back onto her high horse. She had decided to stay, but she wasn't going to put up with even these mild reproaches.

Worn out, Monsieur Bougran didn't dare look at her as she strutted out of the room with insolent pride.

IV

'Not much in the post this morning!'

'No, Huriot, we're falling behind. I had an important piece of business to deal with yesterday, and as I have to do it all by myself, I had to leave the less urgent questions to one side, and the service is suffering in consequence!'

'We're turning into real slackers, as poor old Monsieur de Pinaudel used to say. Did you know him, Monsieur?'

'Yes, old chap, I did. Oh, he was a very able man. He was in a class of his own when it came to composing a tricky letter. Another trusty civil servant who was retired prematurely, like me!'

'Yes, and you should just look at the service these days: young whipper-snappers who have only one thing on their minds – how to have a good time! Ah, Monsieur Bougran, office life isn't what it used to be!'

Monsieur Bougran sighed. Then he dismissed his assistant with a nod and settled back down to work.

Ah, this administrative jargon he had to get right! All those turns of phrase: 'Our client pleads', 'In reply to your kind letter, I have the honour to inform you that', 'As per the opinion expressed in your dispatch relative to . . .' Those customary idioms: 'The spirit, if not the letter of the law', 'Giving all due weight to the importance of the considerations to which you refer in support of this argument . . .' And finally, those formulae intended for the Ministry of Justice, in which reference was made to 'the opinion emanating from His Chancellorship', all those evasive and inconclusive phrases: 'I am inclined to believe', or 'It will not have escaped your notice', or 'I would be most grateful if' – that whole vocabulary and phraseology going back to the age of Colbert, gave Monsieur Bougran a terrible headache.

His head in his clenched hands, he reread the first sentences he had just drafted. At present he was engaged in highly specialized tasks, up to his neck in an appeal to the Council of State.

And he falteringly murmured the inevitable formula of address:

MONSIEUR LE PRÉSIDENT,

The Legal Department has transferred to me, for deliberation, an appeal brought before the Council of State by Monsieur So-and-So, with the aim of annulling as ultra vires my resolution dated . . .

And the second sentence:

> Before moving to a discussion of the arguments brought forward by
> the petitioner in support of his case, I will summarily recall the facts
> motivating the present appeal.

It was here that it started to get difficult.

'I ought to spend some time embellishing it, and not move forward too
hastily,' Monsieur Bougran muttered. 'Monsieur So-and-So's request is
well founded in law. We'll have to try and wriggle our way out of this
dispute, go in for a bit of sharp practice, deliberately overlook certain
points. All in all, the letter of the law gives me forty days to reply: I have
time to think about it, mull it over in my head, not leap blindly to the
defence of the ministry . . .'

'More post!' said Huriot, bringing two new letters.

'*More?* It's been a hard day – and it's already four o'clock! All the same,'
Bougran said to himself, drawing a deep breath of fresh air once the
assistant had gone out, 'it's amazing how that Huriot reeks of garlic and
wine. Just like in the office!' He added with satisfaction. 'And there's dust
everywhere – he never bothers to sweep . . . again, just like in the office.
It's so authentic!'

What was equally authentic, though he barely noticed it, was the growing
antagonism between Eulalie and Huriot. Despite having obtained her fifty
francs per month, the maid couldn't get used to this drunkard, even though
he was obliging and mild-mannered and slept on a chair in the hallway,
waiting for his employee to ring for him.

'Lazy sod,' she would say, shifting her copper pots and pans round.
'When you think that old office skivvy snores away all day long doing
nothing!'

And to demonstrate her discontent to her master, she deliberately spoilt
the sauces, refused to utter a word and violently slammed the doors.

Timidly, Monsieur Bougran would lower his eyes and close his ears to
the terrible rows that occurred between his two domestics at the kitchen
door. Nonetheless, he could not help but pick up the odd phrase in which,

for once united in their opinions, Eulalie and Huriot called him a 'madman', a 'feather-brain', an 'old idiot'.

This filled him with sadness, which had a negative influence on his work. He could no longer settle down and get on with it. Even though he would have needed all the concentration of which he was capable to draw up this appeal, he found that his mind wandered in the most extravagant way: his thoughts kept returning to dwell on those domestic quarrels, on Eulalie's ferocious bad temper, and as he tried to disarm her with the imploring meekness of his sheepish gaze, she stood even more on her dignity, sure of being able to win if she struck hard. And he, in despair, stayed at home by himself in the evenings, chewing on his disgusting evening meal, not daring to complain.

All this aggravation accelerated the infirmities of age that were now starting to weigh him down. He had rushes of blood to the head, found he got breathless after his meals, and at night kept waking in a cold sweat.

Soon he found it difficult to make his way downstairs and leave the building so as to 'go to his office' – but he stiffened his resolve, setting out each morning in spite of everything, taking a half-hour walk before returning home.

His poor head was spinning – all the same, he wore out his strength on this appeal that he had embarked on and from which he could no longer extricate himself. With great tenacity, when he felt his mind clearer, he continued to labour over that fictitious problem he had set himself.

He did resolve it, finally, but he so overexerted himself mentally that his brain gave way and he suffered a fit. He uttered a loud cry. Neither Huriot nor the maid bothered to come. Around evening they found him, slumped over the table, his lips muttering disconnectedly, his eyes vacant. They sent for a doctor, who diagnosed apoplexy and declared that there was no hope for him.

Monsieur Bougran died that night, while his assistant and his maid exchanged insults and tried to dodge each other so that they could slip off and ransack the drawers.

On the desk of the now deserted office lay the sheet of paper on which Monsieur Bougran, sensing that he was about to die, had hastily scrawled the last lines of his appeal:

For these reasons I cannot, Monsieur le Président, but express a negative opinion on the action to be taken in the case of the appeal lodged by Monsieur So-and-So.

Translated by Andrew Brown

OCTAVE MIRBEAU

On a Cure

Before quitting the Pyrenees, I wanted to see my friend Roger Fresselou, who has lived for years and years in Le Castérat, a small village in the Ariège.

It was a long, hard journey. After six days of tough walking and steep climbing, aching and exhausted, I arrived at Le Castérat as night was falling. Picture in your mind thirty or so houses clustering on a narrow plateau surrounded on all sides by black mountains with snowy summits. To begin with the view is majestic, especially when the mist softens somewhat the closed horizon, turning it milky and covering it with gold dust. But this feeling soon vanishes, and faced with these lofty walls of rock, it is replaced by an invasive and dreary sadness, and by a horrid sense of imprisonment.

The village is at such an altitude that the trees are stunted and the only bird is the heavy ptarmigan with his feathery claws. Only a few meagre rhododendrons survive in this stony soil, and the dwarf thistle which opens its large yellow flowers with their pointed and wounding spines only in the noonday sun. On the slopes below the plateau, to the north, grows short, greyish grass, grazed over in summer by cows and sheep and goats, whose bells tinkle incessantly, like the tinkling of the priest's bell in our native countryside, that sounds in the evening as he bears viaticum to the sick. Nothing is sadder, and nothing is less flower-like, than the rare species that scrape a living out of this mean and joyless corner of nature; poor stunted plants with whiteish, hairy leaves, and coarse corollas that have the discoloured, clouded look of dead pupils. Winter with its snowfalls, and all the surrounding gulfs filled with snow, cuts the village off from the rest of the world, from the rest of life. The herds move down to the low valleys, the sturdy men of the village seek work or adventure elsewhere, sometimes far away; the post doesn't even get through . . . For months and months there comes no news from the other side of the impassable snows. No one living is left, merely the half-alive, the old men, and the women and children who go to earth in their houses, like marmots in their holes. They only come out on Sundays, to hear mass in church, which is made up of a little square tower, its stone fissured, with a kind of lean-to up against its side, shaped like a barn. Oh! The sound of that bell muffled by the snow!

This is, however, where my friend Roger Fresselou has made his home for twenty years. A little house with a flat roof, a small, stony garden, and with rough, silent, jealous men for neighbours, miserable and complaining, clad in coarse homespun and mountain headgear. Roger has very little to do with them.

How did he end up here? And above all, how can he live here? In truth I have no idea, and I don't think he really knows either. Every time I ask him why he has exiled himself like this, he replies with a shrug: 'How would I know? . . . That's how it is . . .', offering nothing further by way of explanation.

One curious thing: Roger has scarcely aged at all. Not a single grey hair, not a wrinkle on his face. And yet I scarcely recognize him under his mountain apparel. His eyes have gone dead, not a spark comes out of them. And his face has taken on the ashen colour of the soil. It's a totally different man from the one I used to know. There is an entirely new life within him, about which I know nothing. And I try in vain to puzzle it out.

He used to be enthusiastic, charming, and full of life. Never exactly exuberant in words or acts, he had a melancholy common to all young people who have tasted the poison of metaphysics. In our little circle in Paris, we were fairly confident of his future. He had contributed some literary essays to small magazines which, while not absolute master-pieces, showed ambition, real seriousness, and a curiosity about life. Thanks to his clear mind and his solid, forthright style, he seemed to be one of those destined to break free of the narrow cliques (in which talent can shrink) and reach a wider public. In the domains of art, lit-erature, philosophy or politics he had nothing of the intransigent sectarian about him, even if he held firm both in radicalism and in beauty. There was nothing morbid about him, no abnormal obsessions, no intellectual bugbears . . . His intelligence was built on solid foundations . . . And then we learned, a few months later, that he was living in the mountains.

Since I have been with Roger we have not once spoken about literature. Many times I have tried to steer the conversation round to a subject he used to love, but every time he has avoided it ill-temperedly. He has asked after no one, and when, pointedly, I mention certain names, once dear to us, and now famous, he betrays not the slightest inner emotion, not so much as a flicker. I sense within him no trace of bitterness or regret. He seems to have forgotten all that, and his former passions and friendships are nothing but dreams, long since blotted out! Of my own work, of my own hopes in part fulfilled, in part disappointed, he has said not a word. And in his house – impossible to find a book, a newspaper, or any kind of image. There is nothing here, and he himself is as empty of intellectual life as his mountain neighbours.

Yesterday, as I pressed him one last time to impart to me the reason for his baffling renunciation, he said:

'How would I know? . . . That's how it is . . . I came here by chance, during a summer holiday . . . I liked the place because of its unspeakable wretchedness . . . or rather, I thought I liked it . . . I came back the following year, with no set plan . . . I thought I would stay just a few days . . . I ended up staying twenty years! . . . That's it! . . . There's no more to say . . . It's quite simple, as you see . . .'

This evening, Roger asked me:

'Do you ever think about death?'

'Yes, I replied . . . And it terrifies me . . . so I try to banish the dreadful image . . .'

'It frightens you? . . .'

He shrugged his shoulders and went on:

'You think about death . . . and you come and you go . . . and you torment yourself . . . and twist and turn in all directions? . . . And you work on ephemeral things? . . . And you fondle dreams of pleasure, maybe . . . and even of glory? . . . Poor little thing! . . .'

'Ideas are not ephemeral things,' I protested . . . 'they can prepare the future, they can steer progress . . .'

With a slow, sweeping gesture he motioned at the circus of black mountains:

'The future! . . . Progress! . . . How can you possibly, faced with that, utter such meaningless words? . . .'

And after a short pause he went on:

'Ideas! . . . Just wind, wind, wind . . . They pass over . . . the tree stirs for an instant . . . its leaves tremble . . . and then they have passed . . . the tree becomes still again . . . nothing has changed . . .'

'You're wrong . . . The wind is full of cells, it carries pollen and winnows seed . . . it fertilizes . . .'

'And creates monsters.'

We remained silent a while . . .

And then I felt, coming from the black mountains opposite us, all around us, with their implacable walls of slate and rock, a stifling, oppressive weight . . . I truly felt the weight of those blocks on my chest and on my skull . . . Roger Fresselou went on:

'When the idea of death suddenly took hold of me, I felt at the same time the pettiness and the vanity of all my endeavours which were using up my life . . . But I procrastinated . . . I would say: "I've taken a wrong turning . . . perhaps I can do something else with my life . . . art is corrupt . . . literature all lies . . . philosophy mere mystification . . . I shall seek out simple men, rough, good-hearted men . . . There must somewhere exist, in pure, remote parts, far from cities, human material from which one might strike a spark of beauty . . . Let us go . . . let us find it! . . ." Alas, no, men are everywhere the same . . . Only their actions differ . . . And even here, on this silent peak where I see them, these actions are disappearing. There is nothing more than a teeming herd which, whatever it does and wherever it goes, jostles on towards death . . . You speak of progress? . . . But progress, swifter and more conscious, is just a big step forward towards the ineluctable end . . . And so here I have remained, where all is ash, charred stone, dried-out sap, where everything has already entered into the silence of dead things! . . .'

'Why didn't you just kill yourself?' I let fly, exasperated by my friend's voice, and seized in my turn by the horrible obsession with death which floats on the mountains and around the summits, gliding over the gulfs towards me, borne along to the sound of those tinkling bells, those tolling bells, on the slopes of the plateau.

Roger answered calmly:

'You don't kill what is already dead ... I have been dead these twenty years, since coming here ... And you've been dead for a long time too ... Why struggle against it? ... Stay where you are now! ...'

I summoned the guide who was to lead me back to the world of men, to life, to light ... Tomorrow, at first light, I shall be gone ...

Translated by Stephen Romer

JEAN RICHEPIN

Constant Guignard

The Guignard spouses, married for love, longed passionately for a son. As if the little soul who was so desired had hastened to fulfil their wishes, he arrived prematurely. His mother died in childbirth and, unable to bear the loss, his father hanged himself.

Constant Guignard had an exemplary but an unhappy childhood. He spent his time at school doing detentions he didn't deserve, receiving thrashings meant for others, and being ill on the days when all the important exams were held. He completed his studies with the reputation of a cockroach and a dunce. When it came to the Baccalaureate, he did his neighbour's Latin translation for him. His neighbour passed, but Guignard was expelled from the exam for copying.

Such inauspicious beginnings in life would have turned a lesser nature vicious. But Constant Guignard had a soul of the higher type, and convinced that happiness is the reward of virtue, he resolved to conquer his ill-fortune by sheer force of heroism.

He entered a house of commerce, which burned down the next day. As the fire raged, he noticed the distress of his employer, and plunged into the flames to retrieve the safe. His hair burned and his limbs suppurated, but he managed, at peril of his life, to break the safe and take the contents out.

But the fire consumed them in his hands. When he emerged from the furnace, two constables grabbed him by the collar. A month later he was condemned to five years imprisonment for having tried to steal, at the opportune moment offered by the fire, a fortune that was quite safe where it was in a fireproof strongbox.

A riot broke out in the high-security prison where he was held. In his attempt to come to the rescue of a warder being attacked, he tripped him accidentally and left him to be massacred by the rebels. So they sent him to Cayenne for twenty years.

Driven by the knowledge of his innocence, he escaped, made his way back to France under an assumed name, and truly believed he had shaken off ill-fortune, and once more set about doing good.

One day, during a fair, he saw a runaway horse dragging a cab straight towards the edge of the rampart. He flung himself at the head of the horse, got his wrist twisted, his leg broken, and had several ribs stove in, but he managed to prevent the dreadful fall. Except that the horse turned round and charged into the middle of the crowd, crushing an old man, two women and three children. There had been no one in the cab.

Wearied by these acts of heroism, Constant Guignard took instead to doing good quietly, humbly devoting himself to alleviating everyday hardships. But the money he gave to families in need was spent by the husbands on drink; the woollens he distributed to poor workers, used to the cold, made them catch pneumonia; a stray dog he rescued gave rabies to six people in the neighbourhood; the military substitute he purchased to get an interesting young man out of the army sold passkeys to the enemy.

Constant Guignard came to believe that money did more harm than good, and rather than spreading wide his philanthropy, he decided to concentrate it on a single person. So he adopted a young orphan girl, not in any way beautiful, but graced with the most loveable nature, and he looked after her with all the tenderness of a father. Alas! He was so good, so devoted, and so kindly towards her, that one evening she flung herself at his feet, declaring that she was in love with him. He tried to make her understand that he had always considered her as his daughter, and that it would be a crime were he to succumb to the temptation she presented. He made her understand, in his fatherly way, that what she took to be love was in fact the awakening of her senses, and he promised her that, taking note of this sign of nature, he would not delay in seeking a husband worthy of her. The next day he found her lying against his door, a knife in her heart.

With that, Constant Guignard decided to give up his missionary role, and swore that from now on he would seek satisfaction simply in trying to prevent evil.

Some time after this, he was apprised by accident of a crime that one of his friends was going to commit. He could have denounced him to the police; but he preferred to try and prevent the crime, and save the criminal. So he became closely involved with the planning, understood all the details, and waited for the precise moment when, having set everything up, he would scupper the whole plan. But the rascal he was trying to save saw through his game, and managed to outwit him, in such wise that the crime was perpetrated, the criminal got away, and Constant Guignard was arrested.

The public prosecutor's requisition against Constant Guignard was a masterpiece of logic. He recalled the defendant's whole life, his miserable childhood, with its punishments and expulsions, the audacity of his first attempted theft, his despicable treachery in the prison riot, his escape from Cayenne, his return to France under an assumed name. From this moment on, the orator rose to the greatest possible heights of legal eloquence. He scourged the hypocritical virtue of the man, who was a corrupter of decent families, who for his own pleasure had sent honest husbands out to drink his money; this false do-gooder who contrived, by giving presents, to attain an unmerited popularity, this monster hidden in the habit of a philanthropist. He dwelt in detail upon the refined perversity of a wretch who rescued rabid dogs only to let them loose on society, of a demon who, in love with evil for its own sake, was prepared to injure himself in order to stop a runaway horse, and why? For the unspeakable pleasure of seeing the animal plunge into the crowd, crushing to death old men, women and children. Such a man would stop at nothing! And there were certainly other crimes to his name as yet unknown. All the evidence pointed to the fact that he was the accomplice of the mercenary who had betrayed France.

And as for the orphan he had raised, and who had been found one morning dead at his door, who else but he could have murdered her? This crime was undoubtedly the bloody end to one of those family dramas made up of shame, debauchery and filth, the like of which was hard to contemplate. After such a list, it was scarcely necessary to dwell on this latest crime. In this case, and despite the impudent denials of the accused, the evidence was incontrovertible. It was necessary, therefore, to condemn this man with the full rigour of the law. The punishment was just, and no punishment could be heavy enough. The defendant was not only a great criminal, he was one of those geniuses of crime, one of those monsters of malice and hypocrisy that make one doubt the existence of virtue and despair of humanity.

Before such a crushing indictment, Constant Guignard's lawyer had no alternative but to plead that his client was mad. He did his best, spoke learnedly of the *compulsion to evil*, portrayed his client as an irresponsible monomaniac, as a kind of unconscious Papavoine, and concluded by saying that such behaviour was more appropriately treated in the asylum at Charenton than on the Place de la Roquette.

The verdict was unanimous: Constant Guignard was sentenced to death.

Men of virtue, driven wild by their hatred of crime, went into transports of joy, and cried hurrah.

The death of Constance Guignard, like his life, was exemplary but unhappy. He mounted the scaffold without fear and without pretence, his face as calm as his conscience, and with a martyr's serenity about him which onlookers took to be the indifference of a brute. At the final moment, aware that his executioner was poor and with a family, he whispered to him that he had left him his entire fortune. The executioner was so moved by this that it took him three attempts to sever his benefactor's neck.

Three months after this, one of Constant Guignard's friends, returning from a long journey, learned of the honest man's sad end. Knowing only the man's merits, he set about trying to repair as best he could the injustice meted out by fate. He purchased a permanent concession, ordered a fine marble tombstone, and composed an epitaph for his friend. The next day he died of a stroke. Nevertheless, the expenses had been paid in advance, so the guillotined man got his sepulchre. But the stone-carver employed to execute the epitaph took it upon him to correct a letter that had been badly written on the manuscript. And the poor virtuous man, misjudged in his lifetime, lies in death with the following epitaph for all eternity:

Here lies Constant Guignard
A Zero

Translated by Stephen Romer

GUY DE MAUPASSANT

The Horla

Doctor Marrande, one of the most eminent psychiatrists in the country, had invited three of his colleagues and four others in the field of the natural sciences to spend an hour at his clinic considering the case of one of his patients. When they were all gathered, he said to them: 'I should like to present to you the strangest and most disturbing case I have ever come across. I shall say nothing ahead of time about this patient, but let him speak for himself.'

The doctor rang and a man entered, accompanied by a member of staff. He was extremely thin, cadaverous even, as some madmen look when they are consumed by an obsession. Their bodies seem ravaged by one sick thought which devours them faster than any disease or consumption. Having greeted the company and sat down, the man spoke.

'Gentlemen, I am well aware of what brings you here. I am happy to comply with Dr Marrande's request for me to give you my history. For a long time he himself believed I was mad. Today he is not so sure. Some time in the near future you will realize that, unfortunately, not only for myself but for you and all the rest of humanity, my mind is as healthy, clear and as lucid as your own. Let me first of all give you the facts.

I am forty-two years old and unmarried. My income is sufficient for me to live a fairly luxurious kind of life. I live in a property which I own on the banks of the Seine at Biessard, near Rouen. I like hunting and I like fishing. Beyond the rocky hillsides behind my house lies one of the most beautiful forests in the whole of France, the forest of Roumare. And in front of the house, which is very large and very old, lies one of the most beautiful rivers in the world. Moreover, the house itself is attractive: it is painted white and stands in the middle of parkland which extends as far as the rocky hillsides I mentioned earlier.

My staff consists, or rather consisted, of a coachman, a gardener, a man-servant, a cook and a laundry-cum-scullery maid. All these people had lived there with me for between ten and sixteen years. They were long familiar with my ways, with the running of the house, with the neighbour-hood, everything. They made an excellent, harmonious team, a point which it is important to bear in mind in what follows.

I should add that since the Seine, as you probably know, is navigable as far as Rouen, on the stretch of it in front of my house I used to see daily all kinds of sea-going vessels from all over the world pass up and down stream, some under sail, some under steam.

Well, about a year last autumn, I suddenly began to suffer inexplicable spells of a strange malaise. To begin with, I was prey to a kind of nervous anxiety which kept me awake for entire nights at a stretch, a kind of hypersensitivity which made me jump at the least little sound. I began to have periods of moodiness and sudden fits of anger for no apparent reason. I consulted a doctor who prescribed cold showers and potassium bromide.

I followed his advice and took a shower morning and evening, as well as the bromide. Quite soon I did in fact manage to start sleeping again, but this time sleep turned out to be even more intolerable than the insomnia. As soon as my head hit the pillow, my eyes closed and I was out. I mean out completely. I fell into absolute nothingness, a void, a total blank. My self became completely dead until I was suddenly, horribly awoken by the most appalling sensation. An unbearable weight was lying on my chest and another mouth was sucking the life out of me through my own. I shall never forget the terrible shock of it! Just imagine a man asleep and in the process of being murdered. He wakes with the knife in his throat. He can hear his own death rattle, feel his own blood ooze out of him. He cannot breathe. He knows he is going to die but not why – that's exactly what it felt like!

I was losing a dangerous amount of weight all the time and suddenly realized that my coachman, a big, solid sort of fellow, was doing the same thing. I said to him in the end, 'Look, Jean, there's definitely something wrong with you. What d'you think is the matter?' 'To tell you the truth, monsieur,' he said, 'I think I've caught whatever you've got. My nights seem to be eating into my days.' I began to think that there was something noxious permeating the house, something poisonous, maybe, emanating from the river.

I had decided to spend two or three months away, despite the fact that the hunting season was in full swing, when something strange happened. I might easily have missed it, so trivial did it at first seem but it led to a series of such unbelievable, fantastical events that I decided after all, to stay.

One night, being thirsty, I drank half a glass of water and noticed when I did so that the carafe on my bedside table had been full up as far as its glass stopper. During the night I had one of those terrible awakenings I just mentioned. Still shaking, I lit my candle and was about to take another drink of water when I noticed to my stupefaction that the carafe was now empty. I could not believe my eyes. Either someone had come into the room or I was acting unconsciously in my sleep.

The following night I wanted to see if the same thing would happen. This time I locked my door to make sure no one could come into the room. I went to sleep and woke up as I did every night. *Someone* had drunk all the water I had seen there with my own eyes only two hours before. But *who*? Myself, obviously, and yet I could have almost sworn that I had made no movement in my deep and painful sleep.

I resorted to various stratagems in order to convince myself that I was not doing these things unconsciously. One night I put next to the carafe a bottle of vintage claret as well as a glass of milk, which I hate, and a piece of chocolate cake, which I love. Both the wine and the cake remained intact. But the water and the milk disappeared. None of the solid food-stuffs had had inroads made in them, only the liquids – the water and milk especially.

I was still in agonizing doubt. Maybe it was still I myself who was get-ting up without any consciousness of it. Maybe it was I who even drank the liquids I detested. My senses could have been so drugged that in sleep they were completely altered. In that state it was possible for me to have shed my former dislikes and acquired new tastes altogether.

I tried another way to catch myself out. I wrapped everything which was likely to be touched in thin muslin, which in turn I covered with the finest linen napkins. Then, just before getting into bed, I rubbed my face, hands and moustache all over with black lead. When I awoke, the materials were still spotless. They had, however, been moved. The napkins lay differently from the way I had placed them, and, more importantly, both the water and the milk had been drained off. This time my door had been locked with an extra security key, the shutters had been padlocked also just in case, and no one therefore could possibly have come into the room. So I had to ask myself the terrifying question of who it was that was in there with me every night.

I see you smile, gentlemen. You have already decided that I am mad, I can see. I have rushed you somewhat. I should have described in greater detail the feelings of a man with a completely clear mind, safe inside his own house, seeing water disappear from his carafe while he's asleep. I should have conveyed to you better the kind of torture I experienced every morning and every evening. I should have described how annihilating the sleep was and how hideous the awakening. But let me continue.

Quite suddenly, these inexplicable occurrences ceased. Nothing was touched in my room. It was over. I began to feel much better in myself. I felt a sense of relief return, particularly when I learned that Monsieur Legite, one of my neighbours, was showing many of my own earlier symptoms. Once more I was sure it must have something to do with our location and that it was something in the atmosphere. My coachman, incidentally, had become extremely ill and had stopped working for me a month earlier.

Winter had passed and it was now early spring. One day I was walking near one of my rose-borders when I saw, I tell you I saw with my very own eyes and right next to me at that, the stalk of one of the most beautiful roses break off exactly as though an invisible hand had plucked it. The flower described the curve which an invisible arm would have made to bring it to someone's face, then hung terrifyingly suspended in mid-air all by itself, no more than three feet away from my eyes. Scared witless, I lunged forward to grab it. Nothing! Gone! I suddenly became furious with myself. No man in his right mind could have hallucinations like that! But was that what it was? I looked for the stem of the rose again and found straightaway where it had been broken off between two other blooms on the same branch. I knew there had been three earlier on. I had seen them.

I went indoors, shaken to the core. I assure you, gentlemen, I am quite clear about this. I do not now and never have believed in the supernatural. But from that moment onwards, I knew as surely as I know night follows day that somewhere near me was an invisible being. It had haunted me before, left me for a while and was now back.

A short while later I had proof.

My staff began to quarrel among themselves every day. It was always over seemingly trivial matters, but for me they were full of significance. One day one of my best glasses, a beautiful Venetian piece, fell for no apparent reason from the dining-room dresser and smashed into smithereens. My manservant blamed the maid who in turn blamed somebody else, and so it continued. Doors firmly locked in the evening were found next day wide open. Every night milk was stolen from the pantry . . . and so on and so forth ad nauseam. What was all this about? What on earth was happening? I vacillated, terrified, torn between wanting to know and dreading what I might learn. Once again the house returned to normal and once more I began to think I must have dreamed the whole thing, until the following events occurred.

It was nine o'clock on the evening of 20 July and very warm. I had left my window open wide and light from a lamp on my table fell on a volume of Musset open at *Nuit de Mai*. I myself was stretched out on a sofa and had nodded off. After about forty minutes or so, awakened by a strange sort of feeling, I opened my eyes again but kept perfectly still. At first nothing happened. Then, as I watched, one of the pages of the book turned over, seemingly by itself. Not a breath of air had wafted through the window. Puzzled, I waited and in another four minutes or so I saw, I saw with my own eyes, gentlemen, another page rise and place itself over the first, exactly as if turned by invisible fingers. The armchair next to it seemed unoccupied but I knew perfectly well *it* was there. I leapt across the room to grab it, touch it, to seize hold of it somehow or other. But before I reached it, the chair, seemingly of its own accord, turned over backwards as if fleeing from me. The lamp also fell and went out, its glass smashed. The window was suddenly flung back against its hinges as if by some intruder making his escape . . . oh, my God! I rang the bell furiously and when my manservant came, said, 'I've knocked all this stuff over and smashed it. Go and fetch another lamp, will you?'

I slept no more that night. Yet I could still have made some sort of mistake. When you wake from a snooze you're always a little bit befuddled. Could it have been I who turned the armchair over and upset the lamp, rushing about like a mad thing? No! Of course it was not! I had not the slightest doubt about that. Yet that was what I wanted to believe.

Now. What should I call this . . . Being? The Invisible One? No, that would not do. I decided to call it the Horla. Don't ask me why. So I was going to be stuck with this Horla indefinitely. Night and day I could feel it there. I knew it was close to me the whole time, yet totally elusive. I also knew for certain that with each passing hour, each passing minute, even, it was drawing the life out of me. I was driven to distraction by the fact that I could never see it. I lit every lamp in the house. Maybe given proper illumination it could be exposed.

Then, finally, I saw it. Believe it or not, I saw it.

I was sitting with some book or other in front of me, not really reading. With every nerve on edge, I was waiting and watching for this being I could feel near me. I knew it was there somewhere. But where? What was it doing? How could I get hold of it? Opposite was my bed, an old oak four-poster. To my right was the fireplace. On the left the door, which I had made sure was locked. Behind me was a very large, mirrored wardrobe before which I shaved and dressed every day. Whenever I passed it I could see myself full length. So there I was, pretending to this presence which I knew was spying on me that I was reading. All of a sudden I felt it reading over my shoulder, brushing against my ear. Leaping to my feet, I turned round so quickly that I nearly fell over. Believe it or not, though the room was bright as day, there was no sign of me in the mirror. It was empty, clear and full of light. But my reflection was not in it, despite the fact that I was standing directly in front of it. I looked at the large glass, clear now from top to bottom. I looked at it in terror. I dared not take a step forward, knowing that this being was in between. I knew that although it would slip away from me again, its own invisible body had absorbed my own reflection. I was so frightened! Then suddenly I saw myself begin to appear from the misty depths of the mirror, rising as if from a body of water. The water itself seemed to shift slowly from left to right revealing, second by second, an increasingly sharper reflection of myself. It was like the end of an eclipse. What was concealing me looked like an opaqueness gradually turning transparent. Finally I could see myself clearly again, as I do when I look in the mirror every day. But now I had seen it. The terror of that moment remains with me and makes me tremble still. The following day I came here and asked to be admitted.

And now, gentlemen, I come to the end of my story. Having been fairly sceptical for some time, Doctor Marrande decided to make a little unaccompanied trip to my part of the world. It transpires that three of my neighbours are now in a similar condition to the one I have described, isn't that so?'

'Absolutely true!' the doctor replied.

'You instructed them to leave out some milk or water in the bedroom every night to see if these liquids disappeared or not. They did. They disappeared just as they did in my house, didn't they?'

With great seriousness the doctor replied, 'They did indeed.'

'So, gentlemen, a Being, some new Being which, like ourselves, will undoubtedly multiply and increase, is now on earth. What? Why are you smiling? Because the Being is still invisible? But, gentlemen, what a primitive organ is the eye! It can barely spot our basic needs for survival. It misses the infinitesimal as well as the infinite. It does not perceive the millions of tiny organisms present in a drop of water. It does not perceive the inhabitants, the plants and the earth of the planets closest to us; it does not apprehend what is transparent. Put it in front of a piece of non-reflecting glass and it fails to notice. We go careering straight into it as a bird trapped inside a house will continue to beat its skull against the window-panes. It fails to perceive solid but transparent objects. Yet these things exist. It cannot see air which is essential to human life; wind, which is the most powerful force in nature, capable of lifting men off their feet, flattening buildings, uprooting trees, and raising the sea into mountains of water which pulverize cliffs of solid granite. Why should we be surprised if it cannot make out a new kind of body to the human, and different from it only in that it does not emit light. Do you see electricity? Yet of course it exists. What is this being, gentlemen? I believe it is what the earth is waiting for, to supersede humanity, to usurp our throne, to overwhelm and perhaps feed on us as we feed now on cattle and wild boar. We have sensed and dreaded it for centuries. We have heard its approach with terror. Our forefathers have been haunted for ever by the Invisible.

'It has come.

'All the legends of spirits, hobgoblins and evil, elusive riders in the sky were about it. It is his arrival which man has been dreading with such trepidation. And you yourselves, gentlemen, all the activities you have been engaged in in the last few years – hypnotism, the power of suggestion, magnetism – all point towards the Invisible. And I tell you he is here. He roams about anxiously, just as primitive man did, ignorant as yet of his full power and potential which will be realized soon enough! Finally, gentlemen, here is an excerpt from a newspaper article which I have come across, published in Rio de Janeiro:

An epidemic of apparent insanity appears to have been raging for some time in the province of São Paulo. The inhabitants of several villages have fled their homes and abandoned their crops in the belief that they are being hunted and eaten by invisible vampires living off their sleeping breath and drinking nothing but water or occasionally milk.

'I should add that a few days before my own first attack of the disease which nearly killed me, I distinctly remember having seen a three-master pass, flying the flag of Brazil . . . I told you that my house is situated near the river bank . . . No doubt he was hidden somewhere aboard that ship. That's all I have to say, gentlemen.'

Doctor Marrande rose to his feet and murmured, 'I am in as much of a quandary as you all. I cannot tell if this man is mad or whether we both are . . . or whether . . . man's successor is already in our midst . . .'

Translated by Siân Miles

GEORGES RODENBACH

The Time

'Barbe, what is the time?'

'A quarter to five,' answered presently the old servant, who had gone to the mantel where, between two old-fashioned vases, stood a small Empire-period clock with four little columns of white marble, bearing aloft a short pinion embellished with gilt bronzes in the form of sinuous swans' necks.

'But I think our clock is slow,' she went on. And with the steady, deliberate tread of people in the provinces who aren't in a hurry, she went to the window, lifted the muslin curtain, and stared out at the nearby tower, the dark tower of the Halles de Bruges, to which is affixed, like a great crown, a vast dial which declines the hour unceasingly to the deserted streets around it.

'Oh, yes! It is slow: it's about to strike five o'clock,' she went on. 'The hands are already in place.'

Sure enough, one minute later the peal went out, and sent a kind of carolling, flustered nest effect into the air; less a song than a plaint, less a snow of flying feathers than a rain of iron and ash . . . Then the great bell struck five times, at regular intervals, slow and solemn, and each time it struck the nimbus of melancholy in the silence expanded, as a stone thrown into the waters of a canal makes rings that shimmer outwards until they reach the banks.

'How long it goes on!' said Van Hulst, falling back among his pillows, wearied from sitting up, even for these few instants, on his bed, to which for weeks now he had been confined by illness.

He had recently entered upon his convalescence, after the attack of typhoid fever which had laid him low. But at least the accesses of the fever had taken from him the sense of time, prostrating him until he lost consciousness, or exalting him in delirium and nightmares whose melting imagery absorbed him. It was only now, when things had grown calmer, that the days had started to drag, divided into the minutes that he had to live through and, as it were, tell out one by one.

And movement, occupation of any kind, was forbidden: and no company was to be admitted to the empty house, to this solitary bachelor's world, crossed only by the silent tread of the old servant, faithful Barbe, who had got him up and seen to his needs, watched over him and restored him with an almost maternal solicitude.

But she could do nothing now to divert him a little: she could not converse, or try reading aloud. And he felt so alone, a prey to the slow, sad passage of time. Especially in the leaden northern twilight, in this late autumn on the quays of Bruges (he lived on the Quai du Rosaire), where a contagious melancholy came in through the windows, settled on the furniture in pallid tones, afflicted the mirrors with a kind of valedictory light . . .

And then there was the impartial little clock in his room, telling out its rosary of minutes without end! During his enforced inaction, empty of event and thought, the patient had little by little become obsessed with the time. He worried about the clock as if it were a living presence. He looked at it like a friend. It made him learn patience. It distracted him with its moving hands and the noise of its workings. It alerted him to the arrival of cheerier moments, when his light meals were served, milk or broth; best of all, to the return of darkness, and with it a good stretch of oblivion, which helped shorten the time. Mesmerizing dial! Other patients use their eyes to count out, mechanically, the number of flowers on the wallpaper or on the cretonne curtains. He engaged in calculations based on the clock. He sought the day when he would be cured, which was already imminent – but still imprecise . . . He consulted the clock, he checked the time, since often, like today, there was a discrepancy between his timepiece and the ancient clock on the tower. When it pealed, he compared one with the other. It became a small diversion for him, seeking the same time on the two dials, as one might a resemblance between two faces.

*

When Van Hulst was better, he carried over from his sickness this pre-occupation with the *right time*. In a town as calm and circumscribed as his own dead Bruges, the tower can be seen, or at any rate heard, in every district, even as far as the suburbs. So the correct time, the official time, so to speak, was given out by this clock. Elsewhere, time is never more than approximate. Everyone keeps their own, and makes do with it. Van Hulst had set his watch against the dial on the belfry, and through the entire period of his illness had never altered it; now, every time he went out, he would check it, and became almost vexed if he remarked it were slightly fast or a tiny bit behind. His timetable, his meals, when he went to bed, when he got up, always at the same time, were synchronized to the minute.

'Gosh! I'm five minutes slow,' he would say sometimes, as if dismayed.

He made sure that his watch and the clocks in his home were always synchronized, not just the little Empire-period clock with the swan's neck bronzes, but the kitchen clock with its dial decorated in red tulips, which old Barbe would consult for her housework chores.

One Friday, market day, Van Hulst, who was still convalescing, was out on one of his gentle strolls; he lingered among the stalls in the main square, and noticed a rather strange Flemish clock. It was half hidden, almost buried, in the miscellaneous chaos covering the pavement. They sell everything at this market: canvas, cotton stuffs, objects in metal, agricultural implements, toys, antiques. A pell-mell patchwork, a turning-out of the centuries. The market is not limited to the stalls, where the sellers display their wares elegantly, underneath pale canvas awnings, shaped into hoods, rather like the winged coifs worn by nuns. Frequently the merchandise is piled or stacked anyhow on the ground, still covered with grey dust, as though issued straight from some inventory, the sale of some missing person's goods and chattels, brought out of a house long since deserted and closed up. Everything is old, dusty, oxidized, rusted, faded, and would look plain ugly were it not for the intermittent northern sun, which suddenly lights up patinas, or Rembrandtian russet golds. It was among such ruins, where occasionally a surprise lies hidden – a piece of furniture, an old jewel, some lacework – but of fine workmanship, that Van Hulst found the Flemish clock, which he instantly wanted to possess. It was made up of a long oak case with sculpted panels, warmly coloured by time, in varnishes and sheen; but its most original feature was the dial. Made of copper and pewter, wrought with taste and imagination, a whole playful cosmography was affixed to it, with a laughing sun, a gondola shaped like a crescent moon, stars that browsed with the bodies of lambkins, moving over the numerals as though they wanted to pick them out like flowers in the grass.

Van Hulst was delighted with this antique clock, which wore its date of birth triumphantly: '1700', incised on to the original metal. But had the mechanism survived, after counting out innumerable years? This was Van Hulst's chief concern, for he desired it less as an antique curiosity than as one more clock which, old as it was, would synchronize with the young clocks in his house.

The merchant assured him that the clock worked perfectly, that even the chiming mechanism functioned accurately; in short, that it had never once gone wrong, throughout all its long years of telling the time.

And chime it did, loudly! Strong-voiced clock, it sang out the hour, in its new home at Van Hulst's. And how thin, by comparison, were the little chimes of the Empire clock and the clock with the red tulips. Rather like children's voices, issuing from clocks that had not yet come of age. But their venerable ancestor lived in harmony with them. Each kept slightly different time; but by an amusing anomaly, it was the old clock that struck the hour first, ahead of the others, as though enjoining them to follow suit. Was this grandmother more solid and indefatigable than her children?

Van Hulst smiled, cheered by the family of clocks that brought his home to life. Nevertheless, it troubled him rather that they were not perpetually in unison. When one lives together, is it not better to think as one!

The obsession with the *right time*, which had come over him during his illness, became stronger since he had added the Flemish clock to his collection. One was fast, the other was slow ... which was right? He synchronized them all with the dial on the tower, that he could see from his windows. Especially when the hour struck. It displeased him that one should ring for longer than the other. When this happened, it was as though they were running after each other, calling each other, losing and seeking each other at all the variable intersections of time.

Little by little, Van Hulst developed a taste for pendulums and clocks. He had acquired others, from the Friday market, from jewellers and auctioneers. Without intending to, he had started a real collection, an interest that started to consume him. No man is ever really happy without an *idée fixe*. It fills his time, the vacancies of his thought, startles his boredom, gives direction to his aimlessness, and sends a brisk, revivifying breeze over the monotonous water of his existence. Van Hulst had access to a subtle joy and to incessant surprises. Now he had a veritable hobby. In the heart of morose Bruges, in the life of this bachelor, which had been free of incident, in which every day had been the same and of the same grey tone as the air of the town, what a change had come about! Now his life was intent, always on the alert for some new treasure! He experienced the collector's lucky find! The encounter with the unexpected, that swells his treasure! Van Hulst already had some expertise. He had studied, sought, compared. He could see at a glance what period a clock was from. He could tell its age, sort the genuine article from the fake, appreciate a beautiful style; and he came to know the signatures of master clock-makers, whose products were works of art. By now, he possessed a whole series of different clocks, scarcely noticing he had done so. He had haunted the antique shops of Bruges. To swell his collection, he had even travelled to nearby towns. He followed auction sales, especially when estates were being sold off, for then one could pick up rare and curious items that had been forever in the possession of dynastic families. His collection became impressive. He had clocks of every type: Empire clocks in marble and bronze, or in bronze gilt; Louis XV and Louis XVI clocks, with curved panels in rosewood, with encrustations and marquetry, showing romantic scenes which enlivened the woodwork like a fan; he had mythological, idyllic, war-like clocks; clocks made out of biscuit, of costly and fragile pastes; Sèvres and Saxe clocks, where time laughs among flowers; Moorish clocks, Norman or Flemish, with oak or mahogany casings, and chimes that whistled like blackbirds or squeaked like well-chains. Then there were the rarities: maritime water-clocks, in which water drops compose the seconds. Finally, he possessed a whole panoply of little table clocks, and ceremonial clocks as delicate and as finely wrought as jewels.

Van Hulst considered that he needed more still. Is this not the subtle pleasure of the collector, that he can perpetually prolong his desire? It is infinite, and meets no limit, and knows nothing of that total possession which can disappoint by its very plenitude. And then there is the excitement caused when he cannot obtain the object he ardently desires! There was, in fact, just such an object, a very old clock that Van Hulst had spotted one day at Walburge's, the richest antique-seller in Bruges, whose shop is situated on the Rue de l'Âne-aveugle, and well known to collectors, and to foreigners who find it mentioned in guides. But the old antique-seller was connoisseur and merchant in equal measure; if he had something special, he would refuse to sell it unless he got a good price. The old clock coveted by Van Hulst was in fact a very rare piece indeed, unique of its kind, marvellously carved, and adorned with painted scenes from the gospels, in the style of prayerbook illumination, and signed by the artist whose name was prized by connoisseurs. Walburge was asking a great deal of money for this clock. Van Hulst would bargain, leave, and then come back. He would have to dig deep, and he hesitated. The merchant stuck to his guns. With his shrewd eye, he could tell how much his client wanted the clock. Every time he entered the shop, Van Hulst would set to and examine the precious thing once more, with the excitement, the feeling in his fingertips that is a kind of pleasure; he had the nervous, sensitive hands of the collector, who are *tactile* by nature, and he would touch, handle, stroke the object of desire. It was as though he already half owned it. But the embrace was incomplete, a half-possession: the caresses of the fiancé who dreams of a full consummation.

Van Hulst had done his sums. He really could not afford the clock. He would never be able to raise the sum against his income, which barely covered his expenses. And he had already used the remainder on his previous purchases. His methodical lifestyle was such that he would never allow himself to eat into his capital, however strong the temptation. He simply had to bargain the price down.

Old Walburge would never have given in; he was one of those hard-headed Flemish types, who digs in his heels for no particular reason, and refuses to budge, rather than be seen to compromise. But by going again and again to the shop, and showing so openly his disappointment and dismay at not being able to buy, he won the heart of Walburge's daughter, a girl of tender age called Godelième. She was the fruit of a late marriage, somewhat too delicate and pale, and she adorned the old widower's home like a large virgin lily.

Van Hulst soon got Godelième on his side. He had started to engage her in conversation, leaning over the loom she worked at to examine the fine lace, playing over it with his fingers as though on a keyboard.

Soon they were joined in a silent, friendly conspiracy against old Walburge. The latter could refuse nothing to his daughter, whom he adored. And the combined force of their two willpowers went to work.

And so it was that one day, pressed yet again by Van Hulst, the antique-seller gave way and accepted his offer. The collector was overjoyed, especially when he took possession of the precious clock and placed it on an old oak table, where it gleamed in a direct ray of light from his windows in the vast room on the first floor which housed his singular clock museum. No sooner was it placed there than the newcomer added its humming, like a small metal bee, to all the others; the strange room was like Time's Beehive.

Van Hulst was not, however, merely interested in having a collection of rare clocks. He treasured them, but not just as still-lifes. Of course, their appearance mattered to him, their structure, mechanism, and artistic merit. But there was another motive behind his assembling so many clocks, and it had to do with his concern for the right time. It was not enough that they should be beautiful. He wanted to consider them as the same, as being of one mind, to think like him, and to keep time, without ever deviating, from the second he had synchronized and set them running. But such a degree of harmonization was a miracle he would never have thought possible up till then. As well ask the pebbles on the beach, come from every corner of the horizon and rolled in the sea by such varying tides, to be identical in size. Yet try he did. Having been initiated by a clock-maker, he now knew the secrets of the wheels, the springs, the cogs, the diamond pins, the workings links, and circuits, every nerve and muscle, the complete anatomy of this gold-and-steel beast whose steady pulse gives the universe its rhythm ... He had acquired all the right tools: the eyeglass, the tiny saws and files, all the minuscule implements needed to take apart, polish, correct and restore such sensitive and delicate organisms. With observation, patience, punctiliousness, by slowing this one and accelerating that one, attending to the weak point in each, he might just attain what was now his obsessive dream: to see them all in unison; to hear them, if only once, strike the hour at the same time, synchronized with the clock-tower; to attain his ideal of harmonizing time.

Van Hulst's compulsion lasted a long while. He never got discouraged. Every afternoon he put in long hours, trying to synchronize all his dials. Whenever he had to go out, he would give careful instructions to his old servant that under no circumstances was she to enter the closed room, where she might upset the weights, brush against the chains, or generally disturb the clocks and thereby upset the result he so desired, which was to get all his clocks to strike the hour in perfect unison. He would remind her of all this, every time he went out. And these days he went out more often. He continued his quest, he remained on the look-out. He was also a frequent visitor at old Walburge's shop, in the Rue de l'Âne-aveugle, to see if a new clock had come in. Mostly it was the gentle Godelière who greeted him. She was always sitting in her place by the window, where the grey day, filtered through curtains, darkened her honey-coloured hair ... She was like a Memling Madonna, with eyes like little mirrors in which you could see yourself, amidst the blues of the sky. She worked unceasingly at her lace-making, and the spindles of the loom played with her fingers, animated her fingers, gave themselves up to her fingers, as though she had tamed them.

When old Walburge was out doing errands, Van Hulst engaged Godelière in long and restful conversations. As a committed collector, he returned to the shop frequently. Little by little, however, he realized that he went there not only in the interests of his beloved museum, but also in part for the girl, who had become dear to him too. Especially since once again she had been unwell. She had grown pale, and thinner still, even though she was already as slender and incorporeal as the Saint Ursula in the Hospital reliquary. Van Hulst was deeply stirred by Godelière's frailty. What was wrong with her? Was there some hidden malady? Or a lack of vitality, something like a death wish?

Before long, he became anxious as well. Perhaps she was fading away from some deep hurt, unavowed even to herself, from some secret too heavy for the delicate soul to bear. She surrounded herself in the mystery of it, in the nimbus of something that was divine in her. And seeing her melancholic, Van Hulst fell in love with her. He had to confess as much to himself. It was for her, to gaze upon her, and to hear her gentle voice – the mysterious voice that canal water has under the bridges – that he stopped by so often at the antique shop. The clocks were merely an excuse. By now he was neglecting his own, being so taken up with Godelième. Is love not an obsession too, one that annihilates all the others, that makes one happier than all the others? And is the lover also not in pursuit of a breathtaking collection of wonderful little nothings: looks, the lowered gaze, the squeeze of a hand, words, declarations, letters, pledges, kisses, that are similarly inventoried and set in order like a treasured collection? And when it is first love, a whole museum comes into being!

Van Hulst, who was already greying, had in fact never experienced real passion. It was as though his heart had lain dormant, dulled by the dead city, with its aimless waters, its empty quays, its silence, Bruges the mystic, given up entirely to the sky.

No access of tender feeling had ever troubled his single life. But here was the old bachelor, chronically stuck in his ways, a victim of his tics and the mad devotion to his clocks, here he was about to betray that devotion, and become someone tender, ardent and loving.

And it was all the more ardent this time, in that his passion could not so easily find satisfaction. Collecting had been child's play, almost instant gratification. But how could he satisfy his passion for the sweet and delicate Godelième! So delicate! She constantly fell ill, and sometimes weeks would pass before he saw her again. But he went on stopping by the antique shop, asking after her, discussing her with her father. The latter was also worried now, concerned by the mysterious malady that no doctor seemed able to fathom. Van Hulst dared not go every day to the Rue de l'Âne-aveugle. But even when he stayed home his sole thought was for Godelième, completely taken up as he was by the girl he had once hoped to make his. He grew alarmed. Perhaps the nameless illness that was eating away at her would end up killing her! The idea sent him into a panic. What if she should slip through his fingers! The collector's instinct within him rose up once more, whetted by the challenge, and he came to desire the object all the more ardently as it escaped him. She was now the wonderful clock that was his heart's whole desire; it was the ticking of her heart that he wanted to hear; it was her face he wanted to set as a guide to his life, that soft dial of flesh with its eyes in enamel, which had gradually led him into neglecting his clocks. The long vigils in his museum were all over, like the dream of synchronized time, the diverting sessions of clock-restoration, identifying all the little malfunctions in the cogs and the springs before him on his bench, with the glass fixed in his eye, pursued with all the patience of laboratory science. He still wound up his clocks and pendulums, but he did it mechanically, merely out of habit, raising the weighted chains, turning the keys, but he was no longer concerned with the dials or the time they showed, he abandoned them to themselves, scattered like a flock the shepherd has set loose, his eye suddenly distracted, gazing from star to star . . .

His single thought was for Godelième. Would he win her one day? He had never dared declare himself. And anyway, what was the good? She seemed reserved for death, rather than as someone's fiancée. On his latest visits to the antique shop he had not seen her. She had taken to her bed. Was it not his great misfortune, to have met Godelième, to have conceived this unattainable love for her, a love that was enough to have spoilt all his earlier joys?

Van Hulst started to brood; he scarcely spoke; his old servant Barbe scarcely recognized her master. It was as though he were always waiting for something. His thoughts grew dark; he imagined the worst.

His fears, as it happened, were only too justified. One Sunday, towards evening, a messenger arrived at his house, sent by Walburge the antiques merchant, one of those messengers they have in Bruges who go from door to door, sent by families when they have to announce a bereavement. Godelième was dead. She had suffocated in a sudden coughing fit that had brought up blood. Hurrying immediately over to his shop, Van Hulst had learned this from old Walburge himself.

And there on a white bed, with a few lilies scattered round the pillow and with her face framed by rivulets of hair, now stilled, in the light of a calmly burning candle, he suffered the grief of gazing one last time upon the young woman he had hoped one day to win, but in a different white dress, and with other lilies.

*

Returning home fairly late in the evening (he had stayed a good while at Walburge's), Van Hulst was startled to find there was still a light in the corridor. Barbe was waiting up, she of all people, who was usually in a hurry to get to bed. He could hear her walking about. Her footsteps seemed to be coming from the first floor, apparently from the room that housed the clock museum. What had happened? Did she not obey him? Did she thus dare to handle and disturb what he had expressly forbidden her to go anywhere near when he was out? But the moment she heard him come in, Barbe leaned over the banister and cried out from the stairwell:

'Monsieur! Monsieur!'

Her voice had a slight quaver in it, as if she had some serious news to impart, which frightened him rather.

Van Hulst hurried up the stairs. Barbe cried out from further off:

'Monsieur! The clocks have struck! . . .'

'What? How?' Van Hulst was baffled.

The servant explained that her master had left open the door of the museum, no doubt accidentally. In the stillness of the house she had suddenly heard a loud noise. As the great clock-tower struck ten, all the chime mechanisms from all the clocks began to strike, all together and at the same time. The result was tumultuous, a strange coppery sound breaking the silence. She had entered the room. All the clocks stopped at the tenth stroke, perfectly in unison, as if in measure, with not a single voice out of line or going over; they were all juxtaposed, and super-imposed, and they all sounded as one. And on all the dials all the hands were opened at exactly the same compass angle . . . Shocked, Van Hulst looked hard. Most of the clocks still showed exactly the same time. A mere twenty minutes had passed since the incredible moment he had dreamed of for so long, and that had come to pass. It would never come again. Little disharmonies were already creeping in. The old Flemish clock began running fast; the little Louis XV pendulum, with its romantic panelwork, was going slow.

Strange skulduggery! The clocks had synchronized themselves, for the space of a minute. They had coalesced, just this once, and they had done so *against him*, to avenge his neglect of them; the very evening that Godelième had died, together they had struck, or rather they had sung the hour, like a conspiracy of abandoned mistresses whose reign, from that moment on, began once more.

The truth dawned on Van Hulst: his plan to harmonize time had been realized, but without him, and without his having been able to enjoy it, punished as he was for coveting love, for having cherished and mourned Godelième, for having abandoned the ideal for reality. The ideal is always jealous, and demands, if it is to be attained, immense, single-minded purpose. Is it not our renunciation of Life itself, that alone makes us fit to attain our Dream?

Translated by Stephen Romer

JEAN LORRAIN

The Man Who Loved Consumptives

—'Ah, here's a new one!' said an elegant black suit sitting in front of me in the orchestra stalls, during the second act of Legendre's play. Smiling into his moustache, he trained his glass on a box to the side, where a slender young woman had just taken her place, extremely pale in a beautiful dress of light blue tulle, which made her look even paler.

It was the middle of the second act, the scene in the chapel, during which Lord Claudio, frowning craggily, his hand on the pommel of his sword, insults Leonato and the candid Hero in the famous Shakespearean apostrophe:

Garde ta fille, elle est trop chère!

Rapt as the audience was by the drama of the scene, and by the dazzling Roybet costumes against the wonderful Ziem watercolour that Porel had mingled with the set design, every eye, and every lorgnette, followed the lead given by the opera glass, so that the fragile creature, leaning now on the red velvet of the box, seemed to reflect in her disturbing and spectral pallor the gaze of all the men and women that had turned their eyes upon her.

Her face was oval, but drawn, with a languid, suffering expression: her eyes, that seemed enlarged, were ultramarine bordering on black. They were unnaturally bright, deep-set in their bruised and blueish rings, spotted with pearl: her delicate nose, with its arched and quivering nostrils, breathed rapidly and shallowly, as if in an atmosphere too thin to sustain her in life, and with her great feathered fan resting against her flat chest, from time to time, with her teeth that shone bright against the red of her mouth, she would bite at the burning purple of her lips, hard enough to draw blood. A man had now taken his place next to her; he was tall and strongly built, flourishing in the prime of health, and very smartly dressed; with the wide silk ribbon of his opera glass threaded through his white evening waistcoat, his sartorial elegance was reminiscent of the Prince de Sagan. He leant towards the pale, fragile woman, whispering in her ear, and now and again offering her from a soft silk bag crystallized Parma violets, which she would nibble at, half-smiling, half-choking.

'She's not long for this world,' sniggered my black-clad neighbour. 'Two months at the outside. That little woman is suffocating, she must be coughing up lungfuls of blood, but I bet she's fired up with fever between midnight and two. She's extremely pretty too, if a little on the thin side.'

He took the lorgnette from his friend's hands, and with both lenses fixed on the box, he described every contraction of the pale blue dress, and every attention proffered by the large white waistcoat.

'All the same, he's got damned strange taste,' the lorgnette went on, 'going for skeletal women; he's a fervent adherent of love's funeral rites.'

'Good old Fauras, I never see him except with funereal Venuses, and they're always different. How many mistresses has he expedited by now?'

'At least three or four in the last two years. It's a kind of monomania, almost as if he collects them from the hospital; illness excites him, especially consumption. We have seen the *hangman's mistress*, now we have the *lover of doomed ladies*; in love with tears and the elegiac, the excellent Fauras, who keeps himself in such good trim, loves only those who are close to death. The frailty of their existence makes them all the dearer and more precious to him. He chokes with their spasms, shivers with their fevers, and listens out for the slightest sigh; attending to their stifling, he spies, like a broken voluptuary, on the progress of their disease, and lives their dying agonies – he's a sybarite, that's what he is!'

'Yes, I know. He's a beast, a kind of sadist prey to macabre ideas, the next thing to a necrophiliac, seeking the last warmth in a cadaver, and in death the last piquancy of love. The Saint-Ouen horror crime re-lived every evening in the privacy of the boudoir. The quest for novel sensations, proof from the sanction of the law because the victim is still just alive.'

'My dear fellow, you could hardly be more wrong! Fauras is a tender-hearted, elegiac soul, obsessed with the exquisite manifestations of sadness, besotted with mourning; he wears black crêpe in his thoughts and has a funeral urn in place of a heart. Deliciously distressed and delighted to be so, he is forever fingering the evergreen cypress of his regrets above his latest loves – a phoenix eternally rising from the ashes!'

'I must confess, I am completely lost.'

'What a lumpish man you are! To love a woman who is doomed to die, to know that with every kiss and caress time is running out, to feel with the rasping of her breath everything ebbing away for ever; to know oneself condemned to despair and yet exalted, to be aware that each fresh pleasure is one step closer to the grave, and that with one's own hands, shaking with horror and desire, one is hollowing out within the love nest the pit wherein you will lay your love to rest, *that* is the piquancy of the thing! A man can never have known the bitter appeal of stolen assignations which may never be repeated, not to understand a passion of this type, with its piercing melancholy, hatched in relationships like this, marked indelibly by Pleasure and Sin!'

'But that's monstrous!'

'And yet absolutely true. Frailty is the great appeal of beings and things, the flower would scarcely move us if it never faded; the faster it perishes, the sweeter the scent, its life is exhaled with its fragrance! The doomed woman is exactly the same; dying, she abandons herself frenziedly to pleasures that fill her with burning life even as they hasten her death; her time is running out; her thirst for love, her need to suffer, burns and flames within her, and she clings to love with the final convulsions of the drowning; and desiring still, she redoubles the force behind her last kiss. Twisted under the hand of Death, she would kill the object of her desperate adoration, were she not expiring herself; and his long, crushing and furious embrace makes her swoon, and die.'

'Voluptuous!'

'Voluptuous, indeed! And Fauras has another advantage; with these consumptive women of his the relationship is never broken off brutally, there are no disagreeable scenes, unavoidable even for a gentleman, there is no vitriolic and sordid settling of accounts: tactful and clear-sighted, Fauras escapes all the predictable disgust and lassitude at the end of such affairs, the dull and wretched conclusion to all such liaisons in which satiety and boredom succeed passion. His love affairs come to an end with the clean white silver-threaded winding sheet in a young woman's coffin, amidst violets and roses in clusters, by candlelight, to the sound of anthems and organ music, with the dead girl laid out like Ophelia. A modern Hamlet, he follows the procession of his own love, and if his heart is wrung, at least it is so within a beautiful setting, with flowers and incense, with music and priestly psalms, in an uplifting scene of apotheosis. His is an artist's grief, in short, but an artist who is also practical and clear-headed, for he has taken death as his notary and his counsel, and he charges the keeper of Montparnasse cemetery with the disposal of his feelings. What is more, the tears he sheds for his mistress are real; now she is dead, he brings her favourite flower to the graveside, and arranges it carefully, and wins the hearts of the family standing by; and so, with a sweet melancholy, embellished with the adored images and the light ghosts of women, his life flows on, between the beloved friend of yesterday, and *the one who is to come*, already perfumed with regret, trembling with echoes, beating with hope, nuanced with memories!'

'The man's a monster, a vile wretch, a . . .'

'. . . great sensualist and a wise man, my dear fellow, for he has contrived to get Death to work for him in the amorous exploits of his life, and he has given body to his dreams by idealizing that nuisance known as Memory. And whatever anyone may say, he is our superior, for he is the only man who mourns his mistresses sincerely, the only man who savours genuine loss, which is the philtre and the poison that killed the legendary lovers of yesteryear. Very few of their kind remain, and they are stranded in this century, this century of unbelief and lucre, in which tuberculosis remains the only killer.'

Translated by Stephen Romer

RACHILDE

The Panther

To Laurent Tailhade

From the underground caverns of the arena, the cage was pulled up slowly, dragging her with it like a thick piece of night. And when the gates opened to the splendid light of the sky and the beast found the mantle of purple-stained golden sand beneath her steps, she basked in the light, believing herself a goddess. Young, dressed in the royal mourning clothes of black panthers, wearing a scattering of enormous topazes all along her limbs, she cast the pure staring gaze of those who encounter for the first time, at the edge of great deserts, their sinister virgin image. Her feline paws, powerful and childlike, seemed to move on drifts of down. In three light leaps, she reached the centre of the ring. There, seating herself with sinuous grace, all other affairs, including the scrutiny of the imperial loge, seemed of little importance to her. She licked her sex.

Near her, quartered Christians hung from crosses red with blood. A dead elephant, like a tumbled colossal wall, blocked off a whole section of the extraordinarily blue sky with its grey mass. In the distance, a strange clamour arose from a cloud of pale forms writhing in the circles of tiered seats. The beast, having finished her intimate toilette, put her muzzle to the ground to seek some reason for these cries of rage. She found them inexplicable; her cold and methodical morals accepted the utility of murder without yet understanding its various hysterias. From over there, she heard the muffled rumble of a sail beaten by the wind, the whining of branches cracking from lightning. She let out a mocking meow in defiance of the storms. Without haste, wanting to show the spectators the gentleness of real wild beasts, she sat down to dine on the flavourful mass of the elephant, disdaining the human prey. She drank leisurely of the steaming liqueur flowing from the monstrous cadaver and cut herself an ample rag of flesh. The feast finished, she planted herself on the remains of her meal and shined her left paw with care. Two days before she had been set free, in the darkness of her prison, they had scattered unworthy meats seasoned with cumin and peppered with saffron to excite the devouring fire of her insides; but the crafty huntress had abstained, having known longer fasts and more dangerous temptations. Hardly ignorant, albeit virginal, she already knew the thirsts of the burning noons of her homeland, where birds cried dirges sighing after the rain; she knew the poisonous plants of great tangled forests where forked-tongued reptiles dripping venom tried to hypnotize her; she knew the fat weight of the sun and the absurd lean-ness of her victims; the anxious vigils under the eye of the treacherous moon that would send her in pursuit of the shadow of prey always just out of reach. From these unlucky hunts, she had kept the instinct of a poor warrior, and asked only for a modest share in order not to be dizzied by this blessed other world in which carnivores, now the brothers of men, seemed to be invited to solemn feasts. She chose her piece without arro-gance, wanting to appear well-mannered in the presence of appetites less natural than her own.

A naked Christian, pathetically armed with a flail, surged over the elephant's hindquarters, driven by unseen executioners. He slipped in the curdled blood and rolled headfirst. Cries rose. He grabbed his flail again and his pale lips twisted into a smile. He did not want to use it, even against the beast who was going to slit his throat. He sat down with his clear eyes fixed on the enemy. She made a playful gesture with her paw, meaning: 'I am satisfied!' And she stretched out, eyes half-closed, whipping her tail in perplexity. In a silent duel of curious gazes, the Christian seeking – despite his expected surrender – the secret of beast tamers, the supreme power of sole will over the brute, and the free beast struggling to deter-mine the power of this species when it is naked.

A clamour roused them from their peculiar daydream. They were now the centre of the bloody revel, and no one, truly, understood this manner of entertainment. A sudden anger invaded the spectators. Bestiarii were called, horses galloped towards the elephant, whose heavy mass was dragged and pulled to its feet; face to face, the two adversaries continued to eye each other. The Christian refused the fight and the panther, no longer hungry, did not feel the need to tear him to pieces. A bestiarius dashed forward, threatening them with his sword. With a single graceful leap the animal avoided the impact, and the Christian kept his melancholy smile. Shouts reverberated from all sides. The storm burst, ghastly. The bestiarii rushed the beast, who declared herself capriciously for the weakest of them. They rested their lances on braziers, brought spears coated with pitch and burning feathers, called dogs trained to cut bulls' hamstrings, filled pots with boiling oil. All their hatred turned in an instant towards the mad young animal, flicking her flanks with her indecisive tail, wondering what all these war preparations meant. The bestiarii left her no time to return to her senses. They swooped down on her and set off a disordered race through a track littered with corpses. The panther fled, taken with superstitious terror. The world was ending! Pell-mell, pursuers and pursued knocked against the bodies of men and animals under the people's immense laughter; this new foolishness amused them. From all sides, they threw rocks, fruits and weapons at the frenzied beast. Patrician women hurled jewels that whistled terribly as they crossed the space, and the emperor himself stood up and stoned her with silver coins. With a last desperate leap, the panther, drunk with rage, bristling with arrows, surrounded by fire, took refuge in her still-open cage. They closed the gate and the dark trap descended below the arena again.

Days and nights flowed by, all atrocious. From time to time, she let out a mournful mew, a call to the sun that she would never see again. She had developed a reputation at the circus and they subjected her to all sorts of torments. A coward, they said, she had refused to fight, and could no longer claim the rank of noble animal. The caretaker of the imprisoned wild animals, a very old slave, took no pity on her even though she had split her mouth open by biting the blade of a sword. He only gave her the scraps from the neighbouring cages, bones that had already been gnawed, foul, rotten things that piled up in the cesspit of her cage. Her fur, soiled with filth, became covered in wounds; young boys had teased her by nailing her tail to the ground until, with a painful effort, she ripped it away from the nail, leaving behind some skin. The old slave amused himself by taunting her, offering her one hand while the other blinded her with a handful of sulphur. He burned off one of her ears with the crackling fire of a torch. Deprived of air and light, her mouth always full of bloody drool, she wailed dismally, looking for a way out, beating the bars of her cage with her skull, tearing at the ground with her claws, and deep inside her, a mysterious ache grew. Because she grumbled in such a sinister way, the order came to let her die of starvation. Worthy deaths, like strangling or a pike to the heart, were no longer for her. The beast understood. She went silent and lay down in one last prideful pose and, pulling her wounded tail in close, crossing her gangrenous paws, closing her fiery eyes, she dreamed while awaiting her agony. Oh! The forests cracking under storms! The enormous suns, the pink moons, the birds crying over the rain, the green spaces, the fresh springs, the young easy prey whose life she could drink in a single swallow, the great rivers spreading out their mirror where wild animals could lean down and be haloed with stars ... Little by little, the dying panther's brain was dazzled by old visions. Oh! Distant happiness, freedom! A movement of mad despair reminded her of her destiny: she saw once more the golden arena sand stained with purple, the grey mass of the gutted elephant, the hard smile of the Christian, and finally the furious cries of the bestiarii, and the torments, all the torments! Her nose resting on her crossed paws, she seemed to be asleep ... perhaps already dead. Suddenly, the darkness of her prison dissipated. A hatch had just slid open above. Descending from heaven into the hell where the damned beast crouched, the svelte white form of a woman appeared. She was carrying a hunk of goat meat in a raised fold of her tunic, and balancing a vessel of water on her shoulder with her right arm. The panther rose up. This creature all in white, she was the old caretaker's daughter.

'Beast,' she said, while behind her was a whirlwind of light as blonde as her hair. 'I have compassion for you. You will not die.'

Detaching a chain, she pushed open the bars of the cage and dropped the hunk of goat meat at the threshold, then set the full vessel down calmly.

So the panther drew back on her haunches, luckily still supple, made herself tiny so as not to frighten the child, watched her for an instant with phosphorescent eyes that had become as deep as chasms. Then she pounced on her throat and crushed her.

Translated by Rachel Tapley

FÉLIX FÉNÉON

Three-line Novellas

Scheid, of Dunkirk, fired three times at his wife. Since he missed each time, he aimed at his mother-in-law: the bullet found its mark.

At des Essarts-le-Roi cemetery, Monsieur Gauthier had buried his three daughters. He wanted them exhumed. One body missing.

Returning to his lodgings, the labourer Vauthier, from Chapelle-au-Bois (Vosges), found his wife drunk and virtuously strangled her.

In front of the druggist who was her lover, a young lady from Toulon killed herself with a bullet to the heart.

Fontanières stabbed Casterès. Replete, like so many Toulousains, with the favours of Mademoiselle Lacombe, they were jealous of each other.

Too poor to care for his month-old son, Triquet, of Théligny (Sarthe), strangled him.

Student Congress in Bordeaux, 1 May 1907. The international question of the equivalence of degree certificates will be discussed.

The gallant Léon Courtescu of Angers was thrown into the Maine, where he drowned, by a husband, Monsieur Brouard.

'Our patriotism does not distinguish between the country and the government it has chosen,' General Blancq declared to the 9th Corps.

Madame Robeis, a farmer with epilepsy of Saint-Jean-les-Jumeaux (Seine-et-Marne), collapsed head-first into a milk churn. Asphyxiated.

Spurned Créteil lover, Claude Cousin, seriously wounded Louise Bisset and Monsieur Richereau who tried to intervene.

In Jobards (Loiret) Monsieur David, furious that his wife did not love him exclusively, killed her with a pitchfork and a rifle.

Lyonnais Monsieur Frechet, bitten by a pug and assumed to be cured (Pasteur Institute), attempted to bite his wife and died of rabies.

Catherine Rosello of Toulon, mother of four children, sought to avoid a freight train. She was crushed by a passenger train.

As she left a Bordeaux hotel with Monsieur Anizan, Léontine Cagnat was on the receiving end of a bullet from the wife of the aforementioned engineer.

His cancer was unbearable. Monsieur Henrion, of Châtillon-Laborde (Seine-et-Marne) slit his throat with a knife and razor.

In a Lille hotel, Monsieur H. Hallynch of Ypres hanged himself for reasons which, according to the note he left behind, will soon become clear.

The Oyonnax stonemasons' strike has ended (they achieved three of their demands). The Agen and Grenoble stonemasons' strike begins.

La Verbeau hit Marie Champion square on the breasts, but burned his own eye, because a bowl of acid is not a precision weapon.

Albert Vallet was beating the landowner Ferrand, from Chappet, with his rifle butt. The shot went off, and the huntsman fell down dead.

The bones discovered at Île Verte in Grenoble belong not to two but to four children's skeletons. Minus two skulls.

In Cozes, 150 soldiers who set out from Rochefort on manoeuvres were unable to move. It was the heat. And they were colonials.

The new prison in Amiens was inaugurated yesterday by little Gourson, who killed his friend Godin, aged 14.

As Poulet, a police officer from Choisy-le-Roi, was trying to arrest him, Marquet seized his sabre and skewered him through both cheeks.

Reconciliation with Artémise Rétro, from Lilas, was Jean Voul's tenderest wish. She would not be persuaded. So he stabbed her.

It was beside the jack that a stroke felled Monsieur André, 75, of Levallois. His pétanque ball was still rolling, but he was no more.

On the roof of Enghien railway station, a painter was electrocuted. His teeth could be heard clacking, then he fell on to the glass canopy.

The septuagenarian beggar Verniot, from Clichy, has died of hunger. Two thousand francs were hidden in his mattress. But let's not generalize.

Translated by Patrick McGuinness

JULES LAFORGUE

Apropos of Hamlet

Far from Paris, far from the French language (the health of which is very dear to me), far from acquaintances, far from Literature and far from Art, on 1st January last, I pondered my solitary presence in Elsinore, on the shore of that sea, the monotone waves of which undoubtedly inspired Hamlet's epitaph on human history:

'Words, words, words.'

It poured down throughout that holy day of the First of the Year, as it had poured down the evening before, as it would pour down, in all probability the next day. Only that morning, I had been in Copenhagen, a meek gawker of the display of official congratulations, of the heavy carriages from the gala lurching on the foul cobblestones, of the grenadiers' tall busbies. Apparently no one, in the coming and going of the court, thought of their ancestor of tomorrow, the unfortunate Prince Hamlet.

You will understand I had no intention of leaving Elsinore without having seen the Lord Hamlet of Shakespearean memory.

The beach was deserted beneath the rain, the sea melancholic as on the bleakest of days, the seagulls attended to their affairs: – around 5 o'clock in the evening, by dint of whistling the triumphant motif of Wagner's *Siegfried* in the wind (but with a mournful tone), I managed to conjure up the unfortunate prince, master of us all.

He was still his psychological age, thirty years old; he was shaved like an actor happily blessed with a liver illness, dressed in black, wearing a cap, with suede gloves. Naturally, he recognized me.

I insisted, without affectation, on having news of his health. We chatted about those little everyday troubles, then about this and that. After a duet of mute reverie facing the sea that lasted an hour, he said to me:

'Have you seen the statue of Irving in my role?'

'Yes, Your Highness, in Berlin. I found that Irving too dramatically concentrated in his mask, taking himself too seriously, something which was absolutely never the case of a distinguished gentleman such as yourself, isn't that so?'

'And in Berlin, did you say? O Germany, O Wittenberg where I studied! O country of Faust, of Faust who unhinged me greatly!'

'Highness – today, it's not like that any more. The condition I will call *faustish* is a condition of the very poor or the excessively rich. The Germans of today are no longer poor and are not yet rich enough. They are living through the crisis of the Parvenu. You would be stricken with black bile in Berlin, Highness.'

'And Paris?'

'In Paris, Highness, as you know, there is, when it comes to your particular legend, Paul Bourget, who cultivates and exacerbates it, with nonetheless enough decency to stop (while feigning to baulk at it) short of Nihilism; there was Arthur Rimbaud who died because of it, after a succession of fits of despair, the marvellous ravings from which have been collected; there is me, who approaches you in good cheer, Highness, in the manner of Yorick, "a fellow of infinite jest, of most excellent fancy" – who approaches you in good cheer because I cannot help myself.'

'And Ophelia? What are they doing to her?'

'It is her that is doing to us, Highness. Ophelia is more irresistible than ever, because of the industrial inventions of some and the hypertrophied arts of others. She is no longer a pious believer. From those altars built of our terrors of the starry sky and of death, she has made an ineffable counter where first she haggles over her beautiful eyes, and then lulls us, with the euphoric exultation of the church organ, into swearing our support and fidelity. With all that, she is no longer so naive, and although her complexion is even more deceptive, it is not cheerful. Those eyes, which will drop at our first word, have examined at their ease, here, there and everywhere, the anatomical charts of existence, charts down to our most famished and most trustworthy artists. A secret museum lives behind Ophelia's violet pupils. It is time that wants it thus. Oh, but she is no less ideal for us, Highness. And absolutely nothing prevails against her sex. And it seems that Nature, albeit unconsciously, has heavily loaded the dice.

As for me, I'm no longer there. This seems to me most obvious and certain:

> From mature lady to young girl,
> I've had a brush with every sort,
> Some were easy, some hard to unfurl,
> It's their watchword that I have brought.
> Flowers of flesh, however dressed,
> For each hour, a proud or lonely air
> No cries or wails can them impress
> We love them. And she remains there.
> Nothing riles them, or ties them down;
> They want us to find them pretty,
> To moan and drone to all around,
> And to treat them accordingly.
> With no use for vows, or for rings,
> Let's suck when they give us a bone;
> Respect can be vague, that's the thing,
> Their eyes are high and monotone.
> Let's pick, without fuss, without hope:
> After the roses, flesh withers;
> Oh! Let's play all the scales note by note.
> It's the truth, nothing else matters.

Hamlet stood up.

'Scales, scales before old age . . .'

He twisted his arm, sniggered fixedly and started to bellow:

'Aux armes, citoyens! There is no reason any more.'

And there he was, letting out desperate and irreconcilable 'Oh, oh's.

His madness won me over, and I began to dance before him, beneath the continual rain of those beaches far from Paris, to dance the step from the *Criterium of Human Certitude*. The step consists of tracing with one's feet the square of the hypotenuse, that Gibraltar of certitude, a simple and immortal figure. A true and immortal figure, but which demands that as we trace the last line of this step, *we know not why*, we inevitably stumble and fall flat on our face.

That is what I did. It was the best possible conclusion to our meeting. And we parted with vague plans to meet, bowing dogmatically.

And yet, this step from the *Criterium of Human Certitude* being primarily symbolic . . .

Translated by Will McMorran

LÉON DAUDET

The Exhibition of Tears

The entrance to the grotto was low and we had to duck down. The labyrinth, formed by a multitude of species chambers, connected to one another by narrow passages, as hatred is to love – an immense labyrinth, according to previous visitors – received very little light, but what did filter through the interstices of the clear and trenchant fissures took on a concentration and an extreme acuity, with the consequence that one could follow its design in the penumbra, shadow upon black shadow. It was sometimes a cone, sometimes a sheet, sometimes a thread as tenuous as a knife edge, according to the whim of the gap.

The tears, like jewels, were arranged in display cases, various in size and gleam, and their disposition seemed to be such that the magnificent luminescence induced by the play of the sunlight struck those pearls of the soul successively.

The man guiding us said: 'It was decided, out of a horror of deception, only to employ natural light. That alone makes true tears glitter. As for false ones, of which you can see sad specimens in the last room, they draw a feeble gleam from little lamps fixed beneath them. Their poor effect makes the incomparable splendour of these stand out even more.'

The speaker was a short, thin man simply dressed in black, with excessively regular features, which gave him a strange, almost geometrical appearance. The straight, narrow nose succeeded the forehead almost without an interval. The impeccable arch of the nose seemed cruel. The clean-shaven chin added a full stop to the profiled phrase: hope no more. His dry and unmoving eyes disconcerted us with their harsh gaze, adding a sentiment of necessity to his curt speech. His only gestures were extensions of a pale hand towards the display cases, and an occasional suspicion of a courteous bow.

'These are the innumerable tears of lovers.'

They were displayed on a slight slope. From the rocky ceiling to a floor sprinkled with fine sand. Blinded by their scintillation, we could not distinguish anything at first. Then our gazes adapted, and I admired their cut and their limpidity.

'Lean over. Each of them reflects the image of the male or female weeper.'

I examined one of the fixed droplets for a long time. Like a memory gradually rising up to consciousness from the tenebrous depths of the mind, the face of a woman, melancholy and beautiful, emerged from the crystalline water. I saw the tender oval and the blue eyes that had shed the faithful gem in question. Thus, dolour kept its form through eternal duration. By virtue of a strange sympathy, I associated myself with that distant suffering: abandonment, despair, the monotonous trickle of hours detached from the eyelids of time, moistening the heart broken by anguish.

The next was that of a young man: a proud and troubling face, his lips trembling, his chin devoid of the slightest down; something ambiguous, as in Da Vinci's portraits. Only the determined pupils and short hair revealed his sex. I could almost have believed that he was about to speak to me, so sincere was the mysterious miniature. Enclosed in a little diamantine tear, as his distress was enclosed within him, it was perhaps for one of the others who were weeping that he wept himself, so frequent is fatal scorn.

Handsome men and beautiful women, ugly men and ugly women of all the epochs throughout ages, I saw in those 'weepers', as our guide called them, who inhabited the grotto. A strange regret came to me – for being wants being to be complete – of having nothing before me but the vestiges of eyes. Where are the other scraps? That which commences with a sight finishes with a clamour. At first there is a murmur, often under the stars; then, in the ardent and naked night, body speaks to body in its own language. Then, in a solitary room, it concludes with a sob.

'These are the tears of lovers.'

That was a stellar swarm, which a brighter luminous jet separated like a galaxy. Veneration gripped us. We knelt down. It is internal hymns that our soul intones when words have ceased to render their power. Bathed by harmonious pity, therefore, with great respect, I leaned over the nearest pearl. Its radiant gleam extended and stretched as if, detached itself with regret, it were still adhering to white lashes.

I perceived a soft and aged face. Those daughters of maternal love shine purest of the pure, for the redemption of infinite pains.

Then we saw the tears of faith, small in number but still blinding. None bore a face; in their depths a cross was distinguishable. I noticed that, arranged in chronological order, their gleam diminished near the edge of the display case.

'There are phases of dryness,' our guide explained.

He showed us others mounted in swords and crowns. 'These are pride and glory.' They burned the eyes with a vivid flame, but it was immediately forgotten, as if the slaked desire no longer propagated any light.'

A field of larger gems astonished us by its amplitude.

'These are all the physical dolours.'

They too were faceless. With a little attention, we noticed that they did remain motionless, but joined together in various forms, outlining spikes and talons by means of the sudden splashes, and then separated from one another, dividing like a population of agitated droplets.

As we advanced further into the grotto, I distinguished a less distinct streak on the walls, the elements of which seemed rebellious against the light, scarcely translucent, or of a milky, opaline whiteness.

'Ennui, remorse, dread and terror have their damp domain here.'

They enclosed sullen faces, as if ashamed.

Our attention was becoming weary. The exhibitor perceived that and said, with a pale smile: 'You understand my bleak expression now, and the brevity of my speech. When I entered this grotto for the first time it was long ago, as a punishment for an excessive wisdom, which offended the divinity. When I list my treasures, I sometimes add to them, by virtue of the tears I have retained – those that all of you are beginning to know. Since then, my eyelids have dried up. You will thus understand the empty showcase at the entrance, which will always remain empty. But before you go out, to climb up again to the source of life, look over here at those I mentioned to you in the beginning.'

In the depths of a fissure, where hardly any real light penetrated, under an array of dull, livid, surly lamps, we saw the false tears.

Translated by Brian Stableford

MARCEL SCHWOB

The Sans-Gueules

They found them lying next to each other on the burned grass, and gathered them both up. Their clothes had been blown off in shreds. The explosion had burned out the numbers and shattered the metal identity tags. They were like two pieces of human clay. The same fragment of shrapnel, flying slantwise, had sliced off their faces, so that they lay on the tussocks like a couple of trunks with a single red top. The Major who had loaded them into the ambulance did so mostly out of curiosity: for the effect was, in truth, most singular. They had neither nose, cheeks, nor lips. Their eyes had sprung out of their shattered sockets, their mouths gaped open in a bloodied hole where the severed tongue still wagged. What could be odder: two creatures of the same height, and *faceless*. Their skulls, covered in close-cropped hair, now had two red sides, simultaneously and identically carved out, with cavities where the eyes had been and three holes for mouth and nose.

In the ambulance they were dubbed *Sans-Gueule* no. 1 and *Sans-Gueule* no. 2. An English surgeon, who was working there voluntarily, was intrigued by the case and took it on. He anointed and dressed the wounds, extracted the splinters of bone, stitched and modelled the mass of meat, fashioning two red, concave hoods of flesh, identically perforated towards the base, like pipes emerging from some exotic furnace. Lying in adjoining beds, the two *Sans-Gueules* stained the sheets with a twin wound, round, gaping and meaningless. The eternal stillness of the wound was frozen in silent suffering: the severed muscles did not even pull against the stitches; the dreadful shock had annihilated the sense of hearing, so the only sign of life left was in the movement of their limbs, and by a twin rasping cry, emitted at intervals from between their gaping palates and the stumps of their tongues.

And yet they started to heal. Slowly and surely they began to control their movements, to develop their arms, to fold their legs so they could sit down, move their hardened gums that still fleshed out their wired jaws. They had one pleasure, which was signalled by some sharply modulated sounds that still had no syllabic content: it was procured by smoking pipes – the stems were held in place in their mouths by pieces of oval rubber, fitted to the dimensions of their mouths. Curled in their blankets, they stank of tobacco, and plumes of smoke escaped from the orifices in their skulls: from the double hole of the nose, from the dark caverns of their eye sockets, and through the torn mouth, between the remains of their teeth. And each plume of grey smoke was accompanied by an inhuman laugh and a sort of gurgling that came from the uvula while the rest of the tongue wagged feebly.

There was a stir in the hospital when a little woman with a mass of hair was brought by the intern to the bedside of the *Sans-Gueules*; she looked at them one after the other, with a terrified expression, and then burst into tears. Sitting in the office of the head doctor, she explained, between her sobs, that one of the two must be her husband. He had been listed among the casualties: but these two mutilated soldiers had no identifying marks, and belonged to a special category. The height, the width of shoulder and the hands recalled the lost man infallibly. And yet she was in a terrible perplexity: which of the two *Sans-Gueules* was her husband?

The little lady was kindness itself: her cheap gown moulded her breast, and due to the way she put up her hair, in the Chinese style, she had a sweet, childlike face. Her straightforward grief and her almost absurd uncertainty mingled in her expression and contracted her features in a way reminiscent of a child that has broken its toy. So much so that the head doctor couldn't stop himself from smiling; and because he had a crude way of talking, he said to the little woman looking up at him:

'Well, what of it! Take them both home! You'll recognize which is which when you try them out!'

At first she was scandalized, and averted her head, like a child blushing for shame: then she lowered her eyes and looked from one bed to the other. The two red mugs rested in their stitches on the pillows, with the same lack of meaning that constituted the whole enigma. She leaned down towards them, and whispered in the ear, first of one, and then the other. The heads did not react at all – but all four hands started to shake – undoubtedly because these two poor bodies whose souls had fled had a vague feeling that a very gentle little woman was close by, who had an endearing manner, and who gave off the sweet smell of a baby.

She hesitated some more, and then asked if they would let her take the two *Sans-Gueules* home for a month. They were transported in a big padded ambulance, and the little woman, seated opposite, wept hot tears unceasingly.

When they got to the house, a strange life began for the three of them. Tirelessly she went to and fro from one to the other, looking for a clue, waiting for a sign. She observed the red surfaces that would never stir again. Anxiously she contemplated the stitches, as one would the features of a beloved face. She examined them in turn, as one might consider different photographs, without being able to choose.

Little by little the sharp grief that wrung her heart, in the early days, when she thought about her lost husband, ended by dissolving into an irresolute calm. She lived like someone who has renounced everything, but goes on by sheer force of habit. The two broken pieces that between them represented the loved one never joined together in her affections; but her thoughts went regularly from one to the other, as if her soul were continually tilting like a balance. She regarded them as her red 'puppets'; they were the two comical dolls that peopled her existence. Smoking their pipes, sitting in the same attitude on their beds, blowing out the same plumes of smoke, and uttering the same inarticulate cries, they resembled more those gigantic puppets brought back from the East, those scarlet masks from overseas, than beings possessed of conscious life that had once been men.

They were her 'two monkeys', her red mannikins, her two little husbands, her burned men, her meaty rascals, her bloodied faces, her holey heads, her brainless bonces. She mothered them in turn, arranging their blankets, tucking in their sheets, mixing their wine and breaking their bread. She led them out into the middle of the room, one on each side of her, and made them caper on the parquet floor; she played with them, and if they became vexed she would slap them down with the flat of her hand. At a single caress they flocked around her, like two famished dogs; and at a gesture of impatience they would double up, cringing like repentant animals. They would rub against her, in quest of morsels; they both had a wooden bowl, and into these, with joyful howlings, from time to time they would plunge their two red muzzles.

The two bonces no longer agitated the little woman as they had before, and no longer fascinated her, like two scarlet wolf-masks superimposed on familiar faces. She loved them equally in her childlike, pouting way. She would say: 'My dolls are asleep; my little men are taking a walk.' She was bewildered when someone came from the hospital to enquire which of the two she was going to keep. The question was absurd, it was like demanding she cut her husband in two. Often she would punish them, the way children do when their dolls have been naughty. She would say to one: 'Look, my little lad, your brother's been bad, he's naughty as a monkey – and so I've turned his face to the wall, and I shan't turn him back until he's said sorry.' And then, with a little laugh, she would turn the poor, penitent body back again, and kiss its hands. Sometimes she would even kiss their dreadful stitches, and then privately wipe her mouth afterwards, pursing her lips. Then straight away she would almost split herself laughing.

Imperceptibly, however, she got more used to one of them, because he was the gentler of the two. Quite unconsciously, since she had long given up any hope of recognition. She preferred him, like a favourite pet that one likes to caress the most. She spoiled him more and kissed him more tenderly. And by degrees the other *Sans-Gueule* grew sad, for he sensed about him less and less of her feminine presence. He would frequently remain curled up on his bed, his head hidden under his arm, like a wounded bird. He refused to smoke, while the other, knowing nothing of his grief, went on exhaling streams of grey smoke through every vent in his purple face, to the accompaniment of little squawks.

So the little woman started to tend to her sad husband, without really understanding his sadness. His head in her bosom would shake with deep sobs that came from his chest; and a kind of harsh groaning would shake his torso. This poor occluded heart was prey to a terrible jealousy, an animal jealousy borne of feelings mingled with memories, it may be, of a former life. She sang him lullabies, as if he were a child, and calmed him by laying her cool hands upon his burning head. When she realized he was very ill, big tears would fall from her laughing eyes on to his poor mute face.

And soon she was prey to a poignant anguish, for she thought she recognized gestures he had made in an earlier illness. Certain movements seemed familiar from before; and the way he held his emaciated hands reminded her of hands that had been dear to her, and which had brushed her sheets, before the great abyss had opened up in her life.

And the wail coming from the poor abandoned one pierced her heart; and in a breathless uncertainty, she once more scrutinized the faceless heads. They were no longer just two purple dolls – one was a stranger – and the other was part of her own self. When the one who was ailing died, all her grief returned.

She now truly believed that she had lost her husband; and she ran, full of hate, towards the other *Sans-Gueule,* and then stopped short, seized by her childlike pity, in front of the wretched red mannikin who was smoking away joyously, uttering his little cries.

Translated by Stephen Romer

MAURICE LEBLANC

Arsène Lupin's Arrest

The strangest of journeys! And yet it had begun so well! I, for my part, had never made a voyage that started under better auspices. The *Provence* is a swift and comfortable transatlantic liner, commanded by the most genial of men. The company gathered on board was of a very select character. Acquaintances were formed and amusements organized. We had the delightful feeling of being separated from the rest of the world, reduced to our own devices, as though upon an unknown island, and obliged, therefore, to make friends with one another. And we grew more and more intimate . . .

Have you ever reflected on the element of originality and surprise contained in this grouping of a number of people who, but a day earlier, had never seen one another, and who are now, for a few days, destined to live together in the closest contact, between the infinite sky and the boundless sea, defying the fury of the ocean, the alarming onslaught of the waves, the malice of the winds, and the distressing calmness of the slumbering waters?

Life itself, in fact, with its storms and its greatnesses, its monotony and its variety, becomes a sort of tragic epitome; and that, perhaps, is why we enjoy with a fevered haste and an intensified delight this short voyage of which we see the end at the very moment when we embark upon it.

But, of late years, a thing has happened that adds curiously to the excitement of the passage. The little floating island is no longer entirely separated from the world from which we believed ourselves cut adrift. One link remains, and is at intervals tied and at intervals untied in mid-ocean. The wireless telegraph! As who should say a summons from another world, whence we receive news in the most mysterious fashion! The imagination no longer has the resource of picturing wires along which the invisible message glides: the mystery is even more insoluble, more poetic; and we must have recourse to the winds to explain the new miracle.

And so, from the start, we felt that we were being followed, escorted, even preceded by that distant voice which, from time to time, whispered to one of us a few words from the continent which we had quitted. Two of my friends spoke to me. Ten others, twenty others sent to all of us, through space, their sad or cheery greetings.

Now, on the stormy afternoon of the second day, when we were five hundred miles from the French coast, the wireless telegraph sent us a message of the following tenor:

Arsène Lupin on board your ship, first class, fair hair, wound on right forearm, travelling alone under alias R—.

At that exact moment, a violent thunderclap burst in the dark sky. The electric waves were interrupted. The rest of the message failed to reach us. We knew only the initial of the name under which Arsène Lupin was concealing his identity.

Had the news been any other, I have no doubt but that the secret would have been scrupulously kept by the telegraph clerks and the captain and his officers. But there are certain events that appear to overcome the strictest discretion. Before the day was past, though no one could have told how the rumour had got about, we all knew that the famous Arsène Lupin was hidden in our midst.

Arsène Lupin in our midst! The mysterious housebreaker whose exploits had been related in all the newspapers for months! The baffling individual with whom old Ganimard, our greatest detective, had entered upon that duel to the death of which the details were being unfolded in so picturesque a fashion! Arsène Lupin, the fastidious gentleman who confines his operations to country-houses and fashionable drawing rooms, and who one night, after breaking in at Baron Schormann's, had gone away empty-handed, leaving his visiting card:

> ARSÈNE LUPIN
> *Gentleman-Burglar*

with these words added in pencil:

Will return when your things are genuine.

Arsène Lupin, the man with a thousand disguises, by turns chauffeur, opera-singer, book-maker, gilded youth, young man, old man, Marseillese bagman, Russian doctor, Spanish bullfighter!

Picture the situation: Arsène Lupin moving about within the comparatively restricted compass of a transatlantic liner, nay – more, within the small space reserved to the first-class passengers – where one might come across him at any moment, in the saloon, the drawing room, the smoking room! Why, Arsène Lupin might be that gentleman over there . . . or this one close by . . . or my neighbour at table . . . or the passenger sharing my state-room . . .

'And just think, this is going to last for five days!' cried Miss Nellie Underdown, on the following day. 'Why, it's awful! I do hope they'll catch him!' And, turning to me, 'Do say, Monsieur d'Andrézy, you're such friends with the captain, haven't you heard anything?'

I wished that I had, if only to please Nellie Underdown. She was one of those magnificent creatures that become the cynosure of all eyes wherever they may be. Their beauty is as dazzling as their fortune. A court of fervent enthusiasts follow in their train.

She had been brought up in Paris by her French mother, and was now on her way to Chicago to join her father, Underdown, the American millionaire. A friend, Lady Gerland, was chaperoning her on the voyage.

I had paid her some slight attentions from the first. But, almost immediately, in the rapid intimacy of ocean travel, her charms had gained upon me, and my emotions now exceeded those of a mere flirtation whenever her great dark eyes met mine. She, on her side, received my devotion with a certain favour. She condescended to laugh at my jokes and to be interested in my stories. A vague sympathy seemed to respond to the assiduity which I displayed.

One rival alone, perhaps, could have given me cause for anxiety: a rather good-looking fellow, well dressed and reserved in manner, whose silent humour seemed at times to attract her more than did my somewhat 'butterfly' Parisian ways.

He happened to form one of the group of admirers surrounding Miss Underdown at the moment when she spoke to me. We were on deck, comfortably installed in our chairs. The storm of the day before had cleared the sky. It was a delightful afternoon.

'I have heard nothing very definite,' I replied. 'But why should we not be able to conduct our own inquiry just as well as old Ganimard, Lupin's personal enemy, might do?'

'I say, you're going very fast!'

'Why? Is the problem so complicated?'

'Most complicated.'

'You only say that because you forget the clews which we possess towards its solution.'

'Which clews?'

'First, Lupin is travelling under the name of Monsieur R—.'

'That's rather vague.'

'Secondly, he's travelling alone.'

'If you consider that a sufficient detail!'

'Thirdly, he is fair.'

'Well, then?'

'Then we need only consult the list of first-class passengers and proceed by elimination.'

I had the list in my pocket. I took it out and glanced through it:

'To begin with, I see that there are only thirteen persons whose names begin with an R.'

'Only thirteen?'

'In the first class, yes. Of these thirteen Rs, as you can ascertain for yourself, nine are accompanied by their wives, children or servants. That leaves four solitary passengers: the Marquis de Raverdan ...'

'Secretary of legation,' interrupted Miss Underdown. 'I know him.'

'Major Rawson ...'

'That's my uncle,' said someone.

'Signor Rivolta ...'

'Here!' cried one of us, an Italian, whose face disappeared from view behind a huge black beard.

Miss Underdown had a fit of laughing:

'That gentleman is not exactly fair!'

'Then,' I continued, 'We are bound to conclude that the criminal is the last on the list.'

'Who is that?'

'Monsieur Rozaine. Does any one know Monsieur Rozaine?'

No one answered. But Miss Underdown, turning to the silent young man whose assiduous presence by her side vexed me, said:

'Well, Monsieur Rozaine, have you nothing to say?'

All eyes were turned upon him. He was fair-haired!

I must admit I felt a little shock pass through me. And the constrained silence that weighed down upon us showed me that the other passengers present also experienced that sort of choking feeling. The thing was absurd, however, for, after all, there was nothing in his manner to warrant our suspecting him.

'Have I nothing to say?' he replied. 'Well, you see, realizing what my name was and the colour of my hair and the fact that I am travelling by myself, I have already made a similar inquiry and arrived at the same conclusion. My opinion, therefore, is that I ought to be arrested.'

He wore a queer expression as he uttered these words. His thin, pale lips grew thinner and paler still. His eyes were bloodshot.

There was no doubt but that he was jesting. And yet his appearance and attitude impressed us. Miss Underdown asked, innocently:

'But have you a wound?'

'That's true,' he said. 'The wound is missing.'

With a nervous movement, he pulled up his cuff and uncovered his arm. But a sudden idea struck me. My eyes met Miss Underdown's: he had shown his left arm.

And, upon my word, I was on the point of remarking upon this, when an incident occurred to divert our attention. Lady Gerland, Miss Underdown's friend, came running up.

She was in a state of great agitation. Her fellow passengers crowded round her; and it was only after many efforts that she succeeded in stammering out:

'My jewels! . . . My pearls! . . . They've all been stolen!'

No, they had not all been stolen, as we subsequently discovered; a much more curious thing had happened: the thief had made a selection!

From the diamond star, the pendant of uncut rubies, the broken necklaces and bracelets, he had removed not the largest, but the finest, the most precious stones – those, in fact, which had the greatest value and at the same time occupied the smallest space. The settings were left lying on the table. I saw them, we all saw them, stripped of their gems like flowers from which the fair, bright-coloured petals had been torn.

And to carry out this work, he had had, in broad daylight, while Lady Gerland was taking tea, to break in the door of the state-room in a frequented passage, to discover a little jewel-case purposely hidden at the bottom of a bandbox, to open it and make his choice!

We all uttered the same cry. There was but one opinion among the passengers when the theft became known: it was Arsène Lupin. And, indeed, the theft had been committed in his own complicated, mysterious, inscrutable . . . and yet logical manner, for we realized that, though it would have been difficult to conceal the cumbersome mass which the ornaments as a whole would have formed, he would have much less trouble with such small independent objects as single pearls, emeralds and sapphires.

At dinner this happened: the two seats to the right and left of Rozaine remained unoccupied. And, in the evening, we knew that he had been sent for by the captain.

His arrest, of which no one entertained a doubt, caused a genuine relief. We felt at last that we could breathe. We played charades in the saloon. We danced. Miss Underdown, in particular, displayed an obstreperous gaiety which made it clear to me that, though Rozaine's attentions might have pleased her at first, she no longer gave them a thought. Her charm conquered me entirely. At midnight, under the still rays of the moon, I declared myself her devoted lover in emotional terms which she did not appear to resent.

But, the next day, to the general stupefaction, it became known that the charges brought against him were insufficient. Rozaine was free.

It seemed that he was the son of a wealthy Bordeaux merchant. He had produced papers which were in perfect order. Moreover, his arms showed not the slightest trace of a wound.

'Papers, indeed!' exclaimed Rozaine's enemies. 'Birth certificates! Tush! Why, Arsène Lupin can supply them by the dozen! As for the wound, it only shows that he never had a wound . . . or that he has removed its traces!'

Somebody suggested that, at the time when the theft was committed, Rozaine – this had been proved – was walking on deck. In reply to this it was urged that, with a man of Rozaine's stamp, it was not really necessary for the thief to be present at his own crime. And, lastly, apart from all other considerations, there was one point upon which the most sceptical had nothing to say: who but Rozaine was travelling alone, had fair hair, and was called by a name beginning with the letter R? Who but Rozaine answered to the description in the wireless telegram?

And when Rozaine, a few minutes before lunch, boldly made for our group, Lady Gerland and Miss Underdown rose and walked away.

It was a question of pure fright.

An hour later a manuscript circular was passed from hand to hand among the staff of the vessel, the crew and the passengers of all classes. Monsieur Louis Rozaine had promised a reward of ten thousand francs to whosoever should unmask Arsène Lupin or discover the possessor of the stolen jewels.

'And if no one helps me against the ruffian,' said Rozaine to the captain, 'I'll settle his business myself.'

The contest between Rozaine and Arsène Lupin, or rather, in the phrase that soon became current, between Arsène Lupin himself and Arsène Lupin, was not lacking in interest.

It lasted two days. Rozaine was observed wandering to right and left, mixing with the crew, questioning and ferreting on every hand. His shadow was seen prowling about at night.

The captain, on his side, displayed the most active energy. The *Provence* was searched from stem to stern, in every nook and corner. Every state-room was turned out, without exception, under the very proper pretext that the stolen objects must be hidden somewhere – anywhere rather than in the thief's own cabin.

'Surely they will end by finding something?' asked Miss Underdown. 'Wizard though he may be, he can't make pearls and diamonds invisible.'

'Of course they will,' I replied, 'or else they will have to search the linings of our hats and clothes and anything that we carry about with us.' And, showing her my five-by-four Kodak, with which I never wearied of photographing her in all manner of attitudes, I added, 'Why, even in a camera no larger than this there would be room to stow away all Lady Gerland's jewels. You pretend to take snapshots and the thing is done.'

'Still, I have heard say that every burglar always leaves a clew of some kind behind him.'

'There is one who never does: Arsène Lupin.'

'Why?'

'Why? Because he thinks not only of the crime which he is committing, but of all the circumstances that might tell against him.'

'You were more confident at first.'

'Ah, but I had not seen him at work then!'

'And so you think . . .'

'I think that we are wasting our time.'

As a matter of fact, the investigations produced no result whatever, or, at least, that which was produced did not correspond with the general effort: the captain lost his watch.

He was furious, redoubled his zeal, and kept an even closer eye than before on Rozaine, with whom he had several interviews. The next day, with a delightful irony, the watch was found among the second officer's collars.

All this was very wonderful, and pointed clearly to the humorous handiwork of a burglar, if you like, but an artist besides. He worked at his profession for a living, but also for his amusement. He gave the impression of a dramatist who thoroughly enjoys his own plays and who stands in the wings laughing heartily at the comic dialogue and diverting situations which he himself has invented.

He was decidedly an artist in his way; and, when I observed Rozaine, so gloomy and stubborn, and reflected on the two-faced part which this curious individual was doubtless playing, I was unable to speak of him without a certain feeling of admiration.

Well, on the night but one before our arrival in America, the officer of the watch heard groans on the darkest portion of the deck. He drew nearer, went up, and saw a man stretched at full length, with his head wrapped in a thick, grey muffler, and his hands tied together with a thin cord.

They unfastened his bonds, lifted him, and gave him a restorative.

The man was Rozaine.

Yes, it was Rozaine, who had been attacked in the course of one of his expeditions, knocked down and robbed. A visiting card pinned to his clothes bore these words:

Arsène Lupin accepts Monsieur Rozaine's ten thousand francs, with thanks.

As a matter of fact, the stolen pocket-book contained twenty thousand-franc notes.

Of course, the unfortunate man was accused of counterfeiting this attack upon his own person. But, apart from the fact that it would have been impossible for him to bind himself in this way, it was proved that the writing on the card differed absolutely from Rozaine's handwriting, whereas it was exactly like that of Arsène Lupin, as reproduced in an old newspaper which had been found on board.

So Rozaine was not Arsène Lupin! Rozaine was Rozaine, the son of a Bordeaux merchant! And Arsène Lupin's presence had been asserted once again and by means of what a formidable act!

Sheer terror ensued. The passengers no longer dared stay alone in their cabins nor wander unaccompanied to the remoter parts of the ship. Those who felt sure of one another kept prudently together. And even here an instinctive mistrust divided those who knew one another best. The danger no longer threatened from a solitary individual kept under observation and therefore less dangerous. Arsène Lupin now seemed to be ... to be everybody. Our overexcited imaginations ascribed to him the possession of a miraculous and boundless power. We supposed him capable of assuming the most unexpected disguises, of being by turns the most respectable Major Rawson, or the most noble Marquis de Raverdan, or even – for we no longer stopped at the accusing initial – this or that person known to all, and travelling with wife, children and servants.

The wireless telegrams brought us no news; at least, the captain did not communicate them to us. And this silence was not calculated to reassure us.

It was small wonder, therefore, that the last day appeared interminable. The passengers lived in the anxious expectation of a tragedy. This time it would not be a theft; it would not be a mere assault; it would be a crime – a murder. No one was willing to admit that Arsène Lupin would rest content with those two insignificant acts of larceny. He was absolute master of the ship; he reduced the officers to impotence; he had but to wreak his will upon us. He could do as he pleased; he held our lives and property in his hands.

These were delightful hours to me, I confess, for they won for me the confidence of Nellie Underdown. Naturally timid and impressed by all these events, she spontaneously sought at my side the protection which I was happy to offer her.

In my heart, I blessed Arsène Lupin. Was it not he who had brought us together? Was it not to him that I owed the right to abandon myself to my fondest dreams? Dreams of love and dreams more practical: why not confess it? The d'Andrézys are of good Poitevin stock, but the gilt of their blazon is a little worn; and it did not seem to me unworthy of a man of family to think of restoring the lost lustre of his name.

Nor, I was convinced, did these dreams offend Nellie. Her smiling eyes gave me leave to indulge them. Her soft voice bade me hope.

And we remained side by side until the last moment, with our elbows resting on the bulwark rail, while the outline of the American coast grew more and more distinct.

The search had been abandoned. All seemed expectation. From the first-class saloon to the steerage, with its swarm of emigrants, everyone was waiting for the supreme moment when the insoluble riddle would be explained. Who was Arsène Lupin? Under what name, under what disguise was the famous Arsène Lupin lurking?

The supreme moment came. If I live to be a hundred, never shall I forget its smallest detail.

'How pale you look, Nellie!' I said, as she leaned, almost fainting, on my arm.

'And you, too. Oh, how you have changed!' she replied.

'Think what an exciting minute this is and how happy I am to pass it at your side. I wonder, Nellie, if your memory will sometimes linger . . .'

All breathless and fevered, she was not listening. The gangplank was lowered. But, before we were allowed to cross it, men came on board: custom-house officers, men in uniform, postmen.

Nellie murmured:

'I shouldn't be surprised even if we heard that Arsène Lupin had escaped during the crossing!'

'He may have preferred death to dishonour, and plunged into the Atlantic rather than submit to arrest!'

'Don't jest about it,' said she, in a tone of vexation.

Suddenly I gave a start and, in answer to her question, I replied:

'Do you see that little old man standing by the gangplank?'

'The one in a green frock coat with an umbrella?'

'That's Ganimard.'

'Ganimard?'

'Yes, the famous detective who swore that he would arrest Arsène Lupin with his own hand. Ah, now I understand why we received no news from this side of the ocean. Ganimard was here, and he does not care to have any one interfering in his little affairs.'

'So Arsène Lupin is sure of being caught?'

'Who can tell? Ganimard has never seen him, I believe, except made-up and disguised. Unless he knows the name under which he is travelling . . .'

'Ah,' she said, with a woman's cruel curiosity, 'I should love to see the arrest!'

'Have patience,' I replied. 'No doubt Arsène Lupin has already observed his enemy's presence. He will prefer to leave among the last, when the old man's eyes are tired.'

The passengers began to cross the gangplank. Leaning on his umbrella with an indifferent air, Ganimard seemed to pay no attention to the throng that crowded past between the two handrails. I noticed that one of the ship's officers, standing behind him, whispered in his ear from time to time.

The Marquis de Raverdan, Major Rawson, Rivolta, the Italian, went past, and others and many more. Then I saw Rozaine approaching.

Poor Rozaine! He did not seem to have recovered from his misadventures!

'It may be he, all the same,' said Nellie. 'What do you think?'

'I think it would be very interesting to have Ganimard and Rozaine in one photograph. Would you take the camera? My hands are so full.'

I gave it to her, but too late for her to use it. Rozaine crossed. The officer bent over to Ganimard's ear; Ganimard gave a shrug of the shoulders; and Rozaine passed on.

But then who, in Heaven's name, was Arsène Lupin?

'Yes,' she said, aloud. 'Who is it?'

There were only a score of people left. Nellie looked at them, one after the other, with the bewildered dread that *he* was not one of the twenty.

I said to her:

'We cannot wait any longer.'

She moved on. I followed her. But we had not taken ten steps when Ganimard barred our passage.

'What does this mean?' I exclaimed.

'One moment, sir. What's your hurry?'

'I am escorting this young lady.'

'One moment,' he repeated, in a more mysterious voice.

He stared hard at me, and then, looking me straight in the eyes, said:

'Arsène Lupin, I believe.'

I gave a laugh.

'No, Bernard d'Andrézy, simply.'

'Bernard d'Andrézy died in Macedonia, three years ago.'

'If Bernard d'Andrézy were dead I could not be here. And it's not so. Here are my papers.'

'They are his papers. And I shall be pleased to tell you how you became possessed of them.'

'But you are mad! Arsène Lupin took his passage under a name beginning with R.'

'Yes, another of your tricks – a false scent upon which you put the people on the other side. Oh, you have no lack of brains, my lad! But, this time, your luck has turned. Come, Lupin, show that you're a good loser.'

I hesitated for a second. He struck me a smart blow on the right forearm. I gave a cry of pain. He had hit the unhealed wound mentioned in the telegram.

There was nothing for it but to submit. I turned to Miss Underdown. She was listening, with a white face, staggering where she stood.

Her glance met mine, and then fell upon the Kodak which I had handed her. She made a sudden movement, and I received the impression, the certainty, that she had understood. Yes, it was there – between the narrow boards covered with black morocco, inside the little camera which I had taken the precaution to place in her hands before Ganimard arrested me – it was there that Rozaine's twenty thousand francs and Lady Gerland's pearls and diamonds lay concealed.

Now I swear that, at this solemn moment, with Ganimard and two of his minions around me, everything was indifferent to me – my arrest, the hostility of my fellow men, everything, save only this: the resolve which Nellie Underdown would take in regard to the object I had given into her charge.

Whether they had this material and decisive piece of evidence against me, what cared I? The only question that obsessed my mind was, would Nelly furnish it or not?

Would she betray me? Would she ruin me? Would she act as an irreconcilable foe, or as a woman who remembers, and whose contempt is softened by a touch of indulgence – a shade of sympathy?

She passed before me. I bowed very low, without a word. Mingling with the other passengers, she moved towards the gang-board, carrying my Kodak in her hand.

"Of course,' I thought, 'she will not dare to, in public. She will hand it over presently – in an hour.'

But, on reaching the middle of the plank, with a pretended movement of awkwardness, she dropped the Kodak in the water, between the landing-stage and the ship's side.

Then I watched her walk away.

Her charming profile was lost in the crowd, came into view again and disappeared. It was over – over for good and all.

For a moment I stood rooted to the deck, sad and, at the same time, pervaded with a sweet and tender emotion. Then, to Ganimard's great astonishment, I sighed:

'Pity, after all, that I'm a rogue!'

It was in these words that Arsène Lupin, one winter's evening, told me the story of his arrest. Chance and a series of incidents which I will some day describe had established between us bonds of . . . shall I say friendship? Yes, I venture to think that Arsène Lupin honours me with a certain friendship; and it is owing to this friendship that he occasionally drops in upon me unexpectedly, bringing into the silence of my study his youthful gaiety, the radiance of his eager life, his high spirits – the spirits of a man for whom fate has little but smiles and favours in store.

His likeness? How can I trace it? I have seen Arsène Lupin a score of times, and each time a different being has stood before me ... or rather the same being under twenty distorted images reflected by as many mirrors, each image having its special eyes, its particular facial outline, its own gestures, profile and character.

'I myself,' he once said to me, 'have forgotten what I am really like. I no longer recognize myself in a glass.'

A paradoxical whim of the imagination, no doubt; and yet true enough as regards those who come into contact with him, and who are unaware of his infinite resources, his patience, his unparalleled skill in make-up, and his prodigious faculty for changing even the proportions of his face and altering the relations of his features one to the other.

'Why,' he asked, 'should I have a definite, fixed appearance? Why not avoid the dangers attendant upon a personality that is always the same? My actions constitute my identity sufficiently.'

And he added, with a touch of pride:

'It is all the better if people are never able to say with certainty: "There goes Arsène Lupin." The great thing is that they should say without fear of being mistaken: "That action was performed by Arsène Lupin."'

It is some of those actions of his, some of those exploits, that I will endeavour to narrate, thanks to the confidences with which he has had the kindness to favour me on certain winter evenings in the silence of my study ...

Translated by Michael Sims

MARCEL PROUST

The Mysterious Correspondent

'Dear friend, I forbid you to go home on foot, I'll have the horses harnessed, it's too cold out, you could get sick.' Françoise de Lucques had said that just before as she led out her friend Christiane, and now that she had gone she regretted that clumsy phrase, which would have been quite an insignificant one if it had been spoken to another – it was a phrase that might have worried the invalid about her state. Seated near the fire where she was by turns warming her feet and hands, she kept asking herself the question that was torturing her: could Christiane be cured of this wasting disease? They hadn't brought enough lamps. She was in the dark. But now, as she was warming her hands again, the fire illumined their grace and their soul. In their resigned beauty – sad exiles in this vulgar world – one could read the emotions as clearly as in a face's expression. Normally absent-minded, they lay outstretched in gentle languor. But this evening, at the risk of creasing the delicate stem that bore them so nobly, they were painfully spread out like tormented flowers. And soon, tears fell from her eyes in the darkness and appeared one by one the instant they touched the hands that, spread wide before the flames, were in full light. A servant entered: it was the mail, a single letter in a complicated script that Françoise did not recognize. (Despite the fact that her husband loved Christiane as much as she did and tenderly consoled Françoise for her suffering when he noticed it, she didn't want to sadden him unnecessarily with the sight of her tears if he came home unexpectedly, and she wanted to have time to wipe her eyes in the darkness.) And so she ordered that lamps be brought in five minutes, and she moved the letter closer to the fire to shed light on it. The fire was burning brightly enough that Françoise could make out the letters as she bent forward to illuminate it, and here is what she read.

Madame,

For a long time I have loved you but I can neither tell you nor not tell you. Forgive me. Vaguely everything I have been told about your intellectual life, about the unique distinction of your soul, has convinced me that in you alone I would encounter sweetness after a bitter life, peace after an adventurous life, after a life of uncertainty and darkness the path towards light. And you have been my spiritual companion without knowing it. But that is no longer enough for me. It is your body I want, and unable to have it, in my despair and frenzy I write this letter to calm myself, the way one crumples a paper while waiting, the way one writes a name on the bark of a tree, the way one cries a name into the wind or over the sea. To lift the corner of your lips with my mouth, I would give my life. The thought that this might be possible and that it is impossible both set me on fire. When you receive letters from me, you will know that I am experiencing a period when this desire is driving me mad. You are so kind, have pity on me, I am dying for being unable to possess you.

Françoise had just finished this letter when the servant entered with the lamps, giving so to speak the sanction of reality to the letter she had read as in a dream, in the shifting, uncertain gleam of the flames. Now the soft but certain, forthright light of the lamps caused to emerge, from the half-light between the facts of this world and the dreams of the other, our interior world, and gave it something like the stamp of authenticity according to matter and according to life. Françoise wanted first to show this letter to her husband. But then she thought it more generous to spare him this anxiety, and that she at least owed her silence to the unknown person to whom she could give nothing else, awaiting oblivion. But the next morning she received a letter in the same elaborate writing with these words: 'Tonight at 9 I will be at your home. I want at least to see you.' Then Françoise was afraid. Christiane was going to leave the next day to spend two weeks in the countryside, where the cooler air could do her good. She wrote to Christiane asking her to come dine with her, since her husband was going out that evening. She ordered the servants not to let anyone else in and had all the shutters solidly closed. She said nothing to

Christiane, but at 9 o'clock told her she had a migraine, asking her to go into the *salon* near the door that led to her bedroom, and not to let anyone come in. She knelt down in her bedroom and prayed. At 9.15, feeling faint, she went into the dining room to get a little rum. On the table there was a large piece of white paper on which were printed the following words:

Why don't you want to see me? I would love you so well. Someday you will regret the hours I could have helped you pass. I beg you. Allow me to see you, but if you order it I will go away immediately.

Françoise was horrified. She thought of asking her servants to come with weapons. She was ashamed of this idea, and thinking that there was no more effective authority than her own to have sway over the unknown man, she wrote on the bottom of the paper:

Leave immediately I order you.

And she rushed into her room, threw herself onto her prie-Dieu, and prayed fervently to the Holy Virgin without another thought in her mind. After half an hour she went to find Christiane, who was reading at her request in the living room. She wanted to have something to drink and asked her to accompany her into the dining room. She trembled as she went in, supported by Christiane, and almost fainted as she opened the door, then advanced with slow steps, almost dying. At each step it seemed as if she had no strength to take another, and that she would faint right there and then. All of a sudden she had to stifle a cry. On the table, a new piece of paper had appeared, on which she read:

I have obeyed. I will not come back. You will never see me again.

Fortunately Christiane, alarmed by her friend's faintness, hadn't seen the paper, and Françoise had time to pick it up swiftly but nonchalantly and to put it in her pocket. 'You should go home early,' she said hastily to Christiane, 'since you're leaving tomorrow morning. Goodbye my dear friend. I might not be able to come and see you tomorrow morning; if you don't see me it's because I'll have slept late to cure my migraine.' (The doctor had forbidden any farewells, to prevent Christiane from becoming overly emotional.) But Christiane, aware of her state, understood clearly why Françoise didn't dare come and why these farewells had been forbidden, and she cried while saying goodbye to Françoise, who overcame her sorrow till the end and remained calm to reassure Christiane. Françoise did not sleep. In the last note from the stranger the words 'You will never see me again' worried her more than anything. Since he said 'see again', he must have seen her. She had the windows checked: not a single shutter had moved. He could not have come in that way. So he must have bribed the concierge. She wanted to dismiss him then, but the following instant she felt unsure, and decided to wait.

The next day, Christiane's doctor, whom Françoise had asked for news of Christiane as soon as she left, came to see her. He did not hide from her that her friend's state, without being irremediably compromised, could suddenly become hopeless, and that he did not envision any precise treatment for her to follow. 'Ah, it's a great misfortune that she didn't marry,' he said. 'That new life could alone have a salutary influence on her languid state. Only new pleasures could modify such a profound state.' 'Get married!' Françoise cried out. 'But who would want to marry her now that she is so ill?' 'She should take a lover,' said the doctor. 'She will marry him if he cures her.' 'Don't say such awful things, Doctor,' Françoise exclaimed. 'I am not saying awful things,' the doctor replied sadly. 'When a woman is in such a state and she's a virgin, only a completely different life can save her. I do not believe we should; at supreme times like these, worry about the proprieties and hesitate. But I will come back to see you tomorrow, I am in too much of a hurry today, and we'll talk again.'

Françoise remained alone for a few minutes, thinking about the doctor's words, but soon involuntarily began thinking again about the mysterious correspondent who had been so cleverly bold, so brave when it was a question of seeing her, and when he had to obey her, so humbly renunciative, so gentle. The idea of the extraordinary decision he must have made to attempt this adventure out of love for her filled her with joy. Already she had asked herself several times who it could be, and now she imagined it was a soldier. She had always loved them, and old passions, flames that had been denied nourishment because of her virtue, but that had set her dreams on fire and sometimes made strange reflections pass through her chaste eyes, were rekindled. Long ago she had often wanted to be loved by one of those soldiers whose broad belt takes long to unbuckle, dragoons who let their swords drag behind them in the evening at street corners while they look elsewhere and when you clasp them too close on a sofa you risk pricking your legs with their big spurs, soldiers who all hide beneath a too-rough cloth for you easily to feel a careless, adventurous, gentle heart beating.

Soon, just as a wind moist with rain loosens, detaches, scatters, rots the most fragrant flowers, the sorrow of sensing the loss of her friend drowned all these voluptuous thoughts beneath a wave of tears. The face of our souls changes as often as the face of the sky. Our poor lives drift at whim between the currents of a voluptuousness where they dare not stay and the harbour of virtue that they don't have the strength to reach.

A telegram arrived. Christiane had taken a turn for the worse. Françoise left, and arrived the next day in Cannes. At the villa rented by Christiane the doctor did not allow Françoise to see her. She was too weak for now. 'Madame,' the doctor finally said, 'I don't want to reveal any of your friend's life to you; I know nothing about it in any case. But I think I should tell you one fact that might make you, who know her better than I, guess the painful secret that seems recently to be oppressing her, and in that way bring her some appeasement, or, who knows, perhaps even a remedy. She keeps asking for a small box, dismisses everyone, and has long conversations with the box, which always end in a kind of crisis of nerves. The box is there, and I have not dared open it. But given the invalid's extreme weakness, which might at any time become of great and immediate seriousness, I think it might be your duty to see what it contains. In that way we can know if it's morphine. There are no injection marks on her body, but she could be swallowing it. We cannot refuse to give her this box; her emotion when we resist is such that it would soon become dangerous, possibly even fatal. But we would be greatly interested to see what we are bringing her all these times.'

Françoise thought for a few minutes. Christiane had confided no secret of the heart to her, and she would certainly have done so if she had had one. It must be morphine or some similar poison; the doctor's interest in finding out was pressing, immediate. With little emotion she opened it, saw nothing at first, unfolded a paper, remained astonished for a second, let out a cry and fell. The doctor rushed to her; she had only fainted. Near her lay the box that had fallen from her hands, and next to it the paper that had fallen out. On it the doctor read: 'Go away, I order you.' Françoise soon returned to herself, had a painful, violent contraction all of a sudden, then, in a voice that seemed calm, said to the doctor: 'Imagine that I thought I'd see laudanum, in my emotion. I am mad. Do you think,' Françoise asked, 'that Christiane can be saved?' 'Yes and no,' the doctor replied. 'If one could suspend this languid state, since she has no diseased organ, she could recover completely. But there is no way of telling what could stop it. It is unfortunate that we cannot know the sorrow – probably due to love – from which she is suffering. If it were in the power of a person currently living to console and cure her, I think, that person would perform that duty even at great cost.'

Françoise immediately had a telegraph form brought to her. She wired her confessor to come by the next train. Christiane spent the day and night in almost complete somnolence. Françoise's arrival had been hidden from her. The next morning she was so poorly, so agitated, that the doctor, after getting her ready, had Françoise come in. Françoise approached, asked her for news so as not to frighten her, sat down by her bed and gently consoled her with deliberately chosen, tender words. 'I am so weak,' said Christiane; 'bring your forehead close, I want to kiss you.' Françoise had instinctively recoiled, but fortunately Christiane didn't see this. Soon she overcame her emotions and kissed her tenderly and at length on her cheeks. Christiane seemed better, more animated, wanted to eat. But a servant came to whisper a word into Françoise's ear. Her confessor, the Abbé de Tresves, had just arrived. She went out to talk with him in a neighbouring room, cleverly, without letting him guess anything. 'Abbé, if a man was dying of love for a woman, who belongs to another woman and whom he had the virtue of not trying to seduce, if the love of this woman could alone save him from a near and certain death, would it be excusable to offer it to him?' Françoise asked quickly. 'How could you not know the answer yourself?' said the Abbé. 'That would amount to taking advantage of an invalid's weakness, to sully, ruin, prevent, annihilate the sacrifice of his whole life, which he made for the sake of his conscience, and for the purity of the woman he loved. It is a fine death, and acting as you say would be to close the kingdom of God to someone who deserved it for having triumphed so nobly over his passion. That would be above all for the woman too pitiful a fall to join the one who without her would have cherished his honour beyond death and beyond love.'

Françoise and the Abbé were summoned: Christiane, dying, was asking for confession and absolution. The next day Christiane was dead. Françoise received no more letters from the Stranger.

Translated by Charlotte Mandell

Notes

THE HUSBAND AS DOCTOR

(p. 1) *the country of Mischief* The author probably means Picardy or Lorraine.

THE TRUE STORY OF A WOMAN WHO KILLED HER HUSBAND . . .

(p. 12) *a Procne and a Medea* In Greek mythology, Procne was married to King Tereus of Thrace. Tereus raped her sister Philomena and then cut out her tongue to prevent her from speaking of the crime. However, by depicting the event on a tapestry Philomela was able to alert Procne. To avenge her, Procne killed her son Itys, boiled him and served him to Tereus.

The daughter of King Aeetes of Colchis and wife of the mythical hero Jason, Medea was notorious for slaying her two children.

(p. 14) *the thieves that had killed Ibycus* The Greek poet Ibycus was robbed and murdered by bandits. Before dying he implored a flock of cranes passing overhead to bear witness to his killing. Sometime later, on spotting the cranes flying over them, one of the men shouted out: 'There go Ibycus' witnesses and avengers!' His words were overheard, and the murderers unmasked.

(p. 15) *as he made her touch . . . the blood spurted out* Cruentation was one of the medieval methods of finding proof against a suspected murderer. The common belief was that the body of the victim would spontaneously bleed in the presence of the murderer.

MICROMÉGAS

(p. 40) *Blaise Pascal* Blaise Pascal (1623–62) was a French mathematician, philosopher and theologian. Among many other distinctions, he was one of the inventors of the calculator.

(p. 40) *Reverend Derham* William Derham (1657–1735) was an English theologian, scientist, astronomer and philosopher, known for measuring the speed of sound.

(p. 41) *Lully* Jean-Baptiste Lully (1632–87) was a French Baroque composer and a favourite of Louis XIV.

(p. 45) *Father Castel* Louis Bertrand Castel (1688–1757) was a French mathematician and physicist.

(p. 45) *the year . . . new style* The reference is to the change from the Julian calendar to the Gregorian calendar, which began in 1582 and was adopted in England in 1752.

(p. 49) *Leeuwenhoek and Hartsoeker* Antonie van Leeuwenhoek (1632–1723) and Nicolaas Hartsoeker (1656–1725) were Dutch scientists and lens makers. Van Leeuwenhoek was self-taught, and is known as the 'father of microbiology'. The 'seed from which we all grow' to which Voltaire refers is semen, which Van Leeuwenhoek and Hartsoeker were reputed to have been the first to observe under a microscope.

(p. 52) *Swammerdam . . . Réaumur* Jan Swammerdam (1637–80) was a Dutch biologist and entomologist. René Antoine Ferchault de Réaumur (1683–1757) was a French entomologist and meteorologist.

(p. 54) *entelechy* In Aristotle's definition, 'entelechy' is the final form and actualization of a potential concept.

(p. 55) *Malebranche* Nicolas Malebranche (1638–1715) was a French Catholic priest and philosopher, known for the doctrine of 'Vision in God'.

THIS IS NOT A STORY

(p. 65) *Petites-Maisons* The Petites-Maisons was a Parisian asylum founded in 1557 – the Parisian equivalent of Bedlam.

THE NOBLEMAN

(p. 89) *Télémaque . . . Gil Blas Les Aventures de Télémaque* was a 1699 novel by François Fénélon. *Gil Blas*, or *L'Histoire de Gil Blas de Santillane*, was a French picaresque novel by Alain-René Lesage, published between 1715 and 1735.

NO TOMORROW

(p. 114) *the forests of Gnide* A reference to Montesquieu's poem 'The Temple of Gnide' (1725).

JEAN-FRANÇOIS LES BAS-BLEUS

(p. 130) *Cazotte* Jacques Cazotte was the author of 'Le Diable amoureux' (1772), considered one of the earliest tales in the French fantastic genre.

(p. 131) *Bézout* Étienne Bézout (1730–83) was a French mathematician.

(p. 133) *Mesmer or Cagliostro* Franz Mesmer (1734–1815) was a German physician, after whom mesmerism is named. Count Giuseppe Balsamo, known as Alessandro Cagliostro (1743–95), was an Italian occultist and magician.

(p. 135) *Messidor . . . Prairial* Respectively the tenth and nine month in the Revolutionary calendar. Messidor started on 19/20 June and ended on 18/19 July; Prairial started on 20/21 May and ended on 18/19 June.

VANINA VANINI

(p. 137) *Carbonari* The *Carbonari*, or 'charcoal burners', were secret groups of pro-unification revolutionaries, active in Italy between 1800 and 1830.

(p. 147) *Murat* Joachim Murat (March 1767–1815) was a French military commander, brother-in-law of Napoleon and King of Naples.

CLAUDE GUEUX

(p. 213) *Émile, or On Education*, by Jean-Jacques Rousseau, is a 1732 treatise written in novel form on education and human nature.

(p. 216) *Jacques Clément* Jacques Clément (1567–1589) was a Dominican friar and conspirator, assassin of King Henry III of France.

(p. 222) *pede claudo* Roughly translated: 'retribution comes slowly'.

(p. 226) *Farinacci* Prospero Farinacci (1554–1618) was a Roman judge known for the harshness of his sentences.

THE VENUS OF ILLE

(p. 229) "Ἵλεως ἦν δ'... οὕτως ἀνδρεῖος ὤν', 'I humbly beg this statue for mercy, I said, a work of overwhelming humanity' Lucian of Samosata.

(p. 232) *a Roman Terminus* A Terminus was a statue or bust that marked a boundary, named after the Roman god Terminus, god of boundaries.

(p. 237) *the Mora Player* Mora (or Morra) is an ancient game in which players simultaneously hold out their hands and guess the combined number of fingers extended by all players.

(p. 238) *C'est Vénus . . . sa proie attachée!* The line is from Racine's *Phaedra*, in which Phaedra describes herself as being a victim of her love: 'It is Venus entirely fastened to her prey!'.

(p. 238) *Quid dicis, doctissime?* 'What do you say, learnèd one?'

(p. 244) *Manibus date lilia plenis* A line from Virgil's *Aeneid* quoted by Dante in *Purgatory*: 'Give me lilies with full hands'.

(p. 246) *Me lo pagarás* 'You will pay me back for it'.

DON JUAN'S CROWNING LOVE AFFAIR

(p. 259) *The mille e tre* The thousand and three – the number of women Don Juan is supposed to have seduced.

KNOCK DOWN THE POOR!

(p. 323) *Lélut and . . . Baillarger* Asylum keepers who claimed that Socrates was mad.

VÉRA

(p. 346) *Qui verra Véra l'aimera* 'Whoever sees Véra will love her'.

THE MAN WHO LOVED CONSUMPTIVES

(p. 415) *Garde ta fille, elle est trop chère!* 'Keep your daughter, she is too dear!'

THE *SANS-GUEULES*

(p. 434) *The Sans-Gueules* Literally 'the faceless ones'. This was the name given to soldiers so badly disfigured in battle that they could not be recognized.

Author Biographies

PHILIPPE DE LAON is the assumed author of many of the *Cent nouvelles nouvelles*, or *One Hundred New Tales*, from which this story is taken. Written between 1464 and 1467, they have been described as the first French literary work in prose. They have also been described as 'a museum of obscenities'. Bawdy, comical, subversive, and often with a moral kick, the tales are told by multiple narrators within a frame narrative and were compiled at the court of Philip the Good, Duke of Burgundy, in Jemappes, near Brussels. They were first translated into English in 1899 with the subtitle *One Hundred Merrie and Delightsome Stories* by Robert B. Douglas and published in Paris by the English-language publisher Charles Carrington, specialist in erotica, in Montmartre.

MARGUERITE DE NAVARRE (1492–1549), also known as Marguerite of Angoulême and Marguerite d'Alençon, was Queen of Navarre, by her second marriage, and the sister of King Francis I of France. Writer, humanist and religious reformer, she was one of the leading intellectuals of her day, as well as playing a prominent role in affairs of state. *The Heptameron* was published posthumously in 1558. Inspired by Boccaccio's *Decameron*, it was intended to contain one hundred stories but at Marguerite's death only seventy-two stories were complete. Like Boccaccio's *Decameron* and Chaucer's *The Canterbury Tales*, the tales are set into a frame narrative. In *The Heptameron* stranded guests in a Pyrenean abbey are entertained with stories as they wait for the bridge which will give them safe passage home to be built.

FRANÇOIS DE ROSSET (1571–1619) was a poet, prose-writer and translator, notably of Ariosto's *Orlando Furioso* and Cervantes' *Exemplary Tales*. His *Histoires mémorables et tragiques de nostre temps* (*Memorable and Tragic Tales of our Time*), from which the present story is taken, was published in 1614. His stories met with huge success in France and abroad, and were translated into several languages. Brief, dramatic and garish in their excess, a sense of their general disposition can be gleaned from the book's full title: *Memorable and Tragic Tales of our Time, in which are contained the baneful and lamentable deaths of many people, visited upon them by reason of their ambition, illicit loves, schemes, thefts, plunders and other diverse happenings.*

JEAN-PIERRE CAMUS (1584–1652) was a writer, preacher and theologian, and author of a number of spiritual works and works of theological diplomacy that contrast markedly with the story that appears in this anthology. He was named Bishop of Belley in 1609 and, just before his death, was persuaded by Louis XIV to become Bishop of Arras. Like François de Rosset, he wrote in the genre of '*histoires tragiques*': lurid and dramatic tales, collected into volumes with titles such as *Amphitheatre of Blood* and *Spectacles of Horror*.

CHARLES PERRAULT (1628–1703) was a poet, writer and civil servant, whose *Histoires ou contes du temps passé* appeared in 1697. Better known today as *Contes de Perrault*, or *Tales from Perrault*, they include such familiar stories as 'Puss in Boots', 'Mother Goose' and 'Bluebeard'. After losing his senior administrative job in 1695, Perrault took up storytelling to entertain his children and his tales have remained a touchstone of literature, influencing, among others, the Brothers Grimm and E. T. A. Hoffmann. His interest in fables led him to advise Louis XIV to include thirty-nine fountains based on Aesop's fables in Versailles. Perrault was elected to the Académie française in 1671.

MADAME DE LAFAYETTE (MARIE-MADELEINE PIOCHE DE LA VERGNE) (1634–1693) was the author of the first French novel, *La Princesse de Clèves*, published anonymously in 1678. Highly educated and a frequenter of literary salons, she was a pupil of the French grammarian Ménage and a close friend of La Rouchefoucauld. Her work is noted for its psychological depth and emotional delicacy. 'The Countess of Tende' was posthumously published in 1724.

VOLTAIRE (FRANÇOIS-MARIE AROUET) (1694–1778) was the most influential French thinker of his century and the leading philosopher of The Enlightenment. His father was a public official and his mother an aristocrat, and Arouet was educated by the Jesuits at the prestigious Collège Louis-le-Grand in Paris. Danger, controversy and scandal accompanied him throughout his life and though Voltaire made many enemies, he was careful to maintain the right friends. His first taste of the Bastille came in 1717, when he was imprisoned for eleven months for insulting the regent in a Latin epigram. His work remains a challenge to despots, dictators, liars, fundamentalists and dealers in double standards. The story in this anthology, 'Micromégas', appeared in 1752 and is an example both of the '*conte philosophique*', or the philosophical tale, and early science fiction.

DENIS DIDEROT (1713–1784) was one of the leading figures of the Enlightenment in France. Born in Langres, the oldest of seven children, he was initially destined for the clergy, whose corruption he spent many years excoriating. Educated, like Voltaire, by the Jesuits, he was a brilliant but unruly pupil. He threw himself into Enlightenment philosophical battles and, with d'Alembert, founded and edited the *Encyclopédie*. Many of his most famous works, including *Rameau's Nephew*, *Jacques the Fatalist*, *D'Alembert's Dream* and *The Nun*, were published after his death.

MARQUIS DE SADE (DONATIEN ALPHONSE FRANÇOIS) (1740–1814) was a writer, philosopher and revolutionary politician who lived a life as dramatic as any of the stories in this anthology. Born in Paris, he was the only surviving child of the Count de Sade, who abandoned the family soon after his birth, and his wife, Marie-Eléonore de Maillé de Carman. A notorious libertine, Sade was imprisoned several times for a range of offences, from blasphemy to literary obscenity by way of kidnapping and sodomy. He spent several years of his life incarcerated under various regimes, falling foul of the monarchy, the French revolutionary regime and Napoleon. A supporter of the French Revolution, he was accused of 'moderatism' and narrowly escaped the guillotine the day before Robespierre was overthrown. His works include *Justine, or The Misfortunes of Virtue* and *The 120 Days of Sodom*, which was written while imprisoned in the Bastille and not published until 1905. His writings are known for the explicit (and often autobiographical) nature of their sexual content, as well as for their intellectual and philosophical adventurousness.

ISABELLE DE CHARRIÈRE (ISABELLA AGNETA ELISABETH VAN TUYLL VAN SEROOSKERKEN) (1740–1805) was a Dutch aristocrat who wrote in French. Multilingual and polymathic, her output included novels, plays, pamphlets, music and libretti. The story included here, 'The Nobleman', appeared in 1763 when she was twenty-two. Though published anonymously, Isabelle was quickly identified as the author. Her family, embarrassed by this satire on nobility, attempted to prevent dissemination by buying up the entire edition of the magazine in which it appeared.

DOMINIQUE VIVANT DENON (1747–1825) was a writer, artist, diplomat, curator and archaeologist in the reigns of Louis XV, Louis XVI and Napoleon. After accompanying Napoleon on his Egyptian campaign, he was appointed director-general of museums in 1802, and in 1812 Napoleon made him the first director of the Louvre. After the Bourbon Restoration in 1814, he fell out of favour and was replaced in 1816. Though best known for his writings on art and his account of the Egyptian Expedition, *Travels in Upper and Lower Egypt During the Campaigns of General Bonaparte*, his story 'No Tomorrow' has remained a classic of French short fiction.

CHARLES NODIER (1780–1884) was a novelist and prolific writer of novels, novellas, gothic tales and horror stories, and a pioneer of the '*conte fantastique*', or 'fantastic tale'. After several years wandering Europe, including a stint in Ljubljana, then capital of the French Illyrian Provinces, as editor of the French, German and Italian newspaper, *The Official Telegraph of the Illyrian Provinces*, he returned to France in 1813. In 1824, he was appointed librarian at the Arsenal and elected member of the Académie française in 1833. His work was influential on a generation of romantics, including Victor Hugo, Sainte-Beuve and Mérimée. Nodier was an admirer of German and English literature and adapted Dr Polidori's 'The Vampyre' for the French stage. His most famous works include *Smarra* (1821), *Trilby* (1822) and *The Crumb-Fairy* (1833).

STENDHAL (HENRI BEYLE) (1783–1842) is one of the most various and engaging French writers of the nineteenth century. Novelist (*The Red and the Black*, *The Charterhouse of Parma*), autobiographer (*The Life of Henri Brulard*, *Memoirs of an Egotist*), travel writer (*Rome, Naples and Florence*, *A Roman Journal*) and art critic (*History of Italian Painting*), he also wrote biographies of Napoleon, Mozart, Haydn and Rossini.

MARCELINE DESBORDES-VALMORE (1786–1859) was born in France and moved with her mother to the French colony of Guadeloupe when her father's *cabaretier* business collapsed in the revolution. At the age of sixteen, her mother died of yellow fever and Marceline made her way back to France, where she embarked on a career as an actress. She published her first book of poems in 1821 and soon after dedicated herself to writing. Her novel *An Artist's Studio* describes the difficulties of being recognized as a woman artist. Baudelaire admired her poetry and she is the only woman to feature in Paul Verlaine's *Poètes Maudits*, or *Cursed Poets*, where she appears alongside Mallarmé, Rimbaud, Villiers, Corbière and Verlaine himself.

HONORÉ DE BALZAC (1799–1850) is one of the most prolific French writers and author of *The Human Comedy*, a cycle of more than ninety novels, novellas and stories that he billed as 'a natural history of society'. Within *The Human Comedy*, whose title is taken from Dante's *Divine Comedy*, Balzac divided the stories into three genres: 'Studies of *moeurs*', 'Philosophical Studies' and 'Analytical Studies', with further subdivisions based on the stories' locations, subjects and characters. 'Society would be the historian, I would be the secretary', he wrote.

ALEXANDRE DUMAS (1802–1870) also known as 'Dumas *père*', or 'Dumas the elder' to distinguish him from his son Alexandre Dumas, was a popular playwright, novelist and short-story writer. He was a prolific historical novelist, many of whose novels and stories have been made into films, musicals and TV series, as well as a hugely successful playwright (notably his play *Kean* (1836)) and travel writer. His most famous works are *The Count of Monte Cristo* and the d'Artagnan series of novels, which began with *The Three Musketeers* (1844), and *La Reine Margot* (1845).

VICTOR HUGO (1802–1885) was a prolific writer across many genres and whose long career straddled the nineteenth century. Poet, playwright and novelist, he was also a politician and one of the leading public intellectuals of his time. When André Gide was asked who the greatest French poet was, and replied 'Victor Hugo, *hélas*', it was less a comment on Hugo's quality than on the sheer intimidating volume of his *oeuvre* and his personality. The range of his poetry alone is remarkable: from fiery romanticism and exoticism to delicate elegy, by way of proto-symbolism and political satire. His fiction is panoramic and often political, and his novels include *Les Misérables* (1862) and *Notre Dame de Paris* (1831). The story in this anthology, published in 1834, shows Hugo's involvement in one of the pressing social and political concerns of his time: capital punishment.

PROSPER MÉRIMÉE (1803–1870) was a writer, historian and archaeologist, who rose in 1831 to become Inspector-General of Historic Monuments. As well as writing a novel, short stories and novellas, Mérimée was also a translator, notably of Gogol, Turgenev and Pushkin, and an influential promoter of Russian literature in France. In 1844, he replaced Nodier as a member of the Académie française. His most famous works, *Mateo Falcone*, *An Etruscan Vase* and *The Vision of Charles XI*, are staples of the French short story tradition and the story in this anthology, 'The Venus of Ille', is a classic example of the '*conte fantastique*', or 'fantastic tale'.

ALOYSIUS BERTRAND (LOUIS JACQUES NAPOLÉON BERTRAND) (1807–1841) was a poet, playwright and journalist, and is one of several French writers credited with inventing the prose poem. His masterpiece, *Gaspard de la nuit*, appeared in 1842 and sold twenty copies on first publication. Twenty years after his death, Baudelaire described Bertrand's influence on his own conception of the prose poem in *Le Spleen de Paris* and Bertrand became an important figure for the Symbolist poets of the 1880s and 1890s. He was even more prized by the surrealists, who considered him an authentic forerunner. The composer Maurice Ravel wrote three piano pieces based on texts from *Gaspard de la nuit*, including the text that appears here, 'Scarbo'.

JULES BARBEY D'AUREVILLY (1808–1889) was a novelist, short story writer, polemicist and influential critic known as 'The Constable of Letters' for his often vituperative reviews and judgments of contemporaries. *Les Diaboliques* (1874), from which 'Don Juan's Crowning Love Affair' is taken, is his masterpiece and his work blends a fascination with decadence and perversion with reactionary politics and high Catholicism. His essay *On Dandyism and George Brummel* appeared in 1845 and was profoundly influential on writers such as Baudelaire.

XAVIER FORNERET (1809–1884) was a poet, playwright and journalist. A bohemian, eccentric and uncategorizable writer who was marginal in his own lifetime and forgotten soon after, he was recuperated by the surrealists and features in André Breton's *Anthology of Black Humour*. The Prize for Black Humour in his memory has been won by, among others, Raymond Queneau, Patricia Highsmith, Ambrose Bierce (posthumously) and Roald Dahl.

THÉOPHILE GAUTIER (1811–1872) was one of the great French romantic poets and the dedicatee of Baudelaire's *The Flowers of Evil*: '*magicien ès lettres*', 'magician in letters'. He was also a novelist, short story writer and travel writer. His novel *Mademoiselle de Maupin*, whose preface is held to be the manifesto of the 'art for art's sake' movement, appeared in 1835. The story in this anthology is translated by the American writer Lafcadio Hearn, whose translation of Gautier's fantastic tales appeared in 1882.

GUSTAVE FLAUBERT (1821–1880) is one of the greatest French novelists of the nineteenth century. He was born in Rouen, the son of a provincial doctor, and, while still an adolescent, professed himself to be 'disgusted with life'. His most famous novel, *Madame Bovary*, appeared in 1857, the same year as Baudelaire's *The Flowers of Evil*. Both books were prosecuted for offense to public morals. *Sentimental Education* appeared in 1869 and *Three Tales*, his most successful book, in 1877. His other novels include *Salammbô* (1862) and *Bouvard and Pécuchet*, which remained unfinished at Flaubert's death.

CHARLES BAUDELAIRE (1821–1867), is considered the great poet of the nineteenth century and the instigator of modern poetry. *The Flowers of Evil* appeared in 1857 and *Paris Spleen: Poems in Prose* in 1869, from which the story that appears here is taken.

JULES VERNE (1828–1905) is best known for his visionary science-fiction writing, and since the late nineteenth century has been the second-most translated author in the world. As well as science fiction, he wrote essays and scientific studies and maintained a keen and largely positive interest in the ways in which scientific advances would alter human life. Several of the technologies that appear fictionally in his novels anticipate inventions that would later become realities and he is credited with a number of predictions, including the moon landings. In 1989 his novel *Paris in the Twentieth Century* was discovered: set in 1960 in a world where only business and technology are valued and art, philosophy and imagination are disparaged and driven underground, it had been refused by Verne's publisher in 1863 as depressing and unbelievable. It may read rather more believably today.

AUGUSTE DE VILLIERS DE L'ISLE-ADAM (1838–1889) was one of the most brilliant and eccentric writers of the nineteenth century. An impoverished aristocrat from Brittany, he worked variously as sparring partner in a boxing gym, army officer and journalist. His short stories, *Cruel Tales*, appeared in 1883, followed in 1888 by *New Cruel Tales* and *Unusual Tales*. In his extraordinary science-fiction novel, *The Future Eve* (1886), the inventor Thomas Edison creates a female 'android' for his friend Lord Ewald and endows her with a mind and a soul far superior to those of her human admirer. Villiers' writings are influenced by occultism and his 'idealist' play, *Axël* – which contains the famous line 'Living? Our servants will do that for us!' – appeared in 1890, the year after his death.

ÉMILE ZOLA (1840–1902) was a prolific novelist, as well as a playwright and journalist, and the founder of the 'Naturalist' school of writing. Like most writers associated with the creation of an '–ism', Zola's work is far in excess of the theory that is attributed to it. His twenty-volume 'Rougon-Macquart' series of novels, published between 1871 and 1893, is subtitled 'The Natural and Social History of a Family Under the Second Empire'. His incendiary open letter to president Félix Faure, *J'Accuse!*, appeared in January 1898, in which he defended Captain Dreyfus against trumped-up charges of spying and accused the French president, courts and establishment of antisemitism.

STÉPHANE MALLARMÉ (1842–1898) was a poet and critic, and the leader of the Symbolist movement, though no '–ism' adequately accounts for the originality and uniqueness of his poetry and ideas. His poems are known for their musicality and suggestiveness, as well as their playfulness and delicacy. His aim was 'to paint not the object but the effect it produces' and his poems have been set to music, notably by Debussy, Ravel and Boulez. His great experimental work *A Throw of the Dice Will Never Abolish Chance* appeared in 1897.

CHARLES CROS (1842–1888) was a poet, dramatist and inventor, and one of the most unusual figures in a period saturated with eccentrics. A friend of Verlaine and Rimbaud, he published poetry, notably the 1873 'The Sandalwood Coffer', and was known for his witty and topical monologues, which were performed in theatres and cabarets by the actor-director Coquelin the younger. Cros was also an inventor: he invented, but failed to patent, colour photography, on which he wrote a book in 1869, and deposited a sealed patent request in 1877 for the phonograph (which he called the '*Paléophone*', the voice of the past). Among his less far-sighted projects was a proposal to the French government to build a giant mirror with which to communicate with Martians.

JORIS-KARL HUYSMANS (1848–1907) is best-known for his novel *À rebours*, or *Against Nature*, published in 1884 and which has been called the 'Bible of Decadence'. It is the 'yellow book' in Wilde's *The Picture of Dorian Gray* and is one of the most internationally influential books in nineteenth century literature. In fact, Huysmans' views on Decadence were far more subtle and less approbatory than his readers thought, and in the preface, written twenty years after the novel, he made clear that the novel was far from being a 'how-to' Decadent manual. Barbey d'Aurevilly, reviewing the novel when it first appeared, wrote: 'After a book like this, all that is left for the author is to choose between the mouth of a pistol and the foot of the cross.' In the preface, Huysmans quotes Barbey and adds the rider 'the choice is made' – a reference to his conversion to Catholicism.

OCTAVE MIRBEAU (1848–1917) was a prolific novelist, short story writer, critic, pamphleteer, playwright and political activist whose work enjoyed immense success in his lifetime. His novels include *Calvary*, *The Torture Garden* and *The Diary of a Chambermaid*, which was the basis of a film of the same name by Luis Buñuel in 1964. He is also the author of several highly original one-act plays. Mirbeau was politically active during the 1890s and a supporter of anarchism, as well as an ardent Dreyfusard, and promoter of modern writers and artists.

JEAN RICHEPIN (1849–1926) was born in French Algeria and studied at the École normale supérieure. Playwright, novelist and poet, he was at various times soldier, actor, sailor and longshoreman. He had an affair with Sarah Bernhardt and scripted a film scenario for her and was associated with the *Chat noir* cabaret in Montmartre. He was elected to the Académie française in 1908. His works include *Bizarre Deaths* (1877), from which the story in this anthology is taken, *Nightmares* (1892), *Tales of Roman Decadence* (1898) and *Stories without Morals* (1922).

GUY DE MAUPASSANT (1850–1893) is best known for his short stories, though also several of his novels, notably *Bel-Ami* (1885) and *Pierre et Jean* (1888). His preface to *Pierre et Jean* is held to be at once a manifesto of realism and a subversion of the realist project: 'I conclude [. . .] that realist writers of talent should instead be called illusionists.'

GEORGES RODENBACH (1855–1898) was a poet and novelist, born in Tournai in Belgium and died in Paris. He was one of the generation of great Belgian writers that included Verhaeren and Maeterlinck, who defined the Symbolist movement. His novel *Bruges la morte* (1892), an atmospherically decadent novel about death and desire in Bruges, was one of the most successful Symbolist novels and gave rise to a whole trend for dead city tourism. The story in this anthology is an offshoot of his second novel *Le carillonneur*, also set in Bruges.

JEAN LORRAIN (1855–1906) was a poet, playwright and novelist associated with the decadent movement, and is best known for the novel *Monsieur de Phocas* (1901). Known as 'The Ambassador from Sodom', his life was as decadent as his fiction and Lorrain exemplifies the life/art overlap that characterizes the sexually omnivorous dandy. 'He loved his period to the point of detestation,' claimed the critic Hubert Juin – an insightful comment about how *fin-de-siècle* writers inhabited their era.

RACHILDE (MARGUERITE EMERY) (1860–1953) was a prolific decadent novelist and short story writer who described herself as a 'man of letters'. Married to the literary critic and editor Alfred Vallette, she quickly established a reputation as a fearless writer and explorer of human desire, notably from the female perspective. An avowed anti-feminist, her fiction nonetheless radically reconfigures gender politics, explores domination and submission, and subverts traditional narratives of desire. *Monsieur Vénus* appeared in 1884 to huge success and with the kind of scandalized response that helps launch a writer for life. *La Marquise de Sade* appeared in 1887.

JULES LAFORGUE (1860–1887) was born in Montevideo and moved to France at the age of six. Though he died young, his work, like that of Rimbaud, has been of immeasurable influence on twentieth-century poetry. T. S. Eliot claimed that the discovery of Laforgue was a defining moment in his formation as a poet. As well as his poetry, which is ironic, self-lacerating, witty and vulnerable, Laforgue is the author of *Legendary Moralities* (1887), which he described, alluding to two of the great masters of the short story genre, as 'neither Villiers nor Maupassant'. The story that appears here reflects Laforgue's fascination with Hamlet and with the monologue as a poetic resource.

FÉLIX FÉNÉON (1861–1944) was a Swiss-French art critic, curator, journalist and anarchist. A regular attendee at Mallarmé's Tuesday evening gatherings, he was a committed supporter of new artists and coined the term 'Neo-Impressionist' to describe the work of Seurat and his *coterie*. His short study *The Impressionists in 1886* is a classic of art criticism. Fénéon kept up his political activities despite being employed as a civil servant by the war office. He was arrested and tried for conspiracy in the anarchist bombing of the restaurant Foyot in 1894. At his trial he defended himself with panache: 'It has been established that you surrounded yourself with Cohen and Ortoz,' claimed the prosecutor; 'One can hardly be surrounded by two persons; you need at least three,' replied Fénéon.

JULES RENARD (1864–1910) is best known for *Poil de carotte*, or *Carrot Top*, his 1894 semi-autobiographical novel about a red-headed child. His *Histoires naturelles*, from which this story is taken, appeared in 1894. Novelist, short story writer and playwright, his masterpiece is perhaps his *Journal 1887–1910*. Published posthumously, it is fresh, lively, lyrical, confiding, waspish and often extremely funny. 'They call this the age of steam,' he writes, 'in terms of poetry, they are not wrong'.

MAURICE LEBLANC (1864–1941), novelist and short story writer, is today best known as the creator of the gentleman-thief Arsène Lupin. Born in Rouen, he was delivered by Achille Flaubert, Gustave's brother. The first Arsène Lupin story appeared in 1905 and Leblanc continued to write Lupin novels and stories into the 1930s. Arsène Lupin's stories have inspired cartoons, manga, films and television series.

LÉON DAUDET (1867–1942) was the son of the famous novelist Alphonse Daudet (author of *Letters from My Windmill*) and the husband of Victor

Hugo's daughter. Like many French intellectuals of his period, he began on the left and moved quickly to the right, co-founding, with Charles Maurras, the nationalist periodical *Action française* in 1907. His politics remained virulently right-wing and antisemitic, and he was a supporter of the Pétain Vichy regime until his death. His short stories are more decadent in their bent and he was also the author of a number of science fiction novels.

MARCEL SCHWOB (1867–1905) was one of the most original writers of the *fin de siècle*. Born to a Jewish family near Paris, he studied Sanskrit and philology at the École pratique des hautes études under the celebrated linguist Ferdinand de Saussure. Schwob's writing is characterized by imagination and erudition, and among his works are a study of Parisian slang (*argot*), six books of short stories, including *The King in the Golden Mask* and the hugely influential *Imaginary Lives*, and a number of articles, translations and introductions, including to Defoe, Robert Louis Stevenson, François Villon and Shakespeare. Jorge Luis Borges cites Schwob's *Imaginary Lives* as an influence on his *A Universal History of Infamy*.

MARCEL PROUST (1871–1922) is the author of *In Search of Lost Time*, begun in 1909 and finished in 1922, soon before his death. The first volume was refused by Gallimard on the advice of André Gide, and published at the author's own expense by Grasset. Gide later wrote to Proust and apologised, claiming that his rejection was his greatest literary regret. In 1919, the second volume won the Goncourt prize, France's most prestigious literary prize. The story in this anthology was written when Proust was in his twenties and prefigures some of the themes of the later novel.

Acknowledgements

We are grateful to the following for permission to reproduce copyright material:

'Don Juan's Crowning Love Affair' by Jules Barbey d'Aurevilly.
   Translated by Stephen Romer in *French Decadent Tales*, Oxford University Press, 2013, pp.3–20. Reproduced by permission of the Licensor through PLSClear.
'Knock down the Poor' by Charles Baudelaire.
   Translated by Keith Waldrop in *Paris Spleen: Little Poems in Prose*, copyright © 2009. Reproduced by permission of Wesleyan University Press, www.wesleyan.edu/wespress.
'Museum of Tears' by Leon Daudet.
   Translated by Brian Stableford in *Decadence and Symbolism: A Showcase Anthology*, Snuggly Books, 2018, pp.332–336. Reproduced by permission of Snuggly Books.
'No Tomorrow/Point de Lendemain' by Vivant Denon.
   Translated by Lydia Davis in *The Libertine Reader: Eroticism and Enlightenment in Eighteenth-Century France*, Zone Books, 1997, pp.732–747. Reproduced by permission of the publisher.
'The Nobleman' by Isabelle de Charrière.
   Translated by Caroline Warman in *The Nobleman and Other Romances*, Penguin, 2012, translation copyright © Caroline Warman, 2012. Reproduced by permission of Penguin Classics, an imprint of Penguin Publishing Group, a division of Penguin Random House LLC. All rights reserved.
'Véra' by Villiers de L'Isle Adam.
   Translated by Robert Baldick in *Cruel Tales*, Oxford University Press, 1963, pp.11–21. Reproduced by permission of the Licensor through PLSClear.

'La Comtesse de Tende' by Mme de La Fayette.

Translated by Terence Cave in *La Princesse de Cleves*, Oxford University Press, 2008, pp.189–204. Reproduced by permission of the Licensor through PLSClear.

'The Horla' by Guy de Maupassant.

Translated by Sian Miles in *A Parisian Affair and Other Stories*, Penguin Classics, copyright © by Sian Miles, 2004. Reprinted by permission of Penguin Books Limited.

'The Substitute' by Marguerite de Navarre.

Translated by P. A. Chilton in *The Heptameron*, Penguin Classics, translation copyright © P. A. Chilton, 1984. Reproduced by permission of Penguin Books Limited.

'Mr Bougran's Retirement' by Joris-Karl Huysmans.

Translated by Andrew Brown in *With the Flow*, Alma Books, 2020. Reproduced by permission of Alma Books Ltd.

'The Man Who Loved Consumptives' by Jean Lorrain.

Translated by Stephen Romer in *French Decadent Tales*, Oxford University Press, 2013, pp.143–147. Reproduced by permission of the Licensor through PLSClear.

'The Venus of Ille' by Prosper Mérimée.

Translated by Nicholas Jotcham in *Carmen and Other Stories*, Oxford University Press, 2008, pp.132-162, copyright © Nicholas Jotcham, 1989. Reproduced by kind permission of the Estate of the author.

'On a Cure' by Octave Mirbeau.

Translated by Stephen Romer in *French Decadent Tales*, Oxford University Press, 2013, pp.76–79. Reproduced by permission of the Licensor through PLSClear.

'Bluebeard' by Charles Perrault.

Translated by Christopher Betts in *The Complete Fairy Tales*, Oxford University Press, 2010, pp.104–114. Reproduced by permission of the Licensor through PLSClear.

'Constant Guignard' by Jean Richepin.

Translated by Stephen Romer in *French Decadent Tales*, Oxford University Press, 2013, pp.92–95. Reproduced by permission of the Licensor through PLSClear.

'The Time' by Georges Rodenbach.

Translated by Stephen Romer in *French Decadent Tales*, Oxford University Press, 2013, pp.148–158. Reproduced by permission of the Licensor through PLSClear.

'The *Sans-Gueules*' by Marcel Schwob.

Translated by Stephen Romer in *French Decadent Tales*, Oxford University Press, 2013, pp.194–197. Reproduced by permission of the Licensor through PLSClear.

'Vanina Vanini' by Stendhal.

Translated by David Coward in *Oxford Book of French Short Stories*, Oxford University Press, 2011, pp.7–29, translation copyright © David Coward, 2002. Reproduced by permission of Professor David Coward.

'The Panther' by Rachilde.

Translated by Rachel Tapley, http://d7.drunkenboat.com/db23/translation/rachel-tapley-translating-rachilde. Reproduced by permission of Rachel Tapley.

'Death by Advertising' by Émile Zola.

Translated by Douglas Parmée in *The Attack on the Mill and Other Stories*, first published by Alma Books, 2008, reprinted by Oxford University Press, 1984, pp.23–26. Reproduced by permission of the Licensor through PLSClear.

In some instances, we have been unable to trace the owners of copyright material, and we would appreciate any information that would enable us to do so.

NOVELS, TALES, JOURNEYS

Alexander Pushkin

'At that moment it seemed to him that the queen of spades winked and grinned. The extraordinary likeness struck him ... "The old woman!" he cried in horror'

Universally acknowledged as his nation's greatest poet, Pushkin was also a master of prose, whose works expanded the boundaries of Russian storytelling. This collection of his prose writing ranges from satires to comedies, travel narratives to imaginative historical fiction, and includes his greatest stories: the haunting dreamworld of 'The Queen of Spades', the five short *Tales of the Late Ivan Petrovich Belkin* and the novella *The Captain's Daughter*, which has been called the most perfect book in Russian literature.

Translated by Richard Pevear and Larissa Volokhonsky

ISBN: 978 0 24 129 037 8

DEAD SOULS

Nikolay Gogol

'Come now, we're not talking about the living; God be with them. I'm asking for the dead ones ... they're just dust, after all'

Chichikov, a mysterious stranger, arrives in a provincial town and visits a succession of landowners to make each a strange offer. He proposes to buy the names of dead serfs still registered on the census, saving their owners from paying tax on them and to use these 'souls' as collateral to reinvent himself as a gentleman. In this ebullient masterpiece, Gogol created a grotesque gallery of human types, from the bear-like Sobakevich to the insubstantial fool Manilov, and, above all, the devilish con man Chichikov. *Dead Souls*, Russia's first major novel, is one of the most unusual works of nineteenth-century fiction and a devestating satire on social hypocrisy.

Translated with an Introduction and Notes by Robert A. Maguire

ISBN: 978 0 14 044 807 8

WUTHERING HEIGHTS

Emily Brontë

'May you not rest, as long as I am living!
You said I killed you – haunt me, then!'

Emily Brontë's novel of impossible desires, violence and transgression is a masterpiece of intense, unsettling power. It begins in a snowstorm, when Lockwood, the new tenant of Thrushcross Grange on the bleak Yorkshire moors, is forced to seek shelter at Wuthering Heights. There he discovers the history of the tempestuous events that took place years before: the intense passion between the foundling Heathcliff and Catherine Earnshaw, her betrayal of him and the bitter vengeance he now wreaks on the innocent heirs of the past.

Edited with an Introduction and Notes by Pauline Nestor
Preface by Lucasta Miller

ISBN: 978 0 14 143 955 6

THE WOMAN IN WHITE

Wilkie Collins

'In one monent, every drop of blood in my
body was brought to a stop . . . There, as if it
had that moment sprung out of the earth . . . stood
the figure of a solitary Woman, dressed
from head to foot in white'

The Woman in White famously opens with Walter's eerie encounter
on a moonlit London road. Engaged as a drawing master to the
beautiful Laura Fairlie, Walter becomes embroiled in the sinister
intrigues of Sir Percival Glyde and his 'charming' friend Count
Fosco, who has a taste for white mice, vanilla bonbons and poison.
Pursuing questions of identity and insanity along the paths and
corridors of English country houses and the madhouse, *The Woman
in White* is the first and most influential of the Victorian genre
that combined Gothic horror with psychological realism.

Edited with an Introduction and Notes by Matthew Sweet

ISBN: 978 0 14 143 961 7

FIRST LOVE

Ivan Turgenev

'I had ceased to be simply a young boy; I was someone in love ...
my suffering began on that day too'

When the down-at-heel Princess Zasyekin moves next door to the
country estate of Vladimir Petrovich's parents, he instantly and
over-whelmingly falls in love with his new neighbour's daughter,
Zinaida. But the capricious young woman already has many
admirers and, as she plays her suitors against each other, Vladimir's
unrequited youthful passion soon turns to torment and despair.
Set in the world of nineteenth-century Russia's fading aristocracy,
Turgenev's story depicts a boy's growth of knowledge and mastery
over his own heart as he awakens to the complex nature of love.

Translated by Isaiah Berlin
With an Introduction by V. S. Pritchett

ISBN: 978 0 14 044 335 6

AROUND THE WORLD IN EIGHTY DAYS

Jules Verne

'To go around the world ... in such a short time and with the
means of transport currently available, was not only impossible,
it was madness'

One ill-fated evening at the Reform Club, Phileas Fogg rashly bets
his companions £20,000 that he can travel around the entire globe
in just eighty days. The reserved Englishman immediately sets off
for Dover, accompanied by his French manservant Passepartout.
Travelling by train, steamship, sledge and even elephant, they must
overcome kidnappings, attacks, natural disasters and the dogged
Inspector Fix of Scotland Yard – who believes that Fogg has robbed
the Bank of England – to win the extraordinary wager. *Around
the World in Eighty Days* gripped audiences on its publication
and remains hugely popular for its thrilling race against time.

Translated with Notes by Michael Glencross
With an Introduction by Brian Aldiss

ISBN: 978 0 14 044 906 8

NANA

Émile Zola

'Her slightest movements fanned the flame of desire, and with a
twitch of her little finger she could stir men's flesh'

Born to drunken parents in the slums of Paris, Nana lives in squalor
until she is discovered at the Théâtre des Variétés. She soon rises
from the streets to set the city alight as the most famous high-class
prostitute of her day. Rich men, Comtes and Marquises fall at her
feet, great ladies try to emulate her appearance, lovers even kill
themselves for her. Nana's hedonistic appetite for luxury and
decadent pleasures knows no bounds – until, eventually, it
consumes her. Nana provoked outrage on its publication in 1880,
with its heroine damned as 'the most crude and bestial sort of
whore', yet the language of the novel makes Nana almost a
mythical figure: a destructive force preying on a corrupt society.

Translated with an Introduction by George Holden

ISBN: 978 0 14 044 263 2

BEL-AMI

Guy Maupassant

'They had moved closer to one another to watch the dying
moments of the day, this beautiful bright May day'

Young, attractive and very ambitious, George Duroy, known to
his admirers as Bel-Ami, is offered a job as a journalist on *La Vie
francaise* and soon makes a great success of his new career. But
he also comes face to face with the realities of the corrupt society
in which he lives – the sleazy colleagues, the manipulative mistresses
and wily financiers – and swiftly learns to become an arch-seducer,
blackmailer and social climber in a world where love is only a
means to an end. Written when Maupassant was at the height of
his powers, *Bel-Ami* is a novel of great frankness and cynicism,
but it is also infused with the sheer joy of life – depicting the scenes
and characters of Paris in the belle epoque with wit, sensitivity
andhumanity.

Translated with an Introduction by Douglas Parmée

ISBN: 978 0 14 044 315 8

CYRANO DE BERGERAC

Edmond Rostand

'Look at me. Who in the world could love a face like this?
My nose goes everywhere ahead of me!'

Poet and soldier, brawler and charmer, Cyrano de Bergerac
is desperately in love with Roxane, the most beautiful girl in
Paris. But there is one very large problem – he has a nose of
stupendous size and believes she will never see past it to
return his feelings. So when he discovers that the handsome
but tongue-tied and dim-witted Christian is also pining for
Roxane, generous Cyrano offers to help by writing exquisite
declarations of love for the young man to woo her with. Will
she ever recognize who she is really falling in love with? Set
during the reign of Louis XIII, Rostand's *Cyrano de Bergerac*
(1897) was one of the great theatrical successes of its time and
remains as popular today for its dramatic power and, above all,
for its good-natured, passionate and swashbuckling hero.

Translated with an Introduction and Notes by Carol Clark

ISBN: 978 0 14 044 968 6